Ellie

Lesley Pearse was born in Rochester, Kent, but has lived in the West Country for the last thirty-two years. She has three daughters and a grandson. She is the bestselling author of fifteen novels, including *Ellie*, *Georgia*, *Tara*, *Camellia* and *Charity*, all five of which are published by Arrow.

Ellie

LESLEY PEARSE

arrow books

Published by Arrow Books 2007

5

Copyright © Lesley Pearse 1996

Lesley Pearse has asserted her right under the Copyright, Designs and
Patents Act 1988 to be identified as the author of this work

First published in Great Britain in 2006 by William Heinemann
First published in Great Britain in paperback in 1996 by Mandarin Paperbacks
First published by Arrow Books in 1998
Arrow Books
Random House, 20 Vauxhall Bridge Road
London SW1V 2SA

www.randomhouse.co.uk

Addresses for companies within The Random House Group Limited can be
found at: www.randomhouse.co.uk/offices.htm

The Random House Group Limited Reg. No. 954009

A CIP catalogue record for this book
is available from the British Library

ISBN 9780099428046

The Random House Group Limited supports The Forest Stewardship
Council (FSC®), the leading international forest certification organisation.
Our books carrying the FSC label are printed on FSC® certified paper.
FSC is the only forest certification scheme endorsed by the leading
environmental organisations, including Greenpeace. Our
paper procurement policy can be found at
www.randomhouse.co.uk/environment

Typeset in Palatino by Palimpsest Book Production Limited,
Grangemouth, Stirlingshire
Printed and bound in Great Britain by Clays Ltd, St Ives PLC

For Hilda Sargent and Rowneen Phillips,
two very different kinds of women,
but both formative influences in my youth.

Hilda, my stepmother, was a tough old bird,
but it was she who encouraged my love of books,
taught me self-reliance and a great deal more.
Rowneen was a friend's mother,
a lady who knew how to love, laugh
and make the world a brighter place.
Sadly they both died in 1995, within days
of one another. I remember them with a smile.

Acknowledgements

Malcolm Golding for his brilliance with computers and his patience while he brought me into the twentieth century, and apologies to Sheelagh for making her a temporary grass widow.

Jack Hatt in Amberley, Sussex for his help in recreating the past glories of Amberley Station, and Mary Taylor in Rushington who gave me so much information about the war years in Sussex.

Finally, Peter Marsh for his knowledge of the fire service, and for his stoic endurance and help with my research while I lived, breathed and slept the war years.

Chapter One

Stepney, London, 1939

''Ere, Poll! Your bleedin' 'Elayna's broke the bog seat again,' Edna shouted indignantly from the bottom of the stairs. 'She might have a name like an effing duchess, but she don't sit on the khazi like one.'

Polly Forester paused in searching her daughter's long, dark brown hair for nits, and half smiled.

No one ever called Ellie by her real name, 'Helena' – which was intended to be pronounced in the Greek way, with an 'a' sound – not unless they wanted to tease or ridicule her. Edna Ross, their garrulous and often fearsome neighbour, loved to bawl it out as the ultimate, affectionate insult, always adding an extra 'a' or two for special effect.

''Ow can you be sure it weren't Wilf?' Polly shouted back good-naturedly. ''E's got an arse like a rhinoceros!'

''Cos 'e's bin down the pub all bleedin' day,' Edna shot back. 'An' I 'opes 'e stays there all bleedin' night too.'

'I'm sorry, Ed,' Polly called back, spluttering with laughter. 'I'll fix it later.'

'Don't matter.' Edna's indignation was gone now, replaced by wheezy laughter. 'Just tell our Ellie if she's goin' to live wiv toffs, she's got to be'ave like one.'

It was four in the afternoon, August 31st, 1939. On any other warm day, Alder Street, Stepney would be ringing with the sound of children's voices, skipping

1

ropes thumping on the pavement, balls thudding against walls and women gossiping on their doorsteps. But an unnatural, eerie silence had fallen over the street in the last hour, as children were called in to prepare for evacuation tomorrow.

'Ave I got nits?' Ellie asked, wincing as her mother scraped the fine-toothed comb through her hair.

Ellie was described as 'a big girl' by her neighbours, a kindly euphemism for 'fat'. At twelve she was almost as tall and several inches wider than her dainty mother. She escaped being labelled 'plain' simply because of her exuberant personality. Her dark eyes sparkled with ready laughter, wide mouth constantly curved into a smile, and she had the ability to make all those around her laugh too.

But anyone seeing Ellie straight-faced, without witnessing her infectious jollity, could be excused for considering her appearance unprepossessing. Black hair, a sallow big face, too fleshy to see if there might be interesting cheekbones beneath it, a nose too small to add any definition. In a worn, striped, cotton dress, long since outgrown, her puppy fat was all too apparent, buttons strained at the chest, sleeves tight, and the short skirt emphasising dimpled knees.

'Can't see any, ducks, but I'd best make certain,' Polly replied, moving her daughter closer to the window for a better view. Ellie's long, glossy hair was perhaps her best feature and it was a matter of pride to her mother to keep it that way. 'We don't want yer new uncle and auntie to think all us cockneys are lousy, do we?'

'Can't I stay with you, Mum?' Ellie twisted her head so she could see her mother. 'You'll be so lonely all on your own.'

'You must go.' Polly's mouth smiled but her eyes were bleak. 'I'd rather be lonely than worrying about you being 'urt.'

Ellie desperately wanted to find some joke to

2

lighten the mood, but for once nothing came to her. 'I'll be scared you might cop it,' she blurted out. 'Wot if one of them bombs gets you?'

Polly sighed deeply. All her thoughts were channelled into getting Ellie away to safety, drilling her on how to behave and making the most of this opportunity. Until now she hadn't even considered the danger to herself.

'There ain't gonna be no bombs,' Polly said with as much conviction as she could muster. 'That's just scaremongering to keep us on our toes.'

'You ain't scared then?' Ellie slid her arms round her mother, leaning on her shoulder.

Ellie had never seen her mother scared. She might be small and slender but she could chase rats out of the outside lavatory with a broom, stand up to the often formidable actors and actresses at the Empire Theatre in Holborn where she worked as a dresser, and take Edna Ross in her stride.

'Only of not seeing you each day.' Polly hugged her daughter fiercely, fighting back tears. 'But it'll all be over by Christmas, you'll see. Maybe I'll be able to get a better place for us while you're gone. Now get yer bits and bobs together and we'll go up Auntie Marleen's, she said you could 'ave a bath. She's got some supper for us an' all.'

This unexpected treat wiped out Ellie's fears of separation. She disengaged herself from her mother's arms, her customary wide smile splitting her face in two.

'Wot, in that posh place? You said you wasn't never going there!'

Marleen was Polly's oldest and best friend, but from what Ellie had overheard, Marleen had a new fancy man her mother didn't approve of, and until now she'd refused to take Ellie to see Marleen's flat.

'Even I can change my mind for summat special,' Polly sniffed, turning her head away and wiping her

3

damp eyes surreptitiously. 'Besides, Marleen loves you and she'd be mad if she didn't get to say goodbye.'

Polly sat down at the chair by the window as Ellie went into the bedroom to get ready. The forced gaiety she'd been keeping up all day was wearing thin. She was sending Ellie away for more than just her safety: Polly hoped a new home in the country would give her daughter all the things she couldn't even dream of supplying. But for twelve years Ellie had been the centre of her world. How was she going to cope without her?

There was nothing in the small room to reassure Polly that she hadn't failed her child. Two worn fireside chairs, a rag rug on bare boards, a small table with one leg supported by a wedge of cardboard, and on the mantelpiece, two plaster dogs with chipped ears flanking a clock which had long since stopped working. Just looking out of the window was enough to depress her further. The terraced street was so narrow, the sun rarely penetrated it. Soot-ingrained brick, so many windows broken and the panes replaced by cardboard or rags. Edna and Iris were gossiping in one patch of sunshine, headscarves tied over their curlers. Old Mrs Schoebl was sitting in her doorway, legs splayed wide, revealing an inch or two of long pink drawers, her head nodding sleepily down on to her chest. Normally the sound of children playing drowned the hum of sewing machines from the workshop at number 21, but now it filled the air like a swarm of bees. Two boys were sitting listlessly on the doorstep, their haircuts making them look like a couple of convicts. As Polly watched, Alf Meeks came into view, his rag-and-bone cart piled high with goods. Even his horse looked defeated, plodding wearily towards the yard further down Alder Street.

Polly was still a very pretty woman. Not even twelve years in Alder Street had dulled the shine in her coppery, naturally curly hair, or banished the poise and grace of the dancer she'd once been. Although she was thirty-seven, men still cast covetous glances at her trim figure, her upturned nose with its sprinkling of freckles, and wondered why the little widow hadn't remarried.

She had moved into these two tiny rooms above Edna and Wilf Ross when Ellie was born, a desperate, temporary measure. She'd been optimistic then, believing the good times would come back, but before long she realised she was trapped, just as all her neighbours were. Jews, Poles, Irish and native Londoners, their customs and beliefs might vary, but poverty united them all. Whole families huddled in tiny, damp, squalid rooms, on a relentless treadmill of hard work for poor wages and no hope of anything better.

It was for Ellie's sake that Polly hadn't stopped trying to make the best of things. She'd learnt to live with the stink of the outside lavatory, the mess that Edna left in their shared kitchen. To eke out her meagre wages from the theatre she often prepared a meal for her daughter and pretended she'd eaten hers earlier, or put up with the cold all day and lit the fire only minutes before Ellie came in from school. Mice overran the house; there were bugs in the walls. In summer they stifled in the heat, but winters were an endurance test. Making pretty curtains didn't disguise the mould growing on the walls, or the rickety furniture. Only Ellie's presence made it a home.

How was she going to face this place without Ellie? They had shared everything – from the bed, to gossip, chores and laughter. What purpose would there be in her life now?

Polly had seen for herself today that she wasn't alone in loving Ellie. All morning there had been a steady stream of neighbours calling at number 18 to say goodbye to her, many of them bringing small gifts. Old Mrs Schoebl, the Polish woman from across the street, brought a few sweets. Ossie Freidburg brought a length of red flannel for Polly to make into a night-dress and Mrs Green, who ran the paper shop on the corner, offered a couple of comics for the journey.

Ellie was such a gregarious and warm-hearted child, that she assumed her neighbours' kindness was extended to every other mother and child in the street. She had no idea that she'd won a special place in people's affections.

Humour was the traditional way in the East End of dealing with the grimness of life. 'If I couldn't have a laugh every day I'd sooner die', was a remark heard constantly, and Ellie made them roar with laughter. Whether she'd become a comedienne through her close contacts with comics at the theatre, or simply to rise above her size and situation, Polly didn't know, but Ellie's ability to mimic and entertain was appre-ciated by everyone, from her schoolfriends, to the oldest residents in Alder Street.

Ellie was an observer. Whether she was sitting on a bus, in a shop or just in a room full of people, she listened and stored away information. Later she would re-enact the characters she'd studied with fault-less precision, using the simplest props like a head-scarf or a pair of glasses.

'You should put your Ellie on the stage,' Edna often said to Polly when she'd had a few gins. 'She 'ad me laughin' fit to bust.'

Polly was never sure how she should react to this. She felt Ellie was destined for it, believed she had the raw talent to succeed, but yet she knew the pitfalls of such a life first-hand. So she took the easy way out, a smile which could either be translated as accept-ance, or as disbelief. She never let on that Ellie's birth had finished her own career on the stage, or showed how hard she found it merely to dress entertainers, when once she had been out there in the footlights.

*

'I'm ready!' Ellie said from the doorway. Polly turned at her daughter's voice and for a second caught a glimpse of how Ellie might look once she'd lost her puppy fat.

With the light slanting over Ellie's shoulder, Polly could see there were high cheekbones and her own delicate, pointed chin buried beneath surplus flesh. Ellie's eyes were glorious, deep pools, so like her father's. That wide mouth, with a slightly protruding bottom lip, hinted at sensuality and her small nose was perfectly shaped.

Polly wasn't quite comfortable with this sudden flash of Ellie as a woman, especially on the eve of evacuation. Guilt stabbed at her as she remembered she hadn't yet got round to broaching that awkward subject of menstruation.

'You don't need a towel.' Polly took the dingy thin grey one from beneath Ellie's arm, shamed as much by this symbol of their poverty as by failing to have seen how fast her daughter was growing up. 'Marleen's got plenty. Just take your cardigan in case it's cold when we come 'ome.'

Polly swiftly ran a comb through her hair and put on a little lipstick. She was wearing her one and only decent dress, a pale blue crêpe that Marleen had given her. If only Ellie wasn't going away tomorrow, having the night off from work would've been a rare treat. As it was, she felt more like crying than pretending this was a celebration.

Ellie would have walked right past the Gray's Inn Road mansion block. Polly grabbed her arm to stop her.

'Is this it?' Ellie asked, looking up at the elaborate red brick Victorian facade with awe.

Polly nodded, smiling at her daughter's expression. Polly had seen smarter places in her time, but today she saw it through Ellie's eyes.

7

The steps were white marble. A red patterned carpet, similar to the one in the Odeon, softened their footsteps as they plodded up the stairs to the second floor. Maybe it hadn't been repainted in years, perhaps the tenants weren't as aristocratic as those it had been designed for, but compared to 18 Alder Street it was a palace.

'Hello, darlings!' Marleen said as she opened the door, her theatrical greeting matching her appearance. She wore a vivid green and orange long kimono, and her hair was dyed a deep, dark red, arranged in loose curls on the top of her head. 'Come on in, Cyril's just left.'

Ellie felt rather than saw her mother's warning finger on her lips, and smiled to herself.

Although Ellie was young, she knew a great deal more about adult relationships than her mother realised. An intuitive and observant child, she could work out for herself exactly how Marleen, who was too old now to dance, managed to have such smart clothes and live in a place like this.

Marleen and Polly had been friends since joining the same dance troupe at seventeen. Ellie sensed, when the two women spoke of those days, that her mother's past was almost as racy as her friend's. She had seen photographs which gave a glimpse of this thrilling, glittery world. Showgirls in spangled costumes and feathered head-dresses, the pair of them in short 'flapper' dresses and beaded headbands on the arms of men in evening dress, always exuding an aura of glamour and sophistication.

Ellie had to assume, though neither Polly nor Marleen could be drawn on the subject, that it was her birth which finished her mother's ritzy life. Maybe if Polly had married one of those suave gentlemen instead of Tom Forester, they might be living in one of those big houses she saw in the background of those pictures.

*

8

'What'cha think of it then?' Marleen asked as she ushered them along the wide, carpeted passageway into her sitting-room.

Ellie stopped short at the door, gasping in admiration. 'Cor, it ain't 'alf nice, Auntie Marleen,' she said. 'It's like a palace.'

'The only palace I've ever seen was the one in Brighton,' Marleen giggled, looking at Polly. 'Remember that place, Poll? You caught my side too tightly when we did the wheel routine and your nails split my costume.'

Normally Ellie would hang on every word of this sort of reminiscing, but just now she was too taken aback by the room before her.

It was full of sunshine, even though the big windows had thick lace curtains which muted it. It had a carpet too, pale blue with scrolls in a darker colour, which went right up to the skirting boards. A big three-piece suite with floppy feather cushions and the covers all greens and blues. As if that wasn't enough, there were gilt electric lamps, and a low table with lion's feet, so highly polished she could almost see her face in it.

Ellie often parodied Marleen. She would drape a coat over her shoulders, pretending it was her aunt's musquash, and mince around, fluttering her eyelashes and talking in that special posh voice Marleen put on for effect. Yet, young as she was, Ellie knew there was another Marleen hidden beneath the brash, hard exterior. She was generous with love and money, loyal and kind-hearted, and when she hit low spots in her life she laughed about it, picked herself up and started out again. It was typical of her showy, caring aunt that she'd chosen to buy a new blue velvet party dress for Ellie to take away with her, rather than something practical like shoes or a coat.

Marleen was still glamorous. Although her face was thin and her features unremarkable, she made

9

the best of herself. Never a hair out of place, her eyebrows just a thin painted line, skin like a porcelain doll. Like Polly, she still retained that dancer's stance, straight-backed, head up, tummy tucked in. She was always entreating Ellie to copy it.

Ellie explored the rest of the flat with ever-growing amazement. A kitchen almost as big as their entire flat, with proper cupboards all built in and that unheard-of luxury, a refrigerator. The main bedroom was pink, with a silky padded cover right over the big double bed.

'You ain't got married 'ave you?' Ellie said, trying very hard to sound guileless.

'Me get married!' Marleen raised one thin eyebrow. 'That'll be the day, luv! My ship come in, that's all.'

Finally they came to the bathroom. Once again, Ellie was dumbstruck. It had white tiles right up to the ceiling and the bath was big enough for two. Pink soap sat on the wash-basin, there was a fluffy rug on the floor, and the lavatory had a shiny wooden seat. Ellie could only remember ever having had a real bath on three occasions – and all of them had been in Marleen's many different homes. But those had been dingy, cold places, shared by other tenants, not this kind of opulent splendour.

'Want yer bath now?' Polly asked, smiling as she saw the excitement bubbling out of her daughter.

'Yeah, 'ave it now,' Marleen agreed, opening a mirrored cupboard on the wall and taking out a bottle of something pink. 'And for a special treat, a touch of my smellies!'

Ellie watched, fascinated, as Marleen poured a little of the pink liquid into the gushing hot water. Instantly, bubbles began appearing. The whole room smelt of roses.

'Cor, that's the stuff film stars 'ave.' Ellie hugged her aunt impulsively, dark eyes dancing with glee.

'You can practise being one then,' Marleen laughed,

tickling the child's upturned face. 'Now wash your-self properly, mind, and when you come out I want to see if you can still do those dance steps I taught you. Just because you're going away don't mean the earth stops moving.'

Ellie was in seventh heaven as she lay back amongst the bubbles. Her mother and Polly would be attacking the gin, soon there'd be a nice supper, and tomorrow would be a real adventure.

Ellie had only been out of London two or three times in her entire life, and then only to Southend with Marleen. Although she was sad at leaving her mother, this was outweighed by the prospect of the new, exciting experiences before her. Miss Parfitt, her teacher, had assured Ellie there would be plays and school concerts she could take part in.

It was inevitable that Ellie would want to go on the stage. As a baby she'd slept in a wicker costume box, and sometimes even been borrowed as a real-life prop when an act called for one. Actors, actresses, dancers and comics had all become an extended family, and she learnt their lines watching from the wings, noting timing, movements and gestures. Instinct told her which were good and bad performances. But Ellie knew she needed experience of acting to further her ambition, and she would never get that in Bancroft Road School.

'Ellie's a lovely kid,' Marleen said as she took a large swig of her gin, a cigarette poised in her scarlet-tipped fingers. She and Polly were sitting at the kitchen table, a warm breeze from the open window ruffling the white lace curtains. 'You've made a good job of bringing 'er up, Poll, so don't worry about 'er with strangers.'

The two women had shared much more than a dancing career. Their deep, close friendship had been cemented with highs and lows, sorrows and joys since 1917, when they'd taken part in their first concert for a group of wounded servicemen. Marleen had been the ambitious one, grasping opportunities for both of them as the First War ended, when people were hungry for entertainment and fun. Yet it was Polly who had the real talent. She wasn't a mere dancer, but a singer and brilliant comic actress. It was she who coached Marleen and comforted her when the breaks didn't come as quickly as she'd hoped. They had cried on each other's shoulders when love turned sour and supported each other in times of need, and though in those early days it had been Polly who was more often than not the provider, Marleen had reciprocated when Ellie was born.

'I just 'ope they find 'er a good place,' Polly said anxiously. 'I dream of 'er getting set up with some toffs.'

'I 'ope she keeps up 'er acting and singing,' Marleen replied. 'She's got your talent, Poll, a lovely voice and she can take off anyone.'

'I know.' Polly smiled. 'She was being Tommy Trinder this morning and if I 'adn't bin feeling so down in the dumps I'd 'ave wet myself laughing.'

'This bloody war,' Marleen exploded suddenly. She knew Polly would be like a three-legged chair without Ellie around and it grieved her to think she could offer no consolation. 'It ain't even started yet and already I'm sick of it. Cyril was even talking about joining up today and I thought 'e was certain to wriggle out of it.'

Polly shook her head in disbelief. Many of the entertainers had already joined up in the hope they'd get a cushy number rather than waiting for conscription, and she was worried the Empire might close with war coming. If a big shot like Cyril Henches, who ran everything in the East End from sweat shops to clubs, had turned patriotic, it seemed the world was going crazy.

'Where will that leave you if 'e does?' Polly asked. Marleen had been Cyril's mistress for a couple of years and when he set Marleen up in this flat Polly was sure it meant that he intended to leave his wife at least.

'Up shit creek,' Marleen smirked. 'Can't see 'im sending me a few bob every week while e's playing soldiers, can you? Even if I got a job I couldn't manage this rent.'

Polly thought for a moment before replying. 'I could move in with you if push came to shove.'

Marleen's pencilled brows shot up in astonishment. 'Blimey girl, that's a turn-up,' she said. 'Thought you didn't approve of my carryings on?'

'I don't,' Polly said quietly. 'But with Ellie away and Cyril maybe joining up we'll both be alone. I 'eard there'll be well-paid jobs in factories soon. Perhaps it'll be good for both of us to start something new.'

Marleen topped up their glasses. Working in a factory was her idea of hell, but she knew Polly meant well. 'It's a thought,' she said. 'But let's see if Ellie settles in the country first.'

Polly knew what Marleen meant. Marleen couldn't and wouldn't change her lifestyle: there would always be men around her. But though Marleen had few morals, she cared too much for Ellie to expose her to anything potentially damaging.

Marleen wasn't a tart, not in the true sense of the word, anyway. She just didn't waste her time and energy on men with nothing to offer her, and Cyril was the latest in a long line of men. Polly worried about her friend, though. She wasn't getting any younger, she drank too much, and though still attractive, the day would come when she'd be forced to fend for herself.

Polly sighed. 'I've gotta get out of Alder Street,' she said, looking around her with envy. 'It's getting me down. Wilf leers at me when I go to the kitchen or the lav. Edna's always prying. What with them and the mice, it's 'ell. Edna even started digging about Tom the other day.'

'Well, I told you years ago it was daft to take 'is name,' Marleen said tartly, getting up again and flinging thick slices of ham on to three plates. 'You could've called yourself Jones, or Brown, made up a story about 'ow 'e died. I never understood why you picked on Tom.'

'You do,' Polly retorted. 'You know exactly. Besides, 'e would've married me, given 'alf a chance.'

Back in 1926, when Polly found herself pregnant by a married man, she had run away rather than let him be disgraced by scandal. She had known Tom Forester since childhood and he'd always been sweet on her. When she heard he'd been killed in a tragic accident at the docks just a couple of months before Ellie was born there seemed nothing wrong with taking his name. But one lie led to another. She even deceived the registrar by giving Tom's name as her husband when she registered Ellie's birth.

Once the false date and place of their marriage had been entered on her daughter's birth certificate, there was no going back. She had a new identity, a faded photograph of Tom and her together taken at Southend, and some happy memories of the big, kindly man who adored her. Enough, she thought, to stop tongues wagging. The only person who knew the truth was Marleen.

'You're a mug, Poll.' Marleen cut a few tomatoes into slices and scooped them on to the plates. 'You could've 'ad 'elp from you-know-who.'

Ellie padded out of the bathroom with a towel wrapped round her, hair dripping on to her shoulders. She'd forgotten to take her clean underwear in with her and she wasn't sure now where her mother had put the bag. As she approached the open kitchen door she heard Marleen speaking and stopped short, instinctively knowing she was hearing something secret.

'If I'd told 'im, soon other people would've found

out,' Ellie heard her mother reply. 'I couldn't do that to 'im, I loved 'im too much to see 'im ruined.'

Ellie knew it was wrong to eavesdrop, yet she couldn't turn away.

'He loved you an' all,' Marleen said stoutly. 'And 'e was stinking rich. If I'd been in your shoes I'd 'ave grabbed anything I could get.'

This curious revelation, together with the sensation of thick carpet curling round her bare toes, gave Ellie the strangest feeling of having stumbled into an alien, yet luxurious world. She crept closer to the door, curiosity getting the better of her.

'Divorce might be possible wiv an ordinary bloke,' Polly said, her tone oddly wistful. 'But not wiv someone wiv a bleedin' Sir stuck in front of 'is moniker.'

'Get the pickles out.' Marleen's voice was close to the door now and Ellie was forced to retreat. But what on earth was it that her mother couldn't tell 'him', and why hadn't she ever admitted she was once in love with someone other than Tom Forester?

Ellie woke up first the next morning. Her mother was flat out on her back, her mouth wide open, her breath smelling of gin.

It had been a lovely evening. Once the supper had been eaten and a few more gins had gone into her auntie and mum, they were very funny, telling her all those stories she loved, about their time with the travelling dance troupe. Ellie had prompted Marleen to talk about the 'stage door Johnnys' with the hope she might discover where this mysterious titled admirer fitted in. But though Marleen told her about a butcher who gave them a leg of lamb when they had nowhere to cook it, and about 'Dandy Jim', whom they had to climb out of a window to avoid, and Big Frank who serenaded them under the boarding-house window in Margate, there was nothing about a 'Sir' anyone.

A violent storm began just before they left Marleen's – thunder, forked lightning and the heaviest rain Ellie had ever seen. They borrowed an umbrella from Marleen, and Ellie had to catch hold of her mother's waist tightly as they hurried to the tube, because she was quite drunk and unsteady on her feet. When they went out to the lavvy before going to bed, Polly kept singing, 'The boy I love is up in the gallery,' and Wilf shouted for her to shut up. Ellie had been on the point of admitting she'd been eavesdropping when they got into bed, but her mother had fallen asleep the moment her head touched the pillow, and the chance was gone.

Now Friday 1st September had finally arrived. My last morning here, Ellie thought, wriggling closer to her mother's side. Polly was too hot and a bit sweaty but it was the last chance to cuddle her.

Ellie knew why Polly had got so drunk last night: it was the only way of coping with sending her child away. She might keep insisting that Ellie would get a better education, and come back speaking posh with swanky manners, but Ellie knew she was breaking up inside.

Teachers at school had often suggested it was wrong of Mrs Forester to take Ellie to work with her every night. But as Polly always said, 'Better under my nose than under another woman's thumb.' Ellie loved helping get the costumes ready for the cast. She had learnt which stars would bite her head off if they so much as saw her, which ones appreciated her running messages and helping with the hooks and eyes. Perhaps most children would find it tiring, but Ellie had the theatre in her blood and the cast and backstage hands were family.

'What are you thinking, Ellie?'

Ellie turned her face, surprised by her mother waking so soon. Polly's blue eyes were bloodshot, her skin looked as worn as her old nightdress, but there was a softness in her voice that meant she too was holding on to these last precious moments with her child.

'Just wondering whether you'll remember to eat when I'm not here,' Ellie whispered. She couldn't voice her fears that her mother might start drinking like many of the theatre people did. Or admit she had butterflies in her tummy. 'You will, won't you, Mum?'

Polly looked at Ellie's troubled face and her heart seemed to swell alarmingly. 'Of course I will,' she said firmly. 'Now don't you go worrying about me, sugarplum. You just be a good girl and make the best of your new home.'

A lump grew in Ellie's throat. The pet name 'sugarplum' was one she had as a little girl and it evoked all those memories of sitting on her mother's knee, of being bathed in a sink and carried home half-asleep in her arms through dark streets. It meant love, that word they never actually said, but she felt it now, hot and sweet.

'We've never been apart for even one night before,' she whispered, wriggling closer in her mother's arms. 'I've never even slept in a bed without you there.'

'It's all part of growing up, baby,' Polly whispered back. 'And it won't be for long.'

As they reached the junction of Alder Street and Whitechapel High Street there was a sea of mothers and children thronging towards the school. Only a few carried a real case like Ellie's, a leather one which Polly said was once part of a fancy set. Mostly the other children had only oilskin shopping bags, pillow-cases or canvas haversacks, but every one of them had a big brown label with their name on it pinned to their chest and the square box containing a gas mask over their shoulder.

Women pushed prams with as many as three small children inside, bigger children holding on to the handles. There were few men, and most of those old enough to be grandfathers. Some children had entire families clustered round them. Grown-up brothers and sisters, aunts and grannies. Many of the children looked shamefully bedraggled.

Ellie looked down at a girl a couple of years younger than her, whose dress was torn and dirty. The sole of her shoe flapped as she walked. Ellie felt proud of her new blue checked dress and the matching ribbons on the ends of her plaits.

'Don't look like that,' Polly whispered, shaking Ellie's arm. 'She ain't so lucky as you, that's all.'

It was enough to chasten Ellie. She was lucky. Maybe she was fat and plain, but she had the nicest, prettiest mother and she was going off on a big adventure.

'How much longer, Mum?' Ellie looked beseechingly at Polly. It was cooler after last night's storm, but her legs ached from standing. There was a desperate kind of atmosphere in the playground. Some children had dumped their belongings and ran around wildly, others were clinging to their mothers and crying. They'd been waiting for over two hours.

'Not long now.' Polly smiled, sliding an arm round her shoulders. 'Miss Parfitt said she thinks you're going to somewhere in Suffolk. I've been in shows up that way and it's right pretty.'

Miss Parfitt, Ellie's teacher, was flushed, rushing around with a register in her hands. A tall, hatchet-faced woman who normally ruled her pupils with fear, today she seemed to have lost her grip.

'Line up now, in twos,' she shouted, blowing her whistle. 'Say goodbye to your mothers now please and we'll be off.'

Here in the school playground, Ellie had no wish to look like a baby and cry, yet she felt as if someone was pulling out her innards as she gave her mother one last frantic hug. She breathed in her mother's smell deeply, that mixture of face powder and soap, and tried to imprint it on her memory. Never before had her mother's skin felt so soft, her arms so comforting. Even though she struggled to fight it, a tear came rolling out.

'Bye, sugarplum,' Polly whispered, struggling not to cry too. 'Best behaviour mind and write to me soon. I love you!'

The train journey was interminable. Doris Smithers had eaten a whole box of Pontefract cakes and then been sick. Reggie Blythe kept sticking his head out of the window and had black smuts all over his face. Carol Muller hadn't stopped crying since they left Liverpool Street.

Their sandwiches were gone, apple cores and sweet papers littering the carriage floor and it smelt as if someone had done something in their pants.

Ellie was glad she'd got the seat by the window, furthest away from Doris and her sicky smell. At first it had been exciting seeing cows and sheep and the fields of ripe wheat being harvested. She'd marvelled at quaint cottages, rivers meandering through green meadows, and the strangeness of going for mile after mile without one house. But now she was only seeing her mother's face, imagining her preparing for the evening's performance, and she wished she could jump from the train and run home.

'Five minutes!' Miss Parfitt slid back the compartment door and forced a grim smile. She had been run ragged since early that morning and couldn't wait to be shot of her charges. 'Get all your belongings together and wait for the train to stop. On the platform I want you all to line up silently.'

Ellie looked down the station steps at the hordes of children ahead of her and grasped the hand of little Rose James more firmly.

'Stop crying,' she ordered. 'No one will pick you

if you've got a runny nose. I'll look after you.'

Miss Parfitt said this place was called Bury St Edmunds, though that meant little to Ellie aside from it being in the middle of Suffolk. Around four hundred children had got off the train, but many more had remained on it, going on further still.

Rose smiled bleakly and wiped her nose on the sleeve of her cardigan, leaving a snail trail.

Once out in the forecourt, Miss Parfitt and the other helpers marshalled the children into small groups, joined by other, local women. Some of these groups were led to buses and even a couple of lorries standing by, but Bancroft Road children were herded up an incline towards the town.

Ellie's apprehension left her, excitement taking over. The station was big and important-looking, to her eyes almost like a castle. Huge trees, bright flower beds and the clean, fresh air made it seem very welcoming. She had never really been aware of the grime in Stepney before, but now as she saw the whitewashed picket fence, the lush green of the railway embankment, the scarlet poppies and golden dandelions, it was like taking off grime-tinged spectacles and seeing the world anew.

'I want my ma,' Rose bleated, tugging at Ellie's hand, presumably reminded of home by the group of women who stood waiting to view the London children. 'I don't like it 'ere.'

The crocodile came to a halt and Ellie gave the little girl a hug.

Rose was only five, a tiny blonde with a squint, still bearing the tell-tale marks of chicken-pox. But she was better dressed than most of the children, in shiny new sandals and a blue print dress.

'Look, Rosie.' Ellie felt she had to spell it out. 'You've gotta be jolly, or no one will want you. You're pretty and small, all those ladies want someone like that. So cheer up, your mum'll come down to see you.'

Just voicing what she expected potential foster parents would require, reminded Ellie that Rose in fact fell far short of being an ideal candidate. She took her own clean handkerchief out of her pocket, spat on it, and vigorously scrubbed Rose's face clean.

'You lucky people,' she said in her Tommy Trinder voice. 'Here we have one pretty little girl for some lucky, lucky lady. And she's got a 'eart-stopping smile an' all!'

Rose giggled. With one eye on Ellie, the other fixed on somewhere distant, she wasn't so pretty, but she was at least clean.

A stout woman in a beige felt hat led the crocodile across the road, holding up her arms to stop the non-existent traffic. To their right was a huge gasometer behind a terrace of small houses not unlike the ones at home, but they were being led past them, up a hill into a pretty town.

Many women stood in groups on doorsteps watching the children pass. It was a little disarming, the way they eyed the children up like cattle going to market, and even more distressing to hear their disparaging remarks.

'Thass a rumman!' one old lady said loudly, pointing out Michael Bendick who had a built-up boot.

Slowly all the children stopped chattering, listening to remarks about their thinness, pallor and shabby clothes, about 'big boys being a heap of trouble', or more personal snipes like 'Look at 'e with the red hair.'

But as Ellie passed by two middle-aged ladies leaning out through an open window, a remark pointed at her stung like a bee.

'I wouldn't want that fat one. Cost a fortune to feed and she's got sly eyes.'

Ellie was in the habit of calling herself 'fat' or even 'gigantic' when she wanted a laugh. But until today, the only time the word 'fat' had been flung at her was in a light-hearted way in the playground, just as she called other kids snot nose, or big ears. Now she was painfully aware just how much bigger she was than all the other girls, and though she wanted to walk tall, with her tummy held in, as Marleen always entreated her to, she felt like a huge, ugly slug.

If Ellie hadn't been smarting inside she might have been cheered by the bustling town. Quaint cobbled streets, pretty little houses all crammed up together like a picture in a magazine. The shops looked exciting too, with things she'd never seen before like gunsmiths and saddlers tucked in between teashops, milliners and haberdashers. It was all so clean, even though many of the houses were ancient. Whitestoned steps, sparkling windows and brightly striped sun awnings competed with flower-filled window boxes.

They were taken to the Corn Exchange, where bunches of balloons had been tied to the pillars. But although this made the majestic old building look welcoming, the eyes of the women grouped around the door were cold.

Once inside the large hall, faced with a long table covered with plates of cakes and sandwiches, most of the children forgot why they'd been brought here. They broke ranks and darted forward, eyes wide with greed, hands reaching out to grab. Ellie didn't dare join them, even though her stomach was rumbling with hunger. She let Rose go and shrunk back as the townswomen came closer to study them all, avoiding her 'sly eyes' falling on anyone.

Back home in Stepney, married women past twenty-five or so were uniformly shabby and worn-looking. Bad teeth, poor posture and bodies sagging from many pregnancies made them look old before their time. In fact, Polly Forester, with her vibrant colouring, her good skin and teeth, was something of a rarity. The hordes of women here, pressing into the hall to look at the children, were quite different. Even though they fell into three distinct groups, they all shared a robust

22

and healthy look. Yet although Ellie scanned them scrupulously from beneath her lashes, she could see no one she could immediately identify with.

The 'posh' women with the smart hats and costumes were getting the first pick of the children. Some of these were young and pretty, but most were middle-aged. Ellie heard their plummy tones, noted the smarmy false smiles, yet still hoped she'd be picked by one of these because that was what her mother wanted.

The middle group looked more intensely at the children, presumably weighing up which would give them the least trouble. These women were neatly dressed, many in summer frocks, their plump arms brown from the sun. Ellie thought they probably lived in the small houses She'd passed on the way from the station.

The final group stood apart. They were the oddest: all were shabbily dressed, some in trousers and men's boots, with neglected hair and weather-beaten faces, as if they'd tramped in from an outlying farm. There were old ladies in this group too, with bent backs and white hair, wearing clothes from the last century.

Men were outnumbered by ten to one. A couple of red-faced farmers in Norfolk jackets and gaiters, several schoolmaster types, and others, possibly shop-keepers, in suits and ties.

Ellie took everything in. The jovial insincerity of the posh women, the keen anxiety of the organisers and the sharp eyes of those strange women from the farms who looked as if they were sizing up horse-flesh.

A woman in a smart green costume picked out Muriel Francis, a small, curly-haired enchantress. She saw a man in a tweed suit with a plump rosy-faced wife single out Billie and Michael Green. One of the odd-looking women in men's boots took the three Coombes boys, and even gave a cheerful, gummy smile when Ed informed her his youngest brother had wet his pants.

It soon became clear, though, that many of the women gathered here had no intention of taking anyone at all.

Rose was eventually led off by a women in a green felt hat without even a backward glance at Ellie. Doris was selected, despite the vomit stains down her dress. An hour had passed since they had arrived at the hall and one by one children were chosen, and a bag of rations handed over to their new foster mothers. Still Ellie waited.

There were only twenty or so children left. Ellie found herself flanked by Phillip Hargreaves, whose knees and hands were covered in scaly sores, the twin boys with red hair from further down Alder Street, and Alfie Smith, who had clearly messed his pants.

Ellie was a foot taller than any of these boys and she felt like a giant. She who could jump up on a table and do an impromptu tap-dance or a stand-up comic routine lost all her nerve. Worse still, she could hear Miss Parfitt pleading for someone to take her. For the first time in her life she discovered what rejection really meant.

'Can she sew?' A squawky voice came from amongst the cluster of women who had already turned their backs on the remaining children, clearly losing interest.

'Oh yes!' Miss Parfitt's voice rang out crisp and bright. 'Helena is very handy with the needle.'

Ellie peeped through her lashes. A woman was pushing her way through the crowd. She was tall and very thin, wearing a severe dark dress and cloche hat, and even at one glance Ellie knew this woman was a witch.

It wasn't just her thick spectacles, her long nose, or her tight, pursed mouth, but the way the more motherly looking women parted to let this apparition pass through, almost as if they were afraid of her.

'Miss Gilbert,' the woman announced herself, holding out a long, limp hand to Miss Parfitt. 'My brother is an undertaker, but we'll take the girl as long as you can vouch for her good behaviour. We can't be doing with boisterous children in our line of business.'

Ellie gulped at the word 'undertaker'. She had seen dozens of comic routines about such people, and although they always got a laugh, she'd always found them scary. Surely Miss Parfitt wouldn't let her go with this woman?

But Miss Parfitt was smiling, coming over to Ellie and urging her forward. 'Helena, or Ellie as we all know her, is a delightfully composed girl,' she said treacherously, clearly relieved to get rid of another child. 'She knows how to behave under any circumstances. I'm sure you'll get on famously.'

'Please, miss, don't send me with 'er.' Ellie caught hold of Miss Parfitt's arm. 'I don't like 'er.'

'Now Ellie!' Miss Parfitt took her two arms and half shook her. 'Don't be foolish. What would your mother say about such ingratitude?'

'She wouldn't like me being at an undertakers.' Ellie's eyes filled with tears. 'Please, miss, I'll go wiv anyone else!'

'There isn't anyone else,' Miss Parfitt snapped. 'If it doesn't work out you can speak to the billeting officer. Maybe if your mother hadn't filled your head with fanciful ideas you'd be glad to be going to a clean, comfortable home instead of whining at me.'

For a moment or two Miss Gilbert spoke to the billeting officer in the beige hat and Ellie crossed her fingers and hoped for a last-minute reprieve. But to her dismay, Miss Gilbert returned and prodded her in the back.

'Come along then, child,' she said crisply. 'I've got the potatoes on at home and I'll have to add another for you.'

Chapter Two

Miss Gilbert's bony fingers dug into Ellie's arm as they came out of a narrow lane lined with tiny shops. Ellie's heart plummeted down into her shoes as she saw their destination.

It wasn't one of the many pretty little houses that seemed to be Bury St Edmunds's standard, but a grim, grey, almost institutional building, dominated by a large, central shop window. Purple satin was draped in the window, two marble angels stood either side of a large ebony cross and 'Amos Gilbert, Undertaker' was printed in bold, black lettering on the glass.

During the ten-minute walk, Ellie had seen much to like about this bustling market town. Winding alleys, ancient cottages and houses from every period in history, fine Georgian buildings and as many shops as in Whitechapel. Although Miss Gilbert's silence was alarming, Ellie's naturally ebullient character wasn't quite defeated.

But now, faced with this forbidding building, the last strands of optimism fled.

'Today you can enter at the front,' Miss Gilbert said in a tone which implied this was a privilege. 'But in future you'll use the back entrance.'

Miss Gilbert's voice was as unattractive as the house – a shrill, seagull-like squawk which made Ellie wince.

A bell rang as Miss Gilbert opened the door. She put her hand up to it and held the clapper. 'Hurry up child,' she snapped. 'Don't stand gawping.'

It was difficult not to gawp. The room had a

church-like solemnity: a black and white tiled floor, a large, dark, highly polished desk bearing only an arrangement of wax lilies and a leather-bound blotter. The walls were painted a shiny, dark green, with wood panelling below waist level, and a discreet sign in gold lettering saying 'Private Chapel of Rest' hung on one wall.

'Is there bodies in 'ere?'

Ellie shot out the question without thinking. Miss Gilbert rounded on her sharply and waved a long, bony finger at her. 'We never refer to bodies,' she squawked. 'You must remember at all times to show the utmost respect for the dead, and you will never, I repeat, never, poke into any rooms down here.'

Ellie had not the slightest desire to poke into anything, in fact if Miss Gilbert hadn't hurriedly pushed her through another lace-curtained door, she would have made a bolt for the street. The passageway she found herself in was gloomy and narrow, with several firmly closed doors on either side, and smelt peculiar, heightening her fear. But Miss Gilbert pushed her on relentlessly through yet another door to a small hall.

'Sit there,' Miss Gilbert snapped, indicating a wooden settle like a small church pew, and promptly disappeared into what Ellie guessed was the kitchen.

The staircase was opposite Ellie's seat. From somewhere above came muted daylight, just enough for her to see that the wallpaper was a browny pink and the narrow strip of carpet up the middle of the stairs was mud brown, held back by highly polished brass stair rods. The bannisters and the sides of the stairs were varnished the same as all the doors, a murky orangey brown colour. But although this decor had clearly remained unchanged for years, it was spotlessly clean, not one scuff or grease mark anywhere. Two large sepia photographs hung on long chains, one of a hearse drawn by black plumed horses, a tophatted bearded man standing beside it, the other of the same man standing with his bride before a church doorway.

'My brother is engaged in something at the moment,' Miss Gilbert said as she came back through the door. She'd abandoned the small bag she had earlier and had put a white apron over her dress. The removal of her cloche hat made no significant difference to her appearance. Her hair was thinning and fair, secured firmly in a plaited knot at the nape of her neck. Ellie supposed her to be around forty, for although her drab clothes and manner suggested she was older, her face was unlined. 'Come with me, you can wash before supper.'

Miss Gilbert led Ellie to the end of a dark landing. 'This will be your room. I expect it to be kept tidy at all times and I don't hold with sitting or lying on the bed.'

If that remark had been made by anyone else, Ellie would have laughed and asked how she was intended to sleep in it. But Ellie instinctively knew this woman wouldn't understand a joke.

The room held nothing but a narrow bed covered in a dull blue counterpane, a small chest of drawers on long spindly legs and an upright chair. Ellie put her case down by the window and looked out. Close to the house was a small wooden shelter, where headstones were presumably engraved in bad weather. She could see rows of chisels and mallets fixed to an inside wall in leather straps and a half finished stone on a bench. All around this shelter were dozens of marble slabs, monuments and urns, weeds curling up round them as if they'd been there for years.

To Ellie's left the yard was cobbled. Black wrought-iron gates led to the side street and next to them was a big building which looked like a stable. Beyond the row of houses behind she could see the tops of trees.

'You got 'orses?' Ellie asked. She had always liked

to visit Dolly, the rag-and-bone man's horse, to give her a carrot or apple, and the prospect of having one close by was comforting.

'No,' Miss Gilbert said curtly. 'We have a motor hearse. The old stable is my brother's workshop.'

Ellie felt a creeping sensation down her spine. Was that where he kept bodies?

'The bathroom is next to this room,' Miss Gilbert continued, her small mouth pursed as if she couldn't open it. 'You will have a bath tonight, but after that only when I give permission. I expect you to present yourself downstairs each morning ready for the day. I will not allow you to return to this room afterwards, not until bedtime. During the day you use the outside lavatory. The bedcover is to be taken off and folded neatly at night, your bed to be made properly each morning before breakfast. Now let me see your clothes.'

Ellie had no idea what Miss Gilbert was searching for. She watched as the woman set aside her hair ribbons, a pink striped dress, the blue velvet dress and a Fair Isle cardigan in one pile.

'Your mother?' Miss Gilbert sniffed, finding a photograph of Polly.

'Yes.' Ellie snatched it up and held it tightly, afraid the woman was going to take it away.

'Keep it up here,' the woman snapped, examining her underwear and nighties as if searching for something unpleasant. 'You may keep those clothes to wear,' she said, pointing to the grey pinafore dress, cardigan and white blouses. 'The other things are quite unsuitable for wear here. I'll put them away until you go home.'

'But Auntie Marleen bought me the velvet frock,' Ellie cried out in alarm, putting out a restraining hand on the woman's. 'She said it was for Sundays and parties.'

'Parties?' Miss Gilbert peered at Ellie over her

glasses, pale eyes registering extreme shock, her mouth opening just enough to reveal yellow teeth. 'We don't have parties here.'

It soon became clear to Ellie that laughter, friendly chatter and even kindness were all as unknown to Miss Gilbert as parties. First Miss Gilbert came back into the room and caught her sitting on the bed and smacked her leg hard. Later, when Ellie was asked to present her hands for inspection, dirt under a couple of nails brought on a lecture on the evils of spreading disease. When ordered to lay the kitchen table for supper, Miss Gilbert rapped her knuckles with a knife for placing a knife and fork round the wrong way.

Ellie counteracted this hostility by making careful note of everything, intending to put it all in a letter to her mother later that night. She watched Miss Gilbert cut a few slices of bread, then measure the loaf with a piece of string before putting it away, and she also saw her add some water to the milk in a jug.

The kitchen was very warm because of the old-fashioned black-leaded range. Yet despite being a large and scrupulously clean place it was devoid of homely touches, or even splashes of colour. The curtains were plain, unbleached cotton, the plates on the dresser pure white. The wooden hoist up on the ceiling had its airing clothes folded neatly. When Miss Gilbert opened the door of the larder, that too had the same ordered appearance, of jars of jam and marmalade in straight lines; even carrots and onions were arranged carefully on a tray. All this was perhaps very laudable, yet the way Miss Gilbert whipped around the kitchen, wiping and straightening as she prepared the meal, made Ellie feel distinctly uncomfortable.

It was a house of many closed doors. The moment Ellie walked into the kitchen, that door too was closed behind her and she was told to sit at the table. Although it was warm and sunny outside, the kitchen was gloomy, the windows and the door leading out into the yard shut, heightening the feeling of oppression. Ellie had never before had any difficulty in striking up a conversation with anyone, but her attempts to talk to Miss Gilbert were crushed by withering glances and sniffs of disapproval.

Mr Gilbert came in just as Miss Gilbert was putting a dish of boiled potatoes on the table. He paused in the porch outside the kitchen door to remove his boots, frowning at Ellie, then beckoned to his sister to come closer. 'I thought I said a boy!' Ellie heard him say in a low voice, and her heart sank even further.

Ellie's mental picture of an undertaker was of a tall, thin man in black with a chalk-white face and a stuckon black moustache. Mr Gilbert was tall, but there the similarity ended.

Amos Gilbert had more in common with a docker than with the undertakers parodied at the theatre and music halls. He was heavily built, with muscular tanned forearms and a ruddy, fleshy face. Fragments of wood shavings were stuck on his moleskin trousers and grey flannel workshirt and he had ominous red stains on his hands which Ellie thought were blood.

'She can sew,' Miss Gilbert sniffed, her tone suggesting she expected no further criticism. 'So she can help with the trimming, and around the house.'

Mr Gilbert didn't reply. He came right into the kitchen in his stockinged feet, looked hard at Ellie, then as if he didn't like what he'd seen, he turned to wash his hands at the sink. Ellie caught a faint whiff of turpentine and realised, slightly reassured, that the stains were only varnish.

'Your name?' he asked. Grey eyes just like his sister's bored into her as he took a seat at the head of the table.

'Elena Forester,' Ellie said nervously. 'But I'm always called Ellie.'

'How old are you?'

'Twelve, sir.'

He said nothing for a moment, frowning as if pondering on it. Ellie was aware, although she didn't dare check, that Miss Gilbert had become tense.

'Well, Ellie,' he said eventually, his tone a little gentler but no welcoming smile on his craggy face. 'My sister and I aren't used to children. You will do as you are told, and behave in a dignified manner at all times. Is that clear?'

'Yes, sir,' she replied, head bowed. She had no intention of staying here for more than one night. It had to be a terrible mistake. Miss Parfitt, her mother and Marleen had all said she'd live with a nice family. The Gilberts and their weird, smelly house were like something from the spooky serials she'd seen at Saturday morning pictures.

Miss Gilbert pressed her hand on Ellie's neck, forcing her to kneel.

'Say a prayer,' she hissed.

It was Sunday morning. Ellie was sandwiched between Mr and Miss Gilbert in St John's Church, just five minutes away from the house in High Baxter Street. Mr Gilbert looked like an undertaker today, in a dark suit with a high wing-collar, his brown hair slicked back with oil. Miss Gilbert's everyday dark blue dress was replaced by an identical one in pale grey with a matching hat and gloves. She had given Ellie back her pink dress this morning, but made a point of saying it would only be worn on Sundays and that in her opinion it was far too short for such a big girl. She'd also insisted on her wearing a borrowed straw boater hat and white cotton gloves and was appalled that Mrs Forester hadn't considered such items essential requirements for a young lady.

All Saturday, Ellie had waited patiently, expecting a billeting officer or even Miss Parfitt to call at the undertakers. She had a little speech prepared, a polite but insistent demand that she was either moved or sent back home. But when no one arrived, Ellie took this to mean no one cared about her at all.

Ellie knew little about churches, and even less of the procedure of a service. Her mother never had time for such things. It smelt funny in here from something they were burning and she didn't like the gruesome pictures of Jesus carrying his cross. It wasn't even a pretty church: compared with some she'd seen, it seemed too high, chilly and bare. She did know, however, that it was God's house. Since no one else seemed to realise how unhappy she was, perhaps he might be a good person to have on her side.

The prayer she offered up was more of a bargain. 'Get me out of this and I'll do anything to please you.' For good measure she asked that he kept her mother and Marleen safe and that the threatened war wouldn't happen after all.

The first hymn gave Ellie hope. It was 'Fight the Good Fight' – one she knew well from school, which she loved singing. The church was packed, right up to the back pews. She could see little Rose across the aisle between two bigger girls with dark hair. Someone had clearly put her blonde hair in rags as she had fat, shiny ringlets. Ellie didn't dare look behind her, but she'd spotted Doris Smithers and Carol Muller as they came in, and both of them looked happy enough. She wondered where the rest of the children from Bancroft Road had been billeted and whether any of them felt as desperate as she did.

Miss Gilbert had made her stay in the house all day yesterday helping with the cleaning, so Ellie knew nothing more of the town than she did on her arrival on Friday. But glancing around here at the congregation, she thought they looked like the people on the posters in stations advertising 'Bracing Skegness' or

'Wonderful Weston-super-Mare', with rosy scrubbed faces, no missing teeth and straight backs.

Seeing all these healthy, happy families dressed in their Sunday best, Ellie could appreciate why her mother had sent her away. Had she been billeted with the motherly lady in a blue polka-dotted dress with artificial daisies on her straw hat, surrounded by her five children, she'd be more than content. But Miss Gilbert wasn't motherly in any way.

Mr Gilbert had barely spoken to her yesterday, but Ellie felt this was more because he was unused to children than from real nastiness. She had heard him speaking to the stonemason out in the yard and his tone was that of a reserved, private man, not another tyrant. As she had seen so little of him, it was hard to make a real judgement, but she had the distinct impression he didn't like his sister any more than Ellie did.

In Ellie's view Miss Gilbert was not right in the head. Aside from her inability to speak unless she was squawking out an order, she was obsessed by cleaning. She never stopped, scrubbing the table, polishing, dusting as if possessed. She'd given Ellie the cutlery to polish, and even though they were soon gleaming, Miss Gilbert inspected each fork and rejected them all, saying she'd missed parts of the prongs. When that task was done to Miss Gilbert's satisfaction, Ellie was sent to scrub the outside lavatory. Compared to the lavatory in Alder Street, and considering it was used only by the stonemason and Mr Gilbert's apprentice, it was clean enough for almost anyone. But Ellie was ordered to scrub the pan, walls, floor and even the wooden rafters above the cistern with disinfectant. Then she had to cut newspaper into sheets exactly four by six inches and thread them on a string to hang from the door. Unfortunately the newspaper was full of interesting snippets and Ellie had her ears boxed for lingering over the task.

Much of the house was still a mystery. She'd helped change the sheets on Miss Gilbert's bed. This was a large but austere room at the back of the house, with old, heavily polished furniture protected by crocheted cloths. Mr Gilbert slept in one of the front rooms, though she hadn't had as much as a glimpse in there. Aside from the bathroom, there were two more unused rooms on this floor and attics above that, reached by a tiny staircase.

Downstairs there was a living-room, parlour and the shop, but it was those closed doors behind the shop which daunted her most. A surreptitious peep over the yard gates had shown a door leading from the side road into one of these rooms, and as she'd heard muted voices coming from it, this had to be the Chapel of Rest. It made her flesh crawl to think a body was lying in there. Each time she looked at Mr Gilbert she wondered how a man could earn a living dealing with such things.

Worse still than the cleaning and the creepiness of the house, was the hunger. Breakfast at seven was a slice of bread and margarine; at twelve she was given a fish paste sandwich, and the dinner served at five in the evening consisted only of a thin slice of ham, half a tomato and a dollop of mashed potato. She watched hungrily as Mr Gilbert ate four thick slices of ham, a fried egg, mushrooms and a mountain of potatoe, plus almost half a loaf of bread spread with thick butter. When she tentatively asked if she could have a slice of bread, Miss Gilbert raised her eyebrows in horror and said she'd 'had quite sufficient'.

Last night, after being cooped up all day in the stuffy house, Ellie had been unable to sleep. She couldn't read, write a letter home or even look out of the window, as Miss Gilbert had tacked black-out material right over it and made it clear it was never to be removed. Although there was electric light in all the other rooms she'd seen into, this one had none, so the black-out seemed unnecessary. Pinpricks of daylight filtered through it, creating a grey, prison-like gloom.

As Ellie lay there tossing and turning, she could hear children's voices in one of the gardens behind Mr Gilbert's workshop. The sound was so evocative of nights at home in Stepney that she wept into her pillow. Sunday had always been the best day of the week. Polly didn't have to work and they spent the day just enjoying being together. Often on warm days they sat out on the doorstep in the afternoon talking to their neighbours, or took a walk to Victoria Park with a picnic. Sometimes Marleen joined them and came back for a supper of bread and cheese, and occasionally there would be an impromptu party down the street. These parties were always family affairs, with everyone welcome from the smallest child to the old people. Those that couldn't get into the host's tiny rooms spilled out into the street or sat on the stairs. So often Ellie and Polly had gone home at around eleven and lay in bed as the sound of revelry wafted up to them. Edna Ross doing her party piece, 'NEllie Dean', Alf Meeks the rag-and-bone man playing his wheezy piano accordion, and a spirited jig on the fiddle from Joe Flagetty, accompanied by the sound of dancing feet.

As Ellie lay in bed she heard the children's mother calling them in. She wiped her eyes on the sheet, trying hard not to think of the bedroom at Alder Street, of her mother snuffing out the gas light and the whispered conversations they had before they drifted off to sleep. Slowly even the pinpricks of light through the black-out disappeared, and the only sound was her own breathing and the creak of the bedsprings as she tossed and turned sleeplessly.

'Let us pray,' the vicar said suddenly, and Ellie hastily dropped to her knees with everyone else. Her stomach was rumbling ominously and she quickly offered up another prayer that Miss Gilbert would realise she was hungry, without her having to appear greedy and adding another black mark to her chart.

During the sermon Ellie forgot her problems as she became engrossed in watching the vicar. He was very theatrical, flinging his arms out wide to stress a point, then leaning his knuckles on the pulpit and glaring at the congregation as if daring someone to get up and argue with him. His message was lost on Ellie, who was too captivated by his extraordinary mouth to listen to his words. It was wide and loose and he twisted it this way and that. At times his false teeth slipped and his tongue would push them back in. Mum would love an impression like that, Ellie thought, mentally rehearsing it.

Ellie became aware of a slight shift in the congregation. The vicar was still speaking, but now he had moved on to something about men joining up. Glancing around, she noticed one man consulting his fob watch. Even Mr Gilbert, who hadn't moved a muscle for the entire sermon, seemed to be on edge.

The vicar left the pulpit suddenly, hurrying down the few stairs, and crossed the chancel towards a wireless set up on a small table.

A low rumble of whispering, clearing of throats and fidgeting in seats puzzled Ellie. As a loud crackling sound came from the wireless, she turned to Mr Gilbert, hoping he would enlighten her.

All at once the sound of Mr Chamberlain's voice boomed out across the church.

'I am speaking to you,' he said, 'from the Cabinet Room at 10 Downing Street. This morning the British Ambassador in Berlin handed the German government a final note, stating that unless we heard from them by eleven o'clock that they were prepared to withdraw their troops from Poland, a state of war would exist between us.

'I have to tell you now that no such undertaking has been received and that consequently, this country is at war with Germany.'

Ellie was stunned. She knew, of course, as everyone did, about Germany invading Poland. Before she left London everyone had been talking about it. But since arriving here, her own problems had taken precedence and the Gilberts hadn't discussed any further developments in front of her.

Horrified gasps came from every quarter of the church and Ellie heard a sob from someone behind her. The vicar held his hand up to silence everyone, indicating that Mr Chamberlain was still speaking.

'I know you will all play your part with calmness and courage. Report for duty in accordance with the instructions you have received. It is of vital importance that you should carry on with your jobs. Now may God bless you all. May he defend the right. It is the evil things that we shall be fighting against, brute force, bad faith, injustice, oppression and persecution, and against them I am certain that the right will prevail.'

The wireless was switched off, and at once a babble of voices broke the stillness in the church.

Ellie turned to Mr Gilbert. 'Does that mean they'll start bombing now?'

There was no time for an answer. The vicar mounted the pulpit again, urging everyone not to panic and reiterating all that the prime minister had said.

'I look to you all to think of your country,' he said earnestly, looking from face to face. 'Today I ask you to remember that each one of us will be tested in the months to come, not just the men expected to fight. From now on we must each rise above self-interest and pool our resources for the common good. The harvest this year is more important than ever before. We have evacuee children in our midst who must be cared for. I beg each and every one of you to give of your best, to offer help and solace to those in need. To maintain the black-out rigorously and follow the instructions you'll be given in the event of an air raid. But above all, I ask you now to pray. For all our brave men who are prepared to give their lives for England. For God's safe deliverance for all of us.'

The vicar's words were still ringing in Ellie's ears as she stepped outside the church porch between Mr and Miss Gilbert, suddenly aware that this was a momentous day, one she'd remember for the rest of her life.

St John's Church was in a narrow street which led down towards the station. Next to it was a small school. There was no churchyard as such, just a few steps down to the pavement. No one was making tracks for home – they were all standing around in groups chattering nineteen to the dozen but otherwise everything looked so normal. A clear blue sky, bright sunshine, the terraced houses opposite just as tranquil as they'd been for the last hundred years. Was it possible that all these people might have to use those hideous gas masks slung over their shoulders? Would German planes really come flying over here and drop bombs?

Despite the knowledge that Britain was now at war, Ellie still had the same objective she'd set out with this morning: to get herself moved away from the Gilberts'. To her delight, she spotted the large woman who'd met them at the station and led them to Corn Exchange. She was standing across the road, outside a gentleman's outfitters with bow windows, chatting to another couple of women. Even at a glance she was clearly a figure of authority. Her wide-brimmed pink hat wouldn't have been out of place in Regent Street, and her matching dress and jacket stood out amongst the more soberly dressed women.

Mr Gilbert paused to speak to an elderly man with a large stomach and a red face.

'What about you, Amos?' the old man asked. 'Will you be called up? Or do you reckon you'll have your work cut out here?'

Ellie glanced at Miss Gilbert. She seemed confused, clutching her prayer book to her thin chest like a shield against expected Germans, staring into the middle distance.

Ellie grasped the opportunity and slid through the crowd in the road towards the woman in the pink hat.

'Excuse me, miss.' Ellie tugged at her sleeve.

'Yes?' The woman turned to Ellie with a look that showed her displeasure at having her conversation interrupted.

'I'm Ellie Forester,' Ellie said breathlessly, one eye on Miss Gilbert, less than fifteen yards away. 'I've been put with Miss Gilbert.'

Suddenly a terrible noise broke out, a wailing sound which made everyone look around in astonishment, covering their ears.

'Bombs,' someone yelled. 'They're coming!'

Ellie was rooted to the spot in shock. All around her people began to run, some back to the safety of the church, others bolting for their homes, dragging children by the hands. She looked up and saw nothing but blue sky, and at the same time someone pushed her firmly in the back and hissed at her to get in the church.

It was Mr Gilbert who'd pushed her, but once inside he seemed calm. His sister, however, was already cowering in a pew. She had her hands over her head, her face ashen, her lips moving as if gabbling out a prayer.

'I'm quite certain they are only testing the siren,' Mr Gilbert remarked, nudging his sister in a gesture that said she should pull herself together. 'I really don't think the Germans have got themselves organised this quickly.'

Some of the older ladies looked quite faint with shock. The lady in the pink hat, whom Ellie so badly wanted to speak to, was offering her smelling salts around.

The siren stopped, and a few minutes later a different one wailed out.

'That's the "all clear",' Mr Gilbert said knowledgeably. 'You see, I was quite right, they were only testing. But in future, Ellie, you must act as soon as you hear it. Next time it could be the real thing.'

Ellie wasn't concerned with next times. She'd lost her opportunity to speak to the lady in the pink hat and she had a horrible feeling she would be stuck with Miss Gilbert for several days before she got another chance.

'You can sit in the living-room and write to your mother this afternoon,' Miss Gilbert said as she sluiced the kitchen sink round.

They had eaten roast beef for dinner, followed by apple pie and custard, but though it was the biggest meal Ellie had eaten here, she was still hungry. She'd seen Miss Gilbert pour some thick dripping into a stone basin and her mouth had watered imagining it spread thickly on bread.

Mr Gilbert had gone into the parlour, a room at the front of the house which Ellie had been told to keep out of, and for the past hour she had helped with the washing up and yet more cleaning of the kitchen.

Ellie brightened up at the prospect of writing home. It seemed simple: she'd tell her mother the truth about this place and she'd come and get her.

'You're a good cook,' Ellie said, hoping to ingratiate herself with the woman, if only to get some peace until she left. 'We 'ardly ever 'ave roast beef at 'ome.'

'I wouldn't expect a child from the slums to eat such things.' Miss Gilbert pursed her lips and looked pointedly at a gravy stain on Ellie's dress. 'You are a very slovenly girl. Perhaps when you've spent a few hours scrubbing clothes, you'll learn to be more careful.'

Ellie sat at the small table in the living-room scribbling away, happy enough now that Miss Gilbert had left her alone.

It was a small, bare room overlooking the yard. Just two wooden-armed easy chairs either side of an ugly fireplace, a wireless on a shelf and the table she was using by the window. The bookcase offered no entertainment, only a set of encyclopaedias, a large Bible and three or four recipe books. As in all the rooms she'd been into, the walls were dun-coloured. Any design on the paper had long since faded, and the only picture was of the King and Queen at the coronation.

Writing to her mother wasn't as good as talking to her, but it was close. She poured out all that had happened since she arrived, the slaps, the hunger and her conviction the woman was barmy. But spite wore thin after a bit and she moved on to describe the place.

'I'm writing this in the living-room,' she wrote, smiling as she thought of it. 'I don't know why they call it that as it's as dead as the bodies in Mr Gilbert's coffins. They only come in here to listen to the wireless and the chairs are placed just so. The window looks on to the yard and there's a row of headstones and a few urns out there which give me the willies. I think the bodies are in the room across the passage which she said I mustn't poke into. There's a funny pong coming from it. But I'll try and get a peek before I leave. You should see the parlour, Mum! It's packed with the kind of old furniture like in the props room at the Empire. But I'm not allowed in there either, except to dust. The only place I kind of like is Mr Gilbert's workshop. It used to be a stable when he had a horse-drawn hearse and it's still got old bits and pieces hanging up. It smells lovely in there, all different kinds of wood, but I suppose it's a bit spooky with all the coffins standing up on end. Mr Gilbert told me today he's going to start me trimming coffins tomorrow. Is this what you meant about me learning something useful?'

Ellie started to laugh to herself, imagining her mother reading it to Marleen, for a moment forgetting how awful it was here. She moved on, explaining how Miss Gilbert watered down the milk and measured the loaf with string, and her conviction the woman gorged herself in private because two or three times she'd seen her with crumbs round her mouth.

'Please let me come home, Mum,' she finished off. 'I'm no good away from you. We should be together.'

Finally finished, she folded up the three pages, put them in the envelope and sealed it down. She was just addressing it when Miss Gilbert came in.

'Can I go and post it?' Ellie asked. 'Mum gave me a stamp.'

'Go and get it then,' Miss Gilbert said, half smiling, as if pleased Ellie had kept quiet for so long.

Had Ellie been used to devious adults she might have wondered why she was allowed upstairs suddenly. But all she could think of was being allowed out on her own and the chance of doing a little exploring.

She scampered up the stairs, found the stamp she'd been given and even stopped for a moment in the bathroom to dab away the gravy stain on her dress. But as she ran back downstairs and saw Miss Gilbert, her stomach turned over.

The woman was sitting down, the envelope ripped open on her lap. She was reading the letter.

Ellie didn't stop to think as she lunged forward and grabbed it from Miss Gilbert's hands.

'Oih, that's private,' she said. 'You ain't got no right to read it!'

'It's just as well I did.' Miss Gilbert snatched it back, ripping it into shreds. 'How dare you write such slanderous lies?'

'There ain't no lies,' Ellie said, her legs turning to water. 'You know there ain't.'

Miss Gilbert moved quickly, slamming the door and standing in front of it. 'You minx,' she said, eyes narrowing behind her glasses. 'If you think you can laugh at me behind my back and make up stories, then you're mistaken. Hasn't it occurred to you your mother sent you here to get rid of you?'

'No she never,' Ellie said indignantly. 'She sent me away to be safe.'

For a moment there was silence. Ellie was shaken by her own stupidity at not anticipating that Miss Gilbert would find a way to read the letter, but she was also cut to the quick by the woman's last remark.

Miss Gilbert was also shaken, not only by the girl's startlingly incisive, well-written letter, but the knowledge that if this got out in the town she might find herself in trouble.

Grace Gilbert was what her own father called 'a tortured soul'. Even as a child she had never been quite right, a strange, solitary child who hid herself away talking to imaginary friends. Old Mrs Gilbert had blamed a severe attack of impetigo when Grace was eighteen for most of her problems. It may indeed have been the start of her obsessive cleaning, but hardly explained her maniacal fits of temper, or her spiteful and vicious nature. But her father must have been keenly aware of his daughter's instability, for when he finally died he left the house and business to Amos with the proviso that his son was to take responsibility for his sister.

She was forty-five, three years older than Amos, and over the years she'd become more and more cranky, spiteful and bitter. She had no friends and no interests aside from her home and reading this letter had somehow stripped away the illusion she'd clung to that she was better than other people.

'I wanna go 'ome,' Ellie said. She was frightened by the strange intensity in Miss Gilbert's eyes, but she was also just a little ashamed of what she'd written. 'I'm sorry for what I said about you, it weren't very nice. But I'm missing my mum.'

Miss Gilbert thought quickly. She had decided to take in an evacuee first and foremost to raise her standing in the church. Just last week the vicar had told the whole congregation that it was their Christian duty. When she discovered she would get ten shillings a week too, that put a seal on it. She desperately wanted to punish the girl, but she knew if she lashed out now, so soon after the girl's arrival, the billeting officer would soon get to hear of it and before long it would be right round the church and town. Besides, Amos approved of the girl and he might take her part. Perhaps it might be better to overlook this incident for now. The girl was at least useful. There was more than one way of killing a cat.

'We'll get one thing straight.' Miss Gilbert wiggled her finger at Ellie, but she softened her voice as far as she was able. 'We all have to make sacrifices for the war effort. My brother and I took you in to do *our* part. You must do yours by following our rules. Now you'll sit down again and write your mother a proper letter, telling her how pleasant it is here. Do you want to make your mother miserable?'

'Course I don't,' Ellie agreed, although she felt like crying. 'But she wouldn't like me to make out I was 'appy 'ere when I'm not.'

Miss Gilbert sniffed. She had picked this girl because she was fat and plain, assuming she'd be docile and suitably grateful too. But her appearance was deceptive. The girl was sharp as a razor, inquisitive and bold, and she'd need watching continuously.

45

'What have I done to you?' Miss Gilbert rolled her eyes alarmingly. 'You have a nice room, you're fed. Clearly, from what I've read, you are a very greedy girl, and that's why you're so fat. Am I wrong to give you a suitable diet?'

This insult was the last straw. Ellie began to cry. 'But you don't like me. I don't want to be in someone's 'ouse what 'ates me.'

Grace Gilbert was unmoved by the girl's tears and a little baffled by this last statement, as she didn't really know what 'liking' someone meant. In fact Ellie's face disturbed her: those dark eyes were too penetrating, her mouth too wide when she smiled. Amos had already expressed the view that she was 'a happy soul' and that sounded too much like approval.

'You haven't given me a chance to like you,' Miss Gilbert said crisply. 'From what I've seen so far you are a liar, greedy and lazy. You don't even speak correctly. Now sit down and write a proper letter to your mother and let's have no more of this.'

Ellie wanted to defend herself, but at the same time she was relieved no punishment was about to be dished out. 'I'm none of those things, and Mum didn't send me away to get rid of me,' she said stubbornly, wiping her eyes with the back of her hand. 'She hoped I'd have a better 'ome than in London, that's all. And I can't 'elp the way I speak.'

Miss Gilbert half smiled. Inadvertently the girl had shown her the tack she must take. 'Well, my dear, just write and reassure her. I'm sure she's got worries enough without you adding to them. Let me have the letter when you've done and I'll enclose one from myself and my brother too. We'll say no more about this unpleasantness.'

'Might I speak to Ellie in private?' Mrs Dunwoody said, ignoring Miss Gilbert's offer of a chair at the kitchen table. 'Perhaps in your parlour?'

'If you think that's necessary.' Miss Gilbert bristled with indignation, casting a baleful glance at Ellie. 'Though goodness knows what you hope to gain from it.'

Ellie controlled her desire to smirk in triumph. Mrs Dunwoody was the woman she'd started to speak to outside the church, almost a week ago. She had called two days later but Miss Gilbert wouldn't leave them to talk alone. Clearly Mrs Dunwoody was determined not to be put off this time.

'I just wish to get to know Ellie better,' Mrs Dunwoody said diplomatically. 'I'd be derelict in my duties as billeting officer if I didn't try to smooth out any little problems and worries and it's easier on a one-to-one basis.'

'Take Mrs Dunwoody to the parlour then.' Miss Gilbert gave Ellie a scathing look. 'I have work to do anyway.'

Once inside the parlour, Mrs Dunwoody sat down on the settee and patted the seat next to her for Ellie to join her. 'Now my dear, how are things?'

'Please move me,' Ellie whispered. She was intimidated by the parlour, which seemed to reflect Miss Gilbert's character more than any other room in the house. A fussy, over-furnished room, with scarcely space to walk around. Uncomfortable, over-stuffed chairs, highly polished walnut cabinets full of china and glass and dozens of old china figurines, vases and cut-glass bowls, each one sitting on a lace doily. The many pictures were all of biblical scenes. A large aspidistra sitting in an ugly green bowl in the lace-curtained window blocked out most of the natural light.

Ellie blurted out everything, trying hard not to cry and make herself look pathetic.

Since the incident of her letter home, Miss Gilbert had been marginally nicer. She'd slightly increased the size of the meals, she'd suggested Ellie should join the library, and even allowed her out alone for a couple of hours in the afternoons.

The town was fascinating. Just a short walk from High Baxter Street, where she was living, was the old abbey with its beautiful gardens. She'd found an ancient charnel house in the graveyard behind the Norman tower and been spooked by an inscription about a nine-year-old girl struck by lightning. There was a museum called Moyse's Hall full of strange exhibits, including a death mask from 1827 of a murderer called William Corder and his scalp and ear. Along with these thrillingly gruesome remains there were instruments of torture dating back to the time when the place had been the town gaol.

But loneliness was getting Ellie down most. The local children jeered at evacuees, and she hadn't run into any of her old classmates yet. She missed not only her mother but the people at the Empire and those from Alder Street. At home she had only to step out into the street and there was someone to talk to. She had always felt secure and cared for, but here she felt as if she was just waiting for time to pass, ignored and unwanted.

'There isn't anywhere to move you to,' Mrs Dunwoody said with a sigh. Her fingers moved up to fiddle with some beads at her neck. She knew Miss Gilbert was strange: rumours about her were always flying around the town. But she couldn't believe it was as bad as the child was saying. 'We had over seven hundred boys and girls sent to us here, not to mention all the mothers with small children, and I've got problems with some of them which are a great deal more serious than yours. Just give it a little longer, my dear. School will be starting again on Monday. You and the other evacuees will be attending in the afternoons, the local children in the mornings. Perhaps that will ease things a little for you. But Miss Gilbert hasn't any complaints about you, Ellie, and Mr Gilbert stated how helpful you've been to him.'

'I don't mind Mr Gilbert,' Ellie said quietly, afraid Miss Gilbert was listening outside the door. 'I've been 'elping 'im line coffins with scrim and I quite like it. It's 'er!' She jerked her head towards the door.

She couldn't adequately explain how unpleasant it was to feel she was being watched constantly, or how she felt something nasty was about to happen.

'Have you heard from your mother?' Mrs Dunwoody was aware that almost all of the evacuees' problems were just plain homesickness.

'Yes.' Ellie frowned. 'The theatre she was working in 'as closed down and until it opens again she ain't got a job.' Her mother had made light of this, saying she was going to work as a waitress in Lyons Corner House, but Ellie had sensed she was very anxious about money, because she'd said she couldn't manage to enclose any pocket money just yet.

Mrs Dunwoody was the wife of a banker and lived in an elegant detached Georgian house by the Abbey. Until these evacuee children landed in the town her only real contact with the working classes had been her servants. Her eyes had been opened in the last week, though, when she met the children from Stepney. A great many of them didn't even have a change of underwear; they had holes in their shoes; almost all of them were undernourished and they spoke so badly.

Ellie, however, was as fat as butter, had decent clothes and it was obvious from the girl's demeanour that she was not only well loved and cared for, but also sensible enough to appreciate that in an emergency such as this, sacrifices had to be made.

'Well, you mustn't add to her problems,' Mrs Dunwoody said gently. 'I'm sure all the theatres will open again soon, especially as they haven't had any air raids yet in London. Let's see how you feel once you're back at school, eh? Write Mummy a nice cheerful letter and keep your pecker up. If you still want to move in a few weeks' time, I'll see what I can arrange.'

Ellie gave a glum smile. Mrs Dunwoody was kindly enough, but she hadn't really grasped anything she'd been told. She was just another of those rich do-gooders, like the ones who swanned down to the East End and made sympathetic noises about slum conditions. She didn't understand why Ellie resented Miss Gilbert reading both the letters she wrote and received. Or what it felt like to be hungry all the time and treated worse than a Victorian scullery maid. Neither could she understand Ellie's dilemma that even if she could tell her mother the truth about what it was like in this house, she was reluctant to do so because sending Ellie the fare home would strain her mother's finances still more.

'I'd better be going.' Mrs Dunwoody got up. 'I've got so many serious problems to deal with, children wetting the bed, others with lice. Some children won't eat, others are stealing food. As for some of the mothers with babies!' She shook her head, as if baffled by it all. 'Would you believe that one mother complained because it was too quiet here? I don't think it dawns on some people that this country is at war and we have to put up with a few inconveniences.'

Chapter Three

Dagenham, March 1940

Bonny Phillips stood at the top of the stairs, ears pricked up. It was after ten on Friday night, and she'd been sent to bed an hour earlier, but a certain tension between her parents during the evening and now their raised voices had made her creep out of her bedroom to try and discover what was going on.

'I've been over and over it.' Her father's voice sounded weary with exasperation. 'We must do what's right for her, Doris.'

It was pitch dark on the stairs, except for a faint golden glow beneath the living-room door. Bonny shivered in her thin nightdress and the sisal stair carpet prickled her bare feet.

'I don't want Bonny to go, Arn,' her mother replied, her voice strangled as if she was crying. 'She's not quite eleven, just a baby, I couldn't bear being separated from her.'

'Do you think I *want* her to go?' Arnold replied. 'But this isn't sending her off to just anyone, she'll have a good life with Miss Wynter. She'll be safe when the bombing starts and she'll have her dancing lessons free.'

Bonny had never been away from home, not even for one night. Last September, when most of the other children at school were evacuated, she was disappointed when her parents declined to send her too. Home was 88 Flamstead Road on the Becontree estate in Dagenham, a very ordinary council house. When many of the children returned home at Christmas with amazing stories about country cottages and big houses at the seaside, Bonny had felt resentful.

In fact, the war had been a great disappointment in every way so far. Last year, when they'd all been given gas masks and practised going into the air raid shelter in the school opposite, Bonny had thought it was all going to be very exciting. She'd even felt a bit like a heroine staying behind at home, facing danger. But nothing had happened, other than planes droning overhead. Even when the siren went off it was only to practise. It had been an exceptionally cold winter, thick snow, pipes freezing up and shortages of everything. Grown-ups talked about rationing all the time, and now Dad had dug up most of the back garden to grow vegetables. They called it the Phoney War. Almost all the evacuees had come home again to stay. Yet from what her dad was saying, it sounded as if something was going to happen at last.

Bonny Phillips was an exceptionally beautiful child, with long, silky blonde hair, wide, almost turquoise blue eyes and the kind of soft, plump lips that made even the most hardened child-hater weaken. Perhaps if she'd been a little less beautiful, or her parents just a little less obvious in their adoration of her, she might have developed a nicer nature. But as it was, Bonny Phillips had an inflated idea of her own importance and a total disregard for others' feelings. Mrs Salcombe, the Phillipses' next-door neighbour, had a blunt explanation for anyone who cared to mention how spoilt Bonny was. 'Doris and Arnold thought she was a bloomin' miracle, and it's another bloomin' miracle someone hasn't strangled the little bleeder.'

Doris was eighteen in 1907 when Arnold Phillips came to mend the boiler at Dr Freeman's house in Islington where she worked as a maid. She was a dumpy, plain girl with mousy hair, so shy she rarely even spoke to the female staff, let alone a man. But she was taken by the tall, slender young man with blond hair and a thin moustache and when he asked her to walk out with him on her night off she sensed right away that he was the only man for her.

Their romance flourished as they discovered how much they had in common. They both came from large, poor families, Arnold's in Shadwell, Doris's in Bethnal Green, and both had a fierce desire to better themselves. Doris was impressed by Arnold's knowledge of machinery, his gentle, affectionate nature, while Arnold fell for her bright blue eyes, her clear complexion and her ladylike demeanour.

They married two years later, in 1909, and set up home in the same tenement in Bethnal Green where Doris's parents lived. Dr Freeman gave them a bone china tea-set as fine as anything he had in his house and the housekeeper, Mrs Oakes, gave them a set of linen sheets. They had such high hopes then. The two-room flat was only temporary; soon they would have a house of their own and children.

But their dreams were not to be. Doris's first child was still-born. Arnold was called up in the First War, went to France, and returned a different man, haunted by images of the trenches, his teeth rotting and his hair falling out. But they still counted their blessings. Arnold had survived, when so many of his friends had been killed. They had one another and, even if their home was grim, things would get better. A few years later, once Arnold was settled as a fitter in a factory, finally putting the war behind him, Doris became pregnant again. But when their little boy died, at just a few weeks old, they were both so crushed by grief that they gave up struggling to improve themselves.

A glimpse into their home as the New Year bells rang out for 1928 would have shown a forlorn couple, who had nothing more from twenty years of marriage and hard work than a few pieces of shabby furniture. The bone china tea-set Dr Freeman had given them as a wedding present was put away, wrapped in newspaper because they knew now they'd never have use for it. The linen sheets were threadbare. Their wedding photograph on the sideboard was fading, just like their dreams.

They were old beyond their years. Doris's once clear complexion was muddy, her blue eyes weary, her body like a sagging bolster. Arnold was stooped, almost bald, racked by coughing fits he'd suffered from since the war, made worse by the damp flat. That year they hadn't even bothered to put up Christmas decorations, or to go out and join in the New Year celebrations. They'd long since accepted that there was nothing to look forward to: Doris too old at forty even to hope for a child, both sets of parents dead, brothers and sisters scattered. Life was just one long, dreary road which appeared to lead nowhere.

It was just a few days into the new year when they received a letter telling them that the tenement was to be pulled down as part of slum clearance and offering them a council house in Dagenham. After a lifetime of disappointments their delight was tempered with a suspicion that there might be a catch in the offer, but they agreed to see the house anyway.

In later years Doris was to count February 1st, 1928, the day they saw 88 Flamstead Road for the first time, as important an anniversary as her wedding day and every bit as joyful. It was bitterly cold and thick snow had fallen overnight but that made it all the more beautiful and memorable.

It was enough to be given a new start in a three-bedroomed house with back and front gardens, electric light and an inside lavatory. But Flamstead Road overlooked a school surrounded by playing fields. As they looked out of the bedroom window, rosy-cheeked children were playing in the snow, and the air was fresh and clean. All the sadness and disillusionment of the past just faded away.

Their happiness mounted in the next few months. First Arnold got taken on at Ford's Motor Company with better wages than he'd previously earned, and then, unbelievably, Doris found she was pregnant.

That summer and autumn were blissful. Back in the tenement they had shared a lavatory with six other families, and cooked on an open fire. If they dared to hang washing outside on the communal lines, there was a good chance of it being stolen. Rats, mice, bugs in the walls, were all part of life in Bethnal Green, as were drunken fights, noisy neighbours and the stink of drains and uncleared rubbish.

Now they had a gas cooker and a copper to wash their clothes and heat water for the bath. When they opened the windows they weren't subjected to noise and gritty dust, just fresh, clean air. To sit on their own clean lavatory for as long as they liked, knowing no one would bang on the door and ask them to hurry up, or to wallow in a real bath, then just pull out the plug without the burden or mess of emptying it, was heaven.

Arnold's health improved as he tended the garden in his spare time. Doris sewed and knitted for the baby. Each strong kick reassured her nothing could go wrong this time and as each day passed Doris seemed to regain the youth and vitality that had drained away in Bethnal Green.

Their baby was born in April 1929, a small, but healthy, six-pound girl, and although they had intended to name her Hilda after her maternal grandmother, Doris took it into her head to call her Bonny, a name she'd seen in a film magazine.

A great many people suggested that Bonny was pretty because she had been awaited for so long. Behind Doris's back they often spitefully added that her looks wouldn't last, that she'd soon be as ordinary as her middle-aged parents. But Bonny confounded them all by not only retaining her looks, but becoming prettier with each passing year.

Moving to Dagenham and all at once finding their dreams fulfilled had a profound effect on the Phillipses. Doris became house-proud, checking to see her windows were the cleanest in the street, her baby's nappies the whitest. Gradually Arnold was affected by it too, making sure his roses were bigger and the lawn neater than his neighbours'. Doris would walk proudly to the shops with Bonny sitting up in her pram in a sparkling white dress and starched sun bonnet, and even though she observed the effect the Depression was having on some of her neighbours, instead of feeling sympathy for those who had lost their jobs, she began to feel she and Arnold were just a cut above others.

Arnold was fortunate that as well as being a diligent worker, he was liked by his superiors. Although other men were laid off at Ford's, he not only kept his job but was promoted, becoming foreman of his section, and this in turn increased their feelings of superiority. If Arnold sometimes felt saddened that he was no longer 'one of the lads', he kept it to himself and put his energies into working overtime to buy the little luxuries he and Doris had always dreamed of.

Bit by bit, the old shabby furniture in their living-room was replaced by a brown Rexine three-piece suite, an oak gateleg table with matching chairs, an Axminster red carpet with gold scrolls and an elegant standard lamp. They had two sets of curtains – heavy red ones for the winter and flowery cotton ones for the summer – but Doris's pride and joy was a walnut, glass-fronted china cabinet where she could display the tea-set given to them by Dr Freeman and a set of glasses which looked like real crystal.

But Bonny was the axis Doris and Arnold's world spun on. Everything they did was with her in mind.

Arnold never had a pint in the pub on the way home because he had to get back to read Bonny a bedtime story. Doris would stop anything she was doing if Bonny wanted her. Every fine Sunday they took her out for picnics; on summer evenings they took her to the park together; if she was fretful she slept between her parents; if she was naughty they blamed themselves.

By the time Bonny was five and starting school across the road, Doris was already looking ahead, sure that Dagenham didn't have enough to offer their precious daughter. She cringed when she saw how other children played in the streets and saw danger lurking behind every bush and tree.

Without Bonny at home during the day, Doris had so much more free time. When she heard that a woman's group based in Romford were looking for new members to expand their charity work, it seemed the perfect way to break into what she called 'polite society'.

In a year of helping out in soup kitchens for the unemployed, sewing circles, hospital visiting and fund-raising, Doris learned a great deal. She managed to modulate her cockney accent and to dress with a little more style, but above all she discovered that middle-class people gave their daughters dancing lessons.

Arnold was hard to convince. He saw it as a waste of good money to take his daughter to Romford every Saturday morning and pay a shilling a lesson, not to mention buying a uniform and special shoes. But Doris was adamant. Bonny was going to dance.

From the first moment that Bonny put on her ballet shoes and her short, pink tunic, it was clear she was made to dance. Doris would have believed this even if her pretty daughter had thundered about like an elephant, but Miss Estelle the dancing teacher made it quite plain that Bonny Phillips was talented.

One lesson a week turned to two, then three. Doris bought cheaper cuts of meat, only did charity work when she could walk there and made do with her old clothes to find the extra money needed. Once Arnold saw his daughter in her first show, wearing a pink tutu and with flowers in her hair, he wiped away a few proud tears and said no more about the expense.

'Look, Doris, Dagenham's bound to be bombed, it's a sitting target so close to the docks,' Arnold said. 'We kept Bonny home when all the other kids were evacuated because we didn't know where she'd end up. But this is different.'

Bonny sat on the stairs in the dark, her heart pounding with excitement rather than fear.

'But nothing's happened,' Doris said tearfully. 'Most of the children have come back. Mrs Ellis said the woman her boys were billeted with had a stick taken to their backs. Iris Osbourne's girls never got enough to eat.'

'This war won't be phoney much longer,' Arnold said firmly, sucking on his pipe. 'The Germans are advancing all the time. I hear things at work. How would we feel if our little Bonny got hurt? The shelter won't stand up to a direct hit. Miss Wynter won't beat her, or starve her – she *wants* Bonny to live with her. Be fair, Doris, she's a real lady!'

Bonny frowned, thinking hard. The name Miss Wynter rang a bell, but she couldn't think why.

'But Sussex is such a long way,' Doris sobbed. 'We wouldn't be able to see her very often. She might get in with some rough children.'

'Can you imagine any rough children living in a place like Amberley?' her father snorted. 'And don't you think a dancing teacher knows how to control children? Be sensible, Doris, if we turn Miss Wynter down now, she'll take another child and then if the government insists the children evacuate again, we'll have no say in anything.'

All at once Bonny remembered who Miss Wynter

was. She was Miss Estelle's sister. She'd been staying in London at Christmas and come to see the show. A tall, elegant woman in a fur coat, another dancing teacher.

'I don't want porridge.' Bonny's lip curled petulantly as her mother put the steaming bowl in front of her. 'I want a boiled egg and toast.'

'I couldn't get any eggs,' Doris said patiently. 'I queued for two hours yesterday and they'd all gone by the time I was served. Now be a good girl and eat your porridge.'

'No.' Bonny pouted, shaking her head so violently that one lone rag came loose on her head and a springy ringlet tumbled out. 'I hate porridge.'

Doris sighed. Hardly a day went past when her daughter didn't make a scene about something. If it wasn't about her breakfast it would be about the colour of her hair ribbons, or which dress she was to wear. Common sense told her to eat the porridge herself and let her daughter go hungry to teach her a lesson. But Doris couldn't do that.

Deep down, Doris knew that her daughter had some undesirable traits, but she couldn't admit it, not even to herself. When Bonny's teacher complained that she led other children into trouble, Doris and Arnold believed she'd got it round the wrong way. Bonny's many tall stories weren't lies, but signs of 'a vivid imagination'. When she refused food they never saw it as a ploy to gain attention, but as a reminder that she was 'delicate'.

'What about a sausage?' Doris asked, sure Bonny sensed something was going on behind the scenes. 'I had one put aside for Daddy, because he's got the day off, but I'm sure he wouldn't mind you having it.'

Bonny hesitated before replying. Her father always worked on Saturdays; if he had today off it had to be because of what they were talking about last night.

Under the circumstances, it might be better to be more amenable.

'I don't want Daddy's breakfast.' Bonny made this sound rather noble. 'I'll eat the porridge.'

If Bonny were to be asked why she was so contrary with her mother, it was doubtful she'd be able to come up with any sensible answer. She knew she was loved, that she had everything any child could reasonably want, far more than most children on the Becontree estate had. Yet Bonny resented her parents. They didn't allow her to play in the street or the park with other children. Her mother even met her outside the school gates at home time, despite living opposite. In the evenings she could hear other kids playing rounders on the school field until it was dark, but she had to be content with playing Snakes and Ladders with her mother or reading a book. These same kids teased her and called her 'mummy's girl', and imitated the way Mrs Phillips tried to speak posh.

At the same time, Bonny was getting glimpses of another world through her dancing lessons, and it seemed she was excluded from this one too. The girls at dancing had posh voices, their fathers collected them in smart cars, they spoke of ponies, parties and going to Brownie camp. Bonny had seen them look down their narrow noses at her mother's worn coat and on more than one occasion she'd been asked what it was like to live on a council estate.

Bonny didn't fit in either world. She didn't want to be shabbily dressed with a snail trail under her nose and give up dancing so she could belong in Dagenham. Neither did she want to be like the prim goody-goodies of Romford with their swanky manners. But she hated being a misfit.

Today, though, Bonny's behaviour was based on uncertainty. Although being sent away from home sounded exciting, she was frightened of the unknown.

*

'Morning, sunshine!'

Her father's warm greeting made Bonny turn in her seat to smile at him. Although she often felt irritated by her mother, she had no such feelings about him.

'Why aren't you going to work?' she asked innocently.

'Because I want to be with my princess,' he said, kissing her cheek.

'Bristles!' Bonny rubbed her cheek indignantly. He hadn't washed or shaved yet, his braces over his vest. It wasn't often she saw him in such a state – her mother always insisted on the proprieties of at least a shirt, and usually a tie too.

He sat down at the kitchen table. Doris put the sausage in the pan, then turned to pour her husband's tea. Once again, Bonny felt the tension between them.

'Are you taking me to dancing this morning?' she asked her father.

Dancing classes had been halted for a while when war first broke out and some of the pupils were evacuated, but they'd been back to normal for some time because the expected air raids hadn't come.

'You won't be going today,' Arnold said, stirring his tea with more force than was necessary. His smile was strained, accentuating the deep lines on his face, and his blue eyes were washed out and weary. 'We have something to tell you, princess.'

As her father gently explained about Miss Wynter and her cottage in Sussex, unaware that his daughter had heard it all before, Bonny found herself taking in all the familiar details of the kitchen which for so long she'd taken for granted.

The glossy cream walls, the wooden draining-board, scrubbed white by her mother. The copper in the corner, the white enamel bread bin on top, the copper stick, scrubbing board and wooden tongs hanging on hooks beside it. Her father's shaving mug next to his mirror on the window sill, a Reckitt's blue bag resting on a tin lid ready for the next wash. The kitchen cabinet had its flap down, half a loaf sitting on it. All at once these so-familiar things seemed very dear to her.

'Are you listening?'

Bonny blinked and looked back at her father. 'Yes, Daddy,' she said, shocked to see his eyes were glistening with tears. She had often wished her father was younger: she disliked his scraggy neck and his baldness and bad teeth embarrassed her. But she didn't notice those failings now, remembering only that he always had time to talk and play with her. Everything he'd told her sounded like a fairy-tale. To live with a dancing teacher in a beautiful house in the country and have private lessons! She wanted to go, and yet . . .

'But when will it be?' she asked him.

Arnold gazed at his daughter, mentally cursing the Germans for forcing such a dilemma upon him. He didn't think he could stand one day without a kiss from those rosy soft lips. The house would be as silent as a tomb without Bonny's chatter, and Doris would be unbearable with nothing to occupy her.

'Tomorrow,' he said, his voice cracking. 'We'll take you there on the train.'

Lydia Wynter paused at her sitting-room door as she put on her coat, casting her eyes around it to make sure everything was perfect.

The scent from the apple logs on the fire was delightful, mingling with beeswax polish. A vase of early daffodils on the window sill and the sunshine playing on the polished wood floor brought spring into the room. Lydia could guess what little Bonny's home was like: she'd driven through Dagenham often enough to get a picture of tiny, dull rooms behind spotless lace curtains. How would she react to living somewhere so different?

Briar Bank was a house of great character, quite unlike any of the other cottages in the village, which were mainly thatched and tiny. Built into a bank, on street level it had three floors, at the back only two, surrounded by an artfully designed terraced garden. The arrangement and size of the rooms made the house perfect for teaching dancing in. The floor in the lowest room was specially sprung, its walls covered in mirrors, and even with ten or twelve heavy-footed girls practising, the rest of the house remained relatively peaceful. There was also a tiny changing-room and an entrance separate from her living quarters.

A small open staircase led up to the hall. The large, sunny sitting-room took up one side of the house, overlooking the lawn; on the other side, a kitchen, dining-room and a study-cum-music room faced a shrubbery and rockery. Upstairs again were three bedrooms and a bathroom. Lydia's simple yet rather expensive tastes made the house look delightfully bright. Honey-coloured polished wood floors, deep, soft settees and armchairs and plain white walls set off the dozens of beautiful water-colours by her late grandmother.

Lydia Wynter was thirty-five and, although labelled as a 'spinster', which suggested she was to be pitied for her single state, she was in fact blissfully content with her life. She had nothing to gain by marriage, except perhaps insurance against loneliness in her old age. She had a private income, a lovely home, a car and still plenty of admirers, two of whom would marry her at the drop of a ballet shoe.

Even the most cantankerous of old men referred to her as 'a fine figure of a woman'. She was still as slim and shapely as she had been at eighteen, with glossy chestnut hair and a clear, glowing complexion. She stood out from the other women in the village not just because she was taller, slimmer and more expensively dressed, but because of a certain poise and radiance they lacked.

She had never had any maternal feelings. Not once in her life had she ever wanted to nurse a baby or wheel a pram and the thought of pregnancy and child-birth made her feel quite sick. Teaching dancing and music was a different thing altogether. To Lydia, each pupil was like a sculptor's lump of marble; it was her job to chisel away the rough parts, to bring out beauty and grace. Just now and again she produced what she considered a masterpiece, a child who could win a scholarship to a ballet school or music college. But mostly her work was to give children social skills. To play the piano for their family's enjoyment, to give them confidence when they took part in shows, some-times just to learn to do the waltz and the quickstep well enough to pass muster at a ball.

Lydia certainly had no intention of becoming a foster mother when she went to stay with her sister Estelle at Christmas in Romford. Yet for some inexplicable reason the moment she saw Bonny Phillips a strange yearning sensation coursed through her body.

Lydia was helping Estelle to get the girls into their costumes for the first number of the show at the church hall. It was chaos; around twenty girls, ranging from five to fourteen, were all chattering at once, the floor and the chairs were covered in tutus, satin dresses and tap and ballet shoes. Estelle was admonishing one great lump of a girl for eating jam sandwiches and daubing her already creased tunic with blackcur-rant jam.

Then Lydia heard a voice which rang above all the others.

'Don't worry if you forget the steps, Amy. Everyone will be looking at me anyway.'

Lydia turned quickly, astonished at hearing such arrogance, but instead of cutting the girl down to size she could only stare.

The girl was wearing nothing but white knickers and a vest, ringlets cascading over her shoulders like gold springs. She had bright blue eyes and a mouth with the most perfect Cupid's bow Lydia had ever seen.

Estelle pounced on the child and told her off in no uncertain manner, but Lydia noted how the girl merely smiled and shrugged her shoulders, so sure of herself she wasn't shamed in any way.

All through the entire evening's performance, Lydia saw the girl was right. Everyone's eyes were on her. It wasn't so much that she was an exceptional dancer – there were others as good – but she had star quality. Her smile as she danced was real, flashing out at the audience, giving each one of them a high. In the tap sequences she alone had true style, and although she clearly lacked the dedication to become a ballerina, her grace was achingly beautiful.

During Christmas Lydia learned everything her sister knew about the child. Elderly parents, a mother who was something of a social climber, an overindulgent father. Estelle expressed the view that Bonny Phillips was spoilt, a trouble-maker, a liar and something of a bully. But she also said that maybe if someone took Bonny in hand she could go a long way.

It was during a snowstorm in January that Lydia came up with the idea of offering Bonny a home for the duration of the war. She'd often felt guilty that she hadn't volunteered to take an evacuee when war broke out and there was talk in the village that people like herself might have part of their house requisitioned as a billet, or that she might be conscripted to do war work. A child in the house might be the ideal way of avoiding these unpleasant things. She was certain from what she knew of the Phillipses that Estelle would present the idea to them in a way they'd find hard to refuse.

It was not as easy as Lydia had expected. Letters passed between her and the Phillipses and on both visits to London Doris made sure Bonny wasn't present, as if afraid her child would be snatched against her will. It was Mr Phillips who finally talked his wife round.

'On your head be it,' Lydia said to herself in the hall mirror as she tilted her velour hat at a rakish angle. 'You're really too set in your ways to think of being a foster mother. She'll probably scratch the furniture and ruin your social life, and Mrs Phillips will hold you responsible if she so much as catches a cold.'

'Hello, Miss Wynter.' Jack Easton saw the dancing teacher standing on the platform at Amberley station and came out of the waiting-room, grinning engagingly. His hands were black with Brasso from cleaning the fender. 'D'you want to wait in here? The fire's lit.'

'It's hardly worth it,' Lydia replied, looking at her watch. 'Only a few minutes till the train gets in.'

Lydia liked Jack despite his dreadful appearance: flamered hair which stood on end, freckles, a snub nose. He was thirteen and the eldest of three brothers, the only evacuees from last September who hadn't left. They were billeted with Bert and Beryl Baker in the station house and although everyone had predicted Beryl was too old to start again with three such boisterous boys, it appeared she was growing fond of them, despite having had no success in smartening them up. Apart from Jack's black hands, he had a rip down the side of his baggy grey shorts, scabby knees and insisted on wearing a khaki battle-dress jacket intended for a grown man, not a skinny, undersized boy.

Lydia and Jack had struck up an odd kind of kinship because of her car. Jack was impressed that a woman could drive, let alone own a new Vauxhall 10. Although the village was some distance from the station, Jack went out of his way to come past Briar Bank as often as possible. Lydia often saw him running his hands appreciatively over the gleaming paintwork and peering in at the dashboard.

'Are you meeting the girl?' Jack asked.

'Yes, I am.' Lydia was surprised that this piece of information had reached Jack's ears already, but then news travelled fast in Amberley. 'Her name's Bonny Phillips. She's almost eleven, the same age as your Michael, so I'd be grateful if you'd look out for her at school, Jack.'

'Okay.' Jack looked none too thrilled at this request. He hadn't much time for girls and one with a name like Bonny had to be a drip. 'Can I clean your car then?'

Lydia smiled at his bargaining technique. Jack had the soul of a salesman, one favour for another, and she respected him for it. 'To be honest, Jack, I think I'll have to stop driving it soon. I just can't get the petrol.'

Jack's face fell. One by one most of the few cars in the village had been put away in garages and barns for the duration of the war. Alec, who ran the little garage near the station, was turning his hand to brick-laying and odd jobs on farms because he had so few customers.

'Maybe you could help Alec take the wheels off and put it to bed for me?' Lydia suggested. She knew Jack wanted to be a mechanic: according to Alec he was always hanging around the garage, wanting to learn everything.

Their conversation was halted by Bert Baker the station master coming out of the ticket office. As always his uniform was freshly pressed, buttons and shoes gleaming, cap on straight, his flag under his arm.

He kept his station like himself, neat as a new pin. In summer he had tubs of geraniums on the platform, in winter a roaring fire in the waiting-room. Despite losing his porter and ticket collector to the army, with Jack's help standards hadn't dropped an inch.

'Aft'noon. Miss Wynter,' he said, his ruddy face

breaking into a welcoming smile. He took his fob watch from his pocket and glanced down the line. Lydia couldn't actually see the train, just a faint hint of smoke on the horizon. 'Right on time. Me and the missus hopes you get on all right with the little girl.'

'I might be calling on Mrs Baker for advice,' Lydia said. Beryl Baker was the expert on children, having had five of her own, all of whom were now grown up and married. 'I just hope Bonny settles here as well as Jack and his brothers.'

Mr Baker ran an affectionate hand over Jack's red mop and grinned at the boy. 'They're nothing but trouble,' he said. 'Always into mischief, running the missus ragged. But we wouldn't be without 'em now.'

'Cor! Is that 'er, miss?' Jack whistled through his teeth as the little blonde girl stepped out of the train, helped by a man.

'Yes, that's Bonny,' Lydia said, surprised that even a thirteen-year-old boy was affected by the girl's appearance. 'She's pretty, isn't she? Now I must go and greet them.'

Jack went back to the waiting-room to finish his polishing, but he was watching the scene outside on the platform with keen interest.

Only a handful of people had got off the train and he knew all of them by sight, if not by name. But he was only interested in watching the girl, the couple with her and Miss Wynter.

The couple couldn't be the girl's parents. They looked too old. The woman was fat and dowdy in a dark brown coat and a woolly hat, especially next to Miss Wynter in her stylish camel coat. The man was tall but round-shouldered and worn-looking, the way Jack remembered men round Kennington. His grey overcoat was shabby and his trilby hat greasy. As he lifted it to Miss Wynter, Jack saw that he was nearly bald.

Jack never usually gave girls a glance, but he

couldn't take his eyes off this one. She was between the man and the woman, holding their hands, looking up at Miss Wynter. In contrast to the couple she was very smartly dressed in a dark blue coat with a pale-blue scarf and pixy hood, golden ringlets spiralling down beneath it.

It was her face that affected Jack most. Not just her prettiness, her big blue eyes and her pink and white skin, but the expression on it. She was openly appraising Miss Wynter and unless he was mistaken, sucking up to her for all she was worth.

Jack couldn't quite make out if he was repelled or attracted by the girl. But he was fascinated.

'This part of Amberley is called Houghton Bridge,' Lydia explained as she drove out of the station forecourt. Mr Phillips was sitting beside her, Mrs Phillips and Bonny in the back. She waved her right hand towards a high chalk cliff on her right with railway sidings beneath it. 'That's the chalk works. Now I'll just do a slight detour first so you can see the school and river before we go home and have some tea.'

She turned left under the railway bridge and before them was the River Arun.

'Isn't it pretty?' Lydia said brightly, aware that Mr and Mrs Phillips were very tense. 'At Easter the teahouse opens and people come here to take out boats.'

Arnold leaned forward in his seat, and Bonny wriggled into the space between him and Lydia, looking out intently.

It was impossible not to be moved by the scene in front of them: the long, old, grey stone bridge with its many low arches spanning the wide river; a flotilla of swans gently swept along on the current. Rowing boats upturned on the lush grass bank, recently painted for the season, weeping willows, a few oil cloth covered tables and gaily painted chairs – all added to the charm of the view.

'I hope you won't allow Bonny down here alone,' Doris said with a catch in her voice. She was unable to see the beauty, only the danger.

'Of course not, Mrs Phillips,' Lydia said soothingly. 'Now let me show you the schoolhouse.'

She turned left, parallel to the railway line just visible up a bank shielded by trees. Past the Bridge Inn and on up a narrow lane.

'Here we are.' Lydia stopped so they could view the red brick building. 'The boys go in that door, the girls in the other,' she said pointing to the two porches either end of the school. They had sharply sloping tiled roofs, each with a gothic arch.

Lydia had already explained in a letter that the school catered for all ages from five to fourteen, although brighter children often went on to grammar schools in Bognor or even Chichester at eleven. As neither Mr nor Mrs Phillips asked any questions now she turned the car round and headed back to Amberley village.

Bonny's mouth fell open in amazement as Miss Wynter drove past a fairy-tale castle. 'Look!' she squeaked, shaking her mother's arm.

Lydia looked round from the wheel and smiled. 'That's Amberley Castle, Bonny. I'm friendly with Mrs Garside who lives there so I expect we'll be invited to tea soon. She's got a couple of peacocks and they make such a noise.'

Just seconds later, before Bonny had even time to draw breath, they were in the middle of a scene from a chocolate-box lid.

This time Doris gasped too, despite her desire to remain aloof. Almost all the cottages were thatched, with neat gardens bright with daffodils and early blossom.

'Lovely, isn't it?' Lydia sensed a slight relaxation in the two adults. 'Briar Bank was my grandparents' country cottage and when I was Bonny's age I spent some idyllic holidays here. You'll be something of a sensation, Bonny. Many of my neighbours have never even been to London.'

All three Phillipses were silent as Miss Wynter stopped the car and got out. Arnold eyed up the whitewashed cottage, noted the shrubbery, the rockery and the old red brick path, and wished he'd managed to give Doris and Bonny a home like it. Doris saw the sparkling lattice windows, the scrubbed steps to the front door and wished there had been some blemish which she could have used as an excuse to take Bonny back home.

But Bonny caught a glimpse of the dance studio through the low windows, saw her reflection looking back at her in a big mirror, and knew she'd never want to go back to Dagenham again.

'Now I like Bonny to keep wearing her liberty bodice until the end of May,' Doris said sharply. Arnold had gone out into the garden with Bonny, leaving her alone with Miss Wynter to discuss the more personal aspects. 'And I always make her wear two pairs of knickers, white ones underneath her navy school ones. I always put Toddilocks on her hair before I roll it up in rags.'

Lydia glanced at her small carriage clock. She was taking Mr and Mrs Phillips back to the station to catch the half-past-five train and it couldn't come soon enough for her.

She had listened to a litany of instructions, amongst them that Bonny must be made to 'do big jobs' every morning before school. How she didn't like tomatoes, or fat on bacon, and that bottled damsons brought her out in a rash. Doris Phillips was quite the most tedious woman Lydia had ever met. She had absolutely no conversation except about her child.

Lydia just nodded in agreement at everything. She'd heard every detail of the woman's confinement, about her problems with 'the change'. Lydia had hoped to find some clue as to where Bonny got her enquiring mind, her vivacious personality and her looks, but now she was convinced the child must be a changeling.

Arnold, to be fair to him, was easier. He had at least asked about Bonny learning to play the piano, and was interested in gardening. But Doris was impossible.

Even the way the woman sat was irritating. Every bone in her body was tense. She'd taken off her coat, but kept her hat on, and had made a great display of crooking her little finger as she drank her tea, of cutting cake into tiny pieces, then eating them one by one as if afraid of actually enjoying them. She set great store by 'Manners' too, in fact she'd used the word at least a dozen times.

'I think we ought to make a move.' Lydia got up from her armchair and smoothed down her skirt over her hips. 'I'll just make you a couple of sandwiches to eat on the train. It's a long journey home. Shall I fill your flask for you?'

Alone in the kitchen, she hastily made some ham sandwiches. It was the last of her meat ration, but under the circumstances this seemed fair exchange for Bonny. She could see Doris through the window, calling her husband and daughter, her plain, worn face so dejected.

'Just don't break down on me,' Lydia muttered to herself, all too keenly aware that the woman had nothing but the child in her life. 'Why couldn't I have picked a kid with a mother like Jack's?'

It was Arnold who took control at the station. All four of them crossed the footbridge, stopping for a moment to admire the view of the river. It was almost dusk and very cold now the sun had gone.

'Go home now,' he said, turning to Lydia, his eyes

bright with unshed tears. 'Don't stand around in the cold with us, it will be easier.'

Doris opened her mouth to protest, but Arnold took her arm firmly.

'If you're sure.' Lydia shot a grateful look at him. He nodded, holding out his arms to Bonny.

A lump came up in Lydia's throat as the child hurled herself at him, burying her face in his chest.

'Be a good girl,' he said softly, bending over and kissing the top of Bonny's pixy hood. 'Write and tell us everything.'

Lydia averted her eyes as Bonny kissed her mother. She saw the naked grief in the woman's face, but also the coldness in the child's eyes.

'I'll be all right Mummy.' Bonny's voice was tactlessly cheerful. 'I like it here.'

Arnold nodded at Lydia and put his arm round his wife, drawing her close to him.

'I'll care for her as if she were my own.' Lydia felt a little like Judas as she took Bonny's hand. 'I wish you a safe journey home.'

As Lydia and Bonny walked back down from the footbridge, she could hear the train coming up the line. But the clickety-clack didn't quite drown the sound of Doris's sobs and the low murmur of Arnold's voice soothing her.

Bonny snuggled down into the soft bed and smiled with delight. Tomorrow Aunt Lydia was taking her to her new school, and in the evening there would be a dancing lesson. Nobody here knew anything about her, or her parents. She could be anyone she wanted to be.

It was a bit embarrassing when Aunt Lydia had told her off for washing her hands and face at the kitchen sink. How was she to know that posh people always used the bathroom? But she'd soon learn all those things if she watched Aunt Lydia. She'd found the place where she belonged.

Chapter Four

Bury St Edmunds, March 1940

'And what might you be doing?'

Ellie spun round at Miss Gilbert's voice. She tried to hide the blood stains on her nightdress with her hands.

'I th'think I've s'started,' she stammered with embarrassment and fear.

It was the middle of the night. Ellie had woken to find herself all sticky. She'd crept down to the kitchen to investigate because she didn't dare put the light on in the bathroom for fear of waking Miss Gilbert. When she saw the blood she nearly keeled over with shock. Although she suspected this was the thing her mother called 'her monthly', Ellie hadn't expected it to happen to her until she was older.

Miss Gilbert must have crept silently down the stairs, perhaps hoping to find Ellie stealing food or snooping. The woman looked like an escaped inmate from an asylum in her long flannel nightgown, hair loose and straggly and eyes glinting demonically behind her glasses.

'You filthy girl,' Miss Gilbert hissed, her mouth pursed in an expression of absolute disgust. 'It's just what I'd expect from you.'

Ellie burst into tears. After seven months with the Gilberts she had learnt not to expect kindness from this mean woman, but such inhumanity at a time when she desperately needed her mother was too much to bear. 'I couldn't help it,' she sobbed. 'I don't know what to do.'

Miss Gilbert turned away from Ellie and went out into the hall. The sound of the broom cupboard opening alarmed Ellie, afraid the woman was going to get a stick to beat her. She backed towards the kitchen door, so scared she almost wet herself.

'I'm sorry,' she whimpered as Miss Gilbert came back in, instinctively putting her arms up to protect herself. Miss Gilbert hadn't fetched a weapon, though – only an old sheet.

'Cut this up and make pads,' she snapped. 'I shall expect you to wash them when my brother is out of the house. Now get out of my sight you slut.'

Ellie lay awake crying long after Miss Gilbert had gone to bed. She'd had many a night feeling forlorn in this house, but never one quite as bad as this.

It was now March, and although Ellie had asked Mrs Dunwoody to move her to another billet countless times in her first few weeks, when no other suitable place could be found, she'd resigned herself to Miss Gilbert.

Her reasons for this stoic acceptance were mostly because of her mother. Polly had two jobs now: working as a waitress at Lyons Corner House by Trafalgar Square by day and at the Empire in Holborn in the evening. The theatre had closed briefly at the start of the war, but when it reopened, Polly decided to keep both jobs.

When Polly came to Suffolk in November to visit, Ellie intended to tell her the truth about Miss Gilbert and beg to be taken home, but she found she couldn't. Despite her exhaustion, Polly was jubilant because at last she was making enough money to save towards a better home. Ellie hadn't the heart to spoil long-term plans which were all for her benefit.

Instead she told her mother about the good things in Suffolk and made out she was happy.

There were many good things. In fact, if she'd been billeted with anyone other than Miss Gilbert, it might have been idyllic. Bury St Edmunds was like a treasure trove, full of interesting places. The surrounding countryside promised to be glorious now that spring was on its way. She'd made friends and the lady at the library liked her and always kept back special books for her.

But most of all she liked St John's School. It was small and old with the tiniest playground, but it was bright and cosy with only four classrooms. Even in January, when it was bitterly cold with snow several feet deep, the school had been warm. It smelt of polish and disinfectant and the walls were covered in children's artwork. There were no more than eighty children, all told. The varying ages and abilities in each class fostered a family atmosphere as older children helped coach younger ones. To Ellie, each day there was like having a new exercise book: clean, blank pages which she wanted to fill with something worthwhile.

Ellie's teacher, Miss Wilkins, was kind, interesting and patient. Her way of teaching wasn't to bark out facts, but to stimulate their interest with shared projects, making them find out information for themselves, then encouraging group discussions. In six months Ellie had never seen anyone get the cane. All Miss Wilkins had to do when someone was playing up was tap them on the shoulder, look at the child reproachfully and point towards the door. Somehow Miss Wilkins made the child feel they'd hurt her by being naughty. When they were allowed into the class again they were always subdued.

It was the acting classes twice a week after school, though, which finally sealed Ellie's determination to put up with Miss Gilbert. Miss Wilkins shared Ellie's passion for the stage and the productions she directed were as popular with the parents who came to watch them as with the children who took part. Although most of Ellie's schoolfriends saw these classes just as a pleasant diversion from routine, Ellie saw them as training towards her goal of being an actress.

Now, as Ellie lay in the pitch-dark room feeling dirty and shamed, the bad things in her life heavily outweighed the good ones. Being woken at six-thirty by Miss Gilbert, given two slices of bread and margarine for breakfast, and having to make all the beds and clean the bedrooms before school. Cleaning came easy to Ellie – she'd always helped her mother – but here, instead of praising her for her efforts, Miss Gilbert went behind her, checking for dust. After school Ellie helped Mr Gilbert in the workroom and on Saturdays there was a full day of scrubbing, polishing and window-cleaning.

The winter had been long and bitterly cold. Heavy snow had isolated villages, animals had frozen to death in the fields. Because of coal shortages people went scavenging for wood, often cutting down trees. The black-out intensified the misery still further, and batteries for torches were almost impossible to find.

Because of the bad weather and her two jobs, Polly was unable to come and visit again. Although she wrote at least once a week, her funny and warm letters, full of gossip about neighbours and the shows at the Empire, heightened Ellie's feeling of loss. Miss Gilbert used the start of rationing in January as a further excuse for meagre meals. Ellie got chaps on her hands and feet and sore places on the inside of her thighs, and night after night lay shivering in her bed because Miss Gilbert wouldn't give her an extra blanket.

She had come to accept the lack of kindness, the strict regime and the hunger. No one could accuse her of being fat any longer; in fact she was now one of the thinnest girls in her class. But now, faced with this final humiliation, Ellie was at breaking point.

'Ellie, stay behind please!' Miss Wilkins said as the children began to file out of the classroom to get their coats.

Miss Wilkins had noticed Ellie's red-rimmed eyes as soon as she'd come into school that morning. The girl hadn't sung in assembly, just stood there with her head bowed. Throughout the rest of the day she'd remained silent and unresponsive.

The teacher waited until the last child had left the classroom. Some of them were peering over the glass partition from the hall, wondering what was going on, but Miss Wilkins waved them away.

'What's the matter, Ellie?' she said gently. 'Something wrong at home?

Ellie hung her head, wanting to blurt it out, but too embarrassed to speak of anything so personal.

'Missing Mum?' Miss Wilkins asked. Most of the evacuees had gone home for Christmas and never returned, but Ellie hadn't been able to go because of her mother's work. 'She'll be down to see you soon now the weather's improving. I don't think this phoney war's going to last much longer though, Ellie. I wouldn't be surprised if all hell breaks loose soon. You're much better off here.'

When Ellie didn't respond in any way, Miss Wilkins was puzzled. Usually she never missed an opportunity to talk about her mother's latest letter, or the progress of the war.

'Is it Miss Gilbert?' The teacher put one finger under Ellie's chin and lifted it. 'You can tell me, Ellie.'

Miss Wilkins was forty, with a softness about her that suggested she was once very pretty. Her eyes and hair were a warm brown, her skin still delicate despite many fine lines, and although she favoured severe plain clothes and her hair was restrained in a prim bun, she was a very feminine woman. Her father had been the vicar of St John's Church and she'd taught at the school since she was twenty-four, her only qualification being the love of children. Fate had deprived her of any of her own; her sweetheart had been killed in Flanders and she'd never met another man who could take his place. But she hadn't become a sour old maid, despite predictions that she would. She found romance in books, her work at the school fulfilled her and her pupils became her children for a few short years.

From Ellie's very first day in her class, Miss Wilkins was amused by the girl's sense of humour. She had asked Ellie if she was comfortable at the Gilberts'.

'I wouldn't call it "comfortable", exactly,' Ellie replied with a mischievous grin. 'But at least they haven't made me sleep in a coffin.'

Miss Wilkins had found the London children were a tough breed. Many of the locals had been appalled at their lack of table manners, their shabby clothes and symptoms of malnutrition. One distracted foster mother claimed she couldn't get the children into a bed – they'd insisted on sleeping under it, the way they had at home. Yet these children were quick-witted, resourceful and receptive. They soon adjusted to their new life and contributed to the community with their cheerful natures, making some of the local children look very dull in comparison. Ellie, however, had been plump on arrival, with glossy hair and sparkling eyes. Today, faced with her dejected state, Miss Wilkins noticed for the first time how thin Ellie had become, how dull her hair and eyes.

Ellie had a strong personality: she was self-assured, warm-hearted and popular with both children and staff. Time and again Miss Wilkins had seen her entertaining the other children in the playground with tap-dancing, slapstick comedy and song-and-dance routines. She was by far the best actress in the school club too, but now, as Miss Wilkins saw the desolation in the girl's face, she realised to her horror that Ellie Forester had been acting out a role, fooling everyone into thinking she was content and even happy at the undertakers.

'Now listen here.' Seeing that Ellie wasn't about to talk, Miss Wilkins took a tougher line. 'Something is very wrong and I insist on knowing about it. If you won't tell me I'll go to Mr Gilbert.'

Ellie blanched. Mr Gilbert was a decent sort, quite unlike his sister. They had even established a kind of tentative friendship as she helped him trim coffins out in the workshop. If he were to discover what had happened last night she wouldn't be able to live with the shame.

There was nothing for it but to take Miss Wilkins into her confidence.

She blurted it out, her fear, embarrassment and shame when Miss Gilbert called her a slut.

'Oh Ellie.' Miss Wilkins's eyes softened with sympathy at Ellie's whispered explanation, drawing her close and hugging her. She understood completely the girl's trauma of being unprepared for menstruation. Even with a mother to explain and advise, it was still a source of embarrassment to girls. Her heart went out to Ellie, silently cursing the bitter old maid who'd made her feel so ashamed of her femininity. 'It's quite normal, you know, you've just started a bit early. Let me explain it all to you.'

Miss Wilkins sat at her desk deep in thought for some time after Ellie had gone home. She was appalled that Miss Gilbert could betray her own sex by humiliating the girl at such a crucial time. Miss Wilkins had explained, reassured and even given Ellie a packet of proper sanitary towels. Yet during their talk she had sensed that this wasn't an isolated incidence of

80

callousness on Miss Gilbert's part, but a long and vindictive campaign against the girl.

What should she do?

Miss Wilkins knew there wasn't an alternative billet in the town. Many of the people had had bad experiences with their first attempt with evacuees and when the children had gone home they'd refused to try again. Now an influx of RAF wives whose husbands were stationed in East Anglia had descended on the town, filling the remaining places. If she asked Mrs Dunwoody to find Ellie a new home it might be miles away in one of the villages, involving a change of school. Ellie had been emphatic she didn't want that, and neither did Miss Wilkins.

Ellie was the kind of child who made teaching a pleasure. She wasn't academic, but her enthusiasm and desire to soak up knowledge were delightful. Since arriving in the village she'd all but lost her cockney accent, taking pride in learning to speak correctly. On top of that, Ellie's acting ability needed nurturing. She was good enough to have a career on the stage.

Miss Wilkins smiled as she remembered back to last September. She'd got the evacuees to tell the class about their parents and homes back in London, in an effort to show the local children a glimpse of city life.

One by one the evacuee children created a picture of big families living in cramped conditions, noisy street markets, eel and pie shops, the docks, pawnbrokers and second-hand clothes shops. Miss Wilkins opened it up as a class discussion, getting the locals to ask questions and indeed to explain to the London children the differences in their lives. Ellie had taken a big role in all this, being far more articulate than many of the others, and her vivid descriptions of her neighbours back home made all the children laugh.

When Ellie had mentioned that her mother worked as a dresser in a theatre, Miss Wilkins picked up on this.

'Tell us about it,' she suggested.

"Ow d'you mean, tell 'em about it?' Ellie asked in surprise.

It was just half an hour until the bell rang for the end of school. Miss Wilkins usually read to the class at that stage of the day.

'None of us has been backstage in a theatre,' Miss Wilkins said. 'We want to know what a dresser does, how you helped.'

Miss Wilkins didn't expect much from Ellie. Speaking out in a group was one thing, but standing up alone and making it interesting enough to hold anyone's attention for more than a few moments was hard for any child, even one as confident as Ellie.

But as Ellie began to speak, Miss Wilkins found herself being richly entertained.

Ellie began by describing how her mother put out all the costumes with the accessories for each performer. Unconsciously, she soon slipped into acting it out.

She mimed her mother's exertions at lacing a fat singer into a corset, then strutted around being the singer trying out a few tentative notes. She described the chorus girls' pushing and shoving to see in one mirror, acting it out with provocative wiggles and pouts. The children experienced Polly Forester's rush against the clock, darting around the overcrowded dressing-room, putting a fan in one hand, a feather boa on someone's shoulders. Ellie kept up the dialogue, too, the plummy tones of some of the actors and actresses, with her mother's rich cockney voice admonishing them to keep still while she did last-minute running repairs to their costumes. The picture she painted was so vivid that every child in the class was spellbound.

The bell for the end of school ended it all abruptly, but for once not one child leapt to his or her feet anxious to leave.

Since then Ellie had been called on many a time for impromptu performances. She could create a scene on the underground trains, become a market trader bawling out his sales pitch, or a harassed mother with four children in tow. But one memorable sketch Ellie had performed now came sharply into focus: Miss Gilbert preparing a meal, counting out the potatoes and carrots, measuring the loaf with a piece of string in case Mr Gilbert's apprentice was to nip in behind her back to steal a slice. Miss Wilkins had assumed then it was exaggerated for comic effect. Now she was sure the reality was probably worse.

Miss Wilkins had known Grace Gilbert since they were children. Grace had always been odd – a withdrawn, whey-faced girl who peered out through the gates of the undertakers at other children and ran away when anyone tried to befriend her. Since reaching adulthood, there had always been rumours about her. Miss Wilkins didn't believe all these tales, because she knew people whispered about her too, for different reasons. But it was certainly true that Grace Gilbert wasn't entirely normal. She had a well-documented obsession with cleaning, she was a skinflint and she was impossible to like. But if Grace Gilbert was now ill-treating a child in her care, it was time her brother put a stop to it.

Miss Wilkins hesitated at the gates of Gilbert's yard. It was half past five and already dark and the undertakers yard was a daunting place for anyone.

She knew Amos was in his workshop; she could hear the sound of sawing and smell the woodshavings, even though because of the black-out no lights were visible.

A row of tombstones glowed eerily further into the yard. She had no way of gauging how deep the puddle of water in front of her was, and she couldn't call at the shop door as she had no wish to run into Ellie or Miss Gilbert just now. This talk with Amos was intended to be a private matter.

Miss Wilkins crossed the puddle, which wasn't deep after all, and tapped lightly on the door of the workshop.

'Come in,' he called back.

She opened the door, went in and quickly shut it behind her. 'Good evening Amos,' she said.

Amos was making a tiny coffin on his workbench by the light of an overhanging hurricane lamp. Dressed for funerals in a black frock-coat, wing-collar and top hat he was a formidable-looking man, but here he was just a craftsman wearing working-men's clothes, rugged, muscular and comfortably ordinary.

His workshop was a surprisingly agreeable place to be in, despite the many different-sized, half-completed coffins standing on their ends like sentry boxes. A small stove kept it warm, a six-foot cabinet of small glass-fronted drawers held all his handles, screws and other equipment and his planes, saws and chisels were hung on the walls with the kind of care which suggested this was where he was happiest. There was still enough harnessing, bridles and other equipment hanging up on the walls and rough beams to show it had once been a stable. The timber stacked up in the old hayloft filled the air with its pungent smell.

'Well, Dora!' Amos looked surprised but pleased to see her. 'It's a few years since you last came in here.'

The teacher smiled. She and Amos had been close friends as small children. As a boy he'd had a great sense of fun and they'd played together up in that hayloft on many an occasion.

Amos had always been quite different from his older sister. He shared her grey eyes and thin lips, but not her pallor or nature. Even now he still retained his ruddy, wholesome appearance and the same shy, warm smile she remembered.

Here in the workshop, Amos was a carpenter, a job she seemed to remember he would have preferred.

But considering the serious nature of his profession, the responsibility for the family business and the company of Grace, it wasn't really surprising he had become a dour and perhaps lonely man.

Miss Wilkins saw the meticulous care he was taking with the tiny coffin, and felt saddened that his craftsmanship was destined to rot away six foot underground instead of making fine furniture for generations to come.

Amos saw her glance at the small coffin and lifted it from his workbench, putting it down on the floor out of sight. 'The Sawyers' little one,' he said gruffly, his grey eyes compassionate. 'I expect you heard she died. A baby's death is something I never come to terms with, not even after all these years.'

'I don't know how you do it,' she said. 'You were always so adamant you wouldn't follow your father.'

'You were going to be an actress,' he replied. 'Remember us putting on a play up there?' He nodded towards the hayloft. 'You were the Queen and I was Sir Francis Drake.' His words were a gentle reminder that most people's dreams had to take second place to duty.

'We had some good times back then.' Miss Wilkins half smiled at the memory of knighting Amos with a poker as he kneeled at her feet. 'But this isn't a social call, Amos, I came to talk to you about Ellie.'

Amos was always gentlemanly. He pulled a stool out from beneath a bench, dusted it off and offered it to her.

'What's she been up to?' he asked, brushing back his dark hair with one hand. Miss Wilkins noted the way his eyes twinkled and she knew immediately that he liked the girl.

Amos hadn't wanted an evacuee foisted on him. He had no experience with children and Grace had even less. But once Grace knew there was money in it, she was determined to have one. And despite Amos's reservations, he had grown to like Ellie. She was eager to please, nimble-fingered and when they were working alone out here she made him laugh with her impersonations of neighbours. Inside the house he rarely saw her because of the long hours he worked. Grace was always sharp with her, but then she was with everyone.

'Ellie hasn't done anything. It's your sister,' Miss Wilkins said quietly. 'I'm very concerned, Amos, and I'm counting on your help to put things right.'

Amos frowned, sat down on an upturned box and took his pipe out of his pocket. 'Tell me, Dora.'

Dora spoke first of Ellie's weight-loss and general condition, mentioning the girl's work-reddened hands and her suspicions about Grace's ill-treatment of her. It was excruciatingly embarrassing to bring up the tale of last night's events to a man, especially an unmarried one, but she managed it with a few euphemisms.

Miss Wilkins could see by the way his face reddened and his eyes couldn't meet hers that Amos was embarrassed. But there was something more. She sensed she'd struck a sensitive chord in him: she could almost hear his thought processes, and the unvoiced question, Why hadn't he realised what was going on under his own roof?

'Girls at puberty are very sensitive,' she explained. 'Ellie would be mortified to know I'd divulged anything like this to you, but you must take Grace in hand, Amos. She can't be allowed to take out her bitterness on a young girl, especially one as vulnerable as Ellie.'

Amos sucked on his pipe thoughtfully. Grace had never been like others, although Amos, being three years younger, had just accepted her oddness in the way any brother would. She was eighteen and Amos fifteen in the summer of 1912, when Sean O'Leary and Meg Butterworth died. Twenty-eight years on he still hadn't managed to squash those dark suspicions about his sister's part in it.

Grace had blighted his life. As a young lad he'd taken stick from his friends at having such a queer sister. Because of her he'd felt compelled to stick to the family business rather than break away and become a carpenter.

Even if the First War hadn't taken most of the young men from the village, no man in his right mind would have wanted a mean-spirited woman like Grace for a wife. She flew into tantrums about nothing, she drove shopkeepers wild with fury when she picked over their goods, and if Amos hadn't been firm enough to keep her away from bereaved relatives, her abrupt, cold manner might have lost them the family business too. But it was her cruelty that had always concerned Amos. He had seen her once strangle a kitten with her bare hands because it made a mess on the floor and the last apprentice that lived in the house had run away when she flogged him for helping himself to a slice of meat pie.

Because of his profession, Amos saw life from a different perspective to other men. He rarely met his neighbours except under circumstances of grief and distress and his sister's temperament made it impossible to have any kind of social life. He was thirty before he fully realised he was trapped. His father died, leaving him not only the business, but also the burden of Grace. One by one he watched his old classmates get married, but girls shunned Amos not only because of how he made his living, but because of his sister. If he popped into a pub for a drink after a funeral, Grace became hysterical. If he even arranged to play a game of cricket on the long summer evenings, something would be damaged when he got home. Years ago, when Amos had been forced to call the doctor to sedate her during one of her hysterical rages, he'd been advised to have her committed to an asylum. Yet Amos couldn't bring himself to do such a thing to his own sister. Instead he just humoured her and hoped she would improve with age.

'I don't know what to say,' Amos said eventually. 'I rarely see Ellie except when she helps me in here. I like her, Dora, and please believe me, I had no idea Grace was ill-treating her. Why hasn't she complained before?'

Ellie had in many little ways made his life more comfortable. During the bitter winter she often warmed his coat by the stove in the mornings, and many a cold night he'd come home late at night to find she'd put a hot-water bottle in his bed. She helped him clear the snow from the yard, she sorted his drawers of handles and screws, swept up the floor in here and often brought him a mug of tea when he was working, unprompted by Grace.

'I think she felt obligated to keep quiet,' Miss Wilkins said. 'She knew there was no other available billet in the town. She didn't want to make her mother anxious. But above all Ellie's a practical girl, Amos. She likes our school and loves the acting class and perhaps even believes she's doing her duty for the war effort by accepting Grace's tyranny.'

'I wish she'd said something at the outset,' Amos said. 'I hope she isn't afraid of me too.'

'I don't think she's afraid of anyone,' Miss Wilkins said firmly. 'She's a brave, conscientious girl who tries hard to please people. That makes Grace's behaviour even more despicable.'

'What do you suggest I do about it?' Amos asked. He was mortified that he hadn't looked closer. 'Are you saying Ellie should be taken away?' He dreaded more gossip about his sister and he would miss Ellie too.

'I wish I had room to have her with me,' Miss Wilkins said, her soft brown eyes deeply troubled. 'But I haven't, and as childhood friends I don't want you to be shamed further by this getting out. But if Ellie is to stay with you, you'll have to change things.

Ellie must have more food, more freedom to socialise with other girls, and she mustn't be humiliated and used as a slave. Unless I see a dramatic improvement in the next few days, I'll have no choice but to report Grace.'

She stood up, anxious to get home now she'd said her piece. She felt sorry for Amos; his life was bleak enough with such a sister, without her adding to his burdens. But she knew he was an honourable man and she trusted him to act fairly.

'I'll do what I can, Dora.' Amos stood up and held out his hand. 'I'm sorry about all this.'

'We have to pull together.' Miss Wilkins smiled as his big calloused hand gripped hers. It was unfair that people had such aversion to undertakers. There was a great deal more to the profession than a man in a black frock-coat, driving a gleaming hearse filled with flowers. His role was akin to doctors' and priests' as he offered consolation and organisation at the lowest point in people's lives, yet he received no praise or admiration. 'I've got a feeling that this war is going to get tough soon for all of us. The children are England's future and it's vitally important that each one of them is cared for, emotionally as well as physically.'

'I want to talk to you, Grace,' Amos said once the supper things had been cleared away. Ellie had gone into the living-room to do some homework and he'd noted for himself how pale and drawn the girl looked.

'What about?' Grace said sharply. She was taking down some airing clothes from the hoist, and her head jerked round, giving him one of her bird-of-prey chilling looks.

Grace had never been attractive, not even as a child. Her voice was shrill, her features sharp, hair dull and stringy. Even as she slipped into middle age, her body had stayed as flat and unyielding as one of Amos's planks of timber.

'Into the parlour. Now.'

'The fire isn't lit,' she snapped.

Amos took no notice and marched on ahead, fixing the black-out curtains firmly, then drawing the curtains over the top and switching on the light.

Grace followed him, but instead of sitting down, began to fuss with the curtains.

Amos disliked this room intensely. Since his parents' deaths Grace's personality had stolen the warmth it once had and she had acquired still more ugly furniture and ornaments, making it claustrophobic and almost menacing.

'Sit down at once,' he ordered her. 'We aren't entertaining the vicar, this is just you and I.'

'Don't you speak to me like that,' Grace wittered, clearly taken aback by her brother's sharp tone.

She sat down primly on the hard leather *chaise-longue*. Amos was reminded that she was incapable of relaxing. In twenty years he hadn't seen her slip off her shoes, or read anything more than the parish magazine or a newspaper. She was like a loaded gun, cocked ready to fire.

'From what I understand I should have been watching you like a hawk,' he said. 'I've had Dora Wilkins round this evening and I don't like what I've been hearing.'

Grace's face was always the colour of old parchment, but at his words a flush of pink crept up her neck. 'I suppose that girl has been telling lies about me,' she said quickly.

'Ellie has said very little.' Amos tried very hard to control his anger. 'I suspect if she'd told everything we'd have women throwing stones at our windows. How could you treat a child so heartlessly?'

Grace denied everything, just as he knew she would. She counteracted his charges of starving Ellie by insisting the girl had the same size meals as herself; that the only chores she gave her to do were simple ones and that Ellie was bone idle, greedy and stuffed up with self-importance.

'She is none of those things,' Amos said, tempted to slap his sister. 'You on the other hand are crazy, Grace, you always have been.'

'Me! Crazy?' She made a cackling noise in her throat which was the closest she could get to a laugh. 'How can you say such a thing after all I do for you?'

'You know exactly what I mean.' Amos gave her a withering look. 'My memory is almost as sharp as your tongue and if I'd had any sense I should have had you committed to the asylum years ago. You've made my life a misery. But I won't stand by and see you ill-treat a child in our care.'

She flew off the *chaise-longue*, reaching out to strike him, but Amos was too quick for her, catching hold of both her arms and pushing her back into her seat.

'I'm warning you now,' he said, speaking in a low, firm voice. 'You'll start undoing the wrong you've done. You'll give Ellie the same meals as you give me. You'll treat her with kindness, as far as you are capable of it, and she'll have freedom to see her friends after school and on Saturdays. I'm going to speak to her myself and tell her the new arrangements. I shall make it quite clear she is answerable only to me in future. If there is any repetition of this kind of cruelty, I won't think twice. I'll be straight round to see the doctor and get you taken away. Do you understand?'

As Amos looked down at his sister he felt nothing but disgust. Her eyes were wild with fury and she had spittle at the corners of her thin mouth. He wondered if he could trust her not to strike behind his back.

'Have I made myself plain?' he asked.

'Yes,' she muttered. 'I'll do as you say.'

'You'd better,' he said, letting go of her. 'Now go and make a cup of tea for us. I'm going to talk to Ellie.'

*

Ellie had heard raised voices from the parlour but it hadn't occurred to her that the disagreement between Mr and Miss Gilbert had anything to do with her. The talk with Miss Wilkins after school had made her feel better about herself and she'd even begun to think of herself as a woman rather than a child. She looked up in surprise as Mr Gilbert came into the living-room with two cups of tea in his hands.

'Hello,' she said. 'Do you want to listen to the wireless now? I've almost finished my homework.'

It was half-past seven. Miss Gilbert always ordered her to bed before eight, and usually Mr Gilbert went into his office across the passage straight after the evening meal. Miss Gilbert always stayed in the kitchen until it was time to hear the nine o'clock news, but Ellie assumed she was coming in here now too.

'The tea's for you,' he said putting one cup down by her and sitting down at the other side of the table. He cocked his head to one side, listening to the sound of aircraft going overhead. It seemed to him that each night there was more and more activity on the air bases. 'I didn't come in to listen to the wireless, but to talk to you.'

Amos wasn't a man who thought about people's appearance much, but he noted now that Ellie had changed dramatically in six months. Losing so much weight had revealed high cheekbones, and her face was heart-shaped, not round as he'd always supposed. Her dark eyes had always been her most attractive feature, but now she was so much thinner they were huge and dramatic. He could see now what Dora had meant about her hair being dull and the glow gone from her skin, yet despite this she was slowly turning into a beauty, and maybe that was just what Grace couldn't stomach.

He wondered whether he would've made a good father if he'd had children of his own. He couldn't help but think how proud he'd be if Ellie was his.

Out of loyalty to both Dora and Grace he had to pretend he'd observed things weren't quite right himself. Brusquely he said it had come to his notice that she was doing too many chores and she looked pale. 'I'm sorry if it's been hard for you here,' he said, running one finger inside the collar of his shirt nervously. 'I know my sister can be very difficult to please, but neither of us are used to children. But I intend to change things, to make it better for you. I want you to see your friends after school if you want to, and on Saturdays you can please yourself how you spend your time. If you are troubled about anything, come to me.'

Ellie was astounded. It didn't occur to her that Miss Wilkins had intervened on her behalf. 'I don't mind helping you,' she said, sensing something more was troubling him, and wanting him to know he wasn't responsible. 'Or doing things around the house. I just hate it when Miss Gilbert is so nasty.'

Amos looked into Ellie's eyes and saw complete honesty. It pricked at his own conscience and he faltered. 'If you want to be moved, I'll understand,' he said. 'But can we give it another shot first?'

Amos felt a sense of shame as a warm, almost affectionate smile spread across her face.

'Yes please,' she said without any hesitation. 'I'll try harder to make Miss Gilbert like me. And I do like helping you in the workshop, really I do.'

Some kind of current passed between them. It was soothing, comfortable, a kind of silent reassurance that their relationship was going to grow from now on. Amos wished he could find the words to explain how he felt, but he'd always been a listener rather than a talker.

'ITMA's on in a minute,' he said to hide his acute embarrassment. Grace had never allowed Ellie to listen to the programme, but he guessed she would like it. 'Will you stay and listen to it with me?'

The joy in the girl's face was like an electric light being switched on. 'Oh yes,' she said breathlessly. 'I'd love to.'

Grace Gilbert lay awake, every bone in her long thin body stiff with rage. How dare Amos say she should be in an asylum? Hadn't she scrubbed, cooked and sewed for him for years without complaint? It was that girl! She was a she-devil, and she was turning Amos against his own flesh and blood.

Grace had seethed with anger as she heard them laughing at *ITMA* together. How dare he sit in her living-room with that common child and exclude her?

'Just you wait,' she whispered into the darkness. 'I'll get even with you, little Miss Perfect. Just when you least expect it.'

Amos tossed and turned, unable to go to sleep. He switched on the bedside lamp, sat up and reached for a book and his reading glasses.

He read a whole page, yet as he turned to the next he realised he hadn't taken in a word.

With a deep sigh he put down the book, took off his glasses and rubbed his eyes. Should he go downstairs and make himself a drink?

His room was his parents' old one and the only thing he'd replaced was the mattress his father had died on. Both he and Grace had been born in the old oak bed, and he could still see his mother sitting at the dressing-table brushing her hair, laughing as he bounced up and down.

His childhood had been a happy one. Both his parents had been jovial characters, not at all how people supposed undertakers to be. What had happened to make Grace so deeply disturbed? She had been loved just the same as he was.

It had been an odd sort of day. First calling to measure up old Herbert Lucas who had died the previous evening and finding his wife, crippled with rheumatism, struggling to dress him in his Sunday suit. Herbert had treated Mrs Lucas shamefully for sixty years of marriage, beating her, drinking and womanising, yet she still insisted on making him look his best to meet his Maker and was prepared to spend her meagre savings to give him a funeral to be proud of.

Amos had spent the rest of the day in his workshop making the coffin for the Sawyers' baby, brooding as he sawed and planed about why God saw fit to take a small, dearly loved child, yet keep someone like Herbert in rude health till he was over eighty.

Dora's unexpected visit had stirred him up still more. Not just the shame of discovering he had failed to notice cruelty to a child going on right under his nose, but also reminders of what he might have become if only he'd been stronger willed.

His life was built on regrets. For not standing up to his father and refusing to become an undertaker. Even for agreeing to provide for Grace. But above all for not sharing his suspicions about Grace with someone, anyone, all those years ago.

He could still see himself, mutely walking before the black-plumed horses. Everyone in the town turned out for that tragic double funeral, the shops all closed in respect, almost every window draped with black. Amos couldn't think of that day without hearing the sobbing. It came from everyone – relatives, friends, neighbours, even his father when, earlier in the day, he'd had to place those blackened skeletons in the two coffins.

Only Grace had dry eyes. Yet just a few months earlier she'd claimed she loved Sean O'Leary.

Grace was eighteen when she met Sean at a dance in the Corn Exchange. Amos remembered it well, because Grace came into his room when she got home, all flushed and excited, whispering to him that she'd met the man she intended to marry and making Amos promise he wouldn't tell anyone.

Amos was fifteen then, more interested in fishing and carpentry than his sister and her romantic ideas, but he was pleased that at last she was behaving like other girls.

In the next few days Amos found his sister's announcement a little premature. The man she'd set her heart on was a devil-may-care Irish labourer who'd only recently arrived in the area to work on Firth's Farm beyond the abbey, and it seemed every single girl under the age of twenty-five was as captivated by the black-haired, blue-eyed charmer as Grace.

Sean never came to call at the house and Grace didn't make excuses to go out. Nor did she mention Sean again. But one evening Amos went into Grace's room and found her sitting on her bed sketching. She tried to cover it up, but Amos snatched the pad from her. To his surprise she was drawing a wedding dress.

Amos teased her, but for once Grace didn't fly into a rage.

'I told you I was going to marry Sean, and I am,' she said firmly. That was the only time Amos had ever thought Grace looked pretty. She was normally very pale, her features sharp and her body too thin to attract any attention. But that night she was different. Her fair hair was loose and fluffy round her face, she had colour in her cheeks and her grey eyes were lit up.

'You mustn't tell,' she begged Amos. 'We'll have to run away because father won't approve of Sean.'

Amos was confused. He couldn't see how Grace had managed to spend any time with Sean, and rumour had it he was walking out with Meg Butterworth, a sparkling blonde whom any man in his right mind would prefer to Grace. But Amos couldn't voice these thoughts. Grace always chilled him and he didn't want to provoke one of her rages.

It was Frank Butterworth, Meg's younger brother, who informed Amos about Sean and Meg's forthcoming engagement. He said it was going to be announced at Meg's eighteenth birthday party. Mr Butterworth was a butcher, with a fine big shop in The Travers. A big, exuberant man, but tough enough to flatten anyone who threatened his beloved daughter's happiness. It was very unlikely that Sean was carrying on with Grace too.

Amos decided he must tell Grace the news before it reached her from another source. He went into her room that evening and blurted it out.

She was sewing a lace-trimmed white petticoat. At first she seemed not to be taking it in and continued with tiny neat stitches, her thin lips curved into a smile.

'Grace, are you listening?' Amos snapped. 'He's getting engaged to Meg. I don't know how you got the idea he liked you, but you've got to forget him.'

Her reaction was startling. She held up a finger and jabbed it with her needle, like she had taken leave of her senses. Amos stared at her in alarm as a bead of blood swelled up in her finger and dropped on to the petticoat.

'He will marry me, or no one,' she said, her eyes sparking with strange lights. 'He's mine.'

Four days later Meg and Sean were dead, burned to a crisp in Firth's barn, a week before their planned engagement.

The barn's close proximity to the town and its position near the River Lark made it a favourite place for lovers to go on long summer evenings. Amos and his friends had often crept up to it and banged on the old door, then run away to hide when couples came out with dishevelled clothing.

At seven that evening Sean and Meg were seen walking down Mustow Street hand in hand towards the river. At eight-thirty, Stan Beddows, who lived in Cotton Lane, looked out of a bedroom window, saw flames shooting up from the barn and raised the alarm.

At first the police thought it was an accident. That Sean had lit a cigarette and thrown the match carelessly down amongst the dry straw. But later, when the burned-out barn was checked, they discovered that the door had been secured from the outside with a lump of wood across the two latches, and that the seat of the fire was by a small hole in the side of the barn.

After an exhaustive enquiry, the police drew the conclusion that a malicious tramp was responsible. Yet still Amos couldn't be entirely convinced of Grace's innocence. She may have been in her bedroom all evening, yet she alone out of all the women in the town who knew Sean showed no reaction at all – not grief because the man she once said she was going to marry was dead, or even anger that he died in another girl's arms.

Grace got impetigo soon after the funeral and it was curiously convenient for explaining away the obsessive cleaning that followed her maniacal mood swings.

That double murder was wiped from most people's memories now, a bit of dark history best forgotten. But not for Amos. Sometimes when he glanced out of Grace's bedroom window and saw the lean-to shed so close, he thought how easy it would be for someone to go in and out that way without being seen.

Amos turned out his light and lay down again. Perhaps at fifteen he had too much imagination for his own good. It was wicked and unnatural even to consider his sister capable of murder. But she was crazy, as unpredictable as spring weather, and in future he'd be watching her closely.

Chapter Five

Amberley, May 1940

'Step and tap, step and tap,' Lydia called out above the beat of the music. 'Heads up, swing your arms, step and tap and step and tap.'

It was Saturday morning, the main tap-dancing class of the week. Eight girls ranging from seven to twelve, all with flushed faces, all wearing the uniform blue short flared dress and red tap-shoes, but varying enormously in their shapes and heights. Betty was the eldest, a hefty twelve-year-old farmer's daughter who had been coming here for lessons since she was six but still couldn't co-ordinate leg and arm movements. Joanie, the youngest, had taken to tap-dancing well, but she was so short and fat Lydia doubted she would ever look right on a stage. Peggy was so thin her dress just hung like a sack and she was struggling vainly to keep in step with the others. Of the eight girls, Lydia felt that only Bonny had all the credentials for a tap-dancer. The grace, confidence, lightness of step and the looks.

To watch Bonny dance was a pleasure. A smile was switched on the moment the music started, natural rhythm swung her along. Not for her, those admonishments not to look at your feet or to stop chanting the instructions aloud – she was a born dancer.

Bonny had been in Amberley for two months now

and although there had been minor problems at the village school at first, Lydia found she was becoming very attached to the child. Occasionally this worried her – after all, Mrs Phillips could demand Bonny back at any time – but in the main Lydia just enjoyed each day as it came.

'Well done.' Lydia stood up from her piano and took up a position in front of the two rows of girls. 'Now we're going to learn the next part, so watch me carefully!'

Lydia wore a similar dress to the children, but hers was black and slightly longer, worn over a pair of pink ballet tights. It was said that fathers volunteered to collect their children from the Saturday morning class in the hope of catching a glimpse of her shapely legs, but they were usually disappointed to find the teacher had wrapped herself in a loose kimono by the time they arrived.

'Now step, hop, step, to the right,' she said, her arms out in front of her. Step hop, step, to the left and turn.'

Lydia watched the children go through this routine until they'd got it, more or less, then returned to the piano.

'From the beginning,' she said, playing the introduction. 'Heads up, tummies in and smile.'

It was May now: the German Army had entered Holland, Belgium and Luxembourg and was advancing rapidly through France. Chamberlain had resigned, and Winston Churchill was now Prime Minister. His stirring words, 'I have nothing to offer, but blood, toil, tears and sweat,' had won the hearts of the nation, but here in Sussex the war still hadn't affected their everyday lives very much.

Littlehampton was preparing for the summer season. Mr Butlin, who owned the amusement park, had claimed back in March that 'Big business should be done on the South coast. It is a safe area and I am very optimistic' – though he added that the black-out of course presented a problem.

Piles of sandbags lay in readiness, the black-out rigorously maintained and collections of waste materials organised. But even though everyone tuned in their wireless each night at nine to hear the latest news of the *blitzkrieg* of the low countries, for now in Amberley the villagers were more concerned with the threat imposed by land-girls, than with possible bombing or even invasion.

Hordes of khaki-breeched and stout-booted girls had arrived with spring. Their masculine attire and enthusiasm for country life should have appeased farmers struggling to keep things going now that the able-bodied men had been called up, but almost everyone was deeply suspicious of these town girls. After only the sketchiest training these typists, shop assistants and domestic servants, many of whom had hardly even seen a cow before, were expected to milk, to spread muck on the fields, to plough and cut hay. Local girls were jealous because they had competition for the attentions of the lads in the Fleet Air Arm stationed nearby. Farmers' wives were nervous that these more worldly women would seduce their husbands. Most of the old farmers resented the government snatching their experienced labourers and replacing them with novices and they took delight in passing on tales of girls who thought cows only had to be milked once a week and didn't know a hen from a rooster.

Lydia had a great deal of sympathy for these girls. They worked cheerfully from dawn to dusk in all weathers, often living in the most primitive of conditions. She admired the way they adjusted to the lack of baths, hairdressers and praise. They were often homesick, missing their families, shops and entertainment, yet still managed to find the energy to get to the nearest Saturday night dance, often outshining the local girls.

Bonny didn't appear to miss her home and parents. On the rare occasions when she spoke of them it was in an abstract manner, almost as if she'd made up her mind she was never going to return. When Mr and Mrs Phillips had come down to visit her in April, Bonny had seemed strained and somewhat embarrassed by their presence and she'd put her mother's back up with a rather tactless eulogy of how blissfully happy she was with both her new home and Lydia.

Before Bonny's arrival, weekends had been the time when Lydia noticed her single status most. Saturdays were busy with both dancing and music lessons, but seeing parents collect their children and overhearing talk of trips to the cinema, walks or shopping always reminded her she had no one to share such things with. Sundays were often long and empty.

But now weekends were transformed into busy, joyful times. On Saturdays they had leisurely breakfasts, talking over what Bonny had done at school, and when the dancing classes were over they often had afternoon tea at Belinda's Tearooms in Arundel, followed by a film at The Arun. Sundays flew by in Bonny's company. Whether they went for a walk or sat by the fire after lunch with a shared jigsaw puzzle, it had become a relaxing, happy day which Lydia looked forward to all week.

Well-intentioned friends reproached Lydia for making too much of Bonny. They disapproved of the time spent on private coaching and the money she lavished on her. It was true that a kilt she'd bought in Chichester cost more than the week's evacuee allowance. Perhaps too the pink, Bunnies' wool twin set she'd got a neighbour to knit was a little extravagant, considering wool was becoming so difficult to get now, but it gave Lydia such pleasure to give nice things to the child and it was a delight to see Bonny's rapid progress in dancing and to hear how her diction was improving.

Lydia was aware Bonny was no angel. Aside from minor trouble at school, neighbours had complained of her cheeking them, and she had been found by Mrs Garside wandering around inside Amberley Castle uninvited. But this plucky side of Bonny's character appealed to Lydia. Had she been as angelic as she looked, she'd have made a dull companion.

'That's it then for today.' Lydia stood up again from the piano and beamed at her class as she saw a couple of mothers peering through the window. The girls were all perspiring heavily, a reminder that the weather was at last becoming warmer. 'Please try and practise at home, real dancers need more than one hour a week. Now off you go and change.'

Bonny ignored the changing-room and ran upstairs to put her clothes on. She never missed an opportunity to show the other girls that she had special status in this house. Pausing for a moment, she weighed up whether to wear her kilt, a new pink cotton dress her mother had sent, or the red siren suit Aunt Lydia had had made for her.

The siren suit won. It wasn't warm enough for the pink dress and everyone had seen the kilt already. Siren suits had become the latest fashion. They had been designed to slip on in the event of an air raid, a comfortable, all purpose garment which would keep out draughts. Bonny loved the big pockets, the red colour and the fact she could climb trees without showing her knickers.

When she got back downstairs, though, all the girls from her class had left and the first few under-sixes were just arriving with their mothers for their ballet lesson.

'Can I go out?' Bonny asked Lydia, who was arranging some music on the piano.

'It's "may I",' Lydia corrected Bonny. 'Yes you may, but be back at one for lunch.'

Of all the things Bonny liked about living here, freedom was the thing she appreciated most. Back in London she wasn't even allowed to post a letter or go to the sweet shop alone. Even if she went into the tiny garden, her mother would put her head round the door to see what she was doing.

Here she could run through a field singing at the top of her lungs, do cartwheels and handstands, prod cow-pats or crawl on her belly through long grass. Aunt Lydia rarely asked where she'd been when she dawdled coming home from school, she didn't cross-examine her about who she'd talked to and she was happy to allow Bonny to wander about the village, just so long as she didn't go down to the river and came home on time.

Aunt Lydia was relaxed about everything. If Bonny didn't eat what was put in front of her, she got nothing else. If she chose to go out without a coat and got cold it served her right. She didn't ask if she'd 'been' or check to see Bonny was wearing her liberty bodice and two pairs of knickers, and she answered questions truthfully.

Bonny had only been in Amberley for about a week when Mrs Beavis who lived across the road had a new baby. Bonny was mystified how the doctor could get such a large baby in his bag. Lydia laughed, but she sat down and explained the whole thing properly, even drawing a few pictures to make it clearer. After that Bonny felt she could ask Lydia anything and she always got a straight answer.

The village looked especially pretty as Bonny skipped off down the road towards Mr Blundell's grocery shop. A very wet spring had followed the long, bitter winter, but at last the clouds had vanished and the sun was warm. Lilac and laburnum dripped over garden walls, and brilliant blue lobelia and vivid yellow saxifrage vied with clumps of marguerites and towering delphiniums for attention. She stopped for a moment to peer through an arched wrought-iron gate at Mr Wendell's beautiful garden. To her it was an enchanted place, with a lily pond, stone statues and flower-covered archways. Bonny had dragged her parents along to look at it during their visit, expecting them to be as enthusiastic as herself, but to her dismay they were disparaging. Dad had said it looked like a jungle, and Mum pointed out that the cottage windows needed a good clean.

Bonny had felt uncomfortable the whole time her parents were here. They'd been sniffy about everything, almost as if they resented her living in such a nice place. Mum had been quite rude to Aunt Lydia, questioning her closely on who Bonny was friends with, what time she went to bed and what she ate.

Bonny turned away from Mr Wendell's garden, suddenly remembering this morning's objective. She wanted to join Jack Easton's gang, and nothing, not even the fact there were no other girls included, was going to stop her.

Jack Easton fascinated Bonny. Although he was what her mother would call a 'Rough Boy', almost three years older than herself, with carroty hair, she admired him. Jack had charisma. He was tough, cocky and often uncouth, but he was also kind-hearted, funny, brave and quick-witted. It was common knowledge that Mrs Easton had only visited her three sons once since they'd been billeted at the stationhouse with Mr and Mrs Baker last September and that now she'd abandoned them entirely. But the fact that Mrs Baker had become very fond of the three boys and indeed hoped to keep them indefinitely, seemed to prove they weren't all bad.

Jack had gruffly welcomed Bonny on her first day at the village school. Since then he'd stuck up for her on several occasion when some of the local children were nasty. Bonny had no way of knowing whether this was because he really liked her, or just because they were both outsiders, but whatever his motive, she was grateful.

In Bonny's two months in the village she had noted the children fell into three groups. First the goody-goodies who were tidily dressed, worked hard at school and pleased adults. Then at the other end of the scale were the drips, those who were either dim, timid or had some defect like being fat or cross-eyed. In the middle was a tiny group, Jack's gang. She'd spotted these boys building camps and tramping off to secret destinations. They alone seemed to have real purpose and all the fun she craved.

She had already tried hard to convince them she should be a member. Although tree-climbing in the school playground was against the rules, she did it, risking her teacher Miss Thorpe's wrath just to impress them. Going into Amberley Castle had been another attempt. But although Jack often grinned at Bonny as if in approval she was no nearer to getting invited to one of the gang's secret meetings.

Women were queuing right out the door of Mr Blundell's grocery shop, all gossiping, their shopping baskets over their arms, ration books and purses in their hands. Jack usually collected Mrs Baker's order at this time on a Saturday morning, but today he wasn't there.

Bonny paused for a moment outside the shop, considering asking someone if they'd seen him, when she saw Tom and Michael Easton going into the post office across the road.

Tom was the same age as Bonny, Michael just six. They shared their older brother's unmistakable flamered hair and freckles and she assumed Jack was with them too, already inside the shop.

Mrs Miller's post office was a dark, cramped Aladdin's cave of a shop. The post office section, behind its metal grill, took up half of one wall; the rest of the shop was a mishmash of sweets, haberdashery, knitting wool and stationery.

It was Bonny's favourite shop. She loved the glass and wood cabinet which held all the Sylko cottons, the reels of ribbons and laces which hung on wooden poles and the exciting profusion of buttons, hair nets, elastic, hair slides and suspenders. There was no space left free in the shop: packets of knitting wool were stacked in front of the counter, still more in cubby holes on the far wall; boxes of birthday cards and bolts of dress fabric were piled up next to writing materials, tubs of knitting needles and curlers.

Mrs Miller presided over a wooden counter crowded with small tubs of aniseed balls, gobstoppers and jelly babies. Behind her, jars of sherbet lemons, toffees and dolly mixtures shared space with jigsaw puzzles, small dolls and toy cars.

Mrs Miller was very old with snow-white hair. As Bonny walked in, tinkling the shop bell, she looked round from measuring some elastic and smiled at her. She was only distracted for a second, but to Bonny's amazement Tom used that brief moment to reach up and snatch a lone, large bar of chocolate from the almost empty display stand, right under Mrs Miller's nose.

While Mrs Miller continued with her measuring, Tom hastily stuffed the bar in the pocket of his shorts.

Bonny was more astounded that there was still such a large bar of chocolate in existence than by Tom's daring. Before she left London most of the shops had long since run out. She was also surprised to find that Tom and Michael weren't accompanied by Jack.

'There now,' Mrs Miller said as she wound the

elastic round her hand and wrapped it in a twist of white paper. 'Now don't you lose it, Tom, we're getting low on elastic and heaven knows when we'll get some more. That's tuppence please.'

Tom held out the money with his left hand, his right covering the chocolate bar which stuck out like a wing on his hip.

'What would you like, Bonny?' Mrs Miller asked.

Bonny hesitated. The theft had made her mind go blank and she couldn't think of any excuse to be in the shop. Worse still, Tom was looking at her, perhaps wondering if she had seen the whole thing.

The shop door opened again and in came Miss Thorpe, Bonny's and Tom's teacher. 'Hello boys,' she said, smiling at Tom and Michael. Then, turning her head, she saw Bonny standing back in the gloom. 'And Bonny too. What a lovely day it is today, thank goodness it's stopped raining. It feels as if summer is here at last.'

Miss Thorpe's sudden arrival and her warm greeting threw Tom entirely. Bonny saw his face drain of colour and his mouth fall open in alarm as he desperately tried to hide the chocolate with his hand.

Mrs Miller gave a little gasp. To Bonny's horror, the old lady was touching the space where the chocolate had been on the display stand. 'You've taken my chocolate!' she exclaimed indignantly, looking right at Tom.

'I never,' he said, too quickly and with too little conviction.

'You must've taken it you wicked boy, it was there before you came in.'

Bonny weighed up the situation in a flash. It was only a matter of time before Tom was caught out, especially with Miss Thorpe to back up Mrs Miller. She had to do something.

'Let me look,' she said in her sweetest voice, sidling up to Tom and the counter. 'I'm sure Tom wouldn't take it, maybe you've knocked it down somewhere.'

Standing on tiptoe to look over the counter, Bonny used her left hand to pull the chocolate from Tom's pocket and surreptitiously lowered it to the stack of knitting wool in front of her.

'Are you sure it hasn't fallen down by your feet?' Bonny asked, stretching still further over the counter.

'No it hasn't. He's taken it.' Mrs Miller's voice rose accusingly. 'Make him turn out his pockets, Miss Thorpe. I won't have children stealing from me.'

Tom flashed Bonny an odd look, somewhere between suspicion and gratitude, and stepped back a little. 'I ain't taken nothin',' he said, his eyes widening in feigned innocence, pulling the contents of his pockets out and revealing only the small package of elastic, a grubby handkerchief and a pencil stub.

Miss Thorpe moved towards Tom, her hands reaching out to frisk him. 'Tom!' Her voice was like rumbling thunder. 'Hand it over at once.'

Little Michael was frisked next, but he genuinely knew nothing of the theft and looked baffled.

Mrs Miller came round the counter. For an old lady she moved quickly, pushing Bonny out of the way and pulling Tom's jumper up, patting at him angrily. 'Where is it, you naughty boy?' She grasped his ear between two fingers and pulled him nearer the door as if to look at him better.

Miss Thorpe frowned, looking first at Tom, then across to Bonny. 'Did you see anything?' she asked.

'No, miss.' Bonny batted her eyes in feigned innocence. 'But I came in after Tom and Michael, only a minute before you did.'

The chocolate was lying on the brown parcel of knitting wool, in full view of everyone. Only the gloom of the shop prevented it from being noticed immediately.

Tom protested loudly, struggling to get free of Mrs

Miller, who was still convinced he had it somewhere about his person.

The shop door opened again, this time to let in the old man who lived a few doors down from Briar Bank. As clear light came into the shop, Miss Thorpe gasped, pointing to the bar lying in state on top of the wool.

'There it is Mrs Miller. Look!'

Mrs Miller had no choice but to apologise, although she did so with a bad grace and mumbled something about boys being like bulls in china shops.

Bonny left with Tom and Michael, offering up the explanation that she'd forgotten what she wanted to buy.

'Thanks, Bonny,' Tom said gruffly once they were well away from the shop. 'I reckon she'd 'ave killed me if she found it in m' pocket.'

'It's all right.' Bonny tried to look nonchalant. 'You were a bit daft taking that big one. I would've taken one of the small ones she wouldn't miss.' In fact she wouldn't have dreamt of stealing from a shop, and was surprised at herself for covering up his crime.

'You won't tell anyone,' he whispered. His brown eyes were screwed up with anxiety and he didn't look as tough as he did at school. 'If Mrs Baker found out she'd skin me.'

Bonny found she was holding an excellent hand. 'I won't if you let me in your gang,' she said with a casual shrug of her shoulders.

Tom looked at Bonny in consternation.

Everyone was a bit wary of Bonny Phillips. She was a show-off, a teacher's pet and vindictive when she was crossed. But if it wasn't for her Mrs Miller would have him in her back room by now, phoning up not only Mrs Baker but PC Onslow too.

'It ain't for me to say.' Tom scratched his head. 'I'll 'ave to ask our Jack. We're 'aving a meeting this after, per'aps 'e could ask the others.'

'At the goods train?' she asked.

Tom's face grew pale beneath his freckles. He had been attempting to stall her, but now it seemed she knew their secret hideout too.

'I know you meet there.' Bonny grinned, knowing she'd got him backed into a corner. She pushed her hands into the pockets of her siren suit, trying desperately hard not to be too girlish. 'I'll come then and bring some fags.'

His faint smirk was confirmation he couldn't think of a good reason to prevent her arrival.

'I ain't sayin' you can join,' he said after a moment's hesitation. 'We'll 'ave to vote on it. But I'll tell 'em all you was a good sport.'

'I was going to take you to see Shirley Temple in *The Little Princess*,' Aunt Lydia said as they ate soup for their lunch. She was a little disappointed that Bonny didn't seem to want to spend the afternoon with her; their trips to the cinema were usually the thing Bonny looked forward to most. 'But if you'd rather go out to play I suppose we could go another day.'

'It's too nice to be inside today,' Bonny wheedled.

'Well, I have got quite a few jobs to do in the garden,' Aunt Lydia sighed. But seeing the child's bright face she smiled. 'Of course dear, you go out to play, you're quite right, it is too nice a day to be in a cinema.'

Bonny approached the dilapidated goods train at the back of the sidings with some trepidation. Even if Tom was on her side, the other boys were all twelve and thirteen-year-olds who had no time for girls.

She had five Woodbines in one pocket and half a dozen chocolate liqueurs in the other. She'd taken the chocolates from a big box in the sitting-room, which Aunt Lydia had said were given to her last Christmas. The cigarettes were filched from the desk drawer.

She tapped nervously on the sliding door of the train.

'Friend or foe?' a boy called out.

'Friend,' she said.

'If we let you in will you promise on pain of death not to pass on any secrets?' the disembodied voice called out.

'I promise,' she called back, her courage for once almost failing her.

The train door made an echoey rumbling noise as it was pulled back. Her eyes were just level with the floor, and Jack was bending over, offering his hands.

'Put one foot on the wheel,' he said, 'and jump up.'

Aside from the three Eastons, there were another four boys – Eric Turley, Peter Samms, Colin Atkins and John Broom. Jack and Tom looked welcoming enough, and Michael, who was clearly only there because of family connections, grinned, but the other four were distinctly hostile.

She managed to get up without disgracing herself. They had a couple of candles in jam jars and the yellow glow made their faces look sinister.

'We don't allow girls in our gang,' Eric Turley threw at her, folding his arms across his chest as if that was the end of it.

'Sit down,' Jack said. He was embarrassed. Tom had explained what had happened at the shop and Jack agreed in principle that such quick thinking on Bonny's part deserved some reward. But the other boys were totally against girls and as they'd pointed out emphatically, Bonny Phillips was a spoilt brat. 'Look Bonny, we can't have girls in our gang. We does fings what girls can't.'

'Like what?' she said, sitting cross-legged and staring boldly from one face to the other. She knew the four older members only slightly. They were in the top class along with Jack, all in identical grey shorts and grey flannel shirts. Eric had a Fair Isle sleeveless pull-over, the others had plain blue ones. Eric and John were dark, while Peter was blond and Colin had light brown hair, but they all had similarly untidy haircuts, lean pre-adolescent faces, grubby knees and worn-out plimsoles. There wasn't much to distinguish one from another.

'Swimming, climbing, train-spotting,' Eric said with a sneer. His father owned the Bridge Inn and he thought he was 'it'.

'I can do all of those,' she lied. In fact she had never tried to swim and, although she was good at climbing, train-spotting looked as boring as watching grass grow.

As they exchanged glances, Bonny got her gifts out of her pockets. 'I brought you some fags,' she said. 'Sorry there isn't one for everyone, but we can share them. The chocolates have got real whisky in them.'

The liqueurs weren't a great success. Little Michael spat his out immediately, the others pulled faces. But the cigarettes were received by the five older boys with respect. Bonny took a deep drag on one when it was offered to her and managed not to cough.

A lull in hostilities at least gave Bonny a chance to weigh up the opposition. She felt certain Jack and Tom would come down on her side if she could just think of something to impress the others with.

'I can speak German,' she blurted out. 'I bet none of you can!'

'Speak some then,' Peter Samms said.

'*Schildkrotensuppe, rinderbraten, sauerbraten*,' she said quickly.

The shocked expression on their faces made her want to giggle.

Aunt Lydia had taught her those few words. She had been telling Bonny about a holiday she'd had once in Germany and as she mentioned things she'd eaten Bonny got her to repeat the words merely because she liked the sound of them.

'What does it mean?' Jack said, suitably awed.

'If you come any closer I'll kill you,' Bonny said. 'Think how useful that would be if any Germans came here.'

They got her to repeat the phrase several times, each trying it out for themselves.

'We could have it as a club password,' she suggested. 'Please let me join?'

They passed around a bottle of lemonade while they thought about it, each taking four gulps. Bonny wanted to wipe the neck before putting her mouth on it, but she guessed such an action would look too girlish.

'You'll have to do a test,' John Broom said. He was the smallest of the older boys and very thin. Bonny remembered hearing that his father, who had now been called up, used to knock him about. 'We all did one.'

'What sort of test?' Bonny felt a tremor of fear.

'Climbing,' Eric said. 'See how far you can get up the chalk cliff.'

Bonny gulped. The chalk cliff was just twenty yards from the train and as high as four or five houses. She'd attempted to climb it soon after her arrival but couldn't manage more than a few feet.

'No, not the cliff,' Jack said, shaking his head. 'Mrs Baker will see her and she'll go barmy. A tree will do.'

All eight children were just passing the stationhouse when Mrs Baker leaned out of the bedroom window and bellowed at Jack.

Mrs Baker was a good sort: fat, motherly and jolly. But although she was mostly good-natured and kindly, she was fearsome when roused and there was no way they could ignore her.

'Come you here,' she yelled, her tone and red face suggesting she'd discovered something. 'Tom and Michael too.'

'I bet she's found that Red Chief Shag tobacco,' Tom said, looking worried. 'I knew we ought to've brought it out with us.'

'We'll wait down by the river,' Eric said quickly, afraid Mrs Baker might tell his mother. 'I'll test Bonny.'

It was on the tip of Bonny's tongue to say she wasn't allowed by the river, but under the circumstances she couldn't. Without the Easton boys with her for support she felt very vulnerable.

Bonny felt a bit out of it as the boys ran down the hill pretending to be Spitfires. All the boys at school were mad about fighter planes: they collected pictures from magazines and cigarette cards and when one went overhead they went wild with excitement. But not to be outdone, she too spread her arms wide and copied the droning noise the boys were making.

'Cor, the river's high,' John said gleefully as they approached it. 'And look how fast the current is!'

The river had always looked scary to Bonny. Aunt Lydia described it as treacherous and warned her hundreds of times not to go near it. The bridge was very long, with a series of low grey stone arches. Usually there was just enough clearance for a small boat to go beneath them and ducks and swans often rested on the tiny islands of weed growing round each of the supports. But until today it had been raining solidly for almost a week and now the river was so high there was perhaps only a two-foot gap between water and arch. The islands were completely submerged. The fact that there were no ducks and swans swimming suggested that the swift current was too much even for them.

As if further proof were necessary of how dangerous the river was, all the rowing boats were pulled up high on the bank by the teahouse. The grass was sodden and there wasn't anyone taking tea outside, even though the owner of the teahouse had put cloths on the tables hopefully.

'Reckon you can swim in that?' Eric asked Bonny, his narrow face alight with malice.

'It's a bit cold for swimming,' Bonny offered, hoping that sounded as if she might be game for it at a later date.

'Girls are soft,' Eric sneered. 'I've swum in it when it's been higher than that.'

Bonny guessed this was a lie. 'The test was supposed to be climbing a tree,' she retorted. 'Find me one!'

'This'll do,' Peter shouted from over to their right by the bridge, pointing out a sycamore tree growing close to the water's edge.

Bonny sighed with relief. It might be big but it was an easy one, with plenty of low branches.

'Well?' Eric said insolently, fully expecting her to back off.

'Okay.' Bonny shrugged her shoulders. 'How high do you want me to go?'

'Start climbing and we'll say when we're satisfied,' he said.

Bonny ran to the tree, shinned up twelve or fourteen feet effortlessly, then paused as she reached a wide branch to look down at the boys.

All four of them looked stunned. Eric's mouth was hanging open and Bonny felt triumphant.

'Shall I go on?' she shouted down.

Eric scowled in irritation. He sensed John and Colin were coming round to this kid and he knew by the way she'd climbed up that far that she could get a great deal further. 'No,' he yelled back. 'Go right along that branch you're standing on.'

Bonny looked. The branch went right over the water, the leaves on the end reaching the far side of the first bridge arch. She didn't like the thought of going out over water, but the branch was a very thick one.

'Okay,' she agreed.

The need to show-off got the better of her. Instead of sitting down astride the branch and shuffling along, she put out her arms like a tightrope walker and began walking.

Bonny had always had good balance, and since her sandals had crêpe soles there didn't seem to be anything to fear. As long as she didn't look down into the river, she could do it easily.

John Broom looked up at Bonny balancing precariously on the high branch and he felt sick. She was such a little girl, however much she swaggered and showed off. Until Jack had befriended him he'd always been ignored by Eric and Peter and he'd had to do things he wouldn't normally dream of doing to be accepted by the gang. He guessed Bonny was doing this for exactly the same reason and he didn't like it. The branch was bending with her weight, and he guessed how strong the wind was up there by the way her hair was blowing around. One false step and she could fall in.

'Sit down,' he called out. 'It's dangerous.'

'I like danger,' she called back. 'I bet none of you would dare do it.' She felt elated, already imagining this reported back in the playground. The boys were bound to accept her as a new gang member now.

But a gust of wind startled her. She glanced down and saw she was way out over the river. All at once she was scared, wanting to sit down, but there was nothing to hold on to while she lowered herself.

John saw her hesitate and knew instinctively she'd lost her nerve. This wasn't a harmless game any longer, but a very dangerous situation. 'Just stay there,' he yelled out. 'I'll come up and help you back.'

'I told you girls couldn't climb,' Eric sneered as John started to climb up the tree, and walked away in disgust.

Peter and Colin were rooted to the spot. Like John, they could now see the real danger. The river was swirling past the bank at a ferocious speed: if she fell she'd be washed away, however good a swimmer she was.

'Stay still,' Peter called out. 'John's coming up to help you. You done good Bonny, but don't go no further.'

As Eric reached the road he was angry. He wasn't concerned if the kid was stuck in the tree, only that she'd spoilt the afternoon by turning up with her fags and chocolates. He put his hands in his pockets, hunched up his shoulders and began to trudge home.

He was just walking under the railway bridge when Jack came running down from the station.

'Where's the others?' he asked, slightly out of breath.

Eric pointed back towards the river. 'Fancy even thinking of letting a girl join our club,' he spat out. 'She's stuck up a tree now, silly cow.'

'Which tree?' Jack asked, aware if anything happened to Bonny he would get blamed by Miss Wynter.

'The big one near the bridge.'

Jack didn't wait to hear anything more, he just bolted down the road. He knew the tree Eric meant and he remembered how close it was to the river.

By now John had reached the branch Bonny was standing on. He sat down astride it and began shuffling along. 'I'm coming,' he reassured her. 'Just stay very still till I reach you.'

Bonny quivered with fear, her outstretched arms flaying wildly. The branch was vibrating beneath her feet now John was moving along it, but she couldn't turn to him. The wind seemed to be getting stronger, blowing her hair across her face, and the rustling of leaves made her even more aware of how high up she was. The river below looked terrifying, swirling past so fast it made her giddy.

'Don't look down.' John's voice was hoarse with fright. 'I'm nearly there.'

As he grew closer, the branch vibrated, Bonny's arms flayed even more wildly, her body swaying from side to side.

'You're shaking me,' she shrieked, losing her balance altogether. Leaves brushed her right hand and she grabbed at them frantically, but as John moved again in one desperate attempt to grab her body, she slipped and toppled off the branch.

Her scream was cut off suddenly by the splash as her body hit the water. John pushed leaves aside, peering down, but he couldn't see her.

'Get help,' he screamed at his friends below. 'Quick, she'll drown.'

Jack had just reached the grass leading from the road down to the river bank when he heard Bonny's scream and saw the flash of red as she tumbled sideways into the water. He could see Colin and Peter teetering on the edge of the bank, not knowing what to do.

'Get Alec from the Tollhouse,' he yelled as he ran forward. 'Quick!'

He kicked off his plimsoles and leapt into the water without even thinking. He went right under, the water so icy it almost paralysed him, but he bobbed up again struggling for breath, looking around for Bonny. Jack couldn't swim more than a few yards, and he'd only learnt to do that last September when he first arrived in Amberley as an evacuee, but it wasn't necessary to swim now – the current was so fierce it was carrying him along.

Peter bolted for Alec in the Tollhouse. Colin stayed on the bank, not knowing what to do. He was aware Jack wasn't a strong swimmer and he couldn't see Bonny at all.

But then he saw a flash of red by the arch of the bridge.

'Under the bridge,' Colin screamed at Jack. 'Grab her!'

The weight of the water in his shorts was pulling Jack down, the water so cold he could barely move, but blindly he struck out, bobbing his head up to try and see.

He saw what looked like a red cushion just going under the bridge and thrashed towards it. He knocked one hand on the underside of the arch, the current bashed him against the bridge support, and now it was too dark beneath the bridge to see anything.

Jack was terrified. The water was so cold it hurt and he could see nothing but the thinnest arc of daylight ahead as his body was thrown from side to side by the current. A hidden rock beneath the water scraped his leg, the brickwork above him was too slimy to hold on to, and his lungs seemed to be full of water. There was nothing for it but to let the current wash him along. He couldn't see anything, but his hands swept out in front of him, groping for Bonny.

It was only when he reached daylight that he saw the flash of red again. Now free of the confines of the bridge he struck out in a desperate crawl towards her, forcing his frozen body to obey him. With one almighty lunge he reached her, clutching at the red material. With his last vestiges of strength, he jerked her up.

Somehow he managed to turn her on to her back, treading water like mad to keep himself afloat. Their combined weight was sweeping them along even faster, and he was sure she was already dead because her head fell lifelessly back on his shoulder.

'Hold on, son,' Alec's gruff voice boomed out. Only then was Jack able to turn his head far enough to see the man running along the bank holding a long boat-hook in one hand, a lifebelt in the other. 'Try and catch the belt. I'll grab you as you pass.'

Alec tossed in the white ring so that it landed just behind them. Jack let go of Bonny with one hand and hooked his arm through it.

'Good lad,' Alec shouted as Jack managed to get a firmer grip again on Bonny. 'Now try and get closer to the bank.'

The security of the ring tucked beneath his arm gave Jack the impetus he needed and he managed a few frog-like movements with his legs towards the hook held out in front of him.

'That's it, lad,' Alec yelled, catching his hook around the rope on the lifebelt. 'I'll haul thee in.'

Jack's strength left him just at the point when he felt Alec taking over. He felt himself being dragged along, and then a bump as the belt hit the bank.

'Brave lad.' Alec's gruff voice sounded distant, but Jack knew the hand grasping his shirt collar belonged to him. 'I've got thee now, never fear.'

Jack was aware of other hands, felt himself slither up the muddy bank and land like a huge gasping fish on the grass of the meadow.

'Have ye called the doctor?' he dimly heard Alec say as someone wrapped a blanket round him. There were other voices too, familiar ones, yet he was too numb to recognise faces.

'Get the lad into the warm.' Alec spoke again and Jack felt arms lifting him.

Then he saw Bonny. She was lying on the grass, Alec astride her small back, pressing, then lifting her shoulders. Her face was chalk-white and her eyes were closed.

'Is shshshe dead?' Jack asked, his teeth clattering like castanets.

Jack didn't know if there was a reply to his question. He just heard a ringing sound in his ears as he felt his knees go from under him.

*

Alec pumped away at the girl. All he knew of her was that she was an evacuee. He was certain she was already too far gone to resuscitate, but still he kept on.

Alec had lived in Amberley his entire fifty-five years, except for his time in the Army during the First War. He owned the garage, but aside from mending cars and farm machinery, he could turn his hand to anything from bricklaying to first aid.

This little girl wasn't the first he'd hauled out of the river – during July and August there was always someone falling out of a boat. But now the river was still icy from the long bitter winter, and she'd been in there quite some time. He didn't think he could pull her round.

A small crowd had gathered, watching silently as spurts of water came out of Bonny's slack mouth. Someone yelled that the doctor was on his way and then, just as he felt he could do no more, Alec heard a gurgle.

'That's it, little 'un, breathe.' Alec's broad, weather-beaten face broke into a smile. 'Come on, m' little darlin', breathe for old Alec.'

'Oh Beryl, what am I to do now?' Lydia sobbed against Mrs Baker's plump shoulder. 'Should I send her mother a telegram? Should I go up to London and tell them?'

'Now, now,' Beryl said comfortingly, smoothing Lydia's hair back as if she were another of her charges. 'They's all right now, you just calm down and drink that sherry.'

Both Jack and Bonny had been brought to the stationhouse, warmed up in a steaming hot bath and tucked into bed with two stone hot-water bottles apiece. Alec had gone up to the village to get Lydia, but it had taken some time to find her as she was out looking for Bonny.

It was almost nine now. Tom was sharing Michael's bed as Bonny was in his, and Mr Baker was out in the station, waiting for the London train. Lydia had spoken to both Bonny and Jack and pieced the entire story together, but now she was in a state of shock, trembling as she realised how close Bonny had come to death.

Dr Noakes was of the opinion that it was little short of a miracle Alec had managed to resuscitate Bonny, and he was still concerned both children might develop a fever, or other complications.

'What if Jack hadn't been so quick-witted?' Lydia said, tears streaming down her cheeks. 'It doesn't bear thinking about, does it?'

'He was a brave lad and no mistake,' Beryl smiled. 'He's a good kid, best day's work I ever done taking him in. But you mustn't go tormenting yerself with might-have-beens, Miss Wynter. The good Lord saved her today for some reason and she won't be going near no water again in a hurry.'

'I'm a failure,' Lydia said in a broken voice. 'I didn't keep a close enough watch on her. I didn't even ask her who she was going to play with.'

Beryl Baker's heart was as big as she was. She'd raised five boys of her own and she had enough love to spare for twenty more. She excelled in emergencies; she didn't flap, or sit in judgement. Lydia Wynter was hysterical and right now she needed mothering too.

'You can't watch them every minute of the day. I knows that,' Beryl said soothingly. 'Your Bonny's a little monkey and twice as crafty. But maybe when she wakes up tomorrow and don't feel so good, she'll understand why we tell 'em the things we do.'

By Lydia's third large glass of sherry her shaking stopped. Beryl had lit the fire in the parlour and she was insisting Lydia stayed the night too. Bert Baker had looked in for a moment, but then gone out again, down to the Bridge Inn for a pint.

'I should send a telegram,' Lydia said, staring into her empty glass.

Bonny had come round enough before being put to bed to relate in detail how drowning felt. She'd said that she felt she was being sucked into a black hole and however she struggled she couldn't get out.

'I saw Mum and Dad holding out their hands to me,' she said, her eyes huge and terrified. 'I couldn't reach them.'

'I reckon this is one thing you should keep quiet about.' Beryl shrugged her shoulders. 'I mean what good's it gonna do telling 'em? They'll get all worked up, rush down here and take 'er home. Then the way the war's going she might have to be shipped off somewhere else again, and the worry'll kill 'em.'

'But I can't disregard parental rights like that.' Lydia looked horrified.

Beryl half smiled. 'D'you think I worry about what the boys' ma would say each time I clout them? I know Mrs Easton don't give a tinker's cuss about 'em and Bonny's folks think she's the sun, moon and stars. But when they handed over their kids to us, I reckon that gave us the right to make decisions for ourselves.'

'Well, I can't do anything tonight,' Lydia sighed. 'I'll see how things are in the morning.'

'Are you awake, Jack?' Bonny whispered.

She was in Tom's bed, Jack a couple of feet away in his own.

'Sort of,' he replied, his voice heavy with sleep. 'What's up?'

Bonny had been awake for some time. She'd heard Mr and Mrs Baker's bedsprings creaking as they got into bed and she'd just lain thinking about things.

The stationhouse reminded her a bit of her home

in Becontree, with square small rooms and none of the luxury she'd grown used to at Briar Bank. But although Mrs Baker's home was shabby, Bonny sensed something here that she'd never encountered before. A kind of cosiness, a sense that nothing bad could happen, a house where people didn't pretend about things or worry about what others thought of them. For some reason it had made her feel guilty.

'I don't ever want to go in water again,' she whispered. 'It was so horrible. I lied to you when I said I could swim.'

'That don't matter,' Jack said. Bonny could see no more of him than a dark shape but she was glad he was close. 'We all tell fibs sometimes. Can you really speak German?'

'No,' she admitted, explaining those were just odd words Lydia had taught her.

Jack sniggered. 'Fat lot of good it would do saying it to a German prisoner then. He'd think we was gonna bring him some grub.'

Bonny giggled, her fear subsiding. 'Tell me about your mum?' she asked.

'Ain't much to tell really,' he whispered. 'She ain't like yours for a start.'

Bonny listened as he told her about about the basement flat in Braganza Street, Kennington. About his two older brothers who'd left home because of his mother's drinking. The picture he painted, of being left alone to fend for the two younger boys all the time, the lack of food and clothes, made Bonny want to cry.

'I thought I was in 'eaven when I got 'ere,' Jack said. 'Mrs Baker picked us three out because nobody else wanted us. Michael had messed his pants and we all had 'oles in our shoes. I love 'er, Bonny. I wish she was our real ma. I don't ever want to go back to London.'

Bonny found herself admitting that she didn't

either. She spoke of her embarrassment when her parents came to visit.

'Mummy's so dreadful sometimes,' she said. 'She pretends she's posh and she goes on to Aunt Lydia about having me and stuff all the time. She thinks I'm a baby and she won't let me out of her sight. Daddy's okay, but sometimes I feel like I'm being suffocated by Mummy.'

They talked of their plans for when they were grown up. Jack said he wanted to be Alec's apprentice at the garage, and one day he'd have his own one. Bonny said she was going to be a film star, and Jack didn't laugh.

'Thank you for saving me,' Bonny said as her eyelids began to droop.

'It weren't nothin',' Jack replied a little gruffly. 'That's what friends is for.'

'Am I your friend?' she whispered.

Jack had made a reputation for himself by being tough. Back in Kennington he would lie, cheat and steal to get what was needed for him and his brothers. But living with Mr and Mrs Baker had altered things: now he saw that the best things came to those who worked hard for them. It was better to be liked than feared. He'd even torn Tom off a strip today for stealing the chocolate. Bonny was like him in an odd sort of way, full of all that bravado and cockiness, but underneath the spoilt brat there was something kind of sweet and nice.

'Course I'm yer friend,' he said gruffly.

'For ever?' she asked, aware now that she'd never had a real friend.

'For ever,' he agreed. 'Now go to sleep.'

Chapter Six

'Share the joke with me!' Amos Gilbert looked up from sawing a length of timber as Ellie laughed aloud.

They were in the workshop. Ellie had brought Amos a mug of tea on her return from school. Now she was sitting in a patch of sunshine just inside the door on an upturned box, reading her letter.

It was Thursday afternoon in late September. Although it was still warm for the time of year, long shadows and the reddening leaves of the Virginia creeper on the workshop walls suggested autumn was almost here.

'It's another one of Mum's funny stories,' she replied, looking up, her dark eyes full of laughter. 'Max Miller was just ready to leave the dressing-room when she noticed he had a little split in the seam of his trousers. Shall I read it to you?'

'Go on then.' Amos wiped his brow with the back of his hand, perched on a trestle and took his pipe out of his pocket.

This was the time of day Amos liked most – funerals over for the day, Grace out and Ellie sharing tea and chatter with him before she went into the house to prepare the evening meal.

Ellie looked very pretty, he thought, in her candy-striped school dress, her plaits coming loose and wisps of dark hair framing her sun-tanned face.

Since the spring, when Amos was forced to take his sister in hand about Ellie, a great deal had changed, both in his home and the progress of the war.

The 'Phoney War' had come to an end with the evacuation of Dunkirk in June. Paris was captured and occupied by the Germans a couple of weeks later. There had been the Battle of Britain, the first daylight bombing of London, in July, and then the start of the London Blitz in August.

Although the residents of Bury St Edmunds hadn't faced any bombing on their town yet, it had come dangerously close. Back in June, visitors were banned along twenty miles of the East coast, and the beaches were mined and small boats immobilised for fear of invasion. In July, a German Junker caught fire in midair in the middle of the night and crashed down in Bury St Edmunds, causing consternation but also great excitement, particularly amongst the small boys who rushed next morning to see it. Norwich had more than its fair share of suffering, with two raids in July and more in August when some two dozen people were killed.

Spectacular air battles fought overhead in August, as the Germans made a massive synchronised assault on all the East Anglian airbases, brought danger even closer. Martleham, where raiders aimed about thirty bombs, was hit first. A Fairey Battle on the ground caught fire and the bombs on board exploded with such violence that two aircraft hangars were destroyed and the watch-tower demolished.

These assaults on airfields had gone on day after day until mid-September, but now, aside from the odd stray bomber coming inland, the Germans appeared to be concentrating their efforts more on London and the south.

To someone arriving from London, Bury St Edmunds might seem an oasis of calm and serenity: there were no smoking ruins or roofless, windowless houses. But the town had its share of problems. Resources, already stretched by evacuees, at times nearly reached breaking-point as still more strangers flooded in.

Exhausted, battered families turned up almost daily from London: desperate people who could no longer stand the lack of sleep, noise and confusion, some with injuries from shrapnel, burns and broken limbs. Small children with white, strained faces clutched their mothers' skirts, wide, frightened eyes reflecting the horrors they'd witnessed.

Wives and girlfriends arrived in the hope of snatching a few hours with their men at Fighter Command in Duxford, Debden and Coltishall, always afraid it might be their last chance to be together. Many old ladies who before the war wouldn't have dreamed of letting a room to a couple without seeing proof of marriage now let the spirit of romance sweep them along, often wiping tears from their eyes as young lovers parted on their doorsteps.

ATS and land-girls rode in on bicycles from nearby barracks or farms to meet airmen and soldiers. They filled the teashops, cafés and public houses and on Saturday nights they jitterbugged in the Corn Exchange to touring bands in the style of Glenn Miller.

The schools were overcrowded, and the doctor, billeting officers and police were all overworked. Housewives complained that this constant influx of people was reducing their rations of food and making the queues still longer. The old guard of the town said that drunkenness and 'loose behaviour' was rife amongst the young.

The meat ration had been cut again, so the country folk went back to their old ways, shooting rabbits and even blackbirds, which they claimed were better than pheasant. Stocks in shops were depleted, but while most people accepted the food shortages calmly, the lack of everyday things like elastic, batteries, face cream and candles infuriated them.

Yet despite all the problems and shortages, the war

united people. Each East Anglian serviceman killed in action brought it home to people that tomorrow their own son or husband might be added to the ever-growing list. Fear and uncertainty drew different classes together in ways unknown in peacetime.

Land-girls with plummy accents palled up with cockneys. Women who'd lost husbands in the First War offered comfort to those recently widowed. Aristocratic ladies made room in the sewing bees for women they once thought of as 'housemaid' material. Crusty farmers were glad of a pair of extra hands, whoever they belonged to. Loneliness became a thing of the past for the many old people who opened up the doors of their cottages to strangers transplanted by war and suddenly found themselves part of a family again.

Shopkeepers had a brisker trade, the pubs and cafés were busier, and the churches were packed on Sundays. While many of the older folk wished for a return of quiet serenity, the young embraced the changes. Strangers added colour and excitement to their lives. Girls who once expected to stay at home until they married joined the ATS and the WAAF and delighted in taking an active part in the war. Danger brought a new romanticism, heightened by the films and songs. Long drawn-out courtships became a thing of the past. Love was to be savoured now: tomorrow might be too late.

Amos Gilbert had his share of headaches. Petrol was in short supply, and good timber and brass handles were hard to find. Few people found it appropriate to send their relatives off with style, when young men were giving their lives heroically for their country. His apprentice had been called up, and the stonemason was always off drilling with the Home Guard. On top of his own business he had fire-watching duties, and he'd cleared part of the yard to grow vegetables, enough to keep any man busy. But

Amos was a happier man than he had been in years. He was growing increasingly fond of Ellie, and Grace had found a new interest.

Once Grace had discovered from a government leaflet that parsimonious talents such as hers were applauded by men in Whitehall, she made it a crusade to insure no one in the town wasted anything. Whether it was collecting jam jars and bottles, spare cooking utensils and scrap metal, or merely old jumpers to be unpicked and re-knitted as blankets, Grace master-minded the task. Because she had a reputation of being fearsome, people did as she said. It was less taxing to divide waste into separate bins for bones, paper, tins, bottles and food scraps, than have Grace Gilbert telling them they were 'letting England down' by throwing it all in together. Armed with a small cart converted by Amos out of an old pram, with a placard on each side proclaiming 'Save for Victory', Grace Gilbert was to be seen daily making her rounds up and down the streets whatever the weather. She smirked with pleasure when people said 'What would we do without Miss Gilbert', never knowing that she was also referred to as 'Goebbels' behind her back.

This collecting work proved to be the answer to Ellie's prayers. It took Miss Gilbert out of the house for long periods and appeared to have a calming effect on her. She was no longer quite so fanatical about cleaning, and occasionally she would actually sit down in the evenings to knit or sew. She would flare up every now and again about something trivial, but overall, life at High Baxter Street was a great deal more pleasant.

With Grace away from the house so much, Ellie and Mr Gilbert formed a close alliance. Most days they would share the washing up and clerical work for the business and then go into the living-room to listen to *ITMA* or *Much Binding in the Marsh* on the wireless.

Soon Ellie was reading Amos her mother's and Marleen's letters and that brought her on to telling him about her previous life and the characters in Alder Street. It seemed to Amos that Ellie had seen far more of life than he had, despite her tender years. He encouraged her impressions of people, got her to rehearse her parts for the school productions in front of him, and found himself dreading the time when his sister would arrive home and halt such jollity.

It was the laughing together in secret that cemented their friendship, but it was the little kindnesses to one another that laid the foundations.

Amos would clean Ellie's shoes, sneak her a glass of milk and a slice of cake and give her money to go to the cinema. Ellie dried his coat when he'd been out in the rain, and left him a hot drink in a vacuum flask when he came back late from fire-watching. She discovered the meals he liked best, and as far as rationing would allow, she tried to provide them, now that she was regularly preparing supper. Grace had never done such things and Amos was careful not to reveal them, for he sensed his sister was like a coiled cobra, perfectly capable of suddenly striking out in jealousy.

Amos watched Grace carefully. Although on the face of it she appeared more kindly disposed to Ellie, just occasionally he noticed an icy, calculating look in her eyes. She sniffed when the neighbours remarked that the girl was turning into something of a beauty, and when Mrs Forester sent money for a new summer dress, Grace deliberately bought it a size too large. She even insisted Ellie's hair was tightly plaited at all times. But it did no good: anyone could see the girl's beautiful eyes, the child's body gradually turning into womanly curves, and guess at what was to come.

Amos smiled now as Ellie read this latest letter. He guessed that much of the comedy of this story about

Polly Forester pursuing the star of the show with a needle and thread right to the wings wasn't actually written down, as Ellie wasn't following the written word too closely. As usual she had picked up the gist of the story and added her particular brand of humorous embroidery.

All through the year there had been letters from Mrs Forester about the Empire's show, *Haw Haw*. Amos sometimes thought he'd actually seen it: he knew Max Miller's co-stars were Ben and Bebe Daniels, he knew about Gusto Palmer the juggler who purposely dropped the balls, and about each one of the cancan girls. Now *Haw Haw* had ended and *Apple Sauce* had taken its place, but Max Miller was still the star, along with Vera Lynn, and according to the reviews enclosed with Mrs Forester's letters it was even funnier than the previous show.

Since the London Blitz had started, Amos had become almost as anxious about Mrs Forester as Ellie, for she'd had several close shaves. Alder Street got a direct hit one night at the end of August and number 18 and the two adjoining houses were completely destroyed. Fortunately Polly was down in the tube station at Whitechapel, along with Wilf and Edna. In a letter just after this she had described how the next morning they picked their way through the smoking rubble to find their house completely flattened but somewhat incongruously a chair, still with her cardigan slung on the back, sitting there as if waiting for her.

This kind of stoic humour, when she had lost everything she owned, endeared the woman even more to Amos, so much so that he wrote immediately to the theatre and offered her a home here, without even thinking what Grace would say. Fortunately perhaps, Fully didn't take him up on it, as by then she'd moved in with Marleen.

Being in London sounded like the worst kind of

nightmare to Amos. Nights in tube stations, packed in like sardines with little or no sleep, often walking to work because bombing had created havoc with transport. Arriving home to find the water and gas had been turned off. Noises and confusion everywhere.

But still the show went on nightly, although earlier than usual so people could get home before it was dark. Polly had reported how the stage door man stood watching bombs drop in distant parts of London, daring Hitler even to think of dropping one on the Holborn Empire.

'I wish Mum would leave London,' Ellie said suddenly. A break in her voice made Amos look round at her. To his surprise, her eyes were welling up with tears. 'What if she got hurt, Mr Gilbert?'

Ellie no longer ached to go back to London. She'd grown to love this pretty town and found joy in being the star of all the school productions. She was fond of Amos, who'd become the father she'd never had, and she'd even learnt to tolerate Miss Gilbert. If her mother would only come here, life would be just perfect.

'Now, now.' Amos got up and put one hand on Ellie's shoulder comfortingly. 'What would she do in the country?'

He had met Polly Forester just three times, but he liked her very much. Once or twice he had even allowed himself to weave a few romantic dreams of her moving here, of what might come of their shared interest in Ellie. But he was a practical man. Not only was the pretty little widow unlikely to fall for an undertaker, but she'd be like a fish out of water away from the theatre and London life.

'I don't know.' Ellie sniffed and wiped her eyes with the back of her hand. 'But I miss her so much and the war seems to be going on for ever, doesn't it?'

'It does,' Amos agreed. He couldn't admit that for him the past few months had flown by. 'What if we both try and persuade her to come here for a holiday? I could ask George at the Crown to put her up. Maybe if she was here for a while she'd change her mind and want to move.'

Ellie's face lit up. 'Maybe she could come next month when we do the show.' Her voice bubbled with excitement. 'I'll write tonight, Mr Gilbert. Would you really ask George?'

Amos smiled. 'Of course I will. But not a word to my sister, though, not until it's arranged. You know how prickly she is sometimes.'

As Ellie mixed some pastry on the kitchen table she was thinking up a persuasive letter to her mother, rather than concentrating on the few ingredients for the evening meal.

Mr Gilbert had managed to get a rabbit last weekend and they'd been eking out the stew all week. There was only a few tablespoons of it left now, but with a bit of onion, some diced carrots and potatoes there was enough to make three pasties.

One invaluable skill Ellie had brought with her from home was cooking. After years of watching her mother turn the cheapest cuts of meat into something tasty and satisfying, wartime rations were no real challenge. Even Miss Gilbert had been agreeably surprised and almost happily surrendered her former place as cook.

Her culinary skills had been widened still further by reading all the frugal recipes in government hand-outs, and learning from country women about herbs and vegetables almost unknown in London.

Ellie had learnt a great deal in her year here. Her cockney accent was all but gone and she had a broader vision of what she wanted for the future. In another six months she'd be fourteen and able to work, and if she hadn't persuaded Polly to move out of London by then, she'd join her there and find an office job or something until she found a way of getting on to the stage.

It was frustrating just waiting for the time to pass, especially when she knew Mum censored her stories of how it was in London in exactly the same way the newspapers and the BBC did. But then Ellie censored her stories too. She never let on how horrid Miss Gilbert was, or how much she missed her mum.

She supposed everyone was the same. Men in battle didn't whinge about how dangerous it was. Wives didn't witter on about how little food they had. Instead they mentioned the good or happy things, just as she told Polly about Mr Gilbert and Miss Wilkins, and Polly told her all the jokey things that happened in the Empire.

Ellie placed the pasties on a baking tray and put them in the oven, then went to her school satchel to find the apples. They were windfalls: she'd discovered a tree overhanging an alley close to her school and she checked there every afternoon to see what had dropped. Ellie smiled as she cut out the bruised bits and sliced them up. Such economy would silence Miss Gilbert's protests that they 'only had puddings on Sundays'.

It was just after six when planes came screaming overhead, so low that Ellie involuntarily ducked, thinking for a moment they were German bombers. Going to the kitchen door, she looked up at the sky. Mr Gilbert was standing by the workshop, shielding his eyes from the sun. It was a tight formation – six Spitfires speeding across the clear sky, leaving white foam-like traces of smoke behind them.

It was a common enough sight – in the past few months it had gone on incessantly – but for some odd reason, this time Ellie's stomach churned alarmingly, and she clutched her mother's letter tightly in the pocket of her dress for comfort.

'They'll knock out a few Germans for us,' Mr Gilbert shouted across the yard. 'Let's just hope they make it back.'

Despite Miss Gilbert returning home in an unusually pleasant mood and actually expressing pleasure at Ellie's pasties, the gut-churning sensation stayed with her, preventing her eating more than a few mouthfuls. Miss Gilbert was gloating about the huge amount of jam jars and bottles the Brownies had collected in a house-to-house campaign, and then suggesting Ellie should help unpick some old jumpers with her that evening to be re-knitted into blankets.

It was just before the news at nine that Ellie felt ill. She was sweating, her mouth was dry and her heart started to pound. Miss Gilbert was sitting opposite her with the wireless on, surrounded by jumpers, and Mr Gilbert was in his office doing some paperwork.

Instinct told Ellie the symptoms were related to her mother. Even though she knew Miss Gilbert would snort and say she was being stupid, she had to voice them.

'I think something's happened to Mum,' she blurted out, dropping the jumper she had started to unpick. 'I can feel it.'

Miss Gilbert stared at her over her glasses for a moment. She had got thinner still in the past six months, and her face was even more puckered. 'What nonsense!' she snapped. 'Get on with that unravelling and don't go looking for ridiculous things to annoy me with.'

The news droned on. Ellie scarcely listened to it as it was all so vague. They never specified which part of London had been badly bombed or the numbers of people killed or injured. Ellie pulled out clump after clump of wool, winding it round her hand and then into a ball, trying very hard to banish the scene in her head.

But it wouldn't go away. It was so clear, like seeing something at the pictures. She was lying in the double bed back in Alder Street, half asleep. Her mother was in her long nightdress, brushing her hair in front of the mirror, softly humming a tune from the evening's show. The small room was lit by a gas mantle, which concealed not only the stains on the walls, but the shabbiness of that nightgown and the faint lines on Polly's face. Fifty strokes on one side, fifty on the other, a crackle of static and faint sparks flying as Polly's gleaming hair jumped to meet the bristles.

It was a scene Ellie had watched night after night throughout her childhood.

She could hear everything, too. The soft thud as the brush was put down, then the bedsprings twanging as Polly got in beside her.

Ellie smelt a whiff of face powder, her mother's warm breath on her cheek as she leaned over to kiss her good-night and pulled the covers right over her shoulders.

'Night night, sugarplum,' she heard as clearly as if Polly were actually in the room.

Ellie saw her mother's eyes then, just the briefest glimpse before she reached up to turn off the gas. Clear blue, with a hint of violet round the edge of the iris.

Ellie couldn't sleep that night. She heard planes coming back, no brave roaring now, or tight formations, but singly, spluttering, limping back to the airfield.

A montage of jumbled images filled the darkness, vivid yet fleeting moving pictures. Polly and Marleen showing her how they did the Charleston, swinging imaginary beads and kicking their legs. Polly sitting on the doorstep in Alder Street, chatting to Edna on a summer's night. Polly rowing a boat in Victoria Park, laughing because she couldn't do more than make it go round and round. But one image was stronger than all the others that crowded in. Ellie could feel her mother's hand in hers as they stood in front of a lighted shop window in Regent Street. In front of them was one lone, white ballgown, surrounded by hundreds of suspended, glittering stars. It was two Christmases ago, when they'd gone to the West End to see the lights.

'You'll be beautiful when you're grown up,' Polly had said, squeezing Ellie's hand tightly. 'You'll wear dresses like that and I'll be so proud of you.'

Ellie now knew with utter certainty that Polly would never see her in such a dress. She would never feel another good-night kiss, hear the word 'sugarplum' or see those blue eyes again. She turned her face into her pillow and sobbed.

'Swop?' Carol suggested, holding out a piece of bread and dripping to Ellie. She knew something was wrong with her friend. Ellie hadn't interrupted once in class this morning, and had been sort of distant and tense, but Carol sensed it was better not to probe.

Officially all the children went home for dinner, but with so many women doing war work a great many of the children brought sandwiches to school now and stayed in the yard.

'You wouldn't want mine.' Ellie wrinkled her nose at the contents of her one thin sandwich. 'It's fish paste.'

Last night's premonition of disaster had been eased by waking to another fine day. She'd seen the telegram boy ride past on his bicycle, and the only telephone call had been for Mr Gilbert. In the face of any firm evidence, Ellie was doing her best to put her fear aside.

'I like fish paste,' Carol insisted. 'I only ever get bread and dripping and I'm sick of it.'

Miss Gilbert knew Ellie hated fish paste, and so she gave it to her all the more. Bread and dripping was a luxury, especially the way Carol's aunt did it, with thick, fresh, home-made bread and plenty of salt.

Carol had only arrived from London in June when the bombing started in earnest, and couldn't be called a true evacuee as she and her mother were staying with an aunt. Carol was small and timid, with mousy hair and odd slanty eyes, and she could barely read or write because she'd been ill a great deal when she was younger.

Ellie had befriended Carol when the other children started picking on her, but since then it had grown into an enduring and comfortable relationship, based on mutual need. Carol was Ellie's audience; she giggled at all her jokes, and comforted her when Ellie missed her mother. In return, Ellie protected Carol, helped her with her reading and boosted her fragile confidence.

'Go on, swop,' Carol insisted. 'I'm mad about fish paste.'

Ellie felt bound to accept, faced with such a well-intentioned lie. The bread stuck in her dry mouth, but Carol's kindness forced her to grin and pretend she was enthusiastic.

Some younger girls had brought out a long rope. Two seven-year-olds were holding each end, trying hard to turn it high enough for the others to skip in. Ellie saw one of them look to her for help and she was just going to stand up when she saw Miss Wilkins come out on to the steps by the school door.

Just the way she stood, with one hand shielding her eyes as she looked for someone, was enough. Even at a distance of some thirty yards, Ellie could see tension in the teacher's stance.

Ellie's stomach turned over. She dropped the remaining bread and dripping into Carol's lap and stood up.

'What's up?' she heard Carol say. A cold feeling was creeping down her spine as Miss Wilkins began walking through the children towards her.

'Ellie, will you come with me?' Miss Wilkins said as she approached. 'I want to have a word in private.'

The few yards seemed like a mile as Ellie followed Miss Wilkins into the school, her legs turning to rubber, her heart pounding.

Once inside the hall, Ellie could wait no longer. She reached out and clutched at Miss Wilkins's arm.

'It's Mum, isn't it?' she asked, hoping against hope she was wrong. 'She copped it last night, didn't she?'

'Oh, Ellie.' Miss Wilkins dropped her usual brisk manner and took hold of Ellie's two hands, pulling her close.

Ellie looked up before being enveloped in the woman's arms, and saw her teacher's damp eyes. 'I knew,' she whispered. 'I knew last night. Is she?' She couldn't finish the question. A feeling of utter desolation was welling up inside her.

For a second Miss Wilkins didn't reply. Ellie heard her gulp, then a deep sigh. 'Yes, I'm afraid so.' The woman's voice broke. 'She was caught in an air raid, running to the shelter.'

Ellie couldn't cry for some time. She let Miss Wilkins lead her to the headmistress's office, took the offered cup of tea in shaking hands and listened while her teacher told her of the telephone call she'd just received from Marleen.

Ellie pictured the scene. She could hear the warning siren, imagine her mother hurrying others out of the dressing-rooms before she thought of her own safety. Then the dash through the streets of Holborn, a basket with sandwiches and a flask of tea on her arm. Had she gone past the nearest shelter, running instead to the tube where Marleen always kept a place for her?

Ellie knew what bombs did. How the buildings just caved in, dust billowing up and then falling, covering everything like a thrown bag of flour. Then the fires breaking out all around like a scene from hell. But she couldn't imagine her pretty little mother being knocked down, her body crushed by bricks and falling masonry.

There was a vase of chrysanthemums on the headmistress's desk, a tawny red colour like Polly's hair. A few petals had fallen on to the blotter and she had an urge to pick them up and put them back on the flowers.

Everything seemed so normal. The sun was shining in at the window, the noise of children playing as loud as it always was. She caught sight of a Janet and John reading book lying on the window sill and remembered Polly coaching her with a similar one.

'Here is Janet. Here is John. This is Janet and John's mother.' She had learnt the words by heart, not really reading them, but the thing she remembered most about that book was the images it created of cosy ordinary families with happy, smiling faces.

A feeling of intense anger rose up inside her. What right did they have to kill her mother? What did she do to anyone?

She wanted to ask Miss Wilkins but she couldn't. All she could do was look at those petals, remember her mother meeting her at Liverpool Street station back in the summer, holding her arms wide, running towards her. They had laughed as they collided, and Polly attempted to pick Ellie up and swing her round, but discovered Ellie was now the biggest.

Ellie cried then. She didn't make a sound at first, just tears welling up and trickling down her cheeks, growing ever faster. She had no father. No home left. The Germans had bombed that too. Now she had no mother either.

'What will happen to me now?' she managed to get out. She was aware Miss Wilkins had moved her chair right next to Ellie's, that she was encircled by her arms and that a hand was smoothing her hair, yet it didn't comfort her.

'Miss Hathersley, your mummy's friend, is coming down here,' Miss Wilkins said. 'It won't be until tomorrow because the trains are in a mess but she told me to assure you she will get here somehow. For now I'm going to take you back to the Gilberts'.'

'How tragic,' Miss Gilbert said as Miss Wilkins finished breaking the news. 'My dear, I'm so sorry.'

Ellie looked up at the thin spinster. Her words might sound sincere to her teacher, but they couldn't fool Ellie. Miss Gilbert's eyes glinted like flint and her lips quivered, the way they always did when she was secretly pleased.

'Is Mr Gilbert here?' Ellie managed to get out, knowing he at least would feel for her.

'He's gone to Cambridge on business,' Miss Gilbert said crisply. 'Now let me get you both a cup of tea.'

'I've got to get back to the school,' Miss Wilkins said reluctantly after the tea. Twice before, she'd had to make announcements at assembly that one of the children's fathers had been killed. But on both those occasions the mothers had broken the news to their children. Ellie had no other parent, or even grandparent – only this friend of her mother's. She was concerned by Grace Gilbert's cool reaction, too, but Amos would be home soon and she knew he'd handle the situation with the utmost sensitivity. 'Now, Ellie, we'll all be thinking about you. If you need me you know where I am.'

Ellie wanted to beg her to stay, even to ask to go back to school rather than stay alone with Miss Gilbert. But she couldn't. This terrible grief inside her was something she'd have to face alone.

The clock hands seemed to have slowed down to the point where Ellie felt each minute was an hour. Miss Gilbert started on some ironing and each time she spat on the iron to test the temperature, Ellie sensed she had some spiteful remark prepared, just waiting for the right opportunity to air it.

All manner of things went through Ellie's mind. Would she be moved to an orphanage? Would her mother have a proper funeral? Or was she already in one of those cardboard coffins Mr Gilbert mentioned they used in the cities and just shoved into a mass grave somewhere?

'What will happen to me?' she blurted out, unable to keep silent any longer. 'Who do I belong to now?'

As she voiced that last question, she answered it herself. She belonged to no one. From now on, the safety net that had been her mother was gone. There could be no more dreams of them sharing a small flat. She was entirely alone.

Miss Gilbert turned from her ironing, her mouth pursed spitefully. 'I'm sure I don't know,' she said coldly. 'I can't imagine what your mother was thinking of, careering around the streets at night when decent folks are at home in their beds.'

A shaft of light came in as the door opened but Ellie didn't move her head to see who it was. She had been crying ever since she was sent to bed and her pillow was soaked.

'Sit up and drink this,' Miss Gilbert said curtly. 'I can't have that noise going on all night. You're a big girl, kindly behave like one.'

'Has Mr Gilbert come home yet?' Ellie sobbed. She had waited and waited for him, her ears pricked up for the sound of his boots outside in the cobbled yard.

'No he hasn't and even if he had he wouldn't be wanting to know about your troubles.'

'He would.' Ellie sprang up in the bed. Normally she wouldn't dare to answer Miss Gilbert back but she was beyond fear now. 'He's a kind man and he cares about me.'

'He cares about no one but himself,' Miss Gilbert snapped viciously. 'His dinner's spoilt and he hasn't even bothered to telephone me and tell me where he is. Now for goodness' sake take this drink and stop that dreadful noise.'

'I don't want it,' Ellie sobbed. 'Go away.'

'How dare you speak to me like that, you ungrateful wretch,' Miss Gilbert retorted, her voice rising to her usual screech. 'It's a good job Mr Gilbert isn't here to witness such rudeness.'

A feeling of utter desperation welled up in Ellie. She had been alone with this cold-hearted woman from two in the afternoon until she'd been sent to bed at half-past seven. Not one word of consolation had passed the woman's lips, no kindly reminders that she still had a home here. In fact, as the afternoon wore on, Ellie had felt distinctly menaced.

'If he was here you wouldn't dare be so nasty.'

'So you think you've got a champion in my brother?' Miss Gilbert said in a chilling voice.

'Well you've never liked me,' Ellie cast at the woman, hating her for her meanness, her skinny long body and all that bitterness trapped inside her. 'You're glad, aren't you?'

The black-out was firmly over the window, as always, but there was enough light to see Miss Gilbert's face. Her eyes glinted with malice.

All at once Ellie was scared. All year she'd avoided any confrontation with this woman without really understanding why. Now she saw the craziness that people in the town spoke of and wished she'd just taken the drink and kept silent.

'Yes, I am glad,' Miss Gilbert spat at her. 'She was a common floozy and she'd set her cap at my brother. All that play acting she had you doing! If I'd had my way I'd have stamped it out long ago. Well, you're an orphan now, and you'll show a little gratitude for

145

the people that have had you foisted on to them. Now drink this.'

The insult to her mother wiped out Ellie's fear. She sprang out of bed, swiping the cup out of the woman's hands, knocking it to the floor.

'You cow,' she snarled, her hands coming up to claw the woman's face. 'You're evil and cruel. How could you say such things about my mother? Get away from me or I'll kill you.'

Ellie had the element of surprise, but Miss Gilbert reacted like lightning. She caught Ellie by one wrist and twisted it round sharply, with the other hand slapping her hard across the face. 'Kill me, will you?' she shrieked. 'You, you, fiend!'

Before Ellie could strike back she was spun round, both wrists caught behind her back. She struggled to get free, but Miss Gilbert was the stronger.

'I know just the place for you,' the woman yelled. 'And you won't like it one bit. I'll teach you to answer me back.'

Ellie screamed at the top of her lungs as she was pushed out of the door towards the stairs. Miss Gilbert only held her tighter, twisting Ellie's arms up behind her back until they felt as if they were being pulled from their sockets. Down the stairs she was pushed, a knee in the small of her back each time she tried to free herself. When they reached the hall Ellie struggled harder still to escape, but the woman had superhuman strength now, grunting ferociously as she pushed Ellie towards the cellar door.

'No,' Ellie screamed. 'No please. Not in there!'

The door swung open, a black yawning hole in front of her, but though Ellie pushed back against Miss Gilbert and dug her bare toes into the floor, a thrust against the small of her back sent her hurtling forward.

Ellie landed face down at the bottom of the stone steps, momentarily stunned.

A burst of maniacal laughter from above her made her lift her head and she had just a brief glimpse of Miss Gilbert's skinny silhouette against the light from the hall.

'I'll teach you,' she shouted down. 'You'll stay in there till you rot.'

The door slammed and Ellie was left in total darkness.

'No,' she screamed in terror. She was used to a dark room, but this was thick, oppressive blackness. 'No.'

She heard the key turn in the lock, then the sound of feet walking away, back up the stairs.

For a moment Ellie just lay there, her mouth full of coal-dust, her knees and forehead throbbing. But as the cold, stone floor penetrated her thin nightdress and she remembered what this place was like by day, she hauled herself up, groping blindly for the steps.

At the top she pummelled at the door with her fists. 'Let me out,' she yelled. 'I'll tell Miss Wilkins and Auntie Marleen when she comes. Let me out.'

She had no idea how long she banged and screamed for, but it did no good. No light came on. No sound of movement outside. She sank down on to the steps and sobbed.

Ellie knew the cellar well: she had often been sent down there for coal. Twelve steps to the bottom, then about another twelve feet to where the coal was. Even by day, with Mr Gilbert's big torch, it was a scary place. Spiders' webs hung from the beams, and there was a dank, nasty, choking smell. Now she imagined all those unseen spiders watching her in the dark, perhaps edging their way towards her. Aside from the door there was only one other way in, through the round iron hatch into which the coalman emptied his sack from the street. During the day tiny pinpricks of light came in through the hatch, but she knew that even standing on the coal she'd never be able to reach it, much less manage to push it open and climb out.

It was so cold. She pulled her knees up to her chest, drew her nightdress down over them and hugged her knees tightly.

Something touched her cheek and she jumped, brushing it away, terror almost suffocating her. She pressed her back hard against the door, her heart pounding. Icy prickles ran down her legs and arms, and when she put her hands up to her face she found her forehead was sticky with blood.

'Mummy,' she sobbed, but voicing that word felt like a stab through the heart. She hugged her knees harder and tried to think.

'Come home Mr Gilbert,' she said aloud, her voice echoing eerily. She guessed he'd gone straight to his fire-watching duty after returning from Cambridge and he rarely came back from that until morning.

All sorts of strange noises came as she sat there shivering. Part of her mind told her it was only the coal shifting slightly, but the other part thought of rats and mice. Goosepimples jumped up all over her and again and again she thought something was touching her. She closed her eyes, burying her head in her knees, but as something dropped on to the back of her neck, she screamed and leaped up, shaking her nightdress and jumping up and down

Anger got the better of her again. She banged on the door, screaming at the top of her lungs, and swearing too – all those words she'd heard, but until now never dared use.

'You evil bugger,' she yelled. 'You mad, fucking cow. Open this door immediately.'

Sheer terror made her stop, her voice dropping to a mere whimper as she pleaded to be let out.

She heard the sound of heavy boots on the pavement outside. Holding on to the rail, she went down the steps right to the bottom, across to the heap of coal, and yelled again.

'Help me,' she screamed. 'Miss Gilbert's locked me in the coal cellar. Get the police. Help.'

But they couldn't hear. Ellie heard the footsteps fade away into the distance and as she turned to go back up the stairs her foot touched something furry.

Absolute horror made her stumble back up the stairs again, cowering by the door, shaking so much she felt sick.

She heard the clock on the church strike twelve, but it seemed like a whole night before it struck one. Again and again she got up, holding on to the rail and trying to run on the spot just to warm herself, but her knees hurt and the cold, concrete floor on her feet was unbearable. Ellie tried to think of warm things. She imagined the dressing-room at the Empire with all the chorus girls crowding in to change. The parties in Alder Street, when as many as thirty people crammed into one small room, or lying in the hot sun in Victoria Park. But each one of these images only reminded her of her mother, and that she'd never see her again.

The church clock struck four. When she heard the sound of footsteps again she thought she must be imagining it.

She was frozen solid now, so stiff she could barely turn her head, let alone stand up. But the sound came closer and all at once she realised it wasn't from outside in the street, but in the house.

'Mr Gilbert,' she yelled, half turning to bang on the door. 'Let me out. Please, please help me.'

'Ellie?' His voice was questioning. 'Is that you?'

'Yes,' she sobbed, trying hard to explain. 'Just unlock the door and let me out.'

'The key isn't in the door,' he said. 'Hold on – I'll go and get it. Just calm down.'

Ellie's anxiety grew even greater as she heard Miss Gilbert's voice again. She was clearly following her brother down the stairs.

'Leave her in there till morning, she deserves it,' Ellie heard her say.

'Get back upstairs, woman,' he snarled at her. 'You're mad, Grace, completely out of your mind.'

'Let her out and you'll be sorry,' Miss Gilbert shrieked back.

'You'll be sorry.' Mr Gilbert's voice came nearer and nearer to Ellie. 'Now get away from here, out of my sight. Go.'

The key turned in the lock and the door opened, light dazzling Ellie. She was too stiff to move away to allow the door to open fully. She just sat, hunched the way she'd been for hours, looking up at him beseechingly.

Amos Gilbert was not an emotional man, but the sight of the child sitting on the step, blinking in the light, made his stomach churn. She was completely black, aside from two clean channels down her cheeks where tears had washed away the coal-dust.

He manoeuvred himself down past her, lifted her up over his shoulder so he could open the door properly, and carried her out.

Once he got her into the kitchen, it was her temperature which frightened him the most. Her limbs were set, unable to move.

'I'm so sorry, Ellie,' he managed to stammer out as he sat her on the one comfortable chair. 'Let me get you warm again.'

He found a couple of blankets and wrapped them tightly around her, then stirred up the stove and added new kindling until he got a blaze going. He put a pan of water and a pan of milk on to heat up, and while he waited he rubbed her legs with his hands, trying to bring back some movement.

In all this time Ellie was silent, her eyes following him around the room, red-rimmed and swollen against the black soot.

'Can you tell me what happened?' he asked, kneeling in front of her. 'What started it?'

'Mummy's dead.'

Amos heard what she said, but he couldn't believe it. 'No surely not,' he said gently, thinking the night in the cellar had brought on strange delusions.

Haltingly, Ellie croaked out how Miss Wilkins had brought her home from school, and described the events which followed it. As the sickening truth struck home and he heard the pain in Ellie's voice, Amos felt murderous towards his sister.

He gave Ellie the hot milk first, adding a little brandy to it, and gradually he saw movement coming back to her arms and legs.

He knew what she needed, because he'd needed it too when his mother died. But he was afraid to reach out and enfold her in his arms – it was so long since he'd held anyone.

'I don't know what to say,' he admitted as he poured warm water into a basin to wash her. 'I'm so very sorry, Ellie, I'm heartsick. Your mother was a lovely woman, one of the best, and I can't make any excuses for my sister's cruelty.'

Ellie gave a shuddering sigh. As she slowly grew warmer, so she became aware of the pain in her knees and forehead. She was exhausted, drained to the point where she couldn't even voice how she felt.

She let him wash her hands, feet, legs and face. She could feel the tenderness in his touch and it made her want to cry again.

He brought a clean nightdress from somewhere. It was big and thick and she thought it might be his mother's. He turned away as she managed to get out of the soiled one and into the clean one. Then he gave her a thick sweater and bedsocks, and dressed the abrasions on her knees and forehead.

'I wish,' he said, tucking the blanket around her again as he went to make her a second drink.

'What?' she asked.

He sighed deeply, pulling up a chair in front of her, and took her hands in his.

'So many things,' he said, his big rugged face contorting, as if trying not to cry himself. That I'd never let you stay here. That I'd had Grace put away out of harm's way years ago. That I hadn't been so selfish.'

'You haven't been selfish.' She began to cry now. 'You've always been good to me.'

Amos let her cry, offering first a clear, handkerchief, then the hot drink, feeling utterly powerless. He had more experience of death than anyone, yet he still couldn't find the right words to soothe her. He had the justification now to get Grace put away for good and he intended to do it, but that wouldn't help Ellie to forget this night. Neither could he hope that Ellie would ever want to see him again after her mother's funeral.

'I have been selfish,' he said, gently wiping her face for her, aware he must at least try to explain his feelings. 'You see, I so much wanted you to stay here that I chose to ignore what I knew Grace was capable of.'

Ellie looked up at him, eyes wide with bewilderment.

'I'd begun to think of you as my daughter,' he continued, his voice cracking with emotion. 'With your fun and gaiety you filled a big hole in my life. But if I'd been anything like a real father I wouldn't have become complacent about Grace. I've failed you, and your mother, who I think trusted me.'

Such a frank admission comforted Ellie in a way that mere sympathy could never have done. 'You didn't fail me.' She shook her head firmly. 'You didn't.'

'It isn't always enough to just smooth things over,' he said, stroking her hand, his grey eyes looking right into her dark ones. 'That's the weak man's way of dealing with things and I'll have it on my conscience for ever.'

Later, Amos escorted Ellie up to bed.

'This can come down,' he said, ripping the tacked-on black-out material from the window, flooding the room with pale dawn light. It was another reminder of his failure to notice Grace's more subtle forms of cruelty. Even if this was the last time Ellie would sleep in the room, he didn't want her waking and thinking she was back in the cellar.

'Don't worry,' he said, moving over to the bed and bending to tuck her in. 'I won't let Grace come near you and I shall be here all the time until your aunt arrives.'

'Thank you for being kind,' Ellie said in a small voice. 'You and I did have some good times together, didn't we?'

Amos looked down at her and his heart contracted painfully. She was as pale as the pillowcase, except for an angry purple swelling coming up on her fore-head, and her eyelids were puffy. Even her beautiful dark hair had lost its gloss.

'Some of the best times I remember,' he replied, fighting back tears.

She gave a shuddering sigh and her eyes closed.

'Sleep tight,' he said, remembering that was what his mother had always said when he was a small boy sleeping in this very room. 'Call out if you need me.'

Chapter Seven

'Let me 'ave five minutes with your bloody sister and I'll put her away permanently,' Marleen snarled at Amos.

'Believe me, Miss Hathersley, I'm tempted to do that myself,' Amos sighed. 'But further scenes in this house will only be more upsetting for Ellie.'

It was three in the afternoon. Amos had taken the precaution of locking Grace in her room after he put Ellie to bed. Between checking on her and Ellie hourly, he was exhausted.

Ellie was still in bed. She'd woken at eleven, drunk a cup of tea and nibbled at some toast, and then gone back to sleep. Grace was silent and brooding, a danger sign as far as Amos was concerned. She hadn't objected to being locked in, but neither was she repentant, and had merely smirked when Amos told her that the doctor would be coming that evening.

Marleen had arrived at two-thirty with an American airman called Kurt Vorster, a giant of a man with a blond crew cut and features which looked as if they'd been rearranged by other men's fists. The American's tough appearance and the woman's distraught state had made it doubly hard for Amos to explain the events of last night.

Amos knew so much about Marleen from Ellie that he'd formed a picture in his head of a glamorous, bubbly redhead, something like Rita Hayworth. But this woman sitting in his parlour looked gaunt; her hair was almost orange, with dark roots, and her black costume, clearly intended as mourning, was tight and sleazy-looking, particularly when surrounded by Grace's prissy lace cloths and biblical pictures. Worse still, she had the language of a fishwife, and he suspected she was more than capable of rampaging upstairs and dragging his sister out by the hair.

Before she'd arrived, Amos had had it all quite clear in his head what he was going to say. He hadn't for one moment expected it to be easy to explain about his sister, but he had hoped Ellie's aunt would hear him out calmly.

But Marleen Hathersley wasn't a calm woman. She had stalked around the room screaming abuse at him, demanding to know if he was mentally deficient, allowing an evacuee in the house when his sister was unbalanced.

'I had no reason to think she'd do anything like this, and Ellie wanted to stay,' Amos assured her more than once. 'Ellie and I got on very well and she liked her teacher here. I admit my sister has always suffered with her nerves, but I couldn't predict she'd turn like this. No one could.'

Ellie was still asleep upstairs and Amos was determined to make Marleen calm down before she woke.

'Ain't it bad enough 'er mum's dead without some loony attacking her and locking 'er in a fucking cellar,' Marleen yelled at him. 'D'you think she'll ever get over that? That kid's come through 'ard times with 'er mum, but she knew nothing but love till she came 'ere. If I 'ad my way I'd 'ang that woman up by 'er feet in yer bloody cellar and whip 'er till 'er skin comes off in ribbons.'

'Please believe me, I've grown very fond of Ellie,' Amos pleaded with her. 'I liked Mrs Forester too. Only yesterday I was discussing with Ellie the possibility of getting her down here for a holiday. I even hoped Ellie would persuade her to leave London.'

Marleen heard the sincerity in his words, but her grief at losing her best friend made her want to lash out. 'You're a pompous, stupid bastard. That's what you are!' she screamed at him, eyes sparking with fury. 'I've met some bleedin' twerps in my life, but no one to equal you. I'd say dead bodies were the best pals for you. If you liked our Ellie so much why didn't you make sure you found 'er a nice billet? Was it the fucking ten bob a week you wanted?'

'Please, Miss Hathersley.' Amos felt weak at such a verbal onslaught; he'd never heard a woman use such terrible language. 'Speak to Ellie before you pass judgement on me.'

'I will, make no mistake about that,' Marleen said, then sagged suddenly, sitting down and covering her face with her hands. 'Oh God,' she sobbed. 'I can 'ardly bear to face Ellie. She and 'er mum loved each other so much. 'Ow's the poor kid gonna cope with this?'

'Whatcha gonna do then, honey?' the airman drawled. It was clear he'd been press-ganged into driving Marleen to Suffolk. He'd chain-smoked from the moment he walked through the door and the arrogant way he sprawled silently on the settee suggested he cared little about Marleen and even less for her dead friend and her child.

'Take her home with me, of course.' Marleen frowned at Kurt as if he was stupid too. 'You don't think I'd leave her here with a mad woman, do you?'

'Come on, honey,' Kurt said impatiently. 'London ain't no place to take a kid, not now with bombing every night. She ain't your responsibilty.'

Marleen leaped out of her chair, eyes blazing. 'Bloody men,' she roared. 'Ain't my responsibility? Polly was my best mate. Do you really think I'd walk away from her kid at a time like this?'

Amos felt ashamed of himself for doubting that such a woman would be a true friend to Polly. She obviously cared deeply. But at the same time he could see Marleen was swept away with emotion, and hadn't given herself time to think things through.

'I know my opinion must mean little to you after what's happened,' Amos said gingerly. 'But Mr Vorster's right in saying that London's unsafe. And we must think of Ellie's future. She's been doing well at school here and has many friends. Why don't you take her home for a few days, and in the meanwhile I'll talk to her teacher and find her a new home in the town?'

'I don't ever want to come back here.' Ellie's voice came from the doorway behind them, and all three adults turned in shocked surprise.

She was dressed in her school gym-slip, her hair loose on her shoulders, but she didn't look like a child. Her expression was too adult and strained.

'Ellie!' Marleen moved quickly across the room, arms opening to enfold the girl. 'Oh baby. I'm so sorry.'

As they embraced fiercely, both faces streaming with tears, Amos sat still in his chair, head bowed, humbled by their grief. Kurt insolently picked up a piece of porcelain and studied it, the gesture implying he regretted being dragged into this.

'I'll look after you, Ellie,' Marleen said stoutly. 'You can stay with me for as long as you like.'

Amos slipped away upstairs to check on Grace, leaving Marleen to talk to Ellie alone. The airman also went out, saying he'd be back in half an hour.

Grace was sitting in a chair by her bedroom window. 'So dear "Auntie Marleen's" another foul-mouthed strumpet,' she said as Amos came in. 'Such language!'

'She's a far better human being than you are,' Amos snapped. 'Just be glad I haven't dragged you down to meet her. She'd have torn you to pieces. Where's Ellie's suitcase and the clothes you confiscated when she arrived?'

Grace pointed to a cupboard. 'If you tell the doctor

157

anything about me I'll make you suffer,' she said slyly.

Amos pulled out the suitcase and turned back to his sister, an expression of utter disgust on his face. 'You've made me suffer most of my life,' he said coolly. 'But it's over now, Grace. You are going where you belong.'

He left quickly, slamming the door and locking it, and then went into Ellie's room to pack her few belongings.

It was dusk as the airman started up the jeep. Marleen was sitting beside him, Ellie hesitating on the pavement. It had grown very chilly. Amos had put a thick blanket in the back for Ellie to wrap round her, but it would be a long, cold, uncomfortable ride.

'Write to me?' he asked bleakly. 'If you need any help, any time, I'll be there.'

The long day had taken its toll on Amos: all colour had drained from his normally ruddy face and he looked old. Ellie too was very pale, her eyes enormous, sad pools. She had left her hair loose on her shoulders, a brave attempt at defying Miss Gilbert one last time – in fact she'd made a point of going out to the workshop just so his sister would see her from her bedroom window. Her coat was too short, the cuffs and collar worn thin, and her school gymslip hung down beneath it. But even with the angry red weal on her forehead and her schoolgirl clothes, she held herself with dignity.

'I'll miss you,' she said simply, looking right into his eyes. 'I don't blame you for anything. Please say goodbye to Miss Wilkins for me.'

Amos watched until the jeep roared off round the corner, one hand raised in farewell. There was so much more he wished he'd managed to say to her, but it was too late now.

'Let's hope my place is still standing,' Marleen said grimly as they came up the steps from Holborn tube station. 'At least the rain puts out a few fires.'

It was mid-morning and judging by the leaden sky, driving rain and cold wind, autumn was finally here in earnest.

Kurt had left them late last night at a pub in Essex as he had to get back to his base. Marleen and Ellie had spent an uncomfortable night sharing a single bed in a room with another woman and her two small children. They were glad of the bed, however, and a hot meal, as they had seen dozens of what Marleen called 'trekkers' looking for barns or thick hedges to give them shelter away from the bombs. Marleen had explained that hundreds of people did this nightly, rather than stay in the city, most of them too poor even to think of the luxury of a real bed.

Ellie hardly slept at all. Aside from the other woman snoring and Marleen hogging most of the bed, the noise of planes, ack-ack guns and bombing in the distance was scary. It had been a cold, miserable drive from Suffolk. Icy wind blasted through the sides of the jeep and with the headlights taped up Kurt could barely see the road. Marleen kept asking him to slow down, but he took no notice. The night sky first grew pink, and then red as they reached Essex. Marleen said that was how it was most nights, but she thought the docks had been hit yet again.

But now, as Ellie stood with Marleen in High Holborn, she saw for herself the carnage left from the night before. Opposite the tube, a huge building she remembered as having been offices was now just a smoking shell. Desks and filing cabinets, grotesquely twisted and mangled, lay below on a mountain of rubble. Someone's blue coat still hung on a peg on what had once been the top floor; on another a calendar fluttered in the wind. Three fire-engines stood by, and dozens of firemen were still working, their faces black with soot, some re-coiling hoses, others clambering over fallen masonry checking all the fires were now out.

'They're the real 'eroes of this war,' Marleen said reflectively. She had made up her face this morning and with a side-tilted felt hat hiding her untidy hair, she looked much more like her old self. ''Ow they do it night after night defeats me. You can bet not one of 'em's 'ad a proper night's sleep since the Blitz began, risking their lives each time they get a shout.'

More men were clearing rubble from the street, sweeping to one side a sea of broken glass, but while Ellie stared open-mouthed in shock, everyone else was walking past without so much as breaking their stride to look.

'How can people be so calm?' Ellie asked as Marleen began to walk away. Aside from that building, things were relatively normal. Men with briefcases and office girls were all going about their business. A small café had its windows blown right out, but it was still trading, with a blackboard propped outside saying 'More open than usual'.

'That's the way it 'as to be.' Marleen shrugged her shoulders. 'Industry and business gotta keep going. People 'ave to work to feed their families. We've all got a bit casual about it really. Those pot-'oles in the road will be filled by tonight, the glass and rubble cleared up. Chances are there'll be another lot tomorrow, but the milk and post will be delivered, and the typists will turn up to see if their chair's still in place.'

It was dark in Marleen's flat and very dusty.

'The winders went last week.' Marleen pulled back the curtains to show Ellie the boards. 'Look what 'appened to the couch!'

There were tiny jagged cuts all along its back, the stuffing peeping out in places. Elsewhere there were more signs of damage: a burn on the carpet which Marleen said was from a piece of shrapnel, and several deep gouges in the highly polished table, caused by more flying glass.

'It used to be so smart an' all,' Marleen said wistfully. 'Still, I'm luckier than most.'

Ellie broke down when she saw her mother's pitifully small collection of belongings in the spare room. The blue cardigan Polly had retrieved from the bombed house in Alder Street, a couple of dresses and some underwear. An old chocolate box held all of Ellie's letters and an envelope stuffed with photographs.

'She dug and dug down in Alder Street till she found those,' Marleen said of the photographs. 'They're nearly all of you as a nipper. I said, "never mind the snaps, Poll, what about finding a few tins of corned beef?" Know what she said?'

Ellie smiled glumly.

'She said, "My sugarplum's face is worth more than a whole crate of soddin' corned beef."'

Marleen had intentionally avoided talking about Polly all the way home. She sensed once the floodgates of grief were opened she wouldn't be able to control herself. But she knew now that Ellie had to grieve, and that here amongst her mother's things was the right place.

Ellie lay down on the bed, hugging the pillow which still smelt faintly of her mother, and sobbed.

Marleen lay down beside her and took her in her arms. 'My poor lamb,' she said. 'Wish I could take the 'urt away, luv. God knows what either of us will do without her, but we got one another, ain't we?'

They spent the afternoon sobbing and holding each other, reminiscing about Polly.

'She was so proud of you, Ellie,' Marleen said through her tears. 'Last time she come back from seein' you she was on about 'ow well you spoke now and 'ow beautiful you were. She really wanted you to be a famous actress one day.'

'She wasn't just my mum,' Ellie sniffed. 'She was my best friend too. I can't believe she's gone for ever.'

'I can't be all she was to you. But I know she'd want me to try,' Marleen said. Tears had coursed through her make-up, giving her a clown-like look. 'Right now I don't know what to do for the best. Should I try and find you another home safe in the country?'

'No. I'm staying here, if you'll have me, and I'll get a job.' Ellie tried to sound brave but her voice wobbled. She had already realised that her mother had paid half the rent here, and Marleen's job in a West End club couldn't bring in much. 'I'll be fourteen soon, so there's no point in going to school.'

Marleen sat up and wiped her eyes. She hadn't seen Ellie since back in early June when she'd visited London. She'd been stunned then by her slim, womanly shape, the way she spoke and her new maturity. But now, perhaps because of her mother's death, Ellie seemed to have dropped the last traces of childhood.

'You're so like Polly sometimes,' Marleen sniffed. 'She was always so practical and worked so 'ard. I wish I was more like 'er.'

'We always liked you just the way you are.' Ellie smiled weakly. 'Don't worry, Auntie, we'll get along all right.'

They had only just finished eating their tea when the air-raid warning blasted out.

'Come on, love.' Marleen jumped up and grabbed her coat. 'Down the tube.'

Ellie's heart pounded with fear as Marleen handed her a rolled-up blanket and a cushion. The siren's wail seemed to be right inside her head, but still Marleen ran about the kitchen putting things into a basket. Finally she was satisfied and grabbing Ellie's arm, ran down the stairs, out into the street.

Searchlights sweeping across the dark sky gave enough light to see clearly but added more menace to the sirens. Dozens of people were going the same way as Ellie and Marleen – women pushing prams, old ladies and men hobbling arm in arm, children clutching their parents' hands. All looked remarkably unperturbed.

They heard the throb of the bombers long before they reached the tube steps, but Ellie could see nothing above her but the dark shape of a barrage balloon caught in the strobe of the searchlight.

'What's that?' Ellie asked as she heard a sound like the tearing of a sheet.

''Igh explosive bombs,' Marleen said breathlessly. 'Now come on, we can't stand up 'ere and watch.'

People were converging towards the tube from every direction as incendiaries rattled down. Ellie caught hold of the belt on Marleen's coat for fear of being separated and they were swept down the steps by the sheer force of numbers behind them.

Polly had described scenes in the tube to Ellie in her letters, making it sound great fun. But Ellie's first reaction as they reached platform level was horror. People were jammed together like sardines and a hot blast of air from the tunnel brought a terrible smell of excrement.

'Pongs, don't it?' Marleen looked over her shoulder and smiled wanly. 'They go in the tunnel after the electric rail's turned off.'

Ellie felt quite ill as Marleen dragged her along the edge of the platform. She had forgotten in her time in the country how sharp and pale Londoners' faces were. Now they looked sinister in the yellowy lights as they prepared for the night ahead of them. All human life was here: the very old, the very young. Servicemen, a few people in evening dress, businessmen in smart suits, office girls and messenger boys. A woman with a baby at her breast, another trying to change her baby's nappy while yelling at her small children to sit down. An entire family picnicking as calmly as if they were in a park, and workmen, still plastered in mud, trying vainly to sleep.

A train came in and disgorged more people, adding to the confusion. Two nuns put down a mat each and, folding their legs beneath their habits and their hands into their sleeves, sat like a couple of statues.

The noise was deafening. Chatter, laughter, babies screaming, mouth organs, someone playing a fiddle.

'Marleen!' someone yelled. 'Over 'ere!'

It was Marleen's friend, Patsy, who'd saved a place. It was barely large enough for one person, but with a hurried explanation that Ellie was Polly's daughter, suddenly another twelve inches or so were added to it.

'I'm so sorry, love.' Patsy reached up and took Ellie's hands. 'Your ma was one of the best and we'll all miss her.'

Patsy was perhaps thirty, but she looked older, her skin a sulphurous yellow, and a scarf tied turban-style round her head with just a few greasy-looking coils of black hair escaping from it.

She reminded Ellie very much of women she knew back in Alder Street, their bodies made shapeless by childbearing, a poor diet robbing them of their looks too soon. But she had that warmth in her eyes Ellie remembered, and in some way it soothed a little of the grief inside her.

Ellie lay down later. Marleen had spread newspaper under one blanket and with the other one over her and her head on the cushion she was reasonably comfortable. It was easier to pretend she was asleep than answer questions, and once Marleen and Patsy were convinced she had nodded off, their conversation became less guarded.

Patsy told Marleen where she needed to go to sort

out being guardian to Ellie and possibly get some financial help. It seemed that Marleen's job was a problem area, because she was worried about leaving Ellie at night.

'She can come down 'ere wiv me,' Patsy said. 'She ain't no trouble. I expected her to be more of a live wire from wot Polly said.'

'Leave it out,' Marleen said. 'The poor kid's still in a state of shock. She's a funny little bugger usually, brilliant at takin' off people, and she can sing like a bleedin' canary. But you gotta remember her and her ma were real close, it's gonna take some time for 'er to get over it.'

Patsy asked Marleen about Kurt. 'Any future in it?' she said, with a gust of ribald laughter that showed she knew a great deal about the Yank.

'I don't knows that I want a future with 'im, not after yesterday. Talk about insensitive!' Marleen said pointedly. 'I'm okay when I keep 'em at bay, know what I mean? A few nights out, a bit of fun. But soon as I starts to want more it all gets nasty.'

'I like my Sid better now 'e's out my 'air,' Patsy said. 'On 'is last leave it was the best we've ever known, wiv the kids away an' all. But when 'e comes back it'll all start up again, knocking me around, banging me up every year. Sometimes I wonder if there's a man alive that ain't a monster once 'e's got you loving 'im.'

The sound of the two women's voices was soothing. Ellie heard Marleen tell Patsy all about Grace Gilbert and Amos.

''E weren't a bad geezer,' Marleen said reflectively. 'I reckon 'e'd got real fond of our Ellie. Course I tore 'im off a strip, blamed 'im like, but when we was leaving 'e looked real sad. He gave me ten quid to 'elp out, an' all.'

'Good job Poll never knew what 'is sister were like,' Patsy said. 'Funny Ellie never let on!'

'Keeping secrets runs in the family,' Marleen said tartly.

'What'cha mean?' Patsy asked.

Ellie was wide awake now, listening carefully, but she kept her eyes tightly shut, wondering what Marleen was going to reveal.

'Nothin' Patsy,' Marleen replied, in that voice she always used when she thought she'd opened her mouth too wide. 'I don't tell people's secrets either.'

Their voices became muffled after that and Ellie dropped off, wondering what Marleen had meant.

The all-clear signal woke Ellie with a start. Immediately people started to move and pack up all around her.

'All right, love?' Marleen helped Ellie roll up the blankets. 'Grim, ain't it?'

Ellie smiled faintly. She was as stiff as a plank, she felt dirty and she longed for some fresh air. 'Better than being with Miss Gilbert,' she said, wondering if she'd be able to say that truthfully after a week or two of sleeping down here. 'I'd rather be roughing it with you than comfortable anywhere else.'

'You little charmer.' Marleen gave a warm, wide smile. 'Now let's see if we've still got an 'ome out there. After a wash and brush-up we've got to sort out a few things. D'you feel up to that?'

Ellie knew Marleen was talking about her mother's death and getting guardianship sorted out. She wasn't ready for it, but one glance at all these other people packing up intending to go to work regardless of how they'd spent the night decided her.

'I'm up to it.' She attempted a smile. 'As Mum always said, "The show must go on."'

'That's the spirit,' Marleen chuckled. 'And I want you to do the roots of my 'air later on an' all. I look like a bleedin' old tart from Cable Street.'

Chapter Eight

Amberley, June 1943

'I'll just die if they make me go home.'

Jack smiled at Bonny's dramatic statement. He stood up from the engine he was mending, wiped his oily hands on a rag and turned to look at her.

Jack was seventeen and an apprentice mechanic at the Turnpike garage in Houghton Bridge. To his disappointment, he hadn't grown tall. In his first year living with Mr and Mrs Baker he grew three inches, but the rate had slowed down since, making him an unremarkable five foot eight. But his body was lean and muscular, his shoulders wide, and he still had the same irrepressible cheeky grin, and the freckles. His red hair, though subdued a little by Brylcreem, was still spiky fire and Alec Hatt, his employer, often teased him by calling him 'the torch'.

It was a hot Saturday afternoon in June. Bonny had dropped by at the garage on her way to play tennis. She was fourteen now and she'd passed from an outstandingly pretty child to a devastatingly beautiful girl without ever touching on the awkward coltish stage most teenagers endured.

Bert Baker called her a 'heart-breaker'. Five foot six, slender, yet curvy, hair like gold satin and wide, turquoise blue eyes which gave her a curious mix of girlish innocence and womanly sensuality. Her white tennis shorts and blouse showed off her sensational, lightly tanned legs and there wasn't a man in the village who wasn't distracted when she rode by on her bicycle.

Beryl Baker called her 'a minx'. Lydia veered between calling her an angel and a devil. Jack knew she was both, but adored her just the same.

'I don't know why you mind going back to London so much,' he said after a while. He didn't want her to go, but any other girl of her age in the village would give her eye-teeth for the chance to be in London. 'It's got a lot more to offer than here.'

'I want to stay for the same reasons as you,' Bonny pouted.

Jack just laughed. He and Bonny had been inseparable ever since the day he rescued her from the river, but he wasn't blind to her faults. She might pretend to love the country, but when it came down to it her real reason for staying here was pure snobbishness. She was ashamed of her parents, and she couldn't bear the thought of living on a council estate after Briar Bank.

'What's wrong with going to secretarial college?' he asked. This place her parents had found for her in Romford sounded very nice.

'I just don't want to be a secretary,' she said stubbornly. 'You know what I want.'

Jack sighed and turned back to his engine. Bonny was set on going to Hollywood. She'd made him sit through endless Fred Astaire and Ginger Rogers films and was convinced she could do even better. But though she was a brilliant tap-dancer, she couldn't act and her voice, though sweet, just wasn't strong enough.

'It's tough breaking into films,' Jack reminded her. 'It might be better to have something else behind you.'

Bonny had been home to Dagenham for several brief holidays in the three years she'd lived in Amberley. Each visit made the differences between her life with Lydia and that of her parents more extreme. Her parents were so dull and strait-laced.

Her mother could talk of nothing but rationing, war damage and the ingredients for her cakes; her father, his garden and Ford's. Their imagination didn't stretch beyond Bonny getting a nice secure office job, marrying a white-collar worker and settling down in a semidetached house in Chigwell or Romford.

Bonny was consumed with dreams of Hollywood. She saw herself in a spangled costume, dancing her way through spectacular Busby Berkeley routines. If and when she married it would be to someone fabulously rich and she'd set her sights a little higher than Romford.

Four years of war had made everything so grim in London. All the way through the East End there was nothing to see but bomb-sites, roofs covered by tarpaulins, broken windows, walls shored up and gaunt shells of old tenements. Her parents' house in Flamstead Road was so poky and shabby after Briar Bank. She couldn't bear to see her father shaving at the kitchen sink, or watch her mother soaking her corns in a bowl of water. Everything about the way they lived offended her.

She hated having to go into the Anderson shelter in the garden when the sirens went off, with that awful smell of damp earth, the cold and the fear that tonight might be a direct hit. Sitting for hours by candle-light, with her mother knitting and going on and on about neighbours who'd been bombed out.

But it was her parents' mentality that got Bonny down more than anything. They were so old and set in their ways. Everything was so serious to them, and they stuck to regulations as if someone was spying on them. The government said no more than five inches of bath water, so her mother measured it. Every scrap of paper was saved, every bone was washed and dried, every tin flattened religiously. They wouldn't dream of buying anything on the black market, not even for a special occasion. When her mother heard a rumour that a pig was being kept illegally by a group of neighbours, she shopped them.

Aunt Lydia did her bit for the war effort, far more than Bonny's parents, but she didn't make an issue of it. She had joined the WVS two years ago and she did everything from driving mobile canteens to helping out with finding homes for people bombed out in Southampton. Dancing and music lessons had to be fitted in when she was free, as often she was working for twenty-four hours at a stretch. The spare bedroom at Briar Bank was used as an emergency billet for anyone who needed it.

In Sussex there was just enough war to be exciting, yet it was distant enough to be safe. There had been one exciting day back in the August of 1940. It was a lovely hot Sunday and after lunch Bonny had persuaded Aunt Lydia to drive her and the three Eastons into Arundel to see a German plane which had crashed close to the castle walls.

Lydia had only just dropped them at the Great Park gates when they heard the roar of planes coming over from Bognor Regis. Dozens of bombers and an escort of fighter-planes in wing-to-wing formation flew in so close they could see the black and white crosses under their wings. As they watched, the planes wheeled round towards Littlehampton and dived in groups of three. Although the Germans' target was some distance away, the noise of bombs and guns was deafening.

They were used to seeing vapour trails in the sky, indicating a battle was taking place. They heard aircraft overhead, sirens wailing, the rattle of machinegun fire, and sometimes caught sight of a parachutist dropping from the sky or heard the occasional bang of a falling bomb. But until that day in August, 1943 all reports of destruction had been far enough from Amberley for them to be casual about it.

Bonny had no desire to go back to the austerity of London at war. Sussex was just fine, and if she could find a way to stall her parents until she was old enough to join a dancing troupe, then she'd never return to Dagenham.

'What does Miss Wynter think about this secretarial college idea then?' Jack asked from beneath the car bonnet.

'She won't say.' Bonny pouted, swishing back her hair from her face. 'I know she thinks it's still very dangerous in London, but as I'm old enough to leave school next month, I suppose she thinks I'm big enough to leave her too. Can you speak to her, Jack?'

Jack smiled to himself. He had guessed Bonny's arrival at the garage today had some purpose behind it. 'You want me to try and influence Miss Wynter I suppose?' he said drily.

He came out from under the bonnet and just looked at Bonny. He adored her, but there were times when he wanted to shake her. She always thought about herself first. Now he was supposed to back her up, tell Lydia Bonny was breaking her heart about going home, yet afraid to hurt her parents' feelings, when in fact her plans had nothing to do with any of the people who loved her.

'Why do you have to be so devious?' he reproached her. 'The real reason you want to stay here is because Lydia will help you get into shows when the war's over.'

Bonny blushed. Jack knew her better than anyone, but she hated the way he was always so blunt about her motives. 'What's wrong with that?' she snapped back. 'You chose to stay here rather than find work in London and help your mum out.'

Jack shook his head. 'My mum couldn't care less about me, or Michael and Tom. I can do more for my brothers by doing an apprenticeship here than giving Mum money so she can go out and get drunk. Your parents are different.'

Sometimes Jack was very aggravating. Bonny thought he should take only her feelings into account, but he always had to have a broader view.

'Does that mean you won't stick up for me?' Bonny tossed her head arrogantly.

Jack paused before answering.

Bonny saw his indecision and knew she had to persuade him somehow. Aunt Lydia liked and trusted Jack. He could easily influence her into offering some alternative suggestion that would appease her parents.

She moved closer to him. 'Hasn't it occurred to you that I might want to stay here because of you?' she said softly, looking right into his eyes. She could always tell what he was thinking by doing this. They were light brown with amber flecks and they registered anger, hurt, love and disbelief more clearly than anyone else's eyes. 'Don't you know I lie awake at nights thinking about you?'

She saw his expression change from suspicion to bewilderment. She knew how he felt about her and it gave her a charge when she saw it in his eyes.

Jack's heart began to pound alarmingly, sweat breaking out on his brow. He could see the outline of her small firm breasts beneath her thin blouse and he licked his lips nervously.

'Kiss me, Jack?' she whispered, reaching up and cupping his face between her two hands.

Her lips touched his before he could stop her. His hands fluttered at his sides, afraid to touch her because of the dirt on them. But the moist warmth of her lips drove away all reason and his eyes closed involuntarily, his body leaning in towards hers.

The delicious sweetness only lasted for a brief moment. Jack opened his eyes as she moved away from him and found she was smiling.

'Can't you do any better than that?' she teased.

'I – I can't hold you,' he stuttered, his voice hoarse with emotion. 'I'm so dirty.'

'Well, clean yourself up and meet me tonight,' Bonny said, turning away towards the open garage door. 'At seven, by the bridge.'

Jack watched her jump on her bicycle and pedal away. She waved one hand but didn't turn her head. Her hair was flowing back in the breeze and her slim waist and small buttocks made his heart contract painfully.

He turned back to the engine, knowing he must have it finished by five, but his mind was on Bonny and the taste of her lips.

Being evacuated to Amberley had been the making of Jack and his brothers. Mr and Mrs Baker had wiped out all the years of deprivation and their mother's indifference. With Bert and Alec Hatt he'd discovered that real men didn't have to be brutes. They'd encouraged his passion for mechanical things, letting him work alongside them, and taught him to appreciate nature and the countryside.

But it was Bonny who'd really motivated Jack. She had vision. Not only did she see herself on the silver screen, but she made dreams for him too. First an apprenticeship, then a garage of his own. One day he could own dozens up and down the country and get others to work for him. She brought magazines down from Briar Bank, glossy ones with pictures of limousines and flashy American cars, and together they'd lapse into happy day-dreams of Bonny in a mink coat and Jack at the wheel of a Rolls-Royce.

She didn't stop at dreams, either. It was Bonny who wheedled Miss Wynter into persuading Alec to take him on as an apprentice, then set to work on Alec until he thought it was all his own idea.

After that day when Bonny had almost drowned, they'd become closer than brother and sister. They climbed trees together, made camps, swopped comics, went scrumping and explored the surrounding countryside. Everyone in the village shook their heads over this odd friendship. Sometimes they thought Jack felt sorry for the girl because no one else liked her; other times they claimed Bonny just used Jack. What they didn't know was that Jack and Bonny had found something in one another that they couldn't find elsewhere. Jack loved her plucky nature and her imagination. She was more fun than another boy because the two of them didn't have to compete; she was the sister he never had.

To Bonny, Jack was excitement. With him she could do the kind of things her mother would never have allowed, but with the safety net of his protectiveness. He didn't put her on a pedestal, but liked her as she really was. It was Jack who taught her to ride a bike, to whistle, to light fires. In turn, she taught him how to waltz, to play board-games and to use his imagination.

Swimming was the only thing he couldn't persuade her to join him at. Littlehampton's beach was swathed in barbed wire, but even if they had been allowed near the sea he knew she wouldn't do more than paddle. She would sit on the wooden jetty by the river watching him swim, but apart from dipping her toes in the water, she went no further.

It was only since Christmas that Jack had begun to realise his feelings for her were no longer brotherly. He'd gone to watch her dance in a pantomime in Bognor and the sight of her budding breasts under the tight costume had given him an erection. Since then he had fallen asleep nightly thinking about her, torturing himself by imagining holding and kissing her. As the months went by he'd watched her figure changing into a woman's and sometimes when he was with her he was tongue-tied by her beauty.

If she'd been sixteen, as she looked, no one would have said anything about them being sweethearts. But she was only fourteen, and he knew if Miss Wynter was to guess what was in his mind, she'd take a horse-whip to him.

*

174

'I've had it.' Belinda tossed her tennis-racket on the grass and flopped down beside it. 'You're too good for me, Bonny.'

Bonny fastidiously wiped the sweat from her forehead and joined Belinda on the grass.

Belinda was Bonny's only real girlfriend. If Bonny hadn't carefully cultivated her, it was quite possible she would have been as wary of Bonny as the other girls.

Belinda was Dr Noakes's daughter – petite, with dark, curly hair and a sweet nature. The only girl in a family of four boys, she was always grateful for Bonny's company and she invited her round for tennis or parties all the time. Belinda danced too, although she had no plans to make it a career as Bonny did.

Dr Noakes's home wasn't an impressive one: just a plain, Victorian, family house with furniture made shabby by his five children. But the garden was huge, with a splendid view of the river, and although a great deal of it had been put down to vegetables, no one had managed to persuade him to dig up the tennis court.

'It's so hot.' Belinda fanned herself with her hand. 'We had some of our lessons outside yesterday because some of the girls were half asleep.'

'What's it like at your new school then?' Bonny asked. Belinda had been moved from the village school when she was thirteen to a small private one in Arundel.

'Stuffy.' Belinda pulled a face. 'My teacher Miss Hobbs is an ogre. I asked my father if I could get a job when I get my school certificate, but he's dead set on me going to university.'

Bonny saw this as an opportunity to air her problems and launched into her account of the college in Romford.

'I can't see why you have to go there,' Belinda said in surprise. 'Why not go to Mayfield in Littlehampton?'

Bonny looked blank.

'Don't you know it?' Belinda seemed surprised. 'It's

a bit like a finishing school. You know the stuff, good manners, deportment, French and music, but they changed it just before the war when that sort of thing went out of date. Now they do typing and shorthand too. One of my cousins went there.'

'I suppose it's expensive?' Bonny knew her parents were planning to pay for the place in Romford, but this sounded as if it was in another league.

'It can't be that bad, my aunt and uncle aren't rolling in it,' Belinda said. 'Why don't you ask Miss Wynter to get a prospectus? You have to wear a posh uniform. Pink dresses and boaters!'

That decided Bonny. She could just see herself in that outfit.

'Have you ever heard of Mayfield College in Little-hampton?' Bonny asked Aunt Lydia over their tea.

Lydia was wearing her WVS uniform, as she would be driving a mobile canteen later. It should have looked awful on her, a grey-green tweed suit and a beetroot red jumper with the kind of felt hat people associated with Angela Brazil books about posh boarding-schools. But Lydia had the suit altered by a tailor and managed to remould the hat to make it look dashing.

'Yes dear.' Lydia was reading the paper as she ate, and her reply was more courtesy than a real answer. 'How awful, Leslie Howard is dead. The civilian plane he was travelling in was shot down by Germans. What a terrible way for a man like him to die.'

'Yes, dreadful,' Bonny agreed politely. She only remembered the man as the drip Ashley in *Gone with the Wind*. Perhaps he should have had more sense than to travel by plane. 'You do know Mayfield then?'

Lydia looked up from the paper. 'Sorry dear, what was that?'

One of the things which Bonny liked most about Lydia was her diverse interests. Aside from music and dancing, she liked sport, cars and the theatre. She read everything from magazines to literary books and studied the newspapers to keep abreast of world affairs. There was never any danger of her discussing cake ingredients.

'Mayfield College,' Bonny repeated. 'Do you know it?'

Lydia smiled and put her paper down. 'Yes I do. Several of my friends went there as girls. What makes you ask?'

'Belinda was talking about it. She said you can do typing and shorthand there. Is it really expensive?'

'Not terribly,' Lydia said, taking a bit of bread and wincing. 'Ugh, this bread is disgusting. I don't know how they expect us to eat it.'

The national wheatmeal loaf was all they could get now and though it might be more nutritious than white bread, everyone complained about the lumpy bits in it.

'Mayfield sounds nice.' Bonny knew she had to give Lydia something to think about on her long drive tonight, but at the same time make no demands. 'I wish Mum and Dad would let me go somewhere like that rather than Romford.'

Lydia poured them both another cup of tea. 'Are you trying to tell me you don't want to go home?' she asked.

Lydia hated the idea of losing Bonny. She thought of her as a daughter now, despite many ups and downs. London wasn't safe, Dagenham was a wasteland and she was afraid that if Bonny was uprooted now, at such a crucial stage in her life, she might rebel.

'I don't know,' Bonny sighed deeply. 'I want to see Mummy and Daddy, but all my friends are here and there's you.'

Bonny was never one to miss an opportunity for drama. She managed to squeeze out a couple of tears, then rushed away from the table.

Lydia followed her, as Bonny knew she would.

177

'Why the tears?' she said, catching hold of Bonny out in the hall. 'Is there something more?'

'I don't want to go away from you,' Bonny whispered, leaning her head against Lydia's shoulder. 'But I'm afraid of hurting Mummy and Daddy's feelings.'

Lydia held her for a moment. She suspected this might be theatricals, yet she wanted to believe Bonny.

'Look, darling, I've got to go now,' she said. 'But I'll give it some thought tonight while I'm working. Now promise me you'll behave yourself this evening. I don't mind you going out for a while, but be back by nine. Be sure to lock the door behind you, you know how nervous I am at leaving you alone at night.'

Jack was waiting at the bridge, sitting on the parapet smoking a cigarette. The moment he saw Bonny coming down the road he leaped down to meet her.

He had made a great effort with his appearance, but he knew he fell a long way short of smart. His grey flannel trousers were a pair Bert Baker had grown too fat for, but they were still too big for Jack's slim hips. Mrs Baker had made his shirt out of some old sheets but the collar didn't sit right. Only his blazer pleased him. It was a really good quality one, passed on to him by Mrs Garside of Amberley Castle. It had belonged to her son, a Battle of Britain pilot who had been shot down over the Channel while returning to his base at Biggin Hill. There was a faint mark on the breast pocket where his RAF badge had been. Jack was proud to wear a hero's jacket.

'You look nice,' Bonny said touching the lapels of the jacket with approval.

'Mrs Baker was a bit suspicious,' Jack sighed. 'She teased me about going courting. I just hope no one spots us.'

'Why? Are you ashamed of me?' Bonny said flirtatiously.

'Of course I'm not,' he retorted. 'But people will talk because you're so young.'

'But we've always hung around together,' she said, taking his hand and leading him down to the teahouse by the river. 'Why should they think this is anything different?'

She knew it was different. Jack was all clean and tidy, his face scrubbed so hard it looked sore. He'd even managed to get the grease out of his fingernails.

A couple were sitting at one of the tables, but they weren't locals. The man was in an Army officer's uniform and his wife wore a very pretty floral dress and a white hat; they were holding hands across the table, looking intently into each other's eyes.

'Honeymooners,' Jack whispered. 'They arrived this afternoon at the Bridge Inn, and he came over to the garage to ask me to mend his spare tyre. There was confetti all over the inside of his car.'

'Let's sit here too,' Bonny suggested, sitting herself down at the last small table. 'It's very romantic.'

The sun was slowly descending towards the bridge, turning the sky pink. Swans were gliding by regally – many of the ducks had already come up on to the bank by the rowing boats for the night. Jack went into the teahouse and bought them both a glass of home-made blackcurrant cordial.

The drink was too weak to be nice, but it was a pretty colour and Bonny thought it more glamorous than tea. She kept stealing glances at the officer and his wife, wishing Jack would hold her hand like that.

She told him about Mayfield College and Jack told her that Alec had come back just as he was closing up and given him an extra shilling for finishing the car on time, but neither of them could think of anything else to chat about and the silence hung between them like an invisible net.

'Do you still have nightmares about falling in the river?' Jack asked eventually. It was so sluggish now it was difficult to imagine how fast it had flowed that day.

'Not so often now.' Bonny shuddered; talking of that day always had the same effect on her. 'Just think, if Aunt Lydia had told my parents, they'd have taken me home and we wouldn't have become friends.'

That day had been a milestone in Bonny's life. Not just nearly drowning, but somehow discovering what was important to her. She was so scared Aunt Lydia would tell her parents that she'd behaved perfectly for some months afterwards. She'd found Jack too, admitted to him she told lies, and realised just how much Aunt Lydia cared for her. Yet in a way that day had also brought it home to her how little she really needed her parents. She hadn't longed for her mother's arms around her. She had enough here.

Jack couldn't stop looking at Bonny. Her skin was peachy brown, those soft full lips a delectable pink. He longed to reach out and run his fingers through her hair, to take her hand.

It was all so bewildering. A year or two ago she used to let him play with her hair, and he'd do it up in dozens of tiny plaits without ever having these strange and overpowering feelings of wanting to squeeze her or stroke her face.

'Did you mean what you said this afternoon?' he said, blushing until his face was as red as his hair.

'What did I say?' She knew exactly, but she wanted him to repeat it.

'That you don't want to go away because of me?'

'Of course I did.' It was she who blushed now, looking down at her hands. 'I wouldn't have said it otherwise.'

Jack felt bolder now and his hand slid over hers on the table. 'Shall we go for a walk?' he suggested.

The long grass tickled Bonny's legs as they walked along the river bank. When they turned to look behind them the sun was almost resting on the bridge, the sky red now.

'It'll be dark any minute,' Jack said. 'Shall we sit and watch it disappear?'

They watched silently, almost hidden by the tall grass, their linked hands lying in the grass between them. The sun dipped again, and the grey stone of the bridge turned pink too, then slowly the sun was gone, leaving just a faint red glow.

'I've never watched it happen before.' Jack's voice was tinged with wonder. Midges were flying round them and he knew tomorrow he'd have dozens of itchy bites, but he didn't care. 'Are you warm enough?'

Bonny took the cardigan from around her shoulders and slipped her arms into it. Jack helped pull it on, but as his hand touched the skin of her neck, Bonny turned her face to his.

She had a faint moustache of blackcurrant. He could smell her hair, her skin, the sweetness of her breath and he felt almost faint with wanting.

His arm went round her, his other hand cupped her cheek and finally he found the courage to kiss her.

The kiss during the afternoon was too short to give anything but a taster, but now he held her tight, his lips pressed against hers so hard he could feel her teeth.

'You have to do it more gently,' Bonny whispered, taking his face in her hands to control him. 'I've watched them doing it on the films and it's like this.'

Her lips teased his, with the lightness of a baby's finger, sending rivulets of delight down his spine. Soon they were lying back on the grass, arms wrapped around one another, each kiss a little bolder, tongues darting out daringly, both lost in a timeless world of pure pleasure.

Jack pressed closer and closer to her, his hands caressing her back and moving down towards the curve of her buttocks, breath heavy, mouth hungry, wanting more as each second passed.

Thick darkness descended without them noticing.

'I wonder what the time is?' Bonny asked eventually, suddenly aware it had to be well past nine. 'I must find out.'

Jack pricked up his ears at the sound of an approaching train. 'It's ten fifteen. That's the London train.'

They had to run then, back along the river bank, up past the Bridge Inn and under the railway bridge in pitch darkness.

'I hope Aunt Lydia hasn't come home early,' Bonny said as they raced towards the village. 'She'll never let me stay here if she finds out about this.'

Fortunately for Bonny there was no one around to spot them and Lydia's car wasn't outside Briar Bank.

'You must go now,' she whispered as she reached the steps up to the front door. 'Mrs Cowie might be looking.'

Jack looked round nervously at the house across the street. 'One more kiss,' he pleaded. 'That's all.'

It was the sweetest kiss of the night. Two young bodies pressing together, both knowing it would seem like for ever until they saw one another again.

'Come to church tomorrow morning,' she whispered. 'I'll say hello and then I'll wander off so you can speak to Aunt Lydia, ask her something about her car to keep her talking, then tell her how sad I am.'

Bonny watched Jack through the studio window as he walked away. He was just a dark shape in the black-out but his so-familiar, bouncing walk gave her the oddest sensation, like something tugging at her from the inside.

Until now she had been so sure her reasons for not wanting to go home were based purely on ambition and a dread of being suffocated by her parents. Now she had the strangest feeling it might really be Jack she didn't want to leave.

Chapter Nine

June 1944

The banging at the front door became more insistent. Ellie listened from the bedroom, knowing exactly who it was, and more importantly why she shouldn't answer it.

A moment's silence, then a rattling sound. Ellie had a mental picture of short, fat Mr Zacharia, wheezing as he subjected himself to the indignity of bending to peer through the letter-box.

'I know you're in there, Miss Hathersley,' he bellowed. 'You're six weeks behind with the rent and I won't stand for it. I'll be back tomorrow and unless you give me what you owe, you'll be out on the street.'

Ellie waited until his footsteps retreated down the stairs, then crossed the hall to Marleen's room.

She was now seventeen, and the promise of beauty hinted at at thirteen had been more than fulfilled. Although tall and slender, there was no mistaking the womanly curves beneath her worn cotton dress. Her black glossy hair framed a hauntingly lovely face, often likened by people to Hedy Lamarr.

But even a casual observer would observe the anxiety in her eyes, the dispirited stoop of her shoulders and the tell-tale mauve shadows beneath her eyes, and wonder why such a lovely young girl looked so troubled.

The answer was that during the last four years Ellie's and Marleen's roles had been reversed. Ellie was now the provider. While she worked as a cleaner and a waitress, shopped, cooked and cleaned their home, Marleen drank.

Marleen had always liked a drink. In those first few months after Polly was killed, Ellie had been too immersed in her own sorrow, too distracted by the Blitz to notice just how many bottles Marleen got through in a week. When Marleen took a swig from a small flask first thing in the morning and told her it was stomach medicine, she'd been daft enough to believe it.

Living and working in wartime London was a struggle: queues for food, shortages of just about every necessity from candles to soap, the black-out and of course the bombs. It was hard for anyone to keep their spirits up when they emerged stiff and cold from the shelter on a winter's morning to find the windows shattered or the gas and water cut off. But in Marleen's case it wasn't the hardships or the danger which made her drink, so much as a sense of worthlessness. Her looks were fading; she had a series of failed love affairs behind her and nothing to look forward to.

For the first two years while Ellie lived with her, Marleen had her drinking under control and was a slapdash but kindly adoptive mother. By day she worked as a waitress in a city restaurant, by night as a barmaid in a West End pub. There was a string of men friends, Americans in the main, and many nights she arrived home too drunk even to undress herself, but she still got up in the morning and maintained an aura of glamour and her sense of humour.

Marleen never explained why she was fired from her waitressing job, although Ellie suspected it might have been pressure from the restaurant owner's wife. But her drinking accelerated from then on and now it was out of control.

Some days there was no getting her out of bed;

others she disappeared for two or three days at a time, eventually staggering home without a penny, dirty and foul-smelling. She hardly ate anything, and was so thin it was painful to look at her. But worse still, to Ellie's mind, was the way Marleen got her drink money.

Ellie had learnt a great deal about extremes since the war started – about cruelty, kindness, bravery, cowardice, love and hate – but she'd also learned to survive. It was survival which concerned her now, and even at the risk of seeming cruel to Marleen, she had to take action.

'Get up, Marleen,' she said as she opened the bedroom door, wrinkling her nose in distaste at the sour smell. The room was pitch black, although it was mid-afternoon. The windows had been shattered by bomb blasts so often they were now permanently boarded up. 'I know you're awake and you are going to get in the bath now, and then eat something. We can't go on like this.'

'Don't go on at me.' Marleen's voice was muffled by blankets and Ellie could see nothing more of her than a hump in the middle of the bed.

'I won't go on at you as long as you do as I say,' Ellie told her more forcefully. 'I've got something important to talk to you about and I want you cleaned up first.'

As Ellie ran the bath she couldn't help but notice that the bathroom seemed to chart Marleen's downward slide. The first night Ellie had seen it she'd thought it as glamorous and perfect as her aunt. Now there were cracks in the once pristine white tiles, and a black mould grew between them which, try as she might, she couldn't get off. The pink, fluffy mat was long gone, the curtains ripped by flying glass, the big mirror shattered and the toilet seat missing. Ellie had cleaned up so often in here, after Marleen and her drunken men friends, and she was weary of it all.

But how could she leave Marleen like this? Who would look out for her?

After the incessant bombing of London had ended in May 1941, there had been a long, dreary lull. Sometimes as Ellie walked home in the early hours of the morning, encountering nothing more dangerous than a reeling drunk or an overturned dustbin to trip on in the dark, she would think back to the Blitz.

The night sky then had been alight with fire, while searchlights scanned for raiders. There was strewn masonry and broken glass underfoot, and teams of rescue workers and firemen with soot-blackened faces searching through the smoking rubble for survivors. The sounds of fire-bells joined the cacophony of wailing sirens, the 'whang whang' of ack-ack, the growl of bombers, and the whistle and crump of bombs. But worst of all had been to see those dazed people, refusing to be taken to safety until they knew the fate of a loved one who was missing. Time and again Ellie had wept as she saw bodies being carried out. They weren't her relatives, but as they shared the same fate as her mother, she felt as if they were.

Many times in those days Ellie was urged by a warden into a shelter where she spent a sleepless night huddled against strangers. After the raid there was the acrid smell, dust, smoke, charred wood and escaping gas, and the ever-present fear that she might get home to discover that the building had gone, or that Marleen had been killed.

But they'd got through it. Bomb-sites were cleared, windows and roads mended and people picked up their lives again. But oddly they were more depressed now by the austerity than they had been by the severe bombing. Many people were almost sentimental about the Blitz, claiming that they'd been part of the war then, whereas now it was just one long round of shortages and hard work.

London was looking very shabby. Where once there

had been fine buildings, there were now great gaping holes, boarded-up windows, peeling paint. The big parks were scarred with deep trenches, its railings ripped out, allotments where once had been smooth grass.

The progress of the war had been defined during those middle years by events elsewhere than in London. The Japanese bombing of Pearl Harbor and the entry of both America and Japan into the war in December 1941; the turning of the tide at El-Alamein in October 1942; the Germans' siege of Stalingrad collapsing in defeat in January 1943. There wasn't a Londoner who didn't believe the war would be won; the only question was how long it would take.

Joy and optimism had spread through London like wildfire just a few weeks earlier, as news got out of the Normandy landings. Ellie had seen for herself the feverish activity in the docks; the convoys of troops, tank and artillery choking the surrounding roads, trucks bearing chalked-on slogans like 'Look out Hitler' and 'Berlin or Bust'. It was rumoured that huge cages had been built on Wanstead Flats to hold the expected prisoners of war. Churchill's promise that ten tons of bombs would be dropped on Germany for every one that had been dropped on the British Isles seemed about to be fulfilled. Nightly Ellie shivered with delight and exultation as she heard the roar of bombers making their way towards France to blow up the German fortifications and on into Germany itself.

But then just as people were about to think the end was in sight, the V-1s, or doodle-bugs, came.

The first time Ellie heard one, she'd thought it was merely a shot-down enemy plane. There had been an ear-shattering roar of engines, a blast of flame from the exhaust and then silence. A few seconds later came a loud explosion and a pall of smoke and dust rising over the houses. Soon she was to discover that it had really been a pilotless rocket, capable of even greater devastation than the old incendiaries. Suddenly everyone was steeling themselves again. People were fleeing London daily to escape what was perceived as 'Hitler's revenge'. But for Ellie there was no such escape, she had her jobs and Marleen to think of.

'Come on,' she called out impatiently now. 'The bath's ready.'

Marleen staggered out of the bedroom. Without the help of dye her hair had reverted to its natural light brown. She hadn't washed it for at least two weeks and it hung in rat's tails on her scrawny shoulders. Her pyjamas were the ones Ellie had once thought fit for a film star: green, artificial silk with pink embroidered roses across the yoke. Now they were faded and torn, just another reminder of good times gone for ever. But it was Marleen's face that was the biggest tragedy of all. Broken veins spread across her nose and cheeks, giving her an almost clown-like appearance that no make-up could hide. He eyes were bloodshot and dull and she had lost two of her front teeth. Anyone seeing the old photographs of her dancing years would never believe it was the same woman.

'I'll put some clean clothes out for you,' Ellie said, turning her head away as Marleen lurched closer to her. Ellie knew she'd been with a man the night before – she'd come to recognise the putrid, fishy smell – and that disgusted her more than anything. 'And wash your hair. I'll come in and rinse it for you.'

An hour later, Ellie faced Marleen across the kitchen table. He hair was washed and in carlers and she wore the dark blue skirt and jumper Ellie had washed and pressed for her, but although she looked and smelt clean there was no drastic improvement. Nothing on earth could give her back her old glamour.

'That's better,' Ellie said in the approving tone a mother might use. 'Now have the soup while it's still hot.'

The kitchen was as dilapidated as the rest of the flat: the refrigerator no longer worked, cupboard doors hung off their hinges, and the once shiny lino was dull, cracked and burned in places. The air raids were accountable for some of it, but wild parties with American airmen had accomplished the rest. This window and the one in Ellie's room were the only ones still intact, criss-crossed with black tape, but it was raining outside and even daylight did little to cheer the room.

'Eat it,' Ellie insisted, as Marleen merely stirred the vegetable soup. 'It's really nice. I managed to get a ham bone to make the stock.'

She was surprised when Marleen obeyed her. Usually she just walked away, but this time she actually ate it all.

One of the saddest effects of Marleen's drinking was her silence. Sober, she had noting to say. Perhaps this was merely a symptom of a hangover, but Ellie was sure it was shame. Once she'd sung like a lark from the moment she got up, tap-danced down the hall, keeping Ellie in stitches with her jokes. Now she had no interest in anything, or anyone.

'Mr Zacharia called. He's coming to evict us tomorrow unless you pay the back rent,' Ellie said tersely. 'Have you got it?'

Marleen just shook her head.

Ellie had expected this. 'Then we'll do a moonlight, early tomorrow,' she said firmly. 'I know a place that's much cheaper than this one. It's only two rooms, but it will do, and you've got to sober up, because if you don't I'll just leave you.'

Marleen began to cry then. She made no sound, just big tears rolling down her cheeks.

It cut Ellie to the quick to see Marleen's tears. Once this woman had been indomitable, had laughed at disaster, ridiculed people who complained of their lot, was resourceful enough to find a way round any problem.

'I have to be brutal, because I love you,' Ellie went on. 'You're a drunk, a prostitute and if you aren't careful you'll end up in some asylum like crazy Grace Gilbert, and I'm not going to stand by and watch that happen.'

'I'm not.' Marleen whined, rocking herself to and fro. 'I'm not.'

Ellie's stomach turned over. Until quite recently she had refused to believe that Marleen sold herself, even though dozens of people had hinted at it. 'You are, Marleen. I know that's where you get money. You haven't got a job – who'd employ a barmaid who looks as bad as you?'

'Do you have to be so blunt?' Marleen asked pitifully, but she didn't deny it.

'Yes, I do. I've pussyfooted around this for too long already. You're killing yourself, Marleen. Without me around you wouldn't eat, or wash. Someone's got to make you see sense and I'm the only person who cares enough to.'

'I can get round Mr Zacharia, we don't have to leave here.'

There was just a tiny spark of the old Marleen left, but that saddened Ellie still more. 'You can't. He won't listen to anything but the rustle of banknotes in his hand. Besides, we have to make long-term plans and get you back on your feet again. The new place is cheap enough for me to pay all the rent, and when you've pulled yourself together again maybe you can get a real waitressing job, or something in a factory. Now let's try, shall we?'

Marleen hung her head. She had an awful hangover and she'd give anything for a drink. But sober, she knew everything Ellie said was true. The high rent had been a problem ever since Polly was killed and she hated seeing Ellie working so hard and worrying so much. She loathed herself too for resorting to prostitution, and knew she was on the slippery slope to the gutter.

'I should've made you stay in the country,' she sobbed. 'I've let Polly down, and you.'

Ellie got up from her seat and went round to Marleen, putting her arms round her and hugging her tightly.

She still hadn't come to terms entirely with her mother's death. The pain of it was like a nagging toothache. Marleen, for all her faults, was so important to her: she was her last link with the past.

Marleen had been so comforting in those first few terrible months. She'd fed and clothed her, talked and listened, made her laugh. All those nights in the shelter when she'd persuaded Ellie to do comic duets with her, making her keep her dreams alive, giving her back her self-esteem and confidence.

'You never, ever let Mum down,' Ellie said firmly. 'She always said that. Remember all the times you bought us things – clothes, food, money for outings? I haven't forgotten that and I never will. You didn't let me down either: you gave me a home and taught me how to cope with life. That's why I'm so tough now. But I'm grown up now and it's my turn to look after you. Just help me by not drinking so much. Can you do that?'

'I'll try,' Marleen sniffed, wiping her nose on the back of her hand. Sometimes these days she confused Ellie with Polly. Polly had been bossy too, telling her off when she went too far, worrying about things like rent and what they ate. But Ellie was even tougher than her mother and Marleen had no doubt that she meant everything she said. 'Okay. I'll try.'

Ellie pricked up her ears. She could hear the droning noise of aircraft in the distance. As it came closer she froze, recognising it as a doodle-bug. Her ears, like all Londoners', had quickly become very sensitive to this sound. This one must be south of the river. The engine cut out, a few moments' silence, then the distant explosion.

'Miles away.' She patted Marleen's shoulder re-assuringly. 'I've got to get to work now. Try and pack up some of your things while I'm gone. But please, please don't get drunk again tonight because we're going to have to get out of here as soon as it's light tomorrow.'

'You're a good kid,' Marleen said, her narrow, gaunt face breaking into a weak smile. 'I won't let you down this time.'

Ellie arrived at the chambers of Sinclair, Forbes and Alton in the Temple, on the dot of six. She was pleased to find the outer door locked as this meant everyone had gone home. Usually at least one of the lawyers was working late and that always slowed down her cleaning. She let herself in with her key, hung her coat in the broom cupboard, and climbed the narrow, winding stairs to start on the rooms on the top floor.

Patsy, Marleen's friend, cleaned at Mr Alton's home in Regent's Park and she'd recommended Ellie for this job soon after her arrival in London. Patsy claimed it was easy work cleaning offices, but Ellie didn't agree. The place was like a rabbit warren: on each of the three floors was a central hall with half a dozen rooms going off from it. In the winter she had to rake out the fires and lay fresh ones in readiness for the morning: the rubbish had to be collected, floors swept, furniture dusted and polished and glasses or cups washed and dried. This might have been easy if the lawyers and their clerks left things tidy, but there were always mountains of papers lying around on desks, huge files dumped on floors, to say nothing of heavy leather-bound law books strewn everywhere. When she'd finished each of the floors, the stone steps had to be scrubbed from top to bottom. But on the plus side it was warm, she could work at her own pace, and she got a pound a week.

Until quite recently Ellie had worked by day too,

waitressing in a café at Holborn. She'd given up that job in favour of one as a cocktail waitress in the Blue Moon night-club. With the tips she got more money, she had her days free and it felt like a step nearer to her goal of somehow getting on to the stage.

Ellie worked fast, cleaning the top floor in record time and moving down to the next. She had to finish here by nine-thirty to get to the Blue Moon, otherwise she'd have to come back again in the early morning.

'Hi, Ellie.' Brenda, one of the three other waitresses, looked round as Ellie came into the changing-room at the club. 'I'd steer clear of Jimbo tonight if I were you – he's in a steaming mood.'

Brenda was an attractive, tall blonde with a husband in the army and a small son evacuated to her mother's in Middlesex. She stood no nonsense from anyone; she was capable of slapping any man who made a pass at her and Ellie had once seen her pour a pint over an airman who insulted her.

'About me?' Ellie's eyes widened with fright, afraid her boss had discovered she'd lied when she said she was eighteen.

'Why should he be mad at you?' Brenda flicked a brush through her hair. 'He's just sore because the singer's cancelled. She's joined up with ENSA.'

The Blue Moon was situated in a cellar in a narrow alley just off Charing Cross Road. As it was the first and only night-club Ellie had seen she had no idea how it compared with others, but Brenda called it 'a dive'. There were three vaulted chambers linked by arches, the whitewashed rough brick walls stained yellow with cigarette smoke. The largest held a small raised platform, barely large enough for the four-piece band. In front of this was a dance floor which doubled as the stage for any cabaret acts, and tables and chairs filled the remaining area. The bar was in the back chamber opposite the club door, a plush affair with tiffany stained-glass lamps and brass rails.

On a good night the club was packed shoulder to shoulder with servicemen who didn't seem to mind the extortionately priced drinks, spivs from Soho and theatre people. It was the last of these that had made Ellie lie her way into the job. Whether they were back-stage people, dancers, actors or actresses, she felt certain that by mingling with them and keeping her ears open, one day she might get a chance to show what she could do.

The owner, James Jameson, known universally as 'Jimbo', was a well-known comedian from the music halls and he endeavoured to put on some sort of act every night to encourage the customers to sit and drink rather than just dance to the band. Since Ellie had been there she'd seen all kinds of acts come and go – exotic dancers, stand-up comics, jugglers, singers, fire eaters and magicians.

Ellie flung down her coat, unbuttoned her dress and pulled it off over her head. The changing-room was a tiny, dirty place with only one bare bulb over the cracked mirror, a few hooks on the walls for clothes and wall-to-wall black mould.

'What on earth do you do before you come here?' Brenda looked at Ellie's dirty knees in astonishment.

'Cleaning.' Ellie grinned. She liked Brenda, who was as friendly as a girl of Ellie's own age, yet moth-erly with it.

'Chimneys?' Brenda's right eyebrow rose question-ingly as Ellie ran some water in the sink to wash them. She had a bony, rather haughty face, which belied her warm nature. 'Sometimes I wonder about you, my girl!'

Ellie said nothing about her private life to anyone. She worked, looked after Marleen and their flat, and if at times she felt desperately lonely, she hid it. Sometimes she wished she could go out dancing with other girls of her own age, or find a boyfriend, but she had neither the clothes nor the money for these things. Just occasionally, she felt a little bitter that she seemed to have drawn a short straw in life, but she would counteract such thoughts by reminding herself she had talent, she was young, people said she was pretty and the war would be over one day soon.

'I suppose Jimbo will just spin out his routine,' Brenda said, getting up to zip Ellie into her uniform dress. 'Though everyone's sick to death of his jokes.'

It had turned quiet when the doodle-bugs first arrived, so quiet that Ellie was afraid Jimbo would sack her. But this lull only lasted a few days. People seemed to need entertainment, music and laughter more than the comfort of home and as the club was beneath the ground, to many people it was a safer alternative.

Ellie looked at herself critically in the cracked mirror. The slinky midnight-blue dress suited her dark colouring. When she came for the interview she was wearing Marleen's only decent dress and so she'd been relieved to find she would be given this to wear. It had a *diamanté* half-moon brooch pinned just above her right breast, and the sweetheart neckline was very attractive. Dressed like all the other girls, she felt she was their equal.

'Shall I do some seams for you?' Brenda asked, picking up an eyebrow pencil. 'I see you still haven't got any stockings.'

Ellie blushed. Brenda had lovely underwear and silk stockings. 'I can't afford any,' she said in a small voice.

'You want to cast those lovely eyes at someone,' Brenda laughed. 'Now hop up on a chair. I'll soon give you a pretend pair.'

The seams were painted on quickly; then Ellie turned her attention to her hair. She had always wished for curls and even been tempted to try a home permanent wave, but Brenda had managed to convince her that sleek, shiny hair like hers was far more attractive than frizz.

'Pin it up at the sides,' Brenda suggested, offering a pair of *diamanté* hair-slides. 'You've got such a lovely face, it's a shame to hide it. Besides, it makes you look eighteen!'

Ellie blushed.

'Your secret's safe with me,' Brenda laughed, doing Ellie's hair for her. 'One of these nights we must find time to have a chat. I'm very curious about you.'

Five minutes later, both girls went into the club. No one ever arrived to drink until around half past ten and empty, the club felt chilly and smelt musty. The other two waitresses, Hilda and Alice, were helping Cyril the barman polish glasses at the bar. Jimbo was talking heatedly to the musicians up on their platform.

As he saw Ellie and Brenda he broke off for a moment and his sharp look made Ellie nervous.

Jimbo was said to be over fifty, but he didn't look it. Ellie thought he looked like a tailor's dummy: he wore sharply tailored suits and his dark hair was slicked back with oil. He was a small, slim man with tiny bright eyes, but he had a curiously mobile face which he could contort at will to impersonate almost anyone.

'Put the candles out, girls,' he called across the empty room, his voice echoing around the cave-like interior. 'We've got no singer tonight, so if the punters start leaving you two will have to go home.'

Brenda raised one blonde eyebrow to Ellie. When Jimbo talked of sending girls home early it was always a bad sign, meaning he was worried. That affected his act, drying him up, and he usually blamed someone else for it.

Ellie collected the small glass lamps, put a fresh

nightlight in each and placed them on the tables. Jimbo had resumed his conversation with the four musicians; he was trying to persuade Roy the pianist to phone a singer friend of his.

'She won't come,' Roy said, shaking his head. He was in his sixties, and like all the musicians, looked permanently weary. 'She's fed up with being used as a stopgap. You told her she sang flat last time, remember?'

Ellie pricked up her ears. Few of the singers Jimbo used were really good. By all accounts, Jimbo's reputation for paying poorly and being rude meant he was always scraping the barrel.

'Do I pay you to stand about doing nothing?' Jimbo suddenly rounded on Ellie. She'd finished putting the lights on the tables and had been so intent on their conversation that she'd forgotten to be discreet about it.

'I'm sorry.' Ellie blushed furiously. 'It was just that –' she paused, not daring to say what was in her mind.

'Just what?' he snapped rudely, frowning with irritation.

'Well, I can sing,' she said, twisting her hands together nervously. 'If you're really stuck.'

Jimbo was staggered. He was a bumptious little man, so full of his own importance he rarely noticed his staff unless they did something wrong. Mostly he couldn't even remember their names.

'You! Sing?'

'I can,' she said, suddenly feeling bolder. 'Try me now before anyone comes in?'

Jimbo turned to Roy, shrugging his shoulders in a gesture of disbelief.

'Can't lose by trying her out,' Roy said, grinning at Ellie. He wasn't a bit surprised: many a night he'd noticed her body swaying to the music in quiet moments, her dark eyes lit up with the kind of passion that could only come from a frustrated performer.

'What numbers do you know?' Jimbo sneered at her, half expecting her to falter.

'Almost anything Roy can play,' Ellie said calmly. 'Why not try me with "White Cliffs of Dover"?'

Ellie preferred more pacey songs – she wanted to say 'Chattanooga Choo Choo', but was aware that she'd need rehearsal for that.

'Go on then.' Jimbo waved his hand towards the small stage. 'If you're lousy I'll send you home for wasting my time.'

Ellie might have concentrated all her energies on mere survival in the past four years, but she hadn't stopped practising singing, dancing and acting. Marleen in her sober moments was a good coach, particularly with dancing. Nights down in the tube during the Blitz had honed her comic routines, as anyone who could offer a few moments of entertainment was soon persuaded to forget any bashfulness.

As Roy began the introduction, Ellie took a deep breath. She was aware she would only get this one chance, that Jimbo was nasty enough to carry out his threat. But she wasn't going to fail.

She began to sing, lifting her head and filling the club with her voice. The words sounded almost prophetic after the scene with Marleen. That thought gave more emotion to her voice and her nervousness just faded away.

In her mind she was back at school in Suffolk, Miss Wilkins playing the piano. She saw Jimbo sit down on a chair, and Brenda, Alice and Hilda standing still beneath the arch listening, and she knew she hadn't lost the ability to entertain that she'd learnt as a child in Alder Street.

Never had the words of the song – joy, laughter, peace ever after – meant so much to her. She looked right into Jimbo's eyes, imagined it was her mother sitting there, and all at once she saw he was smiling.

Jimbo was not a nice man. He'd got where he was

by backstabbing, conning people and using them. He guessed the girl was under-age, otherwise she would be in the WAAFs, or the ATS. He'd taken her on just because she was pretty and when she turned out to be a good worker that was a bonus. But as he heard her rich, contralto voice, he got a tingle down his spine. The Yanks would love her, he wouldn't have to pay her much and she'd be so bloody grateful to him she'd never be any trouble.

'Bravo,' he called out as she finished and a chorus of clapping came from the other waitresses. 'Two sets tonight. One before I go on, the other after. Sort out some numbers, Roy!'

'Well you're a dark horse.' Brenda grinned as Ellie came back to the bar to join the other girls. 'Where'd you learn to sing like that?'

'I've always sung,' Ellie said shyly, stunned that singing one number to Jimbo had resulted in her suddenly being pushed into the limelight. 'Was I really okay?'

'Okay? You were marvellous.' Brenda patted her back. 'But don't count your chickens yet, love. You know what the punters in here can be like!'

The club was packed, so full of smoke Ellie could scarcely breathe. There was a different balance to the crowed tonight, fewer servicemen as so many had gone to Normandy, but more businessmen and theatre people. There were a couple of Americans in one corner who Brenda thought were deserters as they weren't in uniform and looked decidedly shifty. For her own sake, she hoped the MPs or 'snowdrops' as the men called them because of their white helmets, didn't choose to raid the place tonight. There were also a great many more of the Soho spivs back at the bar and she wondered if Jimbo was in fact a black marketeer himself.

Ellie squeezed through the tiny gaps between

chairs, holding her tray of drinks high over the customers' heads. She didn't know whether her churning stomach was from terror or excitement. She did know, however, that she'd got to calm down enough to take drink orders without making any mistakes.

'Hi there.' A brawny American airman tried to catch hold of her hand as she took the drinks off the tray and handed them round to his five friends. 'Come and sit with us, babe?'

'I can't, I'm working.' Ellie flashed a big smile and put the bill in front of him.

'Hell! Surely you don't work all the time, honey?' he said as he took his wallet out and handed over a note. 'Can't I walk you home later?'

Ellie just laughed and shook her head, even though he had bright blue eyes and a warm smile. She never knew quite how to handle advances from men – she was drawn to them, yet scared too. Sometimes she thought she was the only girl of her age in London who'd never been kissed.

'Keep the change, honey.' His hand lingered on hers.

Ellie blushed. She wasn't sure if it was caused by the big tip, his blue eyes, or the touch of skin on skin.

'You're a very pretty girl,' he drawled, his eyes fixed on hers. 'Change your mind about joining me, and I'll be right here.'

Just before eleven, she slipped out to the changing-room to check her hair and put on some more lipstick. She was quivering with nerves and the quiet of the changing-room made it worse. Over the din from the club she could hear that the band had stopped playing and Jimbo was telling jokes. She took a deep breath and walked back into the club.

'Tonight I've got a treat for you,' Jimbo said, catching sight of her standing beneath the archway. 'A lovely young lady who's been hiding her light behind my very own bar. I give you "Our Ellie".'

Ellie had to push her way through the crowd. Her legs felt as if they were made of rubber. Roy smiled encouragingly at her and patted the piano to indicate she should come and sing by him.

He began the introduction of 'Shine on Harvest Moon', before she actually reached him, perhaps guessing that it was better to push her into singing immediately, before she had time to look at the audience and panic.

Ellie could see no further than the tables right by the dance floor. The rest of the club was full of swirling smoke and shadowy shapes, punctuated here and there by a brilliant white shirt and the red glow of cigarette ends.

Her nervousness faded with the first line. Singing always made her feel good, lifting her from reality. Around halfway through the song she realised everyone had actually stopped talking and with that her confidence grew. The next number was 'I'm Going to Get Lit Up' and she let go of the edge of the piano and quite unselfconsciously began to move with the music. By the third number, which had been her choice, 'The Thingummy-Bob Song', she was acting it out.

They loved it. She could hear people tapping their feet, see heads nodding, and as she got to the last line, wild applause broke out.

'She's bloody good,' one of the spivs back at the bar said to Jimbo. 'Where's you find 'er?'

Jimbo looked at the slender, dark girl up on the stage and a shiver of pleasure went down his spine. She had magnetism, the kind of stage presence he associated with Marie Lloyd and other great music hall stars.

'Right under my nose,' Jimbo grinned. 'And that's where I'm gonna keep her.'

*

It was some time after two when Ellie left the club and she was so full of excitement she felt like whooping with joy. Jimbo had offered her a regular spot on Friday nights for which he'd give her an extra five bob on top of her wages and he'd also said he'd use her as a stand-in if other entertainers let him down. As she slipped down the deserted back streets towards High Holborn she was humming 'The White Cliffs of Dover', hearing again the whistles, the clapping and stamping of feet.

Nothing mattered any more; not her shabby dress, not having to do a flit from Gray's Mansions in a few hours, not even Marleen's drinking. She was on her way: she felt it with utter certainty. Tonight maybe it was only a handful of songs in a seedy dive, but she had a lot more up her sleeve to show people. One day she would look back on June 21st, 1944 as the day her career started.

She looked up at the sky as she walked and smiled. Marleen had once pointed out a bright star and said that was Polly looking down on them and the thought had comforted Ellie on many a dark night.

'Did you hear me, Mum?' she whispered to herself. 'Were you proud?'

Ellie laughed aloud then, hugging to herself the shock in the airman's eyes after her first set, Brenda's praise and even Cyril the barman's laconic 'You ain't just a pretty face'.

She was on High Holborn, nearly at Gray's Inn Road, when she heard the roar of a doodle-bug coming from the direction of Blackfriars. She stopped in her tracks looking up, paralysed by fear. It seemed to be coming right for her, a blast of flame from its exhaust making the bark of the engine even more menacing.

'Get to the shelter!' she heard a man yell from somewhere behind her and in that moment she was overcome with the strangest feeling of *déjà vu*. She was only yards from the place where Polly had been killed running for the shelter of the tube.

The rocket was right overhead now, and the roar of the engine louder than a dozen motor bikes revving up. She wheeled round, not knowing which way was the safest to run. She didn't dare look up: boarded windows were rattling and a pub sign cranked to and fro, squeaking in protest. Diving into a shop doorway, she crouched down, arms protecting her head.

The engine cut out. It was like being suspended in space, every muscle tensing as she waited for the explosion and death.

'Not me, not now,' she whimpered.

The boom was so close she felt the ground shudder beneath her and it was some minutes before she dared remove her arms from her head and open her eyes.

To her surprise, there was no sign of any damage around her and no sign of any other person, but she could hear fire-bells in the distance, coming closer with every second.

Relief flooded through her. She even smiled at how frightened she'd been. Only this evening she'd over-heard someone saying they could swear their heart stopped for a moment under similar circumstances, and now she knew just what they meant.

The clamour of fire-bells filled the air and as she resumed walking home, a fire-engine hurtled towards her, screaming left into Gray's Inn Road. Ellie ran then, suddenly acutely aware of Marleen. A thick pall of billowing dust blew into her face as she turned the corner, obscuring any view of what was going on further up the street.

'Don't let it be our place,' she whispered as she ran.

Another two fire-engines overtook her, bells clanging, then a truck with helmeted rescue men in the back.

Ellie saw the tree first. It was the one just across

the street from their flat, which Marleen jokingly said ought to be cut down so she could spy on her neighbours. It had been stripped of its leaves, suddenly winter-bare. The fire-engines had stopped beside it.

Her blood seemed to turn to ice in her veins, the dust making her choke and her eyes run. Gray's Mansions had a direct hit.

Ellie stopped short, her mouth falling open in horror. The mansion block looked as if a giant fist had thumped down on its centre, crushing the central eight flats, yet leaving both ends intact. The marble steps and the porch were still standing but a dense fog of dust and mortar was billowing from the building.

She rubbed her eyes, willing it not to be true. But it was. Their flat was gone with the others – just a mountain of smoking rubble, with papers and bits of curtain fluttering above it like so many small birds.

Her senses were assaulted from every direction. Screams from one quarter, shouted orders from firemen already advancing on the rubble, dragging hoses. Small bursts of flame leaped up, turning the scene into an image of a thousand candles lit in a dark shrine. She could smell escaping gas, feel dust settling on her face and hair and taste mortar on her lips.

A woman wearing only a nightdress suddenly appeared from nowhere, screaming at the top of her lungs as she ran mindlessly up and down. Only then did the full impact hit Ellie. Unless Marleen had disobeyed her, she was in that rubble!

Ellie ran to the nearest fireman. 'My aunt's in there!' she screamed at him. 'Get her out!'

'We'll get everyone out,' he said calmly. 'Did you live here too?'

'Yes,' she said, looking wildly back at the ruined building. 'On the second floor.'

'Look. Go back over there.' The fireman pointed to

where a team of rescue workers were getting shovels from the back of a truck. 'You can help by telling one of the men all you know of the other tenants in the block. Try not to worry about your aunt. She might have gone down to the shelter.'

Ellie watched and waited, willing Marleen to appear, staggering drunkenly up the road. She saw tenants from the part of the block left intact being brought out and shepherded away to safety. Other neighbours came out to watch, coats over their nightclothes, some of the men joining the rescue workers.

She saw two bodies lifted on to stretchers and carried carefully down, but although she ran forward, she was prevented from seeing them by a policeman.

'It's the people from the top flat,' he said gently.

Ellie retreated to the other side of the road, sobbing as she remembered the kindness that old couple had shown her when she first came to London. Next they found Mr Grace from across the landing to the Hardings. He was a widower and as deaf as a post and she heard someone say he was found still in his bed. They found two more bodies from the top floor, but Ellie didn't recognise their names.

It was so frustratingly slow. She watched as men eased up beams and took brick by brick away, all the time calling and listening. There were no serious fires, but with the overpowering smell of escaping gas the firemen were taking no chances, damping down as they tunnelled their way into the debris.

'We do find people alive,' a fireman said as he came over to Ellie with a cup of tea from a mobile canteen. 'Quite often they're trapped under tables, even in wardrobes sometimes. Why don't you let one of the WVS ladies take you to a rest centre?'

He indicated a couple of women who'd been shepherding people from the rest of the flats away to safety.

'I can't go,' Ellie said. 'I've got to stay.'

He seemed young, although his face was almost concealed with dust. She noticed one of the silver buttons on his uniform was covered with black cloth, a sign he was in mourning.

'I know how you feel.' His voice was husky and gentle. 'But you're cold and in shock.'

'I can't leave.' The sympathy in his voice made tears spring to her eyes. 'If you find her and she's still alive, she'll want to see me straight away.'

Charley King had joined the fire brigade when war broke out. Like all firemen, he'd faced death night after night during the Blitz and he'd seen so many terrible sights he thought he had gone beyond being affected by a girl's tears. But just two weeks ago he'd heard his brother Eddie had been killed in Normandy and so he knew exactly how she felt.

'What's your name?' he asked, putting one hand on her shoulder and wishing he had the nerve to give her a comforting hug. 'When we find your aunt I can say you're waiting.'

'It's Ellie,' she sniffed. 'Ellie Forester. My aunt's called Marleen.'

Charley patted her shoulder. 'I'll see if I can get a blanket for you.'

The first rays of dawn light did nothing to cheer Ellie. She sat hunched up on the steps of the flats opposite Gray's Mansions, wrapped in the blanket, watching and praying for a miracle.

There had been so many people milling around all night, some just to watch, others to help, but now at dawn people were coming down the road to go to work. Groups of nurses with their capes over their uniforms, stopping for a moment to offer help, cleaning ladies off to do their stint at offices in Chancery Lane and Holborn, bus drivers, porters and all those other people who scurried about their business when Ellie was usually fast asleep. She was exhausted now, dropping off for odd moments, then jerking up at each sudden noise or voice.

'Poor kid.' Fred Barratt prised up a heavy lump of masonry with a lever, looking over to where Ellie sat on a step, hunched in the blanket. 'I don't reckon she's got another person in the whole world.'

'I tried to get her to go to the rest centre,' Charley King replied, slipping a rope round a metal beam and signalling for the others to start hauling. 'She won't go.'

The two firemen had been on duty since six the previous morning and in twenty-four hours they'd attended at three other jobs. Exhaustion was their biggest enemy now; working in poor light, one wrong move could bring down rubble and kill not only buried survivors, but rescue workers too. Each brick and timber had to be taken out carefully; it was too dangerous to use heavy lifting equipment. Although they knew replacement men were on their way to relieve them, as always when people were unaccounted for, they were loath to leave.

'Did you hear something?' Fred suddenly dropped to his knees, putting his head down into the hole they'd just excavated.

Charley joined him, straining his ears above the sound of traffic. 'Tapping!' he exclaimed, grinning at Fred. 'There's someone down there!'

'We can hear you,' Fred shouted. 'We're trying to reach you. Tap again if you can hear me.'

The two men grinned as an answering tap came back.

'Is it Marleen?' Charley yelled.

Again a faint tap.

'Ellie's here,' Charley shouted down. 'She's safe and waiting for us to get you out. Hang on.'

The shrill whistle woke Ellie out of her torpor. She saw it was blown by the young fireman who'd given her the blanket and she jumped to her feet. She dodged through the rescue equipment and on to the site.

'Have you found her?' she called out, clambering over the rubble.

Charley leaped to his feet. 'Go back, its not safe,' he yelled, climbing down towards her.

They met halfway up the pile of rubble.

'It is your aunt,' he said. 'She's alive, she was tapping.'

Ellie's eyes flew open, wide with delight.

Charley put one warning hand on her shoulder.

'Go and wait down there,' he said firmly. 'You'll only get in the way. She might be badly injured and anything could happen while we dig down to her. But I told her you're here.'

'Bless you.' Ellie was so overcome with joy she impulsively kissed his grimy cheek.

Ellie had no choice but to stand back as the entire force of rescue workers and firemen concentrated on getting Marleen out of her tomb. She mentally lifted each stone, brick and piece of timber herself. It began to rain but she didn't feel it. New firemen arrived to replace the ones that had been working all night, but she was touched to see that 'her' fireman refused to leave.

A crane arrived on a truck and a couple of sniffer dogs with their handlers joined more rescue men. Now at last the pace seemed to be speeding up.

Ellie felt faint with a mixture of exhaustion, cold, hunger and anxiety, but still she stood resolutely in the rain until at last she saw one of the firemen signal to a man who was standing by.

Ellie couldn't wait another moment. She was up on the rubble faster than a scalded cat.

As she reached the edge of the hole the men had cleared she saw Marleen, or rather the legs of her silk pyjamas. Pale green, yet soaked with blood.

Her stomach contracted violently and her legs collapsed beneath her.

Strong arms lifted her and she felt herself being carried back down to the road.

'Sit here, don't come back up.' She opened her eyes to see it was the young man again. His face beneath his helmet was too grimy to read an expression, but his voice was sympathetic. 'She's trapped by a beam across her back,' he said gently. 'Her head seemed to be protected by a low table. One of the rescue workers is slipping a tube into her mouth to give her some sodium bicarbonate solution to counteract shock. A doctor will be here any minute.'

'Is she going to be all right?' Ellie's croaked out.

Charley didn't know what to say. He suspected the woman's back was broken and when he'd shone his torch on her face it had looked like a side of raw beef.

'I'm no doctor,' he replied. 'But I promise you I'll get her out.'

Chapter Ten

The casualty department of University College Hospital was quiet, considering it was midday and that three V-1s had fallen in the surrounding area in the last twelve hours. Around twenty or so patients waited to be seen, some with emergency dressings over wounds, still caked in dust and grime, staring mindlessly as if unable to comprehend what had happened to them.

Charley King glanced around the waiting area anxiously. He had left Gray's Mansions soon after they freed the woman Marleen, leaving the replacement watch to finish searching for further bodies. But although he'd gone home to bed he found he couldn't sleep for thinking about the girl.

It was that remark Fred had made. 'She don't look as though she's got anyone left in the world.'

'Have you seen a Miss Forester?' he asked a nurse as she hurried by.

She paused, frowning. 'A patient?'

'No. She's a relative of a woman brought in with back injuries early this morning. A young, tall girl with black hair,' Charley explained.

'Oh yes. She's in the waiting-room.' The nurse pointed back along a corridor. 'We've asked her to go home several times but she just won't.

Her somewhat callous report irritated Charley. 'Perhaps that's because she hasn't got one,' he said tersely, and wheeling round, made for the waiting-room.

All the firemen in Charley's watch had nicknames,

often heartlessly cruel ones relating to some peculiarity like sticking-out ears, or bad teeth. Charley's was Shirley Temple. This wasn't meant as a slight to his masculinity, just a leg-pull because he had blond curly hair and an almost pretty face. Practical jokes, affectionate abuse and leg pulling was the way firemen dealt with their dangerous and often traumatic job. Charley was every bit as tough as the next man, and his emotions were rarely tugged in the line of duty, but as he looked through the glass pane on the waiting-room door and saw Ellie asleep in a chair he felt a pang of almost unbearable tenderness.

She looked so young and grubby. Her bare legs, face and dress were daubed with dirt; even her hair was grey with dust. Aside from an old man, also asleep, she was alone, a small handbag and her shabby coat beside her, clearly all she had left in the world.

The door creaked as he opened it and she woke up with a start.

'I'm sorry to wake you,' Charley said. 'I just wondered how things were with your aunt.'

He saw her frown and realised she didn't recognise him.

'I'm Charley King, the fireman,' he said, a blush creeping up his neck. Even through the dirt he could see she was beautiful – huge, dark, sad eyes, a wide soft mouth and such long thick eyelashes. 'The one who got you the blanket.'

'The one who stayed behind.' She attempted a smile, but her eyes were dead. 'You look different without your uniform.'

All she remembered of this man was his kindness to her, but even in her present dazed and forlorn state she couldn't help but be cheered a little by his appearance. He had an open, boyish face, with springy blond curly hair and gentle brown eyes. His open-necked shirt was worn and old, but a dazzling white, his grey trousers, equally worn, were well-pressed, but the overall impression was one of strength and robust health.

'I hope you don't mind me coming here,' he said, taking a seat opposite her, looking down at his hands nervously. 'I just wanted to know how your aunt is and if you've got somewhere to stay.'

Ellie was touched by his compassion. She couldn't fault the care the doctors and nurses had shown Marleen, yet not one of them had shown the slightest interest in herself. This young fireman who'd been working all night had found it in his heart to spare a thought for her.

'That's very kind of you,' she said. 'My aunt's in a bad way. But you don't need to worry about me. I'll sort something out.'

Charley looked hard at Ellie. On the face of it she seemed in control, in fact the bald statement about her aunt's state could be construed as 'Go away, I don't need any help'. But Charley remembered only too well that he'd reacted just this way when he heard the news of his brother's death in Normandy, even so far as insisting he did his shift that day. Twelve hours later he'd been sobbing in his mother's arms like a baby.

Did Ellie have someone to comfort her?

'Let me take you to a café and get you something to eat,' he suggested. He didn't want to pry, but he couldn't just walk away and forget her without being sure she could cope. 'There's one just along the road.'

Ellie had thought she was beyond breaking down. Her savings, the money she'd intended to pay for the new flat, was buried in the rubble of Gray's Mansions along with her clothes. She'd made up her mind to wait here until six, go down to her job at the Temple where she could wash in the cloakroom and collect her week's money, then on to the Blue Moon for the evening. Maybe Jimbo would even let her sleep in the changing-room until she found somewhere else.

But this young fireman with his golden curls, his sun-tanned face and his kindness pricked through her defences, and tears welled up.

Charley saw her face crumple and he moved over to sit beside her, drawing her into his arms as if he'd known her all his life. 'You poor kid,' he said, holding her tightly. 'Suppose you tell me all about it?'

'Her back's broken,' Ellie sobbed. 'She's paralysed from the waist down and she was blinded by the glass. She's only forty-two and if she doesn't die now from shock she might have to lie for years in a hospital bed in total darkness, unable to do anything for herself.'

The old man continued to sleep. Nurses and doctors scurried past the door and emergency bells rang as yet more casualties were brought in from ambulances.

'Marleen would prefer to die than live like that,' Ellie sobbed. 'They let me see her for a minute or two and all she said was "Forget me, Ellie, get on with your life. I've been too much trouble already." We were going to leave that flat this morning. If only I'd made her go last night.'

Charley pieced the picture together as Ellie spoke of her mother's death, her jobs, her savings buried in the rubble. There were points about Marleen he didn't quite understand; nor could he make out quite why Ellie was so adamant about going to work tonight at this club. But he knew she'd seen just as much hell in this war as he had.

'I'm taking you home to my house,' he said firmly. 'Mum will sort you out some clothes and you can have a bath and a sleep. I'll phone your jobs and tell them what's happened. You don't have to go to work tonight.'

'I have to go to the club.' She sniffed defiantly. 'I can't risk losing that job.'

Annie King patted her son's cheek affectionately. Although he was due twenty-four hours off, the flying bomb raids were so severe he'd been ordered in again. All he'd had since bringing the girl back with him was a cat nap in a chair, but his sense of duty was stronger than his need for sleep.

Both Charley and Annie stiffened as they heard the roar of a doodle-bug. The window frames began to rattle, lightly at first but growing stronger as the bomb came nearer. The cups on the dresser joined in, tinkling against one another and the kettle on the stove jumped up and down. As it grew louder and louder, Annie clutched her son's arm fearfully.

'It's okay, it's going past,' Charley said.

The roaring continued for another minute or two, but it was less intense now and the vibration in the room gradually slowed. As the roaring cut out and they waited for the explosion, Annie's fingernails dug into her son's arm.

The explosion was subdued. Charley, with his trained ear, reckoned it to be in Camden Town.

'I'll look after Ellie,' Annie said, instantly behaving as if nothing had happened. 'If she insists on going to that club I can't stop her. Just you come home in one piece.'

'I don't like the thought of her going to Soho,' Charley said stubbornly. He knew he was in for a bad night and although most of these bombs seemed to be bypassing the West End, that could change at any time. 'I know that club's in a cellar, but we still dig people out from those.'

'Look son, she isn't your girl,' Annie said. 'From what she's told us both I'd say she was born adult and maybe her singing is all she has left now. Remember when you were little and brought home that bird with a broken wing?'

Charley smiled. He knew exactly what his mother meant. He had mended the wing, fed the bird by hand, petted it, loved it and when it was better it just flew away. 'That's a warning, is it?'

Annie put his tin of sandwiches into his hand. Her plump face was soft with concern. 'I suppose it is,' she said. 'I like her too, Charley, and you did right to bring her home. Just don't get carried away.'

'Do you think her aunt will survive?' Charley asked.

'I don't know, son.' Annie shook her head. From what she knew of spinal injuries it was a living death, lying in plaster in a home for incurables until such time as infection released her from misery. 'I can't help feeling it might be better if she didn't, for both of them.'

Annie waved from the basement window as Charley went up the outside stairs, then turned back to the pile of clothes she was sorting out on the kitchen table.

She was a widow of fifty-eight. Her hair was grey and she was short and stout with bad varicose veins in her legs, but she had the sparkle and energy of a much younger woman. To her neighbours in Coburgh Street in Euston, Annie was known as a 'brick'. She was the one they ran to with their troubles, someone who would sit them down, give them a cup of tea and sort them out. Over the years she'd acted as nurse, priest, teacher and friend to countless people. She didn't gossip or backbite, she didn't sit in judgement, she could turn tears to laughter. As her own doctor said on more than one occasion, 'If he could bottle Annie King, he'd have the wonder-cure.'

Even though it was only two weeks since she heard that Eddie, her eldest of five sons, had been killed in France she could still put aside her own grief to help someone else cope with theirs. But then Annie King had huge reserves of compassion: she had experienced more than her share of hardship.

Annie was fourteen in 1900 when she came to work for the widowed Mrs King at number 33. It was a big lodging-house for gentlemen boarders with three floors and a basement. Although she was taken on as

a maid, Mrs King expected her to do everything –
cleaning, laundry, laying fires, preparing meals and
washing up. She was given the tiny room at the back
of the basement where Ellie was sleeping now, a
uniform, her food and two shillings a week.

It was more than a job to Annie, it was a chance
to better herself. As one of nine children, it was the
first time in her life she'd had a bed to herself, enough
to eat or even a tidy dress. Her father had disappeared
some years earlier and her mother had turned to drink
and prostitution. She'd seen two younger sisters die
of tuberculosis and her brother Mick had his hand
torn off by a machine in a factory when he was only
ten.

For two years Annie willingly worked like a slave
for Mrs King. She came to love the house for its elegant
Georgian windows, its highly polished furniture and
the air of comfort it exuded. Coburgh Street was only
a stone's throw from the slums of Somers Town and
not grand like the places up by Regent's Park, but it
had a quiet sedateness about it, even if the brickwork
was engrained by soot and their neighbours were
tradesmen and clerks. Annie was a friendly girl who
enjoyed meeting the many boarders and Ted, Mrs King's
only son, was the kind of man she wanted as a husband.

He was twenty-eight, a nice-looking man with
blond curly hair and soft brown eyes who worked
for the railways. He was rather pompous, perhaps,
but she felt this was understandable as he was dominated by his tyrannical mother who had brought him
up to think he was a cut above his neighbours.

Annie knew she was no beauty. Her fair hair was
limp and she had freckles across her snub nose. She
knew too she fell far short of the kind of genteel lady
Mrs King would approve for her son, but Annie had
youth, persistence and a quick mind in her favour.

For two more years she set to work to make
herself indispensable. She learned every aspect of

housekeeping from Mrs King: how to lay tables properly, how to cook, clean and sew. She listened to how the old lady spoke and copied her, and when Ted came home from work she was always attentive, listening to his complaints about his colleagues, soothing him when his mother made endless demands on him.

By eighteen, Annie was transformed from the undernourished little waif who'd arrived four years earlier. Her fair hair was neatly coiled at the nape of her neck, her body was well curved and she held herself with dignity. Even the mean-spirited Mrs King became anxious that someone would poach this girl who now ran the house so well, though she never praised Annie to her face.

Fate took a hand later that year when old Mrs King fell on the basement steps. Already frail, now she needed constant nursing. The woman's reputation for being bad-tempered and mean meant she was unlikely to get anyone as competent or as willing as Annie to care for her and the house. Banking on this, Annie put her proposition to Ted.

She had to be blunt, there was no other way. She stated simply that only marriage would make her stay and care for his mother.

For the first and only time in his life, Ted stood up to his mother's objections. Annie knew it wasn't out of love for herself, only convenience, but on their wedding day she was convinced she could make him happy.

Many times in those first few years Annie doubted the wisdom of having settled for security rather than love. Old Mrs King never accepted her as anything more than a servant and Ted, once he'd slipped the wedding ring on her finger, proved to be a great deal more demanding than she'd expected. Not only did he insist she ran the boarding-house and nurse his mother unaided, but he had a powerful sex drive. Night after night he insisted on having his way with her without the slightest tenderness or affection.

Edward was born ten months after their wedding, and James, Michael and William followed at yearly intervals. If a meal was five minutes late, or if a shirt wasn't ironed just so, Ted would ask what she'd been doing all day. Sometimes she felt as if she would drop dead with exhaustion. His mother became totally bedridden and incontinent. There were piles of soiled linen to wash, mountains of food to be prepared, small children under her feet and always a baby in her arms. Ted's pomposity increased as he was promoted to station master at Euston, but he was tight-fisted with money and he still refused to get her any help in the house.

War in 1914 brought more problems. Ted enlisted, as did every able-bodied man, and the boarders who stayed during those war years were no longer the sedate gentlemen Annie had grown used to. Old Mrs King grew increasingly difficult and money was tight with four fast-growing boys to feed.

Early in 1918, old Mrs King died. Annie found it hard to manage even one tear for her, for in seventeen years she had never shown the slightest gratitude for all Annie had done. Ted was given a few days' leave for the funeral, the first in two years. To Annie's surprise, the war had changed him drastically. His old pomposity had gone and on his first night home he took Annie in his arms and apologised for being such a hard, uncaring husband.

In fourteen years of marriage he had never said he loved her. But he did then, and made love to her with such tenderness that the past was wiped out completely.

Annie's last memory of Ted was of winding a scarf around his neck, down in the kitchen. It was a raw January morning, still dark outside, and the boys were still in bed. Ted caught hold of her two hands, pressing them to his lips, his eyes bright with unshed tears.

'You and the boys mean everything in the world

to me,' he said, his voice cracking with emotion. 'I'm ashamed of how I've treated you, you deserved better. But when the war's over I'll make it up to you, my darling.'

The telegram telling her of Ted's death in France arrived just days after she had written a long, loving letter announcing the news that she was expecting another child.

Charley was born in October of that year. On November 11th, as bells rang out all over London for Armistice Day, Annie nursed her new baby and cried.

Yet her stoic nature refused to be bowed down by finding herself a widow with five boys to care for. She had the house and a tiny widow's pension, and at thirty-two she was young and resourceful enough to manage.

In those first years after the Great War came times of hardship almost as bad as she'd experienced in childhood. Boarders were so scarce that sometimes she and the boys huddled round the fire in the kitchen with nothing but a couple of slices of bread each for their suppers. But slowly Annie's natural warmth and kindness attracted lodgers who came and stayed. The basement of 33 Coburgh Street rang out with the boys' laughter, permeating the entire house. Old Mrs King would have been appalled to find her fine linen sheets and dainty china used by working men. Doubtless she would turn in her grave at the robust stews and roasts Annie seduced her lodgers with. But Annie found real happiness, and she had time to lavish on her boys. As they grew into manhood each one of them was honest, diligent and a credit to her.

Now, when Annie looked back at over forty years of living in this house, she understood why she'd felt that sense of deep gratitude on her first night here. Her fate was marked out that day and she didn't regret a moment of it. Her boys were scattered now: Bill married and living in Australia, James in the army,

Steven in the airforce, Eddie buried in France. But she still had Charley to hold on to. She busied herself by helping her neighbours and offering temporary accommodation to those bombed out. During the Blitz her basement was open house to anyone who needed shelter.

Yet although she maintained a calm front to her neighbours and sons, Annie fretted about Charley. All through the Blitz, when he didn't come home for days on end, she half expected each knock on the door to be a senior officer with the news he'd been killed. So many times he staggered in too exhausted to even speak, his eyebrows and lashes singed, eyes red-rimmed. He made light about the holes in his under-wear, or the time his rubber boots had melted, but she knew he was haunted about friends who had lost their lives and by the bodies he hauled out of burning houses.

Now Annie was afraid for Charley again, for a sixth sense told her the young girl along the passage was going to cause him pain. She'd seen that light in his eyes when Ellie came out of the bathroom in his pyjamas, her hair all shiny and clean, her skin pink from her bath, and Annie guessed it was already too late to attempt to divert fate.

Annie was ironing a dress on the kitchen table when she heard the door along the passage creak.

'Is that you, Ellie?' she called out. It was almost six in the evening, and she'd just been considering waking her with some tea.

Ellie came into the kitchen. She was still wearing Charley's pyjamas and she looked apprehensive.

'Sit yourself down.' Annie stood the iron up on its end and crossed the kitchen to fill the kettle. 'I'll make us a cup of tea.'

Ellie sat in an easy chair by the fireplace. When she'd arrived here with Charley she'd taken in little more than that it was a big house on several floors. She'd been so tired she'd willingly let Mrs King run her bath and tuck her into bed, but when she woke again to find herself in a gloomy small room with bars over the windows, she'd had a moment or two of pure panic.

'I expect you're feeling a bit strange,' Annie said gently as she lit the gas under the kettle. 'And worried about your aunt and the future.'

Ellie felt exactly as she had on the day she was evacuated. This house wasn't creepy like the Gilberts' and Mrs King was kind, but nevertheless she felt marooned and scared.

The kitchen was very homely, despite being in the basement. Bright curtains hung at the window, and a shaft of late afternoon sun shone down through the railings from the pavement above. Photographs tacked to the walls above the fireplace showed all five boys from babies to manhood. Letters were stuffed behind the clock, and old toys, games and children's books still remained amongst pretty china on the old dresser.

'I'm very grateful to you and Charley,' Ellie said hesitantly. 'But I can't stay here.'

Annie guessed what lay behind that remark. She sat herself down at the kitchen table and smiled at Ellie. 'Let's just look at what we've got here,' she said. 'You've lost your home, your money and you haven't any family. Worse still is the uncertainty about your auntie. Now Charley and me are rattling around in this big house. You won't be in the way because I've always had lodgers. Isn't it best to stay with us, at least until we get more news of your aunt?'

Put like that, Ellie could only nod her head in agreement.

'Well, that's settled,' Annie said. 'I took the liberty of getting you some clothes from the WVS. We can sort out things like a new ration book in a day or two.'

'But –' Ellie started to protest, but to her dismay she began to cry again.

'But you're scared?' Annie asked, reaching out and

221

taking one of Ellie's hands. 'You're quite safe here, ducks. I'm just an ordinary woman whose boys are all scattered by the war and I'll be glad of your company. Now shall we look at these clothes?'

She put a handkerchief in Ellie's hands and stood up. 'Some of the things they gave me are awful,' she smiled. 'I wouldn't put a refugee in them, much less a pretty girl like you. But there's a couple of really nice frocks and some camiknickers good enough for the Queen of Sheba.'

'You are kind,' Ellie said tearfully, heartened by the woman's sincerity. 'I just don't want to be any trouble to anyone.'

'Look at this.' Annie held up the apple-green crêpe de Chine frock she'd been ironing. 'I should think this one came from one of those rich women in Regent's Park, look at the quality.'

Ellie's unhappiness was eased by the dress. It was cut on the bias, the way good dresses always were before the war, and it had a corsage of darker green embroidery from one shoulder to just above the bust line. She liked everything about it – the little shoulder pads, the covered buttons and its nipped-in waist.

She held it up to herself. 'It's lovely.' She smiled. 'I really like it.'

'Look at these, then.' Annie made a scandalised face and held up some dainty pink camiknicker by their narrow straps. 'I wish I was slim enough to wear them. Why don't you try them on?'

Ellie took the underwear and the dress through to the room she'd slept in and pulled off her pyjamas. All her underwear had been old, worn and poor quality. These silky camiknickers slid over her hips like a caress, instantly making her feel beautiful. She didn't need a mirror to know she looked as desirable as Brenda at the club in them. If it had been Marleen in the kitchen next door instead of Mrs King she would have pranced in to show them off.

The frock was an even bigger thrill. It fitted as if it was made for her. She could hardly believe anyone would throw it out.

'How does it look?' she asked Annie shyly, standing in the kitchen doorway.

Annie smiled. The dress suited Ellie just as she'd known it would: the colour threw a pink glow on her skin and it flattered her curvy shape.

'Perfect,' she said. 'How about the undies?'

'They're lovely.' Ellie blushed.

Annie could see why Charley had reacted so quickly to this girl. It wasn't just her sultry looks, but a kind of glow that came from deep within her.

'Well there's a lot more things we might be able to use,' Annie said. 'Come and look with me and see what you think.'

It was quite the cosiest evening Annie had had for some time. They ate Spam and fried potatoes and discussed the clothes. A skirt needed taking in, and another big, warm dress had enough material in its skirt alone to make a more simple one. A huge, voluminous cotton nightdress would make three or four pairs of knickers.

Several times they heard bombs, but they were mainly to the south, probably on the other side of the river.

'I've never had anything as nice as this dress,' Ellie admitted later, turning to look at herself in the mirror.

'Do you know, the first decent dress I ever had was my uniform when I came here to work,' Annie said, taking a trip down memory lane and remembering how she'd stood admiring herself in just the way Ellie was now. She told Ellie how it was for her at fourteen at her dreadful home in Poplar, and how she became determined to stay here at all costs.

'I know she was my mother,' she said with a shrug of her shoulders. 'But she'd have sold me into prostitution if she'd got the price of a drink for me.

Sometimes we have to be ruthless and just think of ourselves. Now and again I wonder what happened to my brothers and sisters; sometimes I even feel a little guilty. But if I'd hung about Poplar for much longer I'd have been sucked into it too.'

In turn Ellie told her about the Gilberts, about Amos's kindness and Grace's passion for cleaning and collecting waste. Quite unselfconsciously Ellie lapsed into her impersonations, giving a hilarious performance of Grace measuring the bread, and even of the crazy way she attacked Ellie that last night and shut her in the cellar.

'Did you ever discover if he got her locked up?' Annie spluttered with laughter. The story should have been a tragic one, but Ellie had made it pantomime.

'He did.' A sad expression flitted across Ellie's face. 'But he's happier now. I've only written a couple of times. I've been too busy working and there didn't seem to be much point in keeping in touch.'

As Ellie moved on to talk about Marleen, Annie began to get a fuller picture. Ellie skipped over it, referring to drink and men friends with a blush of shame.

'I love her, though,' she hastily added. 'She couldn't help it. I think she drank so she could pretend she was still young and pretty. She's a good person really, she was always there for me and Mum.'

'Don't judge her by what other people say is right,' Annie said gently. 'Remember all those times she was there for you and forget the rest. It's my belief we all find a crossroads in our life, and most of us gamble on which road to take. For some, like me, the road turned out to be a good one, but I didn't know that when I set out. Your aunt chose the wrong turning, that's all. It could happen to anyone.'

At half past nine, Ellie got up. 'I've got to go to the club, Mrs King,' she said almost wistfully. 'It's important to me.'

Annie knew she couldn't stop her, and now she knew more about Ellie she felt she had no right to attempt it.

'Mind how you go,' was all she could say. 'Nip into a shelter if you hear a doodle-bug, won't you? I'll leave the basement door on the latch for you.'

'Thank you, Mrs King.' Ellie impulsively leaned forward to kiss the older woman. 'For everything.'

Annie caught hold of Ellie and hugged her. 'It's Annie,' she said, her gentle brown eyes, so much like Charley's, alight with concern. 'I think we're going to get on famously, Ellie. I do hope so – I always wanted a daughter, you know.'

Annie dragged her eyes away from Ellie on the stage to watch her son for a moment. He was leaning forward, drinking in every word she sang, totally unaware of his firemen friends at the bar, the pint of beer on the table in front of him or anything else.

Ellie had been living with them at Coburgh Street for almost three weeks now. Marleen, much to Ellie's joy, had been transferred to a new spinal injuries unit called Stoke Mandeville Hospital in Buckinghamshire, where they not only pioneered revolutionary treatment for their patients but aimed to return most of them, despite their profound disabilities, back to the community as useful and respected citizens.

Ellie had become like the daughter Annie had always wanted. It was a pleasure to look after her. Ellie's funny impersonations made her laugh, and the days seemed shorter with Ellie's chatter, and her interest in Annie's family and friends. She was a great help, too. Unasked, she took over whitestoning the front steps, cleaning the brass and the guests' bedrooms. She helped with the washing, prepared the vegetables, and even sat down at the sewing machine one day to mend a whole pile of sheets. When a doodle-bug had flattened number 66, fortunately when the entire family was out, Ellie had rallied round to help with emergency arrangements. Annie had been amazed when she saw Ellie scrabbling over the rubble, salvaging toys and bits of furniture. It said something about the girl's character that she knew a retrieved teddy bear or doll would go a long way to comfort a small child.

Annie was quite sure her son was falling in love with Ellie. Perhaps this should have alarmed her, but it didn't. If she could choose the perfect daughter-in-law, Ellie would be the one.

Tonight, however, was the first time they'd heard Ellie sing in public. From the moment Annie saw Ellie get up on the stage she realised that this was the only rival Charley had.

It had been Charley's suggestion that all three of them went to the Old Duke for a drink. It was the first time since Ellie moved in that her Sunday off had coincided with his.

The four-piece band was playing as they came in and soon after the landlord asked for volunteers to come up and sing.

Doodle-bugs didn't deter people from coming out any longer. As in the Blitz, they managed their work- and play-time round them. Factories and some of the taller offices had spotters on the roofs and they sounded the alarm when a bomb was coming in that direction. The streets could be emptied in seconds – building workers shinning down from scaffolding, mothers rushing with prams – and then everything suddenly started again with the all clear. In the pubs people rarely moved: the windows could rattle, the beer mugs jump on the tables, but the conversation continued. There was a commonly held theory that public houses couldn't be hit.

The three of them had heard one old drunk get up and sing a terrible rendition of George Formby's 'When

I'm Cleaning Windows', quickly followed by a gutsy but out-of-tune version of 'If you were the only girl in the world' by the flower woman from the station.

Charley had pushed Ellie up next. Annie didn't know whether this was to show her off to his friends or out of curiosity about her ability. But whatever his reason, there was no doubt Ellie was a born performer.

She'd sung 'Shine on Harvest Moon' first and the applause was so great the landlord had asked for more. 'Little Steeple Pointing to a Star' came next and then 'The London I Love'. But now she was singing 'Somewhere Over the Rainbow' and there wasn't one person in the bar unmoved by her voice.

Annie felt a chill run down her spine as Ellie sang the last line, her voice husky and wistful. Somehow the lyrics suggested Ellie's ambitions and dreams. Annie knew deep down they weren't about a husband and children.

'Wasn't she great?' Charley shouted to Annie over the raucous applause. 'I never expected her to be as good as that!'

Ellie came back to her vacant seat, her face glowing with perspiration.

'You really can sing,' Annie said, reaching forward to pat her shoulder. 'Charley and I nearly burst with pride. Let's have another drink to celebrate?'

'On me.' Frank the burly landlord had squeezed through the packed tables and was now leaning towards Ellie. 'What'll you 'ave, darlin'?'

'Just a cordial, please.' Ellie smiled up at Frank. She knew his next question would be whether she would sing again on a regular basis; she was just hoping he'd settle for an early slot so she could do a stint here and then go on to the Blue Moon afterwards.

Annie had a port, Charley a pint. Frank offered Ellie five shillings to sing on Saturday nights.

'Make it ten bob and I'll do it,' she said cheekily. She guessed he could easily afford it. The pub was packed on Saturdays, and she'd heard that Frank's only problem was getting enough beer for his regulars.

The drinks arrived, the deal was struck and Frank disappeared back behind his bar. It was only then that Ellie noticed Charley's face had tightened.

She wasn't going to ask him why: she knew. He didn't like the thought of her singing in here when he wasn't around. In one way it was comforting to feel protected, but whether Charley liked it or not, she was determined to sing here or anywhere else they were prepared to pay her.

'I'll make some cocoa,' Annie said later, putting the kettle on. 'What a nice evening it's been. I haven't enjoyed myself so much for years.'

Ellie sat down at the kitchen table, glancing at Charley. He hadn't said much since she made the deal with Frank to sing at the pub and she felt he was brooding about it. She wanted to bring it out in the open, but perhaps it would be better to leave it for now.

'How far is it to Stoke Mandeville?' she asked instead. 'I thought about going to see Marleen tomorrow.'

Ellie had felt an overwhelming sense of relief when Marleen was transferred to Stoke Mandeville. To see her aunt just lying there in a big, noisy ward at University College Hospital, heavily sedated, her face covered with dressings was distressing enough, but the hopelessness of her situation was far worse. In her few lucid moments she lay crying, wishing for death, and who could blame her when all movement and sight was gone. But then Dr Guttmann, the leading spinal specialist, came to see her, offering her a ray of hope.

'I think it might be better if you left it a couple more weeks yet,' Annie said as she took some cups down from the dresser. 'She needs time to come to terms with her injuries and her guilty feelings.'

In many ways Annie was a more genteel version of some of the ebullient women Ellie remembered from Alder Street, big-hearted, funny and very wise. Her insight was little short of astounding.

'I wouldn't want her to think I'd forgotten about her,' Ellie said, surprised that Annie had mentioned guilt.

'She knows you won't forget her,' Annie said soothingly, laying one hand on Ellie's shoulder. 'Write again to reassure her, say how much you miss her, but let her scars heal, her mind clear and give Dr Guttmann time to work on her. It will be better for both of you.'

Ellie saw immediately what Annie meant. Marleen had to accept and adjust to what had happened. To be confronted with the person she believed she'd failed at this stage could set back any progress.

'The trains are disrupted anyway,' Charley said. 'I could probably arrange to borrow a car and drive you there in a couple of weeks.'

'Could you?' Ellie smiled. Such a suggestion was typical of Charley – he was so good at organising things. 'I'd like it if you came too, I'm scared of hospitals.'

'Me too,' Annie agreed. 'Just the smell of them makes me queasy. Now I think I'll take my cocoa up to bed and read for a while. Lock up for me, Charley.'

Another roar of a doodle-bug halted Annie; again the rattle of windows, the tinkling of china. They were becoming so used to it now they rarely moved.

'It's going over St Pancras,' Charley said with a knowledgeable grin. 'What did I say about the trains being disrupted?'

Annie picked up her drink, dropped a kiss on both Ellie and Charley's foreheads and disappeared through the door.

'I ought to get to bed too,' Ellie said, sipping her

cocoa. It wasn't often she and Charley were alone together and she felt just a little apprehensive now.

'Don't go yet,' he said, moving round the table to the chair next to her. 'We never get a chance to talk.'

This was true. Although he worked twenty-four hours on and twenty-four off, he was often called in again during his rest period. When he did finally get a whole day off, sometimes Annie found it impossible to wake him.

Annie had moved Ellie up to an upstairs room. She kept the basement one now as a place to take shelter in the rocket attacks. Few bombs seemed to fall after midnight and Annie saw no sense in leaving Ellie in a miserable damp room when there were good ones upstairs free.

Ellie was so happy to be here. They'd shared her anxiety for Marleen, comforted and supported her and made their home hers too. She couldn't imagine living anywhere else now.

'Are you cross about me taking that job at the Duke?' she asked.

'Not cross, why should I be?' Charley half smiled. 'More worried about you being alone with so many men, I suppose.'

It wasn't done for women to go into pubs unescorted. Some landlords still refused to serve them, regardless of the fact that these same women were driving buses and ambulances and getting less money than their male counterparts. But Ellie, perhaps because of Marleen's influence, didn't really feel intimidated by a male province.

'But there's lots of men at the Blue Moon,' she said. 'No harm comes to me there. Jimbo even sends me home by taxi now.' This was a recent development. She was singing on an average of three nights a week now and could only attribute Jimbo's generosity to her increasing popularity.

'There's a lot of rough blokes get in the Duke,' he

replied, his frown suggesting he knew something he wasn't able to say.

'Don't you think I'm capable of keeping my distance?' Ellie said archly. 'I'm not going there for fun, only for the money.'

'Let's get off this subject.' Charley flashed one of his wide smiles at her. 'I've got no right to tell you what to do.'

'Tell me about you, then,' Ellie suggested. She had tried to get him to tell her about his work lots of times but he rarely opened up. 'Why haven't you got a girl-friend?'

He shrugged his shoulders. 'I suppose I haven't got time to find one.'

'But you must have had some?'

'Well yes.' He looked a bit sheepish. 'A few, but nothing what you'd call serious.'

'Don't be so evasive,' Ellie retorted. 'You know all about me. I want to know what the real Charley King's like. How you came to be a fireman, what it's like. What you did before the war, what your ambitions are.'

Charley hated to talk about his job. He didn't mind discussing racing to shot-down German planes or battling against raging fires in factories and ware-houses, but he drew the line at even thinking about the carnage these flying bombs were causing. Only a few days ago he'd been sent to help when one fell on a trolley bus at Forest Gate. It was crammed with people going home from work. Dismembered bodies littered the road and some of the standing passengers had been flung at the walls of the houses. Charley had almost been sick. He could still hear the screaming of the few survivors in his head.

But he didn't mind talking about his childhood and once he started to describe it he painted a very clear and vivid picture. The youngest child, protected and well loved by his four much older brothers, living in close proximity to the appalling slums of Somers Town, yet with the security of a strong family around him. His teenage years were overshadowed by the depression of the thirties, but he'd found work first in a butcher's and then in a brick factory, and had been taught to drive by his brother Eddie.

'I was driving a truck before the war,' he said. 'Stephen joined up first in the airforce, then Eddie and James went in the army and Bill went to Australia. I couldn't leave Mum on her own, so I went for the fire brigade.'

He just laughed at Ellie's suggestion that it was dangerous.

'It has its moments. In the Blitz it was a bit hairy. But then it was for everyone. When I look back I only remember the funnier things, like the pig we raised.'

Charley could tell a good story – he had a knack of giving enough detail so Ellie could picture it. The pig was called Blossom and he and a group of other firemen kept her in a pen on a bomb-site close to the fire station.

'I got really fond of her,' he grinned. 'I used to hose her down and tickle her ears and I pestered everyone for food scraps for her. But once she was fully grown I hated the thought of her being killed. I came up with the plan to find a mate for her – I thought if she had some babies she'd be saved.'

Ellie laughed as he explained how he got in touch with other fire stations which had pigs, and eventually tracked down a boar out in Essex.

'The other blokes thought I was mad,' he grinned. 'So I had to do it alone. I borrowed a pick-up truck and shoved Blossom in the back. Only trouble was, there was a hole in the partition at the back of the cab and she had her snout through it the whole journey, nuzzling my ear. By the time I got out to Essex I smelt as bad as her.'

'So what did Blossom think of her husband?' Ellie giggled.

'She took fright and scarpered,' Charley said. 'Brawn, he was called, a big, ugly thing. As I let down the tailgate, he reared up in his sty and let out a roar enough to wake the dead. Blossom just leaped out, knocked me over and was off like a dose of salts. Before I'd picked myself up, Brawn had crashed through the fence and was off in hot pursuit.'

'What did you do?'

'Ran after them.' Charley grinned. 'Half the men from the local fire station with me. The pigs ran down the High Street scattering shoppers, women were screaming, someone was blowing a whistle, it was like the Keystone cops. At the end of the High Street was a cricket field. The pigs went over that and into an allotment at the back. People think pigs are slow, but these two went like billy-oh. We finally caught up with them wallowing in a patch of prize leeks. They'd trampled and rolled on just about everything.'

'How did you get them back?'

'Don't ask,' Charley groaned. 'It was a nightmare. Blossom wasn't too bad, she'd had her outing and waving a few cabbage leaves in front of her did the trick. But Brawn was a renegade, he'd had his taste of freedom and liked it. He charged a couple of the men, knocked over a water butt. He was ferocious. But eventually we got a vet to sedate him and I can tell you I was the most unpopular fireman in Essex.'

'So did Blossom have to be slaughtered?' Ellie giggled.

'Well, the most amazing thing was, Brawn must have found time to do the business. A few weeks later we discovered she was pregnant. So she got a temporary reprieve. I was on the carpet, reminded I was a fireman not a pig farmer. Blossom produced eight piglets but the officers at the station insisted they all had to go to farmers. Poor old Blossom ended up on plates.'

'Oh no,' Ellie gasped. 'After all that!'

'The lads still bring it up even now.' Charley grinned. 'They've only got to get a whiff of bacon frying and they say things like "Blossom's frying tonight". I don't think I'll ever live it down.'

It had been just before midnight when they got in from the pub and to Ellie's surprise it was now nearly two. They had talked about so much – Ellie's childhood, her time with the Gilberts. She'd even told him some of the story about Marleen.

'What are you going to do when the war ends?' she asked him.

As they'd been talking, Ellie had found herself being drawn to Charley. It wasn't just his looks, though the combination of his lean, muscular body and his boyish face was very appealing. He had clearly inherited his mother's understanding of people, accepting them without judging. He was honest and modest, able to laugh at himself as readily as he did about everything else.

'I'd like to go to Australia,' he said thoughtfully. 'Bill's got a small farm out there now and he keeps urging both me and Mum to join him. I like the idea of the sun, riding horses and working with animals. There's a real future in Australia, beautiful beaches, wide open spaces.'

Ellie felt a slight pang. She couldn't exactly call it disappointment, or even anxiety – after all she was just a lodger, nothing more – but there was something.

'Wouldn't you like that too?' Charley asked.

The question caught her on the hop. 'I don't know,' she said, biting her lip, unsure if she would want such a thing even if it was offered to her. There were no theatres in the outback; she didn't think they even had a film industry. From what she remembered of the country from school there was nothing but kangaroos and sheep.

'What is it you want, Ellie?' he asked, his voice suddenly very soft, almost as if he were afraid of the answer.

Ellie looked into his eyes and their intensity floored her. All at once she understood why he'd come to her rescue, understood his little kindnesses since she'd been here and those jokes from his friends tonight. But at the same time she realised it wasn't one-sided; she'd had her moments of gazing at him over breakfast, or jumping when she heard his feet on the basement stairs.

'I don't know,' she whispered. She felt strangely dizzy, the way she did when she had a glass of gin. Her heart was going too fast and nothing seemed more important at that moment than his face.

She thought she knew it so well. The golden blush from the sun, the way his curls snuggled round his ears, a small scar over one golden eyebrow, even a slight bump on his nose. But now she was seeing only his mouth. His lips looked plumper and moist, she noticed too how they curled at the corners as if in a permanent grin, and she wanted them to kiss hers.

'Is it me?' he asked, one hand reaching out and covering hers in her lap.

Ellie looked down at that hand, a strong, big hand calloused by dozens of old scars and burns, yet just the touch of his flesh on hers made her insides quiver.

'I wanted you from the first moment I saw you in my pyjamas,' he said, his voice husky and very low. 'It just hit me like a thunderbolt. I never felt that way about anyone before.'

Ellie turned her face to his, leaning towards him. There was absolute silence, not a rattle, not a creak, not a sound left in the world but their breathing, and slowly his lips came down on hers.

She had watched so many long, lingering kisses on the screen, often wondering how the people breathed, or what made them want to stay that way for so long.

Now she understood, for every second of it grew more and more thrilling. Her bones felt like rubber, melting against his body, his arms came round her, crushing her ever tighter and his lips parted, his tongue probing into her mouth in a way that sent new shivers of delight down her spine.

'Oh Ellie,' he gasped, holding her face between his two hands, covering her nose, eyes and cheeks with more kisses. 'What are we going to do now?'

There was no reply to this; they were glued to one another, unable to draw apart. Sitting on two hard, upright chairs, wanting nothing more than the touch, the smell and the taste of one another and all the time a bigger need growing inside them.

It was the first time Ellie had ever been painfully aware of her body. All those whispered warnings from other girls about 'getting carried away' suddenly made sense. Charley's hands were cupping her breasts and she was arching towards him, unable to stop.

Charley drew away first. His face was flushed, lips swollen and his eyes sleepy with longing. 'We mustn't,' he sighed, leaning his head against hers as if it had taken all his strength to pull away. 'It's not right, not like this.'

Only then did Ellie notice the clock. It was almost four in the morning and Charley had to go to work at seven. 'Look at the time,' she said hoarsely.

Late as it was, she couldn't sleep that night. Her body seemed to be on fire, her mind reliving every kiss and touch. It was the first night she could remember when imagining herself on the stage didn't transport her into oblivion. All she could see was Charley's face dancing before her and hear her heart beating too fast.

Chapter Eleven

Amberley, June 1944

'Good morning, Mr Baker.' Bonny smiled at the stationmaster. She was early for the 8.50 train to Littlehampton and he was still in his shirt-sleeves, watering his tubs of flowers outside the booking hall. Bonny always found it ridiculous how he scurried to put on his jacket and cap before passengers arrived. Mr Baker prided himself on being stationmaster and he didn't like people to know he did all the menial tasks too.

It was a beautiful June day, the early wispy mist fast clearing with the promise of heat. Mr Baker didn't subscribe to the wartime motto of 'make do and mend', at least not where his beloved station was concerned. The picket fence and the outside of the booking hall had a fresh coat of white paint and with the tubs of flowers, Amberley was probably the best kept station on the Southern Railway.

'What's got you up this early on Saturday?' Bert asked. He thought Bonny looked lovely in her pink dress and dainty, strappy sandals. 'Something on at your school?'

His missus looked forward with relish to the day when young Bonny Phillips would get on the London train, never to return. She claimed she tortured poor Jack, drove Lydia Wynter to distraction and upset all the other young girls in the village. But Bert had a soft spot for Bonny. She was like his prize-winning lilies, proud and beautiful, and he didn't really believe she was as black as she was painted.

'I'm going for an audition,' Bonny said. She was so excited that even talking to boring old Mr Baker was better than waiting alone for the train. 'It's for a show in Littlehampton.'

'For the summer, is it?' Bert asked.

'Yes, but I hope it might lead to something permanent.' Bonny fluttered her eyelashes at him. 'Maybe even a show in London.'

'Good luck then.' Bert took out his pocket-watch to check the time. 'I've got to see to the signals.'

Bonny went up on the footbridge, hoping to catch a glimpse of Jack down at his garage. It gave her a good feeling being high above everything, the breeze ruffling her hair. The river was like a silver ribbon winding its way through the lush meadows. She could see Alec Hatt hauling his boats down to the water's edge, and Mrs Talbot from the tearooms putting out more chairs by her tables, clearly expecting an influx of holiday makers later on. But there was no sign of Jack. The garage doors were open wide and she could hear the whirr of some machinery, so he was probably inside, working on a car.

Today the view intensified Bonny's impatience. She was bored with looking at green fields, trees and meadows. Bored stiff by a war which seemed endless, a village where nothing happened. Even bored with Jack.

Mayfield College had proved to be a disappointment. It was just the same as school, but without the boys. She had mastered typing, just, but she'd made no real progress at shorthand because her mind was always on something else. At least Littlehampton was more exciting than Amberley, or had been until most of the servicemen disappeared over to France for the Normandy landings. Canadians, Americans, Poles and French, along with British Royal Marines, airmen and soldiers could all be relied on to whistle at the girls from Mayfield, and to offer to buy them tea at the Pavilion. If Aunt Lydia hadn't been so insistent on her coming straight home in the afternoons, Bonny might have been tempted to arrange a date or two.

Her parents harped on in their letters about her finding a 'nice job in the City' once the war was over. Aunt Lydia kept stressing Bonny must pay more attention at Mayfield and get her Pitman's certificate. Even Jack, who she once thought shared her spirit of adventure, just looked hurt these days when she talked about going on the stage.

But Bonny intended to show them all what she was made of. This job as a chorus girl in a seaside variety show might not look much to anyone else, but as far as Bonny was concerned it was a springboard to bigger and better things.

'Which way to the audition?' Bonny asked a man in shirt-sleeves who was sweeping the path up to the Pavilion.

He looked her up and down and smiled. He was at least sixty, with a swirling, military-type moustache, and she recognised him as the man who usually sold tickets for the concerts and dances here.

'Go on in,' he said, pointing towards the café door. 'Someone will tell you when it's your turn. Good luck!'

Bonny had reminded herself several times on her way here that the Pavilion was little more than a long, low hut, without proper tip-up seats or a big stage, and that therefore they wouldn't be too choosy. But to her surprise there were already some thirty other girls waiting in rows in the café, already changed into practice clothes. They were all older than herself, many of them distinctly glamorous.

'Your name?' A woman in a dull, green dress with a frizzy halo of orange hair came towards Bonny, a clipboard in her hand.

'Bonny Phillips,' she whispered, unnerved by the other girls' stares.

'Have you got your music with you?' Again the woman didn't look up, merely ticking off her name on her pad.

'Yes.' She could hear a girl singing next door in the concert hail and she was better than Bonny.

'Change in there.' The woman pointed towards a cloth-covered screen set up in the corner of the café. 'Then wait here until your name is called.'

Bonny emerged from behind the screen some few minutes later feeling despondent. Two other girls who sounded far more experienced than herself were already dressing to go home again, having been dismissed. She had learnt too that so far only five girls had been asked to stay for a second audition.

Her despondency increased as she sat in the café, listening to girl after girl perform. She wondered now if her short flared satin tunic with matching knickers smacked of village dancing classes. Most of the other girls were wearing old, much darned ballet tights and leotards which, although shabby, at least gave them an aura of professionalism, and their whispered conversations revealed that none of them were strangers to auditions. Would Mr Dingle see her as a complete novice and dismiss her immediately?

Mr Dingle, whom she caught a glimpse of every time the concert hall door opened, looked formidable. He wore a beige, linen jacket with a rose in the button-hole, fair hair artistically long, and the expression on his face was one of weary exasperation.

Bonny thought he must be fifty at least, because he'd escaped call-up, but his face was smooth and unlined, and his features rather feminine. Without even speaking to him she somehow knew he would be a hard taskmaster, the kind of man immune to her brand of flirtatious charm. Just the sardonic smirk he gave as he dismissed the girls who weren't up to his exacting standards suggested he'd be cruel too.

Bonny rarely considered herself anything but the best, but as she heard other girls sing, her confidence plummeted. She couldn't see them dance, of course, and she was certain she could give them all a run for their money where that was concerned. But where were the fat, the short, the clumsy that she'd expected? Four out of every five girls here looked like beauty queens!

She squeezed the little black cat Jack had given her. He'd won it at a fair in Bognor at Easter. When she'd put it in her case this morning it had seemed childishly superstitious: she firmly believed she had enough talent not to need luck too. Now she wasn't so sure.

Jack was one of her main reasons for wanting this job. She was certain what she felt for him was love. His kisses were thrilling, his hard body made her tingle from head to toe, and he was the best friend anyone could have. But he was getting so serious, and she felt trapped.

In Amberley Jack was well known and respected. No doubt he would one day own a garage, since he worked so hard. But a small voice inside Bonny kept reminding her that there was a big world outside Amberley, one she needed to explore and taste before committing herself to Jack. She suspected there might be other men who could make her feel the way Jack did, ones with even better prospects and no engine oil beneath their fingernails. A summer job away from him would at least give her some breathing space.

A girl with red hair was belting out 'Chattanooga Choo Choo' and her tap-dancing sounded as good as Bonny's own.

'Thank you, Margaret,' Mr Dingle called out as she finished. 'Stay behind please for a second audition.'

'Bonny Phillips,' the woman with the green dress called out.

Bonny jumped up, dropped the black cat, clutched her music to her chest and ran into the hall. She was beyond wondering if 'Fascinating Rhythm' was a good choice – she'd rehearsed it so often with Aunt Lydia she knew it backwards. She handed the music to the pianist, jumped up on to the small, bare stage and switched on her smile.

Ambrose Dingle winced as the girl began to sing. Her voice was too sugary for his taste and he found it a little presumptuous on her part to choose a number which Eleanor Powell had immortalised in *Lady Be Good*. She was much too young too.

But as he watched the girl he began to forget her tinny voice. She could dance and she had the kind of confidence he liked. He glanced at the list in his hand. Only fifteen, as he'd suspected, no experience except in panto and village dancing displays. But she did live locally.

Ambrose Dingle had begun his theatrical career as a song and dance man in music hall. During the thirties he'd taken a chance and gone to America, intent on getting into a Broadway show. He never made it to Broadway, but he did become the dancing partner of Lois Lombard and toured America with her during the Depression. Lois was spotted by a talent scout and became one of Busby Berkeley's chorus girls. Ambrose took the only job on offer, as a stage-hand.

In 1938 Ambrose came back to England, his dreams of becoming a Hollywood star shattered. All he had in his favour was the knowledge of what made a spectacular show, a firm grounding in choreography and the determination to make the name Ambrose Dingle as well known as Busby Berkeley's.

The war had been his saviour, yet a curse. People wanted glamorous variety shows, yet dancers who met his Hollywood standards were hard to find. He'd staged small shows like this up and down the country, collecting girls with talent as he went. When the war was over he intended to get his 'girls' on to the West End stage and forget these provincial concert halls for ever.

This blonde had the makings of a real showgirl. Long, slender legs, dramatic large eyes, and a perfect body. Perhaps he could just give her a try.

'Thank you, Bonny,' he said as she finished. 'Wait here for the second audition.'

'I've got it!' Bonny burst into the Tollgate garage, dropping her vanity case to the oily floor. 'I've got it, Jack!'

Jack was lying flat on his back under a car, but at Bonny's excited shriek he hauled himself out. The double doors were folded right back to let in the fresh air, but the smell of oil, exhaust fumes and rubber tyres in such a small place was overpowering.

'Well done,' he said, getting to his feet and grinning at her. Deep down he'd hoped she wouldn't get it, but the excitement in her voice and eyes shamed him into being pleased for her. 'I'd like to hug you, but I'm filthy.'

'You're always filthy,' she said, torn between disgust at his oily hands and grimy face and a desire to kiss him regardless. 'Can't you wash and come and have a cup of tea with me to celebrate?'

'What, now?' Jack looked scandalised. 'I can't knock off in the middle of a Saturday.'

Bonny pouted and perched on a high stool by the garage door. 'I want to tell you all about it,' she said. 'I can't in here.'

She'd overheard Sally, one of the other dancers, say she was being taken out to lunch to celebrate getting the job and seen her swanking away down the promenade on the arm of a Royal Marine. Bonny felt she should have similar attention.

'Bonny, I'm dying to hear about it.' Jack sighed

deeply. 'But I can't break off from this job, I've got to have it finished in a hour. Go on home and tell Miss Wynter. I'll take you into Arundel tonight if you like and you can tell me everything then.'

It was no secret any longer that they were sweethearts. When it got out last year, Miss Wynter had read him the riot act, warning him she would get him locked up if she discovered there was any 'hanky panky', as she called it, but she seemed to accept Jack's intentions were honourable. Jack wanted to keep her approval and he'd lose it pretty quickly if he was seen to be a conspirator in Bonny's latest plan.

Jack was eighteen now and he loved Bonny with a passion that often terrified him. Just a touch of her hand made him tremble, a day without seeing her seemed like a month and she was on his mind every waking hour. But there was no peace in loving her. She wound him up, teased him, played with his feelings, belittled him and wounded him; yet each time she put her lips on his, pressed her body against his, he was lost.

He looked at her now, sitting on the stool, and he wanted to crush her into his arms. She sat provocatively, legs crossed showing just enough honey-coloured thigh to enflame him still further, her arms folded, pushing up her breasts, and her lovely mouth pursed in reproach. He had learnt a long time ago that he had to stand against her demands, but it was so hard.

'I don't know that I *want* to go to Arundel with you,' she said peevishly. 'I might ring Belinda and see if she wants to go to the dance tonight.'

Jack turned away, sickened by her manipulations. 'Go home and tell Miss Wynter your news,' he said. 'I'll ring you when I've finished work.'

'I might not be there.' Bonny jumped down from the stool and picked up her vanity case. 'I may have found someone by then who is interested in my job.'

'Bonny, I *am* interested.' Jack's voice rose in anger.

'You know that perfectly well. But I have to get this job finished. Don't be so childish!'

'Childish, am I?' She put her hands on her hips and looked scornfully at him. 'Well, I wasn't too childish to be picked out of two hundred girls. Mr Dingle said I was the best dancer he'd ever seen.' In fact there were no more than sixty girls and Mr Dingle hadn't singled her out in any way from the ten he'd finally chosen, but Bonny always added a great deal of embroidery to every story.

'I'm really glad for you.' Jack lowered his voice again. 'I want to take you out and celebrate. I want to hear every last thing about the audition. Please be reasonable.'

'I'll think about it.' She turned away and walked off.

Jack stood for a moment, tempted to run after her, but he looked back at the car and decided against it. Bonny Phillips wasn't reasonable. She probably never would be. Perhaps it was as well that he'd had his call-up papers today. As Mrs Baker had said, 'A spell away from that young minx will do you a world of good.'

'Ambrose Dingle is an excellent choreographer,' Lydia said reluctantly. She didn't know him personally, only by reputation. 'But he's a hard, difficult man, Bonny. I'm glad, of course, that you've been chosen, but I think you're too young still for this.'

Lydia had guessed Bonny had something up her sleeve when she disappeared this morning, but it had never occurred to her she might go to an audition without talking about it first. Now Bonny was saying she'd not only been taken on but would have to stay in digs once the show left Littlehampton and moved on to Bognor and Worthing. And she wanted to leave Mayfield right away to start rehearsing.

'But it's what I want,' Bonny said indignantly. 'Some of the other girls are my age too.'

'Have you thought about what your parents will say?' Lydia asked, imagining Mr and Mrs Phillips arriving on the next train, blaming her. 'I don't think they'll be happy about you living in digs. And what happens at the end of the summer? You can't just go back to Mayfield when you feel like it.'

'I don't want to go back there.' Bonny folded her arms and looked insolently up at the ceiling. 'I'm a dancer, not a shorthand typist. When this show's over I'll find another job.'

'Now look here.' Lydia felt anger rising. She loved Bonny, but at times she didn't like her one bit. 'You are only fifteen, and I'm responsible for you in your parents' absence. They've paid good money for you to go to college and they'll be bitterly disappointed if you don't finish your course. You think you can run rings around me, them and everyone else, but it's high time you stopped being so selfish and gave a moment's thought to those who care about you.'

'It's my life,' Bonny said, walking away from Lydia towards the door. 'I'm going to do what I want with it.'

Lydia felt deeply for Mr and Mrs Phillips. She had helped in Southampton during the bombing and she'd experienced first-hand the terror, the loss of life, homes and dreadful injuries that city dwellers had to endure. Bonny's parents had been bombed out twice, returning to their house in the middle of winter with just a tarpaulin over the roof until it was mended. Looters had taken many precious belongings, furniture damaged by fire and broken glass. Mr Phillips not only worked by day but stayed behind at Ford's to fire-watch, and in one raid he'd been burned so badly he was hospitalised. On top of the lack of food, and the shortages of everything that made life bearable, they were separated from their only child. Yet Mrs Phillips strained her eyes nightly making dainty underwear for Bonny, all their clothing coupons were used for things Bonny needed, and they'd saved every penny for her future.

The war had hardly touched Bonny. Aside from bombers flying overhead, a few explosions in Littlehampton when mines on the beach blew up in bad weather and reports of bomb damage in Chichester and Bognor, she knew little. The closest she'd come to the war was on one trip home to Dagenham when her parents had insisted she spent the night in their Anderson shelter. Even a bus ride out through the devastated East End of London hadn't really brought home the hardships city people suffered. Bonny was well fed, and she had pretty clothes and dancing lessons when other girls her age were hunting for fire-wood on bomb-sites, or queuing for rations. She knew nothing and cared less.

'Don't be like this,' Jack pleaded with Bonny as they got off the bus in the village. She had been silent all the way home, refusing even to hold his hand. They had gone into Belinda's Tearooms in Arundel and failed to notice the time as they were talking. By the time they got to the cinema all the seats for *Clive of India* were taken. 'We can go and see it some other time. I didn't realise you wanted to see it so badly. It's an old film anyway.'

'I didn't,' she snapped. 'But seeing drippy Ronald Coleman is better than talking to you. All you've done is take Aunt Lydia's part and throw cold water on everything. Now you tell me you've been called up. What am I supposed to do?'

It had never occurred to Bonny that Jack might want to go in the army. As an apprentice he could probably get out of it. But to her surprise, Jack actually welcomed conscription, believing he would gain valuable experience working on army transport and help his country at the same time.

Jack caught hold of her shoulders, pushing her gently towards the shelter of the churchyard wall. It was still light and people were out in their gardens. Jack was very much aware that his every last move was reported back to Miss Wynter.

'I don't want to leave you,' he said, looking right into her eyes, trying hard to articulate all the conflicting emotions inside him. 'You know I love you, but everything's against us right now because you're so young. I'm not pouring cold water on your dancing job either. I only tried to point out your parents won't like it any better than Miss Wynter. Please kiss me and say you aren't mad with me?'

'I'll kiss you if you come in with me now and try and talk Aunt Lydia round,' Bonny sniffed.

'Okay,' Jack said wearily. He didn't believe he could influence Miss Wynter, but perhaps she'd see his call-up as a sign that one of her problems was shortly to be solved.

Bonny softened the instant Jack's lips touched hers. She adored kissing and hours and hours of practice had made her very good at it. Hardly a night went by with Jack when she wasn't deeply tempted to let him go further, especially on those warm evenings out in the fields when no one was about.

Jack groaned softly as Bonny pressed herself closer to him. He wanted her so badly that at times it consumed him. How many more nights could he stand the torture of constant arousal with no relief?

Bonny opened the door and went into the hall. The sitting-room door was open but Lydia wasn't there.

'She must've gone out.' She turned to Jack, hovering nervously on the doorstep. 'Come in anyway, maybe she's left a note.'

Jack shut the door behind him and followed Bonny. A note was propped up on the sofa table.

'I've been called out to Bognor,' Bonny read aloud.

'Lock the door but don't bolt it. I can't say what time I'll be back so don't wait up.'

'I'd better go, then,' Jack said, knowing Miss Wynter might be angry if she found him there when she got back.

'No.' Bonny's eyes sparkled, her tongue flickering across her lips. 'You've got the perfect excuse for being here. If she turns up we'll just make out we've just come in and you want to tell her your news.'

Jack knew it wasn't a good idea, but Bonny was already pulling over the black-out and curtains. 'Just for a short while, then,' he said reluctantly. 'If she isn't home within half an hour I'd better go.'

They rarely had the comfort and privacy of a softly lit room. As Bonny snuggled into his arms, Jack soon forgot about Miss Wynter and the promises he'd made to her. Within minutes they were lying together on the big sofa and passion flared up like fire in dry hay as one long kiss led to another.

'I love you,' Jack whispered, his finger fumbling at the buttons on the front of her dress, reaching in to cup one full breast in his hand. 'You are so beautiful, I want you so badly.'

She had allowed him to stroke her breasts on many an occasion, but he'd never seen them naked before. He looked down at the small hard nipple between his fingers and squeezed it gently. Her eyes were closed and her mouth open slightly, soft moans of pleasure coming from deep in her throat. Jack moved down to take her nipple in his mouth and her moaning grew louder, her hand reaching out to stroke his head and neck, urging him closer still.

'That's wonderful,' she gasped. 'More.'

Jack forgot all the warnings. The taste and smell of her skin drove out all thought but to possess. He sucked on her nipples, his hands roaming down her body, fingers pressing into all the soft, hidden places. Even through her dress he could feel the heat of her,

her thighs yielding to his touch, opening enough to let his hand in.

She drew his face back to hers, her lips hot and insistent, tongue probing sensuously against his. Jack's hand rested for a second on her knee, then slowly slid up her thigh under her dress.

He expected her to stop him, but instead she moaned again, arching her body against his. Slowly his hand crept up, stroking and smoothing the hot silkiness of her inner thighs until it reached satin knickers.

Jack could hardly contain himself as he rubbed her there. The combination of silky damp satin, the triangle of soft pubic hair and the soft womanly folds of skin that he'd dreamed about for so long was unbearably erotic. But instead of Bonny stiffening as he expected, her thighs parted further, urging his fingers deep inside her.

Jack's knowledge of women's bodies came only from crude male jokes. He hadn't expected it to be so hot and slippery or to feel such awe and tenderness all at once. He found as he slipped his finger in and out that Bonny's moans grew louder and his desire to please her was greater than his own need. He grew bolder as she writhed under him, pulling her knickers to one side and experimentally stroking her all over. The musky smell of her, the whispered cries for more, her darting tongue against his, her hard nipples against his chest were inflaming him to such a pitch he had to unbutton his trousers.

'Hold me,' he begged her, pushing his fingers deep within her, hoping that she wouldn't suddenly push him away. 'Please hold me.'

'I love you, Jack,' she whispered huskily in his ear. 'It's so wonderful.'

Her hand closed round Jack's penis willingly, but she was insinuating her body towards it too, drawing him on to her.

'No,' Jack whispered with little conviction. 'No, we mustn't.'

'But I want you, Jack,' she said, her hands reaching down the back of his trousers and cupping his buttocks. 'Please!'

Nothing on earth was as wonderful as the moment when he thrust himself deep inside her. It was like the thrill of driving a motorbike at full throttle down an empty road, the blast of heat on opening a furnace door, and yet the sweetness of stepping into a garden after a summer shower.

'I'll love you for ever,' he heard himself call out at the moment of eruption and all at once he was crying.

'What's the matter?' Bonny whispered, lifting his face from her shoulder to kiss him. She wiped away his tears, her blue eyes troubled.

'I don't know,' Jack whispered.

Bonny had never looked more beautiful, her hair tousled, lips swollen with kissing, her face rosy. But it was the tenderness in her eyes which affected him the most. She'd never looked quite that way before.

'We shouldn't have done it,' he said hoarsely. 'You're under-age. We should've saved it till we got married.'

The purr of a car engine outside startled them. Jack leaped up, fastened his trousers and tucked in his shirt. Bonny was quicker still. She buttoned her dress, smoothed down her hair and pushed her feet back into her sandals all in one swift movement.

They had just plumped up the sofa cushions as Lydia opened the front door.

Lydia saw Bonny sitting sedately on the sofa as she came into the hall and didn't immediately notice Jack in an armchair tucked behind the door. It had been a long, weary evening, trying to sort out a home for a young, pregnant woman with two small children who had turned up in Bognor after her house in London had been bombed. On the drive home Lydia had thought long and hard about Bonny and she had come reluctantly to the conclusion that it would serve no purpose to oppose the girl about this dancing job.

'Still up?' She smiled warmly. 'Was the film good?'

Lydia took a step closer, about to suggest they had some cocoa. When she saw Jack, her smile faded.

'Jack came back to tell you his news,' Bonny said too quickly. 'He's got his call-up papers. He's joining the Royal Army Service Corps.'

Lydia didn't need any sixth sense to tell her what had been going on. Jack's eyes were puffy, he was very flushed and his eyes didn't meet hers. Bonny's dress was a mass of creases and there was a faint odour in the room which Lydia instantly recognised.

'What have you two been doing?' she asked. She was wearing her WVS uniform. She withdrew a long hat-pin and put her hat down on the coffee table.

There was a highly charged atmosphere between them. Jack looked guilty, standing awkwardly at the fireplace like a burglar interrupted mid-job. Bonny was too calm; normally when she was with Jack she was giggly and restless.

'Just waiting for you,' Bonny said innocently. 'We haven't been in long.'

Lydia looked at the clock. It was half past eleven, so this last remark was a lie. 'From what I can see it's just as well Jack's got his call-up papers.' She turned to look directly at him. 'I'm not a fool, Jack, I know what's been going on here tonight. I trusted you. How could you do such a thing?'

Jack blanched. He had visions of Miss Wynter calling a doctor to examine Bonny, then having him run in to the police.

'We haven't done anything.' Bonny stood up, her eyes flashing defiantly. 'What do you mean?'

Lydia knew Bonny would continue to lie to her last breath. 'Go to bed,' she snapped at her. 'I'll talk to you in the morning.'

Jack sidled towards the door.

'You can sit down.' Lydia pointed towards the chair. 'I'll talk to you alone.'

Bonnie flounced out, without so much as a backward glance. Lydia waited until she heard her footsteps overhead. She took out her cigarettes, took one herself and handed one to Jack. Once he'd lit them both she sat back in her chair and looked hard at him.

Jack was normally a very relaxed lad, but now his hand trembled, his knees were braced as if ready to spring out of the chair and his brown eyes were wide with alarm. Lydia had a great deal of affection for Jack. He was endearingly ugly with his squashed-looking nose, red spiky hair and those freckles. Anyone meeting him for the first time could be pardoned for assuming he was a thug – his shoulders rippled with muscle, his hands were like two great hams. An unfortunate appearance for someone with so many fine qualities.

'Don't lie to me, Jack,' she said. 'Bonny lies easier than she breathes, but I expect better of you. Have you had relations with her tonight?'

Jack blushed scarlet at such a direct question. It was tempting to deny it but he knew Miss Wynter better than that. 'We didn't mean to,' he mumbled. 'It just happened.'

Lydia nodded; she'd had her own moments of being carried away in the past. His honesty was at least admirable. 'Setting aside the law, which makes it a crime to have relations with an under-age girl,' she said coolly, 'perhaps you should consider that such an act might lead to pregnancy.'

Jack gulped. 'I'd marry her,' he said immediately. 'I want to anyway.'

Lydia shook her head, her expression one of pity now rather than anger. 'Jack! Bonny's fifteen. A spoilt, selfish girl who is no more capable of looking after a baby than I am of stripping down an engine. I've grown to love her,' Lydia sighed. 'But I'm not blind to her faults. We'd better both pray hard she isn't pregnant, because I can't think of anyone who'd make a worse mother.'

'But I love her, Miss Wynter,' Jack protested. 'And she loves me.'

'I believe you truly love her,' Lydia said sadly. 'But I don't believe Bonny loves anyone but herself. I'm telling you this, Jack, because I care for you, not to be spiteful. She may change as she grows up – I certainly hope so. But for now she is a mass of contradictions with the body of a woman, but the mind of a child.'

To Jack's shame, he began to cry. He tried to prevent it but tears just cascaded down his cheeks.

Lydia got up and went over to him, laying one hand on his shoulder. 'Poor Jack,' she said softly. She could guess what he was feeling; one moment a glimpse of paradise, the next cruel reality. Tom between the army and being close to Bonny. But she had to warn him. In her heart Lydia knew Bonny was just using him for practice, that in a few months he would be discarded like yesterday's news. 'Go off to the army, Jack, look around the world and enjoy your youth and freedom. Maybe one day it will work out for you and Bonny, but don't count on it.'

'Link arms, step and kick,' Ambrose shouted from below the stage. 'Get those legs higher, head up and smile. Now break arms and turn, faces towards the audience and high kicks again.'

The girls held on to each others' waists and kicked their way into the wings.

'Come back,' Ambrose yelled again. 'To make this look right *all* your legs must reach the same height. At the moment you look like a drunken centipede. From the beginning again. This time I want it right.'

The pianist pounded the introductory bars yet

again. Once more the girls lined up to repeat the entire routine.

Bonny's back ached, her legs were stiff and her face felt set in a permanent false smile. This was nothing like Lydia's lessons, it was torture. She could do the high kicks effortlessly, but she wasn't used to dancing as a team. She was soaked in sweat, she was hungry and thirsty and they still had another two hours of rehearsal.

'Ten-minute break,' Ambrose yelled, just as she thought she might keel over. 'Outside, get some fresh air.'

Out in the tiny yard behind the café the girls sank on to the many empty crates and boxes. One of the café girls brought out mugs of tea on a tray and a pile of damp, grey sandwiches.

'They're all we've got,' she said apologetically. 'Corned beef again.'

Bonny leaned back on the wall and closed her eyes. Right now she wished she was back at Mayfield, fresh and clean in her pink and white frock, doing nothing more arduous than tapping a business letter into the typewriter.

She had achieved her objective of being one of 'The Cover Girls', but somehow she felt she'd lost something precious in the process.

Her parents had eventually reluctantly agreed, just as they did to all her demands, yet their obvious disappointment in her had taken the edge off her pleasure. Aunt Lydia was still cool and had made some very stinging comments that Bonny didn't choose to dwell on. Worse still, the other girls in the troupe seemed hell-bent on breaking her confidence.

Bonny realised too late that sucking up to Ambrose Dingle was a mistake. It hadn't made him nicer to her and now the girls went out of their way to show her up. Most of them were better singers than her, many of them danced just as well and she'd learnt to her cost that an inexperienced dancer with no friends was in for a rough ride.

'Stop whining,' one girl said to her when she dared to complain at being kicked in the shins.

'Ambrose will keep you practising till your feet bleed.' Another grinned maliciously when a blister the side of a half-crown came up on her heel.

The afternoon sun slanted down into the yard, hitting Bonny squarely in the face, but every patch of shade was taken by the other girls. They had all formed tight little groups – one of the six girls who'd toured with Ambrose before, the remaining nine split into two more – but Bonny was excluded from all of them. Their laughter and chatter, the smell of shared cigarettes, wafted over her, making her feel isolated and vulnerable, and she hadn't the least idea how to go about gaining acceptance.

On top of this was Jack. Next week he would be off to Aldershot and it might be months before she saw him again. Aunt Lydia had been so cruel about her and Jack. First spelling out in graphic detail what pregnancy meant and then accusing Bonny of playing with Jack's emotions. Fortunately her period had turned up, but she didn't really understand what Aunt Lydia meant about playing with emotions. Surely the way Bonny felt now was love? She couldn't stop thinking about what they did that night, she kept imagining his hands on her body, she wanted him. If that wasn't love, what was it?

'Are you all ready?' Ambrose Dingle walked along the line of girls, looking them up and down. Sally, a statuesque brunette who led the sixteen girls, was right in the wings, waiting for the cue to lead them on. The line went right back to the dressing-room. Bonny was in the middle, a position she was secretly convinced had been given her because she was the prettiest. 'Now, please remember to smile, smile,

smile. They'll forgive you if you stumble but not for looking sour. Forget that this is the dress rehearsal – there's fifty wounded servicemen out there all trying to forget what they saw in Normandy. Dazzle them!'

Bonny looked down at her costume. The opening number of the show was 'Lullaby of Broadway'. She could only suppose that the flimsy chiffon shifts worn over skin-tight shorts and sequinned bra tops were supposed to look somewhere between evening gowns and nightdresses, but to her they were just plain tacky. Worse still, they were so old her shorts had been patched and she shuddered to think how many times they'd been worn and never washed.

Jack was out there tonight, with Beryl Baker and Aunt Lydia, along with most of the other girls' relatives and the servicemen. Tonight was Jack's last night in Sussex; tomorrow he'd be in the barracks at Aldershot.

'The orchestra's tuning up.' Frances, the girl next in line to Bonny, turned to her, grinning broadly. In fact there was a pianist, a drummer, two very old violinists, an enormously fat lady playing cello and a saxophonist. 'Are you nervous, Bonny?'

Frances was the only one of the girls who was coming round, but perhaps this was because she was a misfit too. She was just a bit plump, with raven black curly hair, and very posh. Most of the other girls came from quite poor backgrounds and they were suspicious of the way Frances threw money around.

'A bit,' Bonny agreed. She wasn't, in fact, but in two weeks of rehearsals and being left out of everything, she'd learnt not to look too confident.

A whisper was being passed down the line of girls from Sally, who was peeping through a hole in the curtain at the audience. She had been giving a running commentary since they lined up, particularly on the men arriving.

'An awful looking red-haired bloke just sat down with two older women right in the front row,' Frances whispered word for word to Bonny. 'Sal wants to know who he belongs to.'

Bonny's heart sank. It had to be Jack; she'd made sure he and Lydia had seats in the front. She hesitated, blushing furiously. To admit he belonged to her might make her a laughing stock, yet if she passed on the whisper that would be denying him. Until now she'd never considered how Jack looked to others and she'd implied to the girls that her boyfriend was something special.

'Pass it on,' Frances nudged her.

Bonny turned to Muriel, a sharp-faced brunette, and whispered the message, trying hard not to think how hurt Jack would be by her disloyalty.

As the overture struck up, the girls braced themselves and moved closer together, ready to start. Bonny wished she'd gone to the lavatory one last time, but it was too late now.

They strolled on, arm in arm in pairs, singing, swirling their chiffon shifts with one hand.

Once out there, Bonny forgot everything but the joy of singing and dancing in front of the footlights. She caught a glimpse of Jack's rapt face and Lydia's broad smile, but looked right out over their heads and concentrated on the rows of servicemen behind.

Despite all Ambrose's pronouncements that they were the worst troupe of chorus girls he'd ever worked with, somehow the performance was perfect. The high kicks were all uniformly chest high, the girls all turned as one and Bonny, Frances, Mary and Sally, who were the only four tap-dancing, synchronised their steps as they never had in rehearsal. As they swept off to the whispering of *'Good-night, good-night'*, the applause was deafening.

'Brilliant, girls!' Ambrose beamed at them as they came off. 'Well done, all of you.'

Back in the dressing-room it was chaos as they changed for the next number. Sixteen girls in a room some eight by twelve with one small mirror.

'I've got a hole in my tights,' Sally moaned.

'My bow-tie's gone,' yelled Margaret.

'Has anyone got any STs?' shouted another girl. They could hear the singer Larry Lewis singing 'You Can't Run Away from Love Tonight', and half the girls had to be back on stage for his next number. 'Oh You Beautiful Doll', changed into long, slinky dresses.

Bonny wasn't in on that number, so she helped those who were get ready, fastening paste necklaces, fixing feathers in hair and handing them their gloves and parasols.

'Anyone discover who the red-haired horror belongs to?' Sally called out the moment half the troupe had disappeared out the door. 'He was looking at you the whole time, Bonny, is he your fella?'

Bonny wanted the floor to open up and swallow her. If she said no and the girls spotted him waiting for her at the end, they'd be laughing at her for weeks. 'He's my cousin actually,' she said, turning her face away so they wouldn't see her blush. 'He's come with my aunt because he's joining up tomorrow.'

For just a second she knew how Judas must have felt. For two weeks she'd been insisting to herself she was in love with Jack, she couldn't get her mind off making love to him and now she had relegated him to a mere cousin.

'I won't ask if he's got a brother,' Sally laughed. 'Never could stand men with red hair.'

Bonny side-stepped Jack's enthusiastic hug at the Pavilion door and hurried towards Aunt Lydia and Mrs Baker in the car. The other girls were coming out and although the road was pitch black she wasn't taking any chances.

'What did you think of the show?' Bonny asked

Lydia the moment she was in the back of the car, Jack beside her.

'Much better than I expected,' Lydia said thoughtfully. 'The dance routines were very slick, all you girls looked very disciplined. The singer Larry what's-his-name wasn't terribly good and the comedian didn't make me laugh. But the show as a whole was better than average for a summer seaside entertainment.'

Jack saw that Bonny was disappointed in Miss Wynter's opinion. 'I thought it was brilliant, especially you.'

'So did I, love.' Mrs Baker turned to pat Bonny's knee. 'Your little feet twinkled and you looked so nice in that spangly waistcoat in the last number. I can't imagine how you remember all the steps.'

'Mr Dingle's found me digs.' Bonny thought she'd better bring this up while she had Jack and Mrs Baker's support. 'I'll be sharing a room with Sally and Frances. They say the food's not bad. I'll move in tomorrow afternoon.'

'Well, it looks like it's an end of an era, Beryl.' Lydia looked sideways at the older woman as she drove. 'Your Jack off to the army and Bonny to the stage.'

'The village will be so quiet.' Beryl looked round at Bonny and Jack holding hands in the back. Bonny was surprised to see she had tears in her eyes. 'You've been a pair of scallywags and no mistake, but it won't be the same without you both.'

Beryl Baker had put aside her wariness of Bonny tonight because she loved Jack. All through the show she'd been remembering how she'd felt at being separated from Bert in the First War and she was big-hearted enough to hope it would work out for them both.

It was raining hard at eight the next morning as Bonny ran down towards Houghton Bridge. Saying goodbye last night to Jack in the stationhouse with the Bakers and Aunt Lydia looking on wasn't enough. She had to see him one more time, alone.

His train was leaving at half-past nine and she'd slipped out without a word to Aunt Lydia. She wished now she'd thought to bring an umbrella; her old school raincoat was already sopping wet and her hair felt like wet seaweed.

Jack was waiting for her, leaning back against the parapet of the bridge, smoking a cigarette. As he saw her come down the road, he dropped the cigarette and ran to her, the Blakeys in his boots making a cluttering sound.

'I didn't think you'd come in this,' he said breathlessly. 'I was just wondering if I dared come up to Briar Bank.'

'I wouldn't have missed saying goodbye to you,' Bonny said. She didn't mind if he did have red hair this morning, and he didn't look ugly to her. All she could think of was all they'd been to one another for so long. 'I can't really believe that you won't be in the garage any more.'

'It won't be for more than a couple of years.' Jack caught hold of her hand and led her down to shelter under the tree by the water's edge. 'Remember this tree?' he said, looking up at it.

'That's when it all started,' Bonny said in a small voice, afraid she might cry. 'And now you're going away.'

'Look.' Jack led her closer to the trunk and pointed.

There on the trunk a heart was carefully carved. Inside it were the words 'Jack and Bonny. For ever.'

'When did you do that?' she asked.

'Last night. I wasn't tired so I came down here to think about things. I had my knife and a torch, so I just did it.'

Bonny's heart lurched painfully. 'Will it really be for ever?'

The river was as dark a grey and as fast moving

as it had been that day four years ago. Suddenly she felt scared, as if she were being swept away again, this time by her new life and her ambitions. There had been no opportunity to make love since that night. Lydia had made sure they were never alone and they hadn't even spoken of it.

'Of course it's for ever.' Jack pulled her into his arms, hugging her so fiercely she could hardly breathe. 'You mean everything in the world to me.'

'Do you think about what we did that night?' she whispered, burying her face in his neck. He was as damp as her, his old tweed jacket smelling of engine oil, cigarettes and him.

Jack tilted her face up to his, brown eyes looking deep into her blue ones. 'Sometimes I can't think of anything else,' he said huskily. 'Our time will come, Bonny. I'll take you somewhere beautiful and romantic and I'll love you till you squeak.'

He unbuttoned her coat and slid his arms inside it, gently stroking her body as he kissed her. Bonny sensed he was trying to memorise each and every curve and the tenderness in his touch brought tears to her eyes.

'You were made for love,' he whispered, nibbling at her ear, drinking in the smell and feel of her slender body. 'But save yourself for me, Bonny, because I'll never be able to love anyone as I do you.'

The rain splattered down on the canopy of leaves above them, filtering through and damping them still further as they kissed. Passion swept aside in the pain of parting, memories of the past flooding back.

Jack remembered the small sodden body in a red siren suit and Alec pumping the water from her. His mind flittered though scenes of them daring each other to walk on cow-pats and heard again their shrieks of laughter as the crust broke on newer ones. Of roly-polys down the hill at the back of Amberley Castle, of hide and seek in the railway sidings.

Bonny remembered that night when they'd both been tucked into bed in the stationhouse after her near drowning and the feeling she'd had that Jack was all-important. Of his hands pulling her up into trees, of watching him swim in the river as she sat on the bank. Now she would have only his younger brothers to remind her of him. They shared his looks, but not his warmth or sense of fun. Amberley would never seem like home until he came back.

'I love you Jack,' she sobbed, aware now that he was indeed the one person who was important to her. 'Write to me, won't you?'

'I'm not much good with letters.' He bent his forehead against hers, tears running down his cheeks unchecked. 'But I'll try. You'll be in my heart, though, and every bit of leave I get I'll be back to see you.'

'Don't stay to wave me off,' Jack said hoarsely as they walked back later towards the station. 'I might not be able to get on the train and my brothers will be there.'

Bonny took a picture out of her pocket. A press photographer had been to the theatre in the first week of rehearsals and she'd persuaded him to let her have a print. She was only in practice clothes, one leg up on the barre, arms outstretched, but it was the first picture she'd seen of herself where she looked like an adult.

'Keep it close to you.' She pressed her lips once more on his then turned to rush away.

Jack watched her until she was out of sight. He looked down at the photograph in his hand and a tear rolled down his cheek.

Her blonde hair was tied back, but tendrils had escaped, sticking damply to her neck and face. Her beautiful curvaceous body was revealed as clearly as if she were naked, such long, slender legs and tiny waist.

'I love you,' he whispered, tucking it into his jacket. 'For ever.'

Chapter Twelve

London, February 1945

Annie got into her bed wearing a long, faded, flannel nightgown, a cardigan and bedsocks, and as a further precaution against the bitter cold she put a shawl around her shoulders and tucked her hot-water bottle between her knees.

In the days when Annie had been a maid, this small, rather dark room at the back of the ground floor was old-Mrs King's private sitting-room. Annie remembered being summoned by the bell at dusk to light the gas and add more coal to the fire as the old girl sat at her desk going over her household accounts. After Ted was killed, Annie changed it to her bedroom and let out the bigger room on the first floor that she'd shared with her husband. Not only was it warmer, but it put her in a better position for making sure none of her lodgers skipped out without paying her. She'd kept the nicest pieces of furniture: the desk, a small chintz-covered settee, and the glass-fronted china cabinet with its collection of family mementoes. Her few clothes were tucked away in a bow-fronted chest of drawers and a single divan bed gave the room a nice modern touch.

Tonight, however, wind seemed to be coming from all directions at once, rattling the windows, blasting under the door and sending eddies of soot down the chimney into the empty grate. It was cold enough to snow and perhaps that was why there wasn't the usual roar of aircraft overhead on their way to bomb Germany. Annie welcomed the peace and quiet, but she couldn't remember ever being so cold in the house before, or feeling quite so alone.

'Don't be so silly,' she said aloud. After all, it had been a long and bitter winter and she ought to be used to it by now. 'You've got three nice lodgers, and Charley and Ellie. There's letters from the boys, your neighbours. You're just getting old and cranky.'

It was only half past eight, but she'd come up to bed because of the cold. It made no sense keeping a fire going down in the kitchen just for her. When the lodgers came home they'd be straight to their beds and so would Ellie. Charley wouldn't be home until morning.

She flicked through *Britannia and Eve*, looking for a short story she hadn't already read. She paused at a knitting pattern, thinking the short-sleeved jumper would suit Ellie – perhaps she could unravel an old jumper of her own for it. But somehow she couldn't concentrate on reading.

It seemed the war was almost over. The Allies had the Germans on the run, and they were fast approaching the Rhine. Just a few days earlier they'd heard the shocking news about a terrible camp in a place called Auschwitz in Poland where it seemed Hitler was intent on destroying the entire Jewish race. Annie hoped that when the Allies came face to face with that monster they'd string him up by his feet and cut a bit off him every day.

The Home Guard was disbanded. On Febuary 1st, twenty-five thousand part-time firemen were finally released from their duties. The barrage balloon in Regent's Park was brought down for the last time. Railings were going up again round the parks and the Board of Trade relaxed the regulations intended to save material, which had prohibited turn-ups on men's trousers and the number of pockets on their jackets. The black-out had become 'dim out'; some streets in London had at least partial street lighting again. But even if these things did signify the end, the war in the Far East was still going strong, and the menace of the V-2s was still with them.

At first the government had explained away these massive explosions as gas mains blowing up. The men in Whitehall meant well enough: they didn't want panic, or for the Germans to know the damage they were doing with these huge, pilotless rockets. But it had become something of a joke. When people heard the formidable bangs, saw the billowing dust like a vast mushroom over the roofs of their houses they turned to one another, saying 'Another bleedin' gas mains!'

They weren't a joke, though. Annie knew from Charley just how deadly these V-2s were, even if the newspapers kept most people in the dark. He spoke of entire blocks of flats flattened, of people blown out through windows and crushed under mountains of rubble. To make matters worse there was no warning at all.

But it wasn't the war that bothered Annie tonight: she'd grown used to the hardships and irritations that came with it. It was Charley and Ellie that worried her.

On the face of it, life at number 33 was topping. They had three nice business lodgers who went home to their wives most weekends and rarely wanted an evening meal. Charley had a job he loved and the girl of his dreams. With Ellie's help Annie didn't have to work so hard. They had money saved, they ate better than most of their neighbours and they could afford a few treats. But Annie knew her son well and she sensed his deep anxiety, even though he made a good show of hiding it.

Charley was desperately and hopelessly in love with Ellie, and she with him. It shone out of their faces, strong and beautiful. They left each other soppy notes, they mooned over every love song and treasured each spare moment with one another. When Steve and Mike had come home on leave last year they'd both agreed with Annie that it was a match made in heaven. But in the last couple of months it had become evident, to Annie at least, that the happy road the pair of them had set out on together was approaching a crossroad and that unless one of them was to bend to the needs of the other, a parting of the ways was bound to occur.

Charley loved the fire brigade and he was torn between staying after the war and going for promotion, or emigrating to Australia. Although he was a lot less rigid in his outlook than most of his friends, he was still old-fashioned enough to believe the man should be the provider. Yet Ellie was earning more than him now, singing at the Blue Moon almost nightly doing an earlier spot in a restaurant in Greek Street, Soho two or three evenings a week too. Charley stoically accepted that he could seldom have Ellie's company in the evenings. He stayed awake after finishing a twenty-four hour shift just to spend the day with her. He was always encouraging and supportive, and so very proud of her talent too.

But Annie saw Charley's underlying frustration and felt deeply for him. He wanted marriage: romance wasn't enough any more. So many times Annie had come in to a room to find them jumping guiltily apart with flushed faces. She's heard Charley tossing and turning in the night, seen the looks of longing that he gave Ellie, and guessed it was only through the girl's iron will that they hadn't become lovers.

But even though Annie felt for her son, she understood and admired Ellie's steely resolve. Just as Annie had learnt from old Mrs King to speak properly, to lay tables correctly and run a household, so Ellie had ambitions for a better life than she'd been born into.

Who could blame the girl for being cautious when one slip-up could mean being tied to a kitchen sink with a parcel of kids and her dreams down the plug-hole?

Ellie had the courage to go all out for what she wanted. She'd become sophisticated and perhaps a little harder, yet that hadn't changed her warmth, thoughtfulness or generosity. She was always bringing home things she'd bought on the black market – bacon, tinned fruit and chocolate. Just before Christmas she'd used up all her points to buy a tweed coat for Annie when she badly needed one herself. She wasn't one bit selfish, just ambitious.

Annie put down her magazine and slid right down under the covers. 'Charley's got to sort this one himself,' she said to herself. 'He's a grown man now, not your little boy any longer.'

Brenda glanced round at Ellie as she zipped up her dress. Ellie was sitting in front of the mirror, wearing just a pair of silky pink camiknickers and nylon stockings, applying some rouge to her cheeks.

Sometimes Brenda found it hard to believe Ellie was the same girl who little less than a year ago had come in with dirty bare knees from scrubbing floors. She'd had a permanent wave recently and despite Brenda's pronouncements that it would spoil her silky hair, it hadn't. Now she had loose curls piled up on top of her head and cascading over her shoulders, and she'd learnt to pluck her eyebrows into that fashionable look of surprise and to apply just enough vaseline to her eyelids to give a dewy-eyed image.

Brenda glanced at herself in the mirror and winced. Her hair needed peroxiding and her skin was ageing fast. Until a few months ago she'd always looked so classy, but you needed more money than she earned to keep up that image, especially when you had a child to keep.

'Is that a new Teddy?' she asked enviously.

Ellie turned and smiled. 'Yes, do you like it? It's not real silk, of course, just that Viscana stuff, but it's pretty, isn't it?'

Brenda hesitated before speaking. In the year Ellie had been working at the club their positions had reversed. Brenda was no longer Jimbo's 'pet' as she had been before, neither was she queen in the glamour stakes. Quite often it was she these days who couldn't run to a pair of stockings, while Ellie was always beautifully turned out.

'How did you get it, Ellie?' she asked. 'I know it's none of my business, but I don't like to think of you getting in over your head.'

She couldn't really imagine Ellie accepting gifts from black marketeers in return for a few favours, especially when the girl was so wild about her fireman. But plenty of other girls had fallen for the temptation.

'I bought them.' Ellie at first looked surprised, then shocked as it dawned on her what Brenda meant. 'I got them cheap, without points, but not how you're thinking.'

'Sorry, love.' Brenda's pale face blushed a becoming pink. 'It's just you're such a lovely kid and I worry about you. Jimbo uses you, I see you singing your head off night after night and lining his pocket and I get scared you might take a few short cuts.'

Ellie got up, reached for the red evening dress she wore for her singing spot and stepped into it. She knew Brenda wasn't being spiteful, as other waitresses had been. She was too kind-hearted for that and rather maternal.

'I'm not quite as dense as I may look,' she said in a low voice. 'I'm using Jimbo too, to gain experience. The moment I get a chance in a theatre, I'll be out of here. Charley's the only man who figures in my life and even if Clark Gable was to offer me a part in a film in return for sleeping with him, I wouldn't take it.'

'I would,' Brenda laughed. 'I'd sleep with him without the offer of a film.'

Ellie smiled. 'Well, I might be tempted,' she said, her dark brown eyes sparkling with mischief. 'But I'll get the break one day, without selling my soul or anything else.'

Brenda zipped up Ellie's dress for her. She admired Ellie for a great many reasons, but the underlying one was her courage. A great many girls of her age without any family would have floundered by now – heaven knows this club alone was a hotbed of temptation. But Ellie hadn't let her success as a singer go to her head: she helped Charley's mother and visited that poor crippled aunt in hospital whenever she got the chance.

'What happens when you have to choose between your career and Charley?' Brenda asked. 'Do you really believe you can have both?'

Ellie frowned. This was a question never far from her mind and she had no answer to it. 'I'll think about that when the time comes.'

'Spoken like a real trouper.' Brenda smacked Ellie's bottom playfully. 'Now are you going to give me a hand out there for a while, or is the star too big for that now?'

'Of course I'm not,' Ellie grinned. 'Let's go and see what Jimbo's managed to get in the way of booze tonight.'

Alcohol was scarce everywhere now, and most of the pubs had signs up saying 'No Whisky. No Gin. No Brandy.' There was talk of 'bathtub' gin being made in secret, even cases of people being poisoned by home-made 'hooch', but Jimbo's supplies of the real stuff never ran out completely. But then anything was available to those with the right contacts and the Blue Moon continued to be the black marketeers' favourite watering hole.

Ellie was behind the bar polishing glasses as the first customers came trickling in. Brenda and the other two waitresses made their way over to the tables to take orders and as Cyril the barman had slipped out for a moment, leaving her in charge, Ellie turned her attentions to Jimbo and his companion, drinking at the bar.

In the past year Ellie's already keen powers of observation had become even sharper. She didn't even need to speak to people to weigh up their character – the way they spoke, moved or their facial expressions told her so much. The club was a never-ending source of material. She'd seen the whole spectrum of human behaviour here, both good and bad, from the courageous pilots out for a drink before what might be their last mission, to married women having a fling while their husbands were away, and the rats who had made a fortune out of war.

Jimbo was talking to one of these now, a shifty-eyed character who called himself the Doc. Like Jimbo, his suit was hand-tailored, his hands well-manicured. He had a pale, foxy face and Ellie guessed he got his nickname because he could fix anything.

She moved closer to the men, wiping down the shelves at the back of the bar. Although her back was to them she was well within earshot.

'It's a wizard prang,' the Doc said, using the RAF slang which he foolishly thought made people believe he was out of the top drawer. He often forgot himself when he'd had a few drinks and lapsed into pure Whitechapel, which she guessed was where he really came from. 'We buy the name and licence of a club out in the suburbs. There's dozens going begging for around a grand, then we sell it on to someone else in the West End for three or four times as much.'

'The police will soon clamp down on that,' Jimbo said disparagingly. 'I'm not risking my money.'

'There's no risk, not even any outlay,' Doc retorted,

taking a cigarette out of a flashy silver case. 'It's perfectly legitimate. There's dozens of premises perfect for clubs in the West End, men out there with the readies to buy in, the only hitch is getting a licence. I know a lawyer who'll cover our traces. You want to get your hands on a theatre, don't you? It couldn't fail now the war's nearly over and all the boys coming home. But that takes big money, Jimbo! How else you gonna get it?'

Ellie was called away at that point but as she turned she could see from Jimbo's face that he was more than tempted.

It was easy to feel nothing but contempt for these men who grew rich wheeling and dealing while men like Charley risked their lives nightly for a pittance. But on the other hand Ellie felt a surge of excitement at what it could mean for her if Jimbo joined this man.

Singing in a seedy club wasn't going to get her very far: her voice was good, but not exceptional. Ellie knew her real talent lay in musical comedy. The problem was getting the chance to prove it.

'Have I told you the one about the actress and the camel?' Jimbo asked the audience.

The club was packed to capacity. Candle-light created a soft, intimate atmosphere, concealing the shabbiness of nicotine-stained plaster, and cigar smoke masked the musty, damp smell. A lone spot-light played on Jimbo. In his impeccably cut dinner-jacket, starched dress-shirt and bow-tie he looked debonair and almost handsome.

Brenda moved closer to Ellie. 'Yes, five million times,' she whispered.

Ellie grinned. They were both taking advantage of Jimbo's act to sneak a quick drink at the bar. They knew once he'd told his favourite long-winded joke he would launch into his parody of Hitler, which wasn't side-splitting either. But the audience were jovial tonight: a group of Canadian airmen, all with various war injuries, had come in earlier determined to make their last night in London memorable. One of them had insisted on buying drinks all round and now the atmosphere was more of a private party than a club.

'You'd better give them something special tonight,' Brenda said. 'Got anything up your sleeve?'

Ellie made a show of peering up it. 'Only a damp armpit,' she said with a dead-pan face. She had already planned to deviate from her usual routine. The crowd were receptive and she had no wish to sing sad songs with all those boys sitting there with arms in slings, patches on eyes and crutches propped up against their chairs. They needed to laugh and put aside memories of their comrades who didn't make it back from France.

Roy and his band had been primed earlier when Jimbo wasn't watching. They'd even moved the first row of tables back a couple of feet from the stage to give Ellie more room. Jimbo liked her to sing like Vera Lynn, but Ellie's forte wasn't crooning, and tonight she intended to show them what was.

Jumbo Jameson was sitting at the bar when Roy struck up the opening chords of 'I'm Gonna Get Lit Up'. Jimbo frowned, turning on his stool to look towards the stage. He had told Ellie to sing sentimental songs tonight and there she was disobeying him.

'Whisky,' he snapped at Cyril, irritated to see even his barman had stopped working to listen.

Cyril jumped to it. He was nearly sixty and he wanted to keep his job when the war was over. 'You had 'em creased up tonight,' he said in the oily voice he kept specially for his employer. He poured a generous measure of whisky and passed it over. 'Our Ellie's gonna knock 'em dead too, by the looks.'

Jimbo downed the glass in one gulp. He was a

troubled man, unsure of which way to turn next, and whisky was the only thing that took the edge off his anxiety.

When he was honest with himself he knew he was burned out as an entertainer. His jokes were stale, his impersonations tired and dull. The club was making money, but he knew that once the war was over new ones would sprout up like mushrooms, taking away his trade.

As the whisky scorched its way down to his stomach, he found he was warming to the Doc's suggestion. If history repeated itself, the post-war period would be boom time. People would want to dress up again, to see a bit of glamour. He could picture himself running a theatre. Show girls in spectacular costumes, comedians, singers and novelty acts, a slick, fast-moving variety show. With money behind him he could get a decent producer and flashing neon signs ten feet high, pack the crowds in and make himself a fortune.

Jimbo stood up as wild applause broke out, nudging his way through the crowd to find a corner to watch Ellie. Cyril was right, she was knocking them dead – but what on earth was she doing telling jokes instead of singing?

Jimbo had been so immersed in his private thoughts that he'd missed the point of the joke. It seemed to be something about a nurse, a wounded soldier and a bedpan, and to his amazement everyone was roaring with laughter, especially the Canadians up front.

It wasn't the first time he'd been surprised by this bit of a kid. Her ability to hold an audience, the way she responded to them, and her stamina had stunned him more than once. But it was her determination which had endeared her to him above all else. The way she'd turned up night after night, even when her aunt was injured. Her stoicism when he found other singers and pushed her back as a waitress. Even when she found a boyfriend she didn't let that interfere with her work. Night by night her performance had improved, and if he was totally honest he'd be lost without her now.

But as Ellie launched into 'My Baby Just Cares for Me', Jimbo got a jolt down his spine. She had stepped down from the stage and she was out amongst the wounded Canadians, doing the most erotic shimmy he'd seen in years. She was sending up all those 'sweet young things' who normally chose this number, making the men laugh as she perched on laps, ruffling their hair. At one point she even stole an airman's cap and held it over her heart.

Jimbo wasn't in the habit of watching her do more than one number, but now he was rooted to the spot, aware he had underestimated her ability. The numbers she was doing now were old music hall ones, but she was giving them a whole new humorous slant and the punters were captivated not only by her voice, but her dancing too.

It was the laughter and the movement which suddenly brought home to Jimbo just how gorgeous she really was. Singing by the piano she was just another pretty girl with a nice voice; seen moving, she was captivating. Dark eyes flashing, that wide full mouth so expressive and delectable. As for her body . . .

Strange he'd never noticed it before. He'd always thought of her as skinny. Now as she moved he saw the womanly curves, legs as long as any Ziegfeld girl. Another year or so and she'd be a show-stopper.

All at once Jimbo knew he was going to join the Doc in his scam. He'd make a pile, get a theatre and launch Ellie as his protégée.

'You want to take *me* out to dinner?' Ellie repeated Jimbo's invitation, thinking perhaps she'd misunderstood him.

'Yes, dinner.' Jimbo smiled at her surprise. 'It's impossible to have a serious talk here. I'll pick you up at seven tomorrow and take you to Maxim's grill.'

When Jimbo called her over after her performance she'd thought he was going to tell her off. But instead he not only complimented her, but asked solicitous questions about Marleen and seemed pleased to hear she had progressed to sitting in a wheelchair. He was almost fatherly, which was very odd for a man who normally barked out orders. And now this invitation.

Ellie was flattered that her performance had created such unexpected interest in her, but she wasn't sure Charley would approve of her accepting such an invitation. 'I haven't got anything to wear,' she said, blushing with embarrassment.

If Ellie looked well dressed and even glamorous to the other girls at the club, it was because she payed close attention to grooming. No one noticed that she came in nightly wearing the same plain wool skirt and blouse, because they were well pressed, her hair always gleaming, her one pair of shoes polished. Jimbo had supplied the red dress she wore to sing in and although it looked good in dim lighting, it didn't bear close inspection. Everything else she owned was second-hand, perked up by a bit of new trimming or by careful alteration, but not smart enough to wear to a posh place like Maxim's. Even the green dress Annie had given her was looking a little shabby now.

Jimbo's wife always claimed she had 'nothing to wear' when in fact she had more dresses than Marshall and Snelgrove. Jimbo didn't think this was the case with Ellie, though: she was too innocent to consider playing up to a man for a hand-out. 'There's a dress that should fit you in my office,' he said. 'I'll go and get it.'

While Jimbo was gone, Ellie hastily consulted Brenda. The club was slowly emptying now, as transport for the Canadians arrived to take them to their hotel.

Brenda took a slug of gin as she listened to Ellie's hasty explanation. 'I don't think he's after your body,' she said drily. 'If nothing else, he's faithful to his wife. But he's a snake, Ellie, he never does anything for nothing. Just remember that, whatever you decide.'

'Some help you are,' Ellie laughed, but Brenda's words chilled her. 'What would *you* do?'

'With your talent and ambition, I'd go.' Brenda shrugged her shoulders. 'He's obviously got some scheme in mind and you might as well hear him out. Just be careful, that's all.'

Jimbo came back with the dress over his arm. 'Any good?' he asked, holding it up for her to see.

'It's lovely,' she said weakly. It was black, the sort of dress any girl would die for, plain but sophisticated and clearly expensive. She held it up to herself and looked in a mirror. Even without trying it on she knew it would fit. Soft wool crêpe, with a high neckline and long sleeves, the slim skirt softened by stylish drapery over one hip.

'Are you sure?' Ellie asked, wondering whose it was and whether he meant her to keep it.

'Quite sure.' Jimbo smiled at her awed expression. He'd got the dress for his wife through one of his contacts, but she didn't need it. 'That's settled then. I'll call at seven.'

A light dusting of snow had fallen during the evening and it was bitterly cold. Ellie shivered as she let herself into the kitchen. The fire had gone out hours ago and she guessed Annie had gone to bed early.

Now she was home, seeing Charley's best shoes tucked under the dresser and his white newly ironed shirt hanging on the clothes-horse, she suddenly felt guilty. He wouldn't like this arrangement one bit and he would see the black dress as a sinister inducement. Should she say Brenda lent it to her?

Up in her bedroom, she hastily undressed and tried

it on. The mirror was a small one and the light dim, but even so she could see she looked sensational in it. The soft crêpe clung to her figure, the drapery on the skirt was so elegant, giving her that fashionable hour-glass shape. She wanted to wear it, she wanted to have dinner at Maxim's, but she was frightened of telling Charley.

Annie had put a stone hot-water bottle in her bed. The thoughtful act reproached Ellie still further. Why couldn't she be like other girls? Just settle for a nice home and a loving husband. Why did she hanker for bright lights, expensive clothes and fame?

Alone in the dark, the covers pulled right up to her chin, Ellie thought about Charley. She loved him for his kindness, sense of humour, his courage and strength. But there was a physical need too, which she kept a tight lid on. So many nights she'd lain here in a state of turmoil. When he was home she could hear his breathing in the room next to hers and she longed to go in to him, climb into his bed and quench the terrible thirst of wanting. She felt his need each and every time she kissed him; a brush of his hand and her limbs turned to jelly. But all she allowed was kissing and mild petting: she was too scared to let it go any further.

Sometimes she wished she could talk to Charley about it. But although they talked about anything and everything else, somehow that subject was too difficult. Her reticence to make love wasn't exactly a question of morality, although after observing Marleen's behaviour and more recently the other girls at the club, she felt it was sensible to be wary. What she was afraid of was losing control. Down deep inside her she knew that once they'd become lovers the commitment would be too great. Next they'd be married and all her choices would be gone.

Her mother had married a docker and her career as a dancer ended there. Again and again as a child she'd overheard singers and dancers bemoaning the fact that their job was hated by their husbands and saying they wished they'd never married.

Charley would never be content with waiting at a stage door; he'd expect her to slip into the same role as his mother, cooking, cleaning and having babies. Yet what would she do if he got tired of waiting? He was her friend, her love and no other man could ever take his place.

Charley opened the kitchen door and stamped the snow off his boots before going in. It was seven in the morning and the snow had become heavy during the night. He was chilled to the bone, for his uniform had got soaked at a fire, then frozen on him.

'Hello, Mum.' His teeth chattered. 'Blimey, it's cold!'

Annie kissed his icy cheek and winced as she touched his coat. 'Take that off this minute!' she said, undoing the thick leather belt and silver buttons as if he were a child. 'It's a wonder to me you don't get pneumonia.'

She took the heavy coat and hung it up to one side of the fire. Within seconds it was steaming, sending out a pungent smell of wood smoke.

'And the trousers!' she said bossily. 'Was it a big fire?'

'It was hell.' Charley slipped off his trousers. Wearing only his woolly long underwear and his uniform blue shirt he sat down by the fire, holding his hands out to the blaze. 'It was in a warehouse over Camden Town way. We got soaked as usual, our uniforms steaming one moment in the heat, then freezing on us the moment we stepped back. Poor old Fred's hand got frozen on the branch. Tore off a lump of skin when we tried to get him free.'

Annie tutted in sympathy. Charley rarely complained, so when he did, it meant it was truly bad. 'What caused the fire?'

'Don't know. The other shift replaced us before we put it out completely. I tripped over an old paraffin stove when we got in, perhaps they'd left that alight.'

Annie poured him a cup of tea, then dipped some bread in powdered egg and milk and fried it for him. 'I'm going down the market after I've done the break-fast,' she said, bending down to feel if his long pants were damp too. 'I thought I'd try and get some fish.'

'I'll just doze down here.' Charley gave a weak smile through his exhaustion. 'I thought of taking Ellie sledging up on Hampstead Heath, but it's too cold for that. It's her night off tonight so perhaps we'll go to the pictures instead.'

By the time Annie had finished dishing up the lodgers' breakfasts upstairs in the dining-room, Charley was fast asleep in the chair. She covered him up with a blanket, turned his uniform, banked up the fire and put on her coat and hat.

Charley woke instantly at the explosion and ran up the stairs two at a time to the top floor to look out of the windows. From the back was only the view of the railway siding of Euston. It looked quite beautiful with the lines, trains and sheds covered in snow, but Charley could see no craters or dust rising in that direction. He moved quickly to the front of the house, opened the window and peered out.

He saw the tell-tale spiral of black dust rising above the roofs and guessed from experience it was some-where near Lower Oxford Street.

As he glanced at his watch, he groaned. It was ten in the morning: whatever street the rocket had landed in, there would be massive casualties, and if it was Oxford Street it didn't bear thinking about.

'I ought to go and help,' he murmured to himself, yet the thought of what he would see turned his stomach. Just a few days ago he'd been sent out to one in the city and as they approached the site he'd seen a young girl, no older than fifteen, impaled on a wall by a steel girder which had been flung some thirty yards by the force of the blast. She was still alive at that point, her mouth and eyes wide open as if screaming, but no sound coming out. Charley could do nothing but talk to her and hold her hand. She died before they managed to free her.

He made a pot of tea, still weighing up whether he should go or not. He silently cursed the authorities for laying off all the part-timers. The public were so quick to complain at firemen waiting around doing nothing when there were no raids or fires, not so quick to praise them when they toiled for up to forty-eight hours without any sleep under conditions that beggared belief. He was becoming convinced that Australia was the place for him after the war, if Ellie would marry him and come with him. But for now he was a fireman and he must go to help. He couldn't live with himself if someone died under rubble for want of an extra pair of hands digging them out. His uniform was dry again at least. He pulled on his trousers and buttoned them up, flicked up his braces and pulled on his boots.

Pouring two cups of tea, he drank his down in one gulp then taking the other he carried it up to Ellie, his coat over his arm.

'Did I hear an explosion, or was I dreaming?' she said sleepily as he came into her room. She hauled herself up in bed and rubbed her eyes.

The room was gloomy with the curtains drawn, but even so Charley tried to avert his eyes from her breasts. Her thin nightdress was taut against them and her nipples stood out like two succulent raspberries.

'Yes, you did,' he said, putting the tea into her hands, and bent to kiss her forehead. She smelt wonderful, all warm and powdery and it was all he could do not to crush her into his arms. 'I'm off there now, it looks like it's around Oxford Street.'

Ellie's face fell. 'Must you? Oh, why, Charlie? I thought we'd have all day together.'

He looked so tired, his eyes red-rimmed and swollen, stubble on his chin. But his hair was endearingly tousled, with the curls he normally tried so hard to suppress with Brylcreem spiralling on to his forehead and neck.

'You know why.' He smiled as he put on his coat and fastened up the buttons. Ellie was beautiful to him at all times, but there was something special about her face in the mornings without lipstick or rouge, kind of open and innocent like a child's. 'It's been snowing and it's so cold I doubt whether you'd want to go out. If they don't need me I'll come right back.'

At the mention of snow Ellie's eyes opened wide in child-like excitement. She wriggled up into a kneeling position, pulled back the curtains and peered out.

'Oh Charley! Doesn't it look pretty!' she exclaimed at the view. 'All the soot and dirt covered up. I wish it always looked that way.'

Charley wasn't looking at that view, only the one of her buttocks and tiny waist beneath her nightdress. 'A cuddle before I go?' he asked, but before she could reply he moved towards her and slid his arms round her, cupping her breasts in his hands.

'Charley!' she murmured reprovingly, but she didn't move, only leaned her head back against his shoulder.

Just the merest touch from Charley made her heart pound, but the roughness of his coat through her nightdress, his big hands on her breasts and the smell of smoke on him heightened the eroticism. His lips were on her neck, kissing and licking away her shoulder-straps while he squeezed her nipples.

'Annie might come up,' she whispered, but she didn't want him to stop.

'She's gone out,' he murmured against her ear. 'She won't be back for ages. We're all alone.'

This was the first time that Charley had caught her with so little on. Downstairs, fully dressed, it was a lot easier to find excuses to back away, but now his hand was on her belly, moving downwards with determination. Her thin nightdress offered no protection, not from him or her own feelings. Just the position she was in, kneeling up at the window, made her feel even more vulnerable and yet excited. She looked down at his hand, caressing her. It was big and calloused, so strong-looking yet so tender and sensitive and she could feel her resolve waning.

'You've got to go to work,' she reminded him.

'Sod work.' His voice was husky as he turned her around to kiss her.

Ellie had always thought she could call a halt at any stage in petting. But it had never been quite like this before. He was fully dressed right down to his boots, his coat buttoned and his heavy leather belt fastened, but his hands were sweeping up inside her nightdress exploratively, over her stomach, hips and thighs, sweeping away her resistance. Never before had she felt such overpowering passion. His mouth was devouring hers, his breath was hot and heavy and his hands on her naked skin made her tremble with wanting.

'I love you,' he gasped, taking one nipple in his lips, making ripples of exquisite pleasure run down her spine. 'You're so perfect and beautiful.' Ellie wanted to caress his skin too, but he was so tightly wrapped in his uniform all she could do was trace the hard muscle in his shoulders and forearms.

As his hand met her pubic hair she welcomed it, yet at the same time she was afraid and embarrassed by a sudden wetness there.

But his fingers were so gentle, stroking her so delicately she responded wantonly, moaning deeply as he probed deep inside her, opening her thighs wider and clawing at his back, pulling him tighter to her still until the two rows of silver buttons on his coat were digging into her skin.

Nothing had prepared her for this. Until today she had never allowed him to touch her above her knees and she'd always had the vague thought in her mind that it was men who had all the pleasure, not women. Wave after wave of intense, savage delight washed over her. She forgot the snow outside, the threat of bombs or even of Annie suddenly appearing in the doorway, and abandoned herself to Charley.

Often in the past he'd guided her hands towards his penis when they were kissing, but always she'd withdrawn it, shrinking back in fright. But now as she undulated beneath him she could feel it throbbing beneath his serge trousers and she wanted to please him too.

Sliding one hand beneath his coat she found the buttons on his flies, opened them and slid her hand in. Still kissing her passionately he helped her and suddenly it was in her hand. It was alarmingly big, but smooth and warm and as her fingers closed round it, his gasp of pleasure encouraged her.

'Oh Ellie my love,' he moaned, biting her breast and moving against her. 'I've longed for you to hold me.'

His breathing grew hotter and fiercer and in innocence Ellie held him more firmly, pressing herself hard against him.

'I can't hold back,' he murmured and suddenly she felt something hot and sticky spurt against her wrist.

Ellie had only the most rudimentary knowledge of how love-making worked and she was baffled by why Charley was suddenly limp in her hand and lying panting on her chest.

'I'm sorry,' he whispered. 'It was just too exciting. I messed it up.'

She was still burning up inside, every nerve-end tingling. She wanted him to go on petting her, but the way he lay still against her suggested it was over. She was much too embarrassed to guide his hands back to her, or even to speak of it.

'Perhaps you'd better go to work,' she said stiffly, surreptitiously wiping her wrist against the sheet. Just a moment ago she had been perspiring, but now her skin felt icy and she reached for a blanket to pull over her.

Charley lifted his head to look at her, hurt by her tone. A moment ago she had been so eager, so abandoned. Now she wasn't even looking at him and she seemed to be cringing away from him.

'Is that really what you want?' he asked, feeling deeply shamed. He hadn't intended any of this, it had just reared up from nowhere. All he wanted now was to strip off his uniform, get into bed properly with her and cuddle. But she didn't seem to want that.

'You said you had to go.' Ellie turned her face away from his, for some inexplicable reason wanting to cry.

Charley was confused. Was she angry because she thought he put his job before her, or had he offended her by what he'd done. His experience with girls was limited to fumbled petting behind the dance hall or in a parlour with the girl's father upstairs. It had never felt like this. He wanted to tell her how wonderful it had been, but perhaps she thought it was disgusting.

'I won't go if you want me to stay,' he said tentatively, wishing he knew what girls felt at times like this. 'Maybe I'd better go downstairs. Mum might come back. I'll take you out to the pictures tonight.'

'I can't,' Ellie said, without thinking. 'I'm going out to dinner with Jimbo, he wants a serious talk with me about my future.'

Charley was already smarting with a sense of failure, but as Ellie spoke it turned to deep hurt. He leaped off the bed as if he'd been scalded. 'I see,' he said icily as he buttoned up his flies. 'And I was mug enough to think I had a part in your future.'

Ellie was smitten with remorse. She didn't know why she felt let down, or indeed how everything had suddenly turned sour. Now she'd made things much worse by blurting out about Jimbo.

She wanted him to get back into bed with her, to hold her and whisper words of love, but his eyes were so cold she felt as if she'd been slapped.

'I suppose you see that future as me being here whenever it suits you,' she snapped back, sitting up and pulling the covers right up to her neck. 'A quick fumble, then off to do what you want. Well Just clear off to work and don't hurry back.'

Charley turned towards the door and wrenched it open, but as he glanced back at Ellie he saw the black dress hanging on the wardrobe door. 'Oh, I see,' he snarled. 'He's bought you a dress to wear! I suppose he's a better lover too?'

He pounded off down the stairs before Ellie had time to think of a reply. Seconds later she heard the basement door slam behind him, then silence.

She sobbed then, lying down and burying her face in the pillow, anger and remorse welling up inside her in equal measures.

'What on earth's the matter, Ellie?' Annie said at five o'clock. She'd arrived home at one, having stopped off to see a friend on the way back from the market, and it was clear to her by Ellie's swollen eyes that she and Charley had had a fight. As the afternoon wore on the girl's silence, punctuated only by deep sighs and glances at the clock, made Annie agitated. She had heard gossip that a V-2 had demolished an office building round the back of Oxford Street and although it wasn't yet substantiated, dozens of people were reported to have been killed and even more injured. She was proud of her son putting duty before his personal life and a little cross with Ellie if this was what their row had been about. 'He has to go if they need him. You know that.'

Ellie refused to be drawn into any sort of explanation; in fact Annie's assumption that she was cross because Charley put his job first made her even more angry. She wished Charley would come home so she could apologise, maybe even explain herself. But the time was ticking by and she couldn't contact Jimbo to put him off.

What should she do? Jimbo would be angry if she let him down; perhaps he'd forget whatever plan he had for her. But how could she go out without making peace with Charley first?

'There's nothing the matter,' Ellie snapped. She wished she could tell Annie, but how could she talk of anything so private to anyone, least of all to Charley's mother!

At six, when Charley still hadn't come back, she went upstairs to have a bath. It was snowing again, so cold she felt she would never be warm, and the smell of fish cooking for the lodgers' evening meal made her quite bilious.

She felt a sense of righteous indignation as she coaxed her hair into curls with setting lotion. It was just like Charley to stay away: he was probably in the fire station bar, swilling down pints of beer and laughing with his mates, avoiding her. Maybe everything the girls said at the club was true: men only wanted one thing and once they'd got that they lost interest.

Charley was just coming up Melton Street as the car pulled out of Coburgh Street. There was only one dim light on the corner, but the thick blanket of snow and the yellow glow of headlamps was enough for him to recognise the occupants. He slunk back into a shop doorway and watched it cruise past. Ellie was sitting in the front like a duchess, her hair piled up in loose curls, her head turned towards the driver.

Of all the jobs Charley had worked on, today's had been one of the most harrowing. Nearly all the dead were women: young typists, telephonists and office clerks, many of them crushed as they sat at their desks. Coal and paraffin fires had caught piles of papers alight, burning the injured before they could reach them. A mother walking past with a pram had thrown her body protectively over her child and been killed outright, but the baby miraculously survived, screaming lustily beneath not only its mother, but a pile of smoking rubble. Charley lost count of the bodies lying on the pavement under blankets, snow falling on them until they were taken away.

He had been frozen all day, and the only thing he'd had to eat was a couple of Spam sandwiches and luke-warm tea. But he'd managed to keep going by telling himself Ellie would be waiting for him. He was so sure she wouldn't go out, whatever she'd said. It was all so clear in his mind: he'd tell her how wonderful she made him feel and he'd make her talk about it too. Maybe he could even take her away for the weekend somewhere and start all over again.

But he was wrong about her. She didn't love him.

'You bitch,' he muttered. 'You don't care for anyone but yourself. Go and find fame and fortune, but don't expect me to be waiting for you.'

Chapter Thirteen

April 1945

'You don't sound like my Ellie. What's wrong, love?' Marleen asked.

Ellie looked at her aunt sitting in a wheelchair, sightless eye sockets hidden by dark glasses, and she felt suddenly ashamed of having considered herself hard done by.

It was the first of April. On the way down to Aylesbury on the train Ellie had seen lambs in the fields and a green haze of buds on the trees, but she had been so immersed in her own misery at being rejected by Charley and forced to leave Coburgh Street that she'd been unable to take any pleasure in knowing that spring had arrived, or that the war was almost over.

'I'm just tired,' she lied.

They were in a room off the main ward at Stoke Mandeville Hospital. There was little furniture, just a utility table under the window, three or four chairs for visitors and a grey tiled floor, but a few paintings by patients and a vase of daffodils on the window sill gave a cheery, optimistic note to an otherwise drab room.

Marleen's hair had turned grey, cut to the level of her chin, pinned unflatteringly to one side with a hair slide. She was wearing a checked, man's dressing-gown, a blanket over her knees and dark glasses.

Dr Guttmann and his team at Stoke Mandeville had performed miracles. In any other hospital she would probably have died or been tormented by futile operations: urinary infections, renal deficiency and bed sores were all problems common to spinal patients. But here they not only pioneered new treatments to mobilise the natural forces of healing, but believed most patients could be rehabilitated to lead a useful life.

They had rescued her aunt from utter despair and given her back some pride, but even so her situation was still tragic. Marleen would never regain the use of her legs, and neither would she ever see again. She couldn't survive without constant medical attention. One day she might just be moved to a less congenial home for incurables to grow old and bitter surrounded by other casualties of war.

Marleen was one of only three women patients; the others were mostly servicemen wounded in battle. Her cheery, cockney humour had won her a special place in everyone's affections, and her efforts to wash and dress herself, to manoeuvre her wheelchair unaided without sight, were an inspiration to all the other patients.

But while the others were learning new skills and crafts, filling the long days with reading, jigsaw puzzles and writing letters to their loved ones, some even playing table tennis from their wheelchairs, Marleen had nothing to occupy her. To watch her attempting to steer her chair was so sad, for there seemed little point in becoming mobile when wherever she went was dark.

Each of Ellie's visits here upset her. It was a pleasant, bright, single-storey building, surrounded by open space, with everything geared for people in wheelchairs, and it was run with dedication and compassion. But the tragedy of these brave people struggling to rise above such insurmountable problems made her want to cry. The nurses reassured Ellie that Marleen had accepted her disabilities, yet Ellie always left the hospital with the feeling that her aunt was praying silently for death to release her from the need to pretend.

'You've told me all about this 'ere theatre Jimbo plans to get,' Marleen said now, smoothing Ellie's hand between her two. 'I've heard about 'ow well your act is coming along and about the other girls at the club. But you ain't mentioned Annie or Charley once. Now suppose you tell me why?'

'It's over with Charley and me, and I've moved,' Ellie said, realising she couldn't hope to keep up the pretence much longer. 'I've got a room near the club.'

Marleen didn't reply for a moment, but lifted her hand and groped for Ellie's face. When her fingers found tears her lips quivered. 'The whole story, love?' she said gently. 'What 'appened?'

Marleen had put on weight since she'd moved here, but there was a yellowish tinge to her skin and a puffiness which suggested she wasn't as well as she claimed to be. Her hands, which had once been smooth and well manicured, were now a mass of engorged veins.

Ellie blurted out the bare bones, about how Charley was waiting up for her when she got in after dinner at Maxim's.

'It was late,' she said. 'After three, but I hadn't done anything wrong. We were only talking about Jimbo's ideas for a show. He introduced me to some friends of his and they were all drinking; I couldn't rush off like Cinderella at midnight. Charley accused me of being a tart and we had a terrible row. After that night he just avoided me. I had to leave, it was unbearable.'

She couldn't bring herself to say that for three weeks she'd tried to plead with him outside his shut bedroom door, where he hid himself away whenever she was in. Or that in fact it was Annie who eventually said she must go because the atmosphere between them was upsetting both her and the lodgers.

Marleen said nothing for a moment. Since losing her sight she had found compensation in picking up the tones in people's voices. Now she could distinguish half-truths, almost hear thought processes.

'Suppose you tell me 'ow this come about?' she said eventually. 'One little fight don't usually mean the end of the line when two people love each other as much as you two did.'

Ellie told her a little of how life had been before that night. Of the days spent together when Charley was off duty and how rare it was having an evening together. She implied the row was just the end result of growing dissatisfaction.

'Were you lovers?' Marleen asked point-blank. 'I know it's no business of mine, Ellie, but there's more to this than jealousy or lack of time together.'

Ellie had all but blocked out in her mind how it had started; her story for the girls at the club was just that she went out to dinner with Jimbo. She didn't feel she could reveal any intimate details to anyone, but she was so terribly confused and she knew she needed advice from someone experienced in such matters. Marleen, if nothing else, was an expert on men and her advice would be blunt and forthright.

Ellie blushed, squirmed in her chair and at times couldn't find the right words. But Marleen gently prompted her, indeed probed in such an incisive way that Ellie found herself telling her, if not everything, at least enough for Marleen to get the drift.

Marleen's first reaction was relief that Ellie hadn't actually lost her virginity. But her second was shock at the girl's naïvety. It was almost unbelievable that Ellie should get to eighteen, especially when she was so astute about most things, without any real understanding of sexual matters.

'It seems to me,' she said at length, 'that you two need yer 'eads knocking together. Didn't you ever talk about your feelings to one another?'

'How do you talk to a man about such things?' Ellie said plaintively. 'It's so embarrassing.'

292

Marleen gave a dry little laugh. 'You remind me of my mum,' she said. 'D'you know she told me after my dad died that they'd never seen each other naked. She was married to 'im for over twenty-five years and 'ad six kids, but their bodies was still a mystery to 'em.'

Ellie sniggered.

'I don't want to embarrass you, Ellie.' Marleen's voice softened. 'But it seems to me I've gotta duty to explain how it all works. It ain't enough to know sex makes babies. There's millions of women out there who never get to like it and it's mostly because of ignorance. At least I won't die being one of those, Ellie.' She laughed, but it sounded hollow. 'I reckon men get a raw deal too. The poor lambs don't know what we need, and if we don't know, or can't tell them, what are they supposed to do?'

Ellie felt very hot and uncomfortable as Marleen launched into a full and graphic explanation about not only male and female anatomy but love-making and orgasm. Yet despite the embarrassment it was soothing to know the feelings of desire she'd had for Charley were normal and that pregnancy didn't have to be an inevitable end result of loving one another.

'Poor Charley 'ad probably been thinking of nothing else for weeks and suddenly it's 'appening and his fuse was too short. If you'd given 'im a cuddle 'e'd have soon got steam up again.'

Ellie said nothing, just wriggled in her seat.

'Cat got yer tongue?' Marleen said with a flash of her old irreverent humour. 'You got it into your 'ead he wanted to go to work. I doubt he did, it were more likely 'e was waiting for reassurance. But then you 'it 'im with your plan to go out with with another man.'

'But why wouldn't he listen to me?' Ellie retorted. 'Surely he couldn't really believe I'd be doing anything other than talking to Jimbo. He's fifty at least and he's a horrid little man!'

293

'That 'orrid little man is rich and he's got a big car,' Marleen said wisely. 'Poor Charley's already smarting 'cos he didn't do things right. 'E knows 'ow much you want to get on the stage. Can you blame 'im for thinking bad thoughts? I'd say 'e'd have to be a saint, or very stupid to think otherwise.'

'You sound like you're on his side,' Ellie sobbed. 'What about my feelings? What should I have done?'

''Ow can I advise you when I've made such a mess of my own life?' Marleen grinned. Charley and Annie had visited her on occasions with Ellie, and she liked them both. 'If I'd been in your shoes I'd have waited until Annie went out and pushed my way into 'is bed. That's not what yer mum would've done, but she was always saintly. I doubt 'e'd have sent you packing and love-making's a great 'ealer. But now you've left the 'ouse, that road is closed.'

'All roads are closed,' Ellie sniffed. 'I've been round there several times. Charley wouldn't open the door to talk to me and when I did see Annie she was frosty too. I've got nothing now.'

'Tosh!' Marleen snorted. 'You've got your 'ealth and strength, you've got a pretty face and a job. Men are ten a penny.'

'I don't want another man,' Ellie retorted. 'I only want Charley.'

'Well, then you'll have to figure out for yourself what might bring him round.'

'Nothing short of giving up my job,' Ellie said in a small voice.

'Is he worth that much?'

Ellie hesitated before replying. There had been many times in the past weeks where if Charley had appeared at her door she would have promised him anything just to rid herself of the misery inside her.

Marleen noted the hesitation. 'That's the crux of the matter, ain't it?' she said gently. 'Charley knows deep down that 'e'll always come second place to your career.'

'He doesn't,' Ellie sniffed, not liking to think she was so selfish.

'Oh yes 'e does.' Marleen shook her head. 'It was the same for me and your mother, ducks. We lived, breathed, ate and drank the theatre, that's why neither of us settled down with a nice comfortable husband.'

'Mum did,' Ellie said.

When Marleen didn't reply to this, Ellie looked hard at her aunt. Her face was half hidden by the dark glasses, but she was biting her lip and a blush was creeping up her neck. In the past Ellie had observed these as signs that Marleen had inadvertently let something slip.

'Auntie Marleen!' she said. 'Is there something about Mum you haven't told me?'

Marleen swallowed hard. She had kept Polly's secret all these years because she'd promised to. But things were different now; she knew she hadn't got much longer. A lifetime of drinking had taken its toll and her kidneys were on their way out. Was it right to deprive Ellie of the truth, especially when it might help her through this difficult patch?

'Oh Ellie,' she sighed, reaching out for the girl's hand. 'Polly never wanted you to know. But we've been talking about 'onesty and perhaps it's time. In a way it might make things a bit clearer for you about Charley.'

'Tell me, whatever it is,' Ellie whispered. 'Even if it's bad.'

'There was never ever anything bad about Polly,' Marleen said fiercely. 'She was a mug maybe, so soft that she preferred to starve rather than cause the man she loved any grief, but nothing bad.'

'But Tom died.' Ellie was puzzled now.

Marleen took a deep breath. She had to go on. 'Yes, Tom Forester died, but he weren't yer dad, Ellie.'

Ellie's mouth dropped open in shock. 'But Mum had his picture and everything,' she managed to croak out.

Marleen was always frustrated by her blindness,

which she hated even more than her useless legs, but now, unable to see Ellie's expression, she felt intensely angry, both at her disability and at her lack of thought in spilling out something so dramatic.

'Oh darlin', forgive me?' she said, fumbling to find Ellie's hand. 'I should've thought this through before telling you. I'm so sorry.'

'It's okay.' Ellie grasped her aunt's hand tightly. 'I can take it, just explain it all to me.'

'Your father was a man called Sir Miles Hamilton.'

Ellie gasped. The name meant nothing, but it brought back the memory of that intriguing overheard conversation between Polly and Marleen at the start of the war.

'You know who 'e is?' Marleen's head jerked up.

'No,' Ellie said quickly. 'Just I once overheard you and Mum talking about "Sir" someone. I always meant to ask Mum about it, but I never did.'

''E weren't "Sir" when Polly first met him,' Marleen said. ''E was just another gent, a charming, 'andsome man in his thirties, the kinda man any girl'd fall for.'

'Tell me how they met,' Ellie asked, desperately anxious to have the whole story now.

'We was together at a first night party. It was 1924, at the Hippodrome in Catford, south London. Polly 'ad her first solo number in that show and she was fantastic – everyone was talking about her, the producer claimed she'd be another Marie Lloyd. It was 'im who introduced Poll to Miles.'

'Describe him?' Shivers were running down Ellie's spine and she didn't know if this was excitement or dread.

'I just remember him being a toff,' Marleen said haltingly, as if trying to recall the night. 'Tall, black 'air, you favour 'im Ellie, wiv the same dark brown eyes. But that night we knew nothing about 'im, 'e was just another geezer sniffing round yer ma. All us girls in the chorus were dead jealous of the attention she was getting. She didn't say anything much about 'im, but I 'ad a feeling she was smitten straight away, and of course I egged her on a bit when 'e sent 'er some flowers the next day.'

'He was married, wasn't he?'

'Yes.' Marleen's mouth pursed as if remembering something unpleasant. 'If 'e'd told her straight off Poll would've bin more cautious, but she fell for 'im like a ton of bleedin' bricks. She never liked just being 'is mistress, but that was all she could be.'

'I can't imagine Mum doing that!' The word 'mistress' brought all sorts of sleazy pictures into her head that didn't fit her memory of her mother.

'Don't you go getting the wrong idea,' Marleen said sharply. 'It weren't nuffin seedy, they loved each other. When 'is father died in 1925 and he became Sir Miles Hamilton, Poll got real scared. She was getting well known and if it got out she was 'is mistress it would cause a real stink. Polly tried to pack 'im in again and again, but Miles just wouldn't let 'er go and she loved 'im so much she just weakened each time she saw 'im.'

'Poor Mum,' Ellie said sorrowfully, imagining the pain of loving a married man.

'Bleedin' daft!' Marleen retorted. ''E was prepared to buy her a little house, give 'er anything she wanted, but she wouldn't take nothing. She were never a greedy cow like me, Ellie, too bleedin' noble and lovin'.'

'But you said they met in 1924,' Ellie said, all at once realising this wasn't a short-lived affair. 'I wasn't born until '27. It went on all that time?'

'Until she fell for you.' Marleen squeezed Ellie's hand tightly. 'I guessed something was up, but she wouldn't tell me. She just packed 'er bags and cleared off without a word to me.'

'Why didn't she tell you, Marleen?' Ellie was puzzled by this.

'I expect she thought I might persuade 'er to get rid of the baby, or tell Miles. 'E kept coming round to the theatre, you see. But eventually she sent me a letter for 'im. It said she'd fallen in love with someone else and she was marrying 'im.'

'I don't understand why.' Ellie shook her head in bewilderment. 'Miles would've helped her, surely?'

'You do know why,' Marleen retorted. 'Yer mum was one of them women what puts others' 'appiness before 'er own.'

'But what about Tom Forester?' Ellie asked. 'Who was he and why did he marry her?'

'Tom was just a dear old friend of hers. She didn't marry 'im Ellie, although 'e would've. That was just a smoke screen. I wish she 'ad really married 'im. It would've spared 'er a few problems, especially as 'e was killed just before you was born.'

'So this man never found out about me?' Ellie asked. 'Did he try and find Mum?'

'Did he!' Marleen's mouth twisted into a grimace. ''E drove us all mad, turning up asking me questions, waylaying me outside the theatre. But I didn't know where she was either. She never contacted me again until just before you was born. I was in a new show then, down in Bournemouth, and she made me promise I would never tell a soul, especially 'im.'

Ellie wasn't entirely convinced by this story. It was a nice one, but perhaps time and drink had clouded Marleen's memory and judgement. Remembering all the hard times they'd had in Alder Street, it seemed inconceivable that her mother wouldn't have asked this man for help. Yet if it was true, it did throw a little light on so many things she had pondered about. Why her mother never married again, her desire for Ellie to get a decent education and speak properly, the way she always seemed to be directing her towards a more genteel way of life.

It grew dark while they sat talking.

'The saddest thing of all is that Polly gave up the stage,' Marleen said sorrowfully. 'She weren't just an ordinary dancer like me, love, she had a 'uge talent and she threw it away.'

'Because of me?' Ellie's eyes filled with tears.

'No, not because of you,' Marleen said quickly. 'because of *'im*. If she'd appeared on a stage 'e'd 'ave found 'er. She never, ever regretted 'aving you, you was everything in the world to Poll. But can you imagine 'ow cruel it was for her to spend night after night dressing performers, when she knew she was better'an most of them? And to know that if she dared use 'er talent she could get you to a posh school and live in a nice 'ouse.'

'But she never let on to me.' Ellie shook her head. 'The only time she sang was when she'd had a few drinks. I didn't know she was anything more than a dancer.'

'When she made 'er choice, she slammed the door and threw away the key,' Marleen said simply. 'She never wanted you to feel guilty about her lost chances because you was 'er life. But when she saw you 'ad inherited 'er talent she was 'appy. She used to say to me, "Marleen, our Ellie's got what it takes, if I'm not around, make sure you give her a big push in the right direction and put her wise if anyone tries to stop her."'

Ellie felt the sharpness of this last remark. 'Do you think that's what Charley's trying to do?' she said in a small voice.

'I'm not saying that.' Marleen's voice was husky with emotion; talking about Polly had brought back so many bitter-sweet memories. 'All I'm saying is that I don't think you can sacrifice your own dreams to make someone else 'appy. It might 'ave worked for your mum, but I don't think it will for you. She wouldn't've wanted that.'

The train back to London was packed solid, nearly all with mothers and children who seemed to be returning home, convinced the bombing was finally over. Ellie privately thought their jubilation a little premature. On 3rd March over seventy German planes had ventured into British airspace and dropped a dozen or so bombs. Another V-2 had dropped on Smithfield Market just days before, killing a hundred and ten people. But it was good to see so many children, and their rosy cheeks, bright smiles and chatter were soothing evidence that peacetime would soon be here.

One little girl was hunched in a corner reading a comic. She was plump, with dark hair, around eleven or twelve and wearing a shabby, too-small raincoat. It gave Ellie a jolt to think that just five and a half years ago she was like this kid, only being packed off to Suffolk instead of going home.

Since then so much had happened. She'd endured Miss Gilbert, lost her mother and grown into an adult without really noticing the years slipping past.

What did she really want? Was this burning for a career on the stage so important? Would it make up for the desperate loneliness inside her? Suppose she was chasing a dream that could never come true?

As the train chugged into Waterloo station she thought about Sir Miles Hamilton. She wanted to know all about him, where and how he lived, what kind of man he was. She had no intention of making herself known to him. But maybe finding out about him would help fill the hole Charley had left inside her.

It was just after eight when she let herself into the tiny attic room in Stacey Passage. Alice, one of the waitresses at the club, lived downstairs. After Annie's comfortable and welcoming home it was grim, with room for nothing more than a single iron bed and a chest of drawers. The walls were a dingy yellow, marked by dozens of previous tenants, and the view from the draughty window was only of roofs and chimney pots. A grisly bathroom downstairs was shared by everyone in the house, and the only cooking facilities were an ancient cooker out on the landing. But once she'd lit the spluttering gas fire and drawn the curtains, it was cosy, and its cheapness and convenience for the club almost made up for the squalid staircase leading to it.

Ellie made herself a small pot of tea, stirred in some condensed milk and sat down to toast some bread on the fire.

As she stared into its orange glow she was reminded of making toast like this with her mother. It had been a coal fire then, Polly leaning forward holding the long toasting fork, her hair like burnished copper in the fire-light, falling forward around her small face. They had been talking about Sadie Howard from further down Alder Street who was expecting a baby and wasn't married. Edna downstairs had made some damning remarks about her 'carrying on with a married man'.

'Don't you judge people like Edna does when you're grown up,' Polly had said. 'No one knows what love will do to them until it hits them. It turns you inside out, stops you from thinking clearly.'

'Were you like that with my daddy?' Ellie had asked, a little puzzled by the sad look in her mother's eyes.

'Yes I was.' Polly put one hand on Ellie's head and stroked her hair. 'When I look back I sometimes wish I hadn't been so rash.'

'Do you mean you wish you hadn't had me?' Ellie remembered asking.

'Oh no, sugarplum, I've never regretted you for one moment,' Polly said quickly. 'Only that I was so impulsive when I first met him and that I didn't think things through.'

At the time Ellie had thought her mother meant she hadn't visualised being left a widow with a young baby and no money. But now, after Marleen's story, this little memory took on a whole new meaning.

'Tell me what to do, Mum?' she whispered, staring into the fire. 'Guide me!'

*

When Ellie arrived at the club later that same evening she found Jimbo sitting at the bar with the Doc and another man she knew as Big Mike. Just one look at their flushed faces and glazed eyes was enough to know they'd been drinking for some time.

'Here she is, my little songbird,' Jimbo said, slurring his words and opening his arms wide, a full glass slopping in his hand. 'Come here my treasure.'

Ellie walked cautiously closer, but avoided his arms.

'I've got it!' Jimbo's voice rose to an excited squeak. 'I got my theatre! Come and have a drink with us, Ellie?'

'I'm very pleased for you,' she said stiffly, not liking this new familiarity. 'But I won't have a drink, I must get changed.'

'There's plenty of time for that.' Once again Jimbo waved his arms, this time indicating the empty club. As yet none of the waitresses had arrived. 'Give her a large gin, Cyril.'

Cyril smirked at Ellie. His expression said it all: 'Watch out girl, the boss is on the rampage.'

'Just a small one then,' Ellie agreed reluctantly. 'Which theatre?'

'The Phoenix,' Jimbo chortled, rubbing his hands together with glee. 'What could be better, eh? Close by, in good shape, I've even trodden the boards there myself. It's a great place and it'll be even greater soon.'

Ellie sipped the gin slowly. She had only acquired the taste for it recently, and she was apprehensive not only about drinking so early in the evening, but about being alone with Jimbo and his friends. At the same time she was impressed that he'd found such a prestigious theatre and anxious to know his plans, especially her part in them. 'That's wonderful,' she said, more warmly. 'When will you take it over?'

'Any day,' the Doc said. 'Just a few papers to sign, a few deals to be done and Bob's yer uncle.'

By this, Ellie had to suppose the Doc was in on it

too and that didn't please her. He was so slimy and as far as she knew he had no theatrical experience.

But however drunk Jimbo was, he did seem absolutely serious about putting on variety shows. As Ellie sipped her drink he spoke of hiring a producer called Ambrose Dingle.

'He's one of the best.' He banged his glass down on the bar for Cyril to refill. 'He's already got the dancers lined up and he can pull in a few stars. I can't wait to see his face when he sees you tonight, Ellie. He'll be staggered.'

'Tonight?' Ellie was really taken aback by this. 'Is he coming here?'

'Sure is,' Jimbo laughed. 'So best foot forward and all that. Don't you let me down now.'

The arrival of the other girls was a good excuse to slip away. Once in the dressing-room, Ellie hastily told Brenda about the new developments, wishing Jimbo had given her prior warning so she could have washed her hair and rehearsed something special. After visiting Marleen she felt drained and even a bit weepy.

'Ambrose Dingle!' Brenda said reflectively. 'Now he is a name to conjure with. He's good, puts on pretty slick shows up and down the country, I saw one of his a couple of years ago in Brighton.'

This made Ellie even more nervous. Jimbo was drunk, she was unprepared – tonight could be a disaster. 'Oh Brenda! What if I blow it?'

'You won't.' Brenda's grey eyes were kind as she put her arm round Ellie's shoulders and squeezed her. 'Forget Jimbo. I doubt very much that he's bought the theatre, that's just big talk. He's probably only going to be a backer. This Dingle chap might not even turn up, that might be big talk too. Just get up on the stage and do what you always do. If the man comes he'll love you – everyone else does.'

Despite Brenda's soothing advice, as Ellie watched the club fill up she was very nervous. For the last

303

three or four nights a new, raucous set of people had been coming in here, Knightsbridge people who talked in loud voices right through her performance and got so drunk they knocked their chairs and drinks over.

'Get those Yanks to sit right down the front,' she whispered to Brenda as a bunch of GIs came in. Americans got just as drunk as anyone else, but they did tend to be more appreciative of an entertainer.

'Will do,' Brenda hissed back behind her hand and with a switched-on smile and a provocative wiggle made her way towards them.

The band were playing a medley of Gershwin numbers when Ellie saw the man come in some time after eleven. She knew even before Jimbo pounced on him that he was Ambrose Dingle.

He had an almost cherubic face, despite being close to fifty or so: a pink, smooth complexion, fair hair parted in the middle, a little long on the collar of his light coloured jacket. Ellie thought he looked effeminate. He had a silk handkerchief drooping out of his breast pocket, a purple cravat tucked into his open shirt collar and he was brandishing a cigarette in a jade and silver holder.

Ellie took an order for drinks at one of the tables. The club was almost full now; all the tables were taken and a number of men were gathering around the bar. Unfortunately the Knightsbridge set had turned up. Brenda had seated them at a table right at the back, but even now they were braying at one another, the men lurching drunkenly as they moved through the tables to go to the gents.

Jimbo had declined to do his act tonight, whether because he was drunk, or because he thought he might lose credibility in Mr Dingle's eyes, she didn't know, but now he was opening a hoarded bottle of champagne, clearly fawning on the producer.

At half-past eleven, when Jimbo still hadn't moved from the bar to introduce Ellie's act, she made her way through the tightly packed tables and chairs to the stage.

She began with 'You're Getting to Be a Habit with Me', an old number from the thirties which always went down well and which gave her the excuse to go among the audience and tease them a bit. To her surprise the noisy Knightsbridge set fell silent for once, and that gave her a surge of new confidence.

Ellie couldn't see Ambrose Dingle, or Jimbo – they were hidden behind a large group of men at the bar. But as she went on to her second number, 'Chattanooga Choo Choo', she forgot about them.

Halfway through the third number, an obscure music hall song she'd found called 'What Would your Mother Say?' she suddenly felt a ripple of tension. Faces were turning towards the Knightsbridge set and angry voices rose above the music.

She carried on singing, but all at once she saw a burly Canadian leap from his seat and haul one of the Knightsbridge men up by the lapels of his dinner-jacket.

A fight in the club would just about finish the evening and perhaps Ellie's prospects with Mr Dingle too. If she waited until Jimbo had the presence of mind to intervene someone could be hurt.

In a flash of inspiration, Ellie moved to the side of the stage where a spotlight was fixed to the wall. Grabbing it firmly with both hands, she swung it round so its beam fell on the two men locked together at the back of the club.

'This is the show for tonight,' she said huskily into the microphone. The band stopped dead and she half turned to signal to the drummer to play a roll. 'Our friend from Canada is just going to show us how to remove an overgrown schoolboy from our midst and deliver him back to his nanny without causing blood-shed or spilling a drink.'

The big Canadian looked round at Ellie, grinned

broadly at her instructions and in one swift movement punched the other man on the chin. While he was still reeling from the blow, the Canadian stuck his shoulder into his victim's stomach and hoisted him up in a fireman's lift on to his shoulders.

'He's done it.' Ellie clapped loudly, encouraging everyone else to join in. 'Now he's going to deposit our schoolboy out on the pavement.'

As the Canadian carried the man out, Ellie swung the spotlight round across the club. 'Any more trouble makers? Anyone wanting to join our chum on the pavement?'

A titter of laughter and some applause banished the earlier tension.

'Right then,' she said, hand on hips. 'Anyone in here reckon they can sing better than me?'

'No one's better than you, babe,' yelled back one of the Yanks. 'Do "My Baby Just Cares for Me"?'

Ellie felt a surge of power. As a child in the Empire she'd heard people talk about this very thing – the moment when they knew they'd got their audience in the palm of their hand. 'You pipe down, big boy,' she retorted. 'Did I ask for requests?'

Instead she told them a joke Marleen had given her. It was a *risqué* version of the Englishman, Scotsman and Irishman jokes, changed to English, American and German and their sausages.

Laughter boomed out, filling the entire club. Then she turned to the band and signalled for them to start playing again.

'Whatcha think?' Jimbo turned to Ambrose as they watched Ellie from the back of the club. 'Is she great, or what?' He might be a little drunk but to his mind this was the best performance of Ellie's he'd seen yet. She'd averted a fight and stopped the trouble-makers stone-dead, and now she had the audience totally bewitched. She was doing 'My Baby Just Cares for

Me' and judging by the expression on the male faces as they watched her dancing, she'd be featuring in their dreams.

'She's not bad,' Ambrose said cautiously. 'Needs training and polishing, of course, but she *might* do to fill in between other acts. The show rests of course on getting a big star. If I can get Tommy Trinder or Tommy Handley we might be in business.'

'So when can we talk?' Jimbo asked. He had expected Dingle to bite his hand off to produce this show. He was disappointed in his reaction to Ellie, but perhaps his own old knack of spotting fresh talent was fading.

'I'll be in touch next week,' Ambrose said. He was watching the girl's face as she sang 'Somewhere Over the Rainbow', wandering how she'd do in a screen test. 'I've got to weigh things up first.'

'Can't you be more definite?' Jimbo had plied the man with champagne, yet still didn't know if he'd hooked him or not. 'I've got other producers to see.'

'Go ahead.' Ambrose shrugged his shoulders. 'I'm the best around and I'm not rushing into anything blind. Now I must go, it's a long drive back to Brighton.'

As Ambrose took the Brighton Road he smiled to himself. Jimbo Jameson was the answer to his prayers. Enough money to back the show, good contacts throughout the business, and naïve too! If he'd had any sense he wouldn't be risking his money on a West End revue but signing that kid up and becoming her manager!

Ambrose had learnt the hard way to make the most of opportunities. Born in Manchester, brought up above his father's butcher's shop, with the smell of raw meat permeating the whole building, he'd decided at eleven or twelve he wanted a more glamorous life than humping sides of beef and cleaning up blood and bones from the floor. The only thing his parents had given him that he was grateful for were piano lessons, allowing him to escape from the shop after school, and indeed leading him on to tap-dancing.

All those years touring America as Lois Lombard's dancing partner had enabled him almost to forget his origins. Likewise no one here knew that they'd only played in small towns or that he himself was a mediocre performer. He could speak of his days in Hollywood, and without actually lying, convince everyone he'd been a star, rather than the lowly studio assistant he really was. Those hard times had stood him in good stead. He'd seen real talent and he knew how to make the most of it.

Young Ellie had star quality. She wasn't a brilliant singer, not as Jimbo had implied, nor a fantastic dancer. But she had the makings of a musical comedy star. That expressive, beautiful face, her impudence and timing. She was a stick of dynamite and he knew how to light the fuse.

'Sign her up with the other girls,' Ambrose smirked to himself. He'd got a good bunch now, collected up during summer shows, pantomimes and small revues. Sally, the statuesque brunette, Margaret with the fabulous voice. Frances, Muriel, Mary – and, of course, Bonny.

Bonny had been a great deal of trouble, and there were many moments when he'd been tempted to ditch her. Fighting with the other girls, screwing around with every man in uniform, refusing to do as she was told. But she was beautiful and she could really dance. A spell in a London theatre would bring everything together nicely. Before long, Ambrose Dingle's name would be as well known as Florenz Ziegfeld.

Ellie was still up as the first dawn light slipped in through the curtains. A pile of screwed-up pieces of writing paper littered the floor, but at last she'd managed to write a letter to Charley that she hoped would bring him back to her.

She'd set out everything with complete honesty. How she felt she couldn't survive without him, but yet spoke of her need to pursue a career on the stage and her hopes they could find a way around the problems if they loved one another enough. She felt she'd hit the right note, loving but firm, prepared to compromise if he would too.

Again and again tonight she'd been distracted by aircraft. Before they'd bypassed London to avoid the screen of barrage balloons. Now they were screeching directly overhead, screaming towards Germany fully loaded with bombs. For the first time in the war, Ellie felt a little sympathy for the people over there, imagining them not as the enemy, but as mothers, fathers and their children, cowering the way she had done in the Blitz, praying they'd get through the night.

Another month or so and the war would be over. Jimbo had been too drunk to talk about what Ambrose Dingle had thought of her, but he had said she'd definitely get a part in the show.

It did seem that the tide was finally turning in Ellie's favour. If Charley would just agree to try again everything would be perfect.

She got into bed and picked up the photograph of Polly and Marleen she kept on the chest of drawers. It was all she had left from the rubble of Gray's Mansions.

They were arm in arm, in spangled costumes and feathered head-dresses. She knew now that this picture had been taken just days after Polly met Miles.

'I'll make you proud of me,' Ellie whispered, kissing each of the two smiling faces that meant so much to her. 'I'll pay you both back for all the love and care you showed me. Just watch.'

Chapter Fourteen

Ambrose Dingle abruptly stopped playing the piano halfway through the number. Ellie halted her dance and peered down anxiously into the gloom of the orchestra pit. It was so quiet in the empty theatre that her panting sounded like a traction engine. She felt certain she'd failed miserably.

'That's it.' He looked up at her. 'I've seen enough. Come down here, I want to talk to you.'

Ellie was confused by Mr Dingle. It was two weeks since he saw her act at the club. Last night he'd appeared again, nodded to her and then gone into Jimbo's office. He remained in there for some two hours and when he did finally come out, he ordered her to meet him at the Phoenix at ten in the morning.

Jimbo was very terse after Dingle left, so much so Ellie didn't dare ask any questions. She wondered if they'd fallen out about her.

The cleaners were still working when she arrived at the Phoenix this morning. One of them ushered her into the stalls and informed her Mr Dingle was discussing something with the manager.

She sat waiting for an hour, and it seemed like three, especially as it was so dark. She could hear the cleaners chatting as they swept out the gallery, but no one came in to speak to her.

She admired the splendid painted ceiling, noted every chip in the gilt cherubs on the boxes, and counted how many of the red plush seats had torn upholstery. She wondered if she dared climb up on to the stage and peer behind the curtain. The theatre smelt horrid, of stale cigarette smoke and mildew mingled with disinfectant, and she wondered if Mr Dingle had forgotten about her and gone home.

When the safety curtain suddenly creaked up, she jumped. The red velvet curtains swung back and Dingle came down the steps at the side of the stage. He barely looked at her, made no attempt to put her at her ease, just handed her one page of a typewritten script and told her to get up on the stage and read it to him.

She had no time to do more than scan quickly through it and she felt angry that he hadn't had the good manners even to apologise for keeping her waiting so long. But her anger at least banished her nerves.

The script was a soliloquy, spoken by a cockney woman deserted by her husband, who had left her with four children.

Ellie felt she read it quite well. For the past two weeks she'd been waiting anxiously for a response to her letter to Charley. Now she felt he would never contact her again, so the anguish of the abandoned woman was easy to identify with. Mr Dingle made no comment when she finished. Instead, he sat down at the piano in the orchestra pit, began to play a number from *The Quaker Girl* and told her to forget singing it, just to dance.

Ellie felt awkward and inhibited being so unprepared – she wasn't even wearing shoes suitable for dancing. The empty theatre was spooky and her feet made the most terrible noise on the bare boards.

She assumed he was now going to tell her she wasn't good enough. As she walked down the steps she had a good mind to give him a mouthful.

'Sit down there,' he said curtly, gesturing a few seats away from him. Then he turned towards her, silently studying her.

Ellie dropped her eyes to her lap, feeling foolish

now and wishing she hadn't come. Even the angry words that had been on her lips a moment ago dried up.

'Ellie,' he said after a lengthy pause. 'You are a natural actress, you have an agreeable voice and you move well. You have a long way to go before you'll be a musical comedy star. But I believe you have the raw material necessary.'

Ellie's head jerked round in surprise. 'You do?'

'Yes,' he said. 'You seem surprised.'

Ellie shrugged her shoulders. It sounded very much as if he was going to add, 'Come back in a few years.'

'I wasn't prepared today,' she said in her defence. 'I can do better.'

Mr Dingle wasn't like other men, but she couldn't put a finger on why. He had no discernible accent, but the rather stilted, slow way he spoke suggested he could be trying to conceal his origins. His clothes were arty – she'd noticed he wore purple socks – but she put that down to his profession. His fingers were long and tapered, the nails carefully manicured, almost feminine, yet she sensed he was strong and muscular beneath that cream-coloured linen jacket. But it wasn't his physical appearance that made her curious about him, so much as his manner. For some reason she felt he was playing a part, that in time she might find the real Ambrose Dingle was quite different.

'I'm sure you can do better,' he said thoughtfully. 'I purposely didn't give you time to prepare, so I could judge your ability to improvise. From what I've seen this morning I'm satisfied you can handle the part.'

Ellie's eyes shone. Had he been more effusive, she would have been suspicious of him; it was enough for now that she'd scraped by. 'I'm prepared to work hard,' she said, so excited she was trembling.

'You'll have to,' he said drily, his pale blue eyes chilling. 'Performing in a theatre is a great deal different to singing in a cellar club, your voice has to reach the back row of the balcony and you'll need to learn discipline when working with seasoned professionals. But I'm prepared to give you a chance.'

'Thank you sir,' she said humbly. 'I won't let you down.'

Ambrose rarely praised girls he was auditioning; he found they put far more effort into their performance if he kept them at arm's length. In fact he had felt the hairs on the back of his head rise while Ellie was reading the soliloquy, a sure sign as far as he was concerned that she had something special. Not only did she manage the best cockney accent he'd heard in years, but she had captured the correct emotions of fear, anger and betrayal. She had stage presence, something he couldn't teach if he spent twenty years with a would-be actor. Her looks too were the kind that improved with age. Today she was another very pretty girl, but by her late twenties she'd be an outstandingly beautiful woman.

'Your cockney accent was excellent.' He smiled for the first time and it made him almost handsome. 'I just hope you'll be able to manage Irish, French and other ones equally well.'

Ellie was just about to say she was good at cockney because she was one, when she realised this was unnecessary. If he didn't know, it meant she could reinvent herself if she wished. 'I 'ave, 'ow you say? A good ear,' she said in her best French maid's voice, smiling demurely.

He laughed, the first time she'd heard it, and it was a rich bellow that, like his smile, made him nicer. 'I can't put you on the bill as "Ellie",' he said, in a warmer voice. 'It creates nothing but an image of a cockney sparrow. What's it short for? Eleanor?'

'Helena,' Ellie said.

'Helena,' he said thoughtfully. 'Helena Forester, now that's got a nice ring to it. You could be French, Greek or anything with such a name.'

'Fine.' Ellie smiled, knowing Polly would have approved. 'What will I be doing in the show?'

'I'm hoping to get Tommy Trinder as our star,' Ambrose went on, speaking maddeningly slowly. 'I have a magician lined up and an excellent tenor, Riccardo De Marco, but I also have an actor called Edward Manning who I intend to pair you with in a sketch. I also want you to do a singing spot with my dancing girls.'

Ellie digested this, a little perturbed at the thought of working in tandem with a man. 'Is the sketch funny?' she asked.

Ambrose gave her an odd look. 'How funny it is will depend on you,' he said. 'Edward will be playing a typically British upper-class idiotic gentleman. You will be a cheeky, seductive maid. The laughs will come from his inability to see what's going on, and all the innuendoes. I have a copy of the script here.' He reached down and pulled out a sheaf of papers from his briefcase. 'Tonight I want you to learn it carefully and tomorrow you can start rehearsing it with Edward. I shall meet you outside here at nine in the morning, sharp. I've booked a room above a pub nearby where I'll rehearse you for a couple of days.'

'What about everyone else?' Ellie asked tentatively.

'The dancers will be arriving in a day or two when their current venue closes. I have a larger rehearsal room booked for then. The other acts don't need to be here until just a few days before we open. But before we go any further, Ellie, I must get you to sign a contract with me.'

Again he delved into his briefcase and brought out a document.

'This is standard procedure,' he said, smiling at her. 'A mere formality, as I'll be paying your wages, not Mr Jameson. All my girls sign with me. It means you can't up and leave in the middle of a show, and prevents anyone poaching you away from me. Us producers would have a tough time of it if we payed you during rehearsals and you then decided to take off and join another show at the last minute.'

'That sounds fair enough,' Ellie smiled in agreement. 'How much are you going to pay me, though?'

'Four quid a week,' he said.

Ellie was startled more by his slang than by the offer of ten bob more a week than she earned now. Throughout their conversation he had been so correct. She looked at him and smirked. 'Four quid sounds fine,' she replied and had the satisfaction of seeing him blush. 'Where do I sign?'

It was too dark to read it, so she just took his pen and signed Helena Forester with a flourish where he indicated.

'What about the club?' she asked. 'Will Jimbo still expect me to sing there?'

'I've told him you won't be in any more. With rehearsals during the morning, matinée and working the whole evening, you'll have no time for anything more.'

'What about tonight, though?' Ellie looked quizzically at Ambrose. She hadn't expected to end her Blue Moon days quite so abruptly.

'Tonight you'll get to bed early, after you've learnt that script,' he smiled almost paternally. 'Now run along, go and sit in the park and get some fresh air. It's your last day of freedom.'

Ellie sat in Leicester Square in the spring sunshine, reading the script, and her estimation of Ambrose Dingle rose another peg or two. It was absolutely perfect for her and she knew as long as this actor Edward Manning was in step with her it could be hilarious.

It was in the tradition of most farces. A somewhat naïve gentleman, complete with monocle, is shown to his room at a weekend country house party by a cheeky cockney maid. He is clearly a little excited about what promises to be a ripping weekend. While she unpacks his suitcase he boasts of his shooting and riding prowess. The maid pretends not to understand much of what he is saying, turning every statement into something saucy and getting him hot under the collar with glimpses of her cleavage and stocking tops. Finally she has him on all fours on the floor, as he desperately tries to explain a point about riding, while she sits astride his back brandishing his riding crop. The sketch ends with the gong for dinner, when she disappears leaving him totally confused.

Ellie was laughing aloud by the time she'd finished the script. It was silly and vulgar, but very funny, and all at once she was jolted painfully back to thoughts of Charley and his mother.

It was their sort of humour. Ellie could imagine acting it out to them in the kitchen of Coburgh Street. A wave of desolation washed over her. The letter she'd written Charley hadn't changed anything. He hadn't called round. He just didn't want her any more.

There were crowds of people about, office girls in groups sitting on the grass eating sandwiches, shoppers pausing in the square for a rest, a bunch of sailors kicking a football about and eyeing up the girls. A stop-me-and-buy-one ice-cream man, the first she'd seen for five years, was doing a brisk trade with choc ices at 9d each. A couple of young lads with grubby faces, both wearing placards round their necks with the message, 'Be ready for Victory', were selling small hand-held Union Jacks out of a suitcase.

So much optimism suddenly. Just a week ago people had been crying in the streets about President Roosevelt's death. Two weeks before that they'd been sighing over the huge casualties in both the Smithfield Market and Whitechapel rockets attacks. But there had been no rockets since the one in Orpington right at the end of March and the news was that all the rocket bases in Germany were now destroyed. Council workers were out putting back bulbs in street lamps, the shelters in underground stations were closed for good and the bunks removed for ever. Everywhere people were tidying up, removing sandbags, stripping tape off their windows; even the London pubs were getting in stocks of gin, whisky and beer, ready for Victory Day when it came.

Ellie got up and walked back to her room, clutching the script under her arm. She was going to be optimistic too, never mind about Charley. As Marleen always used to say, 'There's as many men in the world as there are fish in the sea, and they aren't so hard to catch.'

'Look out the window, Edward!' Ambrose roared out. 'Don't look round at Ellie as you say your line. It's for the audience to laugh at what she's doing, not you.'

The room above the Fighting Cocks was bare except for a few chairs, tables and a piano. Ambrose had arranged the chairs in the position the bedroom furniture would be in on the real stage.

To Ellie, Edward Manning *was* the Hon Charles De Witt: he didn't have to act. Young, tall and slender, with a plummy, upper-class accent, he wore his grey flannels and blazer with precisely the right air of a man who'd never done a hand's turn in his life.

Ambrose had introduced Edward to Ellie outside the Phoenix and then they'd come straight to Percy Street, off Tottenham Court Road, and begun rehearsing. There was no time to talk and Edward's stiff manner suggested he had no desire to. Now it was almost four in the afternoon and aside from a ten-minute break when the landlord had brought them up corned beef sandwiches and tea, they had been working at the sketch non-stop.

'Gosh! I believe that's Phoebe Bonhill,' Edward said, looking out of the pretend window. 'How absolutely topping, such a sweet gel.'

While Edward was speaking his line, Ellie was lifting up a pair of underpants from a couple of chairs, which were standing in for the bed. She held them aloft, putting her finger through the hole in the front and wiggling it about suggestively.

'I say, Ruby.' Edward turned back towards Ellie. 'I can unpack my underwear myself.'

'I'm sure you can, sir,' Ellie said in a strong cockney voice, rolling her eyes suggestively. 'But it's ever so much nicer when someone does it for you.'

This time they went right through the sketch, without Ambrose stopping them once.

'Much better,' he said as they finished, and for the first time that day he looked pleased. 'That's enough for one day. Be here again at nine tomorrow. Ellie, bring your practice clothes too – I shall be running through your song.'

Ambrose hailed a cab as they came out of the Fighting Cocks, leaped in and was off without a backward glance.

'I wish the public houses were open,' Edward said. 'I could murder a gin and tonic.'

There was something wistful about his remark. Ellie had a feeling it wasn't so much that he wanted drink, but company.

'A cup of tea and a sit down would suit me,' she said. She realised from his manner that he probably wanted male company, but she was curious enough about him to risk a brush-off. 'Fancy joining me?'

Although Edward's speech and manner were typically British, he looked German. His hair were white blond, eyes icy-blue and he had an exceptionally fine bone structure and glowing skin. Over their lunchtime sandwich she had forgotten herself and called him Lord Haw Haw. His only real flaw, apart from his starchy manner, was a weak and petulant mouth. She thought perhaps he had been spoilt as a child, but he had laughed at being called Lord Haw Haw, so he obviously did have a sense of humour.

'Topping,' he said with a smile. She couldn't be certain whether he was still being Charles De Witt, or whether he normally spoke like that.

Sonny's was closest, a grubby little café just off Tottenham Court Road. Edward looked a bit concerned about the stained and peeling oilcloth on the tables and hesitated before sitting down.

There were no other customers. A glass dome on the counter held two rock buns and a blackboard hanging on the wall had the scrawled message, 'No sosages. But bacen.'

'I hope you didn't want a sausage,' Ellie giggled. 'I think it might be dangerous to eat one here anyway.'

'Perhaps it might be better to go somewhere else,' Edward said nervously. A large tabby cat sitting up by the tea urn was looking at him balefully with half-closed eyes. 'There doesn't seem to be anyone serving.'

As he spoke, a woman in a flowery, none too clean pinny and a turban-style headscarf appeared before them, a cigarette dangling between her lips, and muttered something unintelligible.

Edward looked askance at Ellie.

'She said, "What'll you have?"' Ellie interpreted, amused by his shocked expression.

'A pot of tea for two, please,' Edward said. 'Do you have any toasted teacakes?'

Again an unintelligible reply, and the woman turned and walked away.

'What is it?' Edward asked indignantly. 'What did she say?'

'She said, "We only do mugs of tea, and what'cha think this is, bleedin' Lyons Corner House. I'll get you toast."' Ellie spluttered with laughter.

'Tell me about you, Ellie?' Edward asked her, fixing her with his cool blue eyes. 'Have you been an actress

319

long? You're frightfully good. I found it terribly hard not to laugh at you today.'

Ellie was a little in awe of him: he seemed experienced and she was very much aware of the huge divide between their backgrounds. But his flattery and interest warmed her, and she started to tell him about the Blue Moon and her ambitions. Perhaps they could be friends.

'I say! Do you think she's gone all the way to China?' Edward asked, when ten minutes later the tea still hadn't arrived.

'She's probably brewing it up in a bucket out the back,' Ellie giggled. 'But we'd better not complain, she might poison us.'

To Ellie, such cafés were perfectly acceptable. People had grown weary in the last year of cleaning up after bombs, of broken windows, food shortages and the bitter, cold winter. She could laugh at such slovenliness, because she sympathised with the reasons behind it.

'You are a hoot,' he said. 'Most girls I know wouldn't dream of coming in a place like this.'

At that point the woman came back. She slammed down the two mugs of tea with one hand, the toast with the other. Ellie realised she'd heard Edward's remark.

'Ninepence,' she snapped. 'And it's real butter an' all. You don't get nothin' but marge in fancy places.'

'Topping.' Edward at least had the grace to blush as he hastily paid up.

Once the woman was out of earshot, Ellie thought she ought to put Edward straight. 'I always eat in places like this,' she said quietly. 'I can't afford to go anywhere else. I suppose you've got rich folks?'

'Well, sort of.' He looked a little uncomfortable. 'Well, actually they're dead Ellie. They were killed in a motoring accident in France back in thirty-two. My grandmother was my guardian until I came of age.'

With just those few lines Ellie got a clear picture. A boy who had all the advantages of a good education and money, but no family life. 'I'm an orphan too.' She put one hand on his, tentatively. 'It's tough sometimes, isn't it?'

She saw a warmth creep into his eyes and knew then they were going to be friends.

'I'm usually scared of girls,' he admitted with a tight little laugh. 'I'm twenty-two, but I was in a blue funk coming up here this morning. Don't know what to say to them, you see.'

'We're just people,' Ellie said, removing her hand from his and munching into the toast. 'And this *is* butter!'

They stayed in the café for almost an hour. She learned his grandmother lived in Wiltshire, that he was in a sanatorium in Austria when his parents were killed and that afterwards he had a private tutor at his grandmother's until he had caught up enough to be sent to boarding-school.

'I hated every moment of it,' he said with a shrug of his shoulders. 'Except for when we put on plays. I always played women's parts, but I didn't mind that too much. I made up my mind to be an actor and I suppose I was lucky really that the war was on and there was such a shortage of men in the theatre.'

'Why weren't you called up?' Ellie asked. It was something of a rarity to see a man of his age out of uniform.

'Failed the medical.' He grinned. 'The one advantage of being a sickly kid. They wouldn't even take me in ENSA.'

'How did you meet Ambrose?'

'Just a fluke, really.' Edward shrugged. 'We got talking in a bar one night. I was in a play in Bath. Ambrose was passing through. He said he'd be in touch if anything came up. I didn't really expect to ever hear from him, you're always meeting people who say such things. About ten days later he telephoned me at my grandmother's and offered me this part.'

Ellie in turn told him about herself. Her childhood background in the theatre, her mother's death and Marleen's injuries. 'The saddest thing is she won't be able to see the show.' Ellie felt a prickle of tears.

'I won't have anyone rooting for me either,' Edward said sympathetically. 'My grandmother won't come to watch, she thinks dancing-girls are harlots and actors are pansies.'

Ellie wondered if he had a girlfriend, but she didn't like to ask. Instead she told him a little about Charley.

'It's been awful,' she admitted. 'I miss him so much, Edward, but he hasn't called round since I wrote to him. I suppose he just doesn't care enough for me.'

She couldn't bring herself to admit to such a new friend that almost every night she cried herself to sleep and that she didn't believe she could ever get over losing Charley, but it was comforting to have someone to confide in, even partially.

'Being in a show makes it hard to have friends outside the theatre,' Edward said, guessing Ellie was as lonely and friendless as himself. 'We don't seem to speak the same language as outsiders.'

'I think it's time we went,' Ellie said, seeing the woman glowering at them from behind the counter. 'Where are you staying?'

'Ambrose put me in some digs in Camden Town. They're awful, but perhaps I can find somewhere else once the show has opened.'

'Rooms are hard to get,' Ellie told him. 'Now all the evacuees are coming back it's getting worse day by day. My room's awful too, but it's cheap and handy for the Phoenix.'

'Well, I'd better get off there now.' Edward looked at his watch. 'I've missed the evening meal, but judging by the smell last night when I arrived, that's probably just as well.'

'See you tomorrow.' Ellie grinned at Edward as they parted. 'It won't be such an ordeal again, not now we know one another.'

He gave her a curious, wobbly smile and disappeared into the crowd without replying.

Stacey Passage, where Ellie lived, was a narrow alley off Charing Cross Road. Sunshine never found its way down between the tall houses and it had a quaintly Dickensian quality, with small second-hand bookshops and malodorous gloom. All kinds of people lived in the dozens of rented rooms above the shops: Ellie had seen little old ladies, Jewish refugees, musicians, shop girls, and even some of the spivvy types she'd seen drinking at the Blue Moon.

As she turned into Stacey Passage her heart nearly stopped. Charley was standing there, looking up at number four.

He was wearing his best clothes; a tweed jacket, grey flannels and the blue tie Ellie had bought him for Christmas. He'd had his hair cut rather severely and the shorn patch above his collar, coupled with the anxious look on his face, made him look endearingly boyish.

'Charley,' she called out, unable to prevent herself from running to him, tears of delight pricking her eyes. He turned at her voice and the joyful expression on Ellie's face made his resolve vanish.

She was wearing the same skirt and jumper she'd worn for much of the winter, bare legs and white ankle socks, her hair tied up loosely with a red ribbon, but she had never looked more beautiful to him.

He'd almost forgotten how big her dark eyes were. In the split second before she reached him, arms open wide with welcome, he thought he'd sooner die than face life without her again.

'Ellie,' he murmured as her arms wrapped around his neck. 'Oh Ellie!'

There were people hustling through the alley, intent on getting home, but they were both unaware of being in the way, causing office workers to sidestep them as they clung to each other.

'Have you forgiven me?' she asked, warm lips showering his face with kisses.

Only then was he brought up sharply as to why he'd come and his mother's insistence that he told her face to face. 'We've got to talk,' he said, catching hold of her two arms and creating a space between them.

'Come upstairs to my room then.' Her eyes danced, her skin glowed with excitement. She had all but forgotten the misery he'd put her through.

Charley glanced up. He'd been to many houses just like this in fires: rabbit warrens of small, dingy rooms with paper-thin walls. He knew that alone with her he would weaken. 'No, let's go to a café,' he said. 'It's better.'

Ellie sensed he had something to say she wouldn't like. But he was here, and that was enough for now. She let him lead her down to Charing Cross Road and into the cafeteria on the corner of Lisle Street.

'Have you had a meal today?' he asked as they queued at the counter.

Ellie saw piles of soggy golden chips, sausages and shepherd's pie lying there invitingly on the hot plate and she was suddenly starving. 'No. Could I have sausage and chips?'

'I'll get it, you go and find a table.' Charley glanced over his shoulder at the crowded room, glad for once to see so many people.

It was hot and noisy, the sort of place where however hard the staff worked, they never got on top of clearing the tables before someone else grabbed them.

Ellie felt rather pleased with herself at finding a corner table only big enough for two. She dumped the dirty plates on to an already loaded trolley, flicked off the remaining crumbs and sat down.

In all these weeks since she'd moved out of Coburgh Street, she'd almost managed to convince herself that her memory of Charley was distorted. But as she watched him shuffling along the cafeteria counter her heart contracted painfully. The length of his eyelashes, his shy smile as the woman serving him made some cheeky comment, the healthy glow of his skin, all so different to the kind of men who drank at the Blue Moon. She could see the outline of hard muscle beneath his jacket, the big hands holding the tray hard enough to direct a hose at the biggest fire, strong enough to dig people out from mountains of rubble: yet she remembered how sensitive they were when he caressed her.

The curls in his hair were already springing up despite his efforts to tame them. He had a new small scar on his chin, another reminder that he lived with danger. But as he turned towards her with the loaded tray his brown eyes were soft with sorrow. She knew he'd got something serious on his mind.

'How's your mum?' Ellie said once he had sat down across the small table to her. She wanted to keep the tone light until at least they'd eaten and she'd had time to gauge his real feelings.

'She's very busy.' Charley sprinkled his chips with salt. 'She took in a bombed-out family. There's four kids and it's bedlam. But with a bit of luck they'll get one of those new prefabs soon.'

He told her about some of his friends who were also hoping to be re-housed, about builders repairing roofs in the street and plans going ahead for a street party for Victory Day. 'I reckon it will be next month,' he said. 'It's really quiet now at the fire station, all we've been doing is putting out fires on bomb-sites where kids have been messing around.'

Ellie told him her news and how she'd spent the day rehearsing.

'I'm really glad for you,' he said, smiling as she described the sketch. 'I'll come to see it, of course.'

As they finished their meal, Ellie felt she had to tackle him. 'You look as if you've got something to tell me,' she said, reaching out for his hand and stroking it. 'But it isn't something I'm going to like, is it?'

She saw him gulp, his Adam's apple leaping over his shirt collar. His soft lips took on a tighter look and his eyes could no longer meet hers.

'I'm leaving the fire brigade,' he said. 'I'm going to Australia.'

It was as if someone had just given her a push off a cliff and she was falling through space. Why did he have to come if it was only to upset her further?

'When?' she managed to ask.

'As soon as I can get a passage,' he said. 'It may take some time, what with the war still on in the Far East. But I've made up my mind, Ellie. England's got nothing to offer me for the future.'

'So you came to say goodbye then?' she croaked out, tears welling up in her eyes. 'I thought. I hoped –' She broke off, unable to continue.

'I came to ask you to go with me.' He reached out across the table and wiped away her tears with one finger. Ellie looked into his eyes and saw a challenge in them.

'Just like that?' she asked. It felt like she was being backed into a corner. 'You expect me to say yes or no right now without any time to think about it?'

'What is there to think about? You said in your letter you loved me, prove it Ellie.'

Ellie didn't answer for a moment as she tried to regain her equilibrium. This wasn't her gentle, reasonable Charley but a hard-faced version. She wondered who had suggested this plan to him; it didn't sound like he'd thought it up himself.

'I do love you,' she said. 'But even if I wanted to, I couldn't just drop everything. I've signed a contract for the show.'

'You can do the show,' he said, looking directly into

her eyes, daring her to stall or prevaricate. 'Like I said, it might be some time before I can arrange a passage for Australia. But marry me now.'

Ellie felt weak. He was as tense as a coiled spring, sitting bolt upright, his forearms resting on the table.

Once married she would have to obey him, go to Australia, or even China if that was what he wanted.

'You aren't being fair,' she said. 'I don't know whether the show will be a success or sink within a couple of weeks.'

'It shouldn't make any difference.' A chill had crept into his voice. 'If you really loved me that would be all that counted.'

A bubble of anger rose inside her. 'If I really loved you?' she snorted. 'You refused to listen to my apologies and let me leave Coburgh Street without even saying goodbye. You've left me to stew for weeks without a word. Now you expect me to give up everything I've worked so hard for, just because of what *you* want.'

He had the grace to blush at this. 'I have to be tough because I know what you're like.' He shrugged. 'A year from now, two years or even three, it might still be the same. You'll be saying, "Let's see how this works out" or "I've just got an audition for this show." I want to be married now because I can't live with uncertainty any longer.'

This last statement offered her a little hope. Maybe the idea of Australia was just a bluff. 'I'm not against getting married,' she said more gently. 'It's the thought of being whisked halfway across the world. Can't we reach some sort of compromise?'

'By that you mean do what you want to do, and I have to fit my life round it.'

Ellie was faced with a stalemate. 'Why does it have to be this all or nothing stuff?' she snapped back at him. 'I want fun, romance, love and adventure. Why can't we have that?'

Charley smiled sadly. 'I thought that was what I was offering.'

They talked on and on. Charley made Australia sound very attractive. Building a home together, learning to ride horses, the sunshine – a land full of opportunity. But however dreamily romantic it sounded, she knew if they lived on a ranch there would be no dancing, singing or acting, and not even any people.

Ellie told him all her news, especially about Marleen. 'That's another thing,' she pointed out. 'How could I leave her? She hasn't got anyone else.'

Charley fudged that point by saying he'd have to leave his mother, but Ellie was certain that Annie would end up moving to Australia too.

She very much wanted to tell him about Sir Miles Hamilton: the secret had been burning inside her ever since Marleen told her. But under the circumstances it wouldn't be wise. It might look to Charley like another wedge between them.

They walked around the West End for a little until it grew dark, then Charley walked back with her to Stacey Passage.

'Come up with me?' she asked, wanting to be alone with him, to hold him and let him sweep away her doubts.

'No, Ellie.' He shook his head. 'I know how it will be if I go in there. I'm not going to add more complications than there are already. Write or call when you can tell me yes or no.'

He kissed her then, long and hard, holding her so tightly she knew he meant exactly what he said. 'If it's yes,' he said, breaking away, his eyes brimming with tears, 'we'll get engaged on Victory Day.'

He didn't have to say what would happen if her answer was no. Somehow she knew he'd be on the first ship out.

Chapter Fifteen

May 1945

'Stop!' Ambrose yelled, running down the aisle of the stalls, a long raincoat ballooning out behind him.

The pianist's hands paused in mid-air, his last notes echoing as he turned on his stool in surprise. He sensed an electric charge coming from the producer, but in the gloom of the theatre he couldn't tell if it was anger or excitement.

The sixteen dancers on the stage halted their cancan routine, flopping instantly to the floor, glad of a break for whatever reason. Some of them had been working under Ambrose's direction for as long as two years, but they had never been driven quite so hard by him in previous shows.

They had been The Gaiety Girls, The Cover Girls and The Brighton Belles. Now he was insisting on calling them 'The Dingle Belles' a name which alternately made them cringe with embarrassment or giggle helplessly. But whatever they thought of their new name, or of Ambrose as a man, they all had to admit that he'd kept his promise to them. He had got his girls on a West End stage.

'Sally!' Ambrose yelled again, and now, as he moved closer to the stage, they could all see his face was flushed. 'Round up the entire cast. Everyone, stage-hands, performers, the lot.'

Speculative whispers broke out amongst the girls as Sally got up and ran off into the wings. The ones who'd been with Ambrose the longest had seen his ruthless pruning and weeding out of girls. All the girls on the stage were uniformly tall and slender, their fatter and shorter friends long since dismissed. Ambrose was a perfectionist, not just about the choreography, but about their appearance. If a girl had a hole in her tights, her hair or make-up less than perfect, he wiped the floor with her. If her dancing wasn't up to standard she was packed off on the next train home.

'You don't think the show's been cancelled?' Muriel whispered anxiously to Frances.

Muriel, Frances, Sally, Margaret and Bonny were the only girls left of the ones auditioned in Littlehampton. Frances had had to lose her excess weight to stay.

'I don't think he's angry.' Frances twirled a black corkscrew curl round her finger, looking thoughtfully at Ambrose. 'It might be he's got a date for opening at last.'

All the girls were aware that Ambrose had been under a great strain. Opening night had been planned for Saturday 28th April, but the theatre owners had insisted that since peace was so close, the show should open to honour it. The BBC had interrupted a programme the night before to say that Hitler was dead and now, on May 3rd, the whole of Britain was holding its breath, hour by hour expecting the news that peace had been declared.

Rumours had been flying thick and fast amongst the cast during this uncertain time, hysteria affecting them all. They had seen Riccardo, the pompous tenor, walk out twice, only to return some hours later. Jimbo threatened to pull out as a backer unless he had a bigger hand in running the show. There were suspicions that Edward Manning only got the part because Ambrose fancied him. Lorenzo the magician was secretive enough about his real name and background to be a deserter and the Doc, Jimbo's partner, had been arrested, apparently for fraud. On top of all this, costumes for the dancers on loan from another theatre had been lost in transit, and had only finally turned up yesterday.

'What's wrong now?' Lorenzo came on to the stage, his narrow face furrowed by frown lines. He was a very ordinary looking man, small, thin and grey faced. But once dressed in his top hat and tails, pulling white doves out of chiffon scarves, or sawing his willowy assistant Magda in half, he really was The Great Lorenzo, one of the finest magicians in the country.

'I'll give the news when everyone's here,' Ambrose replied from the darkened front of the house.

Ellie and Edward, who had been going through their sketch back-stage, arrived next. Riccardo followed with a couple of the stage-hands he'd been arguing with. One by one they all trailed on to the stage. Buster the comic, wearing a ridiculously large pair of checked trousers wired at the waist and held up by red braces, bounced them to make the girls laugh. Fred, the man who handled the flies, appeared eating a sandwich; the props girl, Ruth, nervously holding her clipboard as if expecting a reprimand.

Ambrose waited for a second, quickly counting heads to make sure everyone was present. They were an ill-assorted bunch. Pretty girls with graceful bodies in leotards, gnarled stage-hands in stained overalls, not one of them under fifty. Fred, with his neanderthal long arms, looked even more bizarre beside Edward's physical perfection. Riccardo, a twenty-stone giant, was resplendent in a bright red jacket, his black hair and moustache gleaming with oil. Next to him stood Angus, the stage-manager, stooped and prematurely aged, in a Norfolk jacket and corduroys.

When Ambrose had been summoned by the theatre owners, he'd assumed they'd decided to call the show-off. Despite all his efforts he hadn't been able to lure

331

Tommy Trinder, only Buster Bradley, who although very funny and on his way up, wasn't exactly a household name. By now Ambrose was so dejected he hadn't even got any counter arguments prepared: in his darkest moments he'd even told himself he could never lick this rag-bag collection of people into anything resembling a slick revue.

But suddenly, with an opening date, he was euphoric. His Dingle Belles were the loveliest girls in the West End, Riccardo's voice would make strong men cry, Lorenzo was a spellbinder and Buster was the funniest man in England.

As he looked at the weary stage-hands and the imbecilic Fred he felt a surge of affection. Ellie and Edward would have the audience rolling in the aisles. It was going to work.

He clapped his hands for quiet. 'I've just been given an opening date,' he announced. 'Wednesday 9th May!'

For a moment there was stunned silence.

'Whoopee,' Sally yelled out, jumping a couple of feet into the air. Fred threw his woolly cap right up into his flies and gave an ear-piercing whistle.

Pandemonium broke out. Cheering, shouting, stamping on the floor and hugs all round.

'Does that mean peace will be declared before that?' Edward bellowed.

'Almost certainly.' Ambrose smiled beatifically. 'As a gesture of good will I'm going to let you all have the rest of the day off. Tomorrow we'll have a full dress rehearsal.'

No one needed telling twice. A half day off was an unheard-of treat from their dictatorial producer. The girls picked up their jumpers and spare shoes and vanished first, quickly followed by the stage-hands who fully expected to be called back.

Ellie saw Edward jump down from the stage to join Ambrose. She paused for a moment, as the thought crossed her mind that the rumours about these two could be true. She and Edward had become good friends and shared a great many confidences, but she had never asked him about his relationship with Ambrose.

But Ellie's attention was suddenly diverted by Bonny. She was hanging back on the stage, and she looked forlorn.

Ellie liked most of the dancers. In the main they were a rowdy, gregarious bunch. Ellie had felt a little intimidated at joining these seasoned professionals for her number from *The Quaker Girl* at first, but they had accepted her, often coaching her privately in odd moments.

Bonny was different from the others, however – cool and occasionally downright hostile. The girls who had been working with her for almost a year claimed she was a trouble-maker, a man-eater, a spoilt brat and entirely self-centred. Maybe all this was true, but Ellie reminded herself that Bonny was the youngest in the troupe. Besides, she didn't like to see anyone looking sad.

'What's up?' Ellie asked. 'You don't look too happy.' She expected a sharp, mind-your-own-business reply, but to her surprise the girl's lip quivered and a tear trickled down her cheek.

There was no denying that Bonny was the prettiest girl in the troupe, and the best dancer. Ellie often sat and watched the girls rehearsing, and it was always Bonny who her eyes were drawn to. Her long blonde hair swung with her graceful body, she had flirtatious, big blue eyes and a show-stopping smile. She was like a hot, dangerous flame on stage, her feet like quicksilver, every muscle tuned to perfection. None of the other girls could match her. Ambrose had given her two tap-dancing solos and Ellie had no doubt that if Bonny's singing had only matched her dancing, it wouldn't be Ellie's name on the programme for the *Quaker Girl* number but Bonny's.

'Tell me.' Ellie instinctively moved to put her arms round the girl. She couldn't bear to see anyone upset and even though she expected a rebuff, she couldn't help herself. To her surprise Bonny didn't move away, but instead leaned on Ellie's shoulder and sobbed.

'I don't know what to do now,' she said, her voice wobbling through her tears. 'They'll all go out together and leave me on my own.'

Ellie knew enough about the politics within the troupe to know this was true. They were split into small tight groups of friends and Bonny was excluded from all of them. But she was surprised this troubled Bonny, who'd always given Ellie the impression this was what she wanted.

'I'll be on my own too today,' she said impulsively. 'We could do something together if you like.'

Bonny drew back from her, the expression on her face somewhere between disbelief and gratitude. 'What about Edward?' she sniffed. 'You're always with him.'

'Only in the theatre,' Ellie said. 'I never see him outside.'

'I thought he was your boyfriend!' Bonny wiped her eyes and they were wary now.

'Not likely,' Ellie grinned, liking the girl more because she didn't seem to share everyone else's suspicions about Edward. 'He's more like a brother. Come on, get changed and we'll find something to do.'

By late afternoon both girls had altered their views on one another, or had at least gained a different perspective.

Ellie had braced herself for an uncomfortable afternoon, fully expecting Bonny to be as chilly as she was in the theatre. Instead Bonny was chatty, clearly pleased to have company, and she had a wicked sense of humour.

Ellie didn't for one minute believe that Bonny's

334

father was a Japanese prisoner of war, or that her Aunt Lydia was a countess with scores of servants. She suspected Bonny was making these things up because her home life was very ordinary. But it was good entertainment, like turning on the wireless and losing yourself in a fantasy.

Bonny, until now, had seen Ellie as a threat. She had a strong voice, she could act, she made people laugh and they liked her. Ever since Bonny had arrived in London for rehearsals, she had been studying Ellie endlessly, hoping to find some way of discrediting her. But warmed by Ellie's kindness in spending the afternoon with her, she found herself not only admiring her, but wanting her as a friend.

They had started out in the same cafeteria Charley had taken Ellie to, where they ate something called 'Victory Pie'. Bonny poked at the grey mass of swede, turnip and the odd fragment of meat and said a better name for it would have been 'Retreat Pie'.

'I'm going to be a Hollywood star,' Bonny announced without any modesty, wolfing the pie down regardless of its content. 'I'm a brilliant dancer and I'm beautiful. I'll be bigger than Ginger Rogers, I bet she looks like a hag without make-up.'

Ellie merely smiled. Bonny's confidence was disarming, especially as she then went on to highlight her shortcomings with equal candour.

'My singing's feeble and I can't act, but when I'm dancing no one can take their eyes off me. That's why the other girls don't like me. I've tried hard to fit in but they can't accept the way I am.'

Ellie was as fascinated by Bonny face-to-face as she had been by her on stage. She had the confidence of a stage veteran and the imagination of a film director. Just an hour or two in her company made Ellie feel as if her own dreams weren't so far-fetched or unreachable.

Later they wandered through Leicester Square and

observed the enormous queue for the film of the Nazi atrocities in Belsen and Buchenwald. They moved on up to Piccadilly, which was as crowded as always, with foreigners taking photographs of one another against the boarded-up Eros. All the news stands carried the message that Hitler was dead and the excitement seemed to have affected everyone. A couple of American sailors stopped the girls and asked if they wanted a walk in Green Park.

'Is that the best you can offer?' Bonny said with a disparaging sneer. 'We're stars in a West End show. We don't walk in parks with sailors.'

'That was a bit rude,' Ellie giggled as they hurried away.

'I'm always rude to men,' Bonny said with her cute little nose in the air. 'They seem to thrive on it.'

They ended up in St James's Park and sat in the sun in a couple of deckchairs while Ellie told Bonny of her predicament with Charley.

It was good to have another girl for company. Edward had become a real friend, but she couldn't share the same kind of confidences with a man as she could with Bonny.

Bonny was as good a listener as she was a talker. 'You can't possibly marry him,' she said with surprising horror. 'You're far too talented to go and live on a farm in Australia. Besides, what do you know about men, if he's the only one you've ever been out with? He sounds just like my boyfriend Jack, wanting to put you in a cage so no one else can get near you.'

Of all the things Bonny had told her in the course of the day, Jack was the only person she'd mentioned who rang entirely true. Bonny had explained how he was down in Aldershot in the army, and that in the last year they'd only been able to see one another on odd nights when he could get a twenty-four hour pass.

'I know just how you feel because no other man

336

makes me feel the way Jack does.' Bonny's eyes clouded over and all at once Ellie saw that she wasn't quite the cold-hearted opportunist she made herself out to be. 'Just thinking about Jack makes me tremble. He's my friend, he's everything. But he's just like Charley, Ellie. He wants me to marry him when he comes out of the army, to settle down in a little cottage and have babies.'

She paused, looking intently at Ellie. 'Sometimes I almost believe I want that too. But there's this stronger side of me that needs luxury and expensive clothes, that wants to see the world and get fame. I couldn't make him happy, Ellie, not for long.'

'Does your mother like him?' Ellie asked. She wanted to cut through Bonny's fabricated background and get a glimpse of the real one.

'Mum thinks he's awful because he's got red hair,' Bonny smirked. 'But then she doesn't believe it's serious because she thinks I'm still a child. I can't talk to her.'

'Where does she live, Bonny?' Ellie probed, wishing she dared say she knew Mr Phillips wasn't really a prisoner of war.

'Dagenham,' Bonny said reluctantly. 'But don't bandy that around, will you? I spent two days with her before I started rehearsals, it was awful.'

Ellie sensed Bonny wasn't ready to talk about her home just yet. 'So what are we going to do about Jack and Charley then?' she said instead.

'Wait and see what happens when the show opens,' Bonny grinned. 'We're a lot alike, Ellie. We can't give up our dreams and settle down just to make them happy. It wouldn't work. Let's let them do all the running!'

Later that night, as Ellie lay in bed, she thought over what Bonny had said about them being alike. It didn't please her to think she might be ruthless or conceited, but then she'd often watched films and thought she could be so much better than Vivien Leigh or Judy Garland, given a chance. Ellie didn't want to be influenced by Bonny; she wasn't even sure she wanted her as a friend. Yet already she had a feeling their destiny was linked in some way.

'What should I do about Charley?' she asked herself.

She wanted his love more than anything. She imagined the adventure of setting off with him on that long boat ride, seeing wide open spaces instead of bomb-sites and slums. Charley could fill that lonely space inside her; there would be his mother and his brothers, then children of their own. Surely all that would more than take the place of being an actress?

What was acting anyway? Pretending to be someone else! What sort of person needed applause rather than love? Surely singing to your own children was just as rewarding as performing for strangers?

The clock hands moved slowly towards nine. It was the evening of May 7th and today's rehearsal had been extended so the entire cast and backstage team could hear the expected news on the wireless together.

They were crowded into the small lobby by the stage door, tension showing in every face, many still wearing their garish make-up from the dress rehearsal, the smell of sweat overpowering in the confined space.

When the dry, precise voice of a man from the Ministry of Information began to speak, they moved closer still, every ear cocked to hear the news they'd been anticipating for so long.

'It is understood that, in accordance with arrangements between the three great powers, an official announcement will be broadcast by the Prime Minister at three o'clock tomorrow, Tuesday May 8th. In view of this fact, tomorrow, Tuesday, will be treated as Victory-in-Europe Day and will be regarded as a holiday. His Majesty the King will broadcast to the people of the British Empire and Commonwealth tomorrow, Tuesday, at 9 p.m.'

For a moment no one spoke, faces turning from one to another, each waiting for something more.

Old Fred broke the silence. 'Bloody hell,' he swore. 'If he meant it's all bleedin' over, he could've put a bit more oomph into it.'

A ripple of laughter broke out, building up into a roar.

Ambrose recovered first. He moved quickly on to the steps leading to the changing-rooms, adjusted his purple cravat and cleared his throat.

'I don't know who was responsible for that uninspired speech,' he said, grinning broadly at all the upturned faces before him. 'But I'm sure Churchill's working on something a little more memorable for tomorrow. Meanwhile I have a few words to say, before you rush off to start celebrating.' He took a handkerchief from his breast pocket and mopped his sweating face. 'The show will open on Wednesday 9th at seven-thirty as arranged.'

Loud cheering broke out all around him. Although they had been working on this date for several days, there had been a real fear it would be put back. For their first night to be at such an auspicious time seemed like a talisman for success.

Ambrose raised his arms for silence. 'You have all worked very hard, under difficult circumstances. I'd like to thank you all for your persistence, your occasional bursts of brilliance and your patience. We have a first-class show, and the timing for its opening couldn't be a better omen. I want you all here on Wednesday for a final dress rehearsal at twelve o'clock sharp. Anyone the worse for their celebrations can expect to be dismissed immediately. Is that clear?'

A nodding of heads signalled agreement. Bonny turned to Ellie and winked wickedly.

'God bless you all.' Ambrose faltered, a little overcome with emotion now that the anxiety and uncertainty was finally lifted. 'Six years of war is over. Now we can all look forward to new happiness and prosperity. Break a leg!'

'What's up?' Bonny darted forward from a doorway as Ellie came out of the phone box. It was tipping down with rain and she held her coat over her head to shelter Ellie.

'Come up to my room,' Ellie said. 'I'll tell you when we get out of this.'

They ran together, dodging through the crowds of people towards Stacey Passage, splashing through the deep puddles.

'Charley's got to work tomorrow,' Ellie said once they'd got in and closed the street door behind them. 'He said all the men have been ordered to stand by because there'll be hundreds of fires.'

Bonny followed Ellie up the steep staircase. 'Never mind,' she said, panting a little. 'We'll have a good time together.'

As Ellie reached her room she looked back at Bonny. Her blonde hair was wet, plastered to her head and her greasepaint-streaked face gave her the look of a street urchin. 'Shouldn't you go home and see your mum?' she asked, opening the door.

'I suppose so.' Bonny faltered for a moment, frowning as she remembered what that would mean. 'There's bound to be a street party.' She followed Ellie into her room, leaving her wet coat outside, suddenly dejected.

Bonny knew exactly what the victory celebrations in Flamstead Road would be like: there would be tables set up, enough food and drink for an army, a piano wheeled out, and everyone would have the time of their lives. Except for her.

Doris was teetotal, and she would sit primly on the

sidelines, getting more and more tetchy as the neighbours got drunk. The party would most likely go on half the night, but her parents wouldn't join in and nor would they allow Bonny to. She'd be back indoors before six o'clock and her mother would spend the whole evening peeping out through the curtains, sniffing with disapproval at the merriment.

'You don't sound too happy about it,' Ellie said impishly. 'I suppose with your dad still a prisoner it wouldn't be appropriate for you and your mum to celebrate?'

Bonny blushed. Ellie was very sharp-witted; she ought to have known better than tell her such a stupid lie. 'He isn't a prisoner,' she said in a small voice. 'I made that up. He works at Ford's. But I can't face going home anyway. I'd rather stay with you.'

Ellie smiled – it was the first time she'd seen Bonny look embarrassed. 'It would be nice to have your company,' she said, making no further comment on the lie. All at once her anticipation of the day ahead drove out the disappointment of not spending it with Charley. 'Let's plan what we'll do.'

The heavy rain prevented them going out again. They decided Bonny should share Ellie's bed instead of going back to her digs with the other dancers in King's Cross. They made toast on the fire and chatted incessantly.

'In another couple of weeks we might really be stars,' Bonny giggled, sitting cross-legged on the bed. 'Men will send us flowers and notes, we might get our pictures in the papers.'

Ellie wanted to tell Bonny she'd decided to marry Charley. She hoped he would put off his plans for Australia and stay in the fire brigade, so she could continue in the show, but her mind was made up: she loved him too much to lose him. It was a shame he'd be working tomorrow – she'd intended to tell him then and make Victory Day a double celebration. But perhaps he'd finish work in time to make the day complete. She couldn't tell Bonny yet. Not until she'd told Charley and Annie.

At twelve o'clock the noise of the storm was drowned by the deep-throated boom of ships' sirens from the docks. They knelt up at the window and saw the sky lit up with searchlights. Car horns, hooters and whistles joined in the cacophony of joyful sounds and the girls opened their windows and added their voices to the din.

'I'll never forget this moment.' Bonny turned to Ellie with shining eyes. 'It's the start of something tremendous, I know it is. We have to remember everything about it so in fifty years' time we can tell our children.'

'I thought you didn't want kids,' Ellie teased her, a little surprised that Bonny was capable of being so emotional.

'Of course I do, one day,' she laughed. 'But first I have to be famous.'

They woke the next morning to the sound of the last all-clear siren, to find the roofs outside the window steaming in the sunshine and the sky as blue and cloudless as Bonny's eyes.

'Our bodies are almost identical,' Bonny said in some surprise as they shared a bath. There was a large mirror on the wall, speckled with brown where the silvering had peeled off but there was still enough of a reflection to see their naked bodies clearly side by side as they stood up to dry themselves. They were the same height, and both had small waists and long legs. The only difference was that Ellie's skin was olive while Bonny's was pink and white. 'That's handy, we can wear each other's clothes.'

'I haven't got anything you'd want to wear,' Ellie said dejectedly. The green dress Annie had given her was still her 'best' dress, and it was getting very shabby.

She was so tired of mending and retrimming second-hand clothes. She'd grown used to food rationing, eking out a stub of lipstick and trying to mend stockings, but she'd give anything for a nice new frock.

Bonny wrapped the towel round herself, shamed because she'd been a little tactless. She had several nice dresses, carefully made by her mother, but until now she hadn't considered how lucky she was.

'We'll soon be in the money,' she said. 'Besides, with faces like ours, no one's going to be looking at our clothes.'

It was twelve noon when they sallied forth into Charing Cross Road arm in arm, aware they made a pretty picture.

They both had jaunty white sailor hats trimmed with red and blue ribbons, their newly washed hair cascading over their shoulders, Bonny's blonde contrasting well with Ellie's black mane. Armed with a striped cardboard hooter and a small flag to wave, smelling strongly of 'Soir de Paris', they were already intoxicated with excitement.

The streets were seething with people, many wearing foolish hats and blowing hooters.

They joined in a conga at Piccadilly with a crowd of American sailors and their girls, kissed countless soldiers, airmen and marines and posed to have their photographs taken dozens of times.

All the pubs had big banners outside, advertising ample stocks of gin, whisky and beer. Music was coming from every direction: pianists in pubs, gramophones in upstairs rooms, buskers playing everything from tin whistles, trumpets, violins and piano accordions. Scores of uniformed men had climbed on to the boarded-up Eros. Buses moved at a snail's pace through the jovial crowd.

The girls were swept along down the Haymarket towards Trafalgar Square.

'Just look at all the people,' Bonny gasped, clinging to Ellie's hand in terror of being separated.

It seemed as if all London was gathered here, a throbbing, seething mass of people spilling out into the surrounding roads, on to walls, steps and even the giant stone lions and still fountains.

Flags fluttered and banners made from sheets bore messages declaring 'Peace For All Time' and 'Victory'. Smiles adorned every face. Uniformed men and women were kissed or patted on the back. Girls in borrowed soldiers' and sailors' caps vied for attention with others in home-made red, white and blue creations. Groups of servicemen and their girls rolled-up their trouser legs and paddled in the fountain.

At three, Churchill's speech was relayed by loud-speaker to the vast crowd. They fell silent as his voice boomed out, hanging on his every word. A huge cheer went up as he announced that as from midnight, hostilities would cease, and another greeted the news that 'our dear Channel Islands' were to be liberated.

At the final point of his speech – 'The German War is therefore at an end' – thousands of flags were waved in triumph and the buglers of the Royal Horse Guards sounded the cease-fire.

Everyone stood to attention at 'God Save the King'. Tens of thousands of people sang with all their heart and soul, many with tears streaming down their faces.

'Isn't it wonderful?' Ellie hugged Bonny, entirely overcome by the emotion of the moment. 'Let's go to the palace now.'

There were times on the way down the Mall when it seemed impossible to get any further. They were packed in on all sides, a teeming mass of humanity shuffling in unison. People were singing now, every-thing from 'Pack Up your Troubles' to 'Roll Out the Barrel', and occasionally bursts of 'Rule Britannia!'. Women trying to push prams stopped, disheartened by the effort, but someone was always there to urge them on. There were old ladies and men staunchly sitting in places they'd bagged early in the morning, undaunted by the fact they could no longer see anything but a forest of legs. Children, goggle-eyed, were lifted aloft on their fathers' shoulders for safety. St James's Park looked like an anthill, the grass all but concealed by the throng milling there.

Ellie had an advantage over many of the people here today, in being used to crowds. Dragging Bonny by the hand, she elbowed her way through, right up to the palace railings, just in time to see the Royal Family step out on to the balcony. The King was in naval uniform, bare-headed. The Queen and Princess Margaret were in blue; Elizabeth wore her ATS uniform. But it was Winston Churchill's day. The moment he stepped out, his fingers raised in his victory salute, the cheering rose to a deafening roar.

'I'm exhausted.' Bonny flopped down on a spare patch of grass in St James's Park. The crowds were dispersing now, the people left looking faintly stunned and unsure what to do next. It was some time after five and they hadn't eaten a thing since breakfast. 'What are we going to do now? We haven't got any money left.'

Ellie lay back on the grass thinking. A tree up above her was just coming into leaf. The sun shining through its branches made each furled leaf look like an emerald.

She was tired too, and felt she ought to go home in case Charley came round, but like Bonny she wanted more. It had been the most special day in her life. Just to slink home would cut it short.

'We can't go to a pub,' she said wistfully. 'I suppose we could go to the Blue Moon later – Cyril will slip us a few drinks. But Jimbo might be funny, I think he's fallen out with Ambrose.'

'Sod Ambrose,' Bonny said. 'And this grass is wet, my dress is getting all creased.' She leaped up and pulled at the hem.

'Hi, girls!'

Ellie was surprised, not by the American voice – they'd been surrounded by both Yanks and Canadians all day – but by the closeness of it.

'Hello boys,' Bonny retorted in the husky voice she invariably dropped into when she saw a man she wanted to flirt with.

Ellie opened one eye, squinting round. It wasn't one Yank but two, and both were very handsome.

'Pardon me if we're intruding,' the man said, so very politely. 'But you two look like we feel and we just wanted to say hi.'

Both men were dark-haired and brown-eyed, with the kind of olive skin that pointed to Italian ancestry. They were in blue-grey uniform, both tall, with wide shoulders and slim hips. The one who had spoken was marginally taller and older, and had a wide, smiling mouth and dazzling white teeth.

'Hi,' Ellie said, getting up. 'How *do* we look?'

'Gorgeous.' He grinned wickedly. 'But a bit pooped.'

Ellie said something about the grass being wet as she picked up her sailor's hat and plonked it back on her head.

'Then let us escort you both to some real seats,' he said. 'I'm Brad Summers. This is Steve Ginsberg.'

'I'm Bonny Phillips,' Bonny said, the bubble of delight in her voice so obvious Ellie knew she wasn't going to be rude to these two. 'This is Helena Forester. We're dancers in a West End show.'

The four of them moved to sit on a bench to chat.

Steve was twenty-one, from Indiana; Brad was from Texas and he was twenty-five. They were stationed out at Ruislip, but they were expecting to go back to Germany any day, taking supplies for the troops over there.

It was quieter now as they sat by the lake. Most of the people left in the park were lovers, entwined in

346

each other's arms on the grass, or strolling arm in arm. There were a few family groups, many with small children in pushchairs, eating sandwiches, but there was an air of expectancy somehow, as if everyone was biding their time until it was dark.

Ellie realised Bonny was attracted to Steve. Perhaps she was only thinking the men might buy them a meal or a few drinks, but she fizzed and sparkled in a way that suggested it was more than that.

Ellie thought of Charley then, a little guiltily. She guessed once it got dark there would be bonfires on every bomb-site and many would get out of control. Even now he was probably wondering what she was doing and what her answer would be about marrying him. He certainly wouldn't approve of her sitting here with these two Americans. Perhaps she ought to telephone the fire station?

'You're cold.' Brad touched Ellie's bare arm lightly, his dark eyes looking right into hers. 'Let's find a bar and get you warmed up.'

It occurred to Ellie some time between her third and fourth gin that however charming, generous and handsome these two men were, she ought to make it quite clear she had a boyfriend. But the atmosphere in the Old King Cole in the Strand was so exciting, she had her fourth gin and forgot about it.

The bar was packed, elbow to elbow, and shouting was the only means of communicating. Someone started to play the piano and everyone sang their hearts out. The landlord did switch on the wireless at nine to hear the King's speech, but after a minute or two of silence while the King stuttered out his message, slowly everyone lost interest and the murmur of drunken voices drowned the last of his speech.

The four of them went out again into Trafalgar Square to see all the buildings floodlit. For Ellie it was an emotional experience: the last time she had seen the National Gallery and St Martin-in-the-Fields lit up like this had been Christmas 1938.

'What's up, honey?' Brad saw a tear rolling down her cheek and tenderly wiped it away.

'Just seeing it again like this,' she said, letting him draw her into his arms. 'My mother always brought me here late on Christmas Eve to see the tree and the lights. It just reminded me of her. But she won't ever share it with me again, she was killed in an air raid.'

'I'm so sorry, honey,' he said, kissing her nose. 'That don't seem much to make up for losing your ma, but happy times are here to stay now, you're all grown up and beautiful and it's a wonderful night.'

Someone started a conga, then it was 'Knees up Mother Brown'. Even the police kept a low profile, only intervening when the merriment got to the point of endangering someone.

Ellie was aware Bonny and Steve were in a tight clinch, but then so were most of the other couples around them. When Brad kissed her she felt as if the searchlight scanning the night sky were right inside her head, and it was a delicious feeling.

The events that happened later were cloudy to Ellie. She remembered they went back to the pub and met airmen friends of Brad and Steve. She vaguely remembered there being an announcement that the bar had run out of drink, and that the one in her hand seemed very large. She and Bonny sang 'I'm Gonna Get Lit Up' at one point, but whether that was before or after the large drink she wasn't sure. Then suddenly they were on their way to a party.

Ellie had no idea where the jeep was taking them. She was crammed into a seat between Brad and Steve, Bonny on Steve's lap. Three other men sat in the front and another two were right in the back. They were all singing and laughing and although they saw hundreds of bonfires and even fire-engines racing by, she was too drunk and happy to give Charley more than a passing thought.

Instinct told her they were out in the suburbs as the jeep stopped. She had an impression of a tree-lined avenue, but all she saw clearly was a keyhole-shaped porch, light blazing out of the open front door, and the sounds of Glenn Miller.

Ellie's experiences of parties were limited to the ones in Alder Street and though the people here were far more sophisticated and smart, the atmosphere was similar. The men were mainly American, outnumbering the rather glamorous women by two to one. In the big room downstairs, several couples were attempting to jitterbug, the men swinging the girls round like rag dolls. People spilled out of the French windows into the garden, the hall, the stairs and the kitchen.

Ellie remembered going up to the bathroom to wash her face and comb her hair. The wash sobered her up enough to think she must ask Brad how they would get home, but once she got back to the kitchen and saw the food, she forgot everything but how hungry she was.

She hadn't seen anything like it, not even before the war. Plate after plate piled high with things she barely remembered: pork pies, legs of chicken, thick slices of ham, great wedges of cheese and sausage rolls. A huge cake decorated with both the Union Jack and the American flag, trifles, fruit flans and apple pies.

'Tuck in, girls.' A burly lieutenant shoved a glass of red stuff in their hands, informing them it was punch. 'We had some trouble getting the grub, and now no one wants to eat it.'

Bonny and Ellie didn't need urging. They loaded food on to their plates and sat down on the kitchen doorstep to wolf it down.

'Where's Brad and Steve?' Ellie asked Bonny after

they'd finished one plateful and began on another. 'We'd better ask how we're going to get home.'

'I don't care if I have to walk,' Bonny said, munching greedily on a chicken leg. 'All I want is to feel my belly burst with food.'

'Look at those two pigs!' A woman's voice some-where behind them halted them in mid-feast. 'Who dragged them here?'

Ellie's head shot round, just in time to see an elegantly dressed woman in red disappearing back into the sitting-room.

'Take no notice,' Bonny sniffed. 'We'll sort her out later. This drink's nice. I wonder what's in it?'

They had eaten their fill and were filling up their glasses with more punch when they heard someone playing the piano. A woman began to sing 'White Cliffs of Dover' and Bonny pulled a face at Ellie.

The singer's voice was out of tune and her breathing so laboured they could hear it in the kitchen. Bonny stuck her head through a hatch into the other room, looked around and pulled it out again.

'It's that cow in the red dress,' she said.

They ladled out some more of the punch and drank it while they listened. The woman was doing 'We'll Meet Again' now and they giggled helplessly.

'What's so funny, girls?' Brad and Steve had come back into the kitchen to look for them. Steve tenderly cleaned chicken grease from Bonny's face with a napkin.

'We're going to do a turn in a minute,' Bonny said. 'Ask the pianist to play "Yankee Doodle Dandy" and lend us your jackets and hats.'

The two men looked at one another and grinned. They were both a little disappointed that the party was waning and this looked like brightening it up again.

'Sure, babe.' Brad unbuttoned his jacket. 'Anything you say.'

Someone had closed the front door now, and the people who had been in the hall and on the stairs had moved elsewhere or gone home. The girls had a two-minute conflab, then pulled off their frocks and slipped on the jackets.

Ellie was too drunk too worry that the lace on her pink camiknickers showed beneath the jacket. She was in the mood for showing off.

Brad's voice boomed out from the other room. 'We've got a star turn for you tonight,' he said. 'Two little honeys direct from the West End stage. Bonny and Helena.'

At the opening bars Bonny jammed a cap on Ellie's head, put one on her own, picked up a walking stick from an umbrella stand and, holding it over her shoulder like a gun, marched into the room.

Ellie couldn't match Bonny's dancing, but she followed her steps gamely, the alcohol numbing any embarrassment. They marched round the room, the crowd shrinking back to the walls to make space.

'I'm a Yanky Doodle Dandy, Yanky Doodle Do or Die,' they sang. Ellie's voice filled the room with its power and they went into a similar routine to the one Ellie did in *The Quaker Girl*, improvising when it didn't quite fit.

They had the satisfaction of seeing the woman in the red dress slink into a corner, her face turning the same colour as her dress, and of knowing that every man in the room was looking at their long, shapely legs.

Bonny broke into one of her fast tap-dances. Even without the proper shoes she was as good as at dress rehearsal. Ellie strutted about singing, stopping here and there to chuck men under the chin and to give the woman in the red dress a smug grin.

The Yanks loved it – they clapped, whistled and cheered. Their women on the whole looked none too pleased, but that didn't bother either Bonny or Ellie.

'You two sure can dance,' Brad said in stunned appreciation when it was over and the girls were back in their own clothes. 'You know, I thought you were pulling our legs when you said you were dancers.'

It occurred to Ellie after her fourth or fifth glass of punch that there was more to it than fruit juice. She could barely move her feet as she shuffled around the floor with Brad and her eyes wouldn't open more than a crack. Bonny was sitting on Steve's lap in a corner and the crowd had thinned out to a mere four or five couples. 'Little Brown Jug' was playing softly on the gramophone, Brad was kissing her neck and she forgot about the rehearsal at noon the next day, Charley, even the show opening in the evening.

'Why don't you lie down on the couch?' she vaguely remembered Brad saying to her. 'I'm just going to the John, I'll be back in a minute.'

The room began to spin the moment she was horizontal, but she couldn't move. She wanted to know where Bonny was but the last thing she remembered was Brad asking her to move over so he could lie down too.

The cold woke her. Ellie's hand groped to find the blankets, but instead it only encountered a hard and prickly settee. Her mouth was so dry she couldn't swallow, her eyes seemed to be stuck together and there was an awful smell somewhere close.

She lay there for a moment, rubbing her eyes. Once they were accustomed to the gloom, she recognised the room she and Bonny had danced in the night before. The entire floor was strewn with empty glasses, beer bottles and cigarette ends.

A sudden realisation that she was naked made her jump up. As she put her feet down on the floor she felt the slime of vomit come up between her toes.

Revulsion ripped away her drowsiness. Stumbling towards the window, she pulled back the curtain.

She gulped hard as the early morning light revealed the mayhem from the party. This wasn't some crazy dream. She was alone in what looked like a war zone, her frock crumpled on the floor amongst the debris. She picked it up, holding it over herself, as an awful suspicion crept into her mind.

The frock was torn across the bodice. Her camiknickers were lying at the end of the settee in a pool of punch, staining them red.

It was so silent. Apart from birdsong from outside and the faint dripping of a distant tap, it sounded as if she was alone in the house. Worse still, there was a strange fishy smell coming from her and she was sticky between her legs.

Utter disgust washed over her as she saw a smear of blood on her thigh. She wanted to believe it was just her period, but as she hastily pulled her frock on she felt soreness too.

'No!' she cried out. 'No, I couldn't have!'

She couldn't remember anything more than Brad asking her to move over. Was that vomit hers? Had he really torn her clothes off, penetrated her, then left?

She sank down on to an armchair, covered her face with her hands and wept with shame. She was disgusted with herself at becoming so drunk she was insensible, and furious that Brad would take advantage of it. But far worse was the knowledge that she'd come to this party of her own free will, without any thought for Charley.

And where was Bonny?

She got up and tentatively peeped through the hatch above the settee. The kitchen was an even worse shambles, with plates of half-eaten food, glasses, bottles and empty boxes all stacked drunkenly on top of one another.

Charley would be coming home from work now; he might even go straight round to her room in Stacey Passage. How could she face him after this?

Creeping upstairs, she felt sick with fear. She had no money and she didn't know where she was. This was all so reminiscent of Marleen, coming home in the early morning unable to remember where she'd been or whom she'd seen and the same unpleasant smell clinging to her.

Someone had been sick on the bathroom floor and the sight of it made her retch. The first room she looked in was empty, although the bed was rumpled.

Who did the house belong to? Were they about to come home?

Bonny was in the big front bedroom. Alone, lying naked across the bed, her face turned into the pillow, her hair covering her shoulders, but her narrow back and small rounded buttocks revealing she was still little more than a child.

'Bonny!' Ellie shook her shoulder. 'Wake up, they've left us here.'

Bonny opened her eyes and then shut them. She groaned and covered her face.

'You must get up, Bonny.' Ellie blurted out what had happened. 'We must get out before someone catches us here.'

Bonny sat up gingerly. She looked at the empty space next to her, then back to Ellie, eyes suddenly wide with alarm. 'Where's Steve?'

'He's gone too, they've both gone.' Ellie began to cry again. 'I don't know how we're going to get home, or even where we are. But we must get out.'

Bonny's pretty face was flushed with sleep, her hair tangled, and she had an angry red bite mark on her right breast.

'Your dress is torn,' she said in a small voice. 'Did Brad do that?'

'I suppose so. But I don't remember anything,' Ellie whispered. 'I just woke up and I was naked. Did you see or hear anything?'

'Steve carried me up here.' Bonny's face began to crumple. 'He said he loved me.'

There was no time for any discussion. Bonny smelt as sour as Ellie did herself.

'We must get cleaned up and out of here,' she said in a strangled voice.

Bonny surprised Ellie. She got off the bed with some dignity and walked to the bathroom. She stepped over the vomit without even commenting on it and turned on the bath taps. 'It's cold,' she said, over her shoulder. 'But it will have to do.'

'Do you know whose house this is?' Ellie asked. Bonny had already stepped into the bath and was splashing water on herself.

'Steve said it belonged to some officer.'

Ellie guessed from the weak sunshine that it was about seven. She stepped into the other end of the bath and began washing too. The cold water was a shock to the system but it cleared her head a little.

'There's only that filthy towel,' Bonny said plaintively. She stepped out, clearing the vomit by inches, and disappeared.

She returned moments later with a clean towel wrapped round herself and handed another to Ellie. 'I'd better try and find something for you to wear,' she added.

Ellie had to admire Bonny. By the time Ellie got back, clean and dry, to the bedroom, Bonny had some underwear layed out on the bed and even managed a weak grin.

'Whoever lives here has good taste. Those are real silk and they're our size.'

The situation was too serious for them to question the morality of helping themselves to another woman's clothes. Ellie slipped into the pretty oyster-coloured French knickers and gratefully accepted the matching brassière. Bonny discarded her own and selected a pale blue set for herself.

The wardrobe revealed a whole host of clothes. Bonny rummaged through it, pulled out a peach-coloured costume with a peplum waist, thrust it at Ellie, and put on a pale green long-sleeved dress.

'Shame she's got such big feet,' Bonny snorted with disgust as she found a pair of green shoes, obviously designed to go with her dress. 'I've got a good mind to leave her a note to show my disapproval.'

Ellie couldn't laugh at the joke; she felt as if she'd never laugh about anything again.

'Go and see if there's any food left,' Bonny said, once Ellie was dressed. 'We might as well take it with us. I'll look around and see if I can find some money.' She took a beige hat down from the shelf in the wardrobe and put it on, then began to rummage again.

Ellie filled a small shopping bag with oddments of chicken legs, pork pies and a bottle of lemonade. She found a full packet of cigarettes and two half crowns in a kitchen drawer, then wrapping up her own clothes, she put them in on top of the food.

'I've found a ten-shilling note.' Bonny came down the stairs just as Ellie had finished. 'I think we're in Uxbridge, or nearby. That's more than enough to get us home.'

'What's in that?' Ellie pointed to a small leather suitcase.

'Just a few things to make us feel a little less used,' Bonny grinned. 'I'll show you when we've got away.'

As they slunk down the garden path, keeping their heads below the level of the privet hedge, the fresh suburban air felt like an instant tonic.

Cherry trees in full blossom almost hid the neat semi-detached houses. Bunting still hung between them and further down some trestle tables suggested there had been a street party yesterday. The clean scent of lilac and laburnum in the gardens heightened the sense of having stumbled into a middle-class ghetto where people peeped from behind lace curtains.

Bonny peered out over the gate, but no one was about. She signalled to Ellie, then the pair of them crept out, trying hard not to run and draw attention to themselves.

They waited until they'd got two blocks away before they stopped for a moment, sitting down on a low stone wall. Ellie handed Bonny a pork pie and the lemonade.

'Suppose the owner of that house calls the police?' she said.

'They won't come after us,' Bonny said with her mouth full. 'Brad and Steve are hardly likely to give our names, not after what they did to us.'

Ellie felt so very strange. Dressed in someone else's beautiful clothes, but feeling bruised and soiled inside. She wanted to know if Bonny felt the same, but she couldn't ask. 'What've you got in the case?' she asked instead.

'A smart outfit each. Another set of undies. A nice silver cigarette box and a diamond ring,' Bonny said casually, her face as angelic as if she'd just left church. 'We'll flog the ring and the box and keep the money for a rainy day.'

'I've never stolen anything before in my life,' Ellie said, a tear trickling down her cheek. 'And I've never –' She stopped, unable to say the words.

Bonny's arm slid round her and drew Ellie's head down to her shoulder. 'It's okay,' she said soothingly. 'We can't put the clock back now and it will serve those two jerks right if they get the blame for the nicked clothes.'

'I feel so dirty inside,' Ellie sobbed. 'Don't you?'

'I feel stupid, not dirty,' Bonny said forcefully. 'I was daft enough to think it was love last night. Steve said he'd take me back with him to the States.'

'I haven't even got that as an excuse,' Ellie

whispered brokenly, seeing Charley's face before her. 'I'm a slut.'

'You aren't.' Bonny held Ellie tightly, refusing even to consider what Jack would have thought of her behaviour. 'It was a moment or two's madness, nothing more, and we're going to forget it. The show opens tonight and we're going to be stars. Nobody else knows about this and we aren't going to tell them.'

'But Charley!' Ellie sobbed. 'I can't possibly marry him now.'

Bonny didn't quite understand that statement, but she was aware Ellie was far more devastated by what had happened than she was. 'Oh Ellie!' She mopped her friend's face ineffectually with her fingers. 'It wasn't your fault.'

Ellie gave a shuddering sigh. It was easy to blame Brad and make out she was a little innocent led astray, but she remembered kissing him, and that dance routine last night. She deserved what she got.

Bonny caught Ellie's distraught face between her two hands and kissed it.

'What's that for?' Ellie asked.

'Because I care,' Bonny whispered. Aunt Lydia had done exactly the same to her the day she'd driven Bonny up to London to start rehearsing at the Phoenix. It was after she was through with giving lectures about visiting her parents regularly and warning her about men 'taking advantage'. Bonny had found it very comforting.

'We'd better get going.' Ellie stood up wearily. 'As my mum always said, "The show must go on."'

'My mum always said I had to wear two pairs of knickers,' Bonny said pointedly, a feeble grin suggesting she wasn't quite as unconcerned as she pretended. 'I see what she meant now!'

Chapter Sixteen

Ambrose stood in the wings watching Ellie and Edward perform and though he knew the script word for word and thought he was beyond surprises he found himself laughing along with the audience.

Ellie, if he wasn't much mistaken, was another Gracie Fields in the making, but much prettier. Each wiggle, wink and ribald innuendo provoked roars of belly laughter from the audience. Edward was the perfect foil for her comic talent, entirely believable as the naïve jackass Charles De Witt. He hadn't fluffed his lines once, and they looked so good together, complementing each other in every way.

It was disappointing to see so many empty seats in the theatre, but that would change if they got good reviews in the morning. Besides, a great many people were still recovering from the victory celebrations.

A terrible dress rehearsal was traditionally a good omen, but Ambrose had been beside himself with rage earlier. It had been a shambles: lines forgotten, cues missed, dancers out of step, almost the entire cast listless and puffy-eyed with hangovers. When he'd looked in the girls' dressing-room an hour before curtain up, three of them were curled up on benches asleep.

Ellie had concerned him most. He had seen her rushing to the lavatories to vomit and when he'd questioned her she seemed distinctly guilty about something.

But now that the show was galloping along without

a hitch, Ambrose was appeased. Whatever Ellie's problem had been she was sparkling now. If she handled her song and dance number with as much vitality, his faith in her would be justified.

Ambrose peeped through the side of the curtain at the audience. Jameson was there in the front row with his wife, along with a group of other people Ambrose didn't know. The men were all in dinner-jackets, their wives in evening dresses and fur stoles. Clearly not one of them concerned themselves with clothing coupons; those weren't made-over dresses like his girls had to wear. There were times when Ambrose wished he'd never got involved with Jimbo Jameson. He was the slimiest, cockiest little runt that ever walked: just looking at the man now, his chest all puffed up with self-importance, made Ambrose want to hurl something at him. He had no doubt the creep would take all the glory if the show was a success, but that if the reviews were less than ecstatic, Ambrose would get the blame.

A barrage of wild applause and the curtain moving beside him made Ambrose aware that the sketch was over. Buster was ambling on to the stage from the left in front of the curtain as if he'd lost his way. Ambrose smiled. Buster was a real find, a genuinely funny man who could ad-lib his way through the Bible and make people laugh. He would be the next big name in comedy.

'Well done, both of you.' Ambrose turned to Ellie and Edward as they came off the stage, flushed with excitement. 'You were excellent. Are you feeling better now, Ellie?'

Ellie blushed. 'Fine, thank you,' she said, her eyes not meeting his. 'It was only nerves.'

'Well run along and get changed for the *Quaker Girl* number,' he said. 'Edward, give a hand with the props.'

Edward glared resentfully at Ambrose's retreating back view. One minute the man treated him like he was special, and the next ordered him about like a stage-hand.

There was no choice but to do as he was told, but the minute the bedroom furniture was cleared from the stage, Edward made his way backstage and shut himself in a storage room.

Sitting on a wicker hamper, surrounded by rails of old costumes, Edward lit up a cigarette. He was elated by the success of his performance tonight and desperately wanted to share it with someone, but it was easier to hide in here than risk a rebuff.

Voices from along the corridor heightened his sense of isolation. Giggling dancers, Riccardo warming up with a few scales, the dresser calling out to Ruth.

Opening night. The sketch with Ellie had been a huge success, but there was no one clamouring to praise his part in it. Why was he always left out?

Riccardo, Lorenzo and even Buster treated him like a simpleton, never including him in drinks at the pub or card games. The girls scared him. In groups they made suggestive remarks, alone they ignored him, and he was frequently acutely embarrassed by the way they flaunted their bodies. Bonny was the worst of all: she'd stripped down to her knickers in front of him earlier today. What had she meant when she said 'Get an eyeful of this then, Edward'? Was she trying to lure him, as she did every other man in the cast, or was it just as Ellie claimed – that she was merely playfully showing off her new underwear?

Women's soft bodies repelled him. Riccardo and the stage-hands all seemed to go out of their way to gawp at the girls. Was he unnatural in not getting excited by them?

Only Ellie was different. She kept provocative behaviour for the stage, never wiggling her breasts at him or giggling about him the way the other girls did. She was interested in him in an unthreatening, sisterly way – his only real friend.

Until a couple of days ago Ellie had always sought him out during breaks, and they often went for walks in St James's Park together. But now she seemed to have switched her allegiance to Bonny.

Aside from missing her company, he was concerned that Bonny would lead her into trouble. He'd gone to Stacey Passage three times yesterday in the hope that she'd be there, but she still hadn't got home at eleven. When he asked her where they'd been and whether she'd seen Charley, she'd nearly snapped his head off.

Edward was no stranger to feeling alone. Even before his parents were killed he was always left with a nursemaid while they were out at parties, the races or country house weekends. When he went to live with his grandmother, she was too old to understand he needed other children to play with.

Edward's acting had started out of solitude. Pretending to be someone else was a comforting form of escape, but with it came the danger of being unable to identify the real Edward Manning. Was he the stereotyped English gentleman, just like the parts he played? The other lodgers at his digs in Camden Town seemed to think so; he often heard them imitating him behind his back. Or was he, as Ambrose had hinted more than once, a nancy boy?

A bell jolted him out of his reverie. He stubbed out the cigarette and leapt to his feet. It was the *Quaker Girl* number and Ellie would be hopping mad if he didn't watch it.

Ellie and Edward linked hands as they took their turn to step forward from the rest of the cast and bow at the curtain call. They looked at one another and smiled with delight at the rapturous applause, which to their ears at least seemed louder than for Lorenzo or Riccardo.

'Bravo, Ellie,' someone yelled from the front row of the dress circle. Ellie glanced up at the familiar voice and to her astonishment saw it was Amos Gilbert. He was standing up, waving his arms in the most uncharacteristic display of exuberance.

The curtain calls seemed to go on for ever, but Ellie's eyes were on Mr Gilbert. She could make out that he had a female companion, also fluttering her hands, and though she couldn't see her face clearly, she was certain it was Miss Wilkins, her old teacher.

'Oh, Edward.' Ellie clutched his arm as the curtain closed for the last time, her voice a squeak of excitement. 'I can't really believe it. The man I was billeted with when I was an evacuee is out there. How can I get to speak to him?'

Edward felt warmed by her delight. Although there was no one out there for him tonight, the joy in her face was infectious. 'Tell Jim on the stage door to let him in,' he said, wishing he had the nerve to hug her. 'He's bound to come round there.'

As Ellie ran up the stairs to take off her make-up and change, her head was reeling with conflicting emotions. The first night had exceeded her expectations and it was absolutely wonderful to think Mr Gilbert had seen it. Yet, besides being puzzled about how he came to be here when she hadn't written for three years, his sudden appearance brought back a rush of painful memories. Could she really cope with a reunion tonight when she was exhausted and riddled with guilt and anxiety?

Bonny had shrugged off the events of last night. By the time they'd arrived back at Ellie's room at ten this morning she was her usual cocky self, thinking of nothing more than how she was going to get through the day with a hangover.

It wasn't so easy for Ellie. A curt little note from Charley was waiting for her on the mat. He said he'd called round several times on VE Day, and suggested rather sarcastically that if she was 'free' perhaps she could meet him at Lyons Corner House on Thursday at eleven. There was no good luck message for the show, although he knew full well it was opening tonight.

What was she going to say to him? Just the sharpness of the note suggested he knew she'd been out all night. What excuse could she possibly offer for not telephoning the fire station yesterday? Now, instead of going home to prepare herself for their meeting tomorrow, she had to slap on a brave face for Mr Gilbert.

The dressing-room was a further poignant reminder of the past. It looked exactly like the scenes Ellie remembered so well in the Empire: all the chorus girls talking at once, flinging down costumes, tossing head-dresses carelessly in one direction, shoes kicked in another, a hot pungent smell of sweat, greasepaint and cheap scent – all that was missing was Polly battling to bring order from chaos. Ellie made her way into the corner, slipped silently out of her *Quaker Girl* dress and pulled on her old skirt and jumper.

'You're very quiet,' Frances commented, her eyes shining like two lumps of jet, stage make-up streaked across her face from emotional tears. 'You were marvellous, Ellie, everyone's talking about you. Are you still feeling ill?'

'A bit,' Ellie lied. Everyone knew she'd been sick several times during the day and although she was over that now she was in no mood for chatter.

'Ambrose reckons we'll get rave reviews,' Sally shouted from the doorway, peeling off her glittering costume at the same time. 'We'll be playing to a packed house every night soon and Mr Jameson has invited us all down to his club to celebrate.'

The noise level grew even higher, with cries of disappointment from some of the girls that they hadn't thought to bring something smart to wear, shrieks of excited laughter and bursts of song.

'Are you coming, Ellie?' Bonny pushed her face through a rack of costumes. She had received two good-luck telegrams during the day, from her parents and from her Aunt Lydia. Jack had posted her a teddy bear wearing a tutu, and sent her a long, loving letter. All of them were planning to come and see the show in the next few days, yet Ellie thought she seemed remarkably indifferent to their loving support.

'I can't come,' Ellie replied. She didn't think she ever wanted another alcoholic drink again as long as she lived and even if Mr Gilbert only stayed to chat for a few minutes, she had no desire to spend another evening with Bonny for a while.

Bonny pouted. 'But you must. We've got to celebrate.'

Ellie explained briefly about Mr Gilbert, adding that she wasn't feeling well enough to meet up later and urging Bonny to go with the other girls.

Bonny's peeved expression seemed to say that she didn't like Ellie having other friends.

'Come with me, Bonny,' Frances piped up impulsively, sensing a prickly atmosphere. She thought Bonny had become marginally nicer since she'd palled up with Ellie, and was generous enough to want everyone to have a good time tonight.

Ellie stopped short on the stairs down to the stage door, stunned for a moment. Mr Gilbert was waiting by Jim the doorman's desk and he really was accompanied by Miss Wilkins. She had never expected to see either of them again; she had tucked her memories of them both away, along with all the other people connected with her childhood, and drawn a curtain over them. But now, as she looked into their beaming, upturned faces, everything they had once meant to her came flooding back.

They looked so different. In her memory Mr Gilbert was a giant of a man, with rolled-up sleeves, smelling of wood shavings. Miss Wilkins had always had tightly drawn back hair, a hand-knitted cardigan and a lace-trimmed blouse. These two people looked so much smaller and very city-fied.

'So it *was* you,' Ellie said weakly. Mr Gilbert was only an inch or two taller than herself, wearing a grey suit with a fancy waistcoat beneath. Miss Wilkins had a Marcel perm and a brown velvet evening coat with a corsage of rosebuds pinned to it. They were both greyer, with more lines on their faces, yet in some strange way they looked younger.

'Oh, Ellie.' Miss Wilkins moved first, stepping forward and taking both her hands. 'It's been such a thrill. All the time I was watching you I could hardly believe you were the same girl I taught six years ago.'

A lump came up in Ellie's throat; she could hear emotion crackling in Miss Wilkins's voice, and sensed that her old teacher was reminded vividly of their last day together.

'Did you like the show?' Ellie didn't want memories of that dreadful day and night to overshadow this reunion. She didn't know whether she should kiss them, hug them, or shake hands and she was staggered that an undertaker and a schoolmistress from the depths of the country could suddenly metamorphose into two such sophisticated city people.

'Like it?' Mr Gilbert chuckled. 'We loved it. Especially you. We just couldn't get over how good you were.'

'But how did you know I was in this show?' Ellie asked, her feelings veering between delight, suspicion and confusion.

'We didn't, not until today.' Miss Wilkins looked at Amos and then back to Ellie, brown eyes warm with pride and pleasure. 'We were just walking down Charing Cross Road this afternoon and we saw your name on the poster outside. We were intending to go and see a play at the Criterion. But of course we changed our plans that very moment.'

*

Pleasure took the place of confusion as Ellie sat between them at a table in a little Soho restaurant. It was so strange to hear their soft Suffolk accents after a diet of harsh London ones, but somehow also very warming to see these two people through adult eyes and to find the good things she remembered about them still very much in place: Miss Wilkins's empathy and warmth; Mr Gilbert's quiet strength. They had believed in her when she was just another cockney kid, encouraged her and taught her so much. Their presence here tonight proved Ellie had been special to them too. That knowledge was truly comforting. But better still was to see the couple were more than mere friends now: the looks they exchanged, the way they touched each other's hands as they chatted, all spoke of love and romance.

'We're going to be married.' Mr Gilbert blushed and smiled, looking almost boyish. 'How about that?'

'I'm *so* happy for you.' Ellie smiled at them both, warmed right down to her toes. 'I can't think of two people better suited. I wish you'd been married when I came to Bury St Edmunds!'

'You were the reason we got to know each other again,' Miss Wilkins said and there was a softness in her eyes which suggested she fully understood what Ellie meant. 'We'd been friends as children, but after Grace went away I often called round to see Amos and one thing led to another.'

'You started the change in my life, Ellie.' Mr Gilbert's grey eyes had so much more fire and life in them now, and there was no longer any similarity to his sister. 'Dora accomplished the rest. I gave up the funeral business, sold the whole premises and bought a small cottage with a couple of outhouses. Now I'm a carpenter.'

'You should see the work he does,' Miss Wilkins said proudly. 'He's made an exquisite table for Mrs Dunwoody and he's got so many further orders. Right now he's working on a round supper table for us, but we hope you'll come down for the wedding and see it all for yourself.'

Ellie just listened. She wanted to ask about Miss Gilbert but couldn't bring herself to. Perhaps Miss Wilkins understood: she gently stated that Grace had died eighteen months earlier following a stroke, and then quickly moved on to happier subjects.

She spoke of neighbours in High Baxter Street and children Ellie had been at school with. She described the cottage Amos had bought so vividly that Ellie could picture it: sun streaming in through tiny windows, lovingly made furniture, colour and warmth, the sort of home two such selfless people deserved.

'But enough of us.' Miss Wilkins was suddenly reminded that Ellie hadn't volunteered any information about how she'd lived before this show. 'Now the last letter you wrote to Amos, you were working in a restaurant. How did you get this part? And how is your Aunt Marleen?'

Ellie hesitated, she didn't want to spoil the evening by relating sad news, but there was no alternative.

'I'm so very sorry,' Amos said gruffly when she'd finished telling them, putting his big hand over Ellie's. 'We only met once, under difficult circumstances, but I know how much she meant to you. It explains too why I didn't get replies to the letters I sent to Gray's Mansions. You poor Londoners had such a terrible war.'

Ellie moved on to explain how she sang at the Blue Moon, came to meet Ambrose and then got her big chance.

'The show's going to run and run.' Miss Wilkins had passion and belief in her voice. 'You have a great talent, Ellie, and I'm proud to think I helped it along.'

'I'm thrilled for you.' Mr Gilbert smiled. 'Dora and I have talked about you so often. We always thought you'd make it one day. We just didn't expect it so soon.'

*

It was after twelve when Ellie waved goodbye to them as they went off in a taxi to their hotel in Bloomsbury, but the bubble of happiness they'd spun temporarily around her burst the moment she opened the door of her room.

The stolen clothes were lying on her bed, along with her torn green dress, and all at once she felt cheap, soiled and unworthy of the admiration Amos and Dora had shown her.

She swept the clothes to the floor angrily and burst into tears. It ought to have been the happiest night of her life, when all her sad memories were washed away by new beginnings, but instead she felt only shame and degradation.

Lyons Corner House was quiet, with no more than ten people on the ground floor and the assistants chatting behind the self-service counter. Charley was sitting at a table by the window, looking out towards Trafalgar Square, so deeply immersed in thought he didn't even glance round as she came in through the door.

His shoulders were hunched, elbows on the table, a couple of newspapers before him, and judging by the cigarette smoke wreathed round him, he'd been there some time.

'Hello Charley.' Ellie managed little more than a whisper as she tapped his shoulder. 'Am I late?'

He jumped up and although he attempted a smile it didn't warm his eyes. 'I got here early,' he said, but even that sounded like a reproach. 'I was reading the reviews, they're good ones. I'll get some tea. Would you like a cake?'

'Just tea,' she said and sat down.

He hesitated for a moment, looking down at her, but then turned and walked away to the counter.

Ellie's stomach felt like someone was wringing it internally. She had been awake since six this morning, going over and over in her mind what she was going to say, but now she'd seen him it was all different. Her life was worth nothing without Charley. She didn't even care enough to open the newspapers and read the reviews.

As she watched him shuffling sideways along the counter putting cups on the tray and then reaching for the pot of tea, she had a sudden, clear vision. She was standing on a dock, a stretch of grey choppy water between her and a huge liner. Charley was standing at the rail of the liner and as it slowly pulled away from the dock, his features slowly became indistinct.

'Will you marry me?'

Ellie started. She'd been so immersed in her vision she hadn't noticed he'd come back to the table. His proposal shocked her back into reality. 'That's a bit sudden,' she said, thrown now, her prepared speech forgotten.

He said nothing, just placed the cups on the table, the milk jug and the teapot, then sat down. Ellie didn't dare look at him. She picked up the milk and poured some into the cups.

'Where were you on VE night?' he asked and she was forced to meet his eyes. They were cold and suspicious, just the way they'd been the night she went out with Jimbo. 'I went to your room half a dozen times and you didn't come back.'

'I went to a party with some of the girls.' She shrugged her shoulders, hoping that would be enough of an explanation.

'Why didn't you phone the fire station, or even Mum's house?' he asked.

'I thought you'd be too busy to speak to me.'

'You didn't even think of me,' he spat at her suddenly. 'That's what really hurts, Ellie. You were out having fun and I never even crossed your mind. It isn't your career that's the problem. It's because *you* just don't care enough.'

'I wish that was true,' she whispered, tears welling

up in her eyes. 'I do care, Charley, far more than you'll ever know.'

'Do you know what happened to us firemen that night?' His voice rose, his face contorted with anger. 'People shouted abuse at us because we put out fires they'd started. A woman actually spat on me and said we were killjoys. Back in the Blitz they said we were heroes. People's memories are short, aren't they? And yours is shorter than anyone's.'

'It's not, Charley,' she pleaded with him, wishing she could find something to take away the hurt in his eyes. 'I haven't forgotten anything, not how you dug out Marleen, or the way you came to the hospital and took me home. Or any of the good times back in Coburgh Street.'

'That's not love, that's merely gratitude,' he said bitterly. 'I'm not good enough for you, am I?'

Ellie thought she'd worked out all his counter arguments in advance, but this was one thing that hadn't even crossed her mind. Now, with so much guilt inside her, it was unbearable. '*I'm* not good enough for you,' she said brokenly. 'I couldn't make you happy.'

'You wouldn't have to *make* me happy. I'd be happy just to have you by my side. Marry me and come to Australia. If you can't do that then there's nothing more to say to one another.'

Ellie closed her eyes. It was so tempting to agree: that tight, suspicious expression would vanish from his face, he would sweep her back to Coburgh Street, she would be welcomed by Annie, everything would be wonderful again and all the preparations for the wedding and immigration would banish her guilt.

She opened her eyes again. He was looking at her with challenge in his eyes, daring her to stall.

An honest, open face, a man who would never lie to her. How could she even consider accepting his proposal without first telling him the truth about her?

'I can't, Charley,' she began. 'I –' she stopped suddenly.

'Go on,' he prompted. 'Why can't you?'

The truth was there on the tip of her tongue, but all at once she knew it would wound him too badly. She must let him keep his pride intact. It was bad enough to let him believe she was turning him down for a life on the stage. But it was kinder than admitting she'd been with another man.

'Because I can't give up my career,' she said in a low voice, fighting against breaking down. 'I don't want to go to Australia.'

He stood up, gripping the edge of the table until his knuckles turned white. 'Well that's it then,' he said, and she saw tears well up in his eyes. 'I'd like to wish you luck, but I can't. I'll just say goodbye.'

Ellie watched him rush out of the door, forcing herself to stay in her seat and not run after him. The show meant nothing now. She would give anything to turn the clock back forty-eight hours and instead of going out with Bonny, be making her way over to Coburgh Street to spend the day with Annie until Charley came home.

Marleen was wrong. Men weren't ten a penny, not like Charley. She would never love anyone like she loved him, and he'd gone for good now, believing she preferred bright lights to him.

'I don't understand,' Bonny said again. She had come round to Stacey Passage to call for Ellie and found her lying on her bed sobbing her heart out. It had taken some time to get the entire story, and although she'd heard it clearly enough, Bonny was baffled about Ellie's reasoning.

'Because I couldn't do anything else,' Ellie sobbed.

Since Bonny had joined Ambrose's dancing troupe, she had pushed Jack into the background. She met him when she needed love and affection, stalled him when there were more exciting things happening. She believed she loved him, no other man excited her so much, but she never felt any guilt about picking him up and dropping him as the mood took her. He would be in the army for some time yet; she would consider him more seriously once he was demobbed.

Until today she had assumed Ellie was the same way about Charley. She hadn't quite grasped that Ellie had a different conception of love, and a very different moral code to her own.

Now, seeing Ellie so terribly upset, Bonny felt a surge of unexpected tenderness. She put her arms round her, cradling her, and this instinctive reaction brought home how important Ellie was becoming to her.

'Don't cry any more,' she murmured, smoothing back Ellie's hair the way she remembered her mother doing. 'Maybe it's for the best. He'll back out of going to Australia, you'll see. He'll come back saying he wants you on any terms.'

'He won't,' Ellie sobbed. 'He's got too much pride. I can't bear the pain, Bonny. I wish I could die.'

Bonny lay back in the steaming bath. Her skin was fiery red, forehead dripping with sweat and the bottle of gin was empty beside her.

'Ger'anover kettle,' she said drunkenly, her mouth slack and her eyes almost closed.

'No more, Bonny,' Ellie pleaded with her. 'This is stupid.'

On VE Day, when they'd compared their identical shapes in the ancient mirror, the bathroom hadn't seemed quite so grim. But the events of that day had tainted everything, like the black smuts flying from out of the old geyser. The window was cloudy with grime, the lavatory caked with brown limescale. It wasn't a place anyone would choose to linger in.

'Jus' do it,' Bonny insisted.

Ellie hesitated before opening the door. She was

afraid to leave her friend in case she passed out and drowned in the deep, almost boiling water, yet at the same time she felt compelled to go along with this barbaric attempt to bring on a miscarriage.

In the days that followed VE night, Ellie had been too distraught about Charley even to think that there might be other repercussions. While she had cried herself to sleep night after night, too tormented by guilt and shame to take an interest in reviews or packed houses, she hadn't even considered that one of them might be pregnant.

When Bonny complained her period was late, Ellie thought it was another one of her tall tales, a ruse to gain sympathy. But when she saw for herself that Bonny's breasts were getting larger and saw how queasy she was in the mornings, she had to take it seriously.

It was now the end of June and Ellie had agreed to help her with the gin and hot bath treatment.

She boiled another kettle upstairs. It was a Sunday afternoon and London was in the grip of a heatwave. Although the window in her room was open wide, there wasn't enough of a breeze to flutter the curtains, or dispel the lingering cooking smells on the staircase.

The sound of violent retching alerted Ellie. She turned off the gas and ran down the stairs, barging back into the bathroom. As she opened the bathroom door she recoiled in horror. Bonny had vomited over the side of the bath, projecting it up the walls and over a clean towel on the floor, and the smell was appalling. Worse still, Bonny was lifeless, only one arm over the side of the bath preventing her from sinking under the water.

Ellie stepped over the mess and pulled out the plug. Grabbing a flannel, she doused it in cold water and wiped her friend's face.

Bonny's eyes opened a crack. 'Tolsho,' she said, her mouth slack and senseless.

Ellie assumed this meant it was working. 'Get up,'

she said, trying to lift her friend under her arms. 'I'll get you into bed.'

Hauling a wet and slippery body from the bath was an endurance test. Time and again Ellie almost got Bonny out, but then lost her grip. By the time she managed to get Bonny hoisted over her shoulder, Ellie's cotton dress was soaked and she'd slipped on the vomit. All the time she was afraid one of the other tenants would come up the stairs and catch her hauling what looked like a dead body up to her room.

Bonny had been in Ellie's bed for less than ten minutes when she was sick again, this time all over the sheets and blankets. Her skin was still fiery red, she was unconscious, and her breathing laboured.

Day slipped into evening, with Bonny waking up now and then to retch into a bowl, before passing out again. Ellie ran up and down stairs, cleaning the bathroom, washing the sheets and bringing bowls of water to sponge Bonny down. The smell of vomit and gin permeated the entire house, but that was nothing compared to her terror that Bonny might have done herself a permanent injury. Her face was green now. When she opened her eyes they were glazed and there was nothing inside her to bring up but bile.

'Speak to me, Bonny,' Ellie urged her, sitting beside her on the bed and stroking back her hair.

'I'll never drink gin again,' Bonny croaked. 'I think I'm going to die.'

By the time it grew dark Bonny was sleeping more peacefully. Ellie had hung the sheets and blankets out of the window to dry and she was exhausted. Only now was she grateful for the heat. There were no more clean sheets and Bonny lay on a towel, covered with a dressing-gown. Ellie rolled-up a cardigan for a pillow, lay on the floor and pulled her coat over her.

'Ellie!'

Ellie woke instantly at the plaintive cry. Enough

weak dawn light was coming in through the window for her to see Bonny was crying.

'I feel terrible,' Bonny whispered. 'I'm so thirsty and hot.'

Ellie got Bonny a drink of water and sat her up.

'It hasn't worked,' Bonny said weakly. 'I haven't even got a tummy ache. What am I going to do now?'

'We'll think of something.' Ellie wiped her brow with a wet flannel. This scenario reminded her of similar ones with Marleen, but Bonny's problem couldn't be solved by telling her to pull herself together. 'Maybe you could ask your parents to help?'

Bonny didn't snap back at her as she'd expected; instead she gave a long, drawn-out sigh. 'I've told you so many lies about them,' she whispered. 'I don't know why I do it, it's so stupid.'

Ellie sat up on the bed and pulled Bonny into her arms, letting her tell her everything. From just one brief meeting with Mr and Mrs Phillips, Ellie had seen enough to guess much of the truth about them, but she let Bonny explain anyway.

Slowly the whole picture presented itself, of a child who felt smothered by her parents' adoration and who, once she'd got a taste of freedom in Sussex, had rejected them entirely.

'I got to hate everything they stood for,' Bonny said in a small voice. 'I love them, but I don't like them. Do you know what I mean?'

'Sort of,' Ellie said, remembering that she'd felt that way about Marleen many times before she was injured.

'While I was at home, Mum made me feel so bad. She kept going on about how all she had in the world was me, how she wanted me back living with them. She can't just be happy that I'm happy, like other mothers. She wants to think for me, wash me, dress me, devour me. To her I'm like a doll. She can't understand I've got my own mind, or that I've got dreams and ambitions of my own. Dad's not so bad. I think he understands, but Mum's impossible. My old bedroom is like a bloody shrine. She's got all my old toys arranged on shelves, my baby clothes are all still in the drawers. It makes me feel trapped, like a pinned butterfly.'

Ellie privately thought it would be comforting to know she had a room like that to go to whenever she felt like it, but she didn't say so.

'They would help me,' Bonny said simply when she'd finished her story. 'But I can't let them. You see I'd be compelled to be what they want. The poor baby would be me all over again; they'd smother it with love and I'd have no say in anything, no life of my own. I'd lose Jack and Aunt Lydia would be so disappointed. I'm going to get an abortion somehow. I can't have a baby, not this Yank's, if it was Jack's it might be different.'

Later Bonny went back to sleep and Ellie lay beside her thinking over everything she had revealed about herself. She wasn't as insensitive as she made out, or as callous. Ellie had a strong feeling that before all this was over both of them were going to be tried and tested.

She turned towards Bonny and looked at her carefully. Despite what she'd been through she still looked so beautiful. Long eyelashes like brushes on her pale cheeks, her mouth soft and childlike in sleep.

She knew she couldn't dissuade Bonny from going through with an abortion; she had an iron will and a lack of fear. But Ellie was afraid. There but for fate it might have been her faced with an unwanted pregnancy.

Now she'd lost Charley, Ellie felt empty and alone. She seemed to be swirling around in a kind of whirlpool, being sucked this way and that by a current she couldn't control. She was scared she wouldn't be able to regain her grip over her own life, terrified she might not achieve success on the stage. But most of all she was scared for Bonny.

Chapter Seventeen

July 1945

Ellie put her head round the door of the men's dressing-room. Lorenzo and Riccardo had left, but Edward was bent over the wash-basin, wearing just a pair of trousers, taking off his stage make-up.

It was July. London was in the grip of a heatwave, and there had only been a very small audience for today's matinée.

'Have you seen Bonny anywhere?' Ellie asked.

Edward groped for a towel. 'She was rushing off as I came up here,' he said, mopping his face. 'That was ages ago.'

'What, *out*?' Ellie looked puzzled. 'She didn't say anything to me. She usually comes back to my place after the matinée.'

'She *was* in a hurry,' Edward said with a smile. 'She hadn't even brushed her hair or cleaned her face properly.'

Ellie shrugged. 'Thanks anyway. Maybe she went shopping, but we usually have tea together on Saturdays.'

'Come and have tea with me?' Edward said quickly. 'It's absolutely ages since we had a chat. It won't take me a jiffy to get dressed.'

'That would be nice.' Ellie smiled, pleased by the invitation. He was right – it was ages since they had a chat. Edward was good company, serene and calming, unlike Bonny, who often made her feel fraught and tense. 'If you're sure you've got nothing better to do?'

'What could be better than tea with you?' Edward said gallantly, picking up a clean white shirt. 'Five minutes and I'll be ready!'

It seemed as if half the population of London had converged on Trafalgar Square as Edward led Ellie down towards Whitehall. Men in uniform perched on walls with their sweethearts, and children were splashing in the fountain, many wearing only their underwear. Younger men in open-necked shirts eyed up groups of giggling shop girls and typists in bright summer frocks, while whole families sat in groups, surrounded by shopping bags, perhaps reluctant to take the train home because of the hot sunshine.

'We can't go in there!' Ellie hesitated as Edward caught her elbow, about to take her up the stairs into the Westminster, just across the road from Big Ben. 'It's too expensive.'

The mahogany doors were open wide and a thick red carpet ran up the middle of its marble stairs. It was the sort of place that cabinet ministers frequented.

'This is my grandmother's favourite place for tea.' Edward smiled at her awed expression. 'And as she's just sent me my allowance, what better place to blow some of it?'

Ellie didn't think her pink cotton frock and bare legs were appropriate for such a place, but Edward looked smart in his white shirt and grey flannels and she supposed he knew best. Besides, she was very hungry.

'That was delicious.' Ellie sat back in the comfortable, velvet-covered chair, sighing with contentment. 'I'll never be able to dance tonight.'

The last time she'd had a tea even remotely resembling this one was before the war in the Copper Kettle out near Epping Forest with Marleen: dainty, crust-less sandwiches, scones with real strawberry jam and wonderful cream cakes on a two-tier silver stand. But the Copper Kettle was little more than an old lady's parlour, with rickety tables and everyone jammed in so tightly you had to mind your elbows. This place was really posh.

Ellie thought about what it would be like to have enough money to come to places like the Westminster all the time. She was impressed by the snowy, thick table-cloths, huge starched napkins, the silver teapots and the vases of pink roses on the window sills – but most of all, by the other customers. All the women wore hats and smart afternoon dresses. There were a few dashing-looking naval officers gazing attentively at their wives as if just home on leave, and all the other men wore stiff collars and dark suits. Edward had been greeted warmly by the head waiter, who'd asked after his grandmother's health. When they were given a good table by the window, Ellie realised she must be even more wealthy and influential than Edward had implied.

'Tell me about your grandmother,' she said. 'Is she very old?'

'Seventy-something and getting a bit frail now.' Edward smiled with affection. 'But she's still very sharp-witted and elegant for an old lady. My grand-father was a barrister. Until he died they had an apart-ment in St James's, they used to come here all the time.'

'Was your father a barrister too?'

'No, he broke the mould, he was a concert pianist, and even though he was very talented and well-known, Grandfather apparently always described him as a "milksop".'

Ellie giggled. The word 'milksop' conjured up a picture of a rather languorous man in a velvet smoking-jacket, blond hair parted in the middle, and a pasty face. 'Did you like him?' she asked.

'I scarcely knew him.' Edward frowned. 'He was away a great deal, and even when he was home, he had little to do with me. The only clear memory I have is of him lying on a couch while I was doing my piano practice, constantly stopping me and making me start all over again. It was a wonder I ever got to like the piano.'

'I didn't know you could play! Are you any good?'

Edward chuckled. 'My grandmother believes I'm as good as Father. I'm not. But I love playing. It's very soothing.'

'So your grandmother dotes on you, then?' Ellie wished he'd be a little more forthcoming; he wasn't very good at creating pictures of his life before she met him, or of his family. So far all she could be certain of was that he'd been a very lonely child.

'I suppose she does,' Edward said thoughtfully. 'Though she isn't one for showing affection demonstratively. Giving me an allowance is her way of saying she loves me, but really I'd prefer it if she forgot the money and came to see me act. I'd rather have her approval.'

'What's her home like?' Ellie wanted to know much more about this elegant, frail woman.

'A rambling, early Victorian place, not far from Chippenham in Wiltshire.' His eyes brightened. 'The garden is glorious – huge trees, wonderful roses – it goes down to a river. It was requisitioned as a convalescent home during the war, which she protested violently about at first, but in the end she not only accepted it, but rather liked having wounded officers sitting around in Bath chairs. "Doing her bit", she called it. She used to read to the men, and watched the nurses constantly for what she called "over-familiar behaviour".'

Ellie smiled. 'And now what does she do? Has she got the house back to herself?'

'Yes, she has, though it needs a great deal of work

doing to it. But you must come with me one day to visit her, she'd like you, Ellie.'

Ellie poured them both another cup of tea and they discussed Edward's awful digs in Camden Town. He was certain his landlady went through his belongings while he was out.

'What is wrong with Bonny?' he suddenly asked. 'She hasn't been quite the ticket for some time. Neither have you, for that matter.'

Ellie gulped hard. She was not only surprised by this abrupt change in the conversation, but by him being so observant. His cool blue eyes were looking right into hers, daring her to lie.

'There's nothing the matter with me,' she said quickly. 'Aside from getting very tired. Bonny's just had some trouble with her parents, she hasn't quite got over it.'

Lying had become a habit lately, something she didn't like one bit, but Edward was very thick with Ambrose and if he got even a whiff of Bonny's predicament, she'd be out on her ear.

Bonny was ten weeks pregnant now and it had knocked the stuffing out of her. Some days even the sight of food made her sick; other days she ate like a pig. Although she still managed to sparkle on stage, backstage she was quiet and morose, given to bursting into tears at the slightest provocation. The problem might ultimately be Bonny's, but that didn't stop Ellie feeling it was hers too.

Edward poured another cup of tea for them both. 'I thought we were chums.' His lower lip curled petulantly, and his eyes said he knew there was more. 'Can't you share your worries with me?'

Ellie felt a little ashamed. Bonny had taken over her life, leaving very little time for anyone else, and there were many times when she regretted ever having got involved with her. Edward's friendship was easy, comfortable and undemanding and she knew she was guilty of leaving him out in the cold since palling up with Bonny.

'I haven't felt myself since Charley and I split up,' she said, blushing because although this was true it wasn't the whole story. 'I know I turned him down because I didn't think I was ready for marriage, but I feel as if he's taken part of me away with him. Can you understand that?'

Edward nodded. 'I think so, though I've never felt that way about anyone yet. But you aren't helping yourself, Ellie, not hanging around with Bonny all the time. I get scared she'll lead you into trouble.'

Ellie laughed lightly, unable to think of any sensible counter-argument. How could she truly explain how she felt about Charley? All those nights of crying, the dull ache inside her, the knowledge she'd smashed something up that was irreplaceable. She wasn't likely to get into any trouble with Bonny: she'd learnt her lesson the hard way.

'Have you heard about the woman who keeps asking for Lorenzo at the stage door?' She changed the subject deftly. 'The girls think she's his wife. For a magician who can make anything disappear, he's not having much luck with her.'

'Nobody tells me anything,' Edward said pointedly. 'Especially you, Ellie, not these days.'

Ellie winced, aware now how she'd hurt him without meaning to. As they'd sat down at their table she'd overheard a woman say what an attractive pair they were. This was probably very true – Edward's Germanic looks, his height and golden skin complemented her more sultry appearance – but it was the word 'pair' which had struck her as appropriate. They were a pair, linked not only by their stage act, but with fundamental similarities. Both orphaned and basically loners, he had only an aged grandmother, she had only Marleen, and the theatre was the mainstay of their lives.

'I'm sorry if it seems that way.' Ellie put her hand over his. 'I do like you very much, Edward. I suppose I feel a bit bruised by men at the moment. Haven't you ever felt that way about girls?'

Whenever Edward looked at Ellie he was touched by her beauty. Her dark, soulful eyes, her plump fleshy lips. Sometimes he felt he wanted to trace those fine, high cheekbones, tilt up her little pointed chin and kiss her perfect nose. But it was something within her which moved him more, her deep understanding of people, her humour and strength. He needed Ellie: she was the only person he trusted, the only one who seemed to accept him just as he was.

'You're the only girl I really like,' he said, dropping his eyes from hers. 'I've never trusted anyone else.'

Ellie sensed there was something more he wanted to say. It hung between them like an invisible veil. 'It takes time to build up trust,' she said softly. 'You have to be bold, ask someone out and get to know them first. I'm sure half the girls in the chorus would like to get to know you better.'

This was entirely true. All the girls thought he was handsome, and they were intrigued by his rather mysterious manner.

Edward took a deep breath. 'Do you know what they say about me?'

Ellie had heard all the whispers, the innuendoes, but she had never given them any more real thought than she did about whether Lorenzo had run out on his wife, or whether Riccardo really did have a mistress tucked away in Knightsbridge.

Edward's eyes caught hers and she saw his pain.

'Is there any truth in it?' she asked gently, squeezing his hand tightly. 'It doesn't make any difference to me, Edward. I like you just the way you are.'

'I don't know if it's true.' His voice dropped to a mere whisper. 'Queer! That's what they call me. A pansy, a nancy boy. But I don't know if I am, Ellie. I wish I did.'

'Oh, Edward.' A lump came up in her throat: she felt moved at his courage in admitting such a thing. 'I don't know about these things. I've had one boyfriend and I don't want another. How can I judge?'

'That's why I'm telling you, because you don't judge,' he said weakly. 'But how am I supposed to find out? I don't feel any urge to have a woman, but then I don't feel that way towards men either.'

'Maybe it's just because you haven't met the right person,' she said comfortingly. 'I never felt anything until I met Charley and I didn't think I was strange. Perhaps for some of us there is only one person in the entire world.'

'Maybe.' Edward felt easier now, as if a burden had been lifted from his shoulders. 'Well, can we be chums until these special people show up?'

'And after,' Ellie laughed. 'For ever, I hope, and don't worry about me and Bonny either. She won't lead me into any trouble. I'm quite capable of finding my own way into it.'

Ellie was leaning out of her window, hanging some washing on the line, when she heard someone coming up the stairs. She'd got back from her tea with Edward just half an hour ago. Her door was wide open to catch a little breeze and dispel the nasty smells that always lingered in Stacey Passage.

'Is that you, Alice?' she called, assuming from the heavy footsteps it was the barmaid from the Blue Moon who lived downstairs. 'Fancy of a cup of tea? I'm off to work soon, but it's ages since I last saw you.'

'It's not Alice, it's me.'

Ellie ducked back in the window at the sound of Bonny's voice. 'Where've you been? I expected you to have tea with me,' she said as she flopped back on her bed.

But she cut her questions short as Bonny came through the door. Her face was white and she was clutching her stomach.

'What on earth's the matter?' Ellie leaped off her bed and reached Bonny in one step. 'Are you ill?'

'I've done it.' Bonny slumped back against the door-post, grimacing as if in pain.

'Done what?'

All at once Ellie knew. The heavy step on the stairs, the hands on the stomach. Bonny's mouth was hanging slackly, she had beads of perspiration on her nose and her eyes were blank.

'You've had an abortion?'

Bonny lurched forward, groping for the bed, doubled up with pain.

Ellie realised this was no time for recriminations, especially as Bonny had insisted for weeks she was going to get one somehow. But it was a terrible shock to find that she'd been out alone to get it done without giving Ellie any warning.

'You'd better get into bed.' Ellie's head reeled; she had no idea what abortion entailed, much less what she should do now. 'Let me help you get your dress off.'

Bonny just sat there, allowing Ellie to undress her to her petticoat. The only effort she made was to kick off her shoes before slumping back on the pillow.

'Bonny, I don't know what this means.' Ellie knelt down by the bed and stroked back her friend's hair. 'Has it gone? What did they do? Where did you go?'

For a moment, Bonny just lay there, staring at the ceiling as if in shock, then slowly she turned her head towards Ellie. 'I had it done in Soho,' she said in a hoarse voice. 'That new girl in the Blue Moon gave me the address. I didn't tell you because I thought you'd try and stop me. But I thought it would be a proper doctor and I'd get to stay there until it was over. He did it then chucked me out. I had nowhere else to go but here, I'm sorry.'

Ellie put her hand gently on Bonny's stomach. 'What do you mean he did it?' she whispered. 'How?'

Bonny's face contorted and a tear squeezed out through her closed eyes. 'He just pushed a sharp thing inside me. It hurt so much I thought I'd never get back here.'

The image of that dirty kitchen was stuck in Bonny's mind. Being held down on a table by a fat, greasy-haired woman with foul breath, while that man prodded at her. She had stupidly thought she'd be in a bed, with some semblance of medical care, but instead the fat woman had just handed her a pad and told her to go home and wait for the baby to come away.

'Oh, Bonny.' Ellie felt sick. 'You mean it's still there? How long will it be before it comes away?'

Bonny felt the warmth of Ellie's hand on her stomach and the comfort made her stronger. 'Not for ages yet,' she said, forcing a faint smile. 'If I could just stay here? You go to work and tell Ambrose I've got a bilious attack. I'll be okay.'

She knew she was bleeding now, but she wasn't going to tell Ellie that and make her worry. With luck it might all be over before Ellie got home again.

'I can't leave you like this!' Ellie's voice wobbled.

It had dawned on Bonny in the past few weeks that she was vulnerable, just like other people. Perhaps it was because of this tiny life inside her, but she'd begun to care about what people thought or said about her. More than that, she'd begun to think about others' feelings, about Jack and Aunt Lydia and even her parents. But mostly she had thought about Ellie, because she saw qualities in her that she wanted for herself. Not her acting or singing ability, that wasn't important, but that caring nature, her generosity and warmth. Right now she felt very guilty that she was imposing on their friendship.

'If you don't go, Ambrose will send someone round,' she said, matter-of-factly. 'Look, I'm fine really. I was just upset at first because I thought I was staying at the place in Soho and had to walk home. I've got some aspirin and pads in my bag. They said it wouldn't be any worse than a bad period.'

Ellie didn't feel right about leaving Bonny, but she could see no alternative. She made her a cup of tea, propped her up with a couple of pillows and a book, and left a bucket by the bed, just in case Bonny couldn't manage to walk downstairs to the lavatory.

'Stop worrying,' Bonny ordered her as Ellie fussed around before departing. 'I'm fine. With my luck it won't even work.'

Ellie looked down at Bonny. She was still chalky pale, but she didn't seem to be in much pain. With her hair loose over her bare shoulders she looked little different to the way she looked on any night when she stayed here.

'Go,' Bonny grinned up at her. 'You're like a bloody mother hen. And mind you don't tell anyone or I'll never speak to you again.'

Ambrose was furious at Bonny not turning up.

'I don't believe she's sick,' he yelled at Ellie. 'She was fine during the matinée. I bet she's got some hot date.'

Ellie felt sickened by his lack of sympathy. She respected Ambrose as a director, but despised his callous attitude to his troupe. She wondered who he thought he was, with his polka-dotted cravat and flower in his buttonhole. In the light of what Edward had told her earlier, she wondered whether Ambrose was responsible for putting those dark thoughts into his head too.

'If you don't believe me, go round to my place,' she snapped at him. 'You might be just in time to empty her sick bucket. Do you think she'd let you down on a Saturday night just for a date? I thought I ought to stay home too and look after her, but I came in because I know you haven't got anyone to take my place.'

'Don't you take that attitude with me, my girl,' he retorted, a flush of anger staining his pale face. 'I can find a replacement for you easily enough.'

Ellie gave the first bad performance ever that night. Several times she forgot her lines and Edward had to prompt her, and she stumbled in the *Quaker Girl* number, almost knocking Sally over. She didn't wait to hear Ambrose's post-mortem after the show, but ran off home still wearing her costume.

The staircase was in darkness as usual. Every now and then the landlord put in new bulbs, but someone always took them. Ellie was just groping her way up the last flight of stairs when she heard a deep groan from her room.

As she switched on the light Bonny lifted her head slightly. She was hunched on one side, clearly in great pain. 'I thought you'd never get here,' she bleated out. 'It's been so bad.'

The room was unbearably hot, with a strange smell Ellie didn't immediately recognise. Bonny's face looked haggard, her eyes swollen, cheeks sunken, and when Ellie touched her forehead she found she was burning up.

'I've lost a lot of –' Bonny gasped out, the last word lost as she writhed in pain.

Ellie stripped back the sheet from her friend, recoiling in horror when she saw the red-stained sheet and petticoat.

'Bonny I'll have to call an ambulance,' she croaked, panic welling up inside her.

'No, Ellie.' Bonny caught hold of her hand fiercely. 'The police will be called and then my parents. I'll be all right soon, I promise you.'

Ellie stripped off her *Quaker Girl* costume and hung it on the back of the door while she thought. It was certainly a criminal offence to give someone an abortion, although she didn't know if you could be charged for having one. But Bonny was right – her parents would be contacted and they'd be devastated.

But what if Bonny died?

Ellie tried to gather herself and look at things logically. The first thing was to make Bonny more comfortable and check just how much blood she was losing. She didn't think another ten minutes or so would hurt either way; after all Bonny was conscious and able to talk.

'I'll wash and change you.' She knelt down beside Bonny and smoothed her brow. 'But if you pass out, or you start to lose too much blood, I'll have to call the ambulance. Do you understand me?'

Bonny nodded, her eyes mere frightened slits.

Ellie filled the bucket with warm water. Then she stripped Bonny, carefully washed her all over, and put a clean pad back. Rolling her over on to one side, Ellie placed newspaper beneath the sheet, folding it in half with the stains inside. The mattress was already disgustingly stained from previous occupants, but Ellie was more concerned with protecting Bonny from its germs than worrying about adding to them.

'That's better now,' she said with more assurance than she felt, and covered her with the top sheet. 'I'll just empty this water and I'll be right back.'

Ellie felt each and every pain as if it were inside her, but all she could do was sit beside Bonny, rub her back, sponge her brow and pray that God would give her some sign if she should get medical help. Bonny was very brave, and didn't cry out during the contractions, although her back arched itself alarmingly away from the mattress and she clung to Ellie's arms until she bruised them. It seemed that they were immersed in this agony for hours, yet each time Ellie looked at the clock only ten minutes or so had passed. She heard other tenants coming in, the banging of doors, the flush of the lavatory. The traffic slowly died to a distant hum, and the sounds of drunks in the street below gradually faded.

'I feel sick,' Bonny whispered, struggling to sit up. It was nearly three in the morning now and Ellie was exhausted by the heat and anxiety. She moved to sit behind her friend, letting her lean back against her chest as she held the bucket, instinctively knowing that a climax was coming and that she couldn't run for help now and leave her.

They were locked together – Ellie supporting and trying to comfort, Bonny retching, and with each spasm the contractions were growing stronger still, bringing spurts of more blood and tissue.

Ellie felt the moment the foetus came away. Bonny's head lolled back lifelessly on to Ellie's shoulder and she was suddenly still.

Wriggling out from behind her friend, and laying her back on the pillow, Ellie hastily covered the mess before Bonny could see it. Tears sprang to her eyes with the knowledge that the tiny embryo could have grown into a child as perfectly formed as its mother, and she hated herself for being a conspirator in its destruction.

At dawn Ellie lost the battle of staying awake. She was sitting on the end of the bed, resting her arms on the window sill, when her head drooped down to them. She had washed Bonny, again changed the bed and put all the soiled linen to soak, but even though she was exhausted and Bonny was sound asleep, she had felt compelled to stay awake and watch over her.

She had been reflecting on the complexities of love and sex. As a child it all seemed so simple. You met a man, fell in love and had babies. But now she saw that she hadn't once been privy to such a state of bliss. Her own mother had brought her child up alone. Marleen, always the mistress, never the bride, had turned to drink to ease the pain. Charley was out there somewhere, filled with bitter thoughts because he'd been cheated. Even his mother had settled for security rather than love. Poor Edward was confused by his sexuality; Ambrose disliked women yet chose to work with them. Night after night at the Blue Moon she'd seen servicemen cheating on their wives, and lonely wives finding comfort with soldiers.

Tonight she'd flushed away the result of celebrations on Victory Day. There were probably countless more all over England passing into the sewers, as well as many babies to be born next January who would never know their fathers, any more than she did.

Bonny woke later and saw Ellie hunched on the window sill. The sight of her friend's bare, slender shoulders and her tousled black hair brought stinging tears to her eyes.

'Ellie, come into bed with me?' she whispered.

Ellie started, turning immediately. 'Are you in pain?'

Bonny saw the deep concern in her friend's eyes and felt humbled. 'No pain,' she said weakly. 'I'm going to be all right. Come into bed with me, you can't stay there.'

Ellie climbed in gratefully; she was chilled and stiff.

For a moment Bonny said nothing. The horror of the night was already fading from her mind, but she would never forget it was Ellie who had pulled her through it. 'Thank you,' she whispered, nestling closer and putting an arm round her friend. 'I love you.'

Ellie looked at Bonny on the pillow next to her and drew comfort not only from those sincere words, but from Nature's ability to heal so fast. Bonny was still pale, but the anguish lines in her face had faded, and her hair against the pillow was as bright as it had been yesterday.

'I love you too,' Ellie said with a deep sigh. 'But don't you ever dare do anything like that again, or you and I are finished.'

'Don't lecture me.'

Ellie smiled. She was glad to see the old spoilt brat was back. 'Go back to sleep,' she said. 'Thank God for Sunday.'

'Now Edward. You *do* know what Ellie and Bonny are up to, and I expect you to tell me,' Ambrose said forcefully.

'They aren't up to anything,' Edward insisted. 'Bonny's had a bad bilious attack, they think it might be food poisoning. When I went round there yesterday Bonny was in bed and she looked half dead. I can't imagine why you don't believe Ellie, or me.'

Edward felt compelled to go along with Ellie's story out of loyalty, but he didn't believe it either. It was true Bonny was in bed, and that she looked pale enough to be recovering from food poisoning. But Edward had weighed up all the clues; Bonny's disappearance on Saturday, Ellie's anxiety that night, the number of sheets and towels hanging on the line outside the window and the subdued state that Bonny had been in for weeks before. Everyone knew Bonny was man-mad. It all added up to an abortion.

'Those two have been in cahoots for weeks,' Ambrose said, his round, shiny face flushed with suspicion. 'They've got something up their sleeve.'

Edward was never quite sure how he felt towards Ambrose. Sometimes he liked him better than anyone else, sometimes he loathed him. One moment he was a bully, yet at other times he was kind and generous. He was grateful to the man because he'd given him his big chance, but didn't like being indebted to him. He admired Ambrose's artistry and knowledge, yet

393

secretly despised the man's pretentiousness. It was confusing, and he hadn't even worked out whether Ambrose really liked him either.

'Have they been for an audition somewhere else?' Ambrose pushed his face up to Edward's and his breath smelt of violet cachous.

Edward wanted to laugh. Ambrose was so transparent sometimes. He huffed and he puffed, but at the end of the day he was just plain scared of losing his grip on people.

It had been a mistake on Edward's part to agree to come to Ambrose's for a 'nightcap'. He couldn't think why he'd agreed; he might have known the man just wanted to pump him for information.

'Why would they audition for another show?' Edward sat down on the arm of a chair. 'They're in the best one in town now. Besides, Ellie was her old self tonight. She was only worried about Bonny on Saturday.'

'Pour us a gin and tonic,' Ambrose said with a dismissive wave of his hand. 'I can smell fish a mile off and if you won't tell me anything I'll find another source.'

Edward wiped his forehead as he poured the drinks. A storm was coming, and it had grown hotter and more muggy all day. He wished he hadn't come here.

Ambrose's flat, or his *pied-à-terre*, as he liked to call it, was on the first floor of a large house in Bloomsbury. It was owned and furnished by a couple living out in India and it reflected their taste and status rather than Ambrose's. Edward had felt at home here the first time he'd seen it, as it had the kind of faded grandeur of his grandmother's house: old Persian rugs, heavy carved furniture handed down through generations, artefacts from all over the world, a baby grand piano, magnificent marble fireplaces. Ambrose, who had a penchant for thirties styling, complained constantly about this place. Edward, whose digs were so grim he could hardly bear to go back there at night, felt the man was a philistine and ought to be truly grateful.

'Sit by me.' Ambrose patted the couch next to him as Edward handed him his drink. 'I want to talk seriously to you and we rarely get an opportunity without flapping ears close by.'

Edward glanced towards the windows somewhat nervously as lightning flashed, and even though he was expecting the clap of thunder which followed it, still he jumped.

'I'd better close the windows,' Ambrose said, getting up and crossing the large room as a gust of wind blew in. 'You must stay here tonight, Edward. I suspect we're in for a heavy storm.'

The windows were only just shut when the rain started, within seconds hammering against the glass with tremendous force. Ambrose pulled the heavy brocade curtains and switched on another side light.

'That's cosier,' he said, sitting down again. 'Now let's get back to you and Ellie. The reason I wanted to know about her is because I have plans for you both.'

To Edward's surprise, Ambrose began to speak about films, saying he had parts for both of them lined up for next year.

'But the show?' Edward asked, gulping down his drink, trying to ignore the storm outside and his nervousness at being expected to stay the night.

Ambrose shrugged. 'It will be finished by Christmas. The theatre-going public are growing tired of revues, they want straight comedy, or drama. But anyway, Edward, the film world is where the money is. Who wants to tramp the boards night after night when a couple of months' filming will bring in as much money as a year in theatre?'

'What sort of film?' Ambrose had hinted more than

once that Edward's looks were perfect for the big screen, but he'd only ever played starchy English gentlemen. He wondered if Ambrose was making it up.

'A comedy, of course.' Ambrose smiled coldly. 'You'll be fine, my lad, I'll make another Ronald Coleman out of you.'

There was something about the words 'I'll make' that worried Edward: they made him sound like a puppet. 'What about your dancers?' he asked. 'Are you getting them in too?'

'Some of the best ones, maybe.' Ambrose looked thoughtful. Edward knew how hard he had trained them, and his plans for being another Ziegfeld. 'There are several who can act. Frances and Sally, to name a couple.'

Edward couldn't help but be cheered by this. Bonny couldn't act to save her life; this might break up the friendship between her and Ellie.

By the time Edward was on his fourth gin and Ambrose was recounting some of his times in America, he was feeling mellow. Even the storm outside had ceased to concern him.

'Why don't you play for me?' Ambrose suggested. 'And don't tell me you can't. I heard you playing one morning in the Phoenix.'

'I'm a bit rusty,' Edward grinned. He was always glad to get an opportunity to play; his grandmother had a beautiful Steinway and he missed it more than anything.

Ironically the score for *Good-night Vienna*, one of his grandmother's favourite musicals, was sitting on the piano, and as Edward began to play it hauntingly, the way she liked it, he imagined her standing behind him, singing along.

The storm outside was forgotten as good memories came back with the music. His grandmother was old and frail now and her once-strong voice wavered, but Edward transported himself back to when he was fifteen or sixteen, and felt again the warm feeling of truly belonging which he only ever had with his grandmother.

He played all her old favourites: 'Barbara Allen', 'North Country Boy', 'Greensleeves'. When he felt a hand on his shoulder he forgot it was Ambrose and began to sing.

'You're a lad of many talents,' Ambrose said as Edward paused after 'Greensleeves'. 'I didn't know you could sing too.'

'I'm not good enough for the public,' Edward smiled. 'And like the playing, the singing's a bit rusty. What would you like me to play now?'

Edward was aware of Ambrose's hand still on his shoulder, his thumb stroking his neck, but it seemed merely an affectionate gesture and he didn't shrug it off.

'No more playing now,' Ambrose said. 'It's late and it might disturb my neighbours. It's time for bed.'

One moment Ambrose was just standing there, looking down at Edward on the piano stool, the next he was bending down to him, kissing first his cheek, his neck and finally his mouth.

It was only as Ambrose's tongue snaked its way into Edward's mouth that he struggled to get free, suddenly realising what this was.

'No.' He pushed him away in alarm. 'Don't do that!'

'Don't be ridiculous and girlish,' Ambrose said, grabbing him tightly to his chest so Edward could barely breathe. 'You know this is what you really want.'

'It isn't.' Edward pushed harder, struggling to his feet. 'Let me go.'

He managed to get free and made a bolt for the door, but Ambrose beat him to it, barring the way. 'Edward, calm down,' he said, his cold blue eyes glinting too brightly. 'It has to happen one day – why not me who cares for you?'

'I'm not like that.' Edward's voice shook. 'I'm not.'

He felt just the way he did when waiting in the wings ready to go on stage, sheer terror clutching at his innards, wanting to turn and run away, yet knowing he couldn't. The same small voice which told him to walk on to the stage was speaking now, telling him this was inevitable, that once he began, the nervousness would fade.

'Deny it to everyone, but not to yourself,' Ambrose said, catching hold of Edward's jacket and spinning him round until their places were reversed and Edward was pinned against the door with Ambrose kissing him again.

This time there was no tongue, just gentleness. The body against his was warm and hard, and it didn't repel him.

'You see.' Ambrose drew back, smiling. 'I don't want to hurt you. I love you, can't you see that?'

Another crack of thunder from outside made Edward start.

'You're safe with me,' Ambrose said very quietly. 'Listen to me. I know what you are because I was lost and alone like you once. I have all you need to make you happy, Edward, just trust me. After tonight you'll understand all those things which puzzled you. Remember, I love you.'

No one had ever said they loved Edward, not even his grandmother. It felt like being tossed a lifebelt in a sea of confusion. The storm outside, the gin and the piano playing had mixed things up in his head. Was Ambrose right? Did he really know what Edward was?

Pansy Manning can't run, can't play rugger. He's queer, the dirty bugger. That cruel rhyme had been thrown at him daily in school, yet he'd never once allowed any of the older boys to touch him as they'd wanted. Was it worth trying to run from it as he had back then? And who would he run to?

'Come with me Edward.' Ambrose took his hand and led him towards his bedroom. 'I care deeply for you. Why do you think I gave you the part with Ellie? I've been so patient with you, we've been good friends. Now we're going to be lovers.'

Edward waited until Ambrose was fast asleep, then sliding out from the arm draped over him, he slowly moved to the side of the bed. He hurt all over, but especially inside.

His clothes were strewn at the end of the bed, where Ambrose had thrown them as he peeled them off. The room was pitch dark, with the curtains tightly closed, so he had to grope for them on his hands and knees.

Five minutes later he was down in the street. It was still raining hard. He turned up the collar of his jacket and began to walk, rain mingling with the tears rolling down his cheeks. He didn't know what direction he was going in, but he hoped it was towards the river.

Chapter Eighteen

'Are you sure about this?' Ellie looked doubtfully at Bonny. She was sitting on the bed, her face still pale and drawn. 'I'm sure I can talk Ambrose into letting you have another couple of days off.'

'I've been in bed for two days.' Bonny shrugged her shoulders nonchalantly and reached for her shoes. 'I feel okay, I must do some practice.'

'You might be able to walk about,' Ellie argued. 'But high kicks? After what you've been through?'

It was Tuesday morning. Bonny had announced her intention of getting back to work late the previous night. Although on the face of it she was none the worse for her ordeal, Ellie was afraid that attempting to dance might set her right back.

'Look! If I feel bad at the theatre at least Ambrose will know I haven't been malingering,' Bonny said firmly. 'I might even ask if I can go to my mum's for a few days if he's sympathetic. I can't stay here any longer anyway. You can't sleep properly with me in that little bed.'

Ellie sighed. In fact she felt as if she hadn't slept for a week. Her room, let alone the bed, wasn't big enough for two people. 'I wish you'd go to a doctor first,' she said. 'Let him check you over.'

'Don't be ridiculous,' Bonny snapped. 'What am I going to say? "Excuse me but I had an abortion at the weekend. Please peer up inside me and check I'm still in one piece?" You are stupid sometimes, Ellie!'

'Will you just talk to Brenda then?' Ellie pleaded.

Her old friend at the Blue Moon had one child and she'd had a miscarriage. She was in a position to know what was normal and what wasn't.

'I'm not talking to anyone.' Bonny tossed back her hair defiantly. 'As far as I'm concerned the whole thing is over. I don't even want you to mention it again.'

'Please yourself then,' Ellie snapped back, putting on her raincoat. 'Don't come crying to me if you have a haemorrhage!'

The girls walked in silence to the theatre, both irritated with one another. Bonny knew Ellie meant well, but last night alone in the room she'd almost been climbing the walls with boredom. She was sure the only way to feel her old self again was by getting back to work.

'How are you feeling?' Frances greeted Bonny as they went in the stage door. She was already in her practice clothes, her curly dark hair tied up in two bunches.

'Weak, but game,' Bonny smirked. 'I feel like someone let out of a cage; my legs are as stiff as planks. Where's Ambrose? I suppose I'd better speak to him first.'

'He's in a foul mood.' Frances looked over her shoulder apprehensively, checking he wasn't within earshot. 'God only knows what's happened. I've never seen him quite as bad as this.'

'He won't send you off to your mum's for recuperation then,' Ellie said drily, looking pointedly at Bonny. 'He'll probably work you till you drop.'

Bonny flounced off up the few stairs towards the stage without replying.

'She looks a bit thin and pasty,' Frances remarked as she and Ellie went up to the changing-room. 'Perhaps that's what I need to lose a bit of weight. Ambrose had a go at me this morning and said I had an arse like a tank.'

Ellie looked at Frances's bottom as she went up the stairs behind her. She wasn't quite as slender as the rest of the girls, but she certainly wasn't fat. Clearly

Ambrose was going to pull out all the stops today to make everyone miserable.

Her expectations were fulfilled. Even as the girls began limbering up, Ambrose started to shout, and before long it was clear this exercise session was going to be a nightmare. Usually he sat out front, merely directing the movements, but today he was purposely selecting the most rigorous routines, making them repeat them again and again and hurling abuse at anyone faltering for even a second.

Although Ellie was having difficulty herself in keeping up, her fears were all for Bonny. Ambrose was picking on her relentlessly, clearly punishing her for daring to have time off.

Bonny was struggling; she was bathed in sweat, her movements laboured and stiff. Time and again she paused to wipe her brow, several times she stumbled and already she looked exhausted.

'Again,' Ambrose yelled at her. 'You're like a blasted cart-horse. When I say plié I don't mean just a slight bending of the knees, I expect you to go *all* the way down. Now do it again properly.'

None of the girls had ever seen Ambrose quite as nasty as he was today. It was as if he hated them all and wanted to make them really suffer. He hadn't shaved, his shirt was crumpled, and for once his gaudy cravat wasn't in evidence. But it was the way he moved that was frightening, pacing around in the stalls like a demented caged bear. All the girls were scared. Every muscle in his body was tense and his mouth was a thin, tight line.

'Bend, touch the floor and stretch,' he yelled. 'Get those legs straight, Bonny Phillips, or you'll be out of here. Again! And again!'

Ellie had always found these exercises hard, but then she wasn't a trained dancer like the others. Now, as she saw Bonny wavering, her face scarlet with exertion, she realised how truly punishing they could be. If she didn't step in, any moment now Bonny really would haemorrhage and then everyone would know she hadn't had food poisoning.

'Stop, Bonny.' Ellie moved over to her friend, who was bent in half. 'That's enough.'

'I'm okay,' Bonny said feebly, but Ellie noticed there was a tell-tale red stain on her tights.

'You aren't. Go,' she said, pointing off-stage.

'Are you suddenly the director?' Ambrose stalked up to the stage, his head just above the footlights. 'No one stops practice until I tell them.'

'Bonny's ill,' Ellie said defiantly. 'Another minute or two and she'll keel over. She shouldn't have come back today. She isn't strong enough.'

A deadly hush fell behind her as all the girls halted their exercises, not even a whisper between them. Bonny wavered indecisively at Ellie's side.

'Who the hell do you think you are?' Ambrose roared, his pale eyes glinting dangerously. 'Who made you Bonny's mouthpiece?'

'She's not well enough to speak for herself,' Ellie retorted. 'Just look at her, will you? She should be in bed.'

Ellie pushed Bonny towards the wings. 'You must go,' she whispered. 'You're bleeding and he'll see it.'

'What did you say?' Ambrose yelled, leaping up on to the stage with unusual ease.

Ellie quaked. Ambrose's face was puce, angry dark veins standing out on his forehead. 'I said it's madness to stay.'

With that Bonny disappeared, clearly deciding discretion was the better part of valour.

'Get her back this minute.' Ambrose strode towards Ellie and struck her hard across the cheek.

'How dare you?' Ellie's hand flew up to her stinging face, anger giving her new courage. 'You animal!'

They stood face to face, glowering at one another.

'You have no right to tell one of my dancers to leave,' he snarled.

'If you were a real human being you'd see she wasn't well enough to dance,' Ellie snarled back. 'Apologise this instant or I go too!'

Ellie sensed every one of the dancers stiffening as they waited to see the outcome of this piece of bravado.

'Apologise!' Ambrose sneered. 'Get back in your place immediately or you'll find yourself out of a job.'

Ellie took a step back from Ambrose and turned to the other girls. 'He has no right to treat any of us like this,' she said, her voice shaking. 'Will you back me up?'

There was understanding in every pair of eyes, but fear too. To her dismay she read their body language, the nervous shuffling from foot to foot, eyes dropping from hers.

'I have to walk out,' Ellie pleaded, her eyes travelling down the two rows of girls. 'Come with me? It could be one of you he turns on next!'

'You don't think they'd support you?' Ambrose jeered. 'They know when they're fortunate.'

Ellie took a deep breath and began to walk off, silently praying for the others to follow. Her footsteps rang out in the silent, empty theatre. She didn't think she'd ever heard such a lonely, desolate sound.

'You see, you can't bank on their loyalty!' Ambrose crowed with delight from behind her. 'Come on back and don't be so damned silly.'

Ellie didn't dare hesitate. She was shaking with anger, hurt by the others' lack of support, and she was too proud to back down.

'I can find dozens of girls to take your place,' she heard Ambrose roar. 'Walk out now and you'll never work in a theatre again.'

A heavy shower cut Ellie's walk short and she turned back towards Stacey Passage.

Bonny had lost a great deal of blood earlier, but

she'd finally fallen asleep around four in the afternoon. Ellie had come out to get some fresh air and some time alone to think. She felt as if she was being manipulated by unseen hands and she was desperately afraid.

Since becoming friends with Bonny, everything seemed to have gone wrong. She'd lost Charley, her tiny room had been taken over, and now, unless she went back and grovelled to Ambrose, she'd lost her career too. She understood why the girls hadn't supported her – after all, they'd worked long and hard to get to the West End – but she felt bitter that not one of them had popped around after practice to apologise.

'Damn you, Bonny,' she muttered as she made her way through the narrow alley towards home. 'Why couldn't you have listened to me and stayed in bed today?'

Now they were both snookered. It was inconceivable that Ambrose would take Bonny back. She had no money, and Ellie herself had less than two pounds to her name, and the rent was due on Saturday.

As she walked up Stacey Passage, utterly demoralised, she saw Edward. He was leaning on her door, writing a note.

Until that moment she hadn't given him a thought; she'd been much too preoccupied with her own problems. But now, seeing him, she was reminded that unless Ambrose found a replacement for her quickly, he'd be out of a job too.

Her heart sank even further. He was bound to be angry that she'd walked out over Bonny. His warning about their friendship had been almost prophetic.

'If that's a note to order me back, you're wasting your time,' she called out angrily.

Edward wheeled round. 'Why aren't you at the theatre?' he asked.

This surprising question, and his appearance, threw Ellie. He hadn't shaved, his wet hair was plastered to his head and his eyes seemed strangely dead.

'Because I walked out, of course,' she said. 'Didn't Ambrose send you?'

'No,' he said. 'I was just leaving you a note to say I'm going home to my grandmother's.'

'I'm sorry I messed things up for you,' she said.

Edward frowned, looking down at his note, then back at her. 'I said much the same in my note.' He passed it to her. 'We seem to be at cross purposes.'

Ellie read it, puzzled.

Dear Ellie,
    I'm sorry I've left you in the lurch. I hope you won't hate me for it. Maybe one day I can explain, but not now. Think of me sometimes.
        Your friend Edward.

Ellie put her hand on his arm, aware that something had happened today aside from her problems. But as she touched his jacket she found it was wet through.

'You're soaked,' she said. 'Look, we must talk. I'd like to ask you up to my room, but Bonny's there. Can we go to a pub?'

'I can't go to a pub.' Edward's voice faltered and Ellie looked at him in surprise. His lips were quivering. She wasn't sure whether he was cold, or on the point of bursting into tears.

'Well we can't talk out here in the rain,' she said evenly, opening the front door, assuming he meant he was too upset to talk in public. 'Look, Edward, just wait down here in the passage. I'll run up and see if Bonny's okay first. Don't go away, will you?'

He nodded, stepping into the hall, and leaned wearily against the wall.

Ellie was less than two minutes. As she got back downstairs Edward was sitting hunched on the bottom step in the gloom.

'She's okay, reading a book,' she sighed, sitting

down beside him. 'You can come up if you like, she's quite decent. Let me dry your jacket?'

'No.' Edward shook his head. 'I couldn't face Bonny. I didn't expect to see you either. Tell me what happened?'

Ellie told the story as simply as possible.

'I had to walk out. I had no choice, he struck me, Edward.'

Edward sighed deeply, leaning his elbows on his knees, his head in his hands. 'It was my fault he was angry today,' he blurted out. 'We had a row and I left. I didn't think he'd take it out on you girls though. I'm so sorry, Ellie.'

'What was the row about?' she asked.

He didn't reply, just covered his face with his hands. 'Tell me, Edward?' Ellie put her arm round his shoulder, trying to draw him closer to her.

'I can't. I've got to go, the train is at eight,' he said, his voice muffled by his hands. 'I'll write in a day or two when I can think straight.'

'Try and explain now,' Ellie wheedled, guessing this was something serious. 'Don't leave me worried about you too. I've got enough on my plate with no job and Bonny ill.'

He put his hands down and sat up straight. 'She had an abortion, didn't she?'

Ellie couldn't see his face clearly in the gloom, just the proud line of his nose and the curl of his lips, but once again she was struck by his keen perception. 'Yes. Do you understand why I couldn't tell you?'

'You thought I'd tell Ambrose.' His voice was hoarse. 'I wouldn't have, not any more than you'd tell people what you know about me.'

That last line was like a shaft of light penetrating the gloom. 'Was your row with Ambrose something to do with that?' she whispered.

He nodded.

Ellie knew then that it wasn't just a row which had

caused Edward's present state, it was something far more dramatic. His manner had striking similarities to the way she'd been after VE night.

'He did something you didn't like?' she whispered, putting her arm around him and drawing him towards her shoulder. 'Was that it?'

Edward turned his face into her neck, clinging to her like a small boy, and told her just the bare bones of what had happened.

Ellie knew nothing of homosexuality, it wasn't something she'd encountered before. Any disgust she felt was directed at Ambrose, not Edward. He had preyed on Edward's vulnerability, in just the same way that American had plied her with drink. The two men had destroyed both Edward's and Ellie's trust and innocence for ever.

'I understand just how you feel,' she said, stroking his cheek tenderly, wishing she could find the right words to show him she too knew about degradation and shame. 'I did something once which made me feel the way you do. But it does fade, Edward, I promise you.'

'I hate myself,' he whispered. 'I can't bear being a freak. I almost threw myself in the river early this morning, but I hadn't even got the guts to do that.'

He wished he could pour it all out. How at first when Ambrose had caressed him he'd felt absolute joy, wild unashamed passion. All the conflicting emotions which had made him so confused before seemed to disappear; it felt pure and natural. Ambrose was so tender and loving, whispering endearments, promising him so much. But it all changed into something dark and bestial when Ambrose penetrated him. Pleasure turned to pain so intense he screamed out in agony, clawing at the sheets, struggling to get free. Ambrose slapped him hard to shut him up, all trace of tenderness gone, biting his shoulders, pressing down on his neck until Edward thought it would break under the pressure, and grunting like a rutting boar.

It seemed like hours before Ambrose released him, shoving him aside contemptuously without the least concern for his pain.

When Edward had stood by the river early this morning, it wasn't so much death he'd wanted, as the desire to rid his mind of those terrible images. Ellie's unjudgemental attitude comforted him a little. Few people would be so liberal.

'Nothing and no one is worth killing yourself for,' Ellie said, holding him tightly. 'You aren't a freak, Edward, and Ambrose is a cruel and twisted man to prey on you.'

Edward let himself be comforted by her arms. He knew in days to come he would probably regret his confession, but for now she was easing the torment inside him.

'I must go now,' he said eventually, knowing that staying would only encourage him to spill out more. 'I'm so ashamed, Ellie, but I guess I'll get over it in time.'

'You will,' Ellie said soothingly. 'You're just over-wrought and confused right now; a hot bath and a good night's sleep will put you right.'

'Bonny's lucky having a friend like you to lean on,' he said, standing up and smoothing down his trousers. 'Say goodbye to her for me. I hope she feels better soon.'

Ellie stood up and impulsively hugged him tightly.

'All three of us are in a mess,' she murmured into his damp neck. 'All the more reason why we should keep in touch.'

Edward took her arms and drew back from her. As he looked into her dark, compassionate eyes he realised he hadn't comforted her for the loss of her job, or even praised her for defending her friend. Nor had he found it necessary to ask her not to divulge any of this to anyone.

'You're my only friend,' he said simply. 'I'll write

in a day or two. Maybe then I'll be able to tell you exactly what you mean to me, Ellie.'

Ellie smiled wanly. 'You're my friend too and I won't forget you. Maybe all three of us can get in another show together.'

Edward kissed her cheek, unable to find the words he wanted to say. 'We had some good times, didn't we?'

'We will again too.' Ellie smoothed his cheek. 'Don't dwell on the bad parts, Edward, just the good bits.'

'I think I'll go down to Aunt Lydia's,' Bonny said two days later. 'Can you lend me some money?'

'I can't.' Ellie tried to quell her mounting irritation with Bonny. It seemed that their predicament hadn't sunk into her head yet. 'I've only got the rent, that's all. Surely you've got some money. You got a taxi to get your clothes yesterday!'

'That was the last of it,' Bonny said airily. 'Can't you go down and ask Ambrose for our back pay?'

Ellie rolled her eyes in exasperation. 'Do you really expect me to do that after everything that's happened?' she snapped. 'You're impossible sometimes. Look at this place! I can't move for all your stuff. I've got to go out and find a job. I can't afford to send you off for a holiday in Sussex. Why can't you just visit your parents?'

Bonny had two suitcases full of clothes. They filled the narrow strip between bed and wall, lids open, the contents strewn where she'd rummaged through them.

'Because Mum will pry, as you well know,' Bonny said sulkily. 'Besides, Aunt Lydia might know of another job for us and I can see Jack if he gets some leave.'

Ellie could say nothing more. Bonny picked people up and dropped them when it suited her. Now it was Jack's turn again, and she hoped he'd have the sense to hold her at arm's length.

'I know, I'll pawn that ring I found at Uxbridge.'

Bonny's face lit up with glee, completely unaware Ellie was cross. 'I can get enough for my fare and some spare. Now where is it?' She bent down to rummage again, creating still more chaos.

Ellie leant into the open train window and kissed Bonny's cheek. 'Behave yourself,' she said wearily. 'Don't come back until you're strong again. Maybe I'll have recovered by then too.'

'I will write to Mum and Dad,' Bonny said in an effort to appease her. 'Don't you move out without letting me know where.'

The guard blew his whistle and Ellie moved back, raising her hand to blow Bonny a kiss. Sometimes she wished she'd never set eyes on Bonny, but all the same she felt a stab of sorrow at seeing her go.

The pistons moved, steam belched back down the train and the noise prevented any further words. Bonny leaned out of the window, waving until her bright hair was just a small flag in the distance and Ellie turned to go home.

Ellie heard feet coming up the stairs, but she assumed it was merely another tenant. Bonny had been gone for two days now and Ellie had spent the time looking for a job. She hadn't found anything, not even waitressing or cleaning and this morning she'd been so dispirited she had just stayed in bed.

A knock on her door made her sit up. She thought perhaps it was the landlord. 'Who is it?' she called out. She had just enough for the rent, but it would leave her very short.

'It's only me, Ellie,' Frances called back.

Ellie bounded out of bed. She assumed the dancer was feeling bad about not backing her up. Frances was a decent sort; maybe if Ellie hadn't palled up with Bonny they'd be closer friends.

'What a nice surprise. I didn't expect to see anyone

from the show again,' Ellie said as she opened the door, pulling a cardigan over her nightdress. 'I was lying in bed feeling sorry for myself.'

Frances came in and sat down on the unmade bed. She looked pretty, her black, curly hair loose on her shoulders, wearing a pink frock.

'We're all so sorry about what happened,' she said, looking a little uneasy, as if expecting Ellie to snap at her. 'Ambrose was awful to you, and we should've supported you.'

'It doesn't matter,' Ellie said. It was enough that Frances had come now. 'I'll make some tea and you can tell me all the gossip.'

While the kettle boiled on the stove out on the landing, Frances gave her a run-down of events. 'Ambrose is still being horrible,' she said. 'Did you know Edward left too? All the girls think there was something going on between them.'

Ellie said nothing. For Edward's sake it was better to pretend she hadn't seen him. 'How are you managing without me?' she asked.

'Sally's doing the *Quaker Girl* number, but she isn't as good as you. Ambrose is auditioning people for some act to replace the sketch, and for another couple of dancers. Where's Bonny? Is she still ill?'

'Gone to her aunt's in Sussex,' Ellie said. 'I've been looking for another job.'

'That's really what I came about,' Frances said. 'I heard of something, if you're interested.'

Over tea, Frances explained that her parents had come up to London last night to see the show.

'Mum's younger brother puts on shows all along the east coast,' she said. 'Apparently he's finding it hard to get performers. He asked Mum if I was free, or if I knew of anyone. I thought of you and Bonny immediately.'

Ellie cheered up immediately. 'Oh Frances.' She grinned broadly. 'I'll do anything! What sort of show?'

'It's not in the same league as a West End show,'

Frances warned her. 'Just a seaside revue, you can't expect it to be very slick or polished. From what Mum said I think most of the cast are old, or just girls straight out of school.'

'I don't care, it's work,' Ellie said excitedly. 'Just as long as I get paid enough to live.'

'Telephone my uncle tonight.' Frances opened her handbag and took out a scrap of paper. 'His name is Archie Biggs. I'll phone him first to tell him how good you are. I expect he'll want you to start almost immediately, he'll get you digs. He'll probably even pay your fare down there.'

'Would he take on Bonny too?' Ellie wasn't totally sure it was a good idea to include her friend – after all she was nothing but trouble – but she was missing her.

'He's bound to.' Frances smiled warmly. 'I bet he'd take Edward as well, if you know where he is.'

Ellie had a feeling Frances had her taped. She blushed and averted her eyes.

'It's okay.' Frances put one hand on Ellie's arm. 'I shan't pass any of this on to Ambrose. He's still breathing fire about all three of you. This is my little way of getting a bit of revenge.'

'Thank you Frances.' Ellie smiled. 'And give the other girls my love. I miss them.'

'We miss you too,' Frances said reflectively. 'Jimbo went mad at Ambrose when he found out you'd left, we all heard them rowing. Keep your head down for a while, remember you signed a contract with him and he might make things difficult for you. But I must go now, we've got yet another rehearsal this morning. I almost wish I'd walked out with you.'

Ellie felt as if a heavy weight had been lifted from her shoulders. Leaving London for the seaside would be as good as a holiday. There would be no painful reminders of Charley, and maybe in a town that wasn't littered with bomb-sites she could begin to forget all the hardships and tragedy the war had brought her.

Chapter Nineteen

The old man's phlegmy cough made Ellie wince. She closed the heavy book, put her notepad in her bag and got up from the library table.

She had a great many fond memories of Bethnal Green Library. It had been a warm, cosy sanctuary on many a cold day when she was a child. She could remember coming here as young as four with her mother to choose picture books. In later years she had spent whole Saturday mornings tucked into a corner by a radiator, transported into a world where girls had large tuck-boxes sent to their posh boarding-schools for midnight feasts, where they rode ponies and spent summer holidays having amazing adventures.

The library had grown shabbier. Once the wood floor was varnished, so shiny it looked wet, the paint-work and brass on the doors gleamed, and there were flowers on the counter. The floor was dull now, all trace of varnish gone, and a smell of disinfectant had replaced polish. There seemed to be fewer books, and all of the popular fiction was dog-eared from continuous borrowing during the war. The wooden armchairs didn't appear so large, although the seats were as slippery as she remembered. But Ellie was certain that the grey-haired, sharp-nosed lady on the desk was the same one who had pounced on children who sniffed or dared speak above a whisper.

Ellie had forgotten that the library was a haven on a wet day for the old, the sick and for tramps who on fine days sat out in 'Barmy Park'. Now they sat dozing over newspapers and magazines, their damp clothes steaming, coughing and spluttering, the odours from their unwashed bodies creating a thick, pungent fug.

'Did you find what you were looking for?' the grey-haired lady whispered as Ellie came past her desk. She wasn't often faced with requests for *Burke's Peerage* and she was curious as to why the black-haired, pretty girl should be so assiduously copying something from it.

'Yes, thank you,' Ellie replied, tempted to show what she'd found to the woman and ask her opinion on what some of the abbreviations meant, but afraid she would be asked why she wanted to know. 'I might come back again another day when it isn't quite so crowded.'

After Frances had left, Ellie had been so excited at the prospect of joining another show, and the real possibility of leaving London and all its painful memories behind, that she'd been unable to stay indoors and wait until evening to telephone Mr Biggs, even though the grey sky looked as if it promised rain.

She caught the bus to Whitechapel in a moment of nostalgia, wanting to look again at all her old childhood haunts, perhaps even to see some faces she remembered.

But the Blitz had altered everything. Gaps in rows of shops, the space between them still piled high with rubble and dumped rubbish, large beams shoring up adjoining buildings. Even the shops remaining were nothing like those she remembered. Where was the one which stocked fancy wedding dresses? Or Uncle Solly's, the pawnbrokers, whose windows were a glimpse into Aladdin's cave, stuffed with everything from ice-skates to gentlemen's hip flasks. Had Solly died, or merely taken his booty to another less dangerous area? Had people managed to get back their best table-cloths, their sets of false teeth or their wedding rings?

The shops she did recognise were smaller and sadder than the picture she'd kept in her head. Norah's Woolshop had a partially boarded-up window and merely three or four skeins of wool grouped around some ancient-looking knitting patterns. Lasker's, the baker's, had only bread and a few currant buns, not the mouth-watering display of fancies, meat pies and sausage rolls she had once drooled over on her way home from school.

Once in the back streets, it was hard to get her bearings. Complete terraces were gone, and the increased daylight and space confused her. Only the first four houses in Alder Street were still habitable. Another four were shored up, windows boarded over; then came a huge gap where her home and its neighbours had been. Weeds grew waist-high over rubble, and a group of shabbily dressed children were making a camp with some sheets of corrugated iron. Ellie guessed the spot they had chosen was once the back yard of number 18.

'I used to live here,' she called out as she clambered over to the children. She hoped to find they were younger brothers and sisters of her old playmates. 'Do any of you know what happened to Edna and Wilf Ross? They lived downstairs to me.'

The children's response was disappointing. In Ellie's time in Alder Street a friendly question from a stranger would have created instant interest and a great deal of unsolicited information and cheek. But these children merely halted their play and stared at her with cold, suspicious eyes.

'Never 'eard of 'em.' One gangly ten-year-old boy with closely cropped hair took a couple of steps towards her, his expression suggesting he thought it was more likely she was a truancy officer than someone with a genuine enquiry.

It began to rain then. The children scuttled off and Ellie went back to Whitechapel Road, then turned into the back streets towards Bethnal Green. As she walked, her raincoat becoming sodden, the sights grew more and more depressing. Demolition men seemed to be working everywhere, thick grey dust covering the weeds that sprouted up through debris, the gutters turning to small streams because the drains were blocked. Some of the badly damaged houses were still inhabited, cardboard and rags shoved into broken windows, tarpaulins spread over roofs. The children Ellie saw looked healthier than their counterparts before the war – food rationing for these kids meant a far better diet than their parents had ever had. But there seemed to be an air of despondency now, which this area, for all its deprivations, had never shown before.

Perhaps she was being sentimental, but where was the vibrancy, the bustle? A few men huddled in a group, smoking under the shelter of a church porch, but there was no laughter. They were all shabbily dressed, greasy cloth caps pulled down over grey, sullen faces. Not one of them turned to look at her, much less whistle or smile. A queue of women waited outside a butcher's shop, their turban-style head-scarves and pinnies already wet through. They were silent, all eyes locked into the interior of the shop, as if afraid any distraction would prevent them from getting their fair rations.

She wished she hadn't come. In the West End it was possible to believe recovery was just round the corner, even if food queues were just as long and there were still terrible shortages of even the most basic of necessities. Suburban housewives flocked to the shops, searching for new clothes, men with demob money in their pockets crowded the pubs and dance halls. Cleaning up was going on all around, and there was optimism in the air.

Here in the East End, Ellie was right up against the real aftermath of war: widows, men who would never work again, homes unfit for human habitation, children who had run wild while the bombs dropped. These people had taken the worst of the bombing, lost family members, their homes and possessions. What was the government doing about them? Kensington, Chelsea and other wealthy areas would soon be put right, but who cared about the poor people's needs?

Ellie could now see for herself why it was thought that Labour would be voted in at next week's general election. On VE Day it had seemed inconceivable that England would ever stop following Winston Churchill, but if the plight of the working classes here in the East End was mirrored elsewhere in Britain, who could blame them for wanting to see a party in power who would do something for them?

It wasn't just the heavy rain which drove Ellie into the library; more a stab of anger that her mother had had no choice but to live in poverty with her child, that she hadn't lived long enough for Ellie to help make her life more comfortable. She would find out about this Sir Miles Hamilton, if only to lay a few old ghosts and understand her mother more fully.

As Ellie rode back to the West End on the bus, she considered what she had learnt.

Miles Hamilton was born in 1890. He served in the Coldstream Guards in the First World War, and was mentioned twice in dispatches. He had two younger brothers, Guy Timothy, and Richard Martin. He was educated at Marlborough, and then Sandhurst. He had married Mary Lucy in May 1920, the only daughter of Frederick and Louise Outwell of Romsey, Hants. His home was Awbridge Hall in Hampshire and he had no children.

There was a great deal more – companies he was

a director of, his family coat of arms – but she didn't recognise the company names and she had no idea what the Latin motto '*Paratus*' meant. Only one small item suggested it was possible he was her father: Sir Miles's grandmother was named Helena too, and she had died in 1924, the year Miles and Polly had met.

'You can't go sniffing around Hampshire,' she said to herself as the bus passed the Tower of London. 'Forget him and think about what you're going to say to Archie Biggs. That's far more important.'

Jack and Bonny walked down the slope to the teashop by the River Arun. Jack was brooding, as he had been since he called for her at Aunt Lydia's. Bonny felt he was building up to say something unpleasant.

Bonny had arrived in Amberley from London four days ago. If Jack hadn't telephoned yesterday to say he'd got a forty-eight hour pass she would have been on the first train back to London this morning, for she hadn't got the warm welcome she believed she was entitled to from Aunt Lydia.

For the last two days it had been warm and sunny, but today the sky was overcast, with a stiff breeze. Nothing in Amberley seemed the same as Bonny remembered. No one seemed interested in her; even Belinda Noakes had said she was 'too busy' to drop in and see her. The river was grey and choppy, the tables on the grass had no table-cloths, and now even Jack was different, treating her with such suspicion.

'Tea and a buttered bun?' Jack asked as they arrived, dusting off a chair for her. 'Are you warm enough, Bonny? We could go inside if you like.'

'I'm fine here,' she said churlishly, buttoning her cardigan over her pink dress. 'It's a shame the weather's changed. I wanted to go to Littlehampton.'

Jack looked hard at Bonny, wondering when she was going to give him a proper explanation. He'd telephoned her digs in London two days ago and discovered she'd left the show over a week before and yet hadn't written to tell him. Perhaps he should have played the same game and ignored her, but instead he'd rung Miss Wynter and discovered Bonny had come here. He'd managed to wangle a spot of leave, but now he almost wished he hadn't bothered, since Bonny was telling him lies again.

'Jack! What a surprise!' Mrs Talbot the café owner came out to take their order, her big face breaking into a welcoming broad smile.

Bonny was irritated further by the woman's delight at seeing Jack and the fact that she wasn't included in the welcome. Jack had nicknamed Mrs Talbot 'the Battleship' when Bonny first arrived in Amberley – she was a formidable, large woman, always doing battle with someone. But she *had* always been very fond of Bonny, admiring her hair and her clothes and keeping sweets for her. Now she barely nodded, and instead gave Jack all her attention.

'What a fine-looking man you've become,' she crowed, patting his broad shoulders almost as if she'd been personally responsible for all that muscle. 'When I think what a scrawny little lad you used to be! The Bakers must be so proud of you. You are staying with them, I suppose?'

Bonny thought Jack looked good too, especially in his uniform. He hadn't grown any taller, or his hair any less fiery, but there was character in that rugged face. So his front tooth was broken, his skin turned red and freckly in the sun, but there was something disarming about the combination of gentle eyes, wide, wide smile and tough, muscular body.

'You're looking pretty good yourself!' Jack grinned engagingly at 'the Battleship'. 'Yes, I'm staying with the Bakers, who else would have me? Another six months or so of the army and I'll be back here permanently. And how's the world treating you?'

As Mrs Talbot launched into an account about her

son, still on active service in the Far East, and her daughter's approaching wedding, Bonny was reminded how much affection everyone in the village had for Jack and how many of the girls wished they could be his sweetheart. She felt bitter that no one put out the flags for her coming home.

Lydia had not believed Bonny's story about having food poisoning, mainly because Bonny wouldn't agree to see Dr Noakes. She tersely asked why Bonny hadn't contacted her parents or gone to the hospital if she was so ill, and pooh-poohed the story of Bonny losing her job through Ambrose's vindictiveness.

Bonny was feeling very down when she arrived, wanting nothing more than sympathy and unconditional love. Lydia's cruel jibe, 'You can lock up from a thief, but not from a liar,' had made her feel even lower.

There was absolutely nothing to take Bonny's mind off the ordeal she'd been through, just endless hours of painful introspection and anxiety about her health. She was still losing blood, and just bending over to do some weeding in the garden made her feel faint. She felt weepy all the time, and when she'd seen a neighbour with her new baby she had become so choked up that she'd had to turn and run indoors. Everything seemed confused in her mind. Why was she getting soppy thoughts about babies now, when only a few weeks ago she saw pregnancy as just a hurdle to be swept away?

Lydia suggested she go into Littlehampton and find a job, but how could she work in a shop or as a waitress when she felt so bad?

Now Jack was freezing her out too.

'Tell me what really happened,' he said once 'the Battleship' had served the tea and sailed back to the café, out of range. 'The whole truth, not the silly story about food poisoning.'

'It's not a silly story,' Bonny retorted indignantly, jumping off her chair. 'I just hope you and Lydia get it one day and find out what it's like.'

Jack jumped up too, catching hold of Bonny's wrists, preventing her from pummelling him. 'I know you too well,' he grinned. 'If you'd been poisoned the whole world would've known about it. You'd even have sent me a telegram so I could bring you grapes. I do believe though that something serious has happened and I want you to tell me, however bad it is.'

Bonny slumped against him, defeated. They were alone on the riverside; the only sound was of water slapping against the moored rowing boats, wind in the trees and an occasional caw of rooks. It reminded her of the days when she had kept nothing from him.

The true story was festering inside her. Each night since arriving back here she'd recalled every minute of her ordeal in that kitchen in Soho, and now she knew she couldn't keep it in any longer.

'I'll tell you if you promise you won't tell anyone else,' she said, her head against his shoulder, an idea already forming in her mind. 'Especially Aunt Lydia!'

'Okay.' Jack let go of her. 'Now sit down and I'll pour the tea.'

The story she told was the truth, except that she skilfully switched Ellie's and her own roles. It wasn't just fear of revealing her own unfaithfulness; more a compulsion to portray herself as a heroine. In the role of friend, nurse and comforter she could heighten the drama of the gruesome back-street abortion, while at the same time winning Jack's respect for standing by Ellie.

'It was so awful,' she whispered, her eyes welling up with real tears as she launched into graphic detail, sparing him nothing. 'Ellie was in so much pain. I thought she was going to die.'

'Oh Bonny.' Jack turned pale. He was worldly

enough to know such abortions were commonplace in big cities, but until now he hadn't known what they entailed. 'You shouldn't have got involved!'

'I had to. She had no one else to turn to. I begged her not to go to the rehearsal so soon afterwards, but Ellie can be very pig-headed and she insisted,' she said, wiping away her tears with the back of her hand. 'I hadn't had any sleep for days, I was exhausted and I could barely manage the steps myself, but I was afraid Ellie would collapse. Ambrose hit me for telling her to go home.'

'He hit you!' Jack's voice rose in indignation and his gentle brown eyes darkened. 'I'll go up there and beat the living daylights out of him!'

'There's no point now.' Bonny put her hand on Jack's arm soothingly. 'I expect I punished him enough by walking out and taking Ellie with me. I didn't want to, but what else could I do?'

'You did right.' Jack sighed deeply. He was shocked by the story: Bonny had painted such a vivid picture he could feel the pain, even smell the blood. 'But where's Ellie now?'

'I packed her off to stay with an old friend of hers,' Bonny lied. 'We hadn't got any more money for her rent. I couldn't stay at my digs once I'd walked out because Ambrose pays for them. I've been feeling so ill too, I keep thinking of that little baby.'

Jack was a great deal more sensitive than his tough appearance suggested and he could well understand how any woman could be traumatised by witnessing such shocking events. Now Bonny's dark-ringed, dull eyes, the tearfulness Lydia had spoken of, the way she'd clung to him last night, at the same time showing no passion, all made sense.

'Why didn't you confide in Lydia? She would've understood.' Jack took Bonny's hand in his, distressed by her obvious grief, yet heartened to find she was capable of feeling another's pain so keenly. It was a dimension of her character he hadn't seen before and he took it as a sign that she was growing less selfish at last.

'Ellie would never forgive me for telling anyone. If you ever meet her you mustn't let on I told you either. You promise?'

'Of course I won't,' Jack reassured her. He was disappointed that he hadn't got to see the show at the Phoenix – this was the first leave he'd had since it started. 'I feel very sorry for her, but it's you I'm most concerned about! You've lost the job that meant so much to you, and you're brooding about it all too.'

'I don't think I'll ever quite get over it. It haunts me, do you understand what I mean?'

Jack sensed she meant it had frightened her off love-making. 'I thought you'd found someone else last night,' he admitted ruefully, blushing when he remembered how jealous he'd been.

They had made love less than a dozen times since Jack went into the army. Aside from two wonderfully memorable occasions when he had managed to get them a room in a guest-house while Bonny was dancing in Brighton, they'd had to make do with fields. Last night Lydia had left them alone in the house while she visited a friend and Jack had been puzzled and angered by Bonny's coolness.

'I couldn't help the way I was.' Bonny dropped her eyes from his. 'I suppose I'm scared now that it could happen to me.'

'But I love you,' Jack said, tilting her face up to his. 'I'd always be careful and even if you did get pregnant you know I'd marry you immediately.'

Jack's loving consideration after such a mammoth deception was almost too much to bear and the tears that trickled down Bonny's cheeks now came straight from her heart.

'I'll be all right soon. It's just shock, I suppose.

Anyway I haven't been a very good girlfriend to you, have I? I don't write as often as I should.'

'I'm not the greatest letter writer either,' Jack said stoutly, refusing to remember just how few letters he'd received from her. She only managed to see him for the odd night when it suited her, rarely putting herself out. 'But it will be different when I'm demobbed. Alec's going to take me on as a partner in the garage.'

'Really? That's wonderful.' She forced herself to sound enthusiastic. 'But aren't you going home to London for a while? What about your mother?'

'I couldn't care less if I never see her again,' he said with a shrug of his shoulders. 'She forgot me and my brothers during the war, never even remembered our birthdays. As far as I'm concerned the only debts I've got are to Mr and Mrs Baker, they've been the ones who stood by us. Tom's off with the railways now, but they've still got Michael till he leaves school and they don't get a penny off Mum for his keep.'

'I'll have to go back to London soon and find another job,' Bonny said quickly. She needed to make it quite clear she wasn't going to wait around here. 'I promised Ellie I'd help her with the rent, and anyway I've left all my things there.'

'I can give you a bit of money to tide you over.' Jack reached into his pocket and pulled out two pound notes, putting them into her hand. 'I saved this intending to take you out somewhere a bit fancy, but it will just have to be the pictures and fish and chips now.'

Bonny looked at the money, relieved she wouldn't have to go back to London entirely empty-handed, and that he seemed to accept her plans. 'I'll pay you back. Next leave you get I'll make sure we have a wonderful time. I'm so sorry I've been awful to you.'

'Bonny, you aren't awful.' Jack smiled broadly, exposing his broken tooth. 'I told you before I'll love you for ever and I will. I love you even more for

425

telling me about your friend, I'm proud of you standing by her. Just don't tell me any more lies, sweetheart, we can't build a future on anything but truth.'

Bonny stood on the platform until the train was almost out of sight and Jack's waving arm just a speck of distant khaki, tears streaming down her face.

'Don't take on now,' Bert Baker said at her elbow. 'It's not long until he gets demobbed.'

'I miss him so much,' Bonny sobbed, allowing Bert to draw her into his arms for a comforting hug. 'There's no one else quite like Jack, he's all I want.'

After their talk yesterday morning it had been such a lovely day. The sun came out at midday and Mrs Baker made them a picnic to take down by the river. All afternoon they'd cuddled and dozed in the long grass, then off to the pictures in the evening. For that short time all her troubles seemed to melt away, and she found herself believing it could be like this for ever if she married Jack and gave up dancing. Maybe she didn't seem to feel quite as strongly about Jack as Ellie did about Charley, but she was sure today she really did love him.

Bert was deeply touched by this unexpected public display of emotion from Bonny. 'It's when you're apart you see how much people mean to you,' he said, patting her slender back. 'Me and the missus hardly speak sometimes when we're at home, but when I gets in, and she's out, the place seems like a bleedin' morgue. Now why don't you pop in to see her? Michael's gone fishing with his pals and I expect she's missing Jack already too. She said this morning how nice it were having you to tea last night.'

Bonny disengaged herself from Bert's arms. She couldn't face Mrs Baker alone; the woman had a way of looking right down into her soul. 'That's very kind of you,' she said, dabbing at her face. 'But I promised Aunt Lydia I would go straight back.'

'Another day eh?' Bert tweaked her cheek, the way he always had when she was small. 'Just don't leave it so long next time.'

Lydia was putting on her hat in front of the hall mirror as Bonny came down the stairs, her suitcase in her hand.

Jack's departure for the barracks at Aldershot the previous morning had left Bonny very tearful. But fortunately Ellie had telephoned during the evening to say she'd landed them both a six-week job in Great Yarmouth, starting in four days' time. Bonny had cheered up immediately, and gone to pack her case, saying she'd better leave in the morning so she had time to go and see her parents before setting off for Norfolk.

Lydia pushed the pearl-ended hatpin in securely and turned. Bonny was wearing a pale green frock, her hair scraped back in a rather unflattering bun.

'Got everything?' she asked, suddenly full of remorse that she hadn't found it in her heart to believe Bonny had food poisoning. Now she wished she'd insisted Dr Noakes examined her, because Bonny really didn't look well. She could hardly fake her pallor or that listlessness. She'd only picked at food in the past few days, and Lydia had observed her clutching her stomach several times as though in pain.

'I think so,' Bonny said in a small voice. She wasn't quite sure how she felt this morning. She was thrilled Ellie had come up with a job for them, but she wasn't sure she was well enough to dance again yet. On top of that she wanted to smooth things over with Lydia before she left and she didn't know how to.

'Take this and put it in your purse,' Lydia said, holding out a five-pound note.

'No, I can't.' Bonny brushed it away. 'I can manage.'

'You won't get paid for another week.' Lydia pushed the note right into Bonny's hand and closed her fingers around it. 'I'd worry if I thought you couldn't afford to eat proper meals. You still look a bit fragile. I'm sorry if I've been unsympathetic.'

Bonny gulped. Lydia wasn't one to apologise, any more than she was herself, and this effort to make things up brought a rush of affection for her aunt. 'I *was* ill Auntie,' she said quietly. 'But I don't blame you for thinking otherwise. I have told you some whoppers in the past.'

Lydia had no desire to launch into a lecture at this late stage, but there were a few points which had to be made. 'I love you, Bonny,' she said, reaching out to draw her close. 'I think I did from the first moment I saw you. But you have a terrible tendency to use those that love you. Me, your parents and Jack. I want you to think about this on your way home. Go and see your parents, write to Jack and come and see me again because you want to see *me*, not just because it's the only place you can think of. Do you understand what I'm getting at?'

Bonny nodded, ashamed of herself.

'That's all, lecture over.' Lydia laughed lightly. 'Drop me a line as soon as you get to Great Yarmouth so I know you're safe. Now let's get to the station. Bert Baker won't hold up the train, not even for you.'

Bonny stopped at the flower barrow outside Becontree station and selected a bunch of dahlias. She had got back to Stacey Passage yesterday afternoon. Today she'd persuaded Ellie to come with her to see her parents.

Ellie looked around curiously as Bonny was paying. She'd never been to Dagenham before, and it wasn't a bit how she'd imagined.

The station entrance was built over the tube lines, and the road sloped down towards a row of shops.

428

Ellie knew this whole vast estate had been built during the twenties to rehouse people from the slums in the East End, and she could imagine how overjoyed people were to be given nice new modern homes. But it had a remarkably soulless feel about it, despite the wide roads and neat houses. Dagenham had had more than its share of bomb damage during the war, but in this part it was only superficial.

'Are you sure your parents won't mind me turning up with you?' Ellie asked as they walked down past the shops. Many still had tired-looking VE Day displays in their windows, probably because there was still a shortage of other goods.

'These will make it all right.' Bonny indicated the flowers, grinning impishly. 'Besides, *you* are my escape route, we can leave as soon as we've had tea.'

Flamstead Road looked pretty. Almost all the front gardens were full of flowers and net curtains at the windows were uniformly sparkling white. A group of children were playing cricket in the street. They paused in the game to watch the girls go by, and one boy of about eleven, with a grubby face and much-patched baggy shorts, whistled cheekily at them.

'Mum never let me play in the street,' Bonny whispered. 'See how close the school is?' She pointed to the low building opposite the house. 'She even used to walk across to meet me!'

Ellie remembered the grim, dark Bancroft Road school and thought Bonny was lucky to have been in classrooms overlooking playing fields. A couple of men were digging and raking. Presumably the grass had been dug up during the war to grow vegetables, and it looked as if they were going to replant it with grass seed now.

'Bonny!' Mrs Phillips's eyes widened in astonishment when she opened the door to find her daughter on the step. 'Why didn't you tell me you were coming? I'd have done some baking.'

Bonny kissed her mother and introduced Ellie, though in fact Ellie had met her briefly once before, when the Phillipses came to see the show at the Phoenix. Then, before her mother could get a word in edgeways, Bonny informed her they couldn't stay long.

Within minutes, Ellie felt for herself Doris Phillips's obsessive adoration of her child. From the moment they got inside the door, Doris never stopped wittering.

She couldn't listen to the answer to one question before starting on another. Why had they left the show? Why did she go to Miss Wynter's instead of coming straight home? How did Bonny know it was safe in Great Yarmouth? What if the digs were dirty?

Doris Phillips seemed an improbable mother for a girl like Bonny. She was short and stout and shared none of her daughter's sparkle. Only her eyes showed her to be Bonny's real mother. Doris's had faded a paler blue, their size diminished by wrinkles and folds of loose flesh, but somehow Ellie knew they were once identical to Bonny's.

Ellie sat in the brown Rexine-covered armchair and studied the living-room as Bonny attempted to get through the fabricated story of her food poisoning and of Ambrose sacking them both for missing performances. The room was full of photographs of Bonny, from a plump, smiling baby sitting on a fur rug, to more recent ones taken at the Phoenix, and all the stages in between. Bonny in a tutu, Bonny at the seaside on a donkey, posed ones from studios in gilt frames, small snapshots in cardboard mounts. Bonny had said her bedroom was like a shrine to her babyhood; this room was a chart of her progress.

Everywhere there was evidence that Bonny was Doris's sole reason for being. Her ballet and tap exam certificates framed on the wall, knitting needles and pink wool sitting on a cardigan pattern which could only be for her. Little cross-stitched mats on every surface, clearly Bonny's handiwork.

Ellie thought wryly that Grace Gilbert would approve of the scrupulous cleanliness of this room. Like everywhere now, it needed redecorating, but Mr Phillips had patched up the wallpaper damaged during the Blitz and the curtains had been starched. Everything was just so – cushions plumped up, highly polished brass ornaments arranged with precision. Even Mr Phillips's pipes, spills, ashtray and gardening books were placed carefully by his armchair. He was still at work. Mrs Phillips kept harping on about how she had kippers for his tea, but she'd have to find something else for them.

'But I still don't understand why you didn't telephone Mrs Parsons and get her to run and get me if you were ill?' Doris's blue eyes were full of reproach as she looked at her daughter.

'Oh, Mum, I didn't want to worry you,' Bonny said, looking at Ellie and winking. 'Besides, Ellie was looking after me.'

Doris looked hard at Ellie. She suspected her of leading Bonny astray, but she couldn't see anything about the girl to confirm this suspicion. She spoke well, with good manners, she was quietly dressed, and she didn't seem to be a trollop. Doris wanted to be reassured by this new friend, the only one aside from Jack she remembered Bonny having for more than a few days, but she felt a little jealous.

'You will look after my Bonny in Great Yarmouth?' she asked. 'Make sure she eats properly and gets to bed early?'

'Of course,' Ellie smiled. 'The sea air will be good for her, she'll soon get over her food poisoning.'

Arnold Phillips arrived home on his bicycle at ten past six. Through the window Ellie saw him remove his bicycle clips from his trousers and take his sandwich tin out of the saddle bag. She thought he looked weary, but as Bonny ran out to greet him, his face broke into a wide smile of pure delight and suddenly he looked younger and less stooped.

Ellie soon realised that she liked Arnold. She had fully expected him to launch into a repeat of his wife's cross-examination, but he didn't. He accepted Bonny's brief story, showed concern that she'd been ill and pleasure that she had another dancing job, and left it at that. Ellie noted how Doris insisted he put on a cardigan once he'd removed his jacket, even though it was hot, and frowned when he attempted to take off his tie, and she felt sorry for him. He was obviously terribly henpecked.

Doris announced tea was ready almost immediately after Arnold arrived home. 'I've been keeping this tin of salmon for something special,' she declared, placing the dish with due ceremony on the table. There was little space left in the room with the folding dining-table opened up, and she had to squeeze round it to get her best tea service out of the sideboard.

Arnold had his kippers and mashed potato, and Doris and the girls the salmon and salad. 'Goodness knows when we'll find such things in the shops again. I was queuing for nearly an hour at the Co-op this morning to try and get a couple of slices of ham for Mr Phillips's sandwiches, but it was all gone by the time my turn came. I think they keep it under the counter for their favourite customers. Mrs Salcombe next door always seems to get what she wants, but then she's a fast baggage.'

Bonny giggled. 'Mum! Mrs Salcombe *fast*? She's at least fifty!'

Doris sniffed. 'You don't know her like I do. While her husband was off in the army she was out every night. She drinks and she plays cards for money.'

'Come now, dear,' Arnold said patiently. 'She was an ARP warden, that's where she went at night, and she was very kind to us when our roof was damaged.'

By the time tea was over, Ellie could understand exactly why Bonny was so reluctant to come home to her mother. She never stopped fussing, forcing Bonny to eat more, urging her to chew her food properly, remarking on her pallor, and constantly firing questions about whether she ate greens, drank enough milk and what time she went to bed. When Bonny said they'd have to leave after tea, Ellie couldn't wait to get out of the door. Not once during their four-hour stay had she heard the woman laugh, and she guessed that if Bonny had come alone, the questions would have been of a very much more intimate nature.

Ellie watched the leaving ceremony with near disbelief. Mrs Phillips had made some sandwiches 'for their journey', and she'd miraculously found some tinned food and half a fruit cake 'to tide them over'. Two pairs of delicately embroidered knickers went into a bag, and yet another dress specially made for Bonny. These gifts were touching, but it was the constant barrage of instructions and warnings that made Ellie cringe.

'Make sure you get in a "ladies only" carriage when you travel to Great Yarmouth. Don't sit on the toilet seat or you'll get germs and don't wash your hair while you're having a period.'

Once she'd run out of warnings, Mrs Phillips began to cry. 'But I don't know when I'll see you again,' she sobbed, clutching Bonny to her plump bosom.

Bonny rolled her eyes at Ellie over her mother's shoulder. 'It's only six weeks, Mummy,' she said between clenched teeth.

Mr Phillips had stood back while all this went on. But as his wife finally let Bonny go, he came forward, hugged Bonny briefly and put a five pound note in her hand. 'Look after yourself, sweetheart,' he said gruffly. 'Write to us won't you? Good luck with the show.'

433

'Phew,' Bonny exclaimed once they had turned the corner and she no longer had to keep looking back to wave to her mother. 'I swear every time I come I won't go back. Aren't they awful?'

'Your mum is a bit much' Ellie agreed. 'But I wouldn't mind a dad like yours, or a real home.'

Once on the train. Bonny fell asleep, her head lolling on to Ellie's shoulder. Ellie thought again about Sir Miles Hamilton and smiled as she imagined how excited Bonny would be if she told her.

But she wasn't going to tell her friend, not tonight, or ever. Bonny couldn't be trusted with a secret as big as that!

They would be off to Great Yarmouth on Monday – a brand new start at the seaside, with no reminders of the past. The pay was awful, just two pounds ten shillings a week, plus their board and lodgings, and three matinées a week on top of the evening performances. Edward would be joining them too; Mr Biggs had been delighted to find a pianist. Everything was going to be just wonderful. She might even be able to forget Charley.

Chapter Twenty

August 1945

Edward played the introduction, the curtain drew back and Ellie and Bonny appeared through an archway before a painted backdrop of a country mansion.

'*We're a couple of swells,*' they sang, dressed as tramps in battered top hats and frock-coats, canes swung over their shoulders with the inevitable red polka-dotted bundles on the end. '*We stop at the best hotels. But we prefer the country far away from the city smells.*'

Edward smiled up at the girls. This, their first number in the show, was always a crowd-pleaser. The Majestic Theatre didn't live up to its name – it was a seedy little place, tucked away in a side street, desperately in need of new seats and redecoration. But tonight, like every night since they'd arrived in Great Yarmouth over four weeks ago, every seat was taken, with people standing at the back.

On the world stage, dramatic events had taken place in the last few weeks. First, in July, Labour had won the general election. Then came news of the Americans dropping atomic bombs on Hiroshima and Nagasaki. There was little sympathy for the seventy thousand Japanese thought to have died in the blasts, only delight in hearing that the Japs had surrendered on August 14th, bringing the Far East war to a close.

Edward and the girls read in the papers that crowds flocked into the West End of London for VJ Day, but here in Great Yarmouth the celebrations were restrained. There were severe shortages of alcohol, and perhaps people on holiday felt no need to break out.

For Edward, Bonnie and Ellie, world events meant little. This show with Mr Biggs was a picnic compared with working for Ambrose Dingle. There was the beach, the funfair, sunshine, and their digs were right on the sea front. They didn't really care what was happening elsewhere.

Edward had discovered he could be happy. Each day here he felt he was moving closer and closer to a state of bliss. Sometimes he had to remind himself that the show had less than two weeks to run and that unless another job like this was offered to him and the girls he might be plunged back into isolation. He often made himself look closely at his tiny room in the attic above Ellie's and Bonny's, and tell himself how frowsy the boarding-house was, that it was only the heady, holiday atmosphere and Ellie which made it fun.

He had so much to thank Ellie for. If she hadn't put his name forward to Mr Biggs, he'd still be stuck in Wiltshire with his grandmother, holding her knitting skeins and mowing the lawn, all the time brooding on his sexuality, wondering if there was a place, anywhere for him, where he wouldn't feel an outcast.

He'd found that place, here. All he had to do now was play the piano: no moments of terror standing in the wings, no endless rehearsals, no disapproval from Ambrose to face. He could laugh along with the rustic comic who gloried in the name of Farmer Pigswill and told jokes about animals mating, with a straw hanging out of his mouth.

He enjoyed the challenge of accompanying Stella and Sydney Smythe, the husband-and-wife team who changed their repertoire of romantic duets almost nightly without warning. This show was in the best seaside tradition: hammy, hilarious and warm. No one felt cheated because the dancers had wobbly thighs, the scenery shook, the singers hit the odd flat note, or the costumes were tawdry. It was cheap, jolly entertainment and if it bore no resemblance to a West End show, so much the better. People on holiday didn't want reminders of city life.

If there was a fly in his ointment, it was only a very small one. Bonny! He tried to like her because Ellie did. Bonny wasn't quite as cutting as she had been in London, nor as self-centred; in fact at times he almost felt himself warming to her. But however much he tried to tell himself she must be a good sort, or Ellie wouldn't care about her so much, he knew deep down he was jealous of just that.

On their arrival here, Bonny had sarcastically remarked that Archie Biggs 'couldn't arrange furniture, let alone choreography'. When she'd seen the dancers, ten plump country girls on loan from the local dancing school with more enthusiasm than talent, she'd curled her lips in disgust and Edward had hoped she'd take off for home.

But Archie didn't put Ellie and Bonny in the chorus line; he paired them together as a singing and dancing duo. It soon became apparent that the man had keen perception and imagination.

Together the girls were dynamite. Ellie had the real voice while Bonny was the brilliant dancer, but from the way they interacted, the audience wasn't aware of either girl's shortcomings – only of grace, beauty and talent.

It was a mystery to Edward why Ambrose hadn't thought of pairing them. Their identical heights, slender figures and long legs were perfectly matched. Ellie's sultry looks complemented Bonny's sugar and spice blondeness and their joy at performing together turned it into a feast for the eyes.

'*The Vanderbilts have asked us up to tea,*' the girls sang in exaggerated falsetto voices, standing back-to-back. '*We don't know how to get there, no siree.*'

Bonny broke into an intricate tap-dance, blonde hair tumbling from under her hat, while Ellie glided around her, posturing comically.

Edward glanced round at the audience. They were loving it, beaming faces everywhere, forgetting that it had been raining constantly for three days, that their fearsome guest-house landladies locked them out after breakfast until tea and that on Monday morning they'd be back working in factories, queuing for rations, trying to save a little for next year's holiday.

Edward often looked at people such as these and wished he was as ordinary. Yesterday afternoon he'd voiced this to Ellie, and once again she'd made him feel special, even loved.

Edward had joined Ellie in her room the previous afternoon because there was no matinée on Thursdays. It was pouring with rain and Bonny had gone off to look at the shops.

Ellie thought her room was heaven, just because it overlooked the promenade and the sea. Edward thought it was the ugliest he'd ever seen, with its violent, salmon-pink wallpaper, its hideous blue curtains and the two beds with horsehair mattresses that groaned when you sat on them.

Ellie was in the process of hanging up all Bonny's clothes, not complaining once about how untidy she was.

Edward lay on Ellie's bed, watching her stop to dust the dressing-table. She was wearing the same old, worn skirt and blouse she put on most days. He felt it was unfair that she had so few pretty things – she deserved better than other people's cast-offs.

It wasn't often Edward got the chance to be entirely alone with Ellie; if Bonny wasn't around there was usually one of the dancers or another member of the cast. They hadn't spoken of that last evening in London since they arrived in Great Yarmouth and he wanted to bring it out into the open.

He began to talk about his grandmother and her increasingly eccentric behaviour. Then he moved on to his parents and admitted how unnatural they had been, always gallivanting around and rarely considering the fact that they had a son who needed them. 'It's no wonder I'm abnormal,' he said, making it sound like a joke rather than a cry for reassurance.

'Who wants to be entirely normal?' Ellie laughed and beckoned him to come over to the window and look out with her. 'That's normal,' she went on, pointing out a couple with a child in a pushchair, hunched up in a shelter, stoically eating a picnic. 'It doesn't look like much fun, does it?'

The rain was like stair-rods, waves breaking over the deserted promenade, the sky an unpleasant, yellowy-grey colour.

'But they are at least married, with a child,' Edward said wistfully. 'If I don't like sex with women, or men, what is there for me?'

'You haven't tried it with a woman yet!' She tweaked his face round to hers and gave him a cuddle. 'But if and when you do and you still don't like it, you'll just have to forget about it and just be Edward Manning.'

'But what is he? A neutered tom-cat?'

'Neutered toms are more lovable,' she laughed up at him. 'Besides, Edward Manning has other talents. He's an actor, a fine pianist, a good friend and a very attractive gentleman. Look at him!' She pointed down to the man in the shelter with his family.

Edward looked. The man was probably younger than himself, wearing a badly fitting demob suit and a battered trilby. He got up as they spoke, standing, hands in pockets, staring dejectedly out at the rain. Even at a distance of some forty yards it was possible to see that his wife was nagging him as she fed their child a sandwich.

'Would you like his life?' Ellie giggled, but Edward sensed she wasn't being entirely frivolous. 'He's come out of the forces expecting everything to be wonderful. But is it? I bet their home's a couple of shabby rooms and he works twelve hours a day just to keep them. His wife doesn't look a barrel of laughs, does she? She's even blaming him for the weather. You must stop thinking you need *someone* to make you happy, Edward. It has to come from within you.'

Edward later decided that Ellie had a point. He was doing a job he liked. He was handsome. He had a private income, his grandmother's money coming to him when she died. No one here made jokes about him being a 'nancy boy'. Priests got by without sex. He could too.

'What are we going to do tonight?' Bonny asked on Friday night as the three of them got to the stage door. It was raining still, just as it had been most of the week. A glance out showed deserted streets. 'We can't go home. It's not even eleven yet.'

'We could go to the Regent,' Ellie said.

Bonny groaned. 'Not that dump!'

'It's the best hotel in town,' Ellie said indignantly. She liked its aura of genteel sophistication and, to be entirely truthful, she got a kick out of being treated like a celebrity by the cocktail bar manager who'd seen the show three times.

'It's stuffy,' Bonny said, picturing the old dears nodding off in their armchairs. 'Besides, the drinks are too dear.'

The three of them rarely went straight home to bed, even though Great Yarmouth had little to offer in the way of night-life. On warm nights they often just sat on the front, watching people, but the weather prevented that tonight.

'What a waste of getting Stella to do our hair,' Ellie said wistfully. Stella Smythe had been a hairdresser before she began singing professionally with her husband Sydney. This afternoon she'd washed and set both girls' hair for them, giving them both the same swept-up style, with artfully arranged curls on top.

Edward looked at both girls appraisingly. They looked so gorgeous, it was a shame to waste it. 'We could've tried that place Marcel told me about,' he suggested. 'But it's a bit out of town – we'll get soaked in this.'

Marcel had been a trapeze artist, but a bad fall had put him off the high wire for good. He incorporated many of the other things he'd learned in the circus in his act – clowning, juggling and a few acrobatics. All three of them were fascinated by the man. He was a womaniser, a gambler and he enthralled them with his circus tales.

'It sounded a bit odd to me.' Ellie popped her head out of the door to see just how hard the rain was, but drew it in sharply. 'He said it was a private house and you could only get in if someone recommended you. I expect it's all old men playing cards.'

'It's not,' Edward insisted. 'Marcel said it's like a party, except you pay for drinks. He wanted me to go with him last Friday. He said I'd have the time of my life.'

'I can't imagine anyone having the time of their life in Great Yarmouth,' Bonny said, an impish grin on her face. 'Mind you, Marcel seems to enjoy himself, so maybe it's worth a try.'

As if in answer to a silent prayer, a taxi cruised down the side road. Taxis were as rare in Great Yarmouth as a good meal at their digs.

'Come on!' Edward leaped out into the rain to flag

441

it down. 'We're meant to go there. If we don't like it we can always leave.'

Ellie expected Vincent House to be something like their own boarding-house. She had a picture in her head of ex-servicemen gathering in a gloomy, smoke-filled room with a few Marleen-type brassy girls swigging gins.

To her surprise, Vincent House wasn't one of those tall, narrow Victorian houses, but a medium-sized country house well out of the town. Set behind an eight-foot wall, with wrought-iron gates and a gravel drive, it looked rather grand. The porch was lit up welcomingly, soft dance music wafted out into the darkness and there were many smart cars. Edward paid off the taxi and ushered them to the door.

At the mention of Marcel Dupont, the man in dinner-jacket and bow-tie on the door dropped his initial haughtiness. 'I will tell Mr Dupont you are here,' he said with an obsequious smirk, taking their rain-coats as if he were handling mink. 'Perhaps you'd like to go into the bar, I'm sure he'll be with you in a few minutes.'

'It's a bit more ritzy than I expected,' Bonny whispered behind her hand to Ellie, noting the wide stair-case, thick red carpet and small, twinkling chandelier. She wondered how they'd managed to keep it so nice when no one else could get paint, and wallpaper had disappeared from the shops at the start of the war.

'Me too,' Ellie agreed. She was impressed that dropping Marcel's name produced such deference from the doorman. The bar was on the right-hand side of the hall and music was wafting out from another room to the left. 'I hope we've got enough money for some drinks between us.'

'I'll get them,' Edward said. The two pounds ten shillings a week they got in wages was soon gone, but he had just got his monthly allowance from his grandmother and he was feeling flush. The bar, with its low couches, subdued lighting and tasteful furniture, was much more to his taste than the sort of pubs they usually frequented.

There were five or six middle-aged men, all smartly dressed, sitting here, two of them chatting to younger, very pretty women. A voluptuous blonde in her mid to late-thirties served them with a drink, informing them that the first was always on the house. Smiling, she said she hoped they would enjoy themselves as there was dancing across the hall.

'I wish you'd suggested this earlier,' Ellie said in a low voice to Edward. 'I'd have put on something smarter.'

Two women were just being helped out of their coats in the hall, and a glimpse of cocktail dresses made Ellie extremely aware that her pink cotton dress was better suited to afternoon tea than a posh club and that her shoes had run-down heels.

But before Edward could reassure her she looked prettier than anyone else, Marcel swept in. 'Well, hello.' His rather high-pitched voice was loud enough to make everyone look up. 'What a surprise! My favourite dancing duo and our talented pianist.'

Marcel's parents were French and although he was as English as Edward, having been sent to boarding-school here, he retained his Gallic charm and appearance, with black hair, olive skin and very white teeth. They were so used to him being in clown make-up and costume that it came as a shock to see him as himself in a dark lounge suit. He wasn't exactly handsome – his eyes were too close together and his nose too large – but he was striking, even though he was now in his forties.

'I hope you didn't mind me bringing the girls?' Edward said quickly, looking a little anxious. 'Perhaps I should've asked first?'

Marcel hesitated for a split second before replying.

Ellie thought perhaps he was worried they were too young to be in such a place.

'Two beauties like these are welcome anywhere.' Marcel took Ellie's hand and kissed it flamboyantly, reassuring her his hesitation was due more to surprise than reluctance. 'You've made my evening, Edward, and I'm sure everyone else's. Now let me introduce you to my friends.'

Twelve o'clock passed, then one, but Ellie wasn't thinking about the time. She was slightly tight; she'd danced with just about everyone and she couldn't remember when she'd last had such fun.

But although not one of the twenty or so men in here seemed anything less than a gentleman, she was wary. She was keeping her eye on Bonny, who was flirting with a tall, dark man. Always observant, she'd noticed enough odd things to know this place wasn't entirely a straightforward drinking club.

The balance between the men and women was all wrong. All the men were middle-aged. The cut of their suits, good leather shoes, their upper-class accents and good manners united them all as being officer class or professional men.

In contrast, the women were much younger, the eldest less than thirty and, with just one or two notable exceptions, working-class girls disguised by expensive clothes, manicures and glamorous hairstyles. Three or four of them were exceptionally lovely. One in particular, who'd been introduced by Marcel as 'Saffron', had dusky skin, jet-black sleek hair and dramatic, dark, flashing eyes.

As Ellie had danced and chatted to the men, albeit in most cases briefly, she'd had the distinct impression that each one of them had come either alone, or with a male friend. Considering that most were probably married, it seemed rather suspicious. Furthermore, they all appeared reluctant to reveal anything personal about themselves, and she had a feeling that even some of the names they gave were false.

Having been brought up knowing how Marleen avoided work yet still had nice clothes, Ellie had to assume the women here tonight survived in much the same way. She wasn't shocked by this, nor did she particularly care if married men were out looking for 'a bit on the side', but it was baffling as to why such a beautifully appointed club didn't attract *any* married couples or groups of friends out for an evening.

Ellie's eyes were drawn to Saffron again and again, especially when Edward began to dance with her. She was very tall and willowy, wearing a floor-length red dress. Most of the women showed a great deal of flesh, but although Saffron's dress was high-necked and long-sleeved, she looked more naked than any of them. The dress was made of a fine crêpe, which clung to her almost feline body like a second skin, leaving little to the imagination and certainly no room for underwear.

Edward was a better dancer than Ellie had expected. She watched him leading Saffron to 'When They Begin the Beguine'. He had lost all his stiffness, his body almost melting into hers. Ellie smiled. He had changed so much since their time in London, was so much more relaxed and happy. She hoped this exotic-looking girl might unbend him a little further.

It was nearly half past one when Ellie came out of the powder room to see Bonny standing alone in the hall, their coats over her arm.

'Can we go now?' she asked.

Ellie had never known her friend to be the first to suggest they went home. Usually she had a job to drag her out, particularly when men were plying her with drinks.

'What's the matter?' Ellie noticed she looked very pale suddenly.

445

Bonny leaned closer to whisper in her ear. 'I've got the curse. My tummy's aching too.'

'Okay, I'll just get Edward,' Ellie said.

'Don't worry about him.' Bonny caught hold of Ellie's arm, digging her nails into it as if in extreme pain. 'He's with that girl in the bar and I don't want to explain. Let's just go, he can get home alone.'

Before Ellie could reply, Bonny was out of the front door and down the steps into the rain.

'Will you tell our friend Edward that we've gone?' Ellie asked the doorman who suddenly appeared again in the hall.

'Certainly.' He nodded, but there was no smile or even an invitation to come again. It seemed odd after his welcome when they'd arrived.

'Bonny, it's not normal to lose that much blood,' Ellie said as she helped her friend into bed, tucking the blankets round her. It was even further home than they'd imagined and they were wet through. Bonny had almost passed out as they came up the stairs and when Ellie had helped her into the bathroom she was horrified to see that her underwear was soaked. 'You've got to see a doctor tomorrow!'

'You're a worry-guts,' Bonny murmured sleepily. 'It would happen though just when I was having such a good time. That man I was dancing with was so nice. He's coming to see the show tomorrow night.'

'He's married,' Ellie said tartly.

'So!' Bonny opened one eye. 'What's that got to do with the price of fish?'

Ellie shook her head in despair. 'Go to sleep,' she said. 'You'll see a doctor before you even think about getting up to anything else.'

Ellie sat at the dressing-table, slowly taking the pins out of her wet, bedraggled hair. She felt quite sober now and very anxious. She felt Bonny's trouble was something more than a bad period, that it must have something to do with the abortion. What if she wasn't well enough to dance tomorrow? They had only another week and a bit in Great Yarmouth before the show finished and although Archie had said he could probably put them in touch with another theatre owner, if Bonny couldn't finish their contract here he might change his mind.

Turning on the stool, Ellie looked at Bonny. She was sound asleep already, her mouth slightly open, one bare arm outside the covers. Bathed in the soft light from a small lamp she looked angelic, her stray wet curls falling loose on to the pillow, her skin as smooth and pinky beige as the inside of a sea shell.

These weeks had been such a happy time, with so much laughing and sharing, from clothes to dreams and money. After the tiny airless room in Stacey Passage it was wonderful to smell sea breezes, to have a bed each, a wardrobe for their clothes and meals cooked for them. But as Ellie looked at her friend, she knew the happiness came from more than just comfort, fun, or even the knowledge of how good they were on stage together. It was the ever growing bond that filled the once-empty spaces in both of them.

Back at the club, Edward was confused how the evening's events had suddenly escalated from drinking and dancing to the point where he'd been relieved of ten pounds by the doorman and shown into this room upstairs with Saffron.

'Let me help you,' Saffron came closer to him and began to loosen his tie, her dark lustrous eyes looking right into his. 'You haven't done this before, have you?'

'What, undressed?' Edward asked.

'No, silly,' she said, her practised hands peeling off his tie and jacket all in one swift movement. 'I meant made love to a girl like me.'

The room reminded Edward of his parents' room, a place he hadn't thought of for years: similar, deep pink walls and an almost identical quilted satin cover on the double bed; a washbasin in one corner; a few cosmetics and perfume bottles on the dressing-table, half a dozen books by the bed. But Edward had the feeling these things had been placed here to create the impression that it was someone's room. There was only one decadent touch: the large, gold-framed mirror almost covering one wall.

He had danced with several women before Saffron, but he'd found himself inexplicably drawn to her. He didn't think he'd ever seen anyone quite so beautiful. Coffee-coloured skin, coal-black eyes, such a sensuous mouth. As they danced her body undulated against his and though close contact with women normally repelled him, there was something about the tautness of hers which was exciting and disturbing all at once. They had gone into the bar at his suggestion, and almost at once he regretted it as he no longer had an excuse to hold her.

But she was as good a conversationalist as she was a dancer. She told him she was Eurasian, her early childhood spent in Ceylon, but that she'd been sent back to school in England and then stayed on with an aunt and uncle. She drew him into talking about the show and confided that she wanted to be an actress. Then suddenly the doorman had come in and said the girls had left. He'd got up to go too, but Saffron had pulled him down again beside her.

'You don't have to go just because they have,' she said in that wonderfully husky voice. 'I expect they did it purposely so we could have more time alone.'

They had another couple of drinks, and continued to chat about the theatre and acting. He was just about to pluck up courage to ask her out to dinner one night, when she asked him if he wanted to take her upstairs.

'Upstairs?' he repeated, struggling to regain his

composure in the face of such a staggering suggestion.

'Yes,' she smiled, stroking his face in a manner which made him feel very odd. 'You sound surprised. Is that because you didn't expect me to be so forward, or you don't find me attractive?'

'Oh no.' Edward blushed furiously. 'You're the most beautiful woman I've ever seen, it's just that –' He stopped short, completely lost for words.

'You're just a bit shy,' she suggested. 'I'll make it less embarrassing for you. I'll go on up first. Speak to the doorman, he'll show you the way.'

There was a moment in the hall when he might have ducked out of the front door, not because he didn't want to pursue Saffron, but from pure fright. But the doorman waylaid him and asked for the ten pounds.

It was pure bravado that made him take out his wallet and pay. He was deeply shocked that a girl as young and lovely should turn out to be a prostitute. But he wasn't going to let on to a mere doorman, or to Marcel, who stood grinning in the doorway, that he was so naïve he hadn't tumbled what the club was. In a way paying made it easier too. If the whole thing was a failure he could always pretend he was too drunk, or that he had a girl at home.

'I've never made love to any woman,' he blurted out now, even though it was the last thing he'd intended to say. 'I expect you find that strange.'

Saffron looked up at him and smiled. Downstairs she had appeared cool and poised, but now she'd taken off her shoes and shrunk three inches, her shingled hair and an impish look in her eyes made her far less formidable.

'Sweet, not strange.' She leaned forward and kissed him briefly on the lips. 'I'll just have to teach you. And it will be a pleasure, Edward, because you are very beautiful.'

'You are beautiful too,' Edward whispered, sliding his arms around her. He could feel her hip-bones pressing against his through her dress and he liked the sensation.

Slowly she unbuttoned his shirt. Edward watched her red-tipped fingers moving so gently and delicately as he held her. Her short dark hair fell forward, partly concealing her face, leaving only her shapely, fleshy lips exposed.

'Mmm,' she murmured, running her fingers over his bared chest. 'Such silky skin, so young and firm.'

His fingers found the zipper on the back of her dress and he lowered it experimentally.

'That's better,' she purred sensuously. 'Now peel it off and you can see what lies beneath it.'

Edward bared her shoulders, marvelling at the colour of her skin. As he bent to kiss it her scent brought on images of waving palm trees, white sand and sarongs.

She moved her arms imperceptibly; her dress slid to the floor and she was naked beneath it. Edward gasped.

'Am I too thin for you?' she whispered, her lovely face clouding with anxiety.

Edward could only shake his head, stunned that at last he was seeing a female form which did excite him. Firm, small breasts, a tiny waist, slim boyish hips, and long slender legs. Even the mound of curly black pubic hair at the base of her flat belly was inviting. He wanted to touch that golden, almost iridescent skin, to see if it was as silky as it looked.

'No,' he said, his voice sounding hoarse to his ears. 'You're just perfection.' He could feel the start of an erection. Hesitantly he put his hands on her breasts, unsure of how he should proceed.

'Kiss me?' she said, moving closer and removing his shirt as if by magic. 'I want to feel my nipples against your chest.'

As he drew her into his arms and felt her warm, soft lips against his, he opened his eyes and caught his reflection in the mirror. The sight of his hands cupping her tight buttocks made his heart pound and his erection grow stronger.

All sense of apprehension left him. The tip of her tongue was teasing his lips, her hands stroking his neck, her small nipples hard against him.

'Lets get these off,' she murmured, a sweet smile curving her lips as she slid her hand down to his flies. 'I think there's someone in there who's dying to get out.'

It was like the sweetest dream. The hand holding his penis was no more alien than his own, a practised touch that sent shivers of delight down his spine.

Edward groaned with pleasure. His trousers and underpants were lying at his feet, yet he was unable to move them for fear she would stop.

But she made him move over to the bed, whisking off the bedspread to reveal sheets below. The bossy manner she removed his trousers, shoes and socks was just enough of an echo of his childhood to be reassuring, but her dusky, naked body kept him hard.

'There now.' She climbed on the bed, kneeling up beside him and opened his legs wider, cupping his balls with one hand, smiling down at his penis. 'That's something to be very proud of.'

Edward was stunned by the size of his erection. He couldn't remember it ever being quite that big before. When he glanced in the mirror, the sight of her dark skin and shiny black hair against his fairness made him tremble with excitement.

Slowly, so slowly, her mouth came down towards him. He was afraid to breathe, sure she was going to take him in that wide, beautiful mouth, but hardly daring to hope for it.

He watched in the mirror; she was on all fours, her buttocks as hard and small as two grapefruits, long slender thighs, her shiny dark hair falling over her face, concealing all but those lips.

'Oh Saffron,' he groaned as her hot mouth closed round him.

Nothing had prepared him for such a sensation. He'd heard men talk of it, he'd even seen pornographic pictures of it, but the feeling he got while masturbating, or even when Ambrose had caressed him, wasn't anything like this.

He was afraid he'd come straight away. He tried to think of something else, like handing out bills for the show, or putting on stage make-up. But he couldn't think of anything except her tongue and lips and it was like he was dying and flying all at once.

When he opened his eyes for a second he saw she had one hand between her own thighs, rubbing at herself, and it halted the magic enough to remember he was supposed to make love to her too.

He reached out, catching her by the back of the neck and drawing her face towards his.

'Kiss me,' he ordered her, intoxicated by his own smell on her face, and as his lips met hers he pulled her on top of him, one hand reaching down beneath her belly to explore her.

'Gently,' she murmured as his fingers forced their way inside her. 'Just gently Edward, like you'd stroke a cat.'

Edward wasn't sure he liked touching her there; it was hot and sticky, and his erection began to fade. But Saffron seemed to like it and as he watched in the mirror, she was undulating herself against him, her boyish hip-bones grinding against his.

The strangest image came to him: that it was Ellie lying on top of him, yet she was the one with the penis and she was pushing it inside him. All at once he was rock hard again and the need for relief was so urgent, he rolled Saffron over, pushed her legs apart and drove himself into her.

He lost himself in the moment. The buttocks he held in his hand were like a young boy's, the flesh on her shoulders smelt of the woods near his grandmother's. He tried to prolong the wonderful, overpowering sensations by imagining playing a scale on the piano, but there was a whole orchestra behind him, building up to a crescendo, and in the second before he came he saw only Ellie's face, those wide, dark, soulful eyes and she was all his.

He held Saffron tightly, tears coursing down his cheeks, wanting to express himself, but unable to find the right words. His body felt like india rubber, as if all his bones had gone. He buried his face in her sweet-smelling hair, smoothing her silky back and the curve of her buttocks, overwhelmed by tenderness for her.

'You'll have to go now.' She wriggled off him, leaning up on one elbow.

Edward swallowed hard. The magic vanished at her reminder that this was a business transaction, not an act of love. He reached out and gently touched her face, desperately wanting her to say something, anything to make him feel he was Edward, not just a faceless man who'd got what he paid for.

But there was nothing in those eyes now; just deep, cool pools without any emotion. She took his fingers and kissed the tips, but it was a tired, meaningless gesture which seemed to say she was anxious to get washed and dressed.

'It was lovely,' he whispered. He couldn't feel angry or cheated. She'd proved to him that he could make love to a woman. That was worth ten pounds of anyone's money.

Chapter Twenty-One

Sheffield, January 1946

Ellie woke with a start at the sound of heavy boots tramping down Marshall Street. She had no need to check the time, she heard the same thing at six every morning except Sunday.

It was January 1946, soon after her nineteenth birthday. Bonny, Edward and herself were in Sheffield, taking part in a pantomime, and those boots belonged to men going off to work at the steelworks.

A sixth sense told her she was alone in the room, even though it was still too dark to see. She pulled the light cord above her head, and sure enough, Bonny's bed was empty.

'Oh, Bonny,' she sighed, snapping the light off again and pulling the covers back tightly over her shoulders. She wanted to go back to sleep; the days were long, cold and miserable enough here in Sheffield without starting so early. But how could she relax enough to drop off again when she was so worried about Bonny?

The night in Great Yarmouth when Bonny lost so much blood had proved to be due to a severe infection in her womb. Somehow she'd managed to limp through another few days, but it had ended in her being rushed off to hospital, where she stayed for almost three weeks.

Looking back, Ellie wished she hadn't listened to Bonny. She should have contacted her parents and let them take responsibility for their daughter. But she hadn't. Perhaps Mr and Mrs Phillips would have been devastated to discover their daughter's troubles stemmed from a back-street abortion, but maybe, with parental guidance, she wouldn't be behaving so badly now.

Ellie and Edward got parts in a play in Lowestoft while Bonny was in hospital. When she came out, she joined them at their digs, and Edward paid for her keep until Bonny was well enough to dance again.

In November all three of them went on to a show in Manchester. Their first reaction to the city was one of dismay. Day after day of living in damp, choking fog, soot-blackened buildings, among dilapidated houses as bad as those in London and uncleared bomb-sites. But the people soon made up for the grimness. They were fun-loving and friendly and every night the show played to packed houses. Everything seemed rosy then, just as it had been back in Great Yarmouth. Edward played the piano; Ellie and Bonny had three good numbers and glamorous costumes. Their digs were shabby but their landlady was an inspired cook, even in the face of further cuts in rations. There were odd undercurrents, even then – Bonny was moody, sniping at Edward and sometimes bursting into tears she couldn't explain.

As the revue drew towards its final couple of weeks, all three of them looked forward expectantly to being offered parts in *Cinderella*, the Christmas pantomime which would tide them over until March.

It was when the producer singled Ellie out and asked her to be the fairy godmother, that things began to turn sour. He had nothing to offer either Bonny or Edward and they were very disappointed. Ellie was caught between two stools. She wanted the part, and wanted to stay in the city she'd grown attached to, but at the same time she didn't want to be separated from her friends.

Bonny selfishly played on Ellie's feelings, sulking and flouncing about making barbed comments like 'I thought we were a double act!' and 'I suppose I'll just have to go home'. Edward, on the other hand, kept urging Ellie to accept the part and think only of her own career.

While Ellie wavered with indecision, another dancer in the show put forward the suggestion that all three of them could get parts in *Aladdin* at the Playhouse Theatre in Sheffield. She knew the manager well: he needed two 'exotic' dancers and he would jump at the chance of a good pianist.

With hindsight, Ellie should have realised that no decent theatre manager in a major city would have left it so late to book his cast, or taken them on sight-unseen, merely on the word of another dancer. But as they had never been auditioned by Archie Biggs in Great Yarmouth and had got their last two jobs through his recommendation, she just assumed the man on the end of the telephone in Sheffield was a similar type.

They arrived in Sheffield in mid-December to find that the Playhouse was well away from the centre of the town, in Attercliffe, and due to be demolished in mid-March. The cast, aside from themselves, appeared to have been scraped from geriatric wards and the script written by a ten-year-old. It was tempting to turn and run away, but it was too close to Christmas to find anything else.

It was bad enough taking part in a fifth-rate, lack-lustre production, and even worse for Ellie and Bonny to freeze nightly in their *Arabian Nights* costumes, which consisted of little more than a few veils stitched strategically to the briefest of underwear, jangling with gold bells and beads. But to top it all, their digs were appalling.

Marshall Street was one of many narrow streets of cheerless back-to-back houses, close to the steelworks where most of the residents worked. Mrs Arkwright, their landlady, owned two adjoining houses. She slept in what would have been the front parlour, while Ellie and Bonny had the front bedroom and Edward shared the back one with Albert Coombes, who played Widow Twanky. Next door housed six more of the cast.

It was so cold the windows froze on the inside. There was no bathroom, just a stinking privy outside, and the food was so gruesome that the moment they got paid they filled up on fish and chips. A permanent yellow fog from the steelworks chimneys hung in the air, staining a white petticoat in just a couple of hours. Noise continued ceaselessly all day, starting with the tramping feet which had woken Ellie that morning, and continuing until after dark. Babies cried, children yelled and women shouted to each other from their doorsteps. It had a great deal in common with Alder Street in many ways. But the people weren't friendly, and they viewed all 'theatre folks' with the deepest suspicion.

Already, in mid-January, the audiences were dropping off so rapidly it looked as if the show would close by the end of the month. They hadn't heard even a whisper of any new shows opening.

But it wasn't the show, the digs or their future prospects which worried Ellie – just Bonny.

She was running wild, shamelessly sleeping with almost anyone who would treat her to a meal, a few drinks or a new frock. Maybe it began out of desperation because everything was so awful here, but it was now out of hand. Night after night she stayed out. By day she squabbled endlessly with Edward. She didn't even seem to have the same commitment to her dancing any more.

Ellie was miserable too. She thought about Marleen a great deal, wishing she was nearer so she could visit her. A nurse wrote Marleen's letters for her and they were unfailingly cheerful, but Ellie suspected this was a smokescreen and that she was far more poorly than she claimed. She still thought about Charley a great deal, wishing she could turn the clock back and start again. Sometimes she was even tempted to write and tell him she'd made a terrible mistake, but how could she? He would think it was only because her career had taken a downturn.

Because of what had happened between her and Charley, Ellie felt badly about the way Bonny treated Jack. She had him on a piece of string, callously writing him love letters while going out with other men. He was due to be demobbed in April. His letters were all full of his plans to go back to Amberley, to take over the garage where he used to work, and his hopes that they could get married in a year or two.

She knew she wasn't really responsible for Bonny but she couldn't just sit back and watch a dear friend who wasn't even seventeen yet ruin herself.

Ellie got out of bed as she heard a car draw up outside, and went over to the window. She rubbed off the ice with the end of her nightdress and saw Bonny getting out of the taxi. Her blue satin cocktail dress and short fur jacket in a setting as dismal as Marshall Street were incongruous even at night, but viewed on a grey, cold, early morning, no one could have been blamed for seeing the girl with tousled blonde hair as a trollop, returning from a night on the tiles.

Ellie wrapped her dressing-gown round her tighter as Bonny came clattering up the stairs. She was already wearing a cardigan over her nightdress and thick wool socks because it was so cold. She wanted to have a wash before Mrs Arkwright surfaced, but just the thought of going down to the icy scullery made her shiver.

'Got an aspirin?' Bonny asked the moment she was in the door, flinging her handbag down on the bed, showing no surprise that Ellie wasn't still asleep. 'I've got such a hangover.'

'Where have you been all night?' Ellie asked. Bonny had gone out straight from the theatre, for supper, she'd said.

'With Stan, of course.' Bonny didn't even look at Ellie, just began rummaging amongst the cosmetics littering the top of the chest of drawers.

'You didn't sleep with *him*?' Ellie's nose wrinkled in disgust.

'Well of course I did,' Bonny retorted. She found some aspirin and popped them in her mouth, grimacing as she swallowed them. She moved over to the mirror and ran her fingers through her hair. Both girls had had a permanent wave last week, but while Ellie's were in a loose, natural style, prompting people to remark she looked like Hedy Lamarr, Bonny's waves were more rigid and she could pass for twenty-one at least. 'What did you think I did with him? Walk on the moors in the moonlight?'

Ellie just stared in horror. Bonny had a new bracelet on her wrist. It looked like real gold. 'How could you, Bonny?' she said in a small voice. 'He's not even nice and he's married.'

'What business is it of yours?' Bonny snapped back. 'Do I criticise you for hanging around with a bloody fairy?'

Ellie decided there was little point in biting back on the insult to Edward before she'd said her piece. 'Sit down and tell me why you're doing this.' This was an order, not a request.

'It's too bloody cold to sit down,' Bonny said, throwing her jacket down, unzipping her dress and dropping it on to the bed. She picked up her dressing-gown and put it on, then climbed into Ellie's bed, which was still warm. 'This is better. But I don't want to talk, I want to sleep.'

'We will talk about you or I find a job on my own

and leave you here,' Ellie threatened. 'I could've had a good part in *Cinderella*, as you well know. But I turned it down so I could be with you. So that gives me the right to ask questions, doesn't it?'

Bonny just crossed her arms and looked at the ceiling with studied insolence.

'It's all to do with what the doctor told you in Great Yarmouth, isn't it?' Ellie sat down beside her, tucking the eiderdown round her knees. 'You've got wilder and wilder since then and it doesn't take a great brain to figure it out.'

'Rubbish. I don't care if I can't have kids,' Bonny said stubbornly, reaching out for a cigarette. 'Who wants them? They're nothing but trouble. I just like having a good time.'

'I think you *do* care about it,' Ellie said carefully, trying hard not to lose patience. 'Deep down you feel worthless – that's why you pick on men you can use. But the more you do this, the worse you'll feel inside.'

Ellie felt a little out of her depth discussing such things when her own sexual experience amounted to an unsatisfying fumble with Charley and relations with an American while she was unconscious. She had no wish ever to try again with another man, not unless she was truly in love, but she realised Bonny was a far more physical person than she was.

'Me, feel worthless!' Bonny snorted derisively, cigarette smoke coming down her nostrils. 'I'm just making the most of opportunities. If you had any sense you'd do it too. Stan offered to set me up in a flat last night, he doesn't like to think of me living like this.' To illustrate her point Bonny waved her hand towards the black mould on the wallpaper beneath the window.

'Stan is over forty, he's got a pot belly, a balding head and three children,' Ellie said coldly. 'Aside from all that stacked against him, he's a crude, loud-mouthed show-off. The only attraction to you is that he's got money. You might as well be a prostitute.'

'He's good fun,' Bonny said indignantly. 'What's more, he's good in bed.'

Ellie shook her head in bewilderment. Stan Unsworth owned a brewery and several public houses in Sheffield. He had brought his children to see the pantomime just after Christmas and being a pushy sort of man he'd taken them backstage to meet the cast. Within a day or two the first bouquet of flowers arrived for Bonny, quickly followed by chocolates, a bottle of champagne and a dinner invitation.

'He *is* good in bed.' Bonny grinned impishly, sure she could make Ellie laugh and forget the lecture. 'It's like having a sex-slave, he does anything I want him to.'

She waited for a moment, sure Ellie was going to ask for details. Bonny was dying to tell her that Stan had given her three orgasms during the night in a lovely country house hotel out near Buxton and that the funniest thing of all was he couldn't even get an erection.

'I don't want to know.' Ellie turned her head away. Bonny loved telling her spicy secrets, but she didn't want to picture that nasty little man slobbering over her friend. 'You've got a serious problem, Bonny, and if you don't face up to it soon you'll end up like my Auntie Marleen.'

'I'm not the only one with problems,' Bonny sniffed, taking another deep drag on her cigarette. 'Look at you! You won't let any man get near you except Edward the queer.'

'Don't call him that,' Ellie riled up. 'He isn't queer.'

'Isn't he?' Bonny smirked, lifting one fair eyebrow. 'I reckon he is! So he gets girls now and then, but haven't you noticed they're always boyish? He wouldn't know what to do with a real woman. I bet he puts rubber gloves on before he touches them.'

'That's a horrible thing to say.' Ellie was sickened

461

by Bonny's cruelty, even if there was a thin thread of truth in what she said. 'Besides Edward and his love-life is nothing to do with you or me.'

Bonny gave a peal of laughter and dropped her cigarette into Ellie's late-night cocoa mug. 'Nothing to do with you or me, eh! It's got everything to do with us. He's obsessed by you, Ellie, and he hates me because he thinks you're the same way about me. A *ménage à trois* is what the French call it. Except none of us is having sex with each other. No wonder I go out and really do it with normal, red-blooded men. You two give me the creeps sometimes.'

Ellie was too shocked to come back with anything.

'Well, answer then!' Bonny was flushed, her eyes almost jumping out of her head.

'I can't. I don't know what to say,' Ellie said weakly. 'You say such wicked, spiteful things, Bonny, and I don't understand why. Edward isn't obsessed with me, we're friends, good friends. And he doesn't think I have some weird thing about you, neither does he hate you. Who paid for you to stay in our digs in Lowestoft until we all got the job in Manchester? Not me Ellie, but Edward. If you remember, I thought you ought to go home to your parents.'

'I'm sick of this.' Bonny turned over on to her side, pulling the pillow over her face.

Ellie snatched it off. Bonny was very good at avoiding things she didn't like. But this time Ellie had no intention of letting her. 'Listen to me,' she ordered her, leaning over Bonny and pressing both her arms down on the bed so she couldn't move. 'I've told you a little about my Auntie Marleen, but not the whole thing. She started out like you, bags of talent, pretty and funny and she lived off men for years. I've never told you what she was like just before our flat was bombed. But I'm going to tell you now.'

Ellie took a deep breath. Marleen might not live for much longer and it didn't seem right to tell anyone about her past. But Marleen would be the first to admit how she'd sunk to the gutter if she might save another girl from going the same way.

'She used to come home too drunk to know what she was doing, brick dust on her clothes from having it off on a bomb-site, smelling like a polecat,' Ellie hissed into her friend's face. 'Sometimes she'd lost her knickers, her stockings were torn and she had vomit on her clothes. I loved her, Bonny, but she sickened me. I learned what the smell of sex is like long before I ever kissed a man. It was enough to put anyone off for ever. You're not even seventeen yet, but you're going the same way. You drink too much already. You've been with at least six different men that I know of just since you had the abortion. Go on the way you're doing and you'll end up just like her.'

Bonny's eyes welled up and spilled over, great round tears rolling down her cheeks, bringing with them sooty mascara.

'I care about you, Bonny.' Ellie began to cry herself, slumping down beside her friend, hugging her tightly. 'I know you're unhappy deep inside you and I want to help. But please give me a chance, tell me what it is you want?'

There was silence for a moment. Ellie heard a horse come clip-clopping up the street. A bell rang, followed by the wheezy cry of 'ragabone'. From downstairs she could hear the sound of Mrs Arkwright scrubbing some clothes against her washboard and the smell of boiling handkerchiefs and shirts. It was a reminder of life in Alder Street, of how as a little girl she used to go to sleep dreaming of singing on a stage, wearing beautiful clothes.

Ellie's dreams were still alive in her. She was singing and dancing now, although she had a long way to go. She wanted to know what Bonny's dreams were, and if they could make them happen together.

'I don't know any more what I really want,' Bonny

said in a strangled voice. 'It used to be to get to Hollywood, but I don't think of that now. It's just faded.'

'But you must've replaced it with something,' Ellie whispered.

'I only think of living in a lovely house like Briar Bank.' Bonny turned her face into Ellie's shoulder. 'One where there's lots of sunshine, the table laid beautifully for dinner and upstairs the bedrooms all sweet and fresh.'

'What about dancing?'

'I don't care about that so much, not any more.' Bonny's voice sounded strangled. 'I like to think of other things, like a little girl outside on a swing and a baby boy in a playpen. I like to imagine a man pulling up in his car and me running out to meet him.'

Ellie didn't snort with disbelief. She instinctively knew this was the truth; all that surprised her was that Bonny wanted something so commonplace. 'Jack?' she asked.

'I wish it was.' Bonny made a little hiccuping sound and wiped her eyes on the sheet. 'But I can't truly love him, can I? Not the way I treat him. Besides, how could I marry him without telling him first that I can't have children? Will any man ever want me as a wife, knowing that?'

Ellie's eyes prickled. As she suspected, the doctor's words in Great Yarmouth were at the bottom of everything. 'That doctor didn't say it was impossible for you to have children, only unlikely. That isn't the same,' she said soothingly. 'And when you find the right man he won't care about your past. You can always adopt a child.'

'Why are you always such an optimist?' Bonny asked, leaning up on one elbow and looking down at Ellie. 'And why don't you admit I've fouled things up for you more than once?'

'Where I came from you had to be an optimist to survive,' Ellie said glumly. 'I remember once Edna who lived downstairs had her window broken by some kid with a cricket ball. She went for him like a mad woman. Mum stepped in to calm things down and do you know what she said?'

'What?' Bonny smiled – she liked Ellie telling her things about Alder Street.

'She said, "Never mind, Edna, think of it this way, luv, you ain't bin able to see out of it fer years 'cos of the dirt on it. Now you've got a clear view of the neighbours." Edna fell about laughing. I thought she was having a fit.'

Bonny giggled, not just at the content of the story but at the way Ellie could revert to a cockney accent at will. 'What gem have you got for me fouling up your life then?'

'You're the kid with the cricket ball.' Ellie smiled affectionately. 'If I hadn't met you I'd probably be married to Charley now. I wouldn't be lying here in this icebox of a room, or wondering where we're going to end up next month. But I've got a view now and I've seen some sights.'

Bonny smiled. She made a mistake in sometimes thinking she knew everything about Ellie. Almost daily she discovered some new facet to her character, or some new story from the past. Ellie could be brave and fiery, like she was that day with Ambrose; she could be as soft as melting butter and yet as tough as Mrs Arkwright's beef stew. To look into her face was to see it all, those passionate dark eyes, the softness of her lips and skin, yet the strength and determination in her little pointed chin.

'Do you still think about Charley?' Bonny asked, all at once aware that she'd rarely concerned herself with her friend's needs or problems.

'Yes,' Ellie sighed, a flicker of pain in her eyes. 'All

the time. But it's done now, just as your abortion is. We have to live with our mistakes, and go on.'

'Should I write to Jack and tell him it's over?' Bonny sat up and drew the dressing-gown round her tighter. 'I think part of the reason I've been so bad is because I felt guilty about him. It isn't fair to let him go on dreaming of a life with me, is it? Not when I know it won't happen.'

'No, it isn't,' Ellie agreed, pleased that on one point at least Bonny was being adult. 'And better to do it now while he's still in the army, he'll have his mates to help him through it.'

'We were such good friends though,' Bonny said wistfully. 'Did I tell you it all started when he saved me from drowning?'

Ellie listened as Bonny told the story.

'We were always an unlikely pair,' she concluded. 'Me so spoilt, him a ragamuffin with a mother who couldn't care less. My mum will be thrilled once she gets the news I've given him up for good. She said once, "But he's so common, and he's got red hair." She's quite forgotten she came from Bethnal Green, and that Jack is a good man just like Dad.'

A week later Ellie got a letter from Frances, posted from her parents' home in Oxford. Her uncle, Archie Biggs, had passed on Ellie's address in Sheffield and she had written not only to pass on gossip about the show at the Phoenix, but also in the hope that Ellie and Bonny might join a new one in Oxford with her.

Ellie read the part of the letter about Ambrose aloud to Edward and Bonny over a cup of tea before they left for the matinée at the Playhouse. 'Jimbo Jameson pulled out as backer not long after you three left,' she read. 'He tried everywhere apparently to get someone else, but no one wanted to know as the audiences were falling off. After Christmas he couldn't pay any of us. Most of us girls stayed on a week, hoping something would turn up, but Riccardo left, and then Buster. Apparently Jimbo's in some serious trouble himself, something to do with the black market, we don't know exactly. Anyway when the second week's wages didn't materialise we all hot-footed it out of there. Ambrose is *savage*! Bankrupt too by all accounts, and I have to say I'm glad, because he was evil to us all.'

'Just deserts.' Edward grinned, but Bonny shrieked with laughter.

'I hope he ends up sleeping under the bridges by Charing Cross station,' she said maliciously. 'Serves him right.'

Maybe if they hadn't had to rush off to the theatre, Ellie might have revealed the rest of the letter eventually that afternoon. But she needed time to think what she was going to say to Edward first.

Frances was going for an audition for a revue at the Arcadia in Oxford the following week, and she had invited Bonny and Ellie to join her as there were sixteen dancers needed. She warmly invited them both to stay at her parents' home, which wasn't far from the theatre, and pointed out they would be found permanent digs immediately if they were accepted.

Bonny felt she must jump at this chance. Oxford was quite close to Stoke Mandeville Hospital, so she could visit Marleen easily. On top of that, no other offers had come their way and *Aladdin* was finishing next week.

Ellie reached the stage-door at ten-thirty that night, just in time to see Bonny, despite her promises, getting into Stan Unsworth's car. It was snowing, and judging by the two-inch blanket hiding the ugliness of the street had been all evening.

'It actually looks pretty for once,' Edward said behind her, then spotting Bonny in the black car just pulling away, he put his hand on Ellie's shoulder.

'She'll never change, that's just the way she is.'

'Well at least she's written to Jack and finished with him,' Ellie sighed. She was in fact relieved that Bonny wouldn't be around tonight. She had to break the news to Edward that there was nothing in the show in Oxford for him, and Bonny was spiteful enough to enjoy it. 'Stan looks as if he deserves a bit of torture. From what I've heard about Jack, he doesn't.'

As they walked home together in the snow, their companionable silence was another reminder to Ellie of how much she would miss Edward, for his self-reliance, dependability and good nature. There were never quiet moments like this with Bonny: she demanded attention constantly as she chattered and giggled. But for some time now Ellie had been aware of the growing animosity between her two friends, and she couldn't stand being pulled two ways by them for much longer.

After the bitter cold outside, the kitchen seemed very warm. The fire was still alight, but they knew it was more than their lives were worth to add more coal to it. This room was very austere, but at least clean. Mrs Arkwright had laid out four mugs on the table, each with a spoon of cocoa and a splash of milk. Four small rock buns sat on a plate, burned on the top and barely edible. The fourth cake and cup were for Albert Coombes, but mostly he got drunk after the evening's performance and didn't come home until the early hours.

'I'll put the kettle on.' Edward hung his coat over a chair, whispering because Mrs Arkwright was in bed in the front room. 'I'm glad Bonny's gone off and Albert's out drinking. I wanted to ask you if you'd like to come home to my grandmother's when the panto finishes, until we find another job?'

Ellie had to tell him about Oxford, then and there, without building up gradually to it.

He was standing by the table, one moment a wide

grin on his face, the next his whole face seeming to sag.

'I'm sorry, Edward,' she said bleakly. 'But I need it, especially as it's so close to Marleen. Maybe you could get a job in Oxford too, playing the piano in a hotel.'

The kettle boiled. He fetched it and poured the hot water into their two mugs, but he didn't say a word. Ellie could see a nerve twitching in his cheek and she was frightened by his silence.

'Speak Edward,' she said, as he stirred the cocoa. 'I know it must seem I'm running out on you. But we always knew we'd get split up some time.'

'I'm not upset about that,' he said at length, slumping down into a chair and putting his head in his hands. 'Though I wish we'd worked on another comic act we could do together. But this will mean you're stuck with Bonny for good. She'll pull you down and destroy you.'

'That's silly.' Ellie put one hand out and touched his shoulder. 'How can she destroy me? Please don't be jealous.'

'I'm not jealous.' He lowered his hands and caught hold of hers, his blue eyes intense and deeply penetrating. 'I would be cheering if you got a good job on your own. But while I'm around Bonny doesn't try to drag you into things with her. The moment I'm off the scene, she will.'

'That's a bit insulting,' Ellie said stiffly. 'Do you really think I've so little character I can't stand up to her?'

'You don't understand, do you?' Edward shook his head. 'She's slow poison, Ellie. She drips it in without you knowing and it makes you think you need her.'

'Rubbish,' Ellie snapped. 'I care about her, I like doing an act with her. But I'm not dependent on her.'

'Then why didn't you stay in Manchester and be the fairy godmother?' he asked. 'I wanted you to, it was a good part. It was Bonny who influenced you against it. She didn't care about you, only herself, and what thanks did you get for it? A month in this hell-hole while she screws every man in town.'

'Don't say such things, Edward!'

'It's all true! Take notice, for God's sake, Ellie, before it's too late,' he pleaded. 'You're only using half your potential doing an act with her. You're a brilliant comic actress, you've also got a wonderful voice. But no one sees that when you're on stage with *her*, they watch her feet and body, Ellie, and your talent is diluted.'

Ellie stood up. 'We can't talk any more tonight,' she said, putting one hand on his cheek in an attempt to say she understood what he meant. 'We'll disturb Mrs Arkwright. Go to bed, Edward. We'll go some-where tomorrow and talk some more, when we've both had time to calm down.'

Ellie lay awake, staring at the ceiling. She'd heard Albert come in minutes after Edward got into bed, waking Mrs Arkwright when he banged the door. He stumbled as he came up the stairs and she guessed he was drunk. Now he was snoring as he always did and she wished Edward would thump him and make him stop.

Some of what Edward said made sense. She was in danger of losing her identity as an actress while dancing with Bonny, and maybe she should talk to Archie about it. But Edward was wrong to think she was being manipulated by Bonny; that much was pure jealousy.

The sound of a creaking door made her sit up. There was a gas light outside the window and the curtains were so thin the room was bathed in soft yellow light. To her astonishment her door was opening and Edward was coming in.

'What is it, Edward?' she whispered. 'Mrs Arkwright will fry you for breakfast if she hears you.'

He crept silently across the floor. He was wearing

striped pyjamas with a sweater over them. 'Let me get in with you?' he whispered. 'Please!'

Ellie moved over and pulled back the covers. Edward got in and wriggled down beside her.

'I'm sorry,' he whispered. 'I couldn't sleep. I was too worried.'

'I told you we'd talk in the morning. I'm not angry with you or anything. I'm not sure you should be doing this.'

She couldn't really imagine Edward making a pass at her, not after all this time. And he was too much of a gentleman just to barge his way into her bed with that on his mind. But Bonny's words a week ago about him being obsessed with her popped back into her head and made her uneasy.

'I'll go back in a minute,' Edward said. 'And I've only got in here because it's cold, in case you think anything else. I just wanted to tell you how I feel about you. By tomorrow I won't be able to find the words.'

Ellie waited. She could almost hear his mind ticking over for the right word to start.

'I love you,' he whispered. 'I don't mean in a romantic way exactly. But it's more than just being a friend. I suppose I am jealous of Bonny, because she'll be with you and I won't.'

'We can still be friends,' Ellie said. 'We can write to each other, spend a holiday together. Just because I'll be working away from you doesn't mean it ends here.'

For a moment he was silent. 'I meant every word I said about Bonny,' he said softly. 'I can't take that back, because it's all true. Just promise me you won't allow her to hold you back from achieving your ambitions?'

'I promise,' Ellie said soothingly. 'Just don't ask me to stop caring about her.'

'Can I cuddle you?' he said. 'Just for a minute.'

He slid his arm round her and drew her head on to his shoulder. She could feel his lips on her forehead and she sensed there was something more he wanted to say.

'Tell me?' she said. 'There's something more, isn't there?'

'Mm,' he murmured. 'I've wanted to tell you hundreds of times.'

'Well, now's your chance.' Ellie wriggled closer. The heat of his body felt good and it was making her sleepy.

'I've found out I can make love to women,' he said against her forehead. 'I'm not queer.'

'What a time to tell me, now you're in bed with me,' she said in mock alarm, lifting her head just enough to see his face. She had grown so used to it she rarely considered how handsome he was. The dim light from the gas lamp in the street showed up his fine cheekbones and straight nose, and the blond hair falling over his forehead gave him a vulnerable look he rarely had by day.

'I don't think I'll ever make a great stud.' He gave a soft little laugh. 'I still don't understand quite why most men think about it all day. Or why I let Ambrose do that to me. But I'm normal, Ellie. I do like women.'

'I'm glad,' she murmured, snuggling down again. 'I'd have liked you just the same, even if you found it was men you liked. But you being happy and comfortable with yourself is what really counts.'

As Edward watched Ellie drifting off to sleep he considered how odd it was that he'd been aroused by three different women with whom he had nothing in common, and yet that now the woman he adored was lying in his arms, he felt nothing but a sense of belonging.

'Jack! How nice,' Lydia said as she opened the door. 'But Bonny isn't here. Did you expect her to be?'

But even as she spoke she saw there was something very wrong with Jack. His eyes didn't meet hers, his shoulders were stooped, he was wringing his cap in both hands – even his hair looked less fiery.

'No, I didn't expect her to be here,' he replied in a growl. 'I had a letter from her today.'

'Come in, Jack.' She opened the door wider and stepped back. Instinct told her what the letter from Bonny contained.

Jack stood awkwardly at the door of the sitting-room. He knew Lydia had increased her dancing classes and piano lessons since the war ended. He thought he might have interrupted one.

'Come on in and sit down.' Lydia gently nudged him through the door. 'I'm all alone.'

Jack sat down in an armchair, looking at the sofa. It brought back memories of the first time he made love to Bonny and a wave of pure agony welled up again.

'Now, Jack, a drink?' Lydia said. 'You look like you could use one.'

She didn't wait for his reply, just poured a large brandy and handed it to him, then pulled up a pouffe in front of him and sat down.

'It's over,' Jack said, his face contorting as he struggled to control himself. 'She said I'd just become a habit she couldn't break, that we had nothing in common and she'd make my life a misery.'

'Poor Jack.' Lydia reached out and took his big rough hand, squeezing it between her two slender white ones. 'I am so *very* sorry. I didn't know she was going to do this. Did you think I might?'

'No.' He shrugged his shoulders. 'I don't even know why I've come here, except you're the only person that loves her as much as me.'

Lydia's heart contracted painfully. She knew exactly what he had left unsaid. Everyone else would say 'Good riddance', 'She wasn't for you Jack'; a grieving

473

man didn't want to hear that. And Jack was a man, a man with a big heart, strong and dependable.

'Did they give you leave?' she asked.

He shook his head. 'No, I just did a bunk. I couldn't face the lads.'

'I'll telephone your commanding officer and explain,' she said quickly. 'You don't want to be put on a charge.'

'I couldn't care less if they locked me in irons and flogged me,' he said wearily, wiping his uniform sleeve across his eyes. 'I can't live without her, Miss Wynter.'

Lydia made him drink the brandy. He winced as he gulped it down and tears sprang to his eyes.

'You *can* live without her, Jack,' Lydia said gently. 'Maybe today it seems that way, but it will get easier.'

'It won't,' he said stubbornly, raising pain-filled eyes to her. 'She's like the sun in my life, take that away and I've got nothing.'

Lydia plied him with more brandy. She called his commanding officer and explained why he'd gone absent without leave, promising she personally would drive him back to camp tomorrow morning. Then she sat down and listened to Jack.

He spilled out so much, so many things she didn't want to hear. Jack's pain became hers, and Lydia wept for the child she loved and yet knew she'd lost too, for Bonny wouldn't come back here again now, not unless she was in trouble. As Jack got drunk he spoke of Ellie having the abortion and Lydia guessed the truth of that story too. But between lies and deceits, childhood friendship and adult passion, one single bright thread stood out.

'You say she influenced you to want more than you were dished out with, Jack,' Lydia reminded him. 'Don't give up on that now because she doesn't want you. Fight, Jack. Get that garage, build it up and make something for yourself. A great many people admire you around here. You are someone for them to look up to. Remember the little lad with holes in his shoes and torn trousers who insisted he wouldn't be parted from his brothers? None of us could forget him! You deserve success and by golly I'm going to see you get it, Jack, if I have to come down to that garage and change tyres with you.'

'But it won't make Bonny love me,' he said bleakly.

'No, but it will make you love yourself, Jack, and there's other girls out there who will give you a great deal more lasting happiness than Bonny ever could.'

'Why couldn't she love me, like I love her?' he said just before passing out on her chair.

Lydia looked down at Jack and sobbed. She knew Mrs Phillips must ask herself that same question. Lydia had even asked it herself too. The truthful answer was that Bonny had been brought up seeing love as chains. She was greedy for freedom, like a bright, beautiful butterfly, only stopping fleetingly to sip on the nectar of love, afraid of being captured and kept in a jar.

Chapter Twenty-Two

Oxford, April 1946

Magnus Osbourne stopped under the shop awning, took off his trilby hat and shook it. It was pouring and he could feel dampness penetrating his raincoat, right through to his suit. It was more than just an April shower; the rain looked set in for the day.

'I should've arranged to meet Basil at my hotel,' he murmured to himself.

All his twenty-year-old student memories of Oxford were bathed in perpetual sunshine. In his mind's eye he saw sunbeams slanting through the leaded panes of his study. Punting down the river wearing a panama hat, shirt-sleeves rolled up, with a couple of giggling girls reclining on cushions. Driving his Alvis with the hood down, playing tennis and rowing on warm evenings. Magnus knew it must have rained on countless occasions, yet he couldn't recall one day in three undergraduate years when Oxford hadn't looked golden.

It wasn't golden today. The university halls were every bit as imposing as he remembered, but a dingy film tinged the yellow stone. The shops were pinched by post-war austerity, badly needing a fresh coat of paint, and the people's faces seemed as grey as the sky. The only cyclists passing were in oilcloth coats, no black, gowns fluttering behind them as he remembered.

Turning towards the window of the bookshop he was sheltering beside, he saw himself reflected clearly, and it wasn't altogether pleasing to observe how clearly the lean youth who'd once bought books in this very same shop was moving into middle age.

Taking off his hat for a moment, he stared at himself. He was forty-one. Ruth claimed he was handsome now, but when they married back in 1929 he had been merely 'interestingly angular'. His hair was still as thick and fair, although a recent severe cut prevented it from having the 'haystack' appearance she so often laughed about. His features were all prominent: a broad nose and forehead, a wide mouth with fleshy lips and a strong chin. His eyes had lost their youthful brilliance; once a bright speed well blue, they had faded and speckled like a wren's egg. But Magnus had never been concerned with his appearance, and his interest in it now wasn't mere vanity, merely a slight anxiety as to whether, at forty-one, he was still physically strong enough to embark on what promised to be a strenuous, new way of life. 'Of course you are.' He grinned at his reflection. At twenty-one he'd been a six-foot weed weighing less than ten stone. He was close on thirteen stone now and it was all muscle and sinew, not an ounce of fat.

'Magnus old chap! How the dickens are you?'

Magnus turned at the booming greeting and grinned at his old chum, putting one big hand on the man's shoulder and squeezing it affectionately. 'All the better for seeing you again.'

Magnus and Basil Lanagan had first met as 'freshers' here in Oxford. Both keen sportsmen, they had rowed and played tennis and cricket together and their friendship had endured, despite only seeing each other every two or three years.

They had both been in the RAF during the war, albeit different squadrons; Basil based in Suffolk, part of a ground crew, Magnus in Kent in reconnaissance. But now Basil was back teaching English and geography in a boys boarding-school close by, and Oxford had been an ideal choice for a long overdue reunion.

'The rain's a damned nuisance,' Basil said, sweeping a hand over his wet hair. 'I thought we'd be tramping around our old haunts.'

Basil hadn't changed much since his student days: a tall, well-built fellow, with glossy black hair, smooth olive skin and flashing white teeth. His six years in the RAF had produced a rather splendid moustache. It suited him, Ambrose thought, and gave him a rather dashing image.

'We could go back to my hotel,' Ambrose suggested without much enthusiasm. 'Though I doubt we'll be able to get anything more than tea.'

Basil looked up at the sky reflectively. 'Tea's better than a soaking!' he replied.

As they made their way back in the direction of the Royal Oxford Hotel, they made small talk about their respective families, aware that the gap of almost three years since they'd last met up left a great deal of trivial catching up to do before they could lapse back into the more comfortable manner of long-term friends.

They might have walked right past the Arcadia Theatre, but for a large board outside, almost blocking the pavement, proclaiming, 'TODAY'S MATINÉE TICKETS HALFPRICE'.

'How about that?' Basil said with laughter in his voice. He wasn't entirely serious, but they both had fond memories of taking part in a student revue at this same theatre. 'Fancy seeing the Great Gonzalis or Ruby Rivers the Northern Songbird?'

Magnus studied the garish posters with some amusement. He knew exactly what this variety show would be like: heavy-footed dancing girls, a thumping piano, ageing comedians and magicians. But the sign declaring that this was the show's sixth week had to be in its favour, and it was one way to while away a couple of hours out of the rain.

'On your head be it,' he laughed. 'Don't complain later that I talked you into it!'

They took their seats just as the musicians were tuning up. It didn't look promising; only a pianist, a drummer, an ancient violinist and a saxophonist.

Looking around him, Magnus saw the theatre was less than a quarter full, mostly of old people, and a sprinkling of those like themselves who'd come in out of the rain. The Arcadia was suffering from the same post-war malaise as shops and houses everywhere in England: peeling paint, upholstery worn and shiny with age, a threadbare carpet. Magnus felt that all too familiar stab of anger again. When were the government going to make a start on getting the country back on its feet?

Magnus knew he was very fortunate. Born into a wealthy, landowning family, he had never known a moment's deprivation in his life, or even the real necessity to work for a living as Basil had to do. Brought up at Craigmore, the family estate in Yorkshire, educated at Rugby and then Oxford, he could have spent his life just as his two elder brothers Frederick and George did, hunting, shooting and fishing. But even as a boy, Magnus had a social conscience. It never seemed right just to fritter his time away, secure in the knowledge that employees ran the estate. Or to whittle away the fortune that previous generations of financially astute Osbournes had left them.

While his brothers concerned themselves mainly with their social lives, to the despair of their father, Magnus took a more active interest in the running of the estate, working alongside the men in his school holidays and vacations from Oxford, learning everything from the art of building drystone walls to carpentry and mending farm machinery.

At twenty-two, with only a second-class degree in English behind him, Magnus regretted not having followed his instincts and chosen architecture or civil

479

engineering instead. He was no academic, but neither was he cut out to be 'just a gentleman'.

Stifled by the social restraints in England and his inability to settle again in Yorkshire, Magnus took himself off, first to America, then on to Canada. His family would have been appalled to discover that in two years away from home he worked in logging camps, on river boats going up and down the Hudson and for a spell as a builder in Vancouver. He might never have come home to Craigmore again, but for his father dying and his mother pleading he was needed, and he certainly wouldn't have stayed but for falling in love with Ruth Tomlinson, a doctor's daughter.

It was clear then, in 1928, that the old order of life in England was changing. The First World War had decimated the young male population and those who remained fit to work wanted more than a life of domestic servitude with the landed gentry. Craigmore was neglected, and Frederick and George, bewildered by suddenly finding themselves expected to take over the running of the estate, looked to Magnus for help.

Magnus agreed to stay, but on his own terms. He intended to marry Ruth and she wasn't a brittle, sophisticated woman like Frederick's and George's wives, or even his own mother. Ruth was gentle, a home-maker, a girl who wanted a real family life and a husband by her side. Above all, Magnus wanted her to have the happiness she deserved.

In return for becoming estate manager, Magnus insisted on having a cash settlement immediately from his father's estate, rather than risk his share being eaten away by his brothers' excesses, as well as the dilapidated gatehouse, free and clear. George and Frederick found their younger brother's requests amusing, and agreed willingly, assuming he'd later regret asking for so little. They continued to treat him like a simpleton as he worked tirelessly on the estate and watched in some amazement as in his spare time he restored the gatehouse into a gracious family home.

In 1929, Magnus married Ruth, breaking a long family tradition in being the first Osbourne not to bring his new bride into the big house. Ruth was delighted with this arrangement; she had been used to living in a small family home and she found the prospect of scores of servants daunting. She had always admired the gatehouse for its elegant proportions, charming arched latticed windows and its position on the road into Harrogate and it meant even more to her now Magnus had restored it for her.

Their marriage was a true love match. They complemented each other in every way: Magnus had the strength of character, the vision and stamina; Ruth smoothed his path, her quiet, loving way giving him the impetus to expand his ideals. Stephen was born in 1930, followed by Sophie some fifteen months later. Ruth didn't subscribe to the idea of nursemaids, cooks or housekeepers, preferring to look after her family herself, and Magnus found real joy in being a husband and father.

Ruth's appreciation and enthusiasm at Magnus's building talent fired him still further. While still managing the estate, he invested his own money in property. He bought small, semi-derelict houses in Harrogate, drew up plans to improve them, then employed local men to do the work, sometimes selling them on when they were finished, sometimes taking in a tenant. Back then he was motivated more by proving to his family that he could make his own fortune, rather than from altruistic ideals of improving people's standards of living, but that was to change.

Despite his background, Magnus was a sensitive man. During the depression years of the thirties, he became acutely aware of the hardship the working classes had to endure. His social conscience pricked at him daily as women knocked on the gatehouse door, begging for bread or a little milk for their children. He saw men who'd lost their jobs in the big shipyards of Tyneside tramping wearily past his comfortable house, looking for any kind of work in any town to keep their starving families.

If it hadn't been for the war, Magnus might have continued to salve his conscience as he had before, by giving the odd day or two's work to needy men, passing on old boots and clothes and letting Ruth give food. But six years in the RAF seeing the wholesale destruction of big cities and mixing with people from so many different walks of life, made his re-evaluate everything. After his demob at the end of 1945, he returned home to Yorkshire realising he had a far bigger duty in life than concerning himself with Craigmore and supporting his indolent brothers.

As Magnus was the youngest son, Craigmore would never be his, or his children's. Frederick had three sons perfectly capable of taking up the reins. There were Yorkshire men returning from the war in need of work who would help them. What England needed now, more than anything, was houses, and Magnus intended to build some of them.

It was estimated that half a million homes had been destroyed or made uninhabitable during the war, while another half a million were severely damaged. The White Paper of March 1945 suggested three or four million new homes must be built in the next ten years, yet now, in 1946, they were dragging their feet, the 'prefab' their only answer to the acute housing shortage.

People were so desperate for homes they were squatting in disused army camps. The council housing waiting lists were so long it could take a man seven or eight years to get his family housed. Magnus knew he could only help a relatively few people to a better standard of living by building, but he had vision and he truly believed that if he led, others might follow, and England could be rebuilt.

*

482

The band struck up 'I've Got Rhythm', the curtain swished back and on pranced the dancers. Magnus sat back in his seat, his lips twitching with suppressed laughter because he was immediately reminded of amateur dancing shows put on at his local village hall in Yorkshire.

The girls weren't co-ordinated, either in their steps or appearance. Half wore top hats, tails and fishnet tights, the other half flowing chiffon dresses. Where it would have made sense to dress the tall ones with good legs in the masculine clothes and the short ones in the dresses, the producer seemed to have given out costumes at random. As they swirled in pairs their weak voices were almost drowned by the band and the tapping of their feet was far from synchronised.

Magnus watched in amusement as the girls linked arms for a high kick routine. One girl was completely out of step with the others, and none of their legs reached a uniform height. The line broke in the middle, leaving gold painted stairs at the back of the stage exposed and as they moved back to form a semi-circle, two more girls appeared at the top of the stairs.

A shiver went down Magnus's spine. These two girls were perfectly matched. One was dark, the other blonde, both in tailcoats and top hats, sensational legs in seductive fishnet.

'Wow!' Basil exclaimed, nudging Magnus's arm.

Magnus was too enthralled to comment. The girls' symmetry dazzled him. Their height, size, even leg length was identical. They came down the stairs tap-dancing, faultlessly in time with each other. Magnus found himself leaning forward, forgetting the rest of the troupe, watching and listening to only these two.

They were both beautiful; slender yet curvaceous, with long legs and tiny waists. The dark girl's face was reminiscent of an old movie star, with angular cheekbones, smouldering eyes, fleshy, succulent lips. The blonde's eyes dominated her face. Even from his seat well back in the stalls he could see the bright blue irises, fluttering thick eyelashes and delicate eyebrows.

By concentrating on each of them in turn, Magnus realised that the dark girl had the best voice, while the blonde was the best dancer. Yet the interaction between them somehow made them as one. Magnus listened to the dark girl's husky, contralto voice, and watched the blonde girl. Her feet moved so fast it was just a flash of glitter, her hair shone like gold satin under the lights, a smile as warming as summer sun. The choreography was disastrous, the band scratchy, yet these two girls managed to pull something remarkable out of nowhere.

When the curtain closed on them Magnus settled back, somehow expecting more surprises in store. But he was disappointed. One sad act followed another and Basil guffawed beside him. It was tempting to get up and leave. But they stayed, nudging each other and sniggering as 'The Great Gonzalis' dawdled over a magic trick that a child of six could see through. They smirked at an awful rendition of 'Danny Boy' from 'The Northern Songbird', and Magnus found himself drifting away from what was on the stage, and thinking instead of the piece of land in Staines beside the Thames he'd bought that morning and the houses he intended to build on it.

It could well turn out to be a disaster. In the last few weeks Magnus had discovered that all builders had to get a licence, then permits for certain materials like timber. On top of these hindrances, the government were insisting that only a certain percentage of new houses built could be sold on the open market; the rest had to be sold back to the local council for people on their waiting lists. Other builders had informed him he would be bogged down by red tape and a mountain of paperwork, because Attlee and his party were trying to prevent speculation in property. But Magnus felt he had to give it his best shot. He wasn't a speculator, he just wanted to build homes.

Both men's interest in the show was re-awakened when the two girls came back singing 'Keep Young and Beautiful'. This time they were in tight spangly shorts with tiny matching tops which gave a tanta-lising view of their flat, firm abdomens. The blonde's costume was midnight-blue, the dark girl's bright red, but as before, it was the way they interacted together which created the magic, not the set or their costumes. Now Magnus could see the dark girl's comic talent as she preened in front of a looking-glass, catching the essence of all those postures women made when they thought they were unseen. The blonde did a faultless string of cartwheels, seemingly with no effort, and her smile remained as vivid throughout the last frenetic tap-dance as it had been at the beginning.

'*Keep young and beautiful*,' Basil droned as they came out of the Arcadia to find it still raining. 'What shall we do now, old bean?' he said, pausing to turn up his raincoat collar.

'My hotel for tea.' Magnus grinned. 'Let's cut out all the banter and talk about the important issues, like how it is for you back in teaching after the rough and tumble of the RAF. And I've got a few plans of my own I'd like to chew over with you.'

It was around ten that night when Magnus and Basil found themselves in the Cabana, a small drinking club above a gentleman's outfitters, just a stone's throw from the Royal Oxford where Magnus was staying. It was reminiscent of many of the clubs in London's Soho: candles in wax-congealed Chianti bottles on each of the bare wooden tables, tarnished gilt-framed mirrors on the tobacco-coloured walls and a half-hearted pianist playing in one corner.

The men propping up the small bar had a striking

similarity to the soldiers and airmen Magnus had drunk with on many a night in London, except they were all in badly fitting demob suits instead of uniforms. Most of them were young and at varying degrees of drunkenness. They leaned on the bar watching a few fresh-faced girls dancing together, from time to time shouting ribald remarks then turning to each other and laughing uproariously.

Both Magnus and Basil were a little tight. They'd had a couple of drinks before dinner at the Royal Oxford, a bottle of wine with their roast beef, then a couple of brandies as they switched back from their plans for the future and their families, to reminiscing about their student days.

It had been Basil's idea to find somewhere else to go. Magnus was happy just to stay drinking in the hotel, then let Basil get a taxi back to his school. But Basil had said, 'What we want is a place with a few fillies and a spot of dancing.'

Magnus had no interest in either 'fillies' or dancing; but when the hotel porter directed Basil to this club, it had seemed a little churlish to refuse, especially when he didn't know when they'd next have a chance to meet again.

Basil was in fine form. He had always been something of a raconteur and the war had given him a whole new fund of hilarious anecdotes. Now as the drink loosened him up still more, he moved on to tales from his school.

'I must tell you about the two little blaggards I found drunk in the gymnasium,' he began – but a sudden hush in the club stopped him short. 'Wow!'

Basil turned first, his face flushing purple in the candle-light. Magnus's head swivelled round; he blinked, then stared open-mouthed.

It was the two dancers they'd seen that afternoon, coming in through the door.

Their entrance had the same confidence as the

afternoon's performance and was as deliberately staged. Not for them a peep round the door, or nervous giggling at finding the club full of men. They merely swept in, leaving the door swinging behind them.

The dark girl wore a cream dress, the blonde an identical black one. They floated across the floor to the bar, seemingly unaware of the dozens of male eyes on them, yet at the same time scanning the crowd.

A little warning bell rang in Magnus's head. He turned back to his drink and tried to pick up the conversation with Basil. He guessed the girls had come here looking for male partners, and though he considered himself far too old to attract their attention, Basil was a good-looking chap and by far the most personable one in the entire club.

'I'll have the brunette,' Basil whispered, leaning across the table. 'I wouldn't say no to the blonde either, but she seems to have set her cap at you, old boy!'

Magnus had been married to Ruth for seventeen years and their marriage was strong enough to withstand even the most cunning of predatory women during the war. But as he turned his head involuntarily and met the blonde's turquoise eyes, looking right into his, it was as if the thinking part of his brain had switched off, leaving only the baser animal instinct.

She was a walking dream. The kind of girl that graced magazine covers, slender, yet curvy and soft. Her mid-calf dress covered those beautiful long legs he'd admired on stage, but it was her face which stunned him. Not just lovely eyes, but a perfect delicate nose and a soft, pouty mouth. Her hair curled on her padded shoulders and her complexion was as clear as a child's.

'I'm Bonny,' she said, putting one hand on his shoulder. 'Can Ellie and I join you? We're celebrating tonight and it would be more fun with company.'

The impudence in her voice warned him to make

excuses and leave, but Basil, always a ladies' man, was already jumping up, pulling out chairs and grinning with delight.

'We saw the show this afternoon,' Magnus admitted after Basil had gone through the introductory pleasantries and bought both girls a double gin and tonic. 'You were excellent. I wish I could say the same for the rest of the show, but I'm afraid you were the only stars.'

Ellie blushed prettily, but Bonny locked her eyes into his. 'It's only been a temporary stopgap,' she said with a dismissive shrug of her shoulders. 'We're off to Brighton next week and then on to another show in the West End.'

She claimed they were both twenty-two. She dropped names of famous show business people into her conversation as if they were personal friends, spoke scathingly of Oxford being 'too provincial' and mentioned shopping in Bond Street as if she never went anywhere else. Although Magnus knew all of this to be a pose, he was intrigued by both girls and the bond between them.

It was no ordinary girlish friendship, but something deep and binding. Although Ellie appeared to take a back seat, Magnus sensed she was an equal partner. They had a curious ability to allow each other equal time in the spotlight, backing each other up, almost as if it were a script they'd learnt together.

Yet Ellie made no wild claims as Bonny did. She made them all laugh with an impersonation of Ruth Rivers the Northern Songbird, holding her throat to get the exact warbling voice, and told a hilarious story about her Aunt Marleen during the Blitz, lapsing into a perfect cockney accent. Magnus noticed she mentioned visiting this aunt in Stoke Mandeville Hospital each week and saw a glimmer of real anxiety in her eyes about moving away to Brighton. But when Bonny told her well-embroidered tales, Ellie's dark eyes glinted with silent amusement.

Seen close up, it was hard to say who was the most beautiful. Bonny was fire and ice, Ellie more earthy; Bonny a doll, Ellie a woman.

Whilst in the gents Basil laughingly likened it to choosing between soft and hard centres in chocolates, both equally desirable, but leaving a different taste in the mouth.

Some time later, while Magnus danced with Bonny, holding her tightly in his arms, breathing in that heady scent of her hair and skin, he thought of her as a strawberry cream, so delicious he could hardly restrain himself biting into her.

The girls had digs in Cowley, and though it made sense for Magnus to walk back to his hotel and leave Basil to escort the girls home in a taxi, then continue on to his school, for some reason Magnus found himself squashed in the back between the two girls.

'Just meet me for lunch tomorrow,' Bonny whispered, her tongue gliding around his ear, sending electric' shocks to his brain. 'Just to say goodbye. I'd like to talk to you when we're both sober.'

The one kiss he gave her was his undoing. He felt like he was seventeen again, flying off into space with a million shooting stars all around him.

'Outside the Black Lion at half past twelve,' she said as she got out of the taxi, then turned to kiss her finger and placed it on his lips. 'Good-night, both of you. It's been a wonderful night.'

Basil was effusive in his praise of both girls as they drove back into town to drop Magnus at the hotel. 'I'd give my right arm to see Ellie again,' he said wistfully. 'But she said she never goes out with married men.'

'Married men': the phrase had meant little to Magnus all evening, but as Basil used it, Magnus's conscience was severely jolted. He could see Ruth's sweet face before him, her brown eyes soft with reproach, and he vowed he wouldn't meet Bonny for lunch.

*

'Weren't they the biggest dishes we've ever seen?' Bonny giggled as Ellie unlocked the front door at their digs. It was well after two-thirty and they were both quite drunk.

Their story about celebrating their new job in Brighton was true. The manager at the Arcadia had recommended them to a friend of his who ran the summer shows on the pier and they were off to start rehearsing next week.

They were both excited about it. To appear in Brighton was a big step up from towns like Oxford. But for Ellie, delight was tempered with sadness. In the six weeks they'd been in Oxford she'd been visiting Marleen regularly and she had seen a fast decline in her health which was very worrying.

'Shh!' Ellie warned her. Mrs Ray, their landlady, was a good sort but she could get very nasty if they woke her. 'Married dishes,' she whispered. 'And Basil was too hearty and old for my taste.'

Bonny's behaviour had improved a little since they arrived in Oxford. At least she hadn't actually stayed out all night. Ellie couldn't be certain whether Bonny was really calming down, or whether it was because Ellie had been persuaded to join her on several double dates and acted as an unwitting 'gooseberry'. Edward sarcastically claimed in his letters it was more likely she hadn't found a man with enough money! He was working in Bristol, playing the piano at tea dances by day and working as a cocktail waiter by night. He sounded very demoralised. There was now a glut of men coming out of the forces and jobs went to them in preference to those like Edward who hadn't seen active service.

'Magnus is a dream.' Bonny took a couple of steps towards the staircase in the dark and giggled as she stumbled.

The light was suddenly switched on and both girls froze, looking up the stairs in alarm.

'I thought you two were never coming home,' Mrs Ray called from the upstairs landing.

'Sorry,' Ellie said quickly. 'We didn't mean to wake you.'

Mrs Ray appeared at the top of the stairs. She was wearing a plaid brown dressing-gown, her hair in curlers. 'I haven't been to sleep,' she said, coming down towards them. 'I've been that worried.'

The house was a thirties-style semi-detached, ordinary enough by Bonny's standards, but Ellie considered it almost heaven to live in a bright, modern house with a real bathroom. Mrs Ray fussed over them in the motherly way Annie King had and Ellie felt guilty when they upset her.

'I'm sorry we're so late.' Ellie tried hard to look sober, bracing herself for a telling off. Mrs Ray's face looked sunken because she hadn't got her teeth in and Ellie resisted the urge to giggle. 'We were celebrating – we've got a new job in Brighton.'

'The hospital telephoned,' Mrs Ray blurted out, taking the last few stairs towards them in a rush. 'It's your auntie, Ellie. They want you to go there.'

For a second or two Ellie could only stare at her landlady stupidly.

'I'm afraid it sounds serious,' Mrs Ray added.

Ellie felt an icy numbness creeping all over her. 'You mean?' She couldn't continue.

'I'm sorry, my dear,' Mrs Ray said gently, reaching out and putting a hand on Ellie's arm. 'They wouldn't have called so late unless –' She paused too, unable to say the word they both understood.

Ellie was suddenly sober. She looked round at Bonny and back again to Mrs Ray. 'I'll have to get a taxi.'

'You can't get one now!' Bonny said, her voice shrill in the silent hallway.

'I'll ask Mr Ray to take you.' Mrs Ray turned back up the stairs. 'He's awake anyway and Bonny's right, you can't get a taxi at this time of night. Just go and make yourself some coffee, Ellie, he won't be a moment.'

Mr Ray was a miserable little man, but he always did what his wife said. He came downstairs pulling a jacket over his pyjamas. He still had the bottoms on – Ellie could see them dangling beneath his trousers as she gulped down the scalding Camp coffee.

'You are *so* kind, Mr Ray,' she said. 'It's about twenty-five miles to the hospital. It would be a fortune in a taxi, even if I could get one.'

He merely grunted and said something about charging her for the petrol since it was still rationed, then bent down to put his shoes on.

'I'll ring you in the morning,' Ellie said, turning to Bonny. 'If I can't get back by tomorrow night someone will have to stand in for me.'

'I'll see to that when you phone.' Bonny hugged her once more, her face soft with concern. 'I'll be thinking about you.'

'She's been waiting for you,' Nurse Symonds said simply as Ellie arrived at the ward, the real meaning of her words obvious. 'She's in a room on her own now, go on in.'

It was so quiet in the hospital, eerie with just the dim, green night-lights glowing through glass doors. Nurse Symonds was a big, raw-faced woman whose wit and often sharp tongue had endeared her to Marleen.

Ellie believed she'd prepared herself for the worst. But as she went into the small room and saw her aunt lying there under a small, dim light, she let out an involuntary cry of distress.

Marleen had been growing thinner and weaker for some months, but now she was almost skeletal. No dark glasses to hide the scarred and empty eye sockets, folds of slack, grey skin revealing sharp cheekbones and her grey hair so thin she looked at least eighty. Her mouth had sunk in, lips cracked and bloodless.

'About time too.' Marleen turned her head slightly towards the sound of Ellie's feet, her voice weak, but with all its usual acerbic sarcasm.

'I came as soon as I heard you were poorly.' Ellie was surprised that Marleen could be aware of time or sense who her visitor was when she looked so fragile. 'I was out when they telephoned.'

'Bin drinking gin, too.' Marleen's nostrils twitched as Ellie bent over to kiss her. 'Wish you'd brought me some.'

The remark was so typical of her aunt's humour that for a moment Ellie thought the nurses and doctor were mistaken about her dying.

'I would've done, if I'd known you were up to it,' she said, taking hold of Marleen's thin scraggy hand and pressing it in both of hers.

An odd noise came from Marleen's chest as she tried to cough. 'I ain't got long now, Ellie,' she wheezed, 'so don't interrupt. I just wanted to say 'ow proud I am of you. Don't reckon I'll end up in the same manor as Poll, but if I do I'll tell 'er all about you.' She paused, struggling for breath.

Ellie took a teapot-like cup from the bedside locker and held it to Marleen's cracked lips. 'Don't try to talk, Auntie,' she urged. 'Save your strength.'

Marleen took one sip, but shook her head impatiently. 'For what?' she said, her voice quavering now, each breath a struggle. 'I done it all, luv. I ain't afraid to die.'

'Please don't talk like that!' Tears ran down Ellie's face.

Marleen fell silent then, the only sound her laboured, wheezing breath. Ellie sat beside her, holding her hand.

Five minutes passed, then ten.

'I love you, Auntie,' Ellie whispered, not knowing whether Marleen could still hear her, but it needed saying.

The hand in hers moved, a weak attempt to prove she'd heard, and Ellie bent her head to kiss it.

'I love you an' all.' Each word came out so slow and tortured Ellie could only stare in horror, clinging to that thin hand, knowing instinctively the moment of death was approaching.

Marleen sunk into unconsciousness, her squeaking breath growing slowly fainter. The nurse came in and sat silently beside the bed.

It had been dark when Ellie arrived, but slowly, grey then pink light pushed away the night, giving Marleen's face a faint blush. A weak, almost imperceptible sound came from her, then utter silence.

'She's gone,' the nurse said softly, taking the hand Ellie was holding and placing it gently with the other across Marleen's chest. 'Rest in peace, Marleen.'

Ellie looked down at the wizened figure in the bed and let her mind slip back to recall her aunt as she wanted to remember her.

A clear picture came to her, of a day at Southend when Ellie was seven. There was a talent competition on the promenade, and Marleen, urged on by Polly, took part. The number she chose was a saucy music hall song, 'He's Got Flirty Eyes'. Ellie could see Marleen so distinctly. Her hair was deep auburn then, a cascade of loose, shiny waves and she wore only an emerald green bathing suit. She could hear the riotous applause, the wolf whistles and calls for an encore ringing in her ears, and see Marleen's broad grin when she won the first prize of two guineas. She insisted on spending every penny of that money on Polly and Ellie. They went on every ride in the fun fair and had candy floss, ice-creams and cockles and then supper before they went home on the train.

But perhaps the most poignant memory of that wonderful day was Marleen's words to Ellie as she kissed her goodbye late at night. 'I ain't so talented,' she'd smiled. 'But I've got nerve, Ellie, and that's all it takes mostly. You just remember that!'

Ellie kissed Marleen one last time, tears rolling down her cheeks. Marleen had kept her nerve, right up to the last moment. Ellie had a funny feeling that when Marleen arrived at the Pearly Gates she'd be demanding the best seat in the house.

'She was such a character,' Nurse Symonds said as she led Ellie out of the room, her arm round her. 'We're all going to miss her, Ellie. Now you come with me, I'll make you a nice cup of tea.'

It was when the nurse brought a bag of Marleen's belongings to Ellie that she really broke down. It was such a pitifully small collection for a woman who had once needed dozens of boxes to shift her belongings from one flat to another and a reminder of how little her mother left behind too. A small teddy bear Ellie had bought her, a bottle of cheap scent perhaps given by another patient, a couple of nightdresses and a cardigan. But in an envelope were a batch of reviews for Ellie's show at the Phoenix. Clearly Marleen had asked people to read them again and again, as they were yellow and dog-eared.

'She was so very proud of you.' Nurse Symonds patted Ellie's shoulder soothingly as she saw her tuck them away again. 'Those meant a great deal to her. She used to say, "Nurse, mark my words, my Ellie's going to be a big star. When you go to the flicks and see her up on the screen, you make sure you clap and stamp your feet for me!"'

Ellie wiped tears from her eyes.

'She'd had enough,' the nurse said softly. 'She put on a brave face here and made us all laugh. But I know she was glad to go.'

The nurse was right, of course. Maybe in a few days Ellie might even be able to voice the same opinion, but for now she could only feel a huge chasm where her aunt had been.

Ellie leafed through the bundle of letters, stopping short when she saw several that weren't from her. The handwriting looked familiar and she opened one to see who they were from.

She was staggered to find it was Annie King – a warm, friendly letter that implied she'd been visiting too.

'Did Mrs King come to visit her?' Ellie looked up at the nurse in bewilderment.

'Yes, dear. She came once a month,' the nurse replied. 'Didn't your aunt tell you? They seemed like very good friends.'

So many times Ellie had thought of visiting Annie, if only to put her side of the story about Charley, but fear of rejection had prevented her and now she felt ashamed she hadn't appreciated how big-hearted Annie was.

'No, she never said.' Ellie shook her head. 'I expect she was being tactful. Annie's son was my old boyfriend.'

'Would you like me to write to Mrs King then?' the nurse asked solicitously.

Ellie hesitated for only a moment. 'No, I'll call on her. I must thank her for her kindness. It wouldn't be right for her to get such news in a letter.'

For the first time in her life, Bonny was on time for a date. She paused in a shop doorway just around the corner from the Black Lion, took out her compact and powdered her nose, frowning at her reflection.

If it hadn't been for Ellie telephoning early this morning with the sad news that Marleen had passed away, Bonny would have dressed to kill in her new blue costume and matching hat. But to wear something so flamboyant didn't seem right, even if her heart was pounding with excitement at seeing Magnus. So she put on her boring navy coat and an

496

ordinary print dress beneath. She'd have to think of some other way of ensnaring him.

Magnus got to the Black Lion just as a church clock was striking the half hour. Vivid images of Ruth had plagued him all morning. He could see her running to him full tilt down the platform at Harrogate station when he was demobbed, arms wide open and tears of joy in her eyes. He felt she knew by telepathy that he had spent the night with erotic dreams of another woman.

Ruth was small, plump, with curly dark brown hair, now, at thirty-seven, sprinkled with grey. She had never been a head-turner; her charm was her keen interest in others, her unselfishness and warmth. In all these years of marriage he'd never wanted anyone else in his arms but her. So why was he waiting here to meet an empty-headed young dancer?

He told himself he was only being polite in meeting Bonny for lunch. He would bore her with his happy marriage and his clever children, then get in his car and leave.

He'd been waiting for less than a minute when Bonny came round the corner. He was surprised by her sensible dark coat – he'd prepared himself for something more dramatic – and a little of his unease left him.

'Hello Magnus.' She tripped lightly towards him, her smile surprisingly hesitant. 'I almost didn't come because I've been so upset. But it seemed awfully rude to just leave you here not knowing what's happened.'

Magnus took her across the road to a small restaurant and over an aperitif she explained how Ellie had gone to see her aunt in the early hours.

'I couldn't sleep for worrying about Ellie.' Her eyes swam and she wiped them with her hanky. 'She rang this morning to say Marleen had died and I've been crying ever since. She hasn't got anyone but me now.'

Magnus was deeply touched by her concern for Ellie. He listened as she explained how Ellie had gone on to

497

London to inform someone else, but that she intended to get back in time for tonight's performance.

'I haven't got anyone either,' Bonny sniffed. 'My parents were killed in the war, just like Ellie's mum.'

Sympathy overrode Magnus's intention to cut this lunch short and be on his way. He ordered soup and lamb chops for them both, and a bottle of wine to cheer her up.

Somehow Magnus didn't get around to talking about his family as he'd intended. He did speak of Craigmore and his childhood on the estate, of his student days in Oxford and his time in the RAF, but not the blissful years tucked in between when Ruth, Stephen and Sophie had been his whole world. Neither did he mention that Stephen was almost sixteen, Sophie thirteen and that both he and Ruth hoped for another child now the war was over.

Bonny was exhilarating company. She painted such vivid pictures of the characters in both this show and previous ones. Her fluffy, girlish dreams and aspirations to get to Hollywood, her enthusiasm for life made him feel unaccountably tender towards her.

Drinking at lunchtime always went straight to Magnus's head, and when Bonny suggested they went for a walk in the afternoon it seemed the only answer if he was to drive to London later. Yesterday's heavy rain had cleared the skies and the spring sunshine was very warm as he took her into the botanical gardens.

'Isn't that beautiful!' She gasped at a magnolia tree in full blossom just inside the gates. 'Its like a – a prayer.'

There was something very touching and unexpected in finding she appreciated nature. Somehow he'd thought her interests wouldn't stretch beyond the cinema and shops.

'I love it here,' she said, smiling with pure delight at a bed of red tulips and forget-me-nots. 'One day I want to have a beautiful garden all of my own.'

When Magnus thought about it later on that day, he wondered how they came to select the most secluded bench in the entire garden. Was it he who chose it, willing something more to happen? Or was it her? Or merely fate that no one else came that way as they sat almost concealed by two large rhododendron bushes?

It was Bonny, however, who instigated the first kiss. 'It turned out a nice day after all,' she said sweetly, half turning on the seat beside him and putting her hand on his cheek. 'Thank you for the lunch and cheering me up.'

Her lips met his and Magnus couldn't and didn't want to avoid them and all at once he had her in his arms, kissing her back with the kind of passion he hadn't felt for twenty years. He was just a boy again, his heart racing, blood pumping at twice the normal speed. Reason, logic and morality had no meaning. He was like a salmon desperately swimming upstream against the current of his conscience, and winning because the need was so great.

Bonny didn't give him a moment to draw breath or consider what they were doing. Her fingers were creeping between the buttons on his shirt, gliding tantalisingly over bare skin, giving him a picture of exactly how it would be if they were in a hotel room.

Magnus's hands slid into her coat, the soft crêpe of her dress making it so easy to feel the contours of her body. When his hand cupped her breast there was no brassière beneath to dull the impact of hardened nipple against his fingers and her gasp of pleasure made it doubly thrilling. Her lips stayed on his, her tongue driving him wilder and wilder until his only thought and need was to possess.

What would make a normally sane, intelligent man of forty plus begin to make love in a public park, even if the girl was the most desirable blonde he'd ever seen? It was Bonny, not him, who pulled her coat over herself as his hand went up under the skirt of her dress. He no longer cared if anyone might see them. She was wet already and so very hot, and as his fingers drew aside her knickers she was arching against him, her need as great as his.

She made soft little moans of bliss as his fingers caressed her, pushing against him for more, and still her lips scorched into his. Her fingers traced the length and width of his erect penis through his trousers, teasing him until he was almost in pain.

'Take me somewhere and make love to me?' she whispered, slowly unbuttoning his flies. 'I want you so badly.'

Bonny knew she shouldn't be doing this, arousing a man purposely just to entrap him. But there was something about his reluctance which excited her. Few men ever even tried to turn her down.

It was only when Bonny's hand reached into his trousers that Magnus knew he was lost. It was either take her here on a park bench and face the possibility of arrest or take her to a hotel. There was no turning back.

Hand in hand, they ran from the gardens, through the busy streets and down towards the Royal Oxford. Magnus had checked out this morning, but he'd left his car in their yard. He was counting on a room being available.

'Of course we can find another room for you, Mr Osbourne.' The clerk smirked knowledgeably at Bonny. 'How nice that your wife came to join you!'

Magnus was convinced he knew Bonny was appearing at the theatre; and surely anyone could read the signs of dishevelled clothing, too bright eyes and swollen lips. But it didn't matter. All that counted was getting into a room, pulling off her clothes and consummating their desire.

It was the sweetest, fiercest love-making Magnus had ever known. Their clothes tossed off at the door, too hungry for one another for even the briefest of foreplay. They fell upon the bed and devoured one another and only in the afterglow of the first frenzied orgasm was there a moment to reflect on how much more they had to give one another.

Magnus knew she was no virgin, even though he expected her to claim she was later. But she wasn't a selfish lover. Her practised hands sought to please him in the manner of a true courtesan.

Love-making with Ruth was always beneath the covers in the dark. Not once in seventeen years had he seen her entirely naked. But Bonny displayed herself without shame or embarrassment, taking him to new heights of pleasure as she wantonly guided his fingers to the seat of her desire. She wound her slender legs around him and clawed at him deliriously, her moans of ecstasy awakening a dormant beast inside him which demanded more and more of her young, firm flesh.

'I'll have to go,' she murmured at half-past six, disentangling herself from his sweat-soaked body. 'Come and see the show again and I'll come back afterwards for the night.'

Magnus couldn't turn her down as he watched her washing herself at the basin. The line of her narrow back and her firm round buttocks were too beautiful and erotic to shut out He briefly argued with himself that one more night couldn't hurt, that it would be cruelly insulting to her if he left her now and went back to London. Yet deep inside him he knew he was lost already.

She turned back to him, a hairbrush in her hand. As she lifted her arms to brush her hair, he gazed at her beauty. Her breasts were pert and up-tilted, her blonde hair showering over her naked shoulders, and her face so achingly vulnerable.

'You do want me tonight? Don't you?' she whispered, those enchanting turquoise eyes swimming with tears. 'Say if you don't. I'll understand.'

'Of course I want you,' he said hoarsely. 'But you must understand I'm married, Bonny, and tonight's all we can have.'

'Bonny, no,' Ellie pleaded with her friend as they waited backstage for their cue, later that day. 'You'll get hurt, Magnus is out of your league.'

'He's not.' Bonny tossed her head defiantly. 'I know he's married, but I don't care. He's the man I want.'

Ellie turned her head away. Her emotions were red raw, she was exhausted from having had no sleep last night and then travelling up to London and back. She couldn't cope with any more scenes now. She wanted to pour out to Bonny how it had felt to lose a woman who'd been a major part of her life since she was born. To tell her how it was to go back to Coburgh Street, and find that Annie King's affection for her was unchanged, despite the way Ellie had hurt her son.

There was the sharp pain she needed to share, of seeing a snapshot of Charley taken on the ship going out to Australia. He was with three or four girls. Could one of them be a new romance?

Ellie had rushed back to Oxford, refusing Annie's offer of a bed for the night, not just because of the show, but because she thought Bonny would comfort her. But Bonny was too wrapped up in this new man to consider Ellie's grief at losing Marleen, or that tonight she might need a friend to pour it all out to.

The band was striking up with 'I've Got Rhythm'. Ellie could hear the other dancers whispering in the wings as they lined up in readiness. As her mother would have said, 'The show must go on.'

There was only one constant thing in her life: her talent. Friends might let ner down, people would come and go, but no one could take her talent away. Ellie knew that, as from tonight, she had to learn to be as single-minded as Bonny.

Chapter Twenty-Three

August 1946

Magnus stood at the ticket barrier at Victoria station, his stomach churning like one of the cement mixers on his building site. He could see the train held up by lights just outside the station and he reminded himself there was still time to turn and run.

But he stayed, oblivious to the throngs of people milling round him or the dusty, choking heat of the station. Porters staggered by with luggage, children clanged buckets and spades, mothers stridently admonished small boys to behave, but Magnus's mind was on Bonny.

It was now August, three and a half months since he'd met her in Oxford. London was in the grip of a heat wave and it seemed today everyone was trying to escape the city. Yesterday, as he'd laid bricks with his workmen in the searing heat, Magnus had thought longingly of Craigmore and Yorkshire. There he could be lounging beneath a shady tree, Ruth bringing him ice-cold lemonade or plunging into the pond with Sophie and Stephen, and at night there would be cool breezes coming off the moors. Today he wondered if the heat were responsible for another attack of middle-aged madness. Why else would a man risk everything he cared for, and lay himself wide open to ridicule?

Four days in Oxford, that's all he'd had with Bonny. Four wonderful, crazy days and nights when he felt he'd danced with the angels, seen the seven wonders of the world, yet made a pact with the devil – all with one woman. Woman! he thought with some cynicism. Bonny wasn't a woman, she was just seventeen, something she'd only admitted after a slip-up. How many more lies had she told him? The week's work in Rome! Would that turn out to be a lie? Was she really an orphan? Could he really believe she felt *anything* for him? Wasn't it more likely she was out to see what she could get, pulling on his string once more, just to check he was still attached?

Magnus had intended to end their affair in Oxford. He took both Bonny and Ellie and put them on the train to Brighton to go on to their next show. Ellie was pale and silent, her eyes still red-rimmed from her aunt's funeral the day before. Bonny had clung to him, tearfully insisting she couldn't live without him. In a moment of weakness, he'd tucked a ten pound note in her hand, along with the address of a friend in London where she could write to him, and rushed away cursing his stupidity.

Yet despite Bonny's fevered declarations of love, she'd only written twice in all this time. Brief, hurried notes, one saying she was going to Rome to dance, another saying she had an audition for a film part. It was odd she didn't send a postcard from Rome, or explain what happened at the audition!

But then, just as Magnus began to think he'd never hear from her again, she wrote to say she was free this weekend. He knew it was folly to see her again, but Bonny had given him something more than a few heady and thrilling memories. That vital spark at the core of her had affected him, given him youthful vigour and a head full of dreams, and he'd charged into his building project like a new man.

Guilt at betraying his marriage vows made long hours of back-breaking work clearing the site preferable to the comfort of home and Ruth's silently questioning eyes. He had no intention of sitting back and watching his men work; he needed the manual labour to feel they were his houses. His labourers' rough ways and crude language helped him forget such things as honour, family pride and his place in society back home

An image of Bonny's flashy taste had influenced the design of his simple houses, giving them something original and almost futuristic. Now the first one was almost completed. Once sold, he'd have tripled his initial stake and have enough capital again to pay for the building of the other five; then on to other similar projects. Maybe he'd discover this weekend that what he thought he felt for Bonny was just a brief infatuation. He hoped so.

The train chugged into the station and doors were thrown open, disgorging passengers. Steam and smoke prevented a clear view down the platform but suddenly Bonny appeared through it like a mannequin.

Magnus's heart thumped alarmingly, his pulse racing. She was wearing a sky blue dress which clung to her legs as she tried to run with her small case in her hand. Her blonde hair swung beneath a tiny veiled pillbox hat and her wide smile said everything Magnus hoped for.

'Oh Magnus,' she squeaked, dropping her case and hurling herself into his arms. 'I thought you'd change your mind!'

Magnus found it hard to keep his eyes on the road as he drove out of London. Just the sight of Bonny's sun-tanned long legs stretched out next to him was making him feel hot under the collar. He'd booked them into a small hotel in Windsor, but they could hardly arrive at eleven in the morning and retire to their room immediately without raising a few eyebrows.

'Would you like to see the house I'm building?' he asked, turning to smile at her. 'It's not quite finished, but it's right on the river and I could hire out a rowing boat and take you to a pub for lunch further downstream.'

'As long as you don't rock the boat,' she smiled, taking off her little hat and tossing it into the back seat. 'I've been scared of water ever since I nearly drowned once.'

'Tell me about it,' Magnus suggested, wondering if this was a tall story too.

'Another time.' She shuddered, as if remembering the incident frightened her. 'I wish I could get over it. It must be nice to take a dip on a hot day like this. I feel as if I'm on fire.'

Magnus was on fire too, but it wasn't because of the weather, only her. 'How's Ellie?' he asked, wishing he could get his mind off the moment when he could undress Bonny. 'Has the show finished? You didn't say in your note how you came to be having a weekend off?'

'Oh, one of the other dancers is taking my place,' she said quickly. 'She wanted the experience of doing a solo. I made out I had to visit my –' She halted suddenly. 'An old aunt.'

Magnus suspected this wasn't the truth, but he said nothing.

'Ellie's okay,' Bonny went on. 'She's got a boyfriend now, so I don't see so much of her.'

Bonny wished he hadn't started asking questions quite so quickly. The truth of the matter was that she'd been sacked from the Brighton show at the beginning of July. She was still living there, sharing a room with Ellie, but there was a certain amount of friction between them. That was why she'd written to Magnus and asked him to meet her this weekend.

'Ellie's getting over her aunt's death then?' Magnus asked, sure Bonny was hiding something.

'It changed her quite a bit,' Bonny admitted. 'We're both doing solo numbers now, not the double act you saw in Oxford. Also Edward, her old friend from the show at the Phoenix, is working in Brighton too, as a pianist in a club. Sometimes Ellie sings with him after the show.'

Bonny's trouble in Brighton all stemmed from her assumption when they left Oxford that she and Ellie would continue to be a double act. But Mr Dyson, the Palace Theatre producer, singled out Ellie to do a couple of solo comedy song and dance numbers and she was relegated to the chorus line again. When Edward turned up there too and began monopolising Ellie, that was the last straw. Looking back, Bonny knew she should have crept round Mr Dyson instead of being difficult, but she was hurt, missing Magnus and jealous of Edward, so she did what she always did when she was unhappy, and found a few older men to make a fuss of her.

'So you get a bit lonely?' Magnus turned, raising one eyebrow questioningly.

'Sometimes,' she said, and Magnus saw she was biting her lip as if this admission troubled her.

'Mind where you step!' Magnus said, taking Bonny's hand and leading her across lumpy soil strewn with building rubble. The almost completed house was in front of them. It had been rendered over the bricks and painted a very pale grey, but it had the graceful appearance of small Georgian houses. Either side were two more skeletons of houses, the brickwork only completed on the ground floor. The foundations were laid for the remaining three, but all work had stopped temporarily until the first could be sold.

'I don't expect you'll be very impressed,' he said as he opened the front door. 'You have to imagine so much at this stage.'

Bonny said nothing as she walked into the main

room, her high heels clip-clopping on the bare floor-boards. She paused for a moment, looking all around, then moved on to peer into the kitchen and dining-room.

She came back into the main room and opened the french windows. There was scrubland down to the river some twenty yards away and although the sunshine made the river itself look beautiful, Magnus had to admit that the six-foot weeds fronting it spoilt the view.

Bonny turned back to him, her eyes glinting. 'It's absolutely lovely,' she said in an awed voice. 'It's like a rich person's house, only smaller. Imagine when that's all lawn down to the river, a couple of small trees and flower beds.'

Magnus was delighted by her enthusiasm, and her understanding of the image he had tried to create. He loathed those awful red-brick houses the councils were so fond of; he felt people deserved better.

'You're so clever,' she went on. 'I love that elegant staircase, the pretty fireplace and the hatch from the kitchen into the dining-room. I'd give my right arm to live here.'

He saw then that the glint in her eyes was caused by tears, but he didn't understand quite why the house moved her so much, unless it was the flashy touches he'd added because of her. She ran upstairs, looking at the bathroom and bedrooms, opening cupboard doors and moving from room to room as if planning the decoration.

'The kitchen will be built in,' Magnus said when she came back down again, showing her a glossy brochure with an illustration of a woman rolling out pastry on a fitted work surface with cupboards above and below. 'It's a new space-saving idea, they have them like this in America.'

Bonny looked at the brochure and with a stab of guilt remembered her parents' kitchen with its ugly boiler, white china sink and the cabinet with an enamel, drop-down flap. She hadn't seen them since she moved to Brighton. They thought she was still in the show too.

'I think it's all marvellous,' she said wistfully. 'I can't imagine anything better than living here.'

It was the sad look in her eyes which made Magnus take her in his arms. 'You'll get married one day and live somewhere like this,' he said. 'Probably somewhere even better. I designed this with ordinary people in mind.'

She turned her face up to his, and the moment their lips met, passion flared up like fire in dry straw.

Her tongue flickered against his, two hungry mouths feasting on one another as he crushed her into his arms. She pulled out his shirt, reaching under it, her fingers clawing at his back, insinuating her hips and belly against his until she felt him grow hard against her.

'Make love to me here,' she whispered, sliding her hand over his erection. 'Now, here on the floor.'

'It's dirty,' he said weakly, glancing round at the bags of plaster, the tins of paint, yet his fingers were already fumbling at the row of tiny buttons on the bodice of her dress.

'I don't care,' she sighed, as his hand cupped round one breast. 'Please, Magnus?'

Magnus knew that any one of his workmen would have taken her against a wall, on a pile of bricks, anywhere, to satisfy their lust. He had always thought he had more respect for women than that, but he couldn't help himself.

A pile of sacks and dust sheets with a few newspapers on top was all he could find. But as he laid them down he saw that Bonny had already torn off her dress and was holding out her arms to him, wearing nothing but a pair of pink camiknickers.

He grabbed her, pressing her up against the wall,

mouth pushing aside the delicate material to suck on her breasts, his spare hand pulling off his trousers in fevered haste.

'Long and hard,' she murmured as his fingers thrust deep inside her. 'I want you to make me scream aloud.'

Memories of making love in the Oxford hotel had tormented him on so very many nights. But when he flung her down on to the makeshift dusty bed, the smell of new paint and plaster seemed to zoom him into an even wilder, desperate plane. She was so hot and wet, clawing at him, rolling on him, begging for more all the time in a way he'd known no other woman do. He knelt between her splayed legs, licking and sucking at her sex until she went into spasms of delirium, tossing her head from side to side, screaming out his name. She rolled him over on his back and slowly slid down on to him, making Magnus gasp with pleasure. She rode him, head thrown back, eyes closing in ecstasy almost as if she were alone with some inanimate, penetrating object. Magnus held her thighs, and wallowed sensuously in the delight of seeing a woman using his body so wantonly.

Her hair smelled of lemons when she finally bent forward to kiss him. He felt he was drowning in the scent, bewitched by the silkiness of her skin, every nerve ending pulsating as she devotec her attentions to pleasing him. He wanted to prolong the total bliss, yet felt himself being sucked into a vortex where he would surrender his life, heart and soul, in exchange for release.

'I love you Magnus,' she screamed at the moment of climax, clawing at his shoulders and grinding herself hard against him.

Magnus looked at her face as she lay curled against him and he felt he'd never seen anything so beautiful in his entire life. Such soft, sweet lips, still swollen from kissing, cheeks with an apricot blush and eyebrows just a glint of gold.

Dust danced in sunbeams through the french windows, playing on her tanned legs and small, white buttocks. She opened her eyes and looked at him. 'You'll always be mine here now,' she said, one finger tracing round the outline of his lips. 'Every time you come in here you'll see me, smell me, feel me.'

Magnus had no reply. He knew she was right. The memory of today would make it harder and harder to return to Yorkshire to be a husband and father. But he loved Ruth too. He could never turn his back on her and his children. He wished he'd never met Bonny and brought this torment on himself, but at the same time he felt so alive inside he knew he couldn't give her up.

Ellie and Bonny were still in their nightdresses, sitting either end of the bed drinking tea, even though it was eleven in the morning and the sun hot outside. It was a week since Bonny had come back from her weekend with Magnus and it seemed to Ellie that she couldn't talk about anything else.

Their boarding-house in Brighton was in Western Road, a tall, narrow, terraced house which had little to recommend it but its position, close to the shops and just a short walk to the Palace Pier and the theatre. Their landlady, an old widow called Mrs Parret, was very fond of telling them about the 'nice families' who came here before the war for their holidays, claiming if she could just get some paint and a man to 'do' the outside of the house, these families would come flocking back. Both girls doubted they would. Practically all the boarding-houses in Brighton had 'Vacancy' signs up, even though it was the high season, and most of them were far nicer houses than this one.

It had a weary, sad look as if it knew it was past its Edwardian prime, clean but shabby: chipped ornaments and saggy chairs in the lounge none of the residents bothered with; the dining-room obsolete because Mrs Parret was too old to feed her guests any longer. Their small room was at the back on the second floor, gloomy because the window overlooked a brick wall, and cramped because it was only intended as a single room. Ellie was trying to control her mounting irritation with Bonny, not only for her untidiness, but for the way she seemed to be living in some fantasy world.

'Magnus won't leave his wife, Bonny,' Ellie said in exasperation. 'I don't doubt he's fallen in love with you. But he loves his wife too and men like him are too responsible to abandon their home and children. You can never be more than his mistress.'

'I can make him leave her,' Bonny pouted. 'He's got all those houses, we could live in one of those.'

Ellie sighed. Bonny had drawn pictures of his houses, raved on about how clever Magnus was. It was all getting so tedious. 'He's built those houses to sell, to make enough money to move on to bigger projects. I can't see a man like Magnus, used to a big country estate, living in suburbia with a girl less than half his age.'

'But they're lovely houses,' Bonny argued. 'What's wrong with suburbia anyway?'

'Nothing, not for people like us who've lived in places with outdoor lavvies and no gardens. But he's what Marleen would've called a nob – they don't go for that type of house. Now, did you tell him you've got the sack from the show?'

Bonny's face darkened. 'Why bring that up?' she snapped, snatching up a pair of shorts from the floor and pulling them on.

Ellie arched her eyebrows. 'Because I can't keep you for ever, Bonny. The show's ending in September. We can't count on getting another job together, not after the way you blew this one. So if I get offered something good in London I'm going to take it and you'll have to look out for yourself.'

Ellie had been feeling very bruised when they arrived in Brighton. She was grieving about Marleen, and thinking about Charley, off to Australia. She found it hard to forget that Bonny hadn't come to Marleen's funeral with her, but spent the day with Magnus instead.

Bonny had acted like a spoilt child when she found they couldn't do a double song and dance act together. If she hadn't been so sulky and rude, Mr Dyson the producer might have come round. But instead she got up to her old tricks again, going out every night after the show, missing rehearsals, being mean to the other dancers and generally making a nuisance of herself until Mr Dyson lost patience and sacked her.

With hindsight, Ellie should have distanced herself and let Bonny sort herself out. The chances were she would have gone back to her parents in London once she'd had to leave the digs Mr Dyson had put them in. But Ellie felt sorry for her, so she left the digs too and rented this room for them to share, fully expecting Bonny to find a job and support herself.

It was just like being back in Stacey Passage, trying to make a meal on one gas ring, sharing a small bed and falling over all Bonny's belongings, while she was out half the night being wined and dined. She had made no attempt to find any work and expected Ellie to provide food as well as paying the rent.

If it wasn't for Bonny, everything would have been wonderful. After quiet Oxford, Brighton seemed as exciting as London. There was the inevitable war damage, the same shortages as everywhere, but the town bustled, the little shops in The Lanes were intriguing, and it was fun to be amongst jolly holiday-makers.

The two solo numbers Ellie had been given were ideal for showing her comic ability, and now Edward was here too. He was playing the piano in The Place, a smart night-club where all the influential people danced and drank. On top of that it had been a glorious hot summer. The barbed wire had been removed from the beaches at last, and the fun fairs stayed open until late at night. Brighton was a fun town. But Bonny had spoilt everything.

She bristled every time Ellie mentioned Edward, or the show. She had droned on and on about Magnus even before she met up with him again last weekend, despite going out with other men continuously. And Ellie was short of money now because Bonny was draining her.

Bonny whisked off her nightdress, pulled on a sleeveless blouse and shoved her feet into sandals. A spiteful, tight expression warned Ellie she was intending to go out and stay out, to make Ellie feel bad about having criticised her.

'Get a part on your own,' Bonny snapped as she flounced off towards the door. 'I can manage without you. But as it happens I was just going to tell you that Magnus has invited us both to a party in London in September. It's some sort of charity do and he wants us to do a turn in a cabaret. Just about everyone who's anyone will be there. Perhaps I'll do it on my own.' She swept through the door, slamming it behind her.

Ellie began to tidy up. She didn't believe a word of what Bonny had said and her indignation grew as she picked up dirty underwear, finding used cups and plates under the bed and an overturned ashtray under a pile of magazines.

It was as Ellie picked up a couple of letters that she found the invitation. It was a thick, expensive-looking card with gold lettering. As it wasn't in an envelope, she had no compunction about reading it.

'You are cordially invited to attend a Gala Evening at the Savoy Hotel on Saturday 18th September, to raise funds for the Red Cross.

Ellie smirked at it, wondering why Bonny hadn't shown her this the moment Magnus sent it. She glanced at it again, reading the smaller print at the bottom.

'*8.00 p.m. until midnight. Buffet, cabaret, dancing, auction and tombola. Tickets two guineas. Black tie. Patrons: Lady Penelope Beauchamp, Sir Roger Turnball and Sir Miles Hamilton.*'

Ellie dropped the invitation as if she'd been scalded as she came to the last name. She sat down on the bed with a bump, so stunned she had to put her head down between her knees for a moment.

Since looking up Sir Miles in *Burke's Peerage*, she hadn't attempted to find out anything further about him. Had she found herself anywhere near Hampshire she might have gone to look at his house or make some local enquiries, but there had never been an opportunity. Now here, when she least expected it, was an invitation with his name on it.

It was tempting to look for the letter from Magnus that accompanied it. Did he know Sir Miles? Was he really intending them to 'do a turn', or was Bonny making things up again? He was certainly taking a risk in allowing Bonny's name to be linked with his. Ellie felt Bonny was incapable of being discreet about their relationship. It was this aspect of Bonny's nature which had prevented Ellie from ever telling her about her mother and Sir Miles, and she certainly wasn't going to admit it now. But if Magnus really was serious about involving her and Bonny it could be just the perfect way of discovering a little more about her father. He might even be there!

A cold chill ran down Ellie's spine. Romantic little dreams of being embraced as a long-lost daughter were a pleasant way of whiling away a sleepless night. The reality of approaching a total stranger who might not want reminders of the past was something else. 'There's no point in agonising about it,' she told herself as she put the invitation back. 'For one thing, you

515

might not even get to the party. Just wait and see what happens.'

Three weeks later, Ellie was rummaging through her few clothes in the wardrobe, panic rising as she realised nothing she owned was smart enough even to walk through the doors of the Savoy in, much less to catch the eye of a West End producer.

'What am I going to wear?' Ellie turned round to look at Bonny, who was lying on the bed reading a magazine. 'The only evening dress I've got is the red one, and it's so shabby.'

It seemed to Ellie that fate had nudged her towards a crossroads and she was scared of taking the wrong turn. The invitation she had found was real; Magnus really had suggested to the organisers of the Gala that she and Bonny take part in the cabaret. Now, just days before the Brighton show ended, everything, costumes, props and, music, was arranged. They were going to do the 'Keep Young and Beautiful' number from the Oxford show and 'We're a Couple of Swells' and they'd rehearsed them diligently with Edward accompanying them on the piano each afternoon.

While Bonny could see no further ahead than this one glittering night and was thrilled that Magnus had arranged accommodation in London for them, Ellie was afraid.

The accommodation was only temporary, to tide them over between the Brighton show, the Gala and finding another job. Bonny seemed to think their turn at the Gala would shoot them into a West End production overnight, but Ellie was less optimistic. None of the girls she'd been working with had been offered further work; there wasn't even a whisper of auditions for shows coming up. She had only a few pounds saved and she had no suitable dress to wear at the Savoy for before and after their act.

Bonny had a beauty – turquoise chiffon which she

looked sensational in, bought by Magnus. Ellie couldn't bear the thought of putting on the red dress and looking like a poor relation beside her.

'Wear my black one!' Bonny suggested. 'Or go and buy something new. What about that midnight-blue one we saw in The Lanes?'

'I can't afford seven guineas,' Ellie sighed. She needed the little money she had saved to live on until she got another job.

'Well, it will have to be my black one then,' Bonny said with hurtful indifference.

Ellie turned to Bonny, anger flashing up out of nowhere. Bonny was lounging on the bed in a new pink dress her mother had made her. She'd had her hair cut and set that morning and had even bought a new pink lipstick and matching nail varnish, while Ellie could barely afford to buy a bar of soap.

Clothes rationing and post-war shortages didn't affect Bonny. While Ellie altered drab second-hand clothes, mended her underwear and sometimes even put cardboard over the holes in her shoes, Bonny somehow managed to get everything she wanted.

'If you were to pay me back all you owe me I could afford a new one,' Ellie snarled at her. 'After all, you can go and stay with your parents in London if nothing turns up. I haven't got anyone.'

When there was no sharp retort, Ellie felt a little deflated.

'Well? Cat got your tongue?'

'Don't mention my parents while we're in London,' Bonny said in a small voice, her eyes downcast. 'I told Magnus I hadn't got any.'

Ellie was so shocked, her anger faded. She flopped down on the bed, stunned speechless. 'But why tell such a lie?' she managed eventually.

'I don't know.' Bonny shrugged her shoulders.

'But it's such a *wicked* lie.' Ellie was aghast. 'I know

your mother gets on your nerves, but she doesn't deserve that! Was it to gain sympathy?'

Bonny's face crumpled at her friend's sharp tone. 'You don't understand,' she bleated. 'I want Magnus to marry me, I did as soon as I met him. I really do love him, Ellie, and it's tearing me apart. I don't want to be a dancer any longer. I want to be in a little house with him and have babies. I want to cut everything from my past. I want a new start, all bright and shiny.'

'Wanting to marry a man you love is understandable. But I can't see for the life of me why pretending you're an orphan would help it along,' Ellie said tartly.

'I don't know why I said that really, I didn't have a reason. It just came out when your auntie died.'

'It just came out!' Ellie sniffed. 'I can live with you telling people your Aunt Lydia is a countess, making out you're twenty-two instead of seventeen. I didn't even mind when you told me your dad was a Japanese prisoner of war. But I draw the line at killing off two people who love you.'

'I don't lie to you.' Bonny lifted her head. She was beginning to cry and it made her look like a schoolgirl. 'Maybe that's because I know you love me for myself.'

There was a great deal more Ellie wanted to say, but that last line of Bonny's pulled her up sharply. It was true. Bonny didn't lie to her – she had stopped it after her abortion – but Ellie had never considered why that was, until now.

'Then you mustn't tell Magnus lies,' she said. 'Everything is stacked against you two, your ages, his marriage and position. The only thing you've got in common is love. But if you intend to fight to keep him, fight fair, for goodness' sake. Don't tarnish what you feel for him with cheap tricks to try and hold him.'

Once Ellie had gone off to the theatre for the afternoon matinée, Bonny began to think more about her friend's words. She lay on the bed, staring at the ceiling, and wishing she could cut out the piece of her that made her tell lies.

She knew why she did it. She wanted attention, anyhow, any way. The real Bonny wasn't very bright, she came from a dull home and had dull parents. What she did was add colour to an otherwise beige background. Edward could talk about his grandmother, his public school and his parents being killed in a motoring accident. Ellie might have been dreadfully poor but she spent her childhood in a theatre surrounded by talented, amusing people. Everyone Bonny knew had colour in their early lives, except her.

But she'd found colour now. The weekend with Magnus was golden, tinged with scarlet passion. When she looked back it was like looking into a vivid painting, startling in its intensity; the deep green of the overhanging trees as Magnus had rowed her up the river, the water silver in the sunshine, with a canopy of turquoise sky above them.

At dinner in the hotel he'd worn a dark suit and white shirt, his wiry hair suppressed with Brylcreem. To everyone else in that dining-room, he was a sedate businessman. Only she knew the body beneath that suit was deep brown from the sun, rippling with taut muscle. Their fellow diners might look at her and admire her pretty face and hair, but in Bonny's eyes Magnus was the more beautiful. Thick springy hair the colour of butter and tender blue eyes flecked with greeny brown. A broad brown nose and wide forehead, fleshy lips that could soothe with gentle kisses, or in turn be as thrilling and as hard as a savage wild dog. His face and his nature were of a country boy, pure at heart, yet often as tempestuous as the weather. He was strong, yet so very sensitive. No other lover had ever taken her to the gates of heaven as he had, or so completely fulfilled her.

Bonny doubted that Ellie had ever been to that particular paradise, otherwise she wouldn't be pouring cold water on it now. But it wasn't just the making love – that she could probably get with other men. It was the way Magnus made her feel inside, more exciting than being up on the stage in a spotlight; sweet and fresh like seeing the first primrose in spring, yet scary too because it could all be snatched away so easily.

Bonny wanted Magnus for ever. For the first time in her life she wasn't concerned with material things, only the man. Ellie might not fully understand how desperate she felt, but she was right in saying she mustn't tell Magnus lies.

She got up from the bed and began to tidy up, suddenly aware how much she took Ellie for granted. She had been thoughtful and quiet for some weeks now. Was it because she was fed up with her? Or was she just worried about the future?

'It's time you did something for her,' she murmured as she washed the cups and cleaned the wash-basin. Bonny didn't like to think about what would happen to her if Ellie did go off and leave her.

It was as she closed the wardrobe door that Bonny thought of that blue dress Ellie liked. 'Seven guineas!' she muttered. 'I haven't even got seven shillings.'

'Close your eyes!' Bonny giggled as she opened the door to Ellie when she arrived home from the matinée, much later in the day. 'Don't open them till I say!'

'What are you up to?' Bonny's surprises had a habit of being trouble, but Ellie shut her eyes anyway.

'Close the door and turn round.' Bonny's voice trembled with excitement. 'Now you can open them!'

For a moment Ellie thought it was a cruel joke. Bonny was holding up the midnight-blue evening dress to her shoulders. 'You bought it!' she exclaimed. 'What for? You've got the lovely turquoise one.'

'I didn't buy it for me,' Bonny said indignantly. 'It's for you.'

A wide smile spread across Ellie's face, but it faded again as a thought crossed her mind. 'Where did you get the money? Did you take it out of my drawer?'

Bonny looked hurt and the corners of her mouth drooped. 'Of course I didn't take your money. It's a present. Though I did nick your clothing coupons. I got the money by selling a couple of bits of jewellery.'

'Not the bracelet Stan Unsworth gave you?' Ellie saw Bonny's wrist was bare.

Bonny grinned. 'It was a lot more valuable than I expected. I got fifteen pounds for it. Now stop nit-picking and try it on.'

Ellie was shaken. Bonny loved that bracelet; she never tired of showing it to people. For her to sell it, to buy a present for someone else, was the equivalent of shaving off her lovely hair or taking a cleaning job. Ellie was so touched at the unexpected generosity she was speechless.

'I d-d-don't know what to say,' she stuttered, a lump coming up in her throat.

'That's not like you!' Bonny grinned impishly. 'Now get it on before I lose patience.'

Ellie pulled off her cotton dress in a second and stepped into the long dress. 'Do me up.' She lifted her hair out of the way and as Bonny finished fastening the tiny buttons, she turned. 'So how do I look?'

'Like my aunt, the countess,' Bonny laughed. 'Oh Ellie, it's so perfect. You look gorgeous.'

Ellie looked at herself in the mirror on the wardrobe and gasped. The deep blue crêpe enhanced her black hair and olive skin in a way no other colour had before. It was strapless, the bodice boned to stay up alone and the skirt cut on the bias so it clung to her hips, then flared out just below her bottom in a fishtail style.

'It's so heavenly,' Ellie whispered reverently. She couldn't really believe what the dress did for her: her bare shoulders looked so sexy and the boned bodice pushed up her breasts so she looked like a film star. 'I've never had anything so beautiful, or so expensive. Oh Bonny!' She took a couple of steps towards her friend and hugged her, a tear rolling down her cheek.

'Now we'll both be a couple of swells at that do,' Bonny said in a curiously croaky voice. 'It's not much good me saying I'm sorry for things I say and do. I'm just made that way. This is all I could think of instead.'

Ellie held Bonny, no more words being necessary. She could understand why men fell under Bonny's spell; there was something so magical about her sometimes. Ellie could feel all her anxiety draining away, and excitement and optimism taking its place.

Now at the Gala she could be confident. Sir Miles might not be there, and she might not get an opportunity to speak to him, even if he was. But none of that mattered now. She was going to make the Gala night work for her. This was the big chance.

Chapter Twenty-Four

September 1946

'Whoever would've believed a kid from Alder Street would end up here!' Ellie whispered to Bonny. They were standing by the window of the Savoy Ballroom watching the guests arrive, trying very hard to look as if they usually came to such posh places. 'Just look at all those jewels! And did you see the furs they've left in the cloakroom? If I had a coat like that I'd be sitting on it, afraid someone would nick it!'

The summer had ended abruptly as they packed their cases to come to London three days earlier, even though it was only mid-September. Tonight it had mercifully stopped raining, but the view of the River Thames from the window was obscured by fog and they could see nothing beyond the lights on the Embankment.

The Savoy was even more grand and intimidating than they had expected. One of the doormen had said it was looking shabby compared with before the war, but Ellie thought it was all too wonderful.

All the guest wore their dinner-jackets and evening dresses with a nonchalance that suggested a gala evening such as this was an ordinary event in their lives. Ellie was aware now that the glass beads at her neck would never fool anyone here into thinking they were diamonds. She could see the real thing every-where, flashing and sparkling from throats, ears and fingers with a brilliance no fake could match. All the women had dainty beaded evening bags and long gloves. Ellie wished she had too, if only to give her something to hold on to.

'Don't speak like that!' Bonny said sharply. 'Someone will hear you and think we're a couple of –' she stopped short, unable to think of an appropriate word.

'Imposters?' Ellie grinned. 'That's what I feel like, or as my mum used to say, "Like a ham sandwich in a synagogue."'

Bonny looked like a film star in her turquoise chiffon, the colour matching her eyes and enhancing her golden suntan. Ellie thought perhaps it was easier for blondes to look expensive. She herself had felt she looked fabulous before they arrived here tonight, but now she wasn't so sure. Black hair, bare shoulders and so much cleavage above the midnight-blue dress was dramatic, but was it too revealing? What if she just looked cheap?

'I feel perfectly at home,' Bonny said, smiling at a short fat man who glanced her way. 'And if you're going to embarrass me I'll find someone else to chat to.'

'Okay, won't mention it again,' Ellie agreed good-naturedly. 'So what do we chat about? Am I allowed to mention that woman is too fat for that dress?'

Bonny giggled, despite her efforts to be dignified.

The woman in question was perhaps fifty and maybe sixteen stone. Her rose-pink taffeta dress had a tight fitted bodice and a full gathered skirt. Not only did the bodice look as if the seams were straining, but she had bulges of puckered flesh breaking out over the top of the low neck and another huge roll at her waist.

'I can't actually see anyone as pretty as us two,' Bonny said immodestly. They had put a lot of effort into their appearance tonight: face masks, manicures, to say nothing of sleeping in curlers and spending a couple of hours on arranging the artful waves and curls which cascaded over their bare shoulders. 'I suppose you've got to be old and ugly to be rich. Maybe you can't have it all.'

The girls lapsed into silence, just observing. The air was rich with scents, French perfume, cigars and flowers. A pianist was playing softly in the background, but he was almost drowned by a buzz of conversation. Gleaming polished wood floor, velvet drapes at the sparkling windows, silver trays clinking with fluted champagne glasses carried by waiters in tailcoats – it was all so luxurious.

Ellie looked up at the huge chandeliers and saw they acted like a kaleidoscope, each sparkling crystal picking up the vivid colours of the women's dresses beneath it. She wondered whether they'd left it there during the war; it must have made such a noise jingling when the doodle-bugs came over. She wondered too who cleaned it and for a moment she imagined herself back in the lawyers' offices in the Temple scrubbing stairs. That seemed like a lifetime ago.

Bonny was right – everyone was old, hardly anyone less than thirty. The men wore their age better than their wives, a few wrinkles and grey hair seemed to give them more character. Yet she wondered, if they were stripped of their dinner-jackets and bow-ties and put into ordinary working men's clothes, whether they'd still manage to look so distinguished.

Ellie thought Magnus looked splendid. He was at the far end of the ballroom, talking animatedly to a small group of men who'd broken away from their wives. She could understand exactly why Bonny was so crazy about him. His height, broad shoulders, bronzed skin and sun-bleached hair were at odds with their anaemic faces and puny physiques. She wondered which of the women was his wife. She could see a tall blonde woman with a bony face looking across at him: if that was Ruth, it was hardly surprising he had a mistress!

Last night, when he called round to the borrowed flat in Pimlico, he'd given them a lecture, warning them Ruth would be there and telling them both to stay well away from her. She had no idea it was he who'd put their names forward for the cabaret, and if anyone else should question them about it, they were to be vague and say they thought it was Mr Dyson in Brighton who had arranged their booking.

Ellie overheard him giving Bonny a further warning later.

'Please just think of it as just a job,' he said. 'I got you it, not to have you close to me, but in the hopes you might get spotted by someone in the entertainment business. So forget me, Bonny, dazzle everyone else and make the most of the opportunity. Don't make me regret it.'

The evening was intended to raise funds to help refugees and people displaced by the war. Earlier the girls had looked at a collection of photographs pinned to a screen of camps set up in Germany by the Red Cross for these people. Ellie had been quite disturbed by the scenes. Somehow until now she'd imagined the people in Germany were no worse off than they were here in England. Now she felt a little guilty that she and Bonny were getting paid for tonight.

'Tables and chairs had been set up around the stage, though as yet most people were just standing in groups chatting. The auction of donated goods would start soon, followed by the cabaret. The girls had taken part in a dress rehearsal in the afternoon. They were to open the cabaret with 'Keep Young and Beautiful'. The comedian would follow them, then the magician, before the girls did their second number.

Maria Dolenze was the star act, a singer who had appeared in many West End musicals, and she was to go on last. Finally, before the tables were moved back for dancing, there was to be a tombola.

Ellie wasn't particularly nervous about their numbers, for they knew them inside out and the band was excellent. But she was growing ever more nervous about Sir Miles Hamilton. She had no idea which of these many middle-aged men he might be, or even how she could find out. Now that she was here, intimidated by posh voices, expensive clothes and the glossy aura these people exuded, she wasn't sure if she had the courage to speak to anyone.

'I thought it would be exciting,' Bonny said indignantly as they made their way off to change. 'But no one took the least interest in us!'

'It will be different after the show,' Ellie said hopefully. She was just as disappointed as Bonny. The only person who'd spoken to them was a waiter and he'd only asked if they'd like a glass of champagne.

'I couldn't work out which was Ruth either,' Bonny said, a flicker of anxiety in her eyes.

'Nor me,' Ellie agreed. 'But stop thinking about her or Magnus. It will just put you off.'

The room they'd been given as a dressing-room was tiny, but grand by their standards, with a washbasin and a well-lit dressing-table. The ballroom was only down the corridor and as they changed they could hear the auctioneer calling out the bids.

'Have I got ten pounds?' they heard. 'Ten over there. Any advance on ten pounds? Ten guineas. Eleven pounds. Any more bids for this lovely bracelet? Surely it's worth more than eleven pounds?'

'I can't imagine anyone bidding for that rubbish,' Bonny said churlishly, sticking out her lip. 'Horrid old paintings, jewellery that looks as if it's from Woolworth's. Who wants that?'

'I don't think any of it's rubbish.' Ellie shrugged her shoulders, guessing her friend was only being spiteful because she was disappointed and worried about Ruth. 'Anyway it's for a really good cause. Imagine if we had to live in one of those camps.'

'Don't get any ideas about refusing our five pounds,' Bonny sniffed. 'We're displaced too. We won't have a job or a home next week.'

'Don't remind me.' Ellie turned her back towards Bonny so she could zip up her costume.

'I look like Shirley Temple.' Bonny stood beside Ellie at the mirror, pulling a silly face at herself. Their costumes were short white tennis dresses with matching knickers. They both had ribbons in their hair and white tap shoes and they looked very young. 'Mum would be proud of me. I'm wearing two pairs of knickers at last.'

Magnus wished he could clap as loudly as everyone else when Bonny and Ellie smilingly curtsied to their audience at the end of their first number. But he didn't dare draw attention to himself with Ruth beside him.

She looked very nice tonight in a green taffeta dress, even though she'd laughingly said she looked like a country mouse compared with these smart Londoners. Green gave her pale skin a luminous quality and he liked the sophisticated chignon the hairdresser had given her; at home she always wore her hair loose. She was thirty-seven now, but to Magnus she had a timeless quality. She would probably look just the same at sixty.

The evening was going very well so far. Ruth knew a few of the other women and she'd found the confidence to leave his side and chat to them. He just hoped Bonny would stick to her side of the bargain after the cabaret.

But Magnus felt very proud of both Bonny and Ellie. They had worked on the act he remembered from Oxford: the choreography was vastly improved and they were slicker, even more self-assured. Bonny's tap-dancing and gymnastics were faultless, Ellie's voice more powerful.

'They were really good.' Ruth tucked her hand through Magnus's arm, her soft brown eyes twinkling with pleasure. 'I thought we'd see stuffy acts tonight, not something like that.'

Magnus gulped hard. One of the things which had attracted him to Ruth when they first met was her lack of guile and her delight in the sort of things his pompous family found 'vulgar'. Over the years it was this quality in her which endeared her to him more than anything. She laughed a great deal, she sang while she worked about the house, she found time for everyone, regardless how busy she was. She was a truly happy person and he loved her; yet he still couldn't help hoping she'd want to go home to Yorkshire on the first train tomorrow morning, so he could have a couple of days in London with Bonny.

The girls swept off their battered top hats, letting their hair tumble down, and bowed deeply at the rapturous applause for 'We're a Couple of Swells'.

'You *are* a couple of swells!' a hearty male voice called out. 'Bravo!'

The girls grinned at this voluble admirer, hitched up their ragged tramps' trousers and bowed again.

'We were sensational,' Bonny said as they skipped off through the wings to change.

'Utterly sensational,' Ellie agreed. 'Bravo!' she added in the upper-crust tones of the male admirer.

'I feel all sweaty,' Bonny giggled as they got inside the dressing-room. 'I hope there's some hot water to wash. I don't fancy dancing with anyone smelling like this.'

'You don't smell too bad to me.' Ellie grinned. 'But then I've got no intention of sniffing round you. Anyway, there must be hot water here, we're not exactly in the pits.'

As Bonny washed they could hear Maria Dolenze singing 'We'll Gather Lilacs'. Ellie began to join her in an exaggerated falsetto.

'Stop it,' Bonny laughed, one foot in the wash-basin. 'I can't bear it.'

'Magnus looked proud of you.' Ellie broke off from removing her stage make-up and tweaked Bonny's hair playfully. She felt exhilarated by their perform-ance, quite giddy and silly. 'I noticed you were a good girl and kept your eyes off him. I hope you can keep it up?'

'The only person I looked at was the tall, dark man by the stage,' Bonny said, drying her feet. 'Did you see him? I like men with moustaches, I might flirt with him later and make Magnus jealous. I think he's on his own.'

'I saw him,' Ellie groaned, remembering the dark, rather serious-faced man who hadn't taken his eyes off them. 'You are incorrigible, Bonny. You'd find a man in a nunnery.'

'I just wish Magnus could creep in here to say hello,' Bonny sighed, her face instantly forlorn. 'It's only his approval I want.'

'You'll get it tomorrow.' Ellie patted her shoulder. 'I think I'll clear off for a couple of days. I don't think I can bear to hear you two at it again!!'

The tombola was over, the chairs and tables moved aside for dancing, and the band playing a foxtrot as the girls swept back into the ballroom.

Two elderly couples had taken to the dance floor, but aside from a few of the older ladies who sat on the sidelines watching, almost everyone else was at the far end of the room where a bar had been opened.

The tall, dark man Bonny had spoken of strode across the empty expanse of dance floor towards them. His purposeful manner suggested he'd been watching for them to emerge.

'Let me get you both a drink?' He smiled at them

both but Ellie knew he was only interested in Bonny. 'I did enjoy your performance. Do tell me which show you are from?'

'We aren't with one. Not at present,' Ellie said quickly before Bonny could make up a story. 'We'd love a drink, thank you.'

As he went off to the bar, Bonny looked at Ellie and smirked wickedly.

'You are a witch,' Ellie giggled. 'He's already spellbound.'

'He might be good for a "reserve".' Bonny wrinkled her nose as she watched his back view at the bar. 'I'll know for certain by what drink he gets us. Did you notice he didn't ask?'

When he came back with two glasses of champagne, Bonny winked at Ellie. He'd passed her test with flying colours.

'I'm John Norton.' He smiled rather shyly. 'I know from the programme your names are Helena Forester and Bonny Phillips, but which is which?'

'Make a guess?' Bonny turned her turquoise eyes on him and fluttered her lashes. She could see Magnus talking to a group of people and guessed he was watching her over their shoulders.

'I think you must be Miss Phillips,' he said, looking right at Bonny, but then glancing almost nervously at Ellie. 'Am I right?'

'You don't think I look "Bonny" then?' Ellie said to tease him.

During the time the girls had been partners, Ellie had seen many men react to Bonny as this man was doing, and she felt for him. She sensed he was a rather staid man who under normal circumstances was too shy and reserved to make a play for a woman. He was very personable, a real gentleman, but most definitely not a 'stage door Johnny' who made a habit of pursuing showgirls. She guessed he was around thirty, and he was almost handsome with soft brown eyes, a generous mouth and a neatly trimmed moustache. Only his habit of frowning, which underlined a serious nature, spoilt him.

'You are both so beautiful,' he said blushing furiously. Ellie knew she'd read him correctly. 'But Bonny just sounds like a blonde's name.'

'Well, you are right,' Bonny said, putting her hand on his arm and looking at him provocatively. 'Now what do you do, Mr Norton? Shall I guess?'

'You won't be able to,' he said gravely.

'I can.' Bonny fluttered her eyelashes. 'You're a lawyer!'

Ellie thought this was a good guess, for it was exactly what he looked like. Very restrained, bookish, careful. She was sure he was single, and that his long tapered fingers certainly never lifted anything heavier than a pen.

'No, not a lawyer, though sometimes I think I ought to be,' he said, smiling now and showing very even white teeth. 'By profession I'm a chemist, but not the sort who dishes out medicine. I'm in the oil business.'

'How interesting,' Bonny said, very insincerely. If she had yawned she couldn't have made it more plain.

'Do you know many people here, Mr Norton?' Ellie asked, wishing to spare him further embarrassment.

'Some of them,' he said. 'Lady Penelope Beauchamp is my godmother and she drags me along to these dos. I see the same faces again and again and know who they are, but I can't say I know many of them well.'

Ellie could sense Bonny was trying to edge away, but she was determined to continue the conversation a little longer.

'Lady Beauchamp is one of the patrons, isn't she?' Ellie asked. 'Which one is she?'

'Over there, in pink.' Norton pointed her out.

Ellie didn't dare catch Bonny's eye: it was the woman they'd laughed about in the too-tight dress.

'Which one is Sir Miles Hamilton then?' she went on quickly. 'Is he here?'

'Let me see.' Norton stood on tiptoe, craning his neck to look over the crowd. 'He is here, I spoke to him and Lady Hamilton earlier. Oh yes, he's over there, by the window. The big man wearing a maroon cummerbund.'

Ellie just stared. Ever since she'd heard of this man's existence she'd imagined someone tall with a black swirling moustache and a top hat. She wasn't sure why she visualised him that way, maybe just because she remembered seeing photographs of her mother and Marleen with men like that. But this man reminded her of Winston Churchill, not just because of his round face and heavy jowls, but the way his head jutted straight out of his neck. He was balding, fat and he had a bulbous red nose. She felt disappointed.

'Why did you want to know about him?' Bonny asked curiously. It seemed to her that Ellie was very intense.

'No real reason.' Ellie managed a light laugh. 'Just the title, I suppose. I've never met a "Sir" anyone.'

'There's a great many people here tonight with titles,' John Norton said. 'But I suspect most of them would willingly swop them for looks and talent like yours.'

'A very gallant compliment,' Ellie teased him, but she was touched by his effort to make them both feel at ease. 'It's been so nice talking to you, Mr Norton, but we ought to mingle a little. Thank you for the drink.'

'Both those girls are so lovely it makes me feel very plain,' Ruth said. 'Just look at them, Magnus!'

A chill crept over Magnus. He could hardly bear to turn his head, guessing immediately whom Ruth was referring to. But he had to look, and to his horror

533

Bonny and Ellie were standing only a few yards from his table, plates of food in their hands.

Magnus had spotted John Norton, an acquaintance of his, talking to the girls earlier, and as John was a bachelor, without a partner tonight, Magnus had hoped he might keep the girls occupied for some time. He didn't think they'd come over near him deliberately; they were just looking for somewhere to sit down.

'You look every bit as lovely,' Magnus replied, willing the girls to move on. Ruth did look lovely, and all his loyalties were with her tonight. He cursed himself for not having realised when he planned this evening that Bonny and Ellie were bound to draw attention from everyone, including Ruth. They were too stunning to be overlooked.

But he hadn't expected evening dresses to make them look quite so sensational. Bonny was radiant, her turquoise dress enhancing her eyes, the delicate chiffon offering tantalising glimpses of the perfect body beneath. Ellie's appearance was even more dramatic and outstanding. She looked regal, yet voluptuous, the twinkling light from the chandeliers sprinkling her dark hair and bare shoulders with gold dust.

Before he could collect his wits, Ruth was on her feet and going towards them. Magnus felt his heart pounding, his mouth dry. It was so typical of Ruth, ever kindly. She'd sensed the girls' predicament and she was going to invite them to their table.

'Come and sit with us,' Magnus heard her say, her Yorkshire accent suddenly very noticeable. 'Both my husband and I enjoyed your act so much. I'd love to know more about you both.'

Magnus stood up involuntarily. His eyes met Bonny's over Ruth's shoulder, wide and confused. He cursed himself again for not anticipating a situation like this.

It was so strange to see the two women he loved together: Bonny, tall, slender and utterly bewitching, Ruth some four inches shorter, dark and twice Bonny's age. Bonny had youthful defiance, a body as yet unspoilt by child-bearing. But that bloom on Ruth, the womanly curves of her body, were all part of her caring, nurturing nature, and every bit as beautiful.

Ellie shot Magnus a 'leave this to me' look. She took a step closer to Ruth, somehow managing to nudge Bonny into the background, and smiled charmingly.

'How kind of you,' she said, her voice low and clear, without any sign of nervousness. 'It's so nice when people tell us they enjoyed our act, and we'd love to join you. But we were actually looking for someone we met earlier. We were supposed to have our supper with him.'

Magnus felt a surge of gratitude to Ellie, but saw too a flicker of disappointment in Bonny's eyes. She was looking hard at Ruth, taking in every last detail. She really was a bitch sometimes. She just wanted to see him squirm.

'Perhaps later?' Ruth said, backing away.

Magnus breathed normally again as the girls slipped off into the crowd, out of sight.

'How nice the dark girl was,' Ruth said as she sat down again at the table. 'But the blonde one had very hard eyes. She made me feel so self-conscious!'

'So that's what she's like,' Bonny said once Ellie had led her well away to the other side of the ballroom and found a spare table by the wall. 'Did you see how fat she was? I bet she's at least forty-two round the hips.'

'No I didn't notice that,' Ellie said tartly. 'I only noticed what a friendly, warm person she seemed.'

*

535

Around an hour later, Bonny grabbed Ellie's arm and squeezed it suddenly. 'Look who's here!' she hissed. 'Look!'

They had 'mingled', or at least attempted to, but Ellie had been thrown a bit by meeting Ruth Osbourne and she was a little nervous that Bonny might try and lead her back in Magnus's direction. Although several people had complimented them on their performance, they hadn't met anyone who really wanted to talk to them or ask them to dance, and certainly no one able to offer them work. To Bonny's further irritation, John Norton was now sitting at Magnus's table, in deep conversation with him and his wife. As John seemed to be the only unattached man here she had already expressed the view that they might as well go home. Ellie still had her eye on Sir Miles, half hoping she might get an opportunity to speak him, but since he was sitting at a table with a whole group of people she didn't think that was likely now.

'Where am I supposed to be looking?' Ellie asked. There were hundreds of people and she couldn't see anything startling enough for Bonny to react so dramatically.

'Over there,' Bonny whispered. 'Oh no! He's seen us.'

All at once Ellie saw whom Bonny meant. It was Ambrose Dingle and he was heading straight towards them.

She sensed this was no chance encounter. The fact they hadn't spotted him earlier suggested he might actually have slipped in without a ticket, perhaps hearing they were performing tonight. Judging by the set expression on his face, he meant trouble.

Ellie's opinion of Ambrose had sunk even lower since learning what he'd done to Edward. His appearance tonight hightened her disgust. He looked decadently foppish, a white carnation on his dinner-jacket, his shirt frilled down the front and his centre-parted hair too long. He had aged, and his face had lost the well-scrubbed look she remembered.

'So you've surfaced at last,' he said as he got closer. 'But if you think you can get work again in the West End, you're mistaken.'

He was flushed, always a sign, as Ellie remembered, that he was about to erupt with anger. Her stomach contracted. She hoped he wasn't going to make a scene. 'We've got nothing to say to you,' she said, more boldly than she felt, taking Bonny's arm and trying to walk on past him.

To her dismay he side-stepped, blocking their path. 'I have a great deal to say to you,' he said in a low, menacing voice, showing his teeth. 'You ruined my show!'

'You left us no alternative but to leave it,' she said quietly. 'But this is hardly the time or place to discuss that.'

His pale blue eyes narrowed. Ellie could smell whisky on his breath. 'You were always too lippy by far.' His thin lips drew back into a snarl. 'You were under contract to me, and you broke it.'

'That was your fault,' Ellie said, aware that Bonny was very tense beside her and that people were turning to look at them, sensing an atmosphere. 'But this is a charity evening, and we don't wish to speak to you. Kindly leave us alone.'

'Leave you alone!' His voice rose an octave. 'Who do you think you're talking to?'

Ellie backed away, frightened by the wild look in his eye. Perhaps he wasn't just drunk – he seemed unstable.

'Don't be ridiculous.' Bonny joined in, her voice squeaky with fright. 'I'll get someone to throw you out!'

'I beg your pardon for intruding,' a deep, almost growling voice came from Ellie's elbow. 'Is this man bothering you?'

Ellie turned to find the voice came from none other than Sir Miles Hamilton and she blushed in confusion, her legs turning to jelly.

She couldn't speak, but Bonny spoke for both of them, perhaps enjoying being the centre of attention. 'He threatened us,' she said indignantly. 'He's drunk and he ought to be thrown out.'

Seen at a distance, Sir Miles was just another tubby, middle-aged man, but close up he was formidable. He was far taller than she'd imagined, perhaps six foot, and despite his weight and thinning hair, power wafted from him.

'Your name, sir?' Sir Miles looked scathingly at Ambrose. 'You have an invitation, I take it?'

Ambrose's hesitation proved to Ellie she had been correct in thinking he'd come uninvited.

'Ambrose Dingle.' He blushed, his voice dropping. 'I, er—' He faltered, clearly unable to think of an excuse.

'Then I suggest you leave, sir,' Sir Miles said evenly. 'This is a charity evening for ticket holders only. If you have anything further to say to these two young ladies, I suggest you find a more gentlemanly approach and a more suitable venue.'

Ellie expected Ambrose to turn and walk away, knowing he was defeated, but instead he puffed out his chest and his eyes became narrow slits of ice blue.

'Who the hell do you think you are?' he said arrogantly.

'Sir Miles Hamilton, one of the patrons and organisers of this event.' Sir Miles put one large hand on Ambrose's chest and pushed at him. 'Now kindly leave before I have you thrown out.'

All at once everyone was edging closer, faces alight with interest. Ellie glanced over to see Magnus behind the crowd, looking very anxious.

As Ambrose took one threatening step towards Sir Miles, two stewards darted forward, grabbing him by either arm. There was a moment's scuffle as Ambrose tried to free himself. Ellie caught hold of Bonny's hand, afraid she might run to Magnus.

'They're scheming guttersnipes,' Ambrose yelled out over his shoulder as he was frogmarched towards the door. 'Just ask them what they did to me!'

Ellie wished the floor could open and swallow her up. She was trembling, feeling cheapened and humiliated. Everyone was looking at her and Bonny, and without a public statement explaining who Ambrose was and why he'd attacked them, these people couldn't be blamed for thinking the worst of them both.

But the impression she and Bonny had made on strangers hardly mattered. It was Sir Miles's opinion she was concerned about.

'I'm so terribly sorry,' she blurted out, catching hold of Sir Miles's sleeve, tears welling up in her eyes.

'My dear, you have nothing to apologise for,' he said. 'Now just come with me and sit down. You both look as if you're in shock. You can tell me all about that unpleasant character over a drink.'

Ellie felt like the unluckiest girl in the world. Ever since finding his name on that invitation she'd thought of little else but meeting this man. Now she was thrown up against him under entirely the wrong circumstances.

She'd never imagined him looking so fierce or old, or that the wife who'd stood in the way of her mother's happiness would have such an endearingly pretty face. But here she was, seated at a table with them both, with Bonny already making the most of the drama by sobbing out her exaggerated version of the story.

A brandy appeared in front of Ellie. The people who'd watched earlier resumed their conversation. Magnus was leaving with his wife. But Bonny was holding court and Sir Miles seemed as enthralled as his wife was, both apparently forgetting Ellie was even at the table.

If nothing else, it gave Ellie the opportunity to study this couple at close quarters. She knew Sir Miles was fifty-six, and guessed his wife was a few years younger. She was overweight, but her elegant black chiffon dress concealed it well and her brown hair, streaked with grey, was swept up into a bun. Her skin was beautiful, still surprisingly taut, like quality writing paper, and her eyes were a tawny brown. The way she listened and nodded at what Bonny was saying suggested she usually took the role of listener rather than talker. Ellie thought she was probably a very gentle person who'd had her fair share of knocks in life, even if she hadn't ever experienced poverty.

Sir Miles, on the other hand, looked stern. He was as interested as his wife in Bonny's story, but there was no sympathy in his eyes. They were dark brown, like her own, but that was the only similarity Ellie could see. It was hard to equate this old, fat man with a bulbous red nose with the tall, dark and handsome one Marleen had spoken of. She wondered, perhaps ridiculously, how he'd react if she suddenly dropped her mother's name. Of course she wouldn't dare do such a thing, but she suspected he'd find a way to freeze her out instantly, and she'd be the one left looking foolish.

'Well, Miss Forester.' Sir Miles surprised her by suddenly turning to her. He was smiling now and he looked less intimidating. 'You haven't had much to say for yourself!'

'I think Bonny's covered the whole story.' Ellie smiled back at him. 'I'd just like to say I'm sorry if we spoilt your evening.'

'You didn't. But I'm sorry that dreadful person had to spoil yours,' he said. 'Miss Phillips tells me you are looking for another show to join. I suggest you contact Bloomfield's Theatrical Agency, I believe they are very good.'

'You were both so *very* talented.' Lady Hamilton leaned forward across the table to speak, her pretty face animated. 'I did enjoy it so much. I'm sure you'll find something else very soon.'

Sir Miles cleared his throat, but added nothing more. Ellie felt it was a signal he'd had enough of talking to them both.

She got up from her seat, looking hard at Bonny to do likewise. 'We'd better go home now,' she said. 'Thank you for being so kind. Maybe we'll meet some other time.'

Sir Miles stood up and shook her hand. He had a strong grip, but his skin felt like dry leaves.

'Good luck to both of you. And thank you for putting on such a good performance tonight.'

Ellie lay awake for what seemed like hours that night, going over and over the events of the evening.

Bonny had laughed all the way home in the taxi about Ambrose being thrown out. She was delighted that Ruth had turned out to be so plain and dumpy and took it as a sign it would only be a matter of weeks before Magnus left her. But perhaps the most irritating thing of all was that she kept crowing about meeting Sir Miles and Lady Hamilton.

Bonny might see the evening as a triumph, but to Ellie it was a disaster. It was unlikely she'd ever get a chance to speak to Sir Miles again. He probably thought she was an empty-headed, irresponsible person anyway.

She had no job, no family, nor even a boyfriend. Where was she going to go from here?

Chapter Twenty-Five

December 1947

'Magnus!' Bonny froze for a second in shock as Magnus looked round the dressing-room door. But she recovered quickly, leaped across the room and flung her arms round him. 'What a lovely surprise! Why didn't you tell me you were coming? Did you see the show? How long have you got?' Her questions came out like rapid gunfire.

Ellie was sitting at the dressing-table, mending a rip in her costume. As she had pins in her mouth she could only raise one hand in greeting.

It was over a year since the gala night at the Savoy. She would be twenty-one in the New Year. Bonny was coming up for nineteen in the spring. They had known each other only two and a half years, but it seemed to Ellie that they'd been together a lifetime.

The last year had had its share of grim moments, but on balance it had been a good year.

Indirectly, they had Sir Miles to thank for finding work. His advice to go to Bloomfield's Theatrical Agency had been their saviour. Harry Bloomfield took on all kinds of acts – musicians, dancers, comedians and actors – and took his percentage for finding them work. Last September all he'd been able to offer the girls was their own spot touring with a music hall show, in which they had to find their own costumes and digs, but they'd taken it as there was nothing else.

At first they had found it very frightening to do their own choreography, find their own music and be entirely responsible for themselves. But they acted on advice from other more seasoned performers who had made a living like this for years, and learned to be self-reliant. Creating an act for themselves was far more fulfilling than merely following instructions, and they won respect and affection from the older comedians, magicians and singers who made up their troupe for the hard work they put into it.

The winter of 1947 was the worst in living memory. Deep snow at the end of January brought the whole country to a standstill. The miners strike and acute shortages of food and supplies meant even more misery. Stuck in grim northern towns, more often than not in dilapidated theatres where the heating didn't reach the dressing-rooms, they learned to shed layers of woollies in the wings, fix a bright smile on their faces, then prance on to the stage in the scantiest of costumes to give the audience something to warm them.

They lived daily with the fear that they wouldn't be able to reach their next venue because of the snow, or that they'd arrive to find the theatre closed down permanently because of dwindling audiences. Sometimes they huddled in railway waiting-rooms for hours for a train which never came. At other times they begged lifts from lorry drivers or travelling salesmen. Often they had nowhere to wash their clothes or even their hair, hot baths were a rare luxury and their digs were so cold they slept in one bed together.

But in April, when the thaw finally came, Bloomfield's sent them for an audition for a variety show opening in Wembley later that month. Ellie and Bonny shared a place at the bottom of the bill with 'Dolores and Mario', a pair of contortionists, but Tommy Handley was the star and the show ran for six weeks before moving on to Hammersmith,

Finsbury Park, then Catford Hippodrome in November. It was lovely to be back in London. Bonny could get to see her parents occasionally, while Ellie sometimes popped over to King's Cross to see Annie King. They were earning a little more money because the show was more prestigious, and even their digs were decent.

They were still in Catford now, with only one more week to run until the end of the show. They were waiting expectantly, hoping that any day Bloomfield's would contact them with news of a pantomime to tide them over until March.

'One question at a time,' Magnus replied, closing the dressing-room door behind him and leaning back on it. 'I've only got one night in London and yes I saw the show. If you're ready I'll take you out and buy you some supper, that little place in Blackheath will still be open. Would you like to come too, Ellie?'

Ellie took the pins out of her mouth and smiled. Magnus was always so thoughtful, but she knew better than to intrude when he had only one night to spare. 'Nice of you to ask,' she said cheerfully. 'But I need an early night. Maybe some other time.'

'I'm almost ready.' Bonny pushed a hairpin in more securely, powdered her nose and put on a little more lipstick, then pushing her feet into four-inch heeled shoes she grabbed her coat from behind the door. 'Don't wait up, Ellie!' she said.

Magnus faltered at the door, looking back at Ellie sitting there sewing. In the twenty months since Magnus had first met the girls, Ellie was the one who had matured the most. She had an aura of calm and true elegance, even though she didn't attempt to compete with Bonny at being fashionable. Her true beauty came from within: those huge, limpid eyes held such deep understanding, and her lovely mouth was so expressive.

'Something more?' Ellie asked. She was thrown by an intense expression on his face which she couldn't read. He had more facial lines now, through working out in all winds and weathers, but despite that and the fact that his hair now needed cutting, she thought he looked more attractive each time she saw him.

'Merry Christmas, Ellie,' he said, to her surprise coming back in and bending to kiss her forehead. 'Happy New Year too,' he said. 'I hope it will be the one when all your dreams come true.'

He was gone before she could reply, the draught from the slammed door making the overhead light swing. Ellie put down her repair, suddenly uneasy. That farewell sounded strangely final!

Bonny had remained stubbornly in love with Magnus, even though until they came back to London in April she had only managed to see him on odd occasions, when Magnus managed to get away from his work for a night. At first Bonny had even stopped finding 'reserves' to wine and dine her in his absence, but she had crept back to that in the last six months.

Ellie had become fond of Magnus herself; he was so charismatic it was hard not to. He worked like a demon alongside his employees, taking a personal interest in each of them, and making them find the same pride in their work as he did. He didn't boast or cut corners to make more money. At heart an altruist, he believed he had a duty to provide people with decent homes at prices they could afford. Although Ellie didn't approve of adultery, at the same time she felt deeply for Magnus and understood he was as much a prisoner of Bonny's as she was herself. As such they had a great deal in common.

In one slightly drunken evening a month or two ago, Magnus had confided in Ellie about Bonny, and she couldn't forget what he'd said.

'She's like a beautiful wrapped parcel, like in a child's party game. Each wrapper I take off I get more

545

and more excited, thinking I'm getting closer to the real Bonny. But each wrapper is different, with a forfeit beneath it. Now I'm beginning to suspect that when I get to the final wrapper there'll be nothing but a booby prize.'

Ellie understood his torment. Bonny played with his feelings, teased him, wound him up and sometimes flung him aside. Magnus believed that she didn't realise what she put him through. But Ellie wasn't so sure. To her it looked like calculated cruelty, a strategy to make him so bewildered that one day he would walk out on Ruth.

Amongst the 'reserves' Bonny held on to for times when she couldn't see Magnus was John Norton, the man they'd met at the Savoy. He had turned up to the theatre at Wembley one night and asked her out to dinner. That date had led to a few others, but they were infrequent as John worked abroad a great deal of the time.

Only Bonny could have the brass neck to let John escort her to a party she knew Magnus would be at, and get a thrill out of seeing his unease. To her disappointment, Magnus hadn't been jealous, perhaps because he didn't believe the serious, rather stuffy John Norton to be a real rival, perhaps because it might allay any suspicions about himself.

Ellie felt a great deal of sympathy for John too when she heard about that night. The poor man was already falling for Bonny; she'd seen that light in his eyes when he came to meet her at the theatre. He wasn't astute enough to work out that Magnus was her lover, or that Bonny wasn't the sweet innocent he believed her to be, and it wouldn't be long before he got hurt too.

Now, after the purposeful way Magnus had just said goodbye to her, Ellie suspected he had come tonight intending to end their affair. Bonny would be impossible if Ellie was right, yet she hoped for his sake, and Ruth's, that he'd find the courage to do it and the strength to stay away.

Ellie had no such complications in her life. She'd had a few dates, but with no one she cared enough about to see them more than twice. She no longer hankered for a big love – she was happy with herself and her life. Edward was still her friend. He had moved a great deal in the last year too, and at present he was in a play in Bath, but they kept in touch with letters and the occasional meeting when he came to London.

Ellie thought less and less about Sir Miles these days too. After the gala evening she had pumped Magnus for a little more information, but was disappointed to discover Magnus knew little about him personally. But he had told her that the company Majestic Inc., which she knew Miles to be a director of, dealt in backing films and plays. Magnus said Miles had a lifetime interest in the theatre, and she couldn't help wondering if her mother had created it!

Quite recently she'd discovered from a mention in a gossip column that Sir Miles had a London home in Holland Park. She went there to take a look, but the house gave little away about him. It was one of the smaller ones in the road, an elegant Edwardian house tucked away behind a walled garden. She peeped through the wrought-iron gate, noted gleaming brass on the front door and the rather regimental small front garden. She could see a grand piano in one of the downstairs rooms, wondered whether it was he or Lady Hamilton who played, and felt a little sad and ridiculous that she had to resort to spying. Ellie felt it was pointless trying to discover anything further about him. She could never get close to him, he might not be her father anyway, and even if he was, a man in his position was hardly likely to welcome the result of an extra-marital affair.

*

547

'You're a bit quiet tonight!' Bonny reached across the table and ran her finger sensuously round Magnus's lips. 'What are you thinking about? Buying more land? Designing bigger and better houses?'

Magnus smiled. Bonny always assumed his mind was stuck on business. It never occurred to her that in any moments of silence he could be reflecting on his impossible position, feeling guilt about Ruth and the children, or wondering why he continued to put himself through so much unnecessary pain.

Bonny clearly never wasted her time on introspection. She was much too concerned with being a fashion plate. While almost every other woman in England struggled to make over old clothes or even cut up curtains to achieve the 'New Look', Bonny somehow managed to have brand new clothes. She deftly changed the subject when he asked how she got the clothing coupons, often claiming she'd 'had this old thing for ever'. Tonight she was wearing a deep plum-coloured wool dress, its padded shoulders, the length of the skirt and the cream lace jabot all too up to the minute to be anything but brand new. Even her hair, put up in a neat roll, looked like the work of a hair-dresser, and as always he wondered how she could afford it.

If only he could make his private life as uncompli-cated and successful as his business! That was going from strength to strength, now that he'd found ways of cutting through the maze of red tape the govern-ment erected to deter all but the most determined builders. Perhaps he shouldn't be buying timber on the black market, or greasing palms in the council, but the ends justified the means. He'd managed to finish the first six houses in Staines just before the big freeze-up came early in the year, and they were all sold immediately. He hadn't made a huge profit: two of the houses had to be sold cheaply to the council to be let to their tenants, one of the many irritating regulations. But he was left with enough capital to buy two further plots of land, with enough remaining for materials and labour costs. Eight houses on these plots were finished now, all pretty little mock-Georgian ones like the first, and a further eight were close to completion. As he now had an excellent, experienced foreman to take over, he had no further reason to stay on in London permanently.

'I'm going to build some houses in Leeds next,' he said, hoping she wouldn't realise how close that was to his home and start a scene. 'But what about you, Bonny? What work have you got lined up?'

'I've had an offer of a job in Paris,' she said. 'In the Moulin Rouge.'

Magnus smiled. She was such an incorrigible story-teller. But this once he wasn't going to pull her up sharply. 'How exciting,' he said, pouring out the last of the wine. 'With Ellie?'

Magnus had brought Bonny to Elliott's Supper Rooms in Blackheath many times since she'd been at Lewisham. In south London there was a dearth of good restaurants and few that were open late at night. Elliott's was tiny and old-world with bow windows and beams in the ceilings, but despite the continuing rationing somehow the owner here not only managed to get decent steak, Dover sole and wonderful fresh shrimps, but he also had a good wine cellar.

'Ellie hasn't been asked,' Bonny said, playing with the wax dripping from the candle. 'That's the reason I haven't agreed yet. She'd be upset if I went alone and she isn't a good enough dancer for this job.'

Magnus found it hard to credit that anyone could lie with such cool ease. She didn't blush, and she could look right into his eyes while she told such whoppers. He couldn't imagine what her motives were. 'You might be doing her a favour,' he said, trying to keep a straight face. 'She could get a straight acting job without you around to hamper her.'

'Why do people always say things like that?' she snapped. 'I carry Ellie most of the time.'

Magnus often wished he'd had the nerve to advise Ellie to branch out on her own. Bonny held her back in more ways than one. Bonny was a brilliant dancer, there was no denying that, but she lacked the drive necessary to become a big star. Recently he'd noticed she had even stopped those fluffy childish dreams of Hollywood which had once been so much a part of her personality. In his opinion her temperament was more suited to being a rich man's plaything than a career girl.

'Let's go back to my room.' Magnus signalled for the waiter to bring the bill. He was glad he'd rattled her a little; she was easier to cope with when she was angry.

Magnus was staying at a small hotel in Prince of Wales Road, overlooking the heath. His intention was to tell Bonny tonight that their affair must end. But although he'd planned to sit her down and talk seriously, Bonny gave him no opportunity even to pour a drink, let alone talk. She tore off her clothes and drew him into making love.

There were times when Magnus seriously considered that Bonny might be a nymphomaniac. She was always ready for sex, whether they were in a car, in a dressing-room, or in a train. In eighteen months he'd seen no gradual cooling of this passion; just a kiss was enough to set her off. When Magnus was away from her this was another thing to be suspicious about, wondering just how she survived without him. But she had only to wind her arms around his neck, to press that beautiful body against his and he was lost, forgetting all the little betrayals, the lies and his own deceit.

Tonight he kept it in his mind that it would be the last time and the pain inside him made it even sweeter. His lips lingered on every inch of her body, breathing in the smell and taste, imprinting it on his mind for all time. But as always she touched his heart as well as his body and at the moment of climax he found himself crying.

'Why the tears?' she asked, snuggling against him, her legs wound tightly round him, her eyes half closed with sleepy satisfaction. 'Was it that special for you too?'

He wiped his eyes on the sheet. Half his brain was demanding that he stalled telling her until another time, but the other half insisted he behaved like a real man and tell her now. 'That was the last time,' he blurted out before he could lose his nerve. 'Never again, Bonny. We have to end this affair for good.'

'But why?' She moved in his arms, her eyes flying open in shock. 'Why now? Because you're going to Leeds?'

'No. I'm moving on to Leeds to be nearer home and to stop myself from being tempted again,' he said. 'Ruth's expecting another baby, Bonny.'

He expected her to jump up, to hit him or start throwing things, but to his surprise her eyes welled up with real tears. 'A baby! You can't have! Not with her!'

'She is my wife, Bonny.' He leaned up on one elbow and stroked her hair. 'I always told you I would never leave her and I could hardly stay but never make love to her. I haven't ever lied to you.'

'But it should be me who's having the baby!' Her tears spilled over, running down her face. 'Not her, she's old!'

'Oh Bonny!' Magnus gulped. He hadn't expected her to say that. He was glad now that he'd always been careful, even when she'd insisted it was a safe time of the month. 'You're not interested in babies.'

'I am, I'd love one,' she sobbed. 'Not just any baby but yours. How could you do this to me?'

'Bonny you are a dancer, a performer. Even if it

551

was possible for me to marry you and for us to settle down, you wouldn't be happy with it for long.'

She didn't reply, but curled up into a ball and sobbed. Magnus lay down beside her and stroked her hair; her pins had all come loose and he removed the last few, letting it tumble down on to her back. This was the side of Bonny he hadn't seen before, but it reminded him poignantly of his own children when they were upset. Even at eighteen, going on nineteen, she was still very much a child and this made him feel even more guilty.

'When's the baby due?' she asked eventually in a strangled, small voice.

'In June.' Magnus sighed deeply. Ruth was so very excited, and Sophie and Stephen were already digging out all their old baby toys for their new brother or sister. Magnus too was thrilled at the prospect of a new child, and hoped it would help to bring back all the idyllic happiness they had as a family before he met Bonny. 'But you have to understand why it has to end now. Not just because I can't bear being torn in two, but because Ruth needs me and she deserves more than I've been giving her for some time. After tonight it's over between you and me.

Bonny sat up slowly, her face crumpled and swollen with tears. She knew he meant it. Magnus never said anything he didn't mean. That was one of the reasons she loved him so much. 'You're wrong about me,' she said putting her hand on his cheek, her eyes looking deep into his and her voice hiccuping with sobs. 'I would've been happy to settle down with you and have children. I don't care about being on the stage. All I want is to live with you and have your baby.'

Magnus saw right through her eyes into her soul. Despite all the lies she'd told him, this time he knew she was speaking the truth. He had a feeling he'd just removed the last wrapper and that this was the real Bonny, naked and truthful. His pain grew ever greater.

'I'm going home now,' she said, reaching for her clothes.

'Not now, not like this,' he said quickly.

She didn't look at him, but slipped on her knickers and a camisole. 'I have to go now,' she whispered brokenly as she put on her stockings. 'If I stay I'll try and force you to change your mind.'

Magnus gulped. Would she exact some revenge? Would she really just go quietly? Just the way she fastened her suspenders, one leg up on the bed, was a reminder of all those sensual, beautiful moments with her. Could he bear to see her walk out of the door?

'I do love you, Bonny,' he said once she was dressed. 'I probably always will. But I have a duty to my wife and children. Do you understand that?'

She wiped her eyes with the back of her hand and tossed back her hair. The forlorn look in her eyes had changed to one of defiant pride. 'Yes. I don't like it, but I understand,' she said. 'I hope you'll be happy, Magnus.'

He expected something more – one last burst of spite or pleading – but instead she just put on her coat and opened the door.

'Wait! Let me get dressed.' He picked up his trousers. 'I'll drive you.'

'No, I'll walk. I need the fresh air.' Her head tilted up proudly. 'Goodbye, Magnus.'

He pulled back the curtain and watched her walking across the heath towards Lewisham. There was frost on the grass and it sparkled like diamonds in the moonlight. She walked so gracefully, almost gliding like a skater, blonde hair standing out against her dark coat, as pale as the moon.

Tears rolled down his cheeks unchecked as he watched her go. There was no satisfaction in knowing he'd done the right thing, no relief that twenty months of deceit and treachery were finished. He felt as if part of him would shrivel and die before the night was over.

Ellie woke to find Bonny getting into her single bed with her.

'What is it?' she whispered, but as she touched Bonny's icy hand, she guessed.

'It's over,' Bonny whispered, a sob in her voice. 'Just hold me, Ellie. Don't ask questions.'

'Bonny won't be able to manage it,' Ellie told Eric, the booking clerk from Bloomfield's on the telephone. He had rung to speak about booking them into a show in Birmingham. 'She's not well and she's going home to her parents until after Christmas at least.'

Ellie held the receiver away from her ear as Eric launched into the expected tirade about being let down at the last minute – 'Did Bonny think she could just work when she felt like it?'

Ellie made suitable sympathetic noises and said it was 'women's troubles'. She guessed that would shut him up, and it did. It wasn't true, of course, but a broken heart could be just as bad as an infected womb. Bonny had managed to struggle through the last week's performance, but now she had her case packed to go home to her mother's, and nothing would make her change her mind.

Eric said he'd look for something else for Ellie alone and promised to phone her back later.

'Was he very angry?' Bonny asked when Ellie got back into their room.

'No, not at all,' Ellie lied. She didn't want to upset Bonny further with what had really been said. She felt Bonny had been through enough: she was pale and listless, and she needed the comfort of being with her parents.

'But what about you, Ellie?' Bonny began to cry

again. She seemed to have been crying incessantly all week. 'I've messed things up for you too.'

'I'll be fine,' Ellie insisted, hoping she would be. 'Eric may find me something. If not I'll take Edward up on his offer to spend Christmas at his grandmother's.'

'You could come to my mum's?' Bonny caught hold of Ellie's hand tightly. 'After Christmas I'm going down to Aunt Lydia's, you'd be welcome there too.'

'You've got a lot of bridges to mend in both those places.' Ellie squeezed the hand in hers. Although Bonny had visited her parents since returning to London, she did it with a bad grace, almost always returning with tales of arguments. Lydia Wynter wrote every week without fail, but Bonny rarely made the effort to write back more than a few lines. 'You don't want me around. Anyway, I'm sure to get something. It's Christmas, after all – someone must want a fairy, a clown, or the back end of a horse.'

Bonny smiled weakly. 'Why don't you ever say "I told you so"?'

'Because it doesn't help.' Ellie tweaked Bonny's small nose. 'I'd rather say "There's someone else out there waiting for you to make miserable". Isn't that a more cheerful prospect?'

'You felt just like this about Charley, didn't you?'

Ellie nodded glumly. She hadn't forgotten one moment of that heartache, the nights spent crying, feeling utterly alone. Sometimes she despaired of ever finding a man to love again. But she wasn't going to tell Bonny that now. 'Yes. But I got over it, and so will you. Now come on. I'll walk down with you to the station.'

Ellie lay down on her bed when she got back from the station, suddenly exhausted. She felt guilty at feeling such a sense of relief now Bonny was gone, but there was only a certain amount of sympathy any one person could dole out and she'd come to the end of the line with hers. She pulled the eiderdown over her and dropped off to sleep.

The telephone ringing woke her with a start.

'Miss Forester, it's for you,' Mrs Wheddle her landlady called out.

'Coming,' Ellie yelled back, stuffing her feet into her slippers and smoothing down her skirt.

It was Eric from Bloomfield's again. Ellie was breathless from running down two flights of stairs. She listened while Eric asked if she thought she could handle being Prince Charming in *Cinderella* at the Little Theatre in Hampstead.

Ellie's heart leaped with excitement. 'Of course I can,' she said gleefully.

Eric sounded a little uncertain. He said that there would be no time for a proper audition, as the original girl chosen for the part had left the company in the lurch in the middle of rehearsals. He asked if she could get there within an hour to meet Kennedy, the producer.

The line went dead before Ellie could ask any further questions. She rushed back up the stairs to brush her hair and collect her dancing shoes.

It was close to four in the afternoon, minutes to go before the deadline, as Ellie arrived at the stage door. She had run from the tube station and she was out of breath. She wasn't in any way dismayed by the Little Theatre being shabby and small; it had a reputation for excellent plays and packed houses.

'I'm Ellie Forester,' she gasped out to the doorman. 'I'm to meet Mr Kennedy here.'

'I 'ope you're the cavalry.' His thin, lined face broke into a wide grin. 'Can't 'ave Cinder-bleedin'ella wivout 'er Prince Charmin', can we?'

Hearing the man's cockney voice was like going home. It seemed like the best of good omens. 'No we bleedin' can't, cock,' she said lapsing into her old way of speaking.

He looked startled for a moment, then burst into laughter. 'Gawd love us,' he said, holding his sides. 'We all thought you was gonna be some snooty bint from up west!' His hand shot forward. 'Alf's the name,' he said, brown eyes twinkling. 'Come on in, ducks. We don't stand on ceremony 'ere. Mr Kennedy's out front now, waiting for yer.'

'Ellie,' she said, shaking his hand. 'And I'm very pleased to meet you.'

As Alf led Ellie into the gloomy theatre a surprisingly young man came forward. He was thin, only a couple of inches taller than herself, with unruly curly brown hair and a boyish, broken-toothed smile.

'Well done, Miss Forester,' he said, shaking her hand as Alf made the introductions. 'When I heard you had to come from south London I thought I was pushing my luck expecting you to be here within an hour.'

'I'd have flown to get here on time.' She smiled, remembering Marleen had always said it paid to look keen, but her stomach was churning with nerves and she wished she'd had time to put on something more attractive than her old checked skirt and a somewhat shrunken jumper. 'I'm usually known as Ellie,' she added.

Kennedy was perhaps thirty; he had a deep, resonant voice and blue-grey eyes. He looked a happy man, very relaxed in an ancient tweed jacket and trousers which needed a press.

'I'm known as Ray to everyone,' he said. 'I am the producer, but in this theatre that's a bit of a misnomer. I'm stage-manager, prompter, and often flunky too.'

Ellie liked Ray on sight. He had an open face and a straightforward, self-deprecating way of speaking which suggested he had a good sense of humour.

'Take this,' he said, handing her a couple of pages

of a script. 'Read it through and get the gist of it. I don't expect you to learn it word for word. Let's face it, we all know the story-line anyway. For now all I want to see is whether you can be a believable prince. I've just got to pop out for ten minutes. Sylvia who's playing Cinderella will acquaint you with my ideas.'

Sylvia was another very pleasing surprise. Ellie felt she'd be the perfect partner. She was a small, quite plain girl of twenty-two with long mousy hair, but her blue eyes were warm and friendly and she grinned engagingly at Ellie as if delighted to meet her.

'I loathed Delia Merchant, the original prince,' she said without any hesitation, leading Ellie up on to the stage. It was bare aside from a few steps at the back; the scenery was still being painted elsewhere in the theatre. There were no spotlights switched on, just a couple of dim bulbs hanging above. 'We're all cheesed off with being left in the lurch halfway through rehearsals. You look nice, Ellie, I hope we can be friends too. So let's get stuck into this and get it all tied up.'

The part of the story they were to run through was the ballroom scene as the clock strikes twelve and Cinderella runs away, leaving her glass slipper behind. Sylvia explained that the entire cast would normally be on the stage but that they'd all gone home for the afternoon.

'Ray will play a waltz for us when he comes back,' she said. 'We have to dance, looking into each other's eyes as if we're falling in love, and try not to giggle. He'll bang on a gong for the striking clock, then I'll be off, leaving one of my size fours on the steps. Don't forget you're supposed to be a man, big strides and all that. When you speak your lines, aim them at the gallery, don't look down at Ray.'

Ellie scanned through the script and ran through it a couple of times with Sylvia, then Ray appeared and sat down at the piano.

'Right, girls!' he shouted up at them. 'From the beginning of the waltz.'

It was good to act again. Ellie shut out the empty theatre, the bare stage and the lack of atmosphere. As she took Sylvia into her arms she imagined the smaller girl in a hooped ballgown, herself in a prince's satin tunic with buckle shoes and tights, and drifted away with the music, gazing into Cinderella's eyes.

The gong boomed out. Cinderella stiffened, gasped in horror, then broke away from Ellie's arms, fleeing up the wooden steps at the back of the stage. By now, Ellie had almost forgotten Ray was sitting at the piano. She was a man in love, stunned by losing her partner so unexpectedly. She strode over to the dropped slipper, picked it up and turned to the invisible audience.

'Search my kingdom for the owner of this glass slipper,' she commanded. 'Every castle, every house, every cottage. I will not rest until you find my love. The girl whose tiny foot fits this slipper will be my wife.'

There was a moment's silence, then Ray clapped down in the orchestra pit. 'Bravo,' he called out. 'You're a natural prince, Ellie. Now let's just run through a couple of the songs, shall we?'

It was after six by the time Ellie left the theatre to go back to her digs in Catford to pack. She was due to start rehearsals at ten the following morning and Ray had promised to get her fixed up in the same digs as Sylvia.

'I hope you'll be happy with us,' he said as he saw her out. 'The pantomime's due to run until the end of February; that gives us plenty of time to get to know each other better.'

On the journey back to Catford, Ellie thought about Ray Kennedy and smiled happily. Things were looking up. She had a leading role, with the chance to let her career take a slightly new direction.

Hampstead was one of the nicest parts of London, and she was free for once to make new friends, away from the often intolerable pressures Bonny put her under. But above all, she had a feeling Ray would be important in her life.

It was a long time since she'd met any man who really interested her. But as Ray spoke she had felt a faint tingle of something special, just the way she had with Charley. He was a little like Charley, now she came to think about it; not just his curly hair, but that openness, the curiosity mixed with eagerness. Maybe she was a bit impudent in imagining a producer could be tempted into a relationship with a relatively inexperienced actress, but it was cheering to find she was capable of thinking of something other than just work.

'Ellie, you're marvellous!' Ray called out from the orchestra pit. 'Let's just run through the scene with the ugly sisters one more time. Let the audience see you pulling faces as they try to force the slipper on, and don't be afraid to ham it up a bit more, that's what panto's all about.'

Ellie had been in rehearsal for five days now and she didn't think she'd ever enjoyed herself so much. She couldn't wait for opening night on Friday. Her satin and brocade costumes suited her admirably, even if close up they were old and patched. She liked every single member of the cast. Monty and Charles, the ugly sisters, had her in stitches all the time. They were a pair of old comics from music hall and she remembered going with Marleen to see them in the Mile End Road when she was eight or nine. They'd spent the war years with ENSA and their stories of those days were hilarious. As for Sylvia, she was fast becoming a very good friend. After all the tumult Bonny created in her wake, it was good to be with someone gentler. Sylvia was uncomplicated, generous and warm-hearted and she wasn't always out to hog the limelight.

'Knock it on the head now,' Ray called out after they'd repeated the scene. 'Be here at ten tomorrow morning for a complete run-through. Then a full dress rehearsal in the afternoon. Ellie, stay behind a moment please.'

Ellie jumped down off the stage into the front of the house. Ray was leafing through some music on the piano. He turned and smiled at her.

Her feelings that Ray was interested in her as a woman rather than just an actress had grown even stronger in the last couple of days. He seemed to go out of his way to talk to her alone. Yesterday he'd kept her back to run through one scene which she knew didn't really call for such personal coaching. They'd had a cup of tea later in his office and talked for over an hour. He'd encouraged her to tell him a great deal about her past and in turn he'd revealed quite a lot about himself.

He was one of four children and his family home was in Orpington in Kent. Ellie surmised, though he hadn't actually said so, that his parents were middle-class and comfortably off. He said he went to grammar school, then on to RADA, but being called up into the army had halted his acting career. During his time in the army, which he laughingly admitted was mainly spent in the stores, he'd been responsible for putting on a few shows. When he was demobbed he came back to London looking for work and the only job he could get was as under-stage-manager in the Haymarket Theatre. After a year there, doing little more than painting scenery and finding props, he got the opportunity to stand in as temporary stage-manager here in Hampstead, while the man who'd had the job before underwent a serious operation. The Little Theatre was struggling to keep going. Ray brought with him new enthusiasm and some good ideas, and when the previous stage-manager found he couldn't return, Ray was offered the permanent job.

'I flannelled my way into becoming producer,' he laughed. 'I had a great many contacts with decent actors and actresses and I was prepared to do anything to put bottoms on the seats. The owners let me have a free hand for a while to see if I could pull things into shape and I managed it, somehow. But I haven't got any illusions about my ability. I'm just good at motivating others, and I've got an eye for embryo talent. Luckily, aside from the panto season, we put on a different play once a fortnight, so if one is awful there's always the next one. I've got quite smart about what the Hampstead crowd want to see, keep them entertained and they come back for each new production.'

Ellie thought Ray underestimated his talent. He was far more professional and creative than any other producers she'd worked with. He got the best out of his cast, he appreciated their talent, he knew when to sit back and let them ad-lib, when to crack down and stick to the script, and he had a knack of drawing out excellent performances.

'Are you enjoying yourself?' Ray asked now, sitting down on the piano stool.

'Very much,' Ellie grinned. She couldn't remember any other producer asking such a thing. If anything most of them seemed to prefer their cast cowed and miserable. She wondered what he actually wanted her for; the relaxed way he was just sitting there implied he'd just called her for a chat.

He was such a nice man. She liked his scruffy clothes, that broken tooth and his wide, warm smile. But most of all she liked his joyful nature. After being used to grouchy performers who thought the whole world was pitted against them it was a tonic to meet someone who could laugh off disappointments and look forward to each day with enthusiasm.

'I love pantomime,' he said, looking faintly sheepish. 'My ambition was to become one of the "*great*" film producers, but I seem to be getting side-tracked by comedy plays, musicals and pantomimes.'

'My ambition is still to be a "*great*" musical comedy star,' she laughed. 'But I don't mind being side-tracked too much if it's like this.'

'You'll get there,' he said, suddenly serious. 'Now you've got people watching over you.'

Ellie smirked. She thought he meant him. 'You're going to produce a musical comedy, then? With me as the star?'

'I wish I could get the chance,' he said with a shrug of his shoulders. 'No, I meant the bigwig behind Bloomfield's.'

'What! Harry Bloomfield?' Ellie was puzzled. 'He isn't the least bit interested in me.'

'Not him, he's just the front man.' Ray frowned, looking at her as if she were slow. 'I'm talking about Sir Miles Hamilton. You must know it was him who suggested you for this part?'

Ellie could only stare blankly. She felt as if she were surrounded by thick fog, Ray's voice coming from somewhere distant.

'You do know who I'm talking about, don't you?' Ray's voice continued. 'Ellie! What's up? You've gone as white as a sheet!'

Ellie groped for a seat, pulled it down and flopped on to it. 'I'm sorry,' she said. 'I felt a bit funny for a moment. I met Sir Miles Hamilton once at a party. He put me on to Bloomfield's, but I didn't know he had anything to do with it.'

'He's one of Bloomfield's directors.' Ray looked hard at Ellie wondering why she should be so shocked by this news. 'He's got fingers in all sorts of pies in the entertainment business. Anyway, he's seen you perform on several occasions. Harry Bloomfield told me this when he made the suggestion I saw you for this part. I wouldn't mind betting Sir Miles will be coming on opening night to see how you're shaping up.'

563

Ellie couldn't think of anything to say to this.

'Well, you might look a bit happier about it,' Ray said, laughter in his voice. 'I'd be grinning like a cheshire cat if I was in your shoes. I hope you can raise a bit more enthusiasm for my next shot.'

'What's that?' Ellie said suspiciously.

'I hoped you might have supper with me tonight.'

Ellie hesitated; she was still floored by the piece of news about Sir Miles.

Ray sighed. 'I suppose you've got a boyfriend?'

'No, it's not that.' She looked down at her feet, suddenly acutely embarrassed.

Ray reached out and tilted her chin up with one finger. He was smiling. 'I'll be honest,' he said, teeth glinting in the gloom of the darkened theatre. 'I've had this terrible, overwhelming desire to kiss you since the first day you came here. And I've had the oddest feeling it might be the same for you too. We aren't in the line of work where people are going to be around for ever, Ellie. So couldn't we have a stab at a bit of romancing, while we've got the chance?'

Ellie had heard many opening lines from men over the years, but this one made her tingle. She did want him to kiss her.

She gave it only the briefest second's thought. So what if he was the producer, or that people would talk. She liked him and life was too hard and short not to take chances. 'That's the most honest approach I've ever heard,' she laughed. 'Okay, supper tonight.'

'You're the most fascinating woman I've met in a long time,' he said, grinning impishly. 'Very direct, funny and warm, yet I get this feeling there's an awful lot of different activity going on beneath the surface.'

'Like a duck's feet?' she laughed.

'I wouldn't like to liken anything about you to duck's feet,' he said. 'But you'd better toddle home to change. I'll pick you up at your digs at seven.'

*

'Happy birthday, Ellie.' Ray pulled the cork out of the bottle and filled up her glass. 'It ought to be real champagne for your twenty-first, but funds wouldn't run to that. At least this is a reasonable imitation.'

It was January 22nd, her twenty-first birthday, and they were in Ray's small, cluttered bachelor flat in Fitzjohn's Avenue, the wide road which led down from Hampstead Village towards Swiss Cottage. All the houses in the road were huge, many of them very dilapidated as it was many years since they'd been purely family homes. Number 25, where Ray lived, was a rabbit warren of small flats and bedsitters. Practically all the tenants were 'arty' types, even the two old ladies who lived on the ground floor.

Ellie had been here only twice before, both times during the afternoon, when she'd been appalled by its squalor. It was just one large room on the first floor with a small kitchen adjoining, and the bathroom was shared by all the other tenants in the house, up another flight of stairs. It was warm and cosy tonight, though: the shutters were closed over the windows, Ray had lit the fire earlier in the evening and now, in candlelight, with the bed made and covered by a thick quilt and all the unwashed dishes and dirty washing cleared away, it looked inviting enough to make her want to stay.

It had been the best month of her life. All the good feelings she'd had right from the day of the audition had been justified. So it was only a pantomime, but all the seats had been sold every night so far, and the local press had praised it to the skies. Her digs in Savernake Road overlooking the heath were among the best she'd ever had, with quite good food, constant hot water and even an electric fire in the room she shared with Sylvia. Quite often they giggled the night away as if they'd known each other from childhood, making toast on the fire and drinking cocoa. All the cast were fun, especially Norman Bounds, who played

565

Dandini. He made no secret of being homosexual, but minced about claiming he was an 'old tart', and he often came into Ellie's, and Sylvia's room late at night for a bit of girlie chatter. At Christmas he'd bought them each a lovely pair of satin knickers, saying he wished he dared wear them himself!

But of all the good things that were happening, Ellie felt most thrilled by Sir Miles's interest in her. He had come with his wife on opening night and called briefly at the dressing-room afterwards to compliment her on her performance. He had asked politely about Bonny, but Ellie felt his curiosity was all centred on her. She still didn't know whether to believe he really was her father. She could see no similarity between them, and sometimes she wished Marleen had never told her about her mother's affair with him. It made her want too much.

Bonny had turned up to see the pantomime with her Aunt Lydia at the start of the new year. Because Lydia was by her side there was no opportunity to really talk, but Ellie felt she was still very distressed by Magnus giving her up. A week later she wrote from her parents' home to say she was joining a dance troupe called The Toppers because otherwise she might strangle her mother. Then she went on to say John Norton was in America but had written to her and that she hoped to see him again when he got back. As Ellie had heard nothing further since then, she had to assume Bonny was recovering.

Then there was Ray.

From that first supper date with him back before Christmas, Ellie had known it was inevitable they'd become lovers eventually. Ray charmed her on every level: he was funny, intelligent and warm, he could chat easily about anything, he was as fascinated by the theatre as she was, in tune with her in every way. The only reason she had held out this long was because she hoped for something more. She wanted him physically, she had from the very start, yet she knew she wasn't in love with him.

'That wonderful meal was enough without champagne,' Ellie smiled, taking the glass of sparkling wine from him and clinking it against his. 'Here's to the abolition of food rationing!'

'I think it's going to be around for a few more years yet,' Ray said, his blue-grey eyes looking seductively sleepy; they'd already drunk two bottles of wine with their steaks in Maria's in Flask Walk. 'I dream of one day going into a shop and being allowed to have everything I want, to load up a shopping bag with pork chops, bacon, ham and twenty different kinds of cheeses.'

'Is there more than one kind?' Since Ellie had been in Hampstead and met many of Ray's rather Bohemian friends she'd become highly aware of her lack of sophistication, and she chose to cope with this by pretending to be even less knowledgeable than she really was.

'My little innocent,' Ray said tenderly, moving closer on the couch. 'There's so many things I'd like to teach you.'

Ray was glad he'd had the foresight to spend this afternoon cleaning and tidying. The fire he'd lit then was roaring away now; he'd even changed the sheets. Ray didn't normally go to so much trouble for his girlfriends – usually a smelly paraffin stove and an unmade bed was all that greeted them – but he was determined to seduce Ellie tonight. He'd even visited the barber's this morning with the sole purpose of buying some sheaths. It was so rare to find a beautiful actress of her age who was still a virgin. Even her kisses were chaste.

'What would you like to teach me?' Ellie put her glass down on the floor and snuggled closer to him leaning into his shoulder. She was just tipsy enough to lose her inhibitions. Ray had put a record on, of lovely dreamy music. She hadn't liked to show her ignorance by asking what it was, but she thought it was Mozart.

'To trust me, for a start,' Ray whispered, nuzzling at her ear. 'To let yourself go and stop thinking about tomorrow, or next week, just the moment.'

He held her face in both his hands, kissing her so lovingly it sent delicious tingles down her spine. Ellie responded to his probing tongue by opening her lips just wide enough to receive it, and the tingles became tremors.

'Mm,' she sighed contentedly. His fingers were already unbuttoning her cardigan. The thought flashed through her mind that maybe she ought to have foreseen something like this tonight and bought some new underwear. Was it dark enough in here by candle-light that he wouldn't notice how shabby they were? How was she going to get her dress off? It had hooks and eyes on the side! And what if she got pregnant?

An hour or so later, most of her anxiety had gone, lulled into a blissful world where nothing mattered more than his kisses. They were lying on the rug in front of the fire. Ray had pulled her dress over her head, all but one candle had burned itself out, her underwear had been slowly removed and surreptitiously shoved by herself under one of the cushions. She'd seen Ray take a packet from his jacket pocket and place it beside him on the floor. The only worry she had now was whether she should instigate him taking his trousers off, or wait for him to do it.

His chest was bare and as endearingly thin and narrow as a young boy's, winter white and entirely free from hair. She ran her fingers through his curls as he sucked at her breasts, wanting to tell him how much he was pleasing her, but yet not knowing how. It was like a delicious dream she never wanted to wake from, wave after wave of sensual delight which she was taking selfishly, offering nothing in return. His fingers were probing into her, finding sensitive spots she hadn't known were there. She wanted it to go on and on for ever.

The music had stopped long ago, the needle scratching in the middle. The fire crackled and groaned as the coals grew smaller, the last candle spluttered and went out and Ellie slid her hands down Ray's back towards his trousers, desire greater now than her anxiety about the proprieties in love-making.

He moaned in delight as her fingers reached for his buttons, his belly arching away from hers to admit her hand. 'I want you so badly,' he whispered huskily. 'You're so beautiful, Ellie, I never want tonight to end.'

'Show me what to do,' she whispered, remembering suddenly that it had been at this point when everything went wrong with her and Charley.

'Just hold me, angel,' he whispered back, pushing his fingers hard inside her making her moan with more pleasure.

Passion welled up more intensely as she felt his hardness. He was wriggling out of his trousers, mouth back at her breasts sucking and biting. He had to be much more experienced than Charley was to have such control, because she was losing all hers.

But even when Ray was naked, he still made no attempt to enter her. He caressed her sex with such delicacy, she felt herself being drawn into a fiery tunnel that made her buck beneath him and clutch him tighter to her. She could hear herself making noises exactly like those she'd overheard from Bonny when she was with Magnus in the flat in Pimlico, but she didn't care any longer, she just wanted to reach the end of that tunnel, wherever it was leading.

'Come, baby, come,' he whispered against her breast. 'Then I'll fuck you and make it happen again.'

Something extraordinary was happening. She was on fire, a burning sensation spreading all over her that made her tremble and gasp in pure delight. Ray's fingers were doing it, it was birthdays, Christmas, first nights and brass bands all at once, then she found herself crying, clinging on to him, shaking from head to toe.

'Nice?' Ray murmured sleepily much later. They had moved into his bed some time ago and made love twice more, and she thought it must be nearly morning now. All the mysteries had been revealed to her – why Bonny couldn't get enough of it, why songs and poems were written about it – and it had exceeded even her wildest expectations.

'It was wonderful,' she whispered, snuggling tighter into his shoulder. Tomorrow she would probably blush when she thought of some of the things Ray had done to her, or recalled the things she'd said. But right now she felt utter peace, her body satiated and complete. 'That was the best birthday present ever.'

Chapter Twenty-Six

September 1948

Wet coats, umbrellas and condensation created a steamy fug in the crowded Hampstead teashop. Rain splattered hard on the bow-windows, the lace curtains fluttering each time yet another drenched person burst in to find refuge from the wet street.

Edward and Ellie were tucked into the furthest corner table. The teapot had long since been drained and the two-tier cake stand was empty aside from one unappetising slice of gingerbread. They studiously ignored the elderly waitress who was clearly hoping they would leave to make room for someone else.

It was mid-September and Ellie had been in Hampstead just over nine months since taking over the role of Prince Charming. The pantomime had run until the last week in February, but Ray Kennedy had kept her on since then in repertory, giving her parts in each new production. She had gained an enormous amount of acting experience during this time, from plays by Ibsen, Shaw and Noël Coward, to the present farce in which Edward had a role as the butler.

Edward had come back to London in March as the resident pianist in Churchill's, a smart West End night-club. Ellie had introduced him to Ray and persuaded him to try Edward out in this part. In all these months Bonny had remained in The Toppers, touring the provinces, and Edward had all but forgotten the influence she once had on Ellie. Now, though, it seemed

Bonny was asserting it again: Ellie was about to join up with her for a double-act in a touring show.

'But why, Ellie? Dancing with Bonny is a step backwards,' Edward argued. 'I don't understand you. You've been making quite a name for yourself in comedy. What on earth made you agree to this?'

'Because I want to keep up dancing,' Ellie said in a low voice, aware that a couple of middle-aged ladies at the next table were listening. 'It won't be any good turning up for an audition in a musical comedy if I'm out of condition. I've been trying to keep up dance practice, but it's impossible when I'm living in digs. My voice is suffering too. A six-month tour will set me up again.'

'Touring's exhausting,' Edward said, leaning back in his seat and lighting up yet another cigarette. He was jealous. He and Ellie had been having such a happy time here in London without Bonny to spoil it. He thought she was being very stupid. 'A week here, a week there, seedy digs, living out of suitcases and all that travelling, what kind of life is that?'

Edward's appearance had gradually changed from that of a very correct English gentleman into a more artistic image in the last couple of years. His blond hair was longer, corduroy trousers and casual jackets replacing his old dark suits and stiff collars. His lifestyle of late nights, lack of fresh air and exercise had given him a slightly haunted pallor, and even his once very correct speech was peppered now with slang picked up in West End clubs and bars.

'It's a good experience,' Ellie said firmly. 'And I like seeing new places. You're just cross because I'll be with Bonny.'

Edward blushed. He hadn't thought he was so transparent. 'I thought she had a new man? Or has that fallen through?'

Ellie bristled a little. She didn't like it when Edward was sarcastic about Bonny. She had no intention of passing on what Bonny had revealed in her letters regarding John Norton. 'No, it hasn't fallen through, in fact he sounds like a permanent fixture in her life,' Ellie said tartly. 'But he's abroad a good deal of the time and anyway, Bonny does make her own living, you know!'

'What about Ray Kennedy?' Edward changed tack. It was a mistake to cast aspersions about Bonny; Ellie was always fiercely defensive of her. 'Does he mind you going away?'

Edward liked Ray. He was intelligent, amusing and a good producer. But Edward couldn't help but be jealous of him too. He didn't actually mind him being Ellie's lover, he just resented the man encroaching on his territory, that of Ellie's best friend.

'Ray's another reason I'm going.' Ellie bent forward across the table, her tone confidential. 'It's not going anywhere with him, Edward. He's good fun and very sexy, and it would be so easy just to stay here and let the months drift by, but I must move on. Six months away will sort out everything, including how I feel about him.'

There were times when she had almost convinced herself she was in love with Ray. They liked the same things, their goals in life were similar – but there was something lacking. She didn't feel that all-consuming passion she had for Charley.

'I suppose you're right,' Edward sighed. He couldn't make out which was worse, Ray's or Bonny's influence on her. Ellie looked very shabby these days. He knew she earned very little, but she was developing a strange Bohemian look that worried him slightly. Her coat appeared to have been made out of tapestry curtains and her brown felt hat brim was pinned up with a vulgar ruby glass brooch. He wished he could be the only person in her life and buy her the kind of clothes that would show-off her beauty. 'Maybe I'm only being a dog in the manger because I'll miss you.'

Ellie often thought that she and Edward were a real pair: two oddballs, who had so much in common. But although she loved him as a brother, there was no sexual chemistry between them. 'Oh Edward,' she grinned. 'We'll always be pals. Besides, you've got Marcia, and Ray's included you in his next two productions.'

Edward was pleased about his roles in the next two plays, but less enthusiastic about Marcia. He'd met her when he was working in Churchill's. She was several years older than himself, a tall, slinky blonde croupier whom he couldn't resist, yet who at the same time disgusted him. She was as voracious in her sexual appetite as Bonny, but common and crude. Although she'd completed his sexual education, he knew there was something dark and unnatural about their relationship. He couldn't tell Ellie this.

'I suppose we'd better go.' Edward looked at his watch. It was nearly four o'clock and he'd arranged to see Marcia at half-past. 'Are you going back to the digs?'

'No, nipping down to see Ray,' Ellie admitted, a naughty glint in her eyes. 'I'll see you at the theatre later.'

Edward turned away to summon the waitress for the bill. He didn't like to picture Ellie in bed with Ray. Not even when he was on his way to screw Marcia.

As Ellie scurried through the rain down Heath Street to Fitzjohn's Avenue she wondered what exactly Ray had that made him so attractive, not only to her, but to many other women.

Such an ordinary face, not one remarkable feature other than his gentle blue-grey eyes and his curly hair. He didn't concern himself about appearances – his broken tooth, or his clothes. She supposed it was purely that his personality shone through. He had such zest for life, always full of enthusiasm, whether it was for a new production, or just a day out. He wasn't a thinker, but a doer. He didn't agonise about the future, the state of the world, or care about making money. He was a well-adjusted man with no hidden complexes who made her laugh and whom she could really talk to. Ray had been good for her: with him she'd learnt so much, to forget her origins and concentrate her energies on living now. She read more, she listened to music and he'd helped her to stretch her abilities on stage. She was going to miss him when she went away.

'You lazy toad,' Ellie said as Ray opened his door to her wearing nothing but a pair of pyjama bottoms. 'Have you been in bed all day?'

Ray had the body of an adolescent, despite being over thirty. Not an ounce of muscle, a puny chest and long skinny legs, yet he was such a sexy man and part of his charm was this boyishness.

'What was there to get up for?' he laughed, pulling her into his arms and slamming the door behind her. 'I did shave though, I didn't want to rough up your tender parts. But why are you so late? I thought you'd be here hours ago!'

Ellie looked over his shoulder at the one big room. As always it was untidy and mucky, strewn from end to end with clothes, books and unwashed crockery, the unmade bed the centre-piece. Ellie sometimes cleaned and tidied it up for him, but within days it was just as bad again. She didn't understand how he could bear to live like it.

'I had tea with Edward,' she said. 'I wanted to tell him about the tour.'

Ray unbuttoned her damp coat and pulled it off her shoulders, tossing it on to a chair. 'Come into bed for a cuddle.' He grinned lasciviously.

'Your cuddles always lead to something more,' Ellie said with a smile, but she let him take off her cardigan too. 'And I hope you've got some supplies of you know what?'

'I've got dozens.' Ray slipped her dress off her shoulders and began kissing her neck, edging her backward towards the bed.

Since the first time Ray made love to her back in January, Ellie had discovered for herself just why Bonny was so addicted to sex. With Ray as an affectionate, enthusiastic and experienced teacher, all Ellie's inhibitions had just floated away and now she often found herself thinking about sex, hardly able to wait for it.

Sometimes, late at night back in her digs, she felt a tiny stab of guilt at behaving with such abandon with a man she knew would never be her husband, but she would dismiss such thoughts by reminding herself that this was what Ray called her 'working-class morality'.

'What would you like me to do to you?' Ray murmured after several long and sensual kisses.

'Pretend you're a doctor,' Ellie giggled.

'Well don't giggle then,' he said reprovingly, his blue-grey eyes twinkling naughtily.

He arranged her as if she were lying on a consulting room couch, then stood up beside the bed.

'Well, Miss Forester, what seems to be the trouble?'

'I've been having pains,' she said, putting her hand low on her stomach.

'Here?' he said, placing his hand on her crutch.

'Yes,' she murmured. 'A kind of burning.'

'I see.' Ray's face was very serious. 'I shall have to examine you. Just remove your underwear.'

Ellie loved these games. It made her feel very wicked, especially stone-cold sober, in broad daylight. Ray had introduced her to them, but she was all too willing to participate. She wriggled out of her knickers, leaving just her stockings and suspenders under her dress.

'Bend your knees and let them fall apart,' he said. 'This won't hurt.'

His touch was every bit as gentle as a real doctor's.

He sat down on the bed beside her and probed into her.

'You seem very hot there,' he said, moving his fingers in and out. 'How long have you had this trouble?'

Ellie was beginning to lose the script for this game. She closed her eyes, her breathing becoming heavy as her excitement grew. 'For ages,' she said weakly. 'Can you do something about it?'

'Let me see your breasts,' Ray said, his spare hand opening the bodice of her dress and pulling her brassière down far enough for one to come free. He squeezed the nipple, at the same time continuing his gentle, erotic probing in her pussy. 'Mm, as I thought, you need my special medicine.'

'But, doctor,' Ellie whispered as his head went down between her legs, 'isn't that a little unconventional?'

She was quivering now, arching her back and opening her legs wider.

'Unconventional methods always work best with my lady patients,' he murmured. 'Just wait and see.'

Ellie floated off into another world as he used his tongue on her. The rain outside, her career, all her little worries were forgotten in sheer bliss. She could feel herself coming and she clutched at Ray's hair, begging him to enter her.

'Come inside me,' she screamed at the point of orgasm. 'Now.'

Ray ignored her pleas and continued to lap at her. Only when the spasmodic jerking of her body had stopped did he move to hold her. 'I shan't trust you visiting a doctor in future.' He grinned, taking her hand and putting it round his hard penis. 'Time for your punishment for being a naughty girl.'

Ray didn't take much in life seriously, except lovemaking. Not for him the quick snack, he made every session a feast. Long, slow strokes, his mouth hungry on hers, stopping now and then to cool himself down before starting again, and after each pause the temperature rising another few degrees.

Ellie was swept along with it, moving beneath him in a delirium of passion, their bodies sticking together with sweat.

'I'm coming,' he groaned, his fingers digging into her bottom. 'It's wonderful!'

He lay on top of her, his breath hot on her neck until the shuddering in his body subsided. But his silence was a reminder of what was missing. She knew in a moment he would get up, remove the sheath and make a cup of tea. What she longed for was some emotion, whispered endearments and tenderness.

'We'd better get moving.' Ray crammed the last of a slice of bread and jam into his mouth and gulped down his tea. 'We'll have to run to get to the theatre on time.'

Ellie was dressing. She turned to look at him.

His hair was tousled, he had jam round his mouth and his trousers hadn't been cleaned or pressed for months. He was still a little boy at heart, who didn't act or think like most men, who would probably never conform.

'Do you ever wish for something more?' she asked.

'More sex! Haven't you had enough?' He made a mock-horrified face.

'I didn't mean sex,' Ellie said weakly.

He went over to the grimy mirror above the mantelpiece, wiped the jam from his mouth and looked back at her in the mirror. He had an odd expression on his face, bafflement, irritation and amusement all mixed together. 'You aren't talking about all that soppy stuff, like in films, the "I'll love you till I die" business are you?' he said.

'Not exactly.' Her voice was faint and she suddenly felt like crying. 'Don't make a joke of it. Ray. There is something missing, isn't there?'

He shrugged his shoulders and began to tie his tie. 'What's brought this on, Ellie? Are you waiting for me to beg you not to go áway?'

'No. But it would be nice if you told me how you feel about it.'

'I'll miss you,' he said, turning back to her. His face was serious now, his eyes as warm as ever, but without any sadness. 'We've had nine months of fun together and it won't be the same without you. Is that what you want to hear?'

Ellie sighed. She knew she was being unreasonable. She felt no more than that herself. If he were suddenly to swear undying love she wouldn't be able to reciprocate truthfully. But she still felt sad.

To her surprise, he came to her then and put his arms round her, holding her close against his shoulder.

'We've given each other some very good memories,' he said softly. 'Isn't that enough?'

'Harder, Edward, fuck me harder!' Marcia screamed out. She was bent over an armchair, supporting herself on the arms, wearing nothing but a garter-belt, a half-cup push-up brassière and black stockings. Edward held on to her waist, still fully dressed aside from his jacket and his opened flies, entering her from the rear.

'Tell me how much you like it, bitch!' he hissed digging his nails into her flesh. 'Is it good?'

'It's the best, it's wonderful, no one can fuck like you,' she whimpered. 'I'm coming, I'm coming.'

Edward closed his eyes and drove himself even harder into her. This was the best part of it, the few seconds before he ejaculated when he felt all-powerful, every nerve in his body throbbing. He could forget he was a third-rate actor, only a passable pianist, or that he only got sexual satisfaction from tarts like Marcia. For a few brief moments he was a real man.

'Ohhh!' Marcia's high-pitched voice brought Edward back to reality. He looked down at her narrow back and eyed with distaste the blotchiness of her skin, the yellow-headed spots on her shoulder. She was still bucking against him, almost as if she hadn't realised it was over.

He withdrew quickly and made straight for the bathroom. He hated the smell after sex and hoped she'd got the lavender soap he liked.

'Would you like a cuppa?' she called out only seconds later, her voice high and nasal.

'No, I'll have to hurry,' he called back, wincing at his appearance in the mirror. There were dark shadows beneath his eyes and his skin seemed to have a yellowish tinge. He needed a holiday.

He washed his cock very carefully, then his hands. Marcia had got the lavender soap, but the bathroom was as mucky as her mind. There was a ring round the bath-tub, the wash-basin had traces of toothpaste stuck to it, and the lavatory stunk.

'You are a slut,' Edward said as he came out, doing up his flies and adjusting his braces before putting on his coat. 'Don't you ever clean up?'

Marcia's flat was a basement in Camden Town. It was gloomy, it smelt musty and there was a rough Irish family living upstairs who sat out on the front steps in good weather.

'I don't get much time, luv,' she replied without a trace of hurt or embarrassment. She had slipped a red satin wrapper over her underwear and her hair looked like a blonde bird's nest. She lit a cigarette and drew in deeply. 'Most fellas don't notice, but I suppose you're different, being a toff an' all.'

Edward glanced around him. Her flat reminded him of some of the worst digs he'd had: stained wallpaper, furniture fit only for firewood, the kind of fairground-type ornaments working-class people always seemed to go for. Everything had a film of dust on it, and there was inevitably washing drying in front of the fire. It looked seedy on arrival, but much worse after sex. If he glanced out of the grimy window the sight of the railings up on the street level made him think of prisons and reminded him that he was a prisoner of his warped sexuality.

He doubted Marcia had ever been pretty – her nose was too long and her lips too thin – but seen at the gaming tables in evening dress with her blonde hair swept back into a sleek chignon, she was steely glamour. Like all the women he was attracted to, she was tall and reed-slim and he overlooked the fact that she was thirty-five because she was grateful for his attention.

'Just clean up before I come again,' Edward said. He wanted to add that the roots of her hair needed retouching, but he didn't dare go that far.

'Can you leave me a few bob for the gas?' she asked, blowing out some smoke towards the ceiling. Edward baffled her. He was such a nasty bastard sometimes, but he was generous, that made up for some of it. 'I'm a bit short.'

Edward turned his back on her, withdrew a ten-shilling note from his wallet and put it down on the table. She wasn't astute enough to become a real prostitute, even though she had the soul of one. The small amounts of money Edward left her and the occasional present appeased them both.

'I'll be off now,' he said over his shoulder. 'I'll phone you.'

Despite the heavy rain, Edward walked to Hampstead up through Chalk Farm, hoping to shake off his black mood before that evening's performance. He couldn't understand why other men were always in a good humour after sex; he just felt tainted.

'It's her,' he said to himself. 'She's a tart and you know you shouldn't be with her. That's all it is.'

But a tiny voice was whispering to him that he was unnatural, that all the women he found were like Marcia, that he picked them specially because he really didn't like women at all.

'Except for Ellie,' he reminded himself. 'She's special.'

Edward knew he'd missed good opportunities by trying to work with or near Ellie. He knew too it was unhealthy to adore a woman to whom he could never be more than a friend. But with Ellie he never felt second-rate or strange. Their friendship was the most important thing in his life.

While Ellie and Edward were both dwelling on their respective flawed love affairs, Bonny was concerned with embarking on a new one, in high hopes it would lead to marriage.

Magnus ending their affair had been the most terrible thing that had ever happened to her. All winter she had been trapped in utter despair, unable even to consider finding a replacement for him. Ellie was miles away in London, by all accounts having a wonderful time not only at the Little Theatre, but with a new man, and with Edward, as ever, on the sidelines.

After the new year, Bonny knew she couldn't stay with her parents. Her mother nagged continually, suffocating her with unwanted attention. A visit to Aunt Lydia's had proved to be almost as bad; there was nothing for Bonny in Amberley now that Jack wouldn't speak to her. In desperation she had joined another dancing troupe, The Toppers, only to find that without Ellie beside her, the other girls treated her with suspicion and even antipathy. It was so dull, the same old routine night after night after night. She didn't need to think about the dance steps. She felt like a clockwork toy: the music was like a key, and when she heard the opening bars she just performed automatically. It made no difference what town she was in, whether Canterbury, Winchester, Yeovil or Exeter: they were all equally boring.

Only John Norton had cheered her a little, with his many warm and interesting letters from America.

When the summer finally came and the tour headed for the seaside towns of Ramsgate, Broadstairs and Margate, Bonny began to recover slightly, aided by John's return to England.

His background was as impressive as Magnus's, even if his family weren't as rich. Lady Penelope Beauchamp was his godmother, a cousin of his had married a count, he himself served as an officer in the Guards during the war and he seemed to know half the socialites in London. On top of that he was a professional man, and he had a house in Somerset. It didn't matter to her that John showed little interest in his more illustrious relations, or that he said the house in Somerset was a near ruin and right in the heart of the country. He looked like a good bet.

Now, at last, Bonny's days with The Toppers were almost over. Ellie had finally become disenchanted enough with being an actress to want to team up again as a double act, and they would be off to open in Manchester in two weeks' time. Six months of touring with Ellie would make everything right again. But meanwhile Bonny was determined to cement her relationship with John firmly: she wanted him for a husband, hopefully within a year, two at the most.

Today, when he came to visit her in Southampton, she'd suggested they went to visit Aunt Lydia. It was Sunday, so there was no evening performance to rush back for. She had no intention of letting him meet her parents until she was forced to. Lydia had style, though, and Bonny knew the moment he set foot in Briar Bank he would be impressed.

'Well, this has been such a lovely surprise,' Lydia said, ruffling Bonny's hair after she'd set down a tray of tea and biscuits on the coffee table. 'I don't see nearly enough of her, John, so thank you for bringing her to see me.'

Lydia thought Bonny had never looked lovelier. Her

hair was set in loose waves, she still had traces of a golden tan, and the blue crêpe frock she was wearing was the height of fashion with its long, slender skirt.

Bonny smiled sweetly, and tucked her arm through John's as they sat on the couch. 'John thought I was exaggerating about how lovely Briar Bank is,' she said. 'So I insisted we came.'

'She does tend to exaggerate.' Lydia looked at John Norton and smiled.

It had been quite a shock to find Bonny at her door this afternoon. At New Year, she'd clearly been deeply unhappy about something, which Lydia had assumed to be a broken love affair, although Bonny couldn't be drawn on the subject. Since then Lydia had only had an occasional postcard from different towns on the south coast, sometimes containing an odd reference to the man who was with her now.

Johh Norton wasn't the kind of man Lydia had expected. Comparing him to Jack was like comparing a terrier to a Red Setter. He was a gentleman: suave, polished and extremely intelligent. But Lydia was warming to this quiet, serious man, and it pleased her to see Bonny looking happy again.

'Well, she didn't exaggerate one bit about you, or your home,' John replied. 'In fact, she omitted to tell me how beautiful you are.'

John had pictured Lydia Wynter older and more stern-faced. She had to be in her forties, but she looked much younger because of her slender figure and chestnut waved hair. Her cashmere twin set and straight skirt were expensive chic, and her vivacious sparkle and lack of spinsterish coyness set her apart from most women of her age.

'Such flattery will get you everywhere,' Lydia laughed. She thought John was handsome, especially when he gave one of his rare smiles. Everything about him was neat: his dark hair, small moustache, slender nose and even white teeth. His dark suit was hand-tailored, he had good shoes, a knife-edge crease in his trousers. His dark eyes, though, were his best feature – kind eyes, which seemed to confirm there was nothing shifty or devious about this man. 'Now let's have our tea and tell me everything. I want to know about the dancing, Bonny, and all about this charming man.'

Lydia listened as Bonny spoke of all the towns she'd danced in during the last nine months, the other girls in the troupe, the terrible digs, and how John had made it bearable by coming to see her when he could.

'He's amazing, Auntie,' she said, eyes dancing. 'He turned up in Canterbury, Margate and Brighton. I don't know how he could bear to see such an awful show over and over again.'

Lydia smiled knowledgeably. John Norton was clearly head over heels in love with Bonny. She just hoped he knew what he was letting himself in for.

'I had business in those towns. Fortunately I get a bigger ration of petrol than most people, and hotel expenses while I'm on company business.' John blushed in embarrassment. 'Besides, the show wasn't awful. I enjoyed it.'

'Bonny described you as a big shot in the oil business? Is there oil in Brighton?' She couldn't resist that little quip, if only to warn him he couldn't fool her.

'I wouldn't call myself a big shot,' John said evenly. 'I'm a chemist by profession, Miss Wynter, I analyse soil and rock samples to enable my company to find oil. But when I'm not out working in the field, I also organise buying tools and equipment for the laboratories. Most of this equipment is bought here in England, then shipped out to wherever we need it. Brighton and Margate are both towns where scientific equipment is made. Canterbury I had to squeeze in on the way to Dover.'

Lydia was suitably impressed by this reply. Obviously he wasn't just a 'stage door Johnny'. 'Bonny says you travel abroad a great deal too. You've recently been working in Texas, I believe?'

'Yes, that's right, my company works with all the big oil companies out there. I shall be doing my usual stuff, making the scientific judgements before they waste time and money on drilling. I'm off to the Persian Gulf soon.'

Lydia wanted to know why he was unmarried still, but she could hardly ask that without sounding impertinent. Perhaps it was the war; a great deal of men seemed to find it hard to settle afterwards. 'So what will you do then, Bonny?' she asked instead, raising one eyebrow questioningly.

'Oh, I've signed up for another tour.' Bonny looked at John in an odd sort of way. Lydia had a feeling she wanted his approval. 'Ellie and I are getting back together again as partners. We go to Manchester next week.'

'Well, that's wonderful.' Lydia had driven Bonny back to London after her visit at New Year and they'd gone to see Ellie's pantomime together. It was the first time she'd actually met Ellie, though she had seen her perform in that ill-fated show at the Phoenix. Somehow she'd always imagined her as very much like Bonny in character and it was a delightful surprise to discover the girl she'd heard so much about was not only very talented, but levelheaded, warm-hearted and seriously ambitious. She felt she was a good influence on Bonny. 'How do you feel about Bonny being back in tandem with Ellie, John?'

'A little relieved,' John said, colouring up suddenly as if he felt he'd let something slip. 'I mean, Bonny's been rather lonely on the last job, some of the girls weren't very pleasant.'

Lydia smiled wryly. She was delighted to see Bonny, but she hadn't forgotten what a little minx she could be.

'Where is your home, John?' Lydia asked after a brief interval of less penetrating questions.

'That's not an easy question to answer.' He smiled as he spoke and she guessed there was a story there. 'I live in hotels most of the time, but when I'm in London I stay with my godmother, Penelope Beauchamp.'

'She's Lady Penelope,' Bonny butted in. She'd been dying to inform Lydia about that.

'But where did you grow up?' Lydia ignored Bonny's boastful remark, but noticed that John blushed at it.

'A tiny Somerset village in the Mendips called Priddy.' John smiled again, as if he liked to recall that. 'I had a wonderful childhood there, roaming the woods and heathlands with my two brothers.'

'Your brothers, do they still live there?' Lydia asked.

'They are both dead now.' John's moustache quivered just slightly, and his eyes dropped from hers.

'I'm so sorry,' she said. 'Was that in action? Bonny said you were in the Guards.'

'Joseph was killed during his platoon's retreat into Dunkirk,' John said. 'Matthew died four years before that of malaria out in India. He was only eighteen.'

'How terrible for your parents,' Lydia said. Maybe this was why John had such kind eyes; grief always seemed to make men more sensitive.

'They coped with Matthew dying fairly well,' John sighed. 'But when Joseph went too, they kind of just gave up. All through the war they became more and more eccentric. Of course I couldn't get home, I was in the army, in France and latterly in Germany, and when I got a rare couple of days' leave it was too far to go. They died within weeks of one another, soon after the war ended.'

'Oh dear,' Lydia said, wishing she hasn't asked so many questions. 'I'm sorry, John.'

'A great deal worse happened to some families during the war.' John shrugged his shoulders. 'They'd had a good life – until my brothers died, a very happy one. I don't think they were sorry to go. They left me the house – it's called "The Chestnuts". As you can imagine, it's surrounded by chestnut trees. It's a lovely old Georgian house, but terribly dilapidated. At first I intended to sell it – it's not the most convenient place to have a home, not in my line of work. But sentimentality got the better of me, and I'm intending to get men in to restore it. I have made a start – the roof is mended and electricity put on – but it's a big job.'

Lydia excused herself later and went out into the kitchen to prepare a meal. She decided she really liked this new man of Bonny's. She sensed he was lonely; perhaps until he'd met Bonny he had nothing in his life but work. Strong, dependable and honest, all qualities she had always looked for in a partner, but rarely found. She hoped he would have a permanent steadying influence on Bonny.

Lydia was just laying the dining-room table when Bonny came and joined her.

'John's looking around the garden,' she said. 'Do you like him, Auntie?'

'Very much,' Lydia replied. She could see John through the window, bending over to look at a patch of cyclamen. The leaves were turning brown on the trees, another week and they'd all be down. Autumn always made her feel a bit sad. 'He's sensitive, serious and very well-mannered. Just about as opposite to you as possible. But more importantly, do you like him?'

'Mmm,' Bonny said thoughtfully. 'I want to marry him.'

If Bonny had hit her with the heavy box of silver cutlery, Lydia couldn't have been more astonished. 'Really! Is this in the air then?'

'Not exactly.' Bonny smirked and twiddled with a strand of hair. 'He hasn't asked me yet. But I'm sure he will.'

Lydia felt sure Bonny was right. She usually got

what she wanted. 'Perhaps this is a good time then to tell you. Jack got married.'

Bonny's mouth dropped open. She had been about to enlarge further on Lady Penelope Beauchamp and the fact that she owned property all over London. She was intrigued by John's godmother, not only because she was titled and rich, but because she was unmarried and was reputed to have been a beauty when she was younger.

'He didn't! Who to?'

'Ginny Meadows. Do you remember her?'

Bonny gave a high, hysterical laugh, an unpleasant, bitter sound. 'What, that ugly kid with hair like dirty straw?'

'Ginny's turned into a very pretty young woman,' Lydia reproved her. 'She made a lovely bride, and they are very happy. I'd like you to be happy for them too, Bonny. Jack is a good man and he deserved a nice wife.'

'So where are they living?' Bonny's face had drained of colour. Lydia wished she'd kept the news to herself.

'In the Tollhouse. Alec moved up here in the village and let them have it. They are struggling to do it up, of course they haven't much money yet. But Jack's prospects look very good.'

The sound of John coming back in stopped any further questions. He put his head round the dining-room door and smiled. 'What a glorious garden, Miss Wynter,' he said. 'No wonder Bonny's so enchanted with Briar Bank. She tells me your grandmother lived here before you?'

Lydia stood outside waving until John's Jaguar had turned the corner by the church. She felt dejected now, regretting her impulse to tell Bonny about Jack and Ginny. It had quite spoilt the afternoon. Bonny hardly said two words during tea and John was clearly puzzled by this sudden mood swing. But why should Bonny be upset, when she threw Jack over?

Lydia sighed. She knew why really Bonny liked to keep everyone in her pocket, just in case. She just hoped John Norton realised what he was taking on!

'Do I have to go back to my digs?' Bonny turned to John as they drove into Southampton. 'Can't I stay in your hotel with you?'

It was an awful night. All day there had been intermittent rain, but soon after they left Amberley to go back to Southampton the rain had become heavier and now visibility was reduced to a few yards. Bonny had been staring silently at the driving rain in the car headlights for some time, brooding about Jack, and she knew that once she was back in the digs with the other girls she'd feel even more miserable.

She hated the thought of Jack living in the little Tollhouse, especially with skinny Ginny. Magnus had gone back to his wife, now Jack was married. Everyone had nice homes and security except her.

'You can't stay with me, Bonny!' John looked utterly shocked. 'What on earth would people think?'

If Bonny hadn't been feeling so depressed, she might have laughed. She didn't care what people thought, ever. 'But I want to be close to you tonight,' she pleaded. 'I don't know when I'll see you again. Please, John!'

'We'll have dinner somewhere nice and then I'll take you home,' he said firmly. 'I'm only human, Bonny, and I couldn't promise to behave like a gentleman if you were to share my room.'

Bonny was stuck for an answer. From the night when John had turned up at the theatre in Wembley, some time after the gala night at the Savoy, Bonny had used John. He was a presentable escort, nothing more. She had teased him and played the part of a timid virgin because she was in love with Magnus.

John had just left for America when Magnus ended their affair, but even if he had been around, she wouldn't have had the heart to embark on another love affair. Yet John's letters had altered her perception of him. Not only were they her only comfort during all those miserable months, but she saw he was worth far more than just a place as a 'reserve'.

He was kind, thoughtful and affectionate, even if he was rather starchy and proper at times. But although she was certain he was in love with her, he hadn't admitted it, or talked even in general terms of their having a future together. Whether this was because he wasn't convinced of her suitability as a wife because of the twelve-year gap in their ages, or whether he doubted her for some other reason, she didn't know. But she suspected his reluctance to make love to her was tied up in this. Perhaps he knew once he'd stepped over that threshold there would be no way back.

'But I'm going away next week, and you're going abroad,' she said, squeezing out a tear. 'I want to be really close to you, John. I've never felt this way about anyone before.' She wriggled nearer to him as he drove, resting her head on his shoulder and putting one hand on his thigh.

'Oh Bonny,' he sighed. 'You are enough to make any man behave foolishly. You're so young and impressionable. I can't take advantage of you, especially just before we're to be separated for a while. When I get back from the Persian Gulf we'll see how you feel then. Now there's a very good restaurant just up ahead. We'll have dinner, then I'll take you home.'

It was still raining hard as John kissed Bonny goodnight outside her digs in Southampton. He was one of the best kissers Bonny had ever met, but tonight she was too irritated by his pomposity to be really aroused. All through dinner he had talked about 'doing the right thing', of not letting emotion 'carry them away'. She wondered if he'd ever done anything in his life without analysing it under a microscope first.

Bonny had learnt a great deal about herself in the nine months of touring without Ellie. She wasn't impervious to pain: there were times when she'd thought she'd die without Magnus. In June, when his baby was due, she'd found herself looking at babies in prams, wanting one herself so badly she burst into tears. Nothing seemed to please her any longer, not dancing, new clothes or even men admiring her. But most importantly, perhaps, she'd faced up to the fact that she would never be a big star.

She's lost whatever it was she had once had. She might be a good dancer, but that was all she was. This tour with Ellie might give her a little limelight again, but it was only a matter of time before Ellie was lured away on a solo career. Bonny couldn't bear being just one of a dancing troupe; she wasn't made for it.

A husband, home and baby was what she wanted. Maybe she didn't feel about John as she did about Magnus, but she'd make him a good wife. She saw herself sitting at a dinner-table with his clients, wearing expensive clothes and jewellery, travelling abroad with him, but most of all she pictured herself in that lovely old house she'd seen pictures of, rocking a baby in a cradle. When she'd got that, she would be entirely happy.

'Write to me?' John whispered, cupping her face tenderly in his hands. 'Try not to forget me?'

Bonny looked deep into his eyes and sighed. 'How can I forget you, John? Can't you see I'm head over heels in love with you? I only live for the times when I can see you.'

'Oh Bonny.' He crushed her to his chest, moved by this unexpected declaration of love. 'I love you too, but it scares me. You're so very young and beautiful.'

Bonny smiled to herself. At last he'd admitted it! Next time she saw him she'd break down his last defences.

John wiped a tear from his eye as he drove away to his hotel, stunned by Bonny's words.

He was a loner. He had been right through university, his spell in the Guards and was even more so now, when his work took him travelling so much. No other woman had ever made him feel as vulnerable as Bonny did. All the defences he'd built around himself came tumbling down when he first met her, and he didn't like the way he couldn't get her out of his head.

Every friend who'd met her had warned him off. They said she was a gold-digger, a self-centred show-off without a heart. He knew Bonny often told him lies, and he suspected that if he hadn't taken her to nice places and given her presents she'd have lost interest in him by now. But now it was proved to him that she'd been truthful about her childhood, and that explained a great deal about her values.

He shuddered at the thought of the callous parents who'd shoved her away to live with a total stranger. Miss Wynter was very charming, her home so very lovely, yet what damage it must have done to a small girl to know she was only there on sufferance, forced to dance or be banished to another home. Bonny idolised the woman, yet Miss Wynter had managed to find something cutting to say to her while he was out of earshot. He'd watched Bonny's face as she hugged the woman before leaving. She was almost in tears, her lips quivering, clearly hoping Miss Wynter would tell her she was proud of her, or better still that she was loved.

How he'd resisted the temptation to take her to his hotel he didn't know. He wanted her so badly it was a physical pain. But he had to be sure of her first. There were too many women out there looking for a free meal ticket and he had no intention of being taken for a ride by Bonny, however much he loved her.

Chapter Twenty-Seven

March 1949

'Four whole days off! Whoopee!' Ellie shrieked, kicking off her shoes and leaping on to the old iron bed. The springs clanged in protest and she laughed and bounced again as if she were on a trampoline, knowing it would bring a howl of rage from Mrs Rolf, their landlady.

Sure enough the voice came from the foot of the stairs. 'Treat that bed with respect,' she yelled. 'It's done me good service and I won't have you flibber-tigibbets destroying it.'

Ellie bounced once more in defiance. She and Bonny were giddy with excitement. They were leaving Birmingham. By midday they'd be in London. Mrs Rolf, her bad food and her lumpy, damp beds would be just an unpleasant memory. True, the next date of the tour was in Coventry, which might very well be as bad as this, but in the meantime she would be staying with Ray and Bonny would be meeting John.

It was March, just one more month before their disastrous tour was over for good. Everything that could go wrong on a tour had: hampers of costumes lost in transit from one town to another; artists disappearing and leaving the rest of the company in the lurch; an influenza epidemic which picked them off one by one between Christmas and the end of January. The whole company were sick of doing the same old routine week after week, the jokes no longer made them laugh, they loathed all the songs and wanted to boo at the magician. It was hardly worth taking their clothes out of the suitcase when at the end of the week they had to pack it all back in.

They were all used to bad digs, but this time they'd discovered new lows. One notable place in Wakefield had an unemptied chamber-pot under the bed and only a candle for light. They put up with snow, ice, rain and hail, dressing-rooms with broken windows, Alfredo the tenor leering constantly at them. Cynthia, an alcoholic assistant to 'the Mighty Marcel' who did a knife-throwing act, chased Bonny with one of his daggers because she thought she had stolen her best wig. In Glasgow Ellie had found a rat in the dressing-room, in Preston a drunk in the audience had pelted the stage with monkey nuts and one of the dancers had slipped and broken her leg. There had been moments of hilarity, but so many more of absolute misery.

Ellie got a sty in one eye which didn't get better for weeks; Bonny caught scabies from a dirty towel. They had fought and cried, been hungry and exhausted, but now it was all put aside, in the joy of going to London.

'I'll give her flibbertigibbets. Look what I've got.' Bonny opened a piece of newspaper and a fishy smell wafted out.

'It's a kipper!' Ellie giggled as her friend drew out the thin, brown fish by its tail. 'What on earth have you got that for?'

'Just watch.' Bonny grinned mischievously. She opened their door and stole out into the gloomy landing. She held one finger up to her lips for Ellie to keep quiet, then still holding the kipper by its tail, she crept over to a heavy chest of drawers wedged in an alcove and slid it down into a tiny gap at the back between the chest and the wall.

Ellie had to cover her mouth to prevent herself

laughing and backed into their room. Mrs Rolf was hateful. She charged them a shilling for each bath, and when the girls had decided to share one, she banned them from bathing altogether. Meals were almost inedible; brawn, tripe and oxtail were her favourite stand-bys. She poked around in their room, she found fault continually, and she insisted they were lucky to be in her cold, cheerless house.

'It won't start smelling really bad until we're long gone,' Bonny giggled, washing her hands at the sink. 'Rolfy will be frantic. She'll never think of looking behind there.'

Ellie picked up her coat and stood in front of the cracked mirror to put her hat on. She had bought it just yesterday from a second-hand shop and she thought she looked like a Cossack in it. It was black Persian lamb, trimmed round with ocelot, and it was wickedly dramatic with the coat she'd bought in a jumble sale.

'You're a fiend, Bonny,' she giggled as she tilted the hat rakishly to one side. The camel coat was huge, but pre-war good quality. She had stitched in shoulder pads, nipped in the waist with a leather belt and now it looked up to the minute. 'But Rolfy deserves it. Just don't leave the newspaper in here, or she'll know we were responsible.'

Bonny put her fur coat on. It was musquash, and like Ellie's coat and hat it too was second-hand. But Bonny managed to look like a film star in it, and they'd been very glad of it on their bed on cold nights.

'That's it then.' Bonny picked up her case and looked around the grim room one last time. 'Can't say I'll ever get nostalgic for Birmingham, not after this house and Mrs Rolf, but I wouldn't mind being a fly on the wall in a week's time.'

'We'll probably be in a worse place by then,' Ellie groaned. She peered under the bed to make sure they'd left nothing behind, then picking up her case, followed Bonny to the stairs.

'You look marvellous.' Ray caught Ellie in his arms when he opened the door to her at his flat in Hampstead. 'God I've missed you!' he said jubilantly as he swung her round.

'You have?' she said in astonishment, pleasantly surprised by such a loving greeting.

He looked different: a few gained pounds had filled out his face and his curly hair was longer than she remembered. But it was more than just that – he looked almost pretty.

'You've had your tooth fixed!' she exclaimed, suddenly aware that the broken tooth was no longer there. 'It changes your whole face!'

'Thank heaven for the new Health Service,' he laughed, opening his mouth and wiggling a plate with two false teeth fitted. 'I went in with raging toothache, expecting to come out with gaping holes, but instead the dentist fitted this.'

'Did you really miss me?' she asked, all at once feeling odd to be back here.

'Well, look how I've cleared up,' he grinned, waving his arm at the flat. 'I don't do that for many people.'

Ellie smiled. He had stacked up books and papers into neat piles, there wasn't any dirty china anywhere in sight, or clothes strewn on the chairs, but it was still dusty and there were balls of fluff on the lino. 'You aren't much of a cleaner,' she commented.

'My Sergeant Major put me off cleaning for life,' he laughed. 'Other men can boast of brave deeds in the war, all I did was scrub floors and hand out stores.'

If Ellie hadn't seen photographs of Ray in uniform she wouldn't really believe he'd been in the army. He wasn't a 'man's man' at all and he loathed taking orders. 'How long have we got before you've got to go to work?' she asked.

Ray looked at his watch. 'Four hours and twenty-five minutes,' he said, grinning wickedly. 'How on earth are we going to fill that?'

'With four hours and five minutes of pure sensat on,' she giggled. 'That leaves you twenty minutes to race up the road.'

'Well, we'd better make a start then,' he said, removing her coat and hat. 'I even put clean sheets on the bed.'

Ellie had missed Ray more than she expected to. She'd had a few dates with other men but she hadn't found anyone who was such good company. Between shows, rehearsals and travelling to new venues there was never time to get to know anyone other than the rest of the company, and late at night, in cold, damp beds she'd often thought longingly of his love-making. As soon as Ray began to kiss her, all the desire and frustration bottled up for five months burst forth.

Every stroke of his hands felt like the first time, each kiss deeper and longer than the one before. He smelt delicious, of soap and toothpaste, and she'd all but forgotten how silky his skin was and how good he was at arousing her.

There were no games now, just the need to possess, to hold and be held. The first time was frantic and Ellie had barely helped him on with a sheath and guided him inside her before he came.

'I will do better,' he sighed, snuggling into her arms. 'Just give me a breather.'

But the second time it was like all the good moments they'd shared in the past, rolled into one. Even more sensual and inventive than she remembered, bringing her to an explosive climax within moments, only to start all over again.

'Oh Ellie, I've missed you,' he whispered, showing all the tenderness which had been lacking in the past. 'I could smell you on the sheets after you left, and it made me feel so lost and empty. I've been so excited

599

about you coming here, I've hardly eaten or slept for the last couple of days.'

It had never been quite as good as this in the past; he seemed to be hanging on, trying to make it last for ever. Long, hard strokes inside her, then moving away just to caress her breasts or stroke her back, then coming back inside her for more.

Ellie came before he did, clinging to him, clawing at his back in abandonment which pushed him over the edge to join her.

'That was the very best,' he whispered as he lay still in her arms. 'I've been such a fool, Ellie, I didn't realise just how much you meant to me until you'd gone away.'

Ray had written a few times during their separation, jokey letters telling her all the news but never with even a glimpse into his heart. Now in the afterglow of lovemaking his tender words meant so much, making sense of the past and promising more for the future.

'I'd better take this thing off,' he said, moving slightly to withdraw from her. 'I'm sorry, it's not very romantic.'

Ellie could remember Ray being far less romantic in the past, and his attempt to upgrade his act was touching.

'Oh shit.' His cry startled her out of sleepiness.

'What is it?' she said, sitting up.

'It's split,' he said hoarsely, kneeling back on his feet and peering intently at the latex dangling on his now soft penis. 'I'm so sorry.'

Ellie could only laugh; he looked so funny and woebegone. 'It's not your fault,' she said, drawing him back into her arms. 'It will be all right, just cuddle me.'

They talked then. Ellie told him just how bad the tour had been. 'It was a mistake,' she said grimly. 'There were times when I actually felt like jacking it all in and getting an ordinary job.'

'It wasn't the same here without you,' Ray said tenderly. 'All the backstage crew missed you, Alf more than anyone. I never knew what to do with myself when I wasn't working. Are you coming back to London once the tour's over?'

Ellie was dying to tell him she was going for an audition on Monday morning to replace the present actress paying 'Aldo Annie' in *Oklahoma*, but she felt it might be a jinx if she told anyone. She hadn't even told Bonny.

Oklahoma had been running for two years at the Theatre Royal, since arriving fresh from Broadway, and the comic role of the flirtatious Annie was one that most of the actresses in England would die for. She thought she'd pretend to go shopping on Monday, then if she was lucky enough to be accepted she could rush back to celebrate with Ray before catching the evening train on to Coventry. If she was turned down, no one would be any the wiser.

'I want to work in London,' she said, cuddling into him. 'I'll have to see if Bloomfield's have got anything up their sleeve.'

They dropped off to sleep for a while and when they woke it was almost time for Ray to leave.

'You stay here,' he said, leaping out of bed. 'You can see the play tomorrow. Have a bath and get dolled up and we'll go out for some supper when I'm finished.'

She lay there watching him dress. To her surprise he put on a dinner-jacket and bow-tie.

'Where d'you think you're off to?' she giggled. 'The Ritz?'

'Part of my new image,' he grinned as he tied the tie. 'The theatre's been smartened up, the owners even put a new carpet in the foyer and mended the broken seats. I thought I'd better do myself up too.'

'I'll come up about ten,' she said sleepily as he bent to kiss her goodbye. 'It will be nice to see Alf and everyone. Is Edward still around?'

Edward hadn't written to her for some weeks. He'd had a lead role at the Little Theatre at that time. She thought maybe he'd written again but that the letters hadn't reached her.

'He's playing the piano in a pub up the road,' Ray said vaguely. 'I'm not his favourite person now because I couldn't offer him another part for a while.'

Ellie left Ray's flat before nine. She had dozed for a bit, and then got up and had a bath and once she was dressed there seemed no sense in staying there alone.

It was a frosty, cold night, the sky studded with stars and a full moon. As she walked briskly up Fitzjohn's Avenue she noticed that a bombed-out house which had been just a shell when she was last here had been pulled down and that a small block of flats was being built in its place. As she got closer to Hampstead village, the dowdy dress shop by Haverstock Hill was transformed by fresh paint, its display of 'New Look' spring suits brightly lit.

Ellie stopped to look, smiling with delight. Clothing coupons had finally been abolished last week and clearly the owners of this shop were expecting good business. Ellie had no money for new clothes herself, but it was exciting to see the years of austerity coming to a close. If she *did* get the part in *Oklahoma* she was never going to wear anything second-hand again.

It was good to see all the old familiar haunts again – the teashop she used to go to with Edward, the pub she often went at lunchtimes with Ray – but though she popped her head round the door of all the pubs she passed, Edward wasn't playing in any of them.

'My word, you look the bleedin' ticket.' Alf's face broke into a broad grin as she came through the stage door. 'Where'd yer get the titter? Bin over to Russia?'

'This is the last word in elegance,' she joked, mincing around the small space between Alf's bench and chair and the stairs that led to the dressing-rooms. 'I got the bleedin' titter in a Birmingham second-hand shop, the coat came from a jumble sale.' She swaggered around, dramatically swinging the skirt of her coat to make him laugh.

'You'll soon be wearing mink,' he insisted loyally. He'd become very fond of Ellie in her time in Hampstead, as most of the backstage crew had. 'You'd better leave me the 'at, then I can flog it once yer famous.'

She stayed talking to Alf for a few minutes about the current play, *Blithe Spirit*. She could hear laughter from the front of the house and the sound, coupled with all the familiar smells of mustiness, greasepaint, disinfectant and cigars made her feel nostalgic, so when Alf was called away by one of the stage-hands, she wandered up to the dressing-rooms.

As she made her way along the corridor, she heard a shrill woman's voice raised in anger.

'You really expect me to stay out of the way until then?'

The voice was coming from the dressing-room which was usually allocated to the leading lady. She didn't recognise it as belonging to anyone she'd ever met.

'Don't be like this, Ruby!'

Hearing Ray's voice took Ellie by surprise. During performances he was always either at the front of the house, or in the wings. She paused, curiosity getting the better of her.

'I did warn you,' he went on. 'You said you understood. It certainly doesn't warrant you refusing to go on tonight. What on earth were you thinking of?'

'You didn't say she was your old girlfriend.' The woman's voice rose another octave, and Ellie was so startled she stepped back in alarm. 'Did you really think I could go on stage tonight knowing you'd been screwing some tart all afternoon? Or spend the next few days twiddling my thumbs while you show this "old pal" a good time?'

Ellie was stunned, not only by the ferocity in the woman's voice but by the sudden realisation that she was the cause of the woman's anger. She stood stock-still, a chill running down her spine.

She hadn't really expected Ray to remain faithful to her in her absence; he was after all a man who was attractive to women and he'd made no promises. But his loving manner this afternoon had given her the idea that he'd thought again about her position in his life. She waited, expecting to hear him put this woman in her place, but as he spoke she reeled back in shock.

'She means nothing. She never did,' he said forcefully.

Ellie knew she ought to run away now – just hearing she meant nothing to Ray was enough – but she couldn't run, she had to hear the rest.

'I love you Ruby, you know that,' he went on. 'Ellie's boring, too naïve and docile for my taste. I told you why I need to keep in with her. She's going to the top soon and I'd be a fool to fall out with her when she might help my career.'

Tears sprang to Ellie's eyes and she turned and ran back downstairs. Alf looked up in surprise, but she didn't stop, just pulled open the stage door and ran out into the night.

She kept running until she was up on the heath. It was very cold – frost was making the grass sparkle, and the moon was reflected in the black water of Whitestone pond – but Ellie was unaware of anything other than her own misery. She only stopped running when she was completely out of breath and a stitch in her side prevented her going on.

The heath was deserted. She sat down on a bench and sobbed bitterly.

'Boring, naïve and docile!' If he had used words like 'too demanding', 'fiery', or even 'too ambitious' she could have lived with it. But he'd made her sound like some humble little nursemaid! How dare he say such things?'

That afternoon was still so fresh in her mind. Why did he agree to her staying these four days with him if he had another woman? How could he make love to her, say such tender things, if he was in love with someone else?

She remembered then the new teeth and the smart new dinner-jacket! Ray had never cared about his appearance before; it had to be the influence of this Ruby!

Ellie felt cheap and used, smarting with shame when she thought of some of the things they'd done together in the past. Ray had taught her everything about love-making, but she would never have been quite so abandoned with him if she hadn't believed he really cared for her. He'd told her once she was the most fascinating woman he'd ever met. Now she was boring!

Rage welled up inside her. She should have stormed into that dressing-room, slapped his face, maybe even smashed something. Why hadn't she?

'Because you are docile,' she told herself. 'You let everyone walk all over you. Go back there now and show them all it's not true. I bet everyone in the theatre knows what's going on, they're probably laughing up their sleeves about you. Even Alf will tell Ray you came running out.'

But she knew she couldn't go back and make a scene. She was too hurt inside to face further humiliation. She dried her eyes and tried to think. It was almost ten now, she had nowhere to go and very little money. On top of that, all her clothes and the things she needed for Monday's audition were at Ray's flat.

Blind panic consumed her. She was freezing, the dark, deserted heath looked threatening and the knowledge there was no one, anywhere to turn to robbed her of clear thought for a moment or two. But instinct made her get up and start walking back towards Hampstead village and as she walked she tried to think of somewhere to go.

There was her old digs, but Mrs Blake would charge her and anyway Ruby might well be staying there. She could go to Annie King's, but calling so late Annie would be bound to ask questions and besides, it was a bit of an imposition. She had just about enough money for the train to Bury St Edmunds, but nice as it would be to see Dora and Amos, there wasn't a train until the morning and she'd have to come back on Sunday to be ready for Monday's audition.

Then suddenly she remembered Edward.

She ran then, down the hill, back past the theatre just as everyone was coming out. She had already checked four pubs on the way up from Ray's earlier, but there were plenty of others.

'We're closed,' the barman shouted as the door of The Feathers opened and Ellie looked in.

Edward was having a last drink with a barmaid. He felt the blast of cold air from the open door and heard Fred shout out, but he didn't turn round.

'I only wanted to ask if Edward Manning plays the piano here.'

Edward spun round instantly at the familiar voice. 'Ellie!' He put down his glass and rushed over to where she stood hesitantly in the doorway. 'What a super surprise!'

She looked like a stranded extra from a film set in her fur hat and heavy military-style coat, but closer inspection showed there were tear stains on her cheeks and her eyes looked desperately forlorn.

'Oh Edward,' she whimpered, lips trembling. 'Thank goodness I've found you.'

An hour later Ellie was feeling a little better. Edward had bought her two large gins in the pub, even though it was past closing time, while he listened to her story, then he'd taken her back to his tiny room in Haverstock Hill. Creeping up the stairs in darkness, smelling that peculiar smell that all rooming houses seemed to have, was so reminiscent of other digs they'd shared, all the good times, that she felt a little less fraught.

Edward jokingly said his room was like a coffin. It was narrow and long with a very high ceiling, but once he'd lit the paraffin stove and poured her another gin from the bottle he'd bought at the pub, it was almost cosy.

'My landlady will throw a fit if she knows I've got a girl up here,' he whispered. 'Thank God she didn't hear us come in.'

Edward was so sympathetic. He admitted he'd seen Ray with Ruby Powers, the new leading lady, on several occasions, but then he'd seen him with other women too. He took the view that Ray was a male Bonny, a man who collected up women who might be of use to him. He promised he would get Ellie's case in the morning, but insisted that for tonight she must stay with him.

'You aren't boring,' he said tenderly. 'Naïve perhaps, and you are sometimes a bit too docile for your own good. But never boring. Ruby Powers is one of those neurotic, hysterical women who I'd call truly boring. Let him stew with her, he deserves her.'

'But why say he was keeping in with me in case I got to the top? I don't understand that.'

'Well, we all know that's just a matter of time,' Edward smiled. He found it amusing that Ellie never fully appreciated how talented she was. 'But perhaps he's heard a whisper about something, he's very thick with Harry Bloomfield.'

Ellie considered this for a moment. Perhaps Ray knew all along she was going for the audition? Could Sir Miles's company be backing *Oklahoma*? It was a cheering idea. She'd barely given the man a thought while she was away, but this brought him sharply back into focus. She half wished she could confide in Edward about him, but something told her it was better to keep it to herself.

The gin made them sentimental. Edward gave her a pair of his pyjamas to put on and they got into the single bed together and reminisced about the good times they'd shared. By the time they'd had a few more drinks they were both very emotional. Ellie started to admit all her failures with men.

'I don't know what I do wrong,' she confided, slurring her words a little. 'But it just never seems to work out. They either think I'll be really "easy" because I'm on the stage and drop me when they discover that isn't so. Or they put me on a pedestal and almost worship me. Why can't I fall in love and have them fall for me too?'

'Part of it's because of the way you earn your living,' Edward said soothingly. 'You can't really blame a chap for trying to get you into bed when he knows next week you'll be moving on. As for the ones who put you on a pedestal! – Well, I can understand that too, Ellie. You're so beautiful, they are bound to be bowled over at first and you aren't around long enough to get to know properly.'

'But I did stay in one place with Ray.' She began to cry again, remembering what she'd overheard. 'It was so lovely with him this afternoon, for a short while I actually thought I'd found what I was looking for. How could a man be that way when he feels nothing?'

'It's hard for me to be objective.' Edward took her glass from her hand and cuddled her. 'I can't understand any man not adoring you, because I do. But I've done my share of dirty tricks with women too, so that puts me in the same camp as Ray.'

'You wouldn't just use someone!' Ellie turned her tear-stained face up to his. 'Would you?'

Edward sighed deeply. 'I do it all the time,' he admitted. 'In fact I'm probably far worse than Ray. I wish I could be different. I don't like myself very much.'

'But why, Edward?' she asked. He had said on the way home that he'd finished with Marcia. He didn't appear to have anyone else. 'Don't you want to be cosy with someone who cares for you?'

Edward did; daily he wished he could meet a girl he felt that way about. He wanted to tell Ellie just how it was for him, to confess everything and be cleansed, but he didn't dare. Ellie's experience was limited to only Charley and Ray and he was absolutely certain that neither of these two had the kind of unnatural urges he did.

'I suppose, like you, I've never met the right person,' Edward said lamely. 'Maybe when we stop looking they'll just pop up.'

'I'll never trust anyone again,' Ellie sniffed.

'We're a pair of emotional cripples,' Edward said, hoping it might make her laugh. He knew it was true of himself, but he couldn't really see her in the same light. 'Go to sleep. Tomorrow it will all look different. It's only your pride that's been hurt. That mends quicker than a broken heart.'

Edward lay looking at Ellie for some time before he turned out the light. She was sound asleep now on his shoulder, one arm across his chest, her eyelashes like sooty brushes on her cheeks, her lower lip quivering as she breathed. He'd held no other woman like this. Even on rare occasions when he had stayed all night with a woman, he always put space between them, hating the enforced intimacy of a bed.

He could feel the warmth and softness of her breasts against him, yet it didn't arouse him. He sensed that the exquisite tenderness he felt now was the kind of emotion a man should feel for a woman after lovemaking. Yet he'd never felt it before, not with anyone.

He turned out the light and buried his face against her hair, tears pricking at his eyelids. Why had he been singled out for torture? What cruel fate had decreed that he should love this woman, yet be unable to make love to her?

As Ellie was dropping off to sleep with Edward, Bonny was dancing along a Durrants Hotel corridor, her high heels in her hand, John Norton a few paces behind her.

She turned as she got to her door, swaying a little unsteadily. She'd had a lot to drink this evening.

'I love hotels,' she said, clamping her hand over her mouth as she realised how loud her voice sounded.

It was one in the morning and all the other guests at Durrants seemed to have gone to bed. This was the best hotel she'd ever been in: it had a quiet sort of luxury, with pale blue carpets, soft wall lights and ivory, silky wallpaper. It was in a road running parallel to Oxford Street, just behind Selfridges. Once an old coaching inn, it still had that old-world charm, with a wood-panelled dining-room and bar, but the bedrooms were comfortably elegant, and hers had its own bathroom, with thick, fluffly towels warmed on a radiator. Magnus had taken her to some nice hotels, but never one as special as this. She was flattered too that John had his own room; she fully intended him to share hers, but it felt good not to be taken for granted.

She giggled as John reached her. 'Anything could happen in a hotel,' she whispered, her eyes sparkling. 'You don't know who anyone is, where they've come from, or where they're going. It's kind of magical.'

John smiled. He didn't see hotels that way; to him they were impersonal, lonely places, though Durrants was far nicer than most. Like Bonny, he was a little drunk. Perhaps he shouldn't have ordered that bottle of champagne in the night-club, not after two bottles of wine with dinner.

He had never seen Bonny looking quite so adorable, her fur coat draped over one shoulder, the other bare and vulnerable, hair coming loose from its pins, and her blue satin evening dress clinging seductively to her hips. 'Go to bed before you wake everyone,' he said as he opened her door for her.

She paused, leaning back on the doorpost. 'Aren't you coming in to say good-night properly?'

John felt himself weakening as he looked at her, suddenly hot all over. Earlier he had felt certain he had enough willpower to kiss her good-night and go back to his own room. Now he wasn't so sure.

'We've got a great many things to see and do tomorrow,' he said weakly. But all he could focus on was the slight curve of her belly beneath her dress. 'I'll just say good-night here.'

John hadn't a great deal of experience with women: a few girlfriends at university, a fling with a laboratory assistant in his first job and casual, short-loved relationships during the war. At heart he was a romantic, believing that for each man there was one true love which should only be consummated in marriage. He had fallen by the wayside in this ideal, especially during his spell in the Guards, but when he met and fell in love with Bonny he became determined to hold out until he was absolutely certain of her. She turned him inside out and upside down. One moment he saw her as a little innocent who needed protecting, at other times he felt it was he who needed protection. He sensed that once he'd made love to her he might lose all control of his emotions. He had a demanding job, and he couldn't work properly if his mind was elsewhere. He wanted her desperately, but at the same time he wanted to retain his mental freedom.

'Okay then.' She reached forward and kissed his

cheek. 'But come in for a moment and unfasten my necklace. I can't do it myself.'

The chambermaid had turned down her bed and drawn the curtains while they were out. One small light had been left on by the bed, and Bonny's nightdress was virgin white against the dark-plum counterpane.

Bonny tossed her coat on to a small chair and kicked off her shoes, then lifting her hair she turned her back to John.

He could barely see the clasp of the necklace in the dim light, but the lovely line of her slender neck, her shoulder-blades above the satin of her dress, were all too visible. His hands trembled as he tried to undo the clasp. Her perfume wafted up to his nostrils and he wanted to bite into that smooth, pink-white flesh.

'Now a proper kiss,' she said, turning as the necklace came away in his hands. 'I'm not going to bed without one.'

Until tonight, all their kisses had been in public places or in his car, but now, with alcohol heightening passion, the soft light and a bed so close to hand, it was quite different. Her lips responded to his hungrily, her tongue insinuating its way into his mouth. He could feel the heat of her body through the delicate dress and he knew there was no turning back.

'I love you, John,' she said, breaking away from his lips for a moment. 'Don't push me away.'

John's resolutions crumbled as she kissed him again. His fingers reached the zipper of her strapless dress involuntarily as she clung to him. As his hands caressed her soft, warm back, so her dress slid down to the floor, leaving her only in stockings, a garter belt and pale-blue, lace-trimmed knickers.

He gasped in wonder as she took a step back from him. Her breasts, which until now he'd stroked only tentatively through clothes, were firm globes with nipples like small raspberries. He was transfixed by her beauty – the cascade of silky hair over her shoulders, the turquoise of her eyes and the plump moistness of her lips – and he grabbed her back into his arms, showering her face and neck with kisses, knowing that he'd passed the point of no return.

'Make love to me, John,' she whispered, holding his face between her two hands and kissing him again. 'All I want is you.' She slowly unbuttoned his shirt and rubbed her breasts against his bare chest, her erect nipples sending shudders of delight down his spine.

John's head told him to take things slowly, but his body reacted violently, with a mind of its own. He pushed her back on to the bed, beyond thinking of anything but his own needs and the passion he'd suppressed for so long. He plunged into her like a dog presented with a bitch in heat, taking his pleasure selfishly, drowning in the scent of her. 'I love you,' he moaned, biting her shoulder fiercely as he came all too quickly. 'Oh, Bonny!'

Bonny smiled to herself as she held John in her arms. He had surprised her. She hadn't expected he would lose control like that. It had been far too quick for her to get any satisfaction, in fact it had hurt, but then she was supposed to be a virgin in this little game.

'I hurt you, didn't I? Oh Bonny, I'm so sorry,' he said, his voice croaking with emotion. He turned her face to his, supporting himself on his elbow. To her further surprise, his brown eyes were swimming with tears.

'Just a bit,' she whispered, taking his hand and kissing his fingertips. 'But it's okay. I think it always hurts the first time.'

Other men had used her just as roughly and she usually despised them for their callousness. But she didn't despise John; in fact she was moved by his distress. He would make an excellent lover with a bit of practice.

'I was like an animal. How will you ever forgive me?' he said, burying his face in her breasts.

She looked down at his back. It was sun-tanned, and his skin was silky smooth. She decided he had a nice body – wide shoulders, firm buttocks, perfectly proportioned and remarkably muscular for a man who didn't do manual work. 'I'll forgive you, if you try again. Gently this time,' she said.

'Only one more night together before I go to the Persian Gulf,' John said sadly as Bonny lay snuggled into his arms on Sunday night. 'I don't know when I'm going to be able to see you again either.'

'I'll be counting the days till you get back,' she said, turning her face up to his and running one finger along his moustache. She could see now why Ellie had said John was handsome, a bit like Ronald Coleman, though it had taken her a long time to acknowledge it. He tended to be so serious and correct, and his unnerving habit of frowning gave the impression he lacked a sense of humour. This weekend she hadn't seen that frown once; his mouth seemed to be curved into a permanent grin, and when he gave one of his rare, deep belly laughs his dark eyes danced and sparkled.

She wished she could make him laugh more often. The boy in him revealed by his laughter was so very appealing. Although she wasn't one to think much about what made people serious or sad, she had found herself pondering on what made him so grave sometimes. Was it his work? Or losing his two older brothers? Or just that he was something of a loner?

She cuddled closer to him, caught by an unexpected pang of tenderness for this man she couldn't quite fathom. 'Oh John,' she murmured. 'It's been such a wonderful weekend. I wish I could be with you all the time.'

John felt his eyes prickle and a lump came up in

his throat. She had said just what he was thinking.

He had been mortified by the way he fell on her on Friday night, but Bonny had just laughed it off. By Saturday morning, John felt he'd mended the fences. They'd made love again for half the night and this time he'd made sure he thought only of pleasing her.

The time had just flown by. On Saturday they had toured the shops in Regent Street and Bond Street, and though John had never liked shopping before, Bonny's girlish excitement had won him over. He wanted to shower her with presents, and he was quite happy to sit back in a chair and watch her try on every dress in the shop. He enjoyed watching her facial expressions, the way she wrinkled her nose when she wasn't sure about something, to see the tip of her tongue emerge from her lips as she scanned through the rails, and her look of triumph when she came out of the changing-room in a dress that was simply stunning. He had fully expected her to be greedy, but she would accept nothing but that one plain black dress.

He wished he could fully explain to her that until this weekend his life had been only work. He might be respected as the top man in his field, travelling the world and seeing sights few other men even dreamed of. But it was a lonely life, and until now, with Bonny beside him, he hadn't fully realised just how empty. He had no immediate family left. His godmother was welcoming enough whenever he came home to London, arranging dinner parties and social events for his benefit, and he had friends too, but there was no one special person waiting for him eagerly.

On Saturday evening they queued for an hour in the cold at the Odeon in Leicester Square to see Danny Kaye in *The Secret World of Walter Mitty*. Just the feel of Bonny's hand in his warmed him. Once inside, laughing along with hundreds of strangers, he put his arm round her and felt like an excited adolescent out on his first date.

Today they'd stayed in bed until eleven, dozing between bouts of sweet, delicious love-making. A walk in Green Park, lunch at the Ritz, then stumbling back here, desperate to be alone together.

'I want to ask you to marry me,' he said hoarsely, the lump in his throat making speech difficult. 'But I can't for a couple of years, Bonny. I've too many important assignments lined up. Will you wait for me?'

Bonny hesitated before answering. This weekend hadn't quite turned out as she expected. She'd come plotting to make this serious, vulnerable man fall for her completely, but although she'd succeeded, somehow he'd turned it around and now she felt vulnerable. Was she falling in love with him? She hadn't thought it could ever happen to her again.

John had surprised her over and over again in the last three days. He was a passionate and tender lover, far more capable of fun than she'd imagined, and so very generous. It felt right being with him; no secrecy, a future together, something she'd never had with Magnus. Now he was finally proposing. It was what she aimed for, what she wanted, but she couldn't wait for two whole years! How could she go back to living in digs, moving from place to place? She wanted to live like this permanently, with a lovely bathroom, good food and soft beds. She'd just wither up and die if she had to spend another winter in places like Rotherham, Scunthorpe and Birmingham.

'Two years is such a long time,' she said, nuzzling into his neck. 'I want to be with you now!'

'I want to be with you too.' He kissed her forehead and sighed. 'But I can't take you to the places I have to go and besides, you still have your dancing.'

'But I don't care about dancing any longer,' she said quite truthfully. After this hotel she didn't care if she never saw another pair of tap shoes. 'I'd much rather be in your house in Somerset.'

John smiled, amused that she thought The Chestnuts was habitable. He wondered what she would have said if she'd seen it as he had just before his parents died. As they became increasingly odd, they'd moved into the kitchen, chopping up the fine furniture for firewood. Chickens had wandered in and out, the bedrooms were littered with buckets and bowls to catch the drips from the leaky roof, and there was food in the cupboards which had gone bad months earlier.

'I don't think you would if you saw the condition it's in,' he said. After visiting Lydia Wynter with Bonny, he had managed to get down once to check on the builders. The roof was repaired, electricity had been put in and the severe problems with damp tackled, but there was replastering to do, many of the window frames had rotted and the garden was like a jungle. 'There are men working on it, but while I'm so far away they don't put their backs into it. And even if I could find the time to chivvy them up a bit, the house is very remote. I couldn't leave you there on your own. We have to wait until we can be together all the time.'

'I'll be afraid you'll meet someone else,' she said weakly. She wasn't really afraid of that, but she was scared that someone might just poison his mind against her in the meantime, that this blissful, dream-like state she was in would suddenly end.

'Don't be silly,' he said tenderly. 'Two years isn't so long. It will give you time to get the stage out of your system, and me time to get my house ready for us.'

Bonny sensed that any pleading would only make him suspicious of her haste. John wasn't like any other man she'd met; he was a thinker and very conservative. Besides, she had another month of the tour to

617

finish. Maybe by that time he'd be missing her so much that he'd change his mind. 'Can I tell people we're engaged then?' she asked wistfully.

John touched her face up to his and kissed her. 'I'll buy you a ring before you catch the train to Coventry,' he said. 'And you've got to promise you'll write to me every day.'

Ellie paused outside the Theatre Royal, looking up at its magnificent façade in awe. It was almost enough just to enter it for an audition, to walk on a stage on which every actor and actress of note had performed, let alone to perform here herself.

There was spring in the air. She'd woken up to find the sun shining and had caught the bus from Hampstead instead of the tube. As it wound its slow way down through Chalk Farm and Camden Town she had seen a green mantle creeping over the many still uncleared bomb-sites, but she'd also seen real evidence of recovery from war. Lots of the shops in Camden Town had been repainted at last, and in Mornington Crescent work had started on building flats where great swathes of old tenements had been cleared. By the time she arrived at busy Covent Garden, she was feeling full of optimism. It was just as she remembered it before the war: the heady perfume of flowers mingling with the astringent smell of oranges and lemons, vivid banks of colour, red and yellow tulips, boxes of spring-bright daffodils, fluffy white clouds of gypsophila, burly red-faced porters shouting and laughing as they rushed around with teetering piles of baskets on their heads, the screech of metal-wheeled trolleys.

She could recall an admiring porter handing her mother a bunch of daffodils here once, and the memory of Polly in her shabby coat blushing with pleasure was enough to remind her there was more at stake today than just a job. Polly had abandoned her dreams for Ellie. Now it was her turn to repay her.

Edward had salvaged Ellie's weekend, soothed her hurt pride, made her laugh and wrapped her in his comforting friendship. He'd even talked his landlady into letting her have a spare room for the rest of the time and had run through her audition piece with her up at the pub where he worked. He believed she was going to get the part today and she had no intention of letting him, her mother or herself down.

She might have been too docile to slap Ray and that uppity Ruby Powers, but she had more than enough spirit to dazzle the producers of *Oklahoma*. Come hell or high water, she was going to get this part, whatever it took!

'I'm here!' Ellie yelled at the top of her voice, leaning out of the train window as Bonny came haring down the platform holding her hat with one hand, her case in the other.

They'd agreed to meet at the ticket barrier for the six-thirty to Coventry, but with only a minute to go before the train left, Ellie had been compelled to get on.

'I thought I was going to miss it,' Bonny wheezed breathlessly, shoving her case at Ellie and leaping in.

The guard blew his whistle and the train began to pull away. Bonny slumped back against the door, wiping her hand across her forehead. She was bright pink, beads of perspiration on her nose.

'There's no—' Ellie halted her sentence as she saw the sapphire ring on her friend's finger. 'Is that what I think it is?'

'Yes.' Bonny's grin spread from ear to ear. 'An engagement ring. John asked me to marry him!'

'I was going to say there's no seats.' Ellie threw her arms round Bonny, ignoring the stares from the two men sharing the small space between carriages. 'But that hardly matters now. Congratulations! Let's see if

619

there's a drink to be had on the train to celebrate!'

'Did you and Ray have a good time?' Bonny asked, still panting.

'Don't even mention his name,' Ellie said with a wide grin. More recent events had all but erased him from her memory. 'But I've got the part of Aldo Annie in *Oklahoma* – I went to the audition today.'

Bonny's mouth gaped open, her eyes wide with surprise. 'Where, when. I mean! Oh, Ellie, I don't know what to say!'

'I'll do the talking,' Ellie grinned. She was shaking still with excitement. Forty-five girls had auditioned for the part, but she'd been selected. They'd even been prepared to wait until she'd finished her contract with this tour. Just as she was leaving the theatre, she'd seen the name 'Majestic Inc.' on a billboard. That meant Sir Miles Hamilton was involved with this production. Had he been instrumental in her getting the part? It gave her a warm feeling to think about it. If she became a big success then maybe one day she might even be able to get close enough to reveal who her mother was. 'Oh Bonny! I've got enough to tell you about this weekend to last all the way to Coventry. Let's look for the bar?'

'From John?' Ellie asked as Bonny came into their room reading a letter.

It was three weeks since their respective weekends in London. They'd played Coventry, then Leicester and now Lincoln for the last week of the tour, the same old faces, the same old routine, just different towns. Ellie was still in bed. Although it was nearly noon, she didn't feel there was anything to get up for, not in a town like Lincoln. Next week she would be starting rehearsals for *Oklahoma*, and she'd been happily imagining her future: curtain calls, bouquets of flowers and her name up in lights.

'Mmm,' Bonny murmured, sitting down on the bed,

still reading. She finished the letter and tossed it aside, pursing her mouth in disappointment. 'He's still in the Persian Gulf, he hopes he can get back in a couple of weeks' time, for a week or so, but then he's going back again.'

Ellie reached out and touched Bonny's arm in silent sympathy. It was clear her friend really was serious about John now. She hadn't even looked at another man in the last three weeks and she never tired of showing off her sapphire engagement ring.

Ellie approved of John, even though she'd only met him a few times, well over a year ago. He might not be as charismatic as Magnus, but he was younger, single and he had a real future to offer Bonny. She had seen a change in her friend since that weekend in London; she was softer, more thoughtful, and she'd been writing to him daily. The trouble with Bonny was she always wanted everything now. She couldn't wait for anything.

'Maybe he won't be there for long,' Ellie said comfortingly. 'Look on the bright side, Bonny, he loves you, he does want to marry you and even your parents won't be able to find fault with such a well set up man.'

Bonny pulled a face and scuffed the heel of her shoe against the lino, making it squeak. 'I wouldn't mind waiting so much if you and I were going to be working together, but you've got *Oklahoma* and all Bloomfield's can suggest for me is a summer season in Margate.'

Bonny had been ecstatic about Ellie getting the part in *Oklahoma*, right from the moment they exchanged their news on the train, all through their three-day celebrations, and the weeks that followed. She hadn't shown even the slightest sign of jealousy, in fact she was still almost as keen on bandying around Ellie's good fortune as she was at thrusting her engagement ring under the rest of the company's noses. She teased

621

Ellie daily by singing, 'I'm Just a Girl who Can't Say No', the big hit from the show. This was the first time she'd even mentioned that Ellie's big break meant the end of the road for their partnership.

'I'm going to miss you so much too,' Ellie said. Bonny had played such an important role in her life for so long, it seemed almost inconceivable that they might never dance together again after this tour. 'But maybe it will turn out for the best. If you haven't got a job, John might bring the wedding forward.'

'I hoped I might be pregnant,' Bonny said. 'John didn't use anything that first night. But no such luck, I came on this morning.'

A cold chill went down Ellie's spine. Until that moment she hadn't even considered her own periods.

'What's up?' Bonny looked round at Ellie, when she didn't reprove her for wishing pregnancy on herself. She was staring into space.

'I can't remember when my last one was,' Ellie said in a faint voice. 'Can you?'

'Your last what?'

'Period.' Ellie could feel her stomach churning.

'It was when we were in Rugby.' Bonny grinned. 'Don't you remember that chemist's we went into to buy some S.T.s? You were too embarrassed to ask the man, and I had to buy them.'

Ellie looked at Bonny in horror. 'That long ago! Before we went to Birmingham!' Her voice rose to a screech. 'That's more than six weeks!'

Bonny looked thoughtful, counting on her fingers. 'It's five and a bit actually. That means you're only a few days late, a week at most. I'm often much later than that, sometimes I don't have one for months. Besides, you must have taken precautions, you're too sensible not to.'

'It split.' Ellie's eyes were now wide with alarm, two red blotches coming up on her cheeks. 'I'd forgotten all about that until now, what with finding out about that Ruby, then getting the part, I didn't even remember,' she gabbled. 'Oh Bonny! What am I going to do?'

It was a rare event to see Ellie getting into a tizzy about anything. Bonny immediately forgot her own preoccupation with John. 'You aren't going to panic for a start,' she said firmly. 'Look! That weekend was like being on a roller-coaster for you! First the business with Ray which knocked the stuffing out of you. Then you passed the audition. After that we were getting tight every night for a week. Your body's just gone a bit haywire.'

Ellie still looked doubtful. 'But what if it isn't just that?'

'We'll cross that bridge when we come to it,' Bonny said sensibly. 'We'll be back in London in a week. If the worst comes to the worst, you can always get rid of it there. But I don't think for one moment you're pregnant. You couldn't be that unlucky. Just think of being on the stage at the Theatre Royal and your name up in lights. That will keep you going!'

Bonny looked out of the window when she heard John's Jaguar pull up outside, but she made no attempt to go down to open the door. She had parted with Ellie on Liverpool Street station three weeks ago. Ellie had gone to find her digs in Islington and to start rehearsals; Bonny had returned home to her parents. A week out in Dagenham with John in the Persian Gulf, no job on the horizon and her mother constantly harping on about her becoming a secretary was too much to bear. Under the pretence of attending a few auditions, she persuaded her father to lend her some money and moved into a room in Notting Hill Gate. Bloomfield's had offered her a place in another dancing troupe, starting next week, but if her plan worked tonight, there would be no need for that.

John had sent her a telegram from Paris yesterday,

623

saying he'd arrive by seven-thirty tonight. He was early, which suited her even better.

Opening the door, she heard the woman on the ground floor speaking to him, telling him to go up to the third floor. As his feet came trampling up the bare wooden stairs, Bonny closed her door quietly and cast one last look around to make sure it looked right.

It was a miserable, cold room, thin curtains barely meeting and peeling paper on the walls. But the bed-spread and table-cloth she'd brought from home, the daffodils in a jam jar and a few framed photographs of her parents and Ellie all gave the impression that she had attempted to make it homely.

At John's knock, Bonny opened the door a crack and made a gasp of alarm at seeing him there. 'I thought you said seven-thirty! I meant to meet you downstairs.'

His bright smile faded. He peered past her into the room, almost as if he suspected she had someone else there.

He was very sun-tanned and was wearing a pale-grey suit. He looked very suave and handsome, completely out of place here in this dingy house.

'What's the matter, Bonny? Aren't you going to ask me in?'

Bonny opened the door and turned away from him. 'I didn't want you to see it, it's so awful. I've been trying to fix it up, but it's hopeless.'

He came in, glanced around, then putting his hands on her shoulders, turned her round to face him. 'I didn't come to see your room, only you,' he said, tipping her face up to his. 'How about a welcoming kiss?'

Bonny let him draw her into his arms for the kiss, then slumped her head against his shoulder.

'Were you intending to tell me fibs and make out it was really nice?' he asked.

Bonny shrugged and bit her lips nervously. 'I suppose so. I don't like you seeing me like this.'

John's eyes swept round the room and he shivered. 'It's cold. Let me take you to a restaurant – you can tell me all about it over a nice meal.'

Once in the warm restaurant, a glass of wine in her hand and a meal on its way, Bonny told him her story. 'There's no work for me just now. Mum and Dad made it quite clear they weren't going to keep me. So I found the room and got a job as a lunchtime waitress. I keep phoning Bloomfield's but they've still got nothing for me.'

'A waitress!' John looked at her in horror. 'I thought you were in the chorus of *Oklahoma*?'

'I never said that,' she said truthfully. 'I only told you about Ellie being Aldo Annie and that I was in digs.'

'But I just assumed . . .' His voice tailed off, thinking back to that letter. He had thought it was odd that she had been so effusive about Ellie's luck and yet not said anything about her own rehearsals or the rest of the chorus. But it hadn't occurred to him she wasn't included. 'You can't be a waitress!'

'It's not so bad,' she said stoically, giving him a weak grin. 'At least I get a free lunch. Something will turn up soon.'

John looked hard at her. She looked pale and drawn and she wasn't as well groomed as usual; in fact her hair needed a wash. He didn't like to think of himself as a snob, but if any of his colleagues were to find out his fiancée was a waitress they'd all be sniggering behind his back. It was very resourceful of her to find another job to fill in, but he couldn't bear the thought of her clearing away dirty plates and living in that grim room alone. 'I'll find you somewhere decent to stay,' he said, putting his hand over hers and squeezing it. 'And you don't need to do such menial work, I'll look after you until you get something else.

How can you attend auditions when you're working each lunchtime?'

'I haven't felt much like dancing anyway.' She dropped her eyes from his. 'I've been feeling poorly.'

Up until now, Bonny had been working to a script she'd prepared over several days, but now he was trying to encourage her about auditions, she knew she'd got to make her story a little more powerful.

'What's wrong, Bonny?'

John's sympathetic and loving tone made her eyes prickle. She knew she should squash the idea forming in her mind, but yet it seemed like the perfect answer to everything.

'I can't tell you, not here,' she whispered, looking around her furtively. 'Someone might hear.'

'Whisper then! Or is it something you don't like to tell a man?' he said, looking very concerned.

She waited, letting tears well up and trickle down her cheeks. 'I think I'm pregnant, John,' she whispered. 'I've been feeling so awful, and I'm very late.'

If she had thrown a bowl of soup at him he couldn't have looked more startled. His face went pale, his mouth fell open and he gave a sharp intake of breath.

'I'm sorry,' she whimpered, terribly afraid she'd gone too far.

John felt as if he were falling through space. He had no regrets about asking Bonny to marry him, or buying her an engagement ring. But always a cautious man who thought things through carefully, he was wary of her haste to get married. Now she was saying she was pregnant! He'd used a sheath except for that first night. Could she be lying to him?

'You're cross, aren't you?' she said, looking at his stricken face. 'I wish I hadn't told you now. I wasn't going to. I was just going to save up enough money and get rid of it.'

'You'll do no such thing.' His voice rose slightly in

indignation. 'Just give me a moment to think it through.'

Bonny lay awake long after John had left her. He had insisted on taking her to Durrants Hotel and booked her into a single room, but he'd gone back to stay with his godmother in Kensington, and he hadn't even attempted to make love to her. She really did feel sick now, not only because she'd told such a colossal lie on the spur of the moment, but because John wasn't such a pushover after all.

It had all seemed like plain sailing after John got over the initial shock. He said he would bring her here, then go home to speak to his godmother, who he thought would help find a decent flat for her, and that he would arrange for them to get married as soon as possible. But then, just when she could almost hear the wedding bells and smell the flowers in her bouquet, he said she must go to see a doctor in Harley Street and have her pregnancy confirmed.

He dressed it up so nicely, saying that she might be mistaken, that even if she wasn't she needed medical advice and attention. But there was something strong and firm in his eyes that silently said until he saw it confirmed in writing there would be no wedding. How on earth could she get round that?

Chapter Twenty-Eight

May 1949

Ellie was in the wings at the Theatre Royal when she got a hissed message from a stage-hand that someone was waiting at the stage door to see her.

Most of the cast of *Oklahoma* were on stage, rehearsing the number 'Out of My Dreams and Into Your Arms'. Ellie wasn't in this scene, and she and Frank Freebody, her partner who played the part of Will, were waiting to be called to run through one of their numbers, 'With Me It's All or Nothing'. They were both in practice clothes: she in tights, ballet shoes and a short tunic.

Ellie had been in rehearsal for three weeks now. If it hadn't been for the gnawing fear that she really was pregnant, this could have been the happiest time in her life. The comic role of the innocent and flirtatious Aldo Annie was perfect for her, she loved the music, the dancing, she got on well with the rest of the cast and she was looking forward eagerly to next week, when she would step into the present Annie's shoes. Betty Noble was leaving for a lead role in a Hollywood film and that seemed a good omen too.

'I won't be a moment' she whispered to Frank. Ellie liked Frank a great deal: he had an impish charm and he made her laugh so much that sometimes she even managed to forget her worries. 'There's someone to see me, call me if they want us.'

She thought it might be Ray wanting to apologise;

she couldn't think of anyone else who would have the audacity to call at a theatre during a rehearsal.

But as she ran back to the steps that led down to the stage door, she was surprised to find that her visitor was Bonny, all dolled up in a blue fitted costume with matching half-veiled hat.

'Bonny! What on earth?' she gasped, looking round nervously. She knew the producer wouldn't appreciate friends just dropping in.

'Can you take a break to talk?' Bonny asked.

'I daren't.' Ellie cocked her ear to the music, looking back in the direction of the stage, half expecting Frank to be beckoning frantically to her. This company were very professional, with punctuality insisted upon, and as the rehearsals were mainly in order for Ellie to learn her role, she had to be on hand at all times. 'I'll be finished at four.'

'Please,' Bonny pleaded. 'I wouldn't ask if it wasn't important.'

Ellie assumed Bonny was in some sort of trouble. Even through her veil she looked pale and strained and she knew better than to interrupt a rehearsal without good reason. 'I'll ask if they can spare me for half an hour,' she said reluctantly, turning to run back up the steps to the stage.

She reappeared a few minutes later, wearing proper shoes. 'I've got fifteen minutes, that's all,' she said, reaching for her mackintosh from a peg by the doorman's desk. 'We'll get a cup of tea in the café next door.'

'I thought I'd just tell you my new address,' Bonny said once they were sitting in a corner with a cup of tea each. It was too early, at eleven-thirty, for the lunchtime trade, and aside from themselves the only other customers were a couple of workmen eating bacon sandwiches. 'John's found me a flat in Harrington Road, South Kensington. You can come there any time you like, it's really nice.'

Bonny was thrilled that John had managed to persuade his godmother to let her use one of her flats. Lady Penelope Beauchamp owned four small serviced apartments above a rank of shops close to the tube station. Normally they were let only to businessmen while they were working in London, and they were very lucky that one was free.

'Where are you working?' Ellie asked, making a note of the address.

'I'm not, I can't find anything,' Bonny said quickly, as if this wasn't important. 'John's helping me out. But I didn't come about that. I wanted to know if you'd come on yet.'

Ellie was touched that this visit was out of concern for her rather than a plea for help. She relaxed slightly, sitting back in her chair, glad to have someone to confide in at last. 'No, I haven't,' she admitted. 'I felt queasy this morning too.'

'You've got to find out for certain.' Bonny leaned closer across the table, frowning with anxiety. 'You can't leave it any longer.'

'I know.' Ellie made a hopeless gesture with her hands. 'But I'm scared of going to a doctor.'

'I'll come with you,' Bonny said, patting Ellie's hand reassuringly.

'All the cast use a doctor in Soho Square,' Ellie whispered, afraid someone might overhear. 'But if I see him, he might tell the producers.'

'There's no need to go to him,' Bonny said. 'I know a good doctor and you could do me a favour at the same time.'

As Bonny launched into explaining the 'favour' she required, Ellie felt a surge of anger erupting inside her.

'That's monstrous,' she gasped, cutting Bonny short. 'You want me to go to this doctor and make out I'm you! I can't believe you'd even think of such a wicked scheme to fool John. And I was mug enough to think you were worried about me!'

Bonny swept her half veil back over her hat, her expression one of shock and hurt, but her eyes gave her away. They were full of her old cunning. 'Ellie I am worried about you. And I didn't mean to lie to John, I just said I was having a baby on the spur of the moment because I wanted him to bring our wedding forward. Once we're married I'll pretend to have a miscarriage, if I'm not already pregnant by then. What harm can it do?'

Bonny had shocked Ellie many times, but never quite like this. On top of her disgust at such an outrageous scheme, the unfairness of their roles sickened her. Bonny had slept with men indiscriminately, while she had only let herself go with one man. Now John was keeping Bonny, making plans for a baby that wasn't even conceived yet, while Ray didn't even care enough to contact Ellie and apologise for that night, much less concern himself that a split sheath might have made her pregnant.

'What harm can it do?' Ellie's voice rose in anger. If they hadn't been in a public place she might have smacked her friend's face. 'Marriage is a serious, important thing. You can't enter into it lying and cheating. It's wicked.'

'It's not,' Bonny insisted, unabashed. 'I love him, he loves me. I'll make him so happy once we're married. I haven't got a job, I don't want to dance any more anyway. I just want to be his wife, that's all.'

Ellie was staggered by such monumental selfishness. 'No, Bonny. I won't do it.' She got up to leave. 'You've got me to lie to men before and I've done it for friendship's sake, but I won't do this.'

'Sit down, Ellie, and listen to me,' Bonny insisted, catching hold of her hand. 'You need to know if you really are pregnant, and if you are you'll need help too. Once I'm married to John, with a nice home, I can help you. You'll need somewhere to go and have an abortion, if that's what you decide. If you have the baby you'll need even more support.'

Ellie swayed on her feet, looking down at Bonny helplessly. She had barely slept for worry since they'd returned to London. Bonny was right on one point; she did need to know for certain.

Slumping back down into the chair, Ellie covered her face with her hands, the enormity of her problem overwhelming her.

'Don't, Ellie.' Bonny tried to remove her hands. 'I know you must think I'm a louse. But I'm not being entirely selfish. You need help. I want marriage and so does John, even though he'd rather wait a bit. Is it such a bad thing I'm suggesting, when it means all three of us get what we really want? I really hope you aren't pregnant, even though that will mean I can't marry John immediately. But if we find you are, then the next step is to decide what to do about it.'

Ellie knew she should refuse to be a party in Bonny's attempted deception, to get up and walk away, but the need to know if she really was pregnant was now foremost in her mind, weakening her resolve. 'I don't like in one bit,' she said weakly. 'I hate it, but okay, I'll do it for me, just so I can stop brooding about it. If there is a God up there, he'll make all the tests negative.'

Bonny sighed with relief. She had really expected Ellie to refuse: she was usually such a stickler for honesty. 'The appointment is tomorrow at five,' she said quickly, opening her bag and getting out a card. She hoped Ellie wouldn't change her mind once she'd had time to reflect on it further. 'I'll come with you, we'll just switch names. John doesn't know this doctor personally and he'll be up north on business, so we don't have to worry about being caught out. You have to bring a sample of pee with you. If you wait outside the theatre at quarter to five, I'll pick you up in a taxi.'

'I loathe you sometimes,' Ellie said as she got up, her face white and strained. She was furious that Bonny had worked this all out, banking on her being desperate enough to collaborate, and she was even more disgusted with herself for being weak enough to agree. 'You'd better make John happy, Bonny, so I don't live to regret my part in this.'

'You can get dressed again now, Miss Phillips.' Dr Rodriguez covered Ellie up with a sheet, pulled off his rubber gloves and smiled down at her. 'We'll have a little chat when you're ready.'

It was quarter to six on May 18th, and it was a warm, sunny day, exactly eight weeks since she had gone to stay with Ray in London. Despite Ellie's acute embarrassment, Dr Rodriguez was a very soothing man. She supposed he must be Spanish, even though he had no accent. He was tall and swarthy, with eyes like melting chocolate and all the charm one would expect from a Harley Street gynaecologist.

The consulting rooms brought home the huge divide between rich and poor. John paying for this consultation meant she was seen at the appointed hour, in luxurious surroundings, with mahogany desks, thick carpets and no stigma attached to her unmarried status. Had she gone to a local doctor, she might have waited for hours in a waiting-room with chronically sick people, treated like a prostitute and dispatched as quickly as possible.

Ellie waited until he had gone back behind the screen, then took off the white gown and dressed again. She knew what the result was, even though he hadn't confirmed it yet, and she wanted to get out of here before she began to cry.

'You are indeed expecting a baby.' The doctor smiled warmly at Ellie as she silently took the seat next to Bonny on the other side of his desk. 'Just about eight weeks, and you can expect your baby at

Christmas.' He laughed softly at the last part of his pronouncement. 'The best present anyone could have.'

Ellie gulped and tried to smile but it was impossible to feel any joy and a tear slid out.

Dr Rodriguez was surprised by her stricken face. He knew, of course, she wasn't married yet, but that engagement ring on her finger and the caring tone of the man Norton who'd made the appointment suggested she would be long before her baby arrived. 'It's quite normal for an expectant mother to feel fraught at this stage,' he said gently. 'Especially if the baby wasn't planned. But mother nature will take you in hand. In no time at all you'll be looking forward to the birth joyfully. You are strong and healthy, Miss Phillips – you'll make an ideal mother.'

Ellie didn't even listen to the rest of what he said. All she could think of was that through one little accident, her career had gone down the pan and she had no one to lean on.

Outside in Harley Street both girls paused for a moment, Ellie holding on to the black painted railings for support.

'Come back to my flat?' Bonny suggested. She was concerned by her friend's pallor and her stony silence. The street was busy with rush hour traffic and she thought Ellie might faint.

'I don't want to go anywhere with you,' Ellie snapped at her, dark eyes cold with disgust. She pulled Bonny's engagement ring off her finger and thrust it back at her. 'Get a taxi, swan off back to the flat John's found for you. Celebrate your "pregnancy" with champagne and plan your damned wedding. Just don't invite me!'

'Don't be like this.' Bonny tried to hold her, but Ellie shrugged her off angrily. 'I meant what I said. I will help you. I can get enough money for an abortion. I'll look after you.'

'Get out of my life, Bonny.' Ellie turned her back

on her friend and walked away. Tears streamed down her face. She didn't think she'd ever felt such utter misery, not even when her mother had died.

John sawed through the partly burnt pork chop, only half listening to Bonny's excited prattle about wedding invitations. He had arrived back in London just two hours ago and he was still a little dazed by Dr Rodriguez's note dated two days earlier, confirming that Bonny was indeed pregnant.

The flat in Harrington Road was clean and comfortable enough, but impersonal, with basic utility furniture. Unlike many of the big houses in the area, which had been converted to flats over the last thirty or forty years, this and the other three in the block had been purpose-built during the twenties. A living-room, one bedroom, a kitchen and bathroom, all decorated in a uniform beige with dark green curtains. Bonny was delighted by such luxuries as a refrigerator, constant hot water and a woman who came in to clean three times a week. Compared to the boarding-houses she was used to, it was heaven. John privately thought it was drab, the constant noise of traffic irritating, and he was a little hurt his godmother hadn't offered to let Bonny stay at her big house in Ennismore Gardens. But then Penelope disapproved of him becoming engaged to a young dancer. She would be even more alarmed and suspicious when he informed her later tonight that the wedding would be taking place as soon as possible.

'A big wedding isn't appropriate,' John said firmly. He was struggling with his conscience; he'd told Penelope a few white lies and soon they would turn to bigger ones. He wanted to do the right thing by Bonny, yet he didn't like this haste or the feeling that he was losing control. He wanted to take her to bed right now, to rediscover all the magic of that weekend they had shared in London, yet his underlying prudishness suggested this was wrong under the circumstances. 'Neither of us have many close relatives. What we have to think about is where the wedding will be. The banns have to be put up where one of us lives. That means if you want it to be in Dagenham or Amberley you'll have to live there for the entire three weeks before.'

Bonny's face fell. She had expected John to be joyful about the news, to sweep her up in his arms and take her either to bed or out to celebrate with champagne. Instead he'd gone down to the shops and bought pork chops for their dinner. He had a dark shadow of beard on his chin, his dark eyes looked wary and he'd already made it clear he would be sleeping at his godmother's, tonight and every night he was in London. He didn't even seem to be enjoying the chops, now she'd cooked them!

Bonny certainly didn't want to get married in Dagenham, and although she liked the idea of the pretty church in Amberley, she didn't fancy spending three whole weeks with Lydia either. She wanted to stay here, for a big London wedding, with write-ups in the *Tatler*, the list of guests reading like a page of *Who's Who*.

'Can't we put up the banns here in London?' she said quickly. 'There's a church just along the road in Queen's Gate, and it would be far more convenient for your godmother and friends and better for my parents than Amberley.'

John pushed away his half-eaten dinner and wiped his moustache on a napkin. Buying chops had been a mistake; Bonny needed a few cookery lessons. 'I must discuss that with your father,' he said. 'Don't you think he'll want you getting married from your home?'

A cloud passed over Bonny's face. 'You know I don't get on with them, John,' she said in a small voice, knowing she had to get over this hurdle at some time. 'I suppose you'll have to meet them, but let's just make the plans and tell them it's all arranged. Daddy couldn't afford to pay for it anyway.'

John mulled this over for a moment. He was very curious about Mr and Mrs Phillips. He couldn't really believe they were as odd as Bonny implied, and suspected she was just ashamed of coming from a working-class home. Yet Bonny's suggestion suited him. It would be easier to arrange the wedding close by, and he had no wish to embarrass either Bonny or his future in-laws.

'Okay,' he said. 'We'll see the vicar tomorrow, then we'll drive out to Dagenham to tell them.'

'Oh John! You are wonderful!' Bonny's face lit up again, relieved he wasn't going to be difficult. 'Where are we going to have the reception? Can I have a lovely dress?'

John smiled. She was such a child, but that made her even more adorable! 'Yes, you can have a lovely dress, and I'll arrange a small reception somewhere smart. But it's not going to turn into a circus. Aside from the fact I've got to go back to finish off my work in the Gulf, which doesn't give me much time to make arrangements if you want to be a June bride, we've also got to consider your condition.'

'It won't be showing that soon!' Bonny said hastily. 'You aren't cross about the baby, are you?'

John got up from his seat, going round the table to kiss her. As he hadn't seriously considered a baby until he saw the doctor's confirmation, he found it hard to assess his feelings. She looked so pretty, her hair tousled becomingly, her face pink from the heat of the kitchen. 'Of course I'm not cross,' he said gently, remembering women needed reassurance at such times. 'I just haven't had time to fully adjust myself to being a father. But the idea's growing on me already.'

'We're going to be so happy.' Bonny jumped up

and flung her arms round his neck, kissing every inch of his face like an excited puppy. She could handle John when he smiled; it was his long silences and deep sighs which worried her. If she could just persuade him to stay a few more hours this evening she'd soon have him as enthusiastic about married life as she was. 'I can't wait to see the house in Somerset. I'm so excited.'

She was terribly excited. Everything was working out as she planned. No more working, living in this nice little flat until the wedding, with nothing more arduous to do than buy a stunning wedding dress and a wonderful trousseau. As John would be working abroad until just before the wedding he wouldn't know if she added a few more guests to the list. Then, after the wedding, there would be the thrill of doing up the house in Somerset. It was all just perfect. Except for Ellie.

Ellie was Bonny's Achilles' heel: the one person who really mattered to her. Although Bonny felt no guilt at fooling John, she was deeply concerned about her friend and the way she'd looked when they parted in Harley Street.

She hadn't forgotten how Ellie stood by her when she had the abortion, and it turned her stomach to think her friend would have to go through the same agony. Bonny had been to the theatre twice, and called round to her digs, but Ellie wouldn't speak to her.

However Bonny looked at it, Ellie was in big trouble. She was tough enough to go and have an abortion alone. But what if she died? If she didn't get rid of the baby her career would be over and family history would repeat itself – a lone woman trying to bring up a baby in poverty.

'What's the matter?' John sensed she was brooding on something. 'Are you worried people might realise you're pregnant at the wedding? Or is it because I've got to go away again?'

'I suppose so.' Bonny nodded, hoping he wouldn't press her further. 'It's just a bit scary sometimes, especially when I'm alone.'

Two weeks after the examination by Dr Rodriguez, Ellie was outside 14 Sussex Gardens in Paddington, looking up at the house in alarm. Sussex Gardens was a notorious area for slums, crime and prostitutes. She hadn't expected an abortionist to live in a nice place, but number 14 was the worst house in the entire terrace. The stone work crumbled around a front door which had huge cracks as if someone had tried to batter it in, stinking rubbish was piled up in the basement area and most of the windows were broken, stuffed up with rags and cardboard. Bright sunshine seemed to emphasise the squalor of the neighbourhood. Sickly-looking children were sitting on doorsteps, mangy dogs lolled listlessly in patches of shade and a couple of tramps were squatting in the middle of a bomb-site, drinking cheap sherry.

Ellie had been sick every morning now for over a week. Just the smell of cigarettes, coffee or fried food turned her stomach, and she couldn't remember when she'd last felt like eating. Everyone in the cast had remarked how pale and gaunt she looked, but they believed her when she said it was nothing but nerves. She made made her début as Annie for the first time in public last Saturday. Everyone had said she was every bit as good as Betty Noble, and one critic had described her as 'a feisty Aldo Annie, as if born for the part'. Sir Miles and Lady Hamilton had come backstage to compliment her, and she'd had good luck telegrams from Edward, Annie King and Amos and Dora. Bonny and John had sent her flowers. She was still so angry with Bonny, she felt like putting them in the dustbin but she hadn't. They were, after all, her first proper bouquet.

Ellie hadn't dared confide in anyone about her

predicament. She'd only managed to find this abortionist through a friend of one of the other dancers, by pretending she was a go-between for someone else. She had been alarmed when the date and time were set by this Mr Cole without first meeting him; she had expected at least an examination before she committed herself. But she was told she was to send 'her friend' here with the ten pound fee and it would be done immediately.

All that had kept her going in the last few days was the knowledge that Bonny had done this and survived. So could she.

Taking a deep breath, she walked up the litter-strewn steps and rang a bell marked 'Cole'. She heard it ring way back in the building and covered her nose so she couldn't smell the rubbish wafting up from the basement.

The door opened a few inches, and a woman peered out. She had curlers in her hair and a crossover pinny, a cigarette hanging out of her mouth.

'I have an appointment with Mr Cole,' Ellie managed to say, her stomach heaving alarmingly.

'You Miss Smith?' the woman said without removing the cigarette. She had a thin, shallow face with slack, bloodless lips. She could have been any age between thirty and fifty.

'Yes,' Ellie croaked.

'You'd better come in then.' The woman opened the door a little further, then immediately turned and went back down the hall, her mules slopping up and down, exposing dirt-ingrained heels.

Ellie went in hesitantly, pausing after she'd shut the door behind her.

'Come on then,' the woman barked back at her.

The hall was gloomy, but not dark enough to hide the filth. An old battered black pram sat at the bottom of the stairs, many of the banister spindles were missing and the cracked lino hadn't been swept, or washed for years. The woman went into a door at the far end of the narrow passageway and turned to beckon to Ellie to follow.

She found herself in what must have been the servants' quarters in Victorian times. A few steps led to a narrow room, sparsely furnished with a table covered in a chenille cloth and a couple of easy chairs. A series of bells hung high up over the fireplace, wreathed in cobwebs. Bare wooden shelves covered one wall, perhaps once used for storing china or cooking pots, but now empty except for a couple of white enamel basins and a few cardboard boxes.

Through a second door ahead, Ellie could see a rusty cooking range and a white china sink. A man with greying, straggly hair was in there, his back to her.

'Won't keep you long,' he called out. 'Just sterilising my equipment.'

He was wearing black trousers and braces over a collarless shirt, slippers on his feet. He moved a couple of feet and Ellie saw a gas ring with a steaming saucepan on it.

The woman looked at Ellie with furtive eyes. 'Got the money?' she said. Ellie opened her handbag and took out the wad of notes. The woman licked her thumb, flicked through them counting, then shoved them in the pocket of her apron. 'You'd better take your things off,' she said, flicking the ash from her cigarette into what looked like a sardine can.

The smell of the cigarette made Ellie feel nauseous. Despite the warm day the window was tightly shut and a heavy, dirty lace curtain covered it, obscuring any view. But she could hear children playing and a ball bouncing close by. She felt they were only yards away.

'How much do I take off?' Ellie put her coat and bag on one of the easy chairs, looking nervously at the table.

'Yer drawers,' the woman said curtly. Going to one of the cardboard boxes, she brought out a sheet which she spread over the table.

As Ellie fumbled beneath her skirt to take her knickers off, Mr Cole came into the room, carrying an enamel kidney dish. In it was a steaming long thin rod and a speculum, very similar to the one used by Dr Rodriguez to open her up and peer inside her.

It wasn't the instruments which frightened her so much, even though they jingled in his shaking hands, but Mr Cole. She'd never seen him before, but she'd seen his type so often as a child, lurching out of public houses. His nose was purple, the same high colour across his cheekbones, unshaven and bloodshot eyes. Even from a distance of six feet, above the smell of stale sweat, she could smell the drink.

'Pull your skirt up,' he said, giving what passed as a smile, showing rotting teeth. 'And hop up on the table.'

'I'm scared,' she whimpered. 'Will it hurt?'

'No more than the cock that got you into this mess,' he said with a leer, as he put down the dish to take hold of her arm.

Ellie looked down at his hand. It was covered in engorged veins, black hair sprouting on the backs of his fingers, every nail ragged and dirty. She thought of those white soft hands of Dr Rodriguez, how gently and reverently they had felt her stomach, and she felt the room spin.

'Don't fuckin' faint on me, girl,' she heard the man say, as if from a distance.

Hands were grabbing her. She didn't know if it was him, or the woman, but suddenly she found herself flat on her back on the table, water splashing on her face.

'I can't breathe,' she wheezed, struggling to get air. The woman was holding down her shoulders, another cigarette in her mouth, the smoke belching into Ellie's face. But worse still, the man was pushing her knees up roughly, and thrusting the speculum into her.

'Keep bloody still,' the woman muttered, gripping Ellie's shoulders.

Ellie submitted to the hot speculum being pushed into her, numbed by shock. Mr Cole was cranking it open, and his breath was hot against her inner thigh. But as she stared sightlessly above her, trying hard to distance herself from the embarrassment and discomfort, she suddenly saw her mother's face as clearly as if Polly was looking down through a hole in the stained ceiling. Her expression was one Ellie remembered so clearly when she'd been naughty, a sad, 'please don't do this' face, one that had always shamed her into obedience.

'Please stop,' Ellie gasped, struggling to get up. 'I can't do this.'

'You silly cow,' Mr Cole said, pulling out the speculum none too gently, clutching her thigh. 'I ain't got time for hysterics. Do you want me to get rid of it or not?'

'No.' Ellie pushed him away from her. It wasn't so much fear of pain that prompted her violent reaction, but a protective instinct for the tiny life inside her. 'I can't, it's wrong.'

'It ain't right to bring a little bleeder into the world when you don't want it neither,' the woman snapped. 'You girls are all the same, open yer bleedin' legs for anyone, then you cry when yer caught out. Now let's get on with it.'

Had there been a little sympathy or reassurance from the couple, Ellie might have changed her mind, but the woman's insulting remark wiped out any hesitation.

'I can't go through with it.' She brushed off the woman's restraining hand on her shoulder and tried to cover herself with her skirt. 'Let me go.'

'You silly bleedin' mare!' Mr Cole sneered at her. 'Gaw on, push off then.'

Ellie was off the table in a second, knocking the kidney dish to the floor as she grabbed her knickers and coat. 'Let me have my money back,' she said.

Mr Cole let out a bellow of derisive laughter. 'Fuck off,' he said, rheumy eyes narrowing. 'There ain't no refunds 'ere.'

'Give it back or I'll go to the police,' Ellie said more bravely than she felt. 'You ought to be locked up for doing this.'

She didn't see him move. One second he was a few feet from her, the next she felt his fist crash into her cheek.

'Get out of 'ere,' he yelled. 'While you still can.'

Ellie took one look at his clenched fists and she knew he meant it. She snatched her handbag from the chair, backed to the door, opened it, and ran.

She was at the end of Sussex Gardens before she realised she was still holding her knickers in her hand. Blood was running down her cheek and she was crying.

'Ellie, open up!'

Ellie lifted her head from the pillow at the sound of Bonny's voice, but she couldn't get up. She had got back from Paddington some two hours earlier; she should have gone straight to the theatre, to get ready for tonight's performance, but she couldn't face it.

'I know you're in there,' Bonny said, her voice coming right through the keyhole. 'And if you don't unlock the door, I'll go and ask your landlady for a key.'

'Go away Bonny,' Ellie said feebly. 'I don't want to talk to you.'

'You'd better,' Bonny said firmly. 'They're going crazy at the theatre because you haven't turned up. I said I expected you were ill and I'd come here to check. If you won't speak to me, you'll have the producer on your back.'

Sighing, Ellie got up and unlocked the door, but went straight back to her bed and slumped down.

Bonny came in, turned on the light and looked down at her friend.

Ellie's Islington digs were good, compared with many they'd shared. Highbury Place was a pleasant wide road overlooking a park, number 4 a well-kept, large terraced house with white stone steps. Ellie had a room of her own with a proper divan, a washbasin, even a bedside rug. But after Bonny's airy and spacious flat in Kensington she found it depressing and wrinkled her nose at the all too familiar seediness and the musty smell.

'What's happened?' she asked, bending over to touch the raw place on Ellie's cheek. 'Who did that to you?'

For a while Ellie wouldn't reply; she just turned over on her stomach and sobbed into the pillow. Bonny sat down on the bed and stroked her hair, urging her to explain.

'I had this feeling something had happened this afternoon,' she said softly. 'It wouldn't go away so I went to the Theatre Royal. When they told me they hadn't seen you and the understudy was going on I was so afraid. Tell me? Please!'

Slowly Ellie told the story, her face still half buried in the pillow, but Bonny caught hold of her and turned her round, drawing her into her arms as if Ellie were a small child.

'You were very brave,' she whispered. 'I'm glad you didn't go through with it. He might have butchered you, like that other man did me. I'll look after you, Ellie, I promise I will. I know I haven't always been a good friend to you, but I won't let you down now.'

It was odd for Ellie to be on the receiving end of comfort, but she let herself be held and sobbed out all her fears. 'How can I bring up a baby? It will be like Mum and me all over again. I didn't want to kill it, Bonny, but how will I manage? And there's Sir Miles too.'

She didn't know why she brought up his name. She hardly knew the man, but since he came to her first night with his wife she'd been thinking about him constantly. She was sure it was Sir Miles she had to thank for the part of Annie. He was most definitely interested in her. She'd even found herself weaving little day-dreams of confiding in him the next time she saw him. It was silly, she knew that, but she hadn't got any other family.

'What's Sir Miles got to do with it? Bonny asked. She understood all Ellie's other fears, but not that one. John knew Sir Miles and Lady Hamilton well, but as far as Bonny knew, Ellie had only met him once, at the Savoy.

'I think he's my father,' Ellie blurted out.

Bonny laughed. She thought Ellie was delirious. 'Oh really? Mine's Winston Churchill!'

It was too late for Ellie to retract it now. She began to cry again, horrified that in a moment of weakness she'd revealed something so potentially dangerous.

'I don't understand,' Bonny said, suddenly aware she'd heard something which was never meant to be told. 'How can he be your father?'

'Promise me you'll never tell anyone, not even John.' Ellie caught hold of Bonny's hand, wringing it in her distress.

'I promise,' Bonny said, disengaging her hand. 'But explain. You can't just come out with something like that and expect me to forget it.'

Ellie sobbed out the story.

'You mustn't ever tell,' she finished up.

'Of course I won't say anything,' Bonny assured her. She was stunned by the news, but even more astounded that Ellie had kept it a secret for so long. 'But he's the answer to your problem, Ellie. Why don't you go to him and ask for help. It's his grandchild, after all. He'll make Ray marry you.'

'I wouldn't marry Ray if he came crawling to me on his knees,' Ellie spat out angrily. 'And I'm certainly not going cap in hand to Sir Miles. Marleen might've been wrong, even if she wasn't, it makes no difference.'

Bonny sighed. If she was in Ellie's shoes she'd use anyone who might make life easier for her. But then Ellie wasn't like that. She was too noble for her own good sometimes. 'You've got to pull yourself together,' she said. 'You don't have to make any decisions just now, it's too soon. All you've got to do for now is look after yourself.'

'Oh Bonny!' Ellie sobbed. 'I feel so dreadful. I'm so scared. I just don't know what to do.'

Bonny held Ellie tightly, rocking her soothingly. She remembered feeling that way when she was pregnant by the American airman. 'Don't be scared,' she implored her. 'I promised I'd help and I meant it. You won't show for ages yet and we'll think of something. Maybe your friends Amos and Dora will help you. If not, once I'm married and living in Somerset, you can come there. We can find someone who'll look after the baby when you're working. When I lived in Dagenham there was a woman down our street who used to take in foster children.'

'Maybe I'll miscarry,' Ellie muttered into Bonny's shoulder. 'If I keep on dancing it could happen.'

'Maybe you will.' Bonny began to undo the buttons on Ellie's dress. 'But for now you're going to bed and I'll ring the theatre and tell them you got knocked down today and were in such shock you didn't think to let them know.'

Ellie looked at Bonny and smiled wanly. 'You always were a good story-teller. I hope you can find a happy ending for this one.'

'We'll think of something.' Bonny kissed Ellie's

cheek. 'And you make sure you come to my wedding, or I'll never speak to you again.'

Jack was driving a customer's car back to Amberley village when he saw a figure ahead of him. Only one girl in the world had such shiny blonde hair and that provocative wiggle and his heart turned a complete somersault with shock.

He had heard from Miss Wynter that Bonny was getting married in a couple of weeks, and been relieved that it would be in London. He should have realised she was bound to visit Miss Wynter before the big day.

At the sound of the car coming up behind her, Bonny turned. She was wearing a slim-fitting pink costume with a matching frivolous hat, and high-heeled ankle strap shoes entirely unsuitable for a two-mile walk.

Had there been a chance for Jack to turn off and pretend he hadn't seen her, he would have taken it. But she was already lifting one gloved hand in greeting. He cursed his red hair for standing out like a beacon.

There was nothing for it but to slow down and stop. He was bound to run into her some time, after all.

'Well, hello Jack,' she said, coming up to the passenger door and bending to look in the window at him. 'How are you?'

'Pretty good.' He tried to look very casual, but, absurdly, wished he wasn't in greasy overalls. 'I hear you're getting married?'

'Happens to the best of us,' she said, her blue eyes even more vivid than he remembered. 'I heard you married Ginny. Now are you going to give the a lift up to Aunt Lydia's? Or are you still sore at me?'

Jack had always sworn to himself that if he ever saw her again he would cut her dead, but one look at that beautiful face which had once meant everything in the world to him weakened his resolve.

'How can I be sore when it all worked out for the best?' He forced a smile. 'I don't think I'd better give you a lift though. Ginny's away for a few days and you were always good at making tongues wag.'

'Don't be daft,' Bonny giggled. 'What could be more natural than giving an old chum a lift, especially when she's only here to make wedding plans? If you're really worried you could drop me off just before the village.'

He cursed himself for having revealed that Ginny was away; he should have said he was just going to pick her up from the shop.

'Okay then.' He shrugged his shoulders. 'Hop in.'

'Is this your car?' she asked as he moved off.

'No, a customer's.' He kept his eyes straight ahead on the road, but he could still see her long, slender legs out of the corner of his eye and it was making him sweat. 'I've got a Ford Anglia myself, things are going really well.'

'I'm glad,' she said and Jack felt she was sincere. 'I didn't get to Hollywood – I don't want that any more anyway. But I'm really happy you got what you wanted.'

'Everything I ever dreamed of,' he agreed, yet to his dismay it sounded like a brave lie. 'A lovely wife, a nice home and my own business. Still got a way to go yet to the string of garages, but I'll get them.'

He pulled up before they hit the first house in the village. 'Sorry I can't take you the whole way.' He leaned across her to open the door. 'Good luck, Bonny. I hope you'll be as happy in your marriage as Ginny and me.'

'Couldn't we have a chat some time before I go?' Bonny slid one leg out of the car, but she didn't attempt to move the rest of herself. 'I'd like to explain properly.'

649

'What's there to explain?' Jack gulped. 'We were just two kids, that's all. We weren't meant for one another.'

'Meet me tomorrow evening?' She fixed him with her eyes. His rugged, endearingly ugly face was stirring up memories. She was sorry she let him down so badly, and now that she was marrying John she had a desire to clean up messes she'd left behind her. 'I was going to catch the six o'clock train back to London, but I could catch a later one. You could just drive me to Three Bridges and we could have a drink on the way and one last chat.'

He shook his head. 'No, Bonny, that's asking for trouble.'

She reached out and put one hand on his cheek. Jack could smell heady, flowery perfume. The touch of her cotton glove evoked a memory of meeting her after evensong in the churchyard and the taste of her lips on his.

'I'll be under the railway bridge at twenty to six. If you don't come I'll understand.' Her voice was soft and sweet and it seemed without guile. 'But I'd like to think we can still be friends.'

She didn't wait for his reply, just got out of the car and walked on. Jack revved up the engine and shot off past her. His throat was dry, his palms were sweating and he knew in that moment that he hadn't entirely cut her out of his heart.

'Promise me you'll work hard at making your marriage work,' Lydia said unexpectedly, just as Bonny was preparing to leave. The sound of girlish giggling was wafting up the stairs from the studio – eight small girls waiting for their class to begin. 'John is a good man and he deserves more than just a decorative wife. Do you understand what I mean?'

Today Bonny had noticed Lydia was suddenly looking older. Her once glossy chestnut hair was peppered with grey, there were lines around her eyes and her chin was no longer so firm. Her figure was still so good it drew attention from her face, but Bonny had observed that she no longer ran lightly up the stairs, or danced with her class with her old exuberance.

All at once she sensed a certain sadness in her adopted aunt. She must be forty-four or five now; perhaps she'd finally come to regret that she never married.

'Yes. I do understand what you mean.' Bonny felt a pang of guilt that she hadn't always shown her appreciation for this woman who'd done so much for her. 'I do love him very much, Auntie!'

To her surprise, Lydia drew her into her arms and hugged her fiercely. 'I don't suppose I'll get to see you very often after the wedding,' she said with a break in her voice. 'Somerset is such a long way away and I expect you'll have children soon to occupy you. But keep in touch and remember I love you, and don't cast your parents off, Bonny, you are all they have.'

'I love you too,' Bonny whispered. 'Thank you, not just for having me now, but for everything in the past.'

'Go on now.' Lydia gently pushed her away. 'I'm sorry I couldn't run you to the station. I'll see you in church.'

Bonny waited under the bridge until ten to six. It had been colder today, with a grey sky, and now she felt distinctly chilly. Jack wasn't coming after all: she could see the garage was all closed up. She looked at her watch again, picked up her case and turned towards the station incline, feeling dejected.

It had been such a nice break being with Lydia, the best time she'd had with her since she left Amberley to dance. Lydia had told her so many funny stories about things Bonny had done years ago, and it was strange hearing an adult version of incidents she'd forgotten. So many of them were connected with Jack. It had brought home just how much he had meant to her.

A car spun round the corner very fast and pulled up with a squeal of brakes. For a moment Bonny didn't recognise Jack: he was wearing a trilby hat pulled well down over his face.

'Hop in, quick!' he hissed. 'And put your head down so no one sees you.'

'Can I sit up now?' Bonny giggled after a few minutes. They seemed to be going very fast, lurching round bends. 'This is like something out of a spy film.'

'I shouldn't have come,' he said, his voice stern. 'I need my head testing.'

Jack drove all the way to Billingshurst before he decided it was safe to stop for a drink. 'My customers come from miles around,' he said. 'And people talk.'

'Village people are so small-minded,' Bonny said airily. 'Why shouldn't two old friends have a drink and a chat?'

'In our case you know exactly why,' Jack said tersely, pulling up beside a small pub, seemingly miles from anywhere. 'I know Ginny wouldn't like it. I doubt your fiancé would either.'

Over the first drink Jack told her how clever Ginny was at doing up their home, how she could knit, sew and cook better than Mrs Baker. By the second drink Bonny was telling Jack how intelligent John was, about his travels and how he'd instructed builders to hurry up and complete the work at The Chestnuts in Somerset so they could move in after their honeymoon. Seven o'clock passed unnoticed as they had a third drink and Jack began to tell her about all the other kids who'd been in his gang.

'Eric Turley married Amanda Nash and they live in Arundel now, expecting their first baby. Peter Samms stayed in the airforce. Colin Atkins was killed right at the end of the war, shot by a German sniper in France. But John Broom went on to university, he's going to be a lawyer.'

They sank back into the past, laughing as they both dredged up old memories, ignoring the time purposely.

'It wouldn't have worked for us,' Bonny said eventually, gulping down her fourth large gin. 'I was cruel the way I broke it off, Jack, but it was the only way.'

She was far too aware of his maleness, exciting, yet disturbing. His big square hands were scrubbed clean, he was wearing a well-made dark suit and good shoes, but the symbols of success were just a thin veneer – scratch it and the rough, tough boy was still there. His plain face was mellowed by age and experience into rugged magnetism and brutish strength. Even though she tried to steer her thoughts away from his muscular body and those big, rough hands, she couldn't help but want him again.

'I don't hold any grudges,' he said, his brown eyes looking right into hers. 'I wouldn't have got where I am today with you, Bonny. You were always too much of a distraction.'

They arrived at the station just in time to see the last train to London chugging out.

Jack looked at Bonny and shrugged. 'I'll drive you. We can talk some more on the way.'

'We're in London now.' Jack shook her to wake her. 'You'd better direct me. I don't know where you live.'

'Fancy me dropping off,' she said, rubbing her eyes. 'I should've found a hotel in Sussex, not made you come all this way.' It was almost half past twelve and she felt a little guilty she hadn't been better company. 'You can sleep on my settee if you like. You can't drive back now.'

Jack didn't reply immediately. He'd had plenty of time on the long drive to think about what might happen when he got to London. Each time he glanced at Bonny's sleeping face his resolve to just drop her at her door weakened. Now he knew he'd lost the battle with his conscience.

'I'll just grab a couple of hours' shut-eye,' he said hoarsely, as Bonny directed him through what looked like a maze of London streets. 'I have to have the garage open at eight.'

Jack's knowledge of London was limited to his childhood memories of Kennington and day-trips to the West End, the former being miserable ones, the latter clouded a little by drink. He was rather impressed by Kensington, with its grand houses and wide streets. Even though it was late at night, shop lights had been left on and there were still a great many people walking about.

When Bonny directed him to pull up outside some mahogany, half-glazed doors between two shops, then led him up a wide staircase with a thick red carpet, he was even more impressed. Tollgate Cottage was pretty, but it wasn't elegant like this.

Bonny shut her flat door behind him, and for a moment they stood looking hesitantly at one another, neither able to speak. A force was flowing between them, pulling them closer. All they had once been to one another surged up, temporarily erasing the images of Ginny and John, and they fell into one another's arms.

It was brutal, rough love-making. Jack pushed her down on to the living-room floor, his hard hands pulling off her clothes in haste. So long ago they had found ways of pleasing each other without full penetration. Tonight was the climax of all those unfulfilling trysts.

Jack forced his way into her, but total domination was what Bonny wanted and she caught hold of his buttocks, revelling in the sheer animal lust. Many men had thrilled her in the past, but this was better and purer. As he savagely bit her breasts, she clawed back at him. He was her Jack and always would be; she wanted him to leave his mark on her for all time.

Much later he picked her up and carried her into the bedroom. Brutality left them now, as the poignancy of first love met the sorrow of knowing this was not a beginning but the finale. Slow lingering caresses, mouth upon eager, tender mouth.

For Bonny it was like returning to fourteen again, rediscovering the heady thrills of lying petting in long grass with Jack, an age of innocence which she regretted passing.

Jack worshipped her body like a man knowing he was on his way to the gallows in the morning. He covered every inch of her skin with kisses, licking at her hungrily, breathing in deeply that sea aroma so he could call it to memory any time in the future when he might need something to assuage the guilt of betraying Ginny's trust.

The first dawn light was creeping through the window when Jack got up. Gently he lifted the covers up and tucked them round Bonny as she lay sleeping. Tears pricked at his eyes; his heart was so very heavy. She looked just as she had when she lay lifeless on the river bank all those years ago, except she had been dressed in a soaked red siren suit then and now she was naked. But the face, without the benefit of makeup, was the same: the clear pink and white skin, the delicate fair eyebrows, the soft, slack mouth.

'I love you,' he whispered. 'But never again, Bonny. Never again.'

He dressed and let himself out silently. He could still smell her on his hands, his face and on his body. He would jump in the river when he got back, swim until he was exhausted. Maybe there he could put this passion to rest, where it had all started.

Bonny walked down Piccadilly towards Fortnum and Mason's. It was just two days since she'd arrived back in London with Jack. She was glad he left before she woke: she could pretend it was all just a delightful, intense dream. She couldn't honestly claim she felt any sense of guilt. Jack was hers long before she knew John; it was as if she had the two men in entirely separate compartments of her life. Perhaps other women might doubt they were really in love with their husband-to-be to allow such a thing to happen.

But Bonny had her own set of rules, and didn't much care what other women did or didn't do.

The sun was warm, the streets crowded with shoppers. Just yesterday she'd had a new permanent wave, and admiring glances from both men and women told her she looked stunning in her pink costume.

There were only ten days to go now to her wedding and her hands were full of shopping bags. John had been so generous, making an arrangement at his bank so she could get money out when she needed it. It was so lucky clothing coupons had been abandoned back in March. Bonny had always managed to get new clothes somehow, whether it was through the black market, gifts from boyfriends or using her mother's carefully hoarded points. But to be able to sweep into shops and spend the money John had left her, that was truly thrilling.

A turquoise dress and jacket from Marshall and Snelgrove's to go away in matched her eyes to perfection. From Bonita's in Regent Street she'd got a delicious frothy hat and three new sets of underwear. Tomorrow she would go for a final fitting of her wedding dress and pick up Ellie's bridesmaid dress.

Ellie was Bonny's only source of anxiety. She just couldn't see any way round her predicament. But John approved of Ellie. They were going to see *Oklahoma* when he got home, and once they were married and settled in Somerset, Bonny was quite sure John would be willing to help her.

She had a couple of baby nightdresses and some booties amongst her other shopping. Half an hour in Selfridges' baby department, cooing over all the pretty things, had made her feel very soft, almost woozy. She was hoping this might be a sign she really was pregnant; that would make her happiness complete. But if not, they'd do nicely for Ellie.

Now she was going to order some special treats to have delivered at the house in Somerset. John had suggested this in his latest letter and indeed listed certain items – strange-sounding things like brie and Gentleman's Relish, along with the more familiar Bath Olivers, Dundee cake and York ham.

A liveried doorman opened the doors for her and Bonny swept in, hoping she looked as if she were accustomed to shopping in such a place.

Never before had she seen so much food, so beautifully arranged. To her right was a huge display of hampers and picnic baskets set amongst straw and flowers, to her left, a glass-fronted counter with handmade chocolates. Further back in the store were marble slabs on which hung brilliantly feathered birds, rabbits, hares and chickens. Another counter had fish curled around wonderful sculptures made of ice, prawns and shrimps and a monstrous-looking, huge fish with fearsome teeth.

Bonny had no idea how to make a start. Her apprehension was increased by the sight of elegant-looking women talking knowledgeably to the assistants in straw boaters.

She stopped by the chocolate stand and watched while a gentleman in a grey morning suit was making his choice, and her mouth watered as one by one chocolates decorated with tiny violets, roses and lemons were placed in a magnificent gold box, as if there were no such thing as sweet rationing.

'Good morning, madam.' A man who looked far too dignified to be a shop assistant came towards her.

He wore a green frock-coat and he had an oiled moustache. 'Can I be of assistance?'

The very fact that he considered her worthy of speaking to made her feel a little less intimidated and she flashed him her most winning smile. 'My fiancé asked me to come and order some things,' she said. 'I have a list; we'd like them to be delivered to our house in Somerset after our wedding.'

Bonny was relieved when he took the list from her hand: she couldn't pronounce many of the items. John, meticulous as ever, had put all his personal details, the address and the date they were required for, at the top.

The man glanced through the list and smiled obsequiously. 'We have all these items in stock, madam, perhaps you'd just like to look around and see if there's anything else you'd like added?'

Bonny had a slight sensation of being tested. As she had no wish to appear unused to shopping in such a place, she agreed to look around with him.

'Perhaps a selection of chocolates,' she said airily. 'I prefer soft centres.'

Several different kinds of preserved fruit went on to the list, chosen more for their appearance than anything else, as well as tins of biscuits and a large cheese in a lovely blue stone pot. But as Bonny approached the wine counter she stopped dead in her tracks, suddenly feeling faint as she recognised an all too familiar back view.

It was Magnus. He was tucked away in a corner, studying a wine label.

'That's everything,' she said dismissively to the assistant. 'You'll make certain it arrives on time?'

'Certainly madam.' The man made a little bow, but Bonny was unaware of anything but Magnus and the hammering of her heart.

Bonny had stored so many memories of him away in her mind, but she rarely let herself open the closed doors and look at them. Now, seeing him again, dressed in a very smart grey suit, his thick, fair hair gleaming under the shop lights, everything she'd ever felt for him came back with a fierce rush of pain.

She had expected to see Jack in Amberley: in her heart she knew she would have searched him out if she hadn't run into him by chance. But she had never expected to see Magnus again, ever. She felt his presence was fate; or maybe the ultimate test.

Taking a step forward, she watched him. He was unaware of her gaze, squinting a little as if he needed glasses to read the small print. He was no longer bronzed as she remembered; the hands cradling the wine bottle were smooth and pale and his face had a few more lines. But his sensual lips, the firm line of his jaw, were just as she remembered.

'Remember me?' she said, reaching out to touch the sleeve of his jacket, unable to walk away, although she knew she should. 'How are you, Magnus?'

Chapter Twenty-Nine

June 1949

Ellie stepped back and looked at her friend in her cream satin wedding dress, and her eyes prickled.

For perhaps the first time in her life, Bonny had understood the principle of 'less is more'. Her dress was simple: a demure high neck, long tight sleeves, the only decoration the seed-pearls along the hem and train. Nothing to distract the eye from her lovely face, perfectly framed by a fluffy halo of curls.

'Just a touch more rouge,' Ellie suggested. 'You're a bit pale. If I didn't know you better I'd think it was nerves!'

Ellie had managed to put aside her guilt in helping to deceive John when in the last few days she'd seen his excitement and happiness at the forthcoming wedding. Bonny seemed different too, as if she'd finally turned into an adult. Maybe the end would justify the means.

'I'm terrified,' Bonny admitted. 'I don't know if I can go through with it.'

'It's too late to change your mind now.' Ellie laughed: she wasn't used to seeing Bonny with stage-fright. 'You'll be fine once you get to the church. Now go careful with the rouge and I'll fix your veil.'

Bonny bent towards the dressing-table mirror and carefully puffed on just a hint of pink. 'Better?' she asked, looking at Ellie's reflection next to her in the mirror.

They had always complemented one another, black hair against blonde, pink and white skin against olive. Today in their roles of bride and bridesmaid, the effect was even more dramatic. Ellie's dress was a deep blue, an Empress style which concealed her slightly thickening waistline. Bonny thought her friend had never looked more ravishing. There was a new bloom to her complexion, and her dark eyes were more lustrous than ever.

'You are perfection,' Ellie grinned. 'But then you know that! Now let's get the veil on.'

'I wish—' Bonny murmured, as Ellie anchored the small seed-pearl head-dress to her hair.

'You wish what? That it was me instead of you?' Ellie joked. For the last couple of days she had forced herself to forget her own predicament, spending her spare time with Bonny in last-minute preparations. An understudy was filling in for her tonight and she relished an evening off from the show.

Her only anxiety today was centred around Sir Miles and Lady Hamilton. She hadn't realised until she learnt they were to be guests that they were such close friends of John and his godmother. Although she was pleased to be able to meet Sir Miles on a social level at last, she wished she hadn't confided to Bonny about him.

'Oh, I don't know what I wish.' Bonny moved her head impatiently as Ellie arranged the veil over her face. 'I suppose I'm a bit ashamed.'

'Can I see you now dear?' Mrs Phillips's voice rang out from behind the closed bedroom door, cutting short any further discussion. 'It should be me helping you. I've washed up the teacups and straightened up in here. Is there anything else I can do?'

'You must let her in,' Ellie whispered. The Phillipses had arrived at the flat some two hours ago. Doris was a terrible, neurotic fusspot, but it seemed very callous of Bonny to exclude her mother from helping her only daughter dress. 'Don't spoil her day, Bonny. She's so proud of you.'

Bonny stuck out her tongue in the direction of the door, but she called her mother in with saccharine sweetness.

Ellie stood back watching mother and daughter, bemused at how Bonny came to be so sparky and vivacious with such a dull, plain mother. Doris had no conversation except about the most mundane things – the continuing food rationing, her knitting, and of course, Bonny. She wondered what the more illustrious wedding guests would make of Bonny's parents. John had made no comment about his meetings with them, but then he was a very tolerant and understanding man.

It was clear Doris was an excellent dressmaker, yet all the work she'd put into her wedding outfit was marred by her choice of a style which merely emphasised her roly-poly shape. The blue crêpe de chine dress had a gathered waist, and the short-sleeved bolero jacket stopped short of a roll of fat. Bonny had been about to tell her this, and only Ellie's timely intervention with enthusiastic compliments for Doris's blue organza hat had averted a potential battle.

'Oh Bonny, you look so lovely.' Doris dabbed at her eyes with the hanky that was permanently in her hand. 'My little girl!'

'You look lovely too,' Bonny said crisply. 'The car will be here any minute, so powder your nose. But please, Mum, don't tell people at the reception embarrassing things about when I was a kid. I hate it!'

A ring at the bell cut short any protest from Doris. She snatched at her daughter's hand in the absence of finding any other part of her accessible and pressed it to her lips.

'Bye my angel,' she whimpered. 'Good luck.'

'I have to go too,' Ellie said as Doris rushed out. Even through Bonny's veil she could see her friend's eyes were wide and frightened, but there was little more she could say to reassure her. 'You'll be all right with your dad. Take a few deep breaths.'

The flat seemed suddenly deadly silent to Bonny once her mother and Ellie left. She walked into the living-room to discover that her father was in the bathroom, yet again. He was nervous about making a speech later, but Bonny was sure he'd be fine when the moment came, and she'd checked it out to make sure he wasn't going to say anything potentially embarrassing. She was glad of a few seconds alone to compose herself, because today guilt was crowding in at her from every direction.

She hadn't really considered her wickedness at fooling John, or even felt guilt at her night with Jack, not until after her encounter with Magnus.

He had taken her to lunch at the Ritz following their meeting in Fortnum and Mason's. At first it was just an innocent and happy reunion. He'd had another son called Nicholas and proudly got baby snapshots out of his wallet to show her. They had one bottle of wine, and then another, both comparing notes on all that had happened since they parted.

She made him laugh with all her best funny stories about the shows, and told him about her forthcoming wedding. He told her of a large old derelict house he'd bought, and his plans to convert it to a luxury country house hotel. They both told each other things had worked out for the best.

Maybe it was because they drank too much that they lapsed into sentimentality. But why did she cheapen herself by persuading Magnus to take her to his room? It would have been enough for most women just to see love still smouldering in his eyes! But no, she had to lure him into bed to test him further. There had been no satisfaction in discovering she could still tweak his chain and make him perform; it was an empty and shallow act which merely shamed her.

Magnus had cried when it was over, saying that he hated himself for betraying Ruth again, but most of all he pitied John.

Later that same evening, alone in her flat, Bonny saw herself as she really was: a scheming, faithless floozy without any redeeming qualities. The living-room was strewn with the wedding presents that had been arriving daily. Every one of them came from John's friends, because she had none of her own, save Ellie. John paid her rent, bought her food and clothes and loved her above all else. She was only twenty, with everything any girl could possibly want before her, yet suddenly all the excitement she'd felt for the wedding plans and her dreams for the future were as flat as a two-day-old glass of champagne.

Suppose she was pregnant? Whose baby would it be? Was she going to have to wait for the birth, not knowing whether it would be dark like John, red-haired, or blonde?

That night, the tears she cried were real. For her parents who loved her blindly. For Aunt Lydia who'd given her so much, for Jack, Magnus and all the lesser men she'd cheated and deceived. And for Ellie, that rock in her life who'd supported her, laughed and cried with her, the one and only true friend who was now in deep trouble herself.

She knew she had wounded them all, using their love and twisting it for her own ends. She hadn't even got the courage to break off this wedding, which was built on trickery and lies. John deserved better than her.

Then John had come home a week later, his lean, usually serious face bright with smiles. Excitement, joy and love bubbled out of him as he produced perfume, silk underwear and a pair of diamond earrings for her from his luggage. All his customary caution was thrown to the wind: he'd arranged a honeymoon in Paris, he took her round antique shops in Bond Street to buy pieces for their house in Somerset, and every plan he made was for her and their baby. She wished she was all he believed her to be.

'Penny for them?'

Bonny was startled out of her reverie by her father coming out of the bathroom, resplendent in a new navy-blue suit and a striped tie. She ran to him, just the way she had as a child.

'There, there.' He held her and stroked her back, his face warm against her veiled cheek. 'Everyone gets last-minute nerves, lovey. John's a fine man. You couldn't have done better, not even if you let me choose him.'

'I'm sorry, Dad,' she whispered. She wasn't ashamed of her father today. He might have no hair, bad teeth and stooping shoulders, but she loved him. 'I haven't give you and Mum much back for all you've done for me, have I?'

He moved her back from his chest, his hands on her shoulders and just looked at her, his lined face and faded blue eyes glowing with love. 'Listen to me, Bonny. You were the best thing that ever happened to me and your mum,' he said, his voice husky with emotion. 'We had given up hope of ever having a child, and when you was born we saw it as a gift from heaven. It's a privilege having a child, you don't expect no thanks, or reward. Love's about giving, not receiving, you just remember that.'

'But I'm so awful sometimes,' she said in a small voice, teetering on a confession.

Arnold didn't view his daughter through the same rose-coloured spectacles as his wife, and at the same time he knew Doris was more than partially responsible for some of Bonny's failings. 'Yesterdays don't matter,' he said firmly. 'Tomorrow is what counts. You go into that church and promise before God to keep the vows you'll make today. Now chin up, and no looking back.'

665

As Bonny walked down to the waiting car holding her father's arm she made a vow to herself. She would start all over again, as from today. She would become the kind of wife John deserved. Faithful, loving and truthful. He would never have cause to regret marrying her.

John turned from the altar to look at Bonny as the organ burst into the first chords of the wedding march. St Michael's was a dank, plain church, still suffering from war damage, with many boarded-up windows, but the profusion of flowers and candles camouflaged the gloom, and his guests in bright colours and pretty hats made it festive.

A lump came up in his throat at Bonny's ethereal beauty. They were all wrong, all those well-intentioned friends who had tried to dissuade him from marrying her.

Mrs Phillips was dabbing at her face already. Miss Wynter, in peach silk, had trembling lips, and Mr Phillips, walking beside his daughter, was bursting with pride. Ellie looked so gorgeous as bridesmaid; it said something about Bonny that her friendship with such a well-balanced, talented girl had endured for so many years.

There might be few people on Bonny's side of the aisle – half a dozen friends from the theatre, that was all – but her life so far had been spent in transit. Soon all his friends would come to know her and love her as he did.

Bonny sat by the bedroom window, staring out on to the rain-washed garden, trying very hard not to cry. It was September, and the three months since their wedding had been the happiest time she'd ever known. Since returning from their honeymoon in Paris, John had been working here in England, rarely staying away for more than a couple of nights at a time and they'd worked together on turning The Chestnuts into a real home. But now John had to go to America for six whole months and she was consumed by guilt, sadness and a feeling that all her lies and trickery were gathering together like a sword above her head which at any minute could come slashing down and destroy everything.

The Chestnuts was a Georgian villa surrounded by a six-foot stone wall and the gigantic trees from which it got its name. The tiny village of Priddy was a mile away, down a winding, narrow lane; Wells, the nearest town, some nine or ten miles further. John's father, an antisocial man who had supplemented his small private income by writing nature books, bought the house in 1900 because of its remote position. Until John was sent away to Sexus School at the age of eleven, he and his brothers rarely went beyond the village, and the rolling hills, woods and heathlands had been their playground.

Bonny had fallen in love with the house on sight, although she had been dismayed at first by its total isolation. While she and John were making wedding plans and taking their honey moon the builders had worked hard to get it ready for them. By the time John carried her over the threshold, the parquet floors downstairs had been sanded and varnished, a new boiler put into the kitchen, the sitting-room, diningroom and kitchen redecorated. But of all the extensive work John had organised it was this bedroom and its adjoining luxurious bathroom which thrilled Bonny most. She hadn't fully grasped then that the pink and cream decor, thick carpet, heavy drapes, fitted wardrobes and the vast film-star-like bed were the work of an expensive London designer, and that quiet, staid John Norton had understood his young bride's character so well that he had cheerfully spent a small fortune to indulge her fantasies.

Bonny had learnt a great deal more about John's

character in three months of marriage, however, and that knowledge had transformed her own. So often she wished she could tell him how he had changed her, but she couldn't, not without admitting exactly what she'd been before.

It was love which had changed her. Day by day, night by night, it had grown, cutting away the calculating, greedy and selfish side of her. John was no longer a meal ticket for life, but friend and lover, a man she never wanted to be parted from. Alone with him she'd found another girl, one she liked a good deal better than the old Bonny. This new person had an entirely new conception of pleasure. To run out barefoot on dew-covered grass to hang out the washing, to plant out flowers and watch them flourish, to share picnics, country walks, cooking and going to bed nightly with a man she knew she would always care for, meant so much more than glamorous living.

Sometimes at night John stroked her belly tenderly and whispered his hopes and dreams for their child and at those times her deceit almost choked her. Another twist of fate was conspiring against her, punishing her in a way she had never anticipated.

In the first few weeks of marriage she'd waited anxiously for a period, intending to use it as a fake miscarriage. When it didn't happen, at first she believed she really was pregnant and almost sank to her knees with prayers of gratitude. But as the weeks slowly passed a sixth sense told her this wasn't so, that her body was merely playing up as it had so often in the past. The absence of periods was a symptom of something fundamentally wrong with her womb, and she couldn't tell John.

John paused now in the bedroom doorway, surprised to find Bonny staring out of the window, her slim shoulders hunched up, one foot tucked beneath her on the window-seat. Their bed was strewn with shirts and underwear, and a half-packed suitcase lay at the foot of the ottoman.

'Such a sad face!' he chuckled. 'I thought you'd be throwing my stuff in it happily, hardly able to wait to get rid of me.'

Bonny turned to him and her eyes were as bleak as the rain-filled sky. 'Everything I put in the case reminded me how long you'll be gone.' Her voice trembled. 'Then I looked out at the garden and saw the summer had gone too.'

John crossed the room and sat beside her, taking her hands in his. He sensed the real meaning of her last sentence and he searched for the right words of reassurance.

He didn't want to go to America, but if the results of the preliminary tests he'd done last year in Texas turned out to be as important as he suspected they were, it would mean huge profits for his company and further promotion for him. He couldn't turn it down: he was in a specialised field and if he refused to go now he would ruin his future prospects. If he went to work for anyone else, he wouldn't be able to keep this house, or maintain the standard of living he'd been used to.

'We've got dozens of other summers ahead of us,' he said gently. 'After this trip I promise I'll wangle it so you can come too next time. I know it's awful that you'll be alone for the baby being born, especially over Christmas, but I can't help it, and we both knew I'd have to go when we set the date for the wedding.'

'But I'm a different person now,' she said, a tear rolling down her cheek. She understood he had to go. His work was very important and a great many other men's jobs would be affected too if he refused. 'I never used to look ahead beyond the end of the week. I didn't expect to find you'd become my whole life.'

John swallowed hard, fighting against an unreasonable desire to telephone his company and tell them he was quitting. Bonny had more than fulfilled his dreams: she'd given him more happiness than he'd ever imagined.

He could hardly credit that the girl sitting beside him, wearing a cotton dress and cardigan, her hair tied up with a blue ribbon, was the same glittering showgirl he'd once been so wary of. All those friends who'd shaken their heads and said he'd regret it were quite wrong. Maybe she hadn't had any skills aside from dancing and looking pretty until their wedding, but she'd learnt so many more now. Downstairs on the kitchen table was a cake cooling from the oven. Furniture gleamed with polish, water-colours she'd found in the attics were hung on the walls. Just looking at the pile of shirts on the bed made him smile. Who would have thought she was capable of washing, starching and ironing shirts and then folding them so they looked as if they came straight from the laundry?

But although these housewifely skills pleased John, they weren't what really made him happy. It was the way she ran to his arms when he came in, her excitement at new challenges, the love she showered on him.

'Your whole life?' he teased her, taking a tendril of her hair in his hand and winding it around his finger. 'That's a bit dramatic, even for you!'

'Bonny tried vainly to smile.

'Don't cry, darling.' John held her close, smoothing back her hair. 'Your parents will come and stay, you only have to ask them. I'm sure your mother would be tickled pink to help you when the baby comes.'

Bonny quaked inwardly. If only she'd pretended to lose this 'baby' right after the honeymoon, regardless of bleeding to back it up! It hadn't occurred to her that John would broadcast the news quite so soon as he did. Now her mother was knitting, posting nasty little cuttings from magazines about preventing stretch marks, varicose veins, cracking nipples and worst of all, piles. It was Bonny's biggest fear that her mother might turn up on the doorstep with two dozen nappies, intending to stick at her daughter's side until the delivery.

What was she going to do? Her mother and Aunt Lydia would be suspicious of her when the news got out she wasn't pregnant after all. She would be five months gone now. Was it feasible to fake a miscarriage at that late date? Surely women had to go to hospital that far on?

'I'll be all right,' Bonny sniffed. She'd think of something in the day or two after John had left. She just wasn't thinking straight right now. 'Women had to put up with their husbands being away for longer than this during the war, I'm just being silly. I don't want my mother here fussing over me, not yet anyway, she'll just get on my nerves. But I will miss you terribly.'

'Well, if you won't ask them, how about getting some help in daily?' John asked, his face soft with concern. 'It's so isolated here. I get worried you might have a fall or be ill.'

'I don't need help in the house,' Bonny scoffed. The Chestnuts was huge by her council house standards, with four bedrooms, three rooms and the kitchen downstairs, but three of the bedrooms were still shut up waiting for redecoration, and anyway, she liked looking after it herself. 'Enoch comes in to do the garden nearly every day, and there's always the telephone. You mustn't worry about me.'

'I can't help worrying,' John said, his brown eyes anxious. 'But if it gets too much for you, ask Mrs Perkins in the post office to find someone for you. And if you want furniture moved, ask Enoch.'

'He's doing a grand job on the garden.' Bonny turned on the window-seat to look at it, glad of an opportunity to change the subject. 'We're going to start putting in daffodil and tulip bulbs next week.'

Bonny had grown attached to the funny old man John had employed as a gardener. He was nearly seventy, spoke in an almost unintelligible Somerset accent and he could neither read nor write. But through him Bonny had found deep pleasure in the garden, watching as he pruned and dug, listening when he told her about the plants. John said he was a substitute for her own father, and perhaps he was right.

'It's beginning to look like it did when I was a boy,' John said thoughtfully. The majestic chestnut trees towered over the grey stone wall. Enoch had dug out brambles, scythed down the long grass and nettles and now at last a lawn was reappearing. John had so many good memories of the garden, of helping his father build the arbour and indeed securing roses to it which were still there, as vigorous as ever. The pond had always been a delight as a small boy, watching tadpoles turn to frogs and the dragonflies shimmering over the surface.

'In London boys would kill for all those conkers.' Bonny pointed out the carpet of them under the chestnuts. 'There was only one chestnut tree in Dagenham and they used to poke it with sticks to get them.'

'Maybe we'll have lots of boys,' John said, putting his hand on her stomach. 'I'll hang a rope for them to swing on like I used to do. Maybe I'll even get around to building a tree house.'

'Don't wish lots of boys on us.' Bonny felt a renewed pang of conscience. His hand felt so warm and loving, and she wished there was a baby in there. 'Two is enough, maybe a girl too.'

'You don't seem to be getting much bigger,' he said, almost wistfully.

'Good job too.' She laughed lightly. In fact she had put on weight. With regular meals and no dancing she was almost two inches bigger round the waist and there was a curve to her belly. 'I'll get fat soon enough. My mum said she didn't show till she was seven months.'

It was John's old-fashioned prudishness which had made it so easy to carry on the deceit. Like so many men of his class he believed pregnancy and the subsequent birth to be an entirely female province. If he knew anything about it at all he was far too gentlemanly to discuss it. Bonny had heard him admit she was in a 'delicate condition' once to a friend on the telephone and that just about summed up his attitude to the situation. Fortunately this meant he also took her word for it that she had attended the doctor in Wells and he never asked for any information.

'I never thought I would hate leaving you so much.' John pulled her into his arms and hugged her fiercely. 'I used to love travelling once. Now I'd rather work as a postman or something just so I could be with you.'

'You wouldn't really like that,' Bonny said and kissed him lingeringly. 'Besides, think how wonderful it will be when you come home again? But I'd better finish your packing or you won't be going anywhere.'

Bonny waved until John's taxi was out of sight, then closed the wrought-iron gate, wiping away her tears. It was eight in the morning and the sun was out, steam rising from the bushes and the puddles in the drive. Yesterday it had seemed as if autumn had set in for good, but now it was glorious summer again.

She paused before going in to clear the breakfast things. She thought her house was the loveliest in England. Large graceful windows with arched tops, two either side of the central porch: such perfect symmetry, like the rather grand doll's house that Belinda Noakes used to have back in Amberley. Wistaria grew up the front and trailed along under the bedroom windows. It had finished flowering by the time their honeymoon was over, but she'd seen one or two blooms, enough to guess how if would look next year. Round the back of the house honeysuckle and jasmine scrambled up everywhere.

It was funny that she'd taken to gardening; when her father had been so proud of his it hadn't meant a thing. But of course there was a great deal of difference between a Dagenham garden and this one. Here nature did what it wanted to, no tidy rows of salvia and alyssum, but clematis winding its way into an apple tree, ivy covering the old shed where John had left his car, clumps of dog daisies jumping up wherever they could find space.

There had been moments since their wedding day when Bonny had half expected to find this was just a wonderful dream, that she'd wake and find herself back in grim digs. She still found it baffling that a city girl who had once believed she couldn't survive without a daily visit to the shops could actually adore such isolation.

Who would have thought she would suggest keeping chickens? But she had, and she fed them and collected the eggs. She had made strawberry and raspberry jam when she discovered a few pounds of sugar stashed away in the pantry, and she got more pleasure hearing Enoch say it was better than the jam his wife made than she used to get from the applause in the theatre.

Bonny hadn't missed dancing at all. Sometimes when John was out working she'd put on her tap shoes, wind up the old gramophone and dance just for fun, but she had no yearning to do it in public any more.

The click of the letter-box and the sight of Ellie's familiar large flowery handwriting on the doormat banished Bonny's intention of scrubbing the kitchen floor. She rushed across the hall to pick the letter up, then returned to the kitchen to sit and read it with a cup of tea. Bonny loved her kitchen almost as much as the bedroom. It was large and sunny, with windows looking out on to the back garden and she'd made dainty blue gingham curtains for them. She had never seen a kitchen with so many cupboards. Some had panels of glass in them and she'd raided the boxes of china up in the attic and displayed pretty plates, jugs and glasses with great care. She often dreamed in here, as she worked through a step-by-step cookery book which John had bought her, of the days when meat rationing would end, when she could cook a lavish meal for some of John's friends and lay the dining-table with all the old family silver.

Since Bonny's wedding, Ellie's letters had been infrequent and short. She said little about her predicament, and it seemed as if she was just taking one day at a time, hoping for some miracle which would solve her problem overnight. Usually her news was all centred on the cast of *Oklahoma* – funny, light-hearted stories about the girls in the chorus, or her digs.

But as Bonny read this letter she grew alarmed, quite forgetting her own worries. She could sense that Ellie was nearly at the end of her tether. Even though she tried to make jokes about it, Bonny knew she couldn't possibly cope in such a situation.

It started off cheerfully enough, a funny story about colliding with a piece of scenery in the middle of 'I'm Just a Girl Who Can't Say No'. But then she began to write about Edward, who had a walk-on part as a butler in a West End play.

'I caught the matinée the other day. I found myself just watching him, wondering if I could tell him about the baby and get him to marry me. I bet he would too! But that's a bit like shooting yourself through the foot. It might save me from disgrace and give the baby a name, but I still wouldn't be able to work.'

From then on the letter became even more disturbing. She spoke of finding a cheap room and eking out her savings with some waitressing or cleaning work until the last possible moment. Then she went on to say how she'd discovered that most hospitals could arrange adoptions, even taking the baby at the moment of birth. There was no agonising over whether she could really bear to do this, just that level-headed acceptance that this was her only possible route.

But finally, at the end of the letter, she dropped all pretence of stoic optimism. 'I just don't know what to do, Bonny. Sometimes I think I'm going to just fall apart with worry. I can't possibly hope to conceal it after October. I'm lacing myself into a tight corset now and sometimes I can barely breathe, let alone sing and dance. I've got to come up with some good reason for leaving. If I just disappear without any adequate explanation I'll never get work again after the baby's born. You were always good at making up plausible stories, work on that one for me!'

'You won't go to a cheap room,' Bonny said aloud as she put down the letter. One of the three spare bedrooms upstairs was in quite good shape, the only one which hadn't been damaged by the leaking roof. She would set to work today and clean it out. 'You'll come here, Ellie Forester. I owe you.'

Ellie clattered down the stairs from the dressing-rooms after the matinée with an enormous sense of relief. It was now the end of September and at lunchtime she'd been in to see the producer with the tale that she had to go to Canada to see an old aunt who was terminally ill. Mr Brascott had been very understanding, asking only that she stayed on another couple of weeks. He had been extremely complimentary and had even suggested she contact him again when she returned to England.

Ellie intended to go and have something to eat, then telephone Bonny to tell her the plan she'd devised had worked, before returning to the theatre for the evening performance. She wasn't absolutely certain about Bonny's idea that she should go and stay in Somerset with her. But she thought she might make for a city like Bristol where no one would know her, find a room and a job and contact a welfare organisation.

She refused to even think of any alternative but adoption for her baby. She didn't dare. If she let herself imagine holding it, she knew she would waver. Being an unmarried mother wasn't just frowned on, but considered almost a crime. Now she fully understood why her mother had taken Tom Forester's name and acted the part of a widow. That really was the only way of protecting her child and herself from malicious gossip.

Ellie didn't immediately see Sir Miles as she reached the stage door area. A group of dancers and several stage-hands had gathered to chat there and the one light was rather dim.

'Miss Forester!' The booming voice made her jerk her head round just as she was about to open the door to leave. 'I'm glad I caught you. Have you got a moment?'

Ellie could never see the man, even from a distance, without feeling a lurch in her stomach. At Bonny's wedding they had spoken briefly, but meeting him at a social event hadn't made things easier. He still addressed her formally, as 'Miss Forester'.

'I was just going to get something to eat,' she said, colouring up.

He was as formidable to her now as he had been at their first meeting. He wasn't a man given to smiling much and his ruddy complexion, heavy jowls and bulbous nose all seemed to speak of a bad temper. Today he wore a rather flamboyant embroidered waistcoat beneath his dark suit. Although it accentuated his big belly, it also suggested he wasn't quite the reserved man she'd initially taken him for.

'Well, let's talk while you eat,' he said. 'I know of a little place quite nearby.'

Ellie was relieved that the place he took her to was only an ordinary café as she wasn't sure whether he intended to treat her to the meal.

'I can recommend the Toad in the Hole,' he said as they sat down at a table by the window. 'I quite often come in here for supper. They make superb gravy.'

'Are you hungry?' Ellie asked. She was surprised that a man in his position ate in such places. It was clean and bright, but not very smart.

He smiled then, as if guessing she would be embarrassed to eat if he wasn't. He looked so much nicer when he smiled; the sternness vanished and his eyes became softer.

'I think I can manage a portion of toad,' he said, patting his fat stomach and looking down at it in mock dismay. 'It's that weakness for food which caused this. But my wife's out playing bridge this evening and I don't relish the cold cuts I'll have left out for me.'

They spoke of general things until their meal arrived, but the moment the waitress had put down their plates he asked her about leaving for Canada.

'You haven't picked a very good time to vanish,' he said, as he cut into the batter surrounding the sausage. 'Your star is just rising, Miss Forester. Is it wise to leave England now?'

Ellie came back with the well-rehearsed excuses she'd offered Mr Brascott: that this was her only living relation, whom she hadn't seen since before the war, that it was a chance to see a little of Canada.

'My Auntie Betty lives in Burnaby, near Vancouver,' she said. 'She was a dancer too, and so anxious to see me again. I can't say no, can I?'

'No I suppose not,' he agreed. 'But make sure you are back before February. I have plans for you.'

It was while he was speaking of a film he intended

to back that Ellie suddenly knew for certain he was her father. It wasn't in his face, or his mannerisms, just the excitement and enthusiasm in his voice. She saw her own character mirrored in that voice. His was deep and growling, each word so perfectly enunciated, yet she could hear herself. It was just the way she spoke when she had a passion about something.

She had read *Soho*, the book the film would be based on. It had been a best-seller for two years after the war, and Ellie had sobbed over it. There were so many parallels with her own life in the character of Megan, a young Welsh girl who leaves the valleys for London and becomes embroiled in the wartime Soho underworld.

'You would be perfect for the part of Megan,' he said. 'I thought of you all the while I was reading the script.'

Ellie forgot the dinner on the table, forgot even the tightly laced corset holding her in and the problems which lay before her. She looked into his face and felt she must be dreaming. 'Are you serious?' she gasped.

'Never more so, my dear,' he said, his eyes twinkling at her astonishment. 'I'm not the only person who thinks the part was written for you. My wife agreed entirely, as do several other interested parties.'

'I don't know what to say.' Her voice seemed like someone else's. She knew she should ask sensible questions but she couldn't think of one.

'Just promise me you'll be back in London by February,' he said, then moved on to tell her casually that the part of Joe Lamprey, the airman who seduces Megan, would be played by Dean Dailey, an American heartthrob. 'It will be a low budget film shot mainly out at Ealing Studios, but all of us involved in it are sure it will be a huge hit. The book was a colossal success, the film can't miss.'

Ellie thought she was being strangled. She couldn't see her assailant's face, but the hands around her neck were squeezing the life out of her. She was struggling to get free, waving her arms helplessly, then suddenly a crash woke her.

She reached out for the string above the bed to switch on the light. The sheet was wrapped around her neck, she was dripping with sweat and fighting for breath. It was one in the morning. She'd only been in bed for an hour.

Throwing off the covers, she got out of bed. The crash had just been a book falling off the bedside table. She hoped she hadn't woken anyone else in the house.

Sitting down by the open window, she looked out into the dark street, waiting for the breathlessness to leave her. Having no one to discuss her symptoms with made the fright much worse. Was it normal to feel that only half your lungs were working? To be so hot all the time, when everyone else was complaining how cold it was getting? Only a couple of days ago Aggie, her landlady here in Highbury Place, had asked how she could bear sitting in her room with the window wide open.

The wind was cold now – it gave her bare arms goose bumps – but it didn't cool her inside. It had been like this at night for weeks now. She would fall asleep, only to wake like this, dripping with sweat, a million nameless horrors filling her mind. This was the first time she'd dreamt she was being strangled, but the dream was nonetheless easy to interpret. She was being strangled by lies and deceit.

Until her meeting earlier in the day with Sir Miles, getting through the next three of four months had been her only concern. Now his offer of the part of Megan had added further complications. It was like glimpsing an island after being cast away at sea for weeks. That island held everything she'd dreamed of since childhood, a chance that might never come again. But the admission fee was so very high.

It was almost like a pact with the devil: everything she desired in exchange for her baby. True, she had always intended to give the baby away, but until now no one had been twisting her arm to do so. How ironic it was that her own father was inadvertently doing the twisting!

'Your mother chose you rather than fame and fortune,' Ellie reminded herself. But would she have done so if she'd known that twelve years later she would still be in Alder Street? Had she hoped that someone would wave a magic wand and that all at once they'd be transported to a pretty house with enough money that they would never go hungry again?

Ellie remembered that hunger sharply: lying in bed listening to her stomach growling, knowing there was nothing in the house to eat; watching the dancers in the Holborn Empire eating fish and chips, hoping against hope that one of them wouldn't be able to manage it all. She could still see Polly picking up bruised fruit and vegetables on her way through Covent Garden, slipping them into her pockets when no one was looking.

'I don't know the first thing about babies,' Ellie murmured, putting her hand on her swollen belly and stroking it tenderly. She could feel tentative flutters of movement inside her, like holding a butterfly in her hand. It brought on a yearning, loving feeling that she hadn't made allowances for and added yet another perspective to her confusion.

'How can I keep you?' she whispered, stroking her stomach soothingly, tears rolling down her cheeks. 'I'd be no good to you as a mother. You'll be happier without me.'

Chapter Thirty

October 1949

Ellie struggled off the train with her heavy suitcase and slammed the door behind her. The guard blew his whistle and the train chugged out, leaving her alone on a deserted, dimly lit platform.

It had been a long exhausting journey from London to Wells, and only the expectation of Bonny waiting for her at the end of it had kept her spirits up. Now, finding herself stranded, apparently miles from anywhere, the tears which had threatened all day welled up and spilled over. She dropped her suitcase and groped in her coat pocket for a hand-kerchief.

'Ellie!'

The figure running towards her down the platform shrouded in a voluminous hooded brown mackintosh bore no resemblance to Bonny, but her voice was unmistakable.

'I'm sorry I'm late. The bus was so slow,' she gasped breathlessly, then as she saw Ellie's stricken face she enveloped her in a clammy, fierce hug. 'You didn't think I'd forgotten, you chump? I've been counting the hours till I saw you.'

'Just a moment of panic,' Ellie sniffed, feeling a little foolish. 'The station looks like something out of a horror film. I half expected Boris Karloff to lurch out of the waiting-room.'

Bonny giggled. 'I'll tell the hunchbacked coach

driver to get lost and take you by taxi to The Chestnuts then. Oh, it's so good to see you again!'

'John won't mind me staying until I get fixed up somewhere?' Ellie asked as Bonny picked up her case and tucked her spare hand through Ellie's arm, leading her towards the deserted ticket barrier.

'I haven't told him.' Bonny grinned impishly. 'As he's in America and you're supposed to be in Canada I saw no point. We'll decide what to do in a day or two.'

Branches swishing against the side of the taxi gave Ellie the impression they were driving through very narrow winding lanes, but heavy rain and darkness obliterated everything but a few feet of road caught in the headlamps. Bonny chattered constantly, mostly about her house and John. Ellie was glad just to sit back and listen. She supposed Bonny was avoiding any conversation that might make the driver prick up his ears, and she was so very tired.

'We're here!' Ellie woke to find Bonny shaking her arm and the car stopped. 'Was I that boring? I should've left the light on in the porch. You can't see anything.'

Ellie sleepily followed Bonny through the rain and darkness. The taxi had already reversed out of the drive. She could hear its engine still, but its lights had vanished. Wet leaves brushed against her legs and she could hear trees creaking in the wind.

'Mind how you go, there's two steps up to the porch,' Bonny called back, her blonde head the only thing visible. 'I'll go on ahead and open the door.'

Ellie heard the tinkle of keys. Just as she reached the steps a bright light lit up the porch.

'So do you like it?' Bonny said impatiently. They had no sooner got in the front door than Ellie had the coat wrenched off her back and was dragged from room to room downstairs, with Bonny putting on every light and drawing curtains, gabbling non-stop.

'It's just wonderful.' Ellie smiled at her friend's exuberance, though she would have appreciated a cup of tea first and the chance to take off her corset. 'Not a bit how I pictured it.'

England was beginning to recover from the war. There was almost full employment at last and the new National Health Service was a great boon to all those people who'd never been able to afford glasses, dentistry or even doctors. But the expected prosperity hadn't arrived yet. There was still an acute housing shortage, some foods and all sweets were still rationed, and paint, building materials and furniture were difficult to find, whether you were rich or poor. Taking into account Bonny's tendency to exaggerate, even in letters, Ellie had expected at best a cosy but shabby cottageyness. Yet, if anything, Bonny had played down the graciousness of her new home.

Polished wood abounded on the floors, doors and the staircase which led off the large square hall. Some of the furniture and rugs might be old, but everything had beauty and elegance. It was funny to hear Bonny keep quoting John – 'John said this Persian rug will last a lifetime . . . John says if you live in an old house you must have period furniture.' In the past she hadn't cared tuppence for men's views and her penchant had always been flashy thirties styling with lots of chrome and glass.

Yet as well as embracing John's taste, Bonny had stamped her own personality on the house. A pretty collection of old perfume bottles was grouped on a shelf beneath a dainty gold cherub lamp. She pointed out four delicate water-colours which she'd reframed in rosewood. There was a large vase of Michaelmas daisies on a low table, a huge stone jar filled with dried flowers and grasses in the hall, and cushions in bright jewel colours on the couch.

Only Bonny's bedroom was entirely true to her character: an extravagant Hollywood dream with its shell-pink carpet, dainty dressing-table with triple mirrors, wall-to-wall wardrobes and a *chaise-longue* strewn with lace pillows.

Ellie felt a stab of envy as Bonny proudly showed her the luxurious *en suite* bathroom, the curtains that opened and closed by the pull of a cord. It wasn't so much jealousy of the ostentatious splendour as being confronted by this testament of John's love and his deep understanding of his young wife's character.

'You are so lucky,' Ellie sighed wistfully, stroking the cream satin counterpane. 'I hope you realise that?'

'I do now,' Bonny said, for once not coming back with sarcasm or a flippant retort. 'John's the best thing that ever happened to me.

Any bitter thoughts that Bonny was still entirely self-centred vanished as Ellie saw the room her friend had prepared for her. Although it was less lavish than her own, the care and thought put into it was every bit as great. A fire was burning in the grate, the pink curtains were already drawn and the old-fashioned bed was covered with a heavy white counterpane.

It was decorated with rose-sprigged wallpaper, against which hung pretty framed prints. On the dressing-table was a tall vase filled with dried flowers and there were books and a lamp beside the bed, fluffy white towels on a wooden stand, even a small easy chair by the window.

'Oh Bonny,' Ellie gasped, wishing she could find the right words to convey that she knew and appreciated the trouble to which Bonny had gone.

'It was lovely getting it ready for you.' Bonny blushed prettily, pleased by Ellie's reaction. 'I found that counterpane and the lace cloths on the dressing-table up in the attic and I put them in the boiler because they were all yellow with age. The trouble was the counterpane weighed a ton when I tried to get it out. I struggled with it for hours, then eventually I had to wait until the water was cold and get Enoch to help me put it through the mangle.'

'Who's Enoch?' Ellie asked.

'He's the gardener, not my lover,' Bonny grinned wickedly, 'and the only person you're likely to see here aside from me. Now let's put your stuff away and then we'll have some food.'

'Can I take this corset off?' Ellie asked, already pulling off her dress. 'It's killing me.'

Bonny stared in horrified fascination as Ellie revealed the tea-rose brocade and whalebone monstrosity. Her mother had had a similar one and she had always thought it looked like an instrument of torture.

'How long have you been wearing that?' she asked.

'For the last six weeks,' Ellie admitted. 'It's been hell changing for the show, I'd have died of embarrassment if anyone saw it. But I couldn't wear it for one more day, not if my life depended on it,' she gasped as she unfastened the suspenders attached to her stocking, then unclipped hooks all down her front. 'Oh, that's better,' she sighed as she slipped it off her shoulders.

Bonny had never seen a pregnant woman without clothes before. Although Ellie still wore knickers, they had slipped down below her protruding belly. She hadn't grown that big yet. With her clothes on she had looked little different to the way she had as a bridesmaid, but seen naked her stomach curved out from beneath her breasts, and it was indented with cruel purple marks from the corset. Her breasts were full and heavy, the aureoles around her nipples a very dark brown.

'Look what you've done to yourself.' Bonny couldn't help herself: she layed one hand on Ellie's stomach and caressed the marks soothingly, stunned by the knowledge a tiny baby was growing within.

Ellie caught hold of her hand and held it firmly in

one place. 'Can you feel him?' she asked. 'He's coming out for exercise now he's got room.'

Bonny's face was a picture. Awe, delight and even confusion passed over it. 'I've always wondered what it felt like,' she said, bending her ear to listen at Ellie's tummy. 'I can hear him too.'

Ellie felt her eyes prickle and a lump came up in her throat. Such an intimate moment, she felt, should be shared by the baby's father, yet she was moved by Bonny's reverence and tenderness. She moved away and put her dress back on, taking some socks and slippers out of her case.

'What have you told the neighbours about me?' she asked, sitting down on the bed to put the socks on. 'We'd better get our story straight.'

'Nothing,' Bonny replied, going to the fire and prodding it. 'There aren't any. The nearest is a mile away.'

'Well, that's one problem less,' Ellie laughed. 'I bought a wedding ring from Woolworth's, I thought I could say my husband was working abroad. Bristol's the nearest big city isn't it? I could get a room there and find a doctor, somewhere near a hospital.'

'We'll have some supper and talk about it then,' Bonny said. 'You need a few days' rest before you go anywhere.'

Eating sausages and mashed potato in the kitchen brought back reminiscences of Stacey Passage and their room in Brighton and Ellie put her questions and concern for her own plight on a back burner for the time being.

'I can cook now,' Bonny giggled as Ellie recalled a night when Bonny had put so much water in the powdered egg that it was like thin soup. 'You just wait until I make a rabbit stew. Enoch brings me one nearly every week. I can't make myself skin them, I get him to do that, but I watch! I can pluck chickens too, and pheasant. I'm getting to be quite the little housewife. My mum would be so impressed.'

They moved into the sitting-room later. It was the biggest room in the house, with windows overlooking the front garden and french windows at the back. With the thick gold velvet curtains and a log fire burning, it was very cosy.

Bonny told Ellie that Lady Beauchamp had given them the dark red brocade three-piece suite, and that the grandmother clock, an ornately carved chiffonier and the two sofa tables had all been bought from an antique shop in Bond Street.

'Utility furniture is so ugly,' Bonny said disparagingly. 'I wouldn't give it house room. How much longer is it going to be before we can buy what we want? The war's been over for four years, we've still got food and petrol rationing. All we've got that's better is the Health Service and everyone's working their socks off.'

'Except you,' Ellie laughed. From what Ellie could see Bonny wasn't going short on anything. She was wearing real nylons, not the lisle ones Ellie had to make do with, and her mid-calf skirt was very fashionable. Since clothing coupons had been abolished back in March, the shops had filled up again with clothes, but few people Ellie knew could afford a skirt and twin set as nice as her friend's.

Just a glance in the pantry had astounded Ellie. It was stuffed with cans, luxuries like salmon, tinned peaches and pineapple. With Enoch supplying such things as rabbit and pheasant she obviously didn't worry too much about meat rationing. Yet marriage seemed to have given Bonny maturity. While they were eating she'd spoken of gardening, reading and making jam. She looked every bit as pretty as before, but it wasn't so contrived now: she wasn't wearing make-up, her hair hadn't been permed again since her wedding, and the twin set and pearls were vaguely reminiscent of Miss Wynter. Was it possible that marriage could make someone who was once so giddy turn into an adult overnight?

Ellie told Bonny about her last couple of weeks in *Oklahoma*, the small party the cast had thrown for her leaving, and about Sir Miles suggesting her for the part of Megan in *Soho* next year.

'I want to do it more than anything in the world,' she admitted. 'I agreed to go for a screen test in early February and he sent round a copy of the script for me to study before I left London. But I'm so confused right now. I really can't look ahead more than one day at a time.'

'Everything will sort itself out,' Bonny said soothingly. 'Will you ever tell him who your mother was?'

Ellie shook her head firmly. 'No. I'm happy that he seems to like me. It might put him off me.'

'Some things are best kept quiet,' Bonny agreed, an odd look passing over her face. Ellie thought perhaps she was thinking about her past.

'Speaking of keeping things quiet, how did John react when you pretended to miscarry?' Ellie asked, suddenly remembering Bonny hadn't mentioned it.

'Would you like some sherry?' Bonny jumped out of her seat and went over to a small cabinet.

A chill went down Ellie's spine. Was Bonny being deliberately evasive? 'I don't want sherry, Bonny,' she replied. 'I want to know what John said.'

Bonny turned and her face was bright pink. 'He didn't say anything,' she said in a faint voice. 'He thinks I'm still pregnant.'

Ellie forgot that just a minute or two ago she'd been admiring Bonny's new maturity. 'Bonny!' she gasped. 'You aren't serious? You'd be six months pregnant. At that stage you can't just claim you flushed it down the toilet.'

'I know,' Bonny whispered.

Ellie looked hard at her friend. There was anguish in those blue eyes, robbing them of their customary sparkle. 'Come and sit down,' she said crisply, determined to get to the bottom of everything. 'There's more, isn't there?'

'Yes,' Bonny admitted wearily. She sunk down on the settee beside Ellie and laid her head on her friend's shoulder. 'You don't know what it's been like, Ellie. I'm so ashamed of myself, I can't begin to explain.'

'Start at the beginning,' Ellie insisted. 'You told me at your wedding that when you got your next period you were going to make out it was a miscarriage.'

'I didn't get one.' Bonny sighed deeply, burying her head against Ellie's neck like a small child. 'I thought that meant I was pregnant after all and I was so thrilled. I even put on weight! But as the weeks passed I sensed I wasn't pregnant, I didn't feel queasy or anything.'

'The old tummy troubles?' Ellie sighed. She remembered Bonny had never been regular and when it did happen she often had very bad pains. 'But couldn't you just fake it?'

'How?' Bonny asked, her eyes wide and troubled. 'Men aren't stupid, Ellie. When someone's sleeping with you night after night they get to know you very well. But that wasn't the only reason.' Her voice was little more than a faint whimper. 'I really do love John, Ellie, not for all this –' she waved her arm, indicating the house and all its contents – 'but for himself.'

Ellie listened carefully as Bonny explained how happy they'd been, how she hadn't wanted to add more lies to the ones she'd already told.

'I was desperate to tell him the truth, but it just got harder and harder because he was so thrilled about the baby. When he said he was going to America, I thought maybe I could do something then, or at least write to him there and admit what I'd done.'

'But you haven't! Why not, Bonny?' Ellie said impatiently.

'Because of what a specialist in Bristol told me,'

Bonny sniffed. 'You see, after John had gone away I thought I'd better have a check-up. He gave me a whole series of tests. He said I definitely wasn't pregnant – what's more I couldn't ever be, because both my Fallopian tubes are severely damaged.'

Ellie was at a loss for words. The doctor in Great Yarmouth had hinted at this, but they'd both been so young then, and they hadn't fully understood the implications. She hugged her friend in silent sympathy and let her go on.

'You can't imagine how stunned and upset I felt, Ellie. You see, I always thought that other doctor back in Great Yarmouth said those things to teach me a lesson because he guessed I'd had an abortion, and babies weren't a priority in my life then. Deep down I didn't really, truly believe it. Now it's been confirmed, it feels like a punishment for all the nasty things I've done. But the more I think about it, the worse it gets. How can I tell John why I can't have babies without admitting the past? Besides, John just couldn't imagine marriage without children, he wants lots. He's always talking about tree houses, sandpits and things. It's bad enough to admit I married him under false pretences, but to have to tell him I can never give him a child, that's just awful.'

'But men don't set such store by children as women do,' Ellie said. The irony of both their situations stung at her. Maybe Bonny deserved a little pain in her life, if only to teach her she couldn't have everything, but it was tragic to think both she and John should pay dearly for a youthful mistake. 'You must tell him the truth, Bonny. At least as far as you aren't pregnant now.'

'I wouldn't have to if I had a baby when he came home.'

Ellie turned in her seat in shock. 'What do you mean?'

Bonny was twisting her fingers nervously. 'Well you've got to give your baby away. Why not give it to me?'

Ellie moved back from her friend, startled by such a ridiculous suggestion. 'This is a joke, isn't it?' she whispered hoarsely. 'You couldn't be serious?'

'Oh I am,' Bonny sighed. 'I've thought of nothing else for weeks since John went away and I got that frantic letter from you. It's the perfect solution for all of us.'

'No, Bonny.' Ellie got up and crossed the room, suddenly so hot she felt faint. 'Never in a million years.'

'Hear me out,' Bonny begged. 'This isn't some crackpot silly scheme, I promise you.'

'I don't want to hear it.' Ellie turned her head away. 'I actually thought you'd grown up.'

'I have. I can work out for myself what it'll do to you when you hand over your baby to a complete stranger. You might go on to become a big star and forget all about it. But it's more likely you'll feel so wretched it will ruin your life.'

'And you think it will make me feel all right about leaving my baby with you? A woman who'd do anything so the lies she's told don't come out?'

'That's not the reason,' Bonny said hotly, her eyes flashing. 'You'd be leaving it with a couple who want a baby more than anything. A couple with a lovely home and money. What guarantee will you get about the couple the hospital find for your baby?'

'They check out people who want to adopt,' Ellie snapped back.

'Like they checked out the homes for evacuees, you mean!' Bonny smirked. 'Suppose your baby ended up with another Grace Gilbert?'

'Don't be ridiculous.' Ellie's voice was raised now. 'That was wartime. It couldn't happen now.'

'Can you be sure of that?' Bonny asked. 'There's orphanages full of kids born illegitimately during the war and after. I heard the other day some have been shipped out to Australia, when their mothers believed they'd been adopted by nice couples. I wouldn't put my faith in a system that lets that happen. Not when I knew there was a better solution.'

Ellie slumped back into a chair. Perhaps Bonny was temporarily deranged after hearing she couldn't have a child. She wished now she hadn't taken her up on her offer of a few days' holiday here.

'Bonny, you know nothing about babies,' she said eventually. 'I know I don't either. But you've never been sensible. You rush into things headlong, then run off when you get tired of something.'

'I'm not like that any more,' Bonny said indignantly. 'Look how I've got this house together! I've learnt to cook and garden. I want a baby too. But you wouldn't be giving it to just me. There's John who you like and trust, there's my parents and Aunt Lydia too, the baby would be shared by all of us. You can be his auntie, maybe his godmother, the perfect excuse for coming here and seeing your baby any time you like. We'd share him.'

Deep down inside, Ellie could feel a tiny spark of wanting what Bonny was offering, and that frightened her more than anything. 'It couldn't be done anyway,' she said impatiently. 'You can't just hand your baby to someone else because you feel like it, or it seems a good solution. What are you going to say to John when he comes home? "Sorry dear, I wasn't having a baby after all. But I've got Ellie's instead"?'

'He would never know,' Bonny said. 'Nobody would.'

'Now you're being preposterous,' Ellie snorted with derision. 'I've got to have my baby in a hospital, its birth gets registered.'

'But in what name Ellie? Your mother didn't tell the truth, did she?'

'That was different, she only lied about her marriage.'

'No one asks you for your birth certificate when

you have a baby,' Bonny retorted, a sly look on her face. 'If you book into the nursing home as Mrs Bonny Norton, why should anyone disbelieve you?'

'You mean I go through a charade like at that doctor's in Harley Street?'

'He didn't doubt you. He was only interested in examining you,' Bonny said. 'I called myself Veronica Smith when I went to the doctor in Bristol. He never questioned it either.'

Ellie looked at Bonny in total amazement. Her friend had always been adept at thinking up schemes to get what she wanted. But this one beat them all.

'Let me get this straight,' she said. 'Do you really believe I could see a doctor, book a bed in a nursing home and have the delivery, all as Mrs Norton? That I calmly give birth, register the baby, pretending to be you? Then one day just disappear, leaving you with the baby? You telephone John and the relations with the good news and everyone sends you flowers and cards?'

'That's about the size of it,' Bonny said calmly. 'Except you'd stay here for a bit until I got used to feeding and changing the baby. There is a tiny nursing home in Wells, that's far enough from here that no one has ever met the real Mrs Norton. There aren't more than four local people who know me anyway.'

'But you're forgetting one important thing.' Ellie felt Bonny was having a brainstorm, perhaps through being alone so long. 'John's going to look at the baby and wonder why it doesn't look like you.'

'He'll think it looks like him,' Bonny said with calm assurance. 'He's got dark brown hair and dark eyes, remember?'

'But supposing it grows just like me,' Ellie said. 'I've got a distinctive face!'

'People see what they want to in kids' faces.' Bonny shrugged her shoulders. 'I don't look anything like either of my parents. I don't think my dad ever considered there was anything odd about that.'

Ellie silently stared into the fire as Bonny went out into the kitchen to make some cocoa. If she'd seen such a plot in a film she'd applaud it for being brilliant, but however attractive Bonny had made it sound, that didn't alter the fact that it was morally wrong, and possibly even criminal.

'Forget it,' she said as Bonny came back into the room. 'It's not right and we both know it. Tomorrow I'll help you write to John and explain.'

Bonny put the cups down on a side table. 'If I tell him the truth I'll have to tell him your part in it, because of the pregnancy test,' she said slyly. 'He's honourable enough to worry about you too. I just hope he doesn't let it slip to Sir Miles some time.'

Ellie felt another cold shiver run down her spine. 'That sounds dangerously close to blackmail,' she said, getting up on to her feet, her voice like ice. 'You reminded me just in time what a bitch you can be, Bonny.'

'I didn't mean it like that,' Bonny said, blushing furiously.

'You did,' Ellie said emphatically. 'I'm going to bed now. And I think it's better if I leave tomorrow.'

'Please don't, Ellie,' Bonny pleaded with her, taking a step forward and grabbing both of her hands. 'I didn't work this out just for myself. Honest I didn't. I'm worried about you. You've got no one but me and I love you.'

Ellie was exhausted, but she couldn't sleep. The bed was the softest she'd ever slept on, the sheets were crisp, sweet-smelling linen and the wind in the trees outside should have been soothing. But she was rigid, stiff with anger that once again Bonny was manipulating her.

There was so much rightness in the idea; that was, if she could put aside the conspiracy against John. This house was so lovely, Bonny was aching for a baby.

Ellie herself would get the best of both worlds, able to continue on the stage, yet see her child grow up.

Ellie knew John would make a wonderful father. If it were possible to tell him everything and get him to agree to adopt the baby, that would be a different matter entirely.

But Ellie knew in her heart that under the circumstances, and because of her part in the initial deception, he'd close his ears to all pleading. In fact he would probably never want Ellie anywhere near his house or Bonny again.

Pictures floated into Ellie's mind, tantalising ones of all those good friends of John's at the wedding – Norman, a dentist and his jolly wife Vera, Bruce, another chemist, and his pianist wife. There was his godmother too, the kindly Lady Penelope Beauchamp, Lydia Wynter, and Sir Miles and Lady Hamilton. Her child could have all these intelligent, caring people as doting aunts and uncles. He or she would be brought up never knowing the seamier side of life.

If Ellie was to keep her baby she'd be ostracised, whispered about, treated as if she were a streetwalker. No dainty crib or well-sprung pram: an unmarried mother and her little bastard could only expect grimy back streets, outdoor lavatories, the butt of everyone's jokes.

What if Bonny was right, if the orphanages were full of children no one wanted? What if she handed her baby over thinking it was going to a good home and instead it ended up somewhere terrible?

But could she live with such a mammoth deception? Could she look John squarely in the eyes and tell him his son or daughter looked just like him?

The tinkling of china woke Ellie. She opened her eyes and saw Bonny at the foot of her bed with breakfast on a tray.

'I boiled you an egg,' she said in a hesitant voice.

'It's only been laid for a couple of hours. I don't suppose you've ever had one that fresh.'

Ellie hauled herself up. Last night's anger had gone; now she just felt confused. Bonny looked about sixteen in her blue fluffy dressing-gown, her hair tousled loose on her shoulders. Her eyes were red-rimmed from crying. Ellie cynically wondered if the tears had been for herself, or for her friend.

'This is a first,' she said. 'You cooking me breakfast.'

Bonny came round to the side of the bed, placing the tray across Ellie's lap. 'Don't go away,' she pleaded. 'I won't fight you about anything, or try to persuade you. I just can't bear the thought of you being alone, frightened and pregnant. You must stay here and let me look after you.'

Ellie felt helpless. One part of her mind said she must leave, but the thought of being alone in a strange city scared her. She was touched by the sincerity in Bonny's words. There was no one else to run to. 'I have to think hard,' she sighed. 'Give me a couple of days, Bonny, I'm so mixed up I can't think straight.'

'I won't say another word about that,' Bonny said, her face crumpling again. 'But I do want to tell you something else.'

'What?' Ellie sighed, expecting more trouble.

'I really am different now,' Bonny said very softly. 'Loving John is part of it. But it's your influence which started it. You've always been so kind and honest. I've been trying to be more like you.'

During the next two days Bonny didn't mention the subject again. The weather improved enough for them to take walks in the surrounding countryside and Ellie was spellbound by the beauty of Somerset. Views from the hilltops were breathtaking, the trees golden, russet and red, lush grass carpeted with autumn leaves. Cottage gardens were still bright with dahlias and

Michaelmas daisies, the hedgerows misty with Old Man's Beard speckled with rose-hips. They picked blackberries, eating as many as they put in their baskets, stole into orchards and helped themselves to the few remaining apples and pears.

Back at The Chestnuts, Ellie helped Bonny plant out winter cabbage and Brussels sprouts. They shared the chores of feeding the chickens, washing and preparing meals, while laughing, chatting and singing together. Enoch was now helping a farmer with his harvest, and aside from the postman and milkman, no one called at the house. At night Ellie drifted off to sleep to the sound of the wind and owls hooting. She knew she wanted this life for her baby.

At four o'clock in the afternoon of her third day, Ellie went out to collect the washing from the line. The sun was a fiery orange ball, almost perched on the garden wall and she buried her nose in a fluffy white towel, breathing in the clean sweet country smell as she unpegged it.

She imagined wrapping her naked baby in such a towel after its bath, and remembered that in London nothing ever smelt that way. She pictured herself as a child taking the slop bucket down the stairs each morning, the stink of that outside lavvy and the kitchen they shared with Edna, always strewn with mice droppings.

London was worse now than before the war for the working classes: uncleared bomb-sites, houses still waiting for repairs, thousands of people still homeless. Where would she end up if she kept her baby? What if a good adoptive mother couldn't be found?

She folded the washing and put it into the willow basket, picked it up and carried it in. Bonny was slicing up bread on the kitchen table and a pot of tea was waiting.

'Even if not many people have met you, they are bound to have heard Mrs Norton's a blonde,' Ellie said, putting down the basket and shutting the back door. 'I'd have to bleach my hair.'

Bonny sat down suddenly, her eyes wide with astonishment. 'You'd do that?' she asked.

'There's no other way.' Ellie's lip quivered. She hated the thought of such drastic action – her hair might never recover – but if that was the only casualty of all this, it was a small price. 'That's the one thing about you which sticks in people's minds. We're the same height, weight and build. If our hair was the same it would fool a stranger.'

That night they planned it all in detail. Tomorrow they would go into Bristol to get Ellie's hair bleached and Bonny would shop for the baby's layette and two identical maternity dresses.

'Don't get blue,' Ellie warned. 'It shows up your eyes. Green's better, it will make us both drabber. We'll have to make certain we're never seen out together after tomorrow. You must pad yourself up, we'll make something. We'll share your mackintosh.'

They thought of everything. Bonny would buy a black wig for when she took Ellie to the nursing home for the birth. She would tell Enoch and people in the village that she had taken in a live-in help until her baby was born, just in case anyone got a glimpse of Ellie.

'Enoch's very shy,' Bonny said. 'He never comes into the house unless I ask him to. Besides, he'll only be here for an odd couple of hours in the mornings now it's nearly winter. You can act it up a bit, you know, call me from upstairs and stuff, so he feels secure about me not being here alone. He doesn't need to see you.'

'I can always put the black wig on to clean windows,' Ellie suggested.

'Seeing the doctor in Wells is going to be the most difficult bit,' Bonny said thoughtfully. 'There's two at the practice, an old doddery one and his son. We'll make for the old one. I'd better come with you in disguise the first time, then I'll know all about him and what sort of things he does and says. I can warn you too if there's anyone there from Priddy.'

On the bus ride home from Bristol, Ellie and Bonny sat right at the back. From time to time they looked at one another and giggled.

'That hairdresser's face!' Bonny whispered. There were only five people on the bus aside from themselves and she knew none of them, but she was being cautious. '"Oh, madam,"' she mimicked. '"Surely not! Your hair is so beautiful, madam. Are you really certain you want to be blonde?" I don't know how I kept a straight face.'

'It makes me feel completely different,' Ellie whispered back. She was wearing a felt hat over her hair now, but in Bristol she had looked at herself in every shop window in amazement.

The hairdresser had done a very good job. It was exactly the same colour as Bonny's, but Ellie felt it made her look cheap: the blonde hair made her olive skin so muddy.

They were weighed down with parcels – nappies, little nightdresses, vests, booties, bonnets and matinée jackets. Baby equipment was in short supply still, but Granger's, one of the bigger shops, had taken Bonny's order for a cot and pram, promising they would deliver them later. Ellie had bought a book on childbirth and caring for babies, as well as the two maternity dresses and identical, sensible lace-up shoes.

'What if your parents turn up unexpectedly?' Ellie asked. 'Have you thought of that?'

'I'll make sure they don't,' Bonny said firmly. 'Once I tell them I've got a maid they'll stop worrying.

Besides, I told them a while ago that I haven't got a room fit for them to sleep in. They wouldn't come all this way from London on the off-chance.'

Old Dr Franklin was doddery. He was small, with snowy white hair, watery blue eyes and a face like crumpled parchment. His surgery was dusty and strewn with books, bottles of pills and medicine, and his patients' notes were dumped in cardboard boxes rather than filed.

'You're a fine healthy girl,' he said after he'd examined Ellie and taken her blood pressure. 'I wish all my young mothers were in such good shape.'

Ellie felt no sense of alarm, despite Dr Franklin's age or the condition of the surgery. Perhaps if she needed an operation she might have been nervous about his shaking hands and the fact that he needed a stick to get across the room, but when he gently prodded her stomach she felt the wealth of experience in those hands and his manner was reassuring.

'I'm not a lover of home deliveries myself, especially for first babies,' he said unexpectedly when Ellie asked about the nursing home. She'd been certain he would try to insist she had it at home like almost everyone else. 'I'll write you a letter to take there. Now just make sure you get plenty of rest and drink lots of milk. If you have any problems later on I can always make a home visit.'

He turned his attentions to Bonny next. As the wig they ordered by post hadn't arrived yet, Bonny had transformed herself into a plain and dumpy lady's maid with the help of a green woolly hat, a pair of spectacles and a shabby, too large coat.

'Make sure Mrs Norton has liver at least once a week, and plenty of green vegetables,' he said curtly. 'Call me if anything unusual happens. As you live some distance from the nursing home I'm sure they can arrange to take Mrs Norton in a couple of days before the expected delivery.'

The weeks sped by as the girls made their preparations. Ellie often felt she ought to be more anxious, but as each day passed she found herself overtaken by a kind of sweet torpor which numbed reality. For the first time in her life she had time to herself. She studied the script of *Soho* Sir Miles had given her before she left London, read the baby book, and rested.

Bonny was like a little mother to her, making sure she ate the right nutritious foods and drank endless glasses of milk and refusing to allow her to help with anything but the very lightest chores. When Enoch worked in the garden, Ellie stayed upstairs out of sight, sewing baby clothes or reading. Occasionally when he was having a cup of tea in the kitchen with Bonny she would yell out questions in the Bristol accent she'd instantly picked up on during their shopping trip.

'Where's the feather duster to, Mrs Norton?' she'd shout over the banisters, or, 'I can't finds any piller cases.'

After Enoch had left, Ellie would have Bonny in fits of laughter with a continuing impersonation of this rather dim, overweight maid whose name was supposed to be Nancy Trotter, or as Ellie called her in more Bristolian style, 'Nancy Trottle'. There was no real sense of wrongdoing now; each day their shared baby bonded them closer and closer.

Before Ellie arrived, Bonny had got a local man to distemper the smallest of the bedrooms in pale lemon. Now together they brought things down from the attic to turn it into a nursery. Ellie sewed a pretty padded lining to the ancient wicker crib which had once been John's, Bonny painted a small chest of drawers white and in the evenings they both knitted small squares of bright wool to join together and make a patchwork blanket.

Letters came from John almost daily and sometimes he telephoned too. These were the only times Ellie really felt guilty, when she overheard Bonny relating her own symptoms, complaining of swollen ankles, shortness of breath and heartburn, and had to retreat out of earshot.

November brought gales. The chestnut trees shed their last leaves and at night they creaked ominously. Once Enoch had gone home, Ellie often went out into the garden to rake up the leaves. She wanted to go for walks, but she was getting too big now to risk being seen.

The long-awaited cot and pram were delivered in early December from the shop in Bristol. Ellie stood back, letting Bonny play at putting in the covers, lifting the hood and fitting the shopping bag into it, reminding herself that by the time the baby was old enough to take for walks she wouldn't be there. But when she went into Wells alone for her second checkup at the nursing home, she bought a brightly coloured beaded toy to stretch across the front of the pram and a small teddy bear.

Ellie was worried about Edward. She wished she had been able to tell him the truth, but she knew what his reaction would be if she had. The only way out was to stick to the same lie she'd told everyone else. Nothing other than an exciting trip away from England would have been a strong enough reason to want to leave *Oklahoma*, and it had to be somewhere far away so neither he, nor anyone else could check up on her.

He had been suspicious at hearing she had an aunt in Canada, when she'd never mentioned it before, and questioned her closely about it. But desperation had made Ellie a plausible liar, and she'd managed to convince him of an old dancing friend of her mother's. Now he would be hurt when she didn't write from Canada, assuming she'd forgotten him in the excitement of seeing a new country. All she could do was read a couple of books of John's on Canada and hope that when she returned, he'd believe her excuse, that her 'Aunt Betty' never gave her a minute to write.

'We'll have to admit I'm here before Christmas,' Ellie said thoughtfully one afternoon as Bonny was dressing a Christmas tree Enoch had bought. It was bizarre to see Bonny dressed identically to her, the cushion they'd made together strapped around her middle under her frock. Bonny had begun unconsciously to copy Ellie's mannerisms and walk. She plodded, often held her back and had a way of perching on things which made her look entirely natural as an expectant mother. 'Suppose you tell John I'm coming back because I'm worried about you. Then we can kill Nancy off for good.'

'Won't Edward wonder why you didn't stop off to see him on the way through London?'

'I'll just write from here and say I didn't like you being alone. That's perfectly understandable,' Ellie said. 'It will appease your parents too. But I don't think you can stay here while I'm in the nursing home. It would blow the whole thing if someone saw you. You'll have to get a room near the hospital.'

'That's the only bit I'm worried about,' Bonny sighed. 'What if Mum and Dad take it into their heads to come down to see me there? After all, it's their first grandchild. Imagine if they just walked in unannounced and found you in my bed.'

'You must write now and make it quite clear they can't come,' Ellie said in alarm. 'Use the excuse no visitors except husbands are allowed and say they can come to stay here once John's home again. Lay it on really thick about how hard it is to find this house, and that I'm in the only room fit for them. That should do it.'

A huge parcel arrived from John on December 20th. Ellie peeped over the banisters to see Bonny putting on a wonderful performance of the helpless pregnant woman for the postman while he carried it right into the sitting-room. Once he'd gone, she waddled downstairs to find Bonny ripping it open with childish glee.

'Just look at all this!' she said, pulling out one gaily wrapped present after another.

'Shouldn't you wait until Christmas Day?' Ellie asked, flopping down breathlessly into a chair to watch. She was getting very tired now, and often fell asleep in a chair during the day.

'I can't wait till then,' Bonny threw over her shoulder as she continued to pull out parcels. 'Besides, we're due at the nursing home on the 27th; there might be food we can eat now.'

Sure enough, halfway down the box was tinned meat, preserved fruit, sweets, chocolates, coffee, dried fruit and several bags of sugar.

'What feasts we can have.' Bonny opened a box of chocolates, stuffed one in her mouth greedily and grabbed a second, then handed the box to Ellie. 'I'd forgotten how wonderful chocolate is,' she added with her mouth full.

The telephone rang before Bonny could open anything else.

'Oh John,' Ellie heard her say from the hall, her voice squeaky with excitement. 'Your parcel has arrived. First Ellie came last night and now this. It really does feel like Christmas now.'

Ellie avoided listening as their conversation grew more intimate, but suddenly Bonny called her. 'John wants to speak to you,' she said, pulling a warning face.

'Hello John,' Ellie said nervously. She had never spoken to anyone abroad before on the telephone, and it was indistinct and crackly. Fortunately he didn't ask any awkward questions about her flight or Canada; his anxiety was all centred on Bonny.

'Is she well?' he asked. 'I've been so worried and it's such a relief to hear you're there now. I was going to send a telegram to her parents and ask them to spend Christmas there with her.'

'Don't do that, John. You know how Bonny is about her mother, they would only end up squabbling and upsetting each other. Besides, she's never been better,' Ellie said quite honestly, smiling at Bonny stuffing yet another chocolate in her mouth. 'I think I ought to confiscate the chocolates, though, before she makes herself sick.'

She reassured him she would take Bonny to the nursing home herself and that she would be staying nearby so she could visit her every day.

'I'll send you a telegram the moment the baby's arrived,' she finished up. 'And I'll stay here afterwards until Bonny's back on her feet and coping. That's the time for her mother to come. I'll get the room ready for her.'

John's last words made her shake with guilt.

'You are such a good friend, Ellie,' he said. 'I can't thank you enough for giving me peace of mind. Happy Christmas.'

Ellie woke the next morning with an ache in her back. She put on her dressing-gown and went downstairs to find Bonny on her hands and knees cleaning out the fireplace in the sitting-room.

'I'm not sure, but I think it's starting,' Ellie said in a small voice. 'It's not how they say in the book, it's just a bit of an ache in my back.'

Over some toast and tea they discussed what they should do.

'Go and have a bath and get dressed,' Bonny said calmly, but her eyes betrayed that she too was scared. 'The book said it takes hours and hours the first time. Enoch will be here in a minute. I'll make some excuse to get rid of him, then call a taxi.'

By twelve, Ellie knew it really was labour. She was all ready, her small case packed, with toiletries and baby clothes, as well as two of Bonny's glamorous nightdresses, dressing-gown, slippers and a framed photograph of John to create the right impression for the nurses. But she was frightened now. They had centered all their plans on her being safe in the nursing home well before labour started.

Enoch was still sawing logs by the side of the house. Until he was gone they didn't dare leave.

The pains were coming every five minutes and were insistent enough to say she must make a move soon. Bonny kept flapping in and out, at a loss as to how to get rid of Enoch without making him suspicious. She couldn't dress herself in Ellie's clothes and the dark wig until he'd gone, and she was beginning to panic.

'He thinks he's doing me a favour.' She shrugged helplessly as she came back upstairs at half-past one after talking to Enoch again. 'He's cut enough logs for the whole of January.'

'Ask him to stop because you want to have a sleep,' Ellie suggested, squirming in her chair as a stronger pain began. 'Tell him the noise is giving us both a headache.'

Ellie watched from behind the curtain as Bonny went out to speak to Enoch. He lifted his cap as Bonny approached him and looked up at the windows when she spoke. Their conversation wasn't a brief one; Enoch kept looking at the house and Ellie sensed he was worried about something. But at last he took his saw to the potting shed and Bonny came back into the house. As Ellie watched from the window, she saw Enoch wheeling out his old rusting bicycle.

From the top of the stairs, Ellie heard Bonny pick up the phone to older the taxi. Then at last she came rushing back up, already unbuttoning her maternity dress.

'Enoch wasn't happy about going,' she said breathlessly, her face pale and strained. 'He said I needed a man around the house at such a time. I had to get a taxi from Wells too. I was afraid to call Blacky in

Priddy because he knows me. It's going to be half an hour. Are you going to be all right until then?'

That nightmarish taxi ride was something Ellie knew she'd remember for as long as she lived, steeling herself against crying out when the pains became strong, so that the driver wouldn't take undue notice of her. Bonny was dressed in Ellie's clothes, wearing the dark wig, babbling away to the driver, playing the part of the visiting friend right up to the hilt.

They weren't a moment too soon. Ellie had hardly got through the door of the nursing home when her waters broke, gushing all over the floor.

Time, place, past or future had no meaning for her as fierce, terrible pain blotted out everything. It was as if she were in a dark tunnel, each pain moving her towards an end which as yet was far from sight.

She heard Bonny insisting she stayed with Ellie. She knew that the hand mopping her brow and the soothing voice belonged to her friend, but sometimes when she opened her eyes and saw a white face surrounded by black hair she lapsed into confusion.

'Remember I'm Ellie,' Bonny whispered once or twice. 'You are Mrs Bonny Norton. Please try to remember, Ellie. It's so important.'

Bonny's words were a reminder there was more at stake than the pain she was drowning in. She felt her friend giving her all to comfort her. It was Bonny's hands rubbing her back, Bonny giving her sips of water, and Ellie felt her love and tender care, even through the searing pain.

'I won't leave you,' she said again and again. 'We'll do this together.'

Other hands touched her too, firmer ones with a voice to match. She thought Miss Gilbert was leaning over her and struggled to get away.

'Can you hear me, Mrs Norton?' a voice said from a great way off. Ellie fought her way through a dense, pain-filled fog, knowing that voice didn't belong to Miss Gilbert after all. She opened her eyes and saw a tall, thin midwife. There was no further similarity to her old enemy.

'You're fully dilated now, Mrs Norton,' she said, cool hands grasping Ellie's feet and putting them on her shoulders. 'I want you to start pushing with the next contraction. Do you understand?'

It was Bonny who repeated the words they'd read together in the baby book. 'Push down with your bottom, hard.' She put her arm round Ellie and supported her against her shoulder, encouraging her with more instructions.

Bonny was beyond wondering what might happen if it was discovered that Ellie wasn't Mrs Norton. All she cared about now was Ellie and the baby that would belong to both of them. With each contraction she remembered how Ellie had pulled her through her abortion and each and every other thing Ellie had done for her in the past.

Ellie's hair was stuck to her head with sweat, her face purple and bloated with pain. It was now nine in the evening and she was clearly exhausted.

'Push for the baby,' Bonny ordered. 'We'll have him very soon, won't we nurse?'

The midwife braced herself as Ellie pushed hard against her and smiled as she saw her first glimpse of dark hair. 'Ten minutes and it will all be over,' she said encouragingly. 'Now push hard, Mrs Norton, you're nearly there.'

Ellie gritted her teeth and pushed with her last vestiges of strength. One agonising pain suddenly ceased as it was replaced by a slithering sensation and Bonny lifted her enough to see her baby eject itself into the midwife's waiting hands.

'It's a girl!'

Ellie slumped back, too exhausted even to speak,

but she heard Bonny cry out, her voice holding all the delight she herself felt but was unable to voice.

'Oh, she's so beautiful,' Bonny cooed. 'I've never seen anything so small and wonderful, she's got a face like a flower.'

As a feeble mewing sound grew to a lusty yell of outrage, Ellie lifted her arms instinctively. 'Let me hold her?' she begged.

'Just a minute or two then,' the midwife said, swaddling the naked baby in a towel. She smiled maternally as she laid the baby into Ellie's arms. 'Then we'll get you both cleaned up.'

Ellie wanted to cry, laugh, sing and shout all at once as she looked down at her baby cradled in her arms, but she remained silent, stunned by the wonder of this tiny scrap which had grown within her.

She remembered seeing neighbours' new-born babies back in Alder Street as a child, and secretly thinking they were ugly, scrawny objects, but she thought no such thing about this one. She stroked her baby's angry red face tentatively. Her eyes were hooded by puffy cheeks, her nose and mouth too tiny for Ellie to tell how they might look in a few months. Ellie bent to kiss the grumpy little forehead and inhaled deeply of that mysterious birth smell trapped in whispy dark hair still congealed by blood and tissue. Tears of joy fell on to her baby's face.

'Isn't she gorgeous?' Bonny whispered reverently beside her, taking one tiny fist in her hand and laughing through tears as the baby's fingers gripped hers. 'What are we going to call her? She doesn't look like any of the names we thought of.'

'Camellia,' Ellie whispered. She wasn't sure why she should suddenly recall that beautiful rose-like flower she'd seen once at Kew Gardens on a visit with Ray, but it seemed so very appropriate.

'Camellia,' Bonny repeated thoughtfully. 'Camellia Norton! Yes, that's perfect for her.'

Chapter Thirty-One

'We've done it!' Bonny whispered, leaning back against the inside of the front door holding Camellia in her arms. 'We've actually done it.'

Ellie tried to smile, but her face seemed to be set in concrete. She was relieved to be back home, released from the burden of being Mrs Norton, but she didn't see her ordeal as over. She knew the real pain was yet to come.

Camellia was sound asleep, wrapped snugly in a shawl. After the constant noise in Bankside Nursing Home, The Chestnuts seemed deathly quiet. It was warm though. Enoch had been in earlier and lit the boiler and the sitting-room fire. His wife had left them a pot of stew for lunch.

'We'd better put Camellia to bed and get ourselves back into our own things,' Ellie said tersely. 'You might get some visitors.'

Bonny hitched Camellia up against her shoulder and with her free hand pulled off the black wig. Beneath it her own hair was tightly coiled and secured with hairgrips.

'You're more than welcome to this,' she sniggered, tossing it across the hall to Ellie. 'It makes your head itch like crazy. I can't believe I've had it on for a fortnight.'

Ellie glanced at the wig. It looked like a curled-up kitten lying on the polished floor. She wanted to retort that having an itchy head for a fortnight was nothing compared to what she'd been through, but she suppressed the remark, knowing she mustn't give way to spite.

'Let me take her up.' Ellie pushed the wig into her coat pocket and held out her arms for Camellia. 'Then I'll get into my own things.'

She saw Bonny hesitate before relinquishing the sleeping baby. In one sense it pleased Ellie, as it showed Bonny's attachment to her, but it irritated her too.

'I'll come up,' Bonny said. 'All the bedclothes are in the airing cupboard and it will be a two-handed job getting them out.'

Two hours later, Ellie sank down gratefully in an armchair in front of the fire and opened a letter from Edward. The house had seemed warm earlier, but now Ellie felt chilled.

The midwife had warned her that it took some time to adjust both physically and mentally to returning home with a new baby, but Ellie hadn't expected to feel quite so low. She was still a little sore, her own clothes felt too tight, she was disoriented and only a step away from bursting into tears. The letter in her hand, as yet unread, would be another reminder of the web of lies she'd spun.

Camellia hadn't woken since they tucked her into her crib, even though her two o'clock feed was almost due. All Ellie could hear was the wind in the trees, the crackle of the burning logs and Bonny's shoes making tip-tapping sounds on the tiled floor of the kitchen.

The stew Bonny was heating up smelt appetising, especially after the bland, stodgy food she'd eaten for the past two weeks, but she wasn't hungry.

All around her was evidence of the carefree days before she went to Bankside, now tinged with melancholy. Holly was withering around pictures, paper chains drooping dejectedly, the Christmas tree she'd helped decorate now shedding its needles. There were sharp reminders she didn't belong here: wrapping paper from John's presents to Bonny spilled out of the waste-paper basket; not one of the Christmas cards on the mantelpiece was for her. In two days' time, on twelfth night, she would doubtless help Bonny pack away the decorations on the tree. Next Christmas, when they were brought out again, Camellia would be one: she might be walking and chattering in baby language.

'I wonder where I'll be?' Ellie murmured to herself, knowing only too well that wherever she was in body, her mind would be in this house.

It had been the worst and yet the best Christmas she could remember. Moments of exquisite happiness as she lay in bed cuddling Camellia, gazing down at that small, flower-like face, examining every inch of her tiny body. She felt Camellia favoured Ray more than her, with fairer skin, and lighter brown hair, but she saw a hint of her own protruding lower lip in Camellia's sweet rosebud mouth. She wondered if those dark blue eyes would remain that colour or turn to brown.

There were seconds of absolute panic when she heard visitors coming down the corridor; any one of them could have been a friend of John's who would raise the alarm that she was an impostor. She'd cried tears of joy on Christmas Eve when three nurses walked in with lanterns singing carols, and bitter tears when she woke one morning to find her breasts overflowing with milk she couldn't give to her baby. There had been a sense of optimism as church bells rang out the New Year: perhaps 1950 would bring prosperity to the nation and banish the austerity of the forties for ever.

Yet there had been merriment too. Bankside was a tiny, privately run maternity home with only sixteen beds, and because of its high fees the atmosphere had more in common with a hotel than the clinical and strict regime of a hospital. As Ellie had a room of her own, they were happy to allow Bonny to come and go as she pleased. One of the nurses jokingly gave her a cap and apron, saying if she wanted to be there so much she might as well make herself useful by emptying a few bedpans and dishing out food. Ellie had been helpless with laughter when she saw Bonny actually doing these menial tasks; she remembered a time when her friend would have considered it well beneath her.

Then there was the terrible emptiness when presents, flowers and cards arrived. She had to look jubilant as she read all those loving messages from people she'd met at Bonny's wedding, and express no surprise that John had friends wealthy enough to post hot-house blooms, baby clothes and toys bought in Harrods.

Only Bonny's devotion to Camellia kept Ellie on an even keel. She watched Bonny constantly, checking and rechecking to make sure she wasn't pretending to enjoy feeding and changing the baby. But even Bonny, for all her wiles, couldn't possibly radiate such tenderness and enthusiasm, not without feeling it. She was content to sit for hours nursing Camellia in her arms, marvelling at her nose, her eyes, each tiny fingernail. She saw it as a major triumph when she got up stubborn wind, even when it brought forth a trickle of vomit down her jumper. She was there each morning anxiously watching as Camellia's weight was checked, crowing with delight when she'd put on an ounce, and she questioned the nurse closely about every kind of problem, from nappy rash to infant diseases.

But above all, Bonny was Ellie's friend and confidante. She listened patiently to all her worries, slipped out to find little delicacies to feed her, turned tears to laughter with her cynical humour.

714

Many times in the last two weeks, Ellie had had the urge to pick an argument with Bonny, wanting to wound her so badly their scheme would just fall apart. They'd had words many times, often resulting with Bonny stalking out, yet she always came back, invariably just when Ellie was regretting the cruel things she'd said.

But now they were home again, Camellia's birth certificate proclaiming her parents were Bonny and John Norton, Ellie felt sick with the enormity of what she'd done. She wished she could look forward to the screen test in February, get excited about seeing people again. But she couldn't. Even if she was to become a big star, be showered with luxury and adulation, she knew she would never be able to forget the price she'd paid for it.

Ellie read Edward's letter quickly. It shamed her further that he hadn't reproached her for not writing from Canada and happily accepted all her lies and instead poured out affection and made jokes about Bonny becoming a mother. He was playing the piano in a smart night-club in Mayfair and he warmly invited her to stay at his new flat in Bayswater when she came back to London.

'The stew's ready,' Bonny said from the doorway, startling Ellie out of her contemplation. 'I'll just nip up and see if Camellia's awake yet. I've made her bottle.'

'I'll go.' Ellie got out of her chair. She felt stiff and awkward and she didn't really know what her role should be now.

'No,' Bonny said, her voice and face resolute. 'I have to learn to juggle cooking, cleaning and looking after her. Besides, you must rest and get your strength back.'

'But –' Ellie started to protest.

'No buts.' Bonny came over to Ellie and put her hand on her arm. 'We haven't really talked about this part, but we both know what's right, don't we? I'm Mummy now and we mustn't confuse Camellia. She's the one who's really important.'

Ellie bit back tears. She knew Bonny was right. But it didn't make it any easier. 'I feel so strange,' she whispered.

'Of course you do.' Bonny drew her into her arms and patted her back maternally. 'But it will get easier, Ellie, I promise you.'

Four days later, John telephoned to say he was coming home on the next flight. The call came on a bitterly cold afternoon when the girls were sitting by the fire with Camellia sleeping in her crib in the corner.

They had devised a routine between them. Ellie prepared the meals, did the lighter jobs and gave Camellia the night feed. Bonny fed and changed her by day and did the washing and cleaning. Camellia was a model baby, sleeping from feed to feed, and although Bonny had insisted on doing the night feed too at first, she had soon discovered how exhausting it was and happily agreed to let Ellie do it as she always woke anyway.

Ellie was feeling better, physically at least. She took herself off twice daily for a brisk walk, the soreness was gone and her appetite had returned. She felt too that she was slowly adjusting mentally. Bonny had proved herself to be a natural mother: she could soothe Camellia as if born to it, she was unflappable and resourceful. Though it hurt Ellie to see her baby responding faster to Bonny's voice than her own, in her heart she knew this was a good thing.

Ellie answered the telephone, just as she had ever since they got back, partially to vet calls, especially the daily ones from Mrs Phillips, but in the main to create the impression that Bonny was still finding it hard to move about quickly. John had sent many loving telegrams to the hospital and telephoned the first day they got back home. But the moment Bonny took the receiver from Ellie's hand, her bright smile vanished and she turned pale.

'The next flight?' she said. 'Oh John you mustn't, your company won't like it.'

Ellie guessed from the expression on Bonny's face that John was claiming his wife and baby were more important than a mere job and although Bonny did her best to sound pleased, she was quivering with fright.

Just the thought of John arriving back so soon made Ellie's heart race alarmingly. She wasn't ready to face anyone yet, especially him. But she and Bonny were in too deep now to change anything, and Ellie knew it was her turn to support her friend.

'We'll manage,' Ellie reassured her, once Bonny had put the receiver down. She put her arm round her and led her back into the sitting-room. 'I know we didn't plan on him coming for some time, but look on the bright side, at least it will deter your mother from coming for a bit. She'd be a great deal nosier than John.'

'But look at you,' Bonny said, touching Ellie's stomach. 'You're tubby, you're still waddling a bit. He'll notice.'

'He won't,' Ellie said firmly. 'I'll wear my corset again, and I'll stop myself from waddling. Besides, he'll only be looking at you and his baby.'

Ellie found it odd that she could talk about John as if he were Camellia's real father, yet found it almost impossible to refer to Bonny as 'Mum'.

'I'm scared,' Bonny sobbed. 'What if I slip up? What about my flat stomach? John's bound to know women's tummies are all wobbly after a baby.'

'You won't slip up,' Ellie reassured her. 'If you can get through two weeks at Bankside without once saying anything suspicious, you can manage it with John. As for your tummy, you just don't let him see

717

it. Wear a big warm nighty. He won't be expecting to make love to you for weeks yet.'

'But your hair, Ellie!' Bonny took hold of a strand, her eyes filling with tears. 'You can't possibly wear that wig, John would know what it was immediately.'

John's concerned, loving voice had reactivated the part of Bonny's brain which she'd chosen to switch off some time ago. For weeks she'd been cocooned in a happy, dream-like state, seeing her own and Ellie's problems as solved to everyone's satisfaction. But now she was reminded of the vow she'd made to herself on her wedding day, and she felt as if that threatening, fiery sword was about to come down from the heavens and strike her for reneging on her promises.

She loved little Camellia as if she were her own, but she loved John too. He knew her so well and he was very perceptive. Did she really think she could fool him with this wicked deception?

'I'll go into Bristol first thing tomorrow and get it put back dark,' Ellie said, sensing a little of what Bonny was feeling. 'Now stop worrying, everything will be fine.'

'I knew you'd regret it madam.' The hairdresser shook her head sorrowfully. 'I couldn't think what possessed you to want to be a blonde when your hair was so beautiful. It's easy enough to bleach hair, but putting it back!' She sighed deeply as if she didn't want to attempt it.

'I had a boyfriend who liked blondes,' Ellie said airily. 'But I've finished with him now. Can you do it?'

Ellie had disliked this woman at their first encounter. She was a hard-faced Marcel-permed, pencil-thin shrew who ordered her assistants around the salon as if they were lower than the off-cuts of hair on the floor.

'I can't just dye it black,' the woman said. 'I have

to take it through several gradual changes, blonde to gold, gold to red, red to brown, otherwise it will turn green.'

'How long will it take?' Ellie asked, refusing to think about ending up with green hair.

The woman shrugged her bony shoulders, her small mouth pursed like a cat's behind. 'All day,' she said. 'And I can't guarantee it will be in good condition at the end of it.'

Ellie felt sick. She was already missing her baby, she hated the smell of perm lotion wafting around the salon and she had a feeling the woman wouldn't try particularly hard to make it perfect. 'Look,' she said, fixing the woman with her eyes in the mirror. 'I'm an actress. I'm about to start filming. If you make a good job of my hair I'll tell everyone you are the best hairdresser in England and give you a good tip. If not . . .' She tailed off, leaving the threat in the air.

'An actress! A film star?' The woman's superior expression changed immediately to subservience. 'Oh, how wonderful!'

'It won't be wonderful unless you give me black shiny hair again,' Ellie said wryly. 'Now, can we start?'

It was nearly seven in the evening when Ellie got off the bus at the bottom of the lane. Once the bus had pulled away she was left in pitch darkness, except for an eerie glow from the frost on the hedges.

As Gloria the hairdresser had said, it had taken all day. Her scalp felt as if it were on fire and the ends were so damaged she'd had three inches taken off the length. But it looked natural, at least, and when she looked in a mirror it was good to see the real Ellie again. The day had taken its toll on her, though, giving her a preview of what she could expect when she finally had to leave The Chestnuts. Camellia had been on her mind every minute, wondering if Bonny had cooled her bottle enough or remembered to put the

719

zinc cream on her bottom; at one point she'd even visualised Bonny falling down the stairs with the baby in her arms.

As she walked up the narrow lane, each and every tree trunk seemed to have an evil, leering face. She felt frightened and terribly alone. Ellie was no stranger to loneliness, but never before had she felt menaced by it as she did now. It made no difference that just half a mile onwards, Bonny was waiting for her eagerly, or that a bright new future was only weeks away. Somehow she knew she would never regain true happiness. This empty feeling she had now was something she would have to live with for ever.

'John's here!' Bonny called up the stairs three days after Ellie had visited the hairdresser. 'Have you braced yourself?'

'Stop worrying about me,' Ellie yelled back. 'Open that front door and run out to meet him!'

Ellie had heard the taxi as she was putting on lipstick. The face that stared back in the mirror was the one she'd seen a million times in dressing-rooms, not the muddy-complexioned blonde who'd given birth to Camellia just twenty-two days ago. Since her hair had been recoloured and cut, she'd mastered the art of rolling it up round a sausage of horsehair, a sophisticated style copied from fashion magazines. Her lipstick was the same crimson as her new mid-calf wool dress, her eyelashes were curled and heavily mascara'd, she'd given herself a fashionable beauty spot on her right cheek and her eyebrows were plucked to a mere pencil line.

She thought she looked the part she intended to play for John: the glamorous actress well on the way to stardom. He wouldn't know her hour-glass figure was held in by the hated corset, or that just yesterday she'd been shuffling around in old slippers instead of these ankle-strapped high heels.

'You're an actress,' she reminded herself, adding just a touch more rouge to her cheeks. 'As Camellia's aunt you must hold back, be a little inept when you pick her up, tease Bonny for being mumsy, even first a little with John. You must never let him see that hunger in your eyes.'

She walked over to the window and watched John embracing his wife out on the path as the taxi drove off. She hoped Bonny could carry off her part too. She had perfected the slightly slovenly look of a harassed new mother. She wore a dark wool skirt which she'd taken in to make too tight, her jumper had a nappy pin stuck into it, she'd tied her hair up with a ribbon so it looked carelessly tousled and left off her makeup. But would she remember that new mothers always had their ears pricked for their baby, that they talked about them incessantly and always put them first?

John looked just as he had at his wedding, in a sober dark suit. His hair was cut very short and neatly parted, his lean face tanned, moustache trimmed just so. The only evidence of his long journey was a shadow of dark stubble on his chin.

'Welcome home, John,' Ellie said as she swept down the stairs, just as he and Bonny came into the house hand in hand. Bonny looked tense, two over bright spots of colour on her cheeks, but John would just put that down to natural anxiety. 'I'm so glad to see you – perhaps Bonny will give me a rest from all the cleaning in your honour. Can I make you some tea, or something to eat? It will keep me occupied while you see your baby.'

Ellie had never thought of John Norton as really handsome, even though she'd told Bonny he was, not until that moment. He normally frowned a great deal, his serious nature colouring his looks. But now his smile was warm and wide, his brown eyes sparkled with excitement and he looked dashing.

'I don't believe you've really been doing cleaning

with those hands,' he laughed, looking at her crimson nails. 'But yes, I'd love some tea, and thank you for being such a good friend to Bonny.'

Ellie stayed in the kitchen, spinning out the tea-making. She could hear John cooing over Camellia in the sitting-room and she steeled herself for the moment when she must go in and join them. She felt hot, then icy cold, and was sure she would trip over in her high heels. She wished she could excuse herself today and rush off to London, but she knew she should hang on until John almost pushed her out.

'She looks like my mother,' John said, as Ellie came tripping in with the tea tray. 'It's her eyes, I think, or maybe the nose.'

'Was your mother impossibly beautiful?' Ellie said lightly. She'd often seen Polly in her baby's face. John was sitting in one of the winged armchairs, holding Camellia awkwardly across his lap, Bonny beside him on a leather pouffe, seeming more relaxed now.

'Not exactly.' John grinned boyishly. 'She always looked weather-beaten and old to me, but there is a likeness.'

'I think she looks like you,' Bonny said, putting one hand on John's cheek affectionately. 'Her eyes are going to be brown and her hair's just like yours.'

'Poor thing,' John said as he smiled adoringly at Bonny. 'Why couldn't she take after you?'

'I'm glad she's not blonde,' Bonny said, glancing at Ellie. 'Brunettes have much nicer natures.'

'Are you really set on calling her Camellia?' John frowned. 'It's a bit grand for a baby.'

Ellie bristled, turning away so John wouldn't notice.

'She'll grow into a grand lady,' Bonny said sweetly. 'And if you think I'm going to call our baby something drippy and common like Susan or Margaret, you're mistaken. Besides, Ellie chose it. She saw a Camellia once in Kew Gardens and she thought it was the most beautiful flower ever.'

John looked at Ellie and smiled. He didn't want to offend her after all she'd done. 'I suppose we could call her "little Ellie" or "Melly" while she's tiny,' he said. 'By the time she's old enough to go to the pictures, her aunt is going to be very famous, I'm told. I bet she'll get a kick out of being named by you.'

Ellie gulped. She loved John for being so big-hearted and despised herself for deceiving him. 'Let me pour the tea,' she said quickly. 'I thought I'd go out for a walk and leave you on your own for a bit. I'm sure you've got a great deal of catching up to do.'

As Ellie walked down the lane wrapped in her coat and scarf, she tried to turn her thoughts to the script of *Soho*. Megan had a baby too, which was taken from her at birth. She knew she'd need little rehearsing for the emotion in that scene.

She thought too of Sir Miles, who'd never known he had a daughter, and who now had a granddaughter too that he would watch grow up, not knowing she was his.

Then there was Edward! She was longing to see him, yet so afraid she wouldn't be able to conceal the sadness within her. Had she learnt enough about Canada from a couple of books to convince him she'd been there? What if he or anyone else asked awkward questions? She'd prepared so many stories about her fictitious Auntie Betty, leaning heavily on memories of Charley's mother, but she'd never been a convincing liar.

Then there were Amos and Dora. She hadn't written to say she'd left *Oklahoma*. She couldn't claim to them she had an aunt in Canada; they knew better.

'When will all these lies be done?' she asked herself.

The wind was strong and icy. Ellie walked fast, for once barely noticing the bare trees and forlorn winter fields. She was reluctant to go back to the house too soon. John and Bonny needed time alone.

*

'Stay another week?' Bonny pleaded.

Ellie put down her hairbrush and turned on the dressing-table stool, looking sadly at Bonny. 'I can't. You know why,' she sighed. 'John's been home a week and I can barely cope with him. Your parents coming will just be too much.'

Ellie couldn't tell Bonny how painful this last week had been for her. John rushed to Camellia the moment she cried and had taken over doing the night feed. There was no place for her now. In the evenings she felt John's need to be alone with Bonny, and she often excused herself and went to bed with a book. He was there while Bonny bathed the baby, he trundled her down to the village in her pram, he even boiled the nappies and put them through the mangle.

Ellie felt she was an impediment to their happiness. Bonny was tense when she talked to John, and he clearly felt left out when she and Bonny were alone together. Ellie was sick of keeping up the glamour-girl routine, weary of watching every word she said. She must walk away from Camellia now, while she still could.

'There'll always be a place for you here,' Bonny said softly, her eyes misty with tears. 'I promise you I'll always be a good mother to her. She means everything in the world to me.'

Ellie went to her bedroom door and opened it. She could hear music downstairs; John was playing some gramophone records he'd brought back from America. Camellia was sound asleep. Ellie shut the door and sat down on the bed beside Bonny.

She was no longer afraid that Bonny wouldn't be a good mother. She had changed immeasurably, bearing no resemblance to the giddy, selfish girl Ellie had met five years ago. All week Ellie had been silently observing her and John, and she knew the transformation in Bonny's character was through love. But it stung to see two people so happy together, to watch their smiles, to hear the little endearments, the loving gestures. They had everything, including Camellia.

'I want you to promise me something more,' Ellie said.

'What?' Bonny's expression was guarded now.

'It won't be right for me to come marching in here several times a year,' Ellie blurted out. 'But promise me you'll write to me once a month, send me snapshots and tell me all about her.'

'Of course I will.' Bonny looked puzzled now; she had expected more.

'Will you promise too that if anything goes wrong you'll let me know immediately? Illness, John losing his job, or you moving, anything important!'

'You know I would.' Bonny frowned. 'You sound as if you aren't ever coming back.'

Ellie hesitated. In her heart she knew she should get out of Bonny's and John's lives for ever, but at the same time she knew she wasn't strong enough for that. 'I can't ever come back, at least not as me. I'll be Aunt Ellie, or Helena Forester the actress. A friend of the family. I'll have to distance myself from you, Bonny, for Camellia's sake.'

'I don't see why.' Bonny pouted. She had a rosy picture in her mind of shared picnics, shopping trips and cosy, girlie evenings together. 'You're being silly.'

Bonny's earlier fears were now replaced with a certain smugness. John was thrilled with Camellia, so loving to her, she had silenced her conscience and told herself she had done the right thing by everyone. All she wanted now to make her happiness complete was for Ellie to revert back to her old jolly, amusing self and stop brooding about everything.

'Maybe you'll understand what I mean better in a few years,' Ellie said gently, taking Bonny's hands in hers. 'We were two feather-brained girls who dreamed up a fairy-tale in which everyone got what they wanted. But we didn't reckon on jealousy, Bonny, and it's lurking in the wings, waiting. I'm jealous of you right now, because you've got the home, the husband and my baby. In a couple of years you might wish you could change places with me.'

'I won't,' Bonny said firmly. 'I've got what I want.'

'I hope so, Bonny.' Ellie drew her into her arms and held her tightly. 'You've got everything that's important.'

'Have you got your things from the bathroom?' Bonny asked, wiping her hands on her apron. The kitchen table was cluttered with baking trays, mixing bowls and the ingredients for a cake. 'Is that dress warm enough for the train? It might be really cold.'

'You sound like your mother,' Ellie said sarcastically. 'Yes, I've got my things. Yes, I will be warm enough. Is John still tinkering with the car?'

Only yesterday John had discovered the engine was frozen up. It had been tucked away in the shed while he'd been in America, shrouded by old blankets, but the frost had penetrated even that. He'd resorted to putting some old stone hot-water bottles on it to thaw it out.

'He's taken it down to the garage in the village.' Bonny looked distractedly at the kitchen clock. 'I hope he won't be long, I don't want you to miss the train.'

'There's plenty of time yet.' Ellie could see Bonny was very tense. It was partly because she was leaving, but mostly anxiety about her mother arriving tomorrow. She was dreading all the intimate questions Doris was bound to ask, and a little afraid she would upset John. 'Let me bath Camellia, then you can get on with making that cake.'

'But you're all dressed up.' Bonny looked at Ellie's red dress almost disapprovingly.

'I'll put the rubber apron on,' Ellie said. 'Come on Bonny, just let me have half an hour with her?'

Bonny opened her mouth to say something,

perhaps that Camellia was still asleep, but was halted by an angry shriek from upstairs.

'Right on cue,' Ellie laughed. 'I'll go and get her.'

As Ellie came back down wearing the green rubber apron with Camellia in her arms, Bonny had the enamel baby bath in front of the sitting-room fire and she was pouring water into it from a bucket.

'She's sopping wet, and stinky,' Ellie said. 'Perhaps she wants to put me off her for good.'

All conversation was difficult this morning and Ellie had tried to make jokes to lighten the mood. But it wasn't really working; everything she said sounded trite, even callous.

Bonny tested the water temperature with her elbow as Ellie sat down and began peeling off Camellia's nightdress and woolly jacket.

'Is it okay?' Ellie asked.

'Perfect.' Bonny's terse tone implied she resented Ellie doubting her, but she disappeared and came back with the basket of baby things, a fresh nappy, towel and some clothes, putting them down on the floor beside Ellie's chair. 'I'll leave you to it then,' she said, turning sharply and shutting the door behind her.

Camellia waved her arms and legs as she lay on Ellie's lap. She had stopped crying the moment she was lifted from her crib, almost as if she knew a bath was imminent.

'You've got porky,' Ellie said once she'd removed the nappy and cleaned her bottom. Camellia was only $5\frac{1}{2}$lb at birth, but she'd put on over a pound since coming home. Sometimes they could almost see her growing. 'And you're a real stinkpot, but I'll soon have you smelling like a little flower.'

Ellie's hands lingered on her baby as she soaped her, caressing each leg and arm, her back and stomach, then holding her firmly, she lowered her into the water.

'Isn't that nice?' she murmured, splashing water over her.

Camellia's head turned towards Ellie, her eyes wide open. Ellie could see now that they were turning brown. Her legs kicked out, she thumped her arms up and down and she grimaced as if trying to manage her first smile.

'I think you're going to be a swimmer, not a dancer,' Ellie said lovingly. 'Just don't let your mum put you off it with her gruesome tale of nearly drowning.'

It wasn't until she had Camellia snuggled up in the warm towel that Ellie began to cry. She had promised herself she wouldn't, not until she was away back in London, but she couldn't hold it back, not once she felt the warmth and sweetness of her baby's face pressing against her breast.

'I love you,' she whispered through her tears, brushing back her baby's spiky hair. 'I'll always be there for you, even if I can only be your Auntie Ellie and never tell you the truth. I wish I'd been brave enough to bring you up on my own.'

Bonny came back just as Ellie finished dressing Camellia. She looked at Ellie's face and put one hand on her shoulder. 'I know how it is,' she said softly. 'But I meant what I said, we'll always share her.'

Bonny was worried about Ellie. She knew her friend so well, yet in the last couple of days she'd been unreachable. She wanted Ellie to leave, to have Camellia all to herself. But her heart ached for her friend.

Bonny could see now how much she owed to Ellie. She could look back and feel shame that she'd taken so much and given so little in return. Without Ellie beside her, she would have been just another tramp, a hard-hearted gold-digger with no love in her heart.

'When I'm in a Hollywood mansion, I'll invite you all over.' Ellie attempted a smile, but it was no more than a there movement of her lips.

728

'You make sure you get there,' Bonny said fiercely, her hand moving to Ellie's cheek and caressing it. 'I want to hear you're driving a Cadillac, that you've got a wardrobe full of furs and ballgowns. Then I won't feel so bad about taking her from you.'

'You haven't taken her.' Ellie looked up and found Bonny was crying too. 'I've entrusted her with you. Keep her safe and love her, that's all I ask.'

'What's this? A wake?' John's voice behind them made Bonny jump away guiltily.

'Just a spot of baby worship,' Ellie said quickly, trying to compose herself.

'Don't tell me you want one too?' John replied with a wide grin. He came round in front of them both and looked from one face to another, wondering about the tears.

'All women want babies,' Ellie said, wiping her eyes with the back of her hand. 'But this one is extra special.'

John leaned down and lifted Camellia out of Ellie's arms. He was highly touched by her devotion to his baby and grateful for all she had done for Bonny. But he thought it almost unhealthy for her to be quite so attached to Camellia.

'She is pretty special,' he said, putting Camellia on his shoulder and nuzzling her head with his lips. 'Especially when she's all clean and dry. But it's time to go now, Ellie. I'm sure you don't want to miss your train for this little darling.'

Ellie made for the lavatory the moment the train pulled out of the station. She knew she was going to break down any minute and she didn't want any witnesses.

She sat on the seat, leant her arms on the wash-basin and let the tears flow, the last glimpse of Camellia imprinted on her mind for ever.

Asleep against Bonny's shoulder, swathed in a

729

patchwork blanket. Bonny's blonde hair bright against the tiny dark head, the picture framed by the grey stone of the porch.

The train chugged on and on, swaying her gently from side to side as she sobbed, her face buried in the sleeves of her coat. She was desolate, the pain in her heart like a red-hot dagger, twisting and turning. She had lost so many people she loved – her mother, Marleen, Charley – but this time the grief was overpowering because of her guilt. What sort of a woman was she that a career and people's opinion of her meant more than keeping her own child?

People tried the door handle but she ignored them. She'd left behind the sensitive girl who cared about other people's needs.

When the well of tears had finally run dry, she sat up and looked at herself in the tarnished mirror above the basin. Beneath her felt hat her eyes were swollen, black mascara forming two lines down her cheeks. She took a clean handkerchief from her pocket, wet it under the tap and held it to each of her eyes, then wiped away the black smears.

'Tonight you'll be with Edward,' she whispered. 'You'll dress up and go with him to his club and you'll get very drunk. You're almost twenty-three, beautiful and talented, and the world is at your feet.'

Taking a compact from her bag, she powdered her nose and put on fresh bright lipstick with bold strokes.

She didn't have to tell herself she'd shrugged off the old, sweet and gentle Ellie. She could already see Helena, a harder, ruthless woman, looking back at her in the mirror.

Standing up, she braced herself against the swaying motion of the train, tilted her hat to one side and forced herself to smile.

'You will be a big star,' she said aloud. 'Nothing and no one will stand in your way.'